Melanie Ifield

I0615607

The Age
of Corruption

A Melanie Ifield book
First published by Melanie Ifield in 2013
All rights reserved
Copyright © Melanie Ifield 2013
www.melanieifield.com
ISBN: 978-0-9922839-3-3

Cover lay out: Shane Seczkowski
Cover image © amok on Bigstock Photos at
www.bigstockphotos.com
Typeset & formatting: Thomas White

No part of this book may be reproduced in any way, in any form, mechanical, electronic or otherwise, without expressed permission from the author.
All characters are fictitious and any resemblance to actual persons, living or dead, is purely coincidental.

Author: Ifield, Melanie
Title: The Age of Corruption / Melanie Ifield
Series: Ifield, Melanie 'A Fiona Page Novel'
Target audience: Adults

I would like to acknowledge everyone who helped make this possible, including Shane, Richard, Thomas, Jane, Danielle and my other Jane. Thanks for helping, and for reading and proofing the material! Any mistakes are mine.

To my parents – thank you for allowing me the time to get this right.

The Age
of Corruption

Chapter One

When I was four, I slipped over in the playground and scrapped my knee. The girl who came to help me was about eight. She sat me down, wiped away my tears and kissed the 'boo-boo'. I followed her slavishly for the whole day.

At twelve I was playing basketball, a riot seeing as I was five foot two and clumsy (nothing has changed). I fell over trying to jump and throw the ball at the same time. One of the senior girls came, took me off the court and patched up the latest scrape. I worshipped the ground she walked on for the rest of her time at school.

At twenty five, I dated a man whose only claim on me was he had changed my flat tyre while out on the Parkway. I wasted a whole year trotting around behind him because he'd saved me. It took finding him 'saving' someone else to make me see reason.

Why this horrid list of my tragic need to be grateful and follow puppy-like wherever my saviour may roam? I'm hoping it'll explain how I ended up standing in the bush one day with a dead man at my feet.

At twenty nine, I hadn't grown up. I was still prone to chasing after those stronger than me: still prone to *needing* those stronger than me. Wanting to be with them to see if what they had could somehow rub off on me. Spending so much time admiring their strength and power, daydreaming over what it would be like to be like them.

Which is why a few short weeks after meeting the latest champion, I found myself down south, watching as a man choked to death on his own blood, my new knife in his stomach.

The only thing I could say in my defence was: I didn't kill him.

I swear I didn't do it. I hardly knew the man. Well, unless you count the fact he kidnapped me only five days before...

"Hello, Fi!" Donald, from No.10, yelled from the other side of my door. "Are you up yet?"

Dragging myself off the couch, I managed to make it to the door. Last night had been heavy going and the fact that I was conscious was starting to throw my system into shock.

Wrenching the door open, I glared at my intruder. Most of my neighbours knew not to disturb me before 1pm. Donald, who had been at the same party as me, looked as bad as I felt.

"Why aren't you sleeping?" This seemed a natural enough question considering the look on his face.

"I was woken up by someone banging around in No.9. I think Wazza and Cherryl won the bet. Lorraine and Simon appear to be moving everything out right now. I reckon they're showing the place to a prospective even as we speak."

I sighed. While Lorraine and Simon could be moving out - who showed new people through at the same time? I turned and headed towards the kitchen, Donald followed. I padded over to the kettle, picked it up and shook. It was, predictably, empty.

"Coffee?" I queried the half-dead man in my kitchen doorway.

"Thought you'd never ask," he grumbled.

I had every modern appliance, but I still drank instant coffee and certainly didn't waste the filtered stuff on my fellow unit mates. But, being the wonderful hostess that I am, I managed to grunt, "Instant okay with you?"

Donald looked at me, and if surprise could register in eyes that severely hung over, then I was sure they were surprised.

"Of course, unless I suddenly warrant the filtered stuff."

He chuckled at his own joke. Everyone in the apartments knew that my filter coffee machine was virginal. But I still asked. A hostess-thing ingrained in me by my obsessive mother who despaired at her daughter's apathetic behaviour and sloth-like existence in general.

I merely growled and went about finding two mugs. I eyed the inside of them and declared them relatively clean – and after all, what more could you want? - dumping a spoonful of coffee in each. What Donald could otherwise see, coffee could cover up. The kettle whistled and I set about filling the room with the glorious morning smell of instant coffee.

Carrying a mug each, we made our way to my lounge room. I'd had the after-party here and the remains littered every available space. Shoving aside empty chip packets, I made room on the couch for Donald, then curled up in my favourite armchair. Muting the Black Eyed Peas, I gave him my undivided attention.

"You're telling me that Lorraine and Simon, after attending our party, are packing themselves off this morning? Unless they intend on moving to Mars they can't get far enough to escape our wrath, especially if they sell to assholes." I contemplated my coffee. "I doubt even Mars could save them then."

Donald was sculling hot coffee like a midnight party fiend. I eyed him warily. When someone was that worse for wear, their judgement was rather impaired. Not that I was a model of sobriety that morning.

But I think that was the point. I wasn't hung over because I was, in all fairness, probably still drunk. And coffee meant less drunk, which meant hang over.

Donald broke into my evil thoughts, gulping the last remnants of coffee. "I could hear Lorraine -" He shrugged.

He had a point. When couldn't we hear Lorraine? As soon as the chick woke up each day she was hard to ignore, unless you were quite happily comatose or watching Video Hits.

"And she was talking to someone, saying 'only can't you see how much space you could have once we take out the furniture?'"

Donald stopped again. His face was a pasty colour and I idly imagined what the coffee was doing to his gastric juices. "I saw a removalists van parked out front. I tell you, they're off. Without as much as a 'see ya', last night. Though how they imagined they would escape with Lorriane's foghorn blaring all morning is beyond me. I wonder if that girl really believes she's whispering?"

We sat in silence. Donald may well have been pondering his own question, but I was marking the inner stirrings of my body. It was finally aware that it was morning and there was no more putting off the moment of sobriety. Conscious and rational thoughts were surfacing, as were strange desires for fried eggs and toilet bowls.

"Donald," I said firmly – well, as firmly as possible – "I think you need to go back to No.10, have a shower and muster the troops. I'll be over … soon."

I wasn't going to put a time on it, as my stomach lurched and complained about the sudden deluge of harsh liquid being tipped into it. I physically pushed Donald out the door; quite a feat considering the physical differences, and launched myself at the spare bathroom.

Once I had eradicated all vestiges of coffee, various varieties of chips and colourful alcoholic beverages from my overloaded system, I felt remarkably sane. Time enough for a quick shower and spruce. I couldn't imagine Lorraine actually packing fast enough to escape quickly. Apart from the fact, I thought uncharitably, stripping off my PJs and adjusting the shower temperature, she probably *wanted* us all out there so she could protest how she didn't want a big fuss and how much we all mean to her and Simon. Of all my neighbours, I liked her the least.

Mainly, because Lorraine really pissed me off if I have to put up with her inane chatter for longer than, well, absolutely necessary really. A small blonde woman (I say from my extreme height of five foot two), with a high-pitched squeaky voice, Lorraine's giggle could cut you to pieces at twenty paces. Simon was an all right sort of bloke. Though I often wondered how the hell he ended up with his crazy wife.

I stood under the pounding water of my o-so *not* water-saving faucet and scalded my skin. Come to think of it, I was kind of going to miss them. We would often have barbecues and pool parties and Lorraine knew how to make the rest of them lighten up and laugh. And Simon was a whiz with steak…

I climbed out of my shower/spa bath, and wrapped a huge bath sheet around myself. Thinking a bit more clearly on the matter - what if we were saddled with old people? We had no say in who bought No.9.

I suddenly felt a little cold. Our happy little block of ten, all joined conspiratorially in parties and drunken orgies, could easily be destroyed by a renegade unit. One unit to complain about the noise, the smell of pot, beer bottles in the pool … I tearily dried myself off, throwing on clothes in a rush to be out there convincing them to stay.

It was quite possible my outpouring of new-found emotion stemmed from the copious amounts of alcohol I'd consumed the night before, but at that stage it didn't matter. We couldn't import someone who could potentially throw considerable spanners in our delicious and heady works.

I stumbled to the door, trying to pull on an ankle boot and grab sunglasses all at once. Somehow the whole ensemble came together and I managed to step out my front door with a semblance of dignity.

Already quite a crowd of us had assembled beside the pool, talking in subdued tones, wearing sunglasses. It had, after all, been one hell of a party. Two burly blokes were swearing and sweating whilst trying to haul Lorraine's piano out the door. It was her pride and joy and sure enough, there she was fluttering around generally making a nuisance of herself.

I felt another pang watching this exodus. Last Christmas had been filled with drunken nights bellowing out carols to Lorraine's accompaniment. What would we do in two months' time when the Season hit us again?

I came up behind Carmen and Kylie, owner and flatmate respectively of No.7. Carmen was muttering, "I can't believe it. Just like that. One day, it's a possibility, the next they sneak out without a word."

"Hardly sneaking, is it?" asked Kylie as Lorraine let out a shriek, a removalist having doinked the side of the piano on the door frame.

"Well…"conceded Carmen. "Sneaking isn't exactly Lorraine's strong point. But it's as good as, you know. There was no word of this last night and it's obviously been planned for a while. You don't hire removalists overnight. Oh, hello Fiona," she added, upon noticing me.

"Hi Fi," came various voices, all tones of weary, resigned, or just plain inebriated.

Once Donald came charging out of No.10, all fourteen members of our neighbours were assembled. Lorraine had the grace to blush. She could see the expressions on our faces. A lot of it was just plain annoyance at being woken obscenely early after a rather large night; with a tinge of betrayal.

Simon came out to join Lorraine in facing the firing squad. He turned at the door and said to someone inside, "No, no, just wander around and have a real good look." He cast us a worried look, then added, "I shouldn't be too long."

There was a general rumble; that's what *he* thought!

Rob, general all-round nice guy, spoke up. "Morning to you two. Mind explaining…" and he waved his hand vaguely in the direction of the disappearing piano.

Such was our general sticky-beakness, this sort of pre-emptory demand wasn't met with a rude 'shove off' from Simon. Rather,

Lorraine squeaked and Simon went a dull red.

"It's really all so embarrassing," Lorraine twittered. "We can't afford to live here anymore dears." (I noticed Simon's increased mortification at this announcement). "I lost my *job* yesterday, just to add to the troubles." She cast a lightening glance at Simon. "We need to *downsize* for a while. It is all a little *too much*. The thought of leaving you all...." she broke off.

I found my new found emotions suffering setbacks. Perhaps, whispered the disloyal little voice in my head, the people who ended up living in No.9 would be *better* than what we had. No need to imagine the worst, after all.

I stood back and listened as the others gave voice to their indignation on how quiet and sneaky the pair had been. I found my slightly glazed gaze wandering to the open doorway of No.9.

There was movement in the shadows and suddenly I had an overwhelming desire to discover who they were hiding in there. I skilfully skirted the crowd badgering Lorraine and Simon and made it to the door.

I was instantly dismayed at the barrenness of the whole place. Obviously the removalists had been going for some time before Donald heard anything. Perhaps Lorraine had upped her usual volume *because* of the lack of attention.

I marched through the open plan living space to the bedrooms and was brought up short by the occupant.

I had been expecting someone. Of course I had.

But it was still weird to actually find them there. Well, her anyway. As Todd would say such a fine specimen of a 'her' as well. Vaguely, deep inside and going totally unacknowledged by my conscious self, I think I felt threatened. There was something menacing and definitely predatory about the woman standing looking out the master bedroom's window. She turned gracefully to see who was disturbing her viewing time. Exquisitely curved brows rose.

I got a long look at who was to become in our language, No.9. I knew this woman was buying. She didn't have 'rental' stamped all over her, she had 'owner' oozing from her immaculately tailored suit.

She was tall. Though considering my lack of extra inches, just about everyone looked tall to me. I'd put her at almost six foot. She had sleek dark hair, pulled back into a tight bun. Her eyes were amazing. I often read in cheap trashy romances about ladies with almond shaped eyes. The woman before me had wickedly shaped eyes the colour of a stormy sea. They tilted exotically at the corners.

To top it all off, she wore a tailored suit with ease and grace, making her look fit and athletic. My mind buzzed with how the male fraternity of our little complex would cope.

I eventually realized the prolonged silence and my staring may be construed as offensive, so I stepped forward and offered my hand.

"Hi, I'm Fiona and I live in No.1. We weren't expecting all this." I motioned at the boxes and general moving chaos that still echoed through the room.

She smiled and my soul shrivelled with jealousy. Could there be too much perfection in one person? Perfect white teeth gleamed from her parted lips.

In a husky voice she said, "I gathered it came as rather a surprise."

She accepted my hand, giving it a firm, warm shake. Her hand felt strong and oddly calloused, so out of place with the image, I nearly let it go. Her lips twitched as though she could read my every thought. I felt my face go red.

I never won at poker either.

"Brakin. The name's Jonelle Brakin." I was about to embarrass myself further by asking rude and obvious questions like, was she going to take the place, when Simon came charging in.

"Fiona! What are you doing in here?"

"Sticking my nose in, of course," I answered, not the least worried about Simon's blustering. If things like that fazed me I would never last in my family. They were always blustering about something.

As usual, Simon didn't know where to go with my honesty.

Jonelle saved him. "It's okay. We were just about to get to the interesting part. I'll take it. That is, if my offer is still acceptable?" She smiled, wolf-like, at me, then toned it down some for Simon. He looked out of his depth.

It's funny how some men don't seem to be able to cope with attractive women. Jonelle was certainly all that.

"I'm sure Lorraine and I can safely accept your terms. Of course, we'll leave all the details to the lawyers." He tried to sound sure. I marvelled. Simon was definitely acting out of character.

The three of us headed back outside. There really was no reason to keep Jonelle a secret anymore. After all, the chances of me keeping my mouth shut were zero.

It was getting quite warm for Canberra in spring and Carmen, Kylie and Julie were seated around the pool, dangling their toes in. Sunnies and hats were out in force, as we were all experiencing some level of dehydration.

The crowd turned to view the outsider. I slipped over to Fernando to catch up on what had gone on while I was inside. He always remembered everything and had a great way of condensing material to its basic facts.

"Well," he said, eyeing Jonelle, probably appreciating the cut of her jacket. "It's like this. They were struggling and when interest rates went up, repayments became difficult. Lorraine losing her job put the last nail in the coffin. They had the place on the market for a while, just to see what sort of nibbles they would attract. They're moving to a rental house in north Canberra. Can't say we'll see much of them, then. Plus, Lorraine's pregnant. They arranged the removalists and this divine creature only about four days ago." That was quite a mouthful, even for Fernando. He swung round to look me in the eye, forcing his gaze to leave Jonelle's peerless suit. "So, is she going to buy it?"

I nodded. My attention had wandered back to Lorraine when Fernando made his extraordinary statement about her pregnancy. It was unusual for Lorraine to have kept such a juicy piece of gossip to herself. It was the sort of news I expected her to be shouting from the roof tops. Perhaps the financial strain of it all had really hit home.

I felt amazed and quietly pinched myself. Both Simon and Lorraine were acting so strange I had to make sure it wasn't all a dream. I could only imagine the pressure was driving them out of their minds. I could sympathize with that – anytime I came in contact with various members of my family I became an incoherent lunatic. They really do manage to bring out the best in me.

Rob and John emerged from No.6 carrying trays with long frosted glasses and jugs full of the hair of the dog. I shuddered. Drinks were served, things settled down and it was just a matter of sobering up in a socially acceptable manner. Shirts were off and sun was being exploited by some, while others wandered back into the welcoming darkness of their units.

I skilfully avoided everyone and slipped back into No.1. I shed sunglasses, boots and shirt on my way to the master bedroom. It was now headed towards 2pm and a great time for a nap. What else did you do on a Saturday afternoon? It wasn't as though I had to work, or study, or basically anything for the rest of forever. This was just as well, because the rich girl lifestyle was addictive.

Of the first twenty nine years of my life, the less said the better. Oh, except I inherited a very large amount of money. For which my family has never really forgiven me.

At the same time as my graduation from university after three years of journalism studying the fine art of how to interview rich men so they'd think I was adorable and marry me, a shockingly wealthy relative popped off his mortal coil and through more luck than anything, I inherited the lot. This, of course, destroyed any budding socialist desire to toil on behalf of the worker and expose the rotting decay of capitalism. I also didn't need to tie myself to some useless guy whose wallet was larger than his IQ, or anything else, for that matter.

As to why this rather nasty old bugger felt the need to leave his accumulated monies to me was debated long and hard at family gatherings.

Now, I lived in an apartment in a young and very upwardly mobile suburb of Canberra, Australia's capital city. My fellow Apartmates – a name we made up - were all in various professions which made them a lot of money, or inherited it like myself, unlike the soon not to be lamented Lorraine and Simon.

There had been nothing in the day's events which could possibly have prepared me for the changes my life was about to undergo. With nothing to even hint at the dangers to follow, the last things I thought of as I slipped into oblivion, were Jonelle's stormy grey eyes and wide, wolfish smile.

Chapter Two

Layers of my darkness peeled back to reveal the pre-dawn light of Sunday morning. It was a good thing I'd had no party plans the night before, because I'd successfully slept my way through it. I was vaguely aware my body was probably trying to tell me something about my lifestyle, but I wasn't one to take hints.

I wiggled my toes, feeling them flex against the sheets. It wasn't a very crisp feeling, which meant I was long overdue for a washing day. I was feeling very relaxed. The long sleep was wearing off and I was filled with a sense of alertness and wondered what had woken me.

There it was again! A noise out of the ordinary. I must have been close to waking for something so faint to stir me.

I swung my legs out of bed and padded to the window. I would like to think that I was very quiet and shadow-like in my stealthy tiptoe to peek over the window ledge. But I have to admit I'm more like the elephant in a china store, than a dainty fairy.

Somehow, I didn't manage to scare away the visitor. I popped my head over the ledge, so my eyes could survey the surrounds. The noise brought my attention to the ground outside my window. I was straining hard to see through the leaves and pale light, when a small figure leapt up on to the outside ledge.

I let out a high pitched squeak and jumped back, my heart nearly throttling me. The shadow leaned againt the gauze and purred. I sat on my butt, spots of fright dancing in front of me.

I was *not* the one to come to in a crisis.

It took a little while for me to realize my assailant was roughly the size of my hand and was so delighted to find human company it was frenzied in joy.

"Bloody little shit," I muttered, even as I peeled open the gauze and allowed my marauder in.

It jumped happily onto the floor and proceeded to march around the room sniffing at everything, before climbing up the sheets onto my bed.

"Oh no, you don't," I said, as it played happy paws on my pillow in preparation of making a nest. "I don't know where you've been and what nasty surprises you're carrying."

With that I plucked it up and took it into the lounge, switching on the lamp as I went.

I took stock of my willing captive. It was a smoky grey in colour, with fur so soft and fluffy I couldn't resist running my fingers through it over and over. A high pitched purr came grumbling out of its little throat. I picked it up and turned it over in an attempt to ascertain its sex, but this indignity was all too much and I received a scratch and bite for my troubles.

"Ungrateful brat," I laughed. "All right. I'll call you Smudge. I wonder where you came from?"

Not really expecting any answer, I dumped my new acquaintance in the laundry and went back to bed. I had turned the lights back off and was lying there, daydreaming about swashbuckling heroes and things of that nature, when I heard another noise originating from outside. I lay there for a moment longer. It couldn't possibly be another kitten, surely?

It wasn't. I slipped back to my peering position, just in time to catch a glimpse of someone coming out of Unit 9.

I knew Lorraine and Simon had totally moved out the previous day. I vaguely remembered overhearing someone say they were staying with her mother for the next two nights until the place they were renting became available. And of course, Jonelle couldn't have moved in overnight (apart from the fact the whole exchange of contracts thingy had to happen yet).

So that left only one option. I hastily backed away from the window. They wouldn't exactly have much to burgle over there at the moment and I felt a little tickle of glee. To risk getting caught breaking and entering only to find the place cleaned out before you – bummer! At the same time, they could move on to another apartment, so I scrambled forward again and pushed my nose against the window. I was just in time to see the figure move from the covering darkness of the doorway and sprint toward the security gate.

Two things hit me at once. One was *hello*, what happened to our security gate? How could this person have gotten through it so easily? And the second was more personal and probably something to do with vanity. This intruder person was sprinting and *not making a sound*. My elephant-like soul shrivelled with jealousy.

The figure reached the gate and pushed it open without a second's hesitation. I jumped up and shot to the front door. It was safe to be heroic now the dangerous person had fled the scene. I could raise the alarm without endangering myself ... or my Apartmates.

I paused a moment on the threshold, one can't be too rash with this sort of thing. The baddie had to have time to make good his, or her, escape. I wouldn't want to go tearing out and run into him coming back the other way.

The early morning was giving over to sunlight and I felt reasonably confident that all baddies would be trundling their way home at this point, leaving innocents to clean up the mess. I stepped out and went to view the damage to our security gate.

There wasn't anything noticeable for someone as inexperienced as myself. I mean, it was open and it wasn't bent, was it? It had its hinges all in place and nothing cut out of it. Having wanted to be an amateur sleuth, I bent down to the lock and did manage to see faint scratches. I immediately deduced that the baddie had picked it. Not a good sign, if it was as easy as all that. Perhaps he had had high tech gizmos that could confound the latest electronic locking mechanisms (though our gate was hardly the 'latest' of anything).

I comforted myself with the idea of a techno whiz kid, then thought better of it, as what techno whiz kid would bother breaking into our places? And then be so stupid as to find the only one that was empty?

I wondered who I could share my interesting news with. Donald's lights came on just as I was going to head for Rob's place, so I changed direction. It was Sunday so it was fairly safe to assume that Donald would not be primping himself for the office (he was currently trying for one of the office girls) so I could go bug him at will.

Donald was the head honcho, majority partner person, in a high powered law firm. Anything I ever wanted, or needed, to do with the law, I did through Donald and a bottle of wine. It was marvellous. Half of the professions a rich sloth like me needed were built into the

Apartmates and for that I loved them.

I tapped on his door and then tried the handle. Unlike me, Donald didn't mind having his space invaded. I often wondered what would happen if he was entertaining, or walking around in the buff when we let ourselves in. The thought of Donald in the buff was both stimulating and scary. The man worked out – a lot. Almost as though he was punishing his body for being so smart it had to be a lawyer.

But on the other hand – he was an Apartmate and my lawyer. I really couldn't go around finding him starkers. Having seen him in a pair of board shorts, making my heart stutter, the full monty would probably give me total cardiac arrest.

Even though it was early on a Sunday morning, Donald was probably reading a brief, or whatever they call them. My knowledge of matters of the law was limited to what I saw on TV.

"Hello," I bellowed as I came all the way into his apartment. "Only me." As if there was any doubt. Though, it might be a surprise, as who would think I knew there was a dawn on a Sunday?

Donald came out of the kitchen, hair still in stuck up all over the place, slept-in mode, coffee in one hand. "Fiona! What do you want at this hour?"

"Hand me a coffee and I'll tell you." My body had just woken up and was letting me know it wouldn't function anymore if I didn't get the prerequisite amount of caffeine into it.

He disappeared for a moment and came out with a steaming mug. I knew it would be freshly brewed. While I may own the most virginal percolator in history, for truly superb coffee, Donald was the man. I could smell the toasty coffee beans. It was heaven.

"You're not going to believe how long I've been up. First, I rescued the cutest little kitty in the world from starvation and loneliness. You have to see him. There is this lovely smudgey thing on his nose, so I called him Smudge and do you think the Apartmates will mind if I make him, like, our mascot?"

Donald rolled his eyes. "What was second thing? Stop waffling, I need to get to work."

I *had* got a teensy bit carried away with my kitten story. But need he be so rude?

"Then I got up again and guess what I saw?" I didn't pause long because I wanted to get to the juicy bit. "Someone was sneaking out of No. 9. The perp busted open our security gate to sneak into the one apartment that is empty! Pretty stupid, hey? I mean, what could he have found for all his trouble?"

Donald wasn't amused. Sometimes I wondered where his funny bone was hidden. He immediately put his mug down and left the house. I trudged along in his wake.

He, too, went straight to the security gate, like it could reveal to us the reason for its failure. It swung idly on its hinges, showing plainly I hadn't latched it after my inspection. Oops. Donald stooped to study the key hole and then moved off to No. 9. I hadn't looked too closely, so I crowded him a bit. Donald shot me a filthy look; then tried the handle. It opened easily.

Now that was weird. I knew Lorraine would have locked it up tight. So it could only mean that the perp (I loved using that sort of know-it-all language) had busted it open as well. Though there was similarly no damage done to the lock; no indication that anything was amiss - except the fact that it was open, for heaven's sake!

"See?" We swung the door fully open to reveal the naked room behind it. The only thing this room had left was a few dust bunnies and grooves in the carpet where the furniture had sat for too long.

"Nothing in there worth stealing. So let's go. We can tell the new girl if we see her later. But now I really need to read these briefs for tomorrow."

"Pfft." I blew my hair out of my eyes. "I'm checking around. What if he left something behind? The clues will have gone all cold by the time Jonelle gets back. She won't be moving in for a few days at least."

We were both tightly pressed against the door, peering into the gloom. So when she spoke from behind us, my heart nearly stopped.

"What are we all looking at? And who won't be moving in?" There was a smile in her tone.

Donald and I jammed ourselves together, knocking heads, trying to get out of the doorway, turning to see her. Why was I not at my best in the mornings, was the first thought that flashed through my head, when I finally got disentangled with Donald and saw Jonelle standing there.

She was looking stunning and so well put together. Everything matched. The white flowing pants, sky blue knitted top, blue band in her hair and white bag. My female self shrivelled in jealousy. It was just past 7:30am on a Sunday morning. You would never find me looking like I'd stepped out of a salon at that hour (well, to be honest, at any hour, unless I *had* just stepped out of a salon).

I was miserably aware of my battered track suit pants and oversized jumper with its frayed sleeves, so long the ends hung passed my finger tips. My hair was only patted into place and I hadn't washed my face. I hated being caught on the hop.

Jonelle flashed me that toe curling smile. The one that said 'I just know what you are thinking and I find it really cute.' At least, I hoped that was what that smile meant. How was I supposed to know? I barely knew the woman.

"Er." I said, as eloquent as ever.

Donald gave me a disgusted look. "There was an intruder this morning, who Fiona spotted. We were just trying to see what possible interest he would have had with an empty unit. It's not like there is anything to steal and from where we were standing there didn't appear to be any malicious damage."

I am afraid to say I giggled. I know, I know. Terribly embarrassing and so bloody girly, but I couldn't help it. "I just love it when a lawyer gets all wordy, don't you?"

Donald and Jonelle shared a look. I mean, right there in front of me, a look passed between them that definitely said 'she's a little strange'. I would have been insulted, except I'd have shared that look too, if they'd let me.

Jonelle didn't stay chummy for long though. Her face, not exactly a wealth of information to date, closed up even further and her lips became a grim line. She pushed us aside, gently, but firmly, and walked into what I guess was about to become her domain.

I didn't know the legalities. They certainly couldn't have settled yesterday, so technically the place still belonged to Lorraine and Simon, but I knew they had washed their hands of it.

I had always imagined myself as a bit of a super sleuth (with no actual evidence of any sleuthing *ever*) and I got a tingling sense that Jonelle wasn't all what she appeared. Exactly what it was she appeared to be was a little outside my scope of things.

Donald shrugged. "You two play detective, or better yet, go wake Amy if she's back and get her to play detective, seeing as she is one. Me? I'm going back to my briefs." And he left me all alone with little miss perfect.

She flicked her gaze at me. "You just going to stand there all day, or are you going to come in? Trust me, even though the paperwork hasn't gone through, this place is mine and no strange person should be skulking around it."

I wondered if she meant me, or the perp?

Guessing at my thoughts again, she added, "Thanks for chasing them off."

Now, here was a dilemma. Did I just let her assume I was this brave morning person who had had enough spunk and brains at that hour to manage such a feat? Or should I confess my pathetic cowardice, admitting I had hidden inside until I was certain our nocturnal visitor had definitely left the building? The twinkle in her eyes kind of helped. I got the impression she didn't really believe I could chase anything away – not even the blues on a rainy day.

"Um, didn't get a good look at the person. It was still pretty dark and he wore black clothes and I was still inside. Hell, I *stayed* inside." That blew my tough girl act. "But I did try to see what he did to the security gate. Hope you didn't buy this place on the grounds that you'd feel safe and sound."

Oops. Maybe she had.

Jonelle was just standing there. Relaxed and looking around her new space. There was the sort of impression that she wasn't paying that much attention to me, but even so, she wouldn't miss anything vital to the conversation, if you know what I mean.

"I don't think I have to worry about a security gate. I can fix it though, if you'd feel better about it all. Why do you say 'he'?" She turned in the centre of the room and grazed me with those wild eyes. Tilting her head that way made her appear very exotic. Like a large bird of prey that had somehow landed here on the way home.

"I'm not too sure. Funny isn't, how we always give the unknown and slightly furtive a male pronoun? Almost as though we're saying only men would be that bad. But the person had a kind of male way of walking. Does that make sense?"

I walked through the apartment as I spoke, watching dust particles dancing in the sun coming through the windows. I made my way from the lounge / open kitchen area into the first bedroom and stopped dead. Jonelle, coming up behind me, only just saved herself from crashing into me.

Stepping around my leaden form, she entered the first bedroom. "Well, it looks like whoever it was came in at least this far."

She was pretty calm about it. I can't say seeing bright red paint on my nice cream walls screaming "Stay out of it Bitch" would have given me that same even tone, but hey, horses for courses.

"I don't think that was for Lorraine." I hardly recognized my own voice. It was kind of hoarse and scratchy.

I'd never seen such a thing and could feel the maliciousness behind the words. The paint had run before it dried, giving the whole thing an impression of dripping with venom. I looked over at Jonelle. Her face was thoughtful.

She walked up to the wall and touched the paint with a finger tip. Rubbing this with her thumb, she contemplated her surroundings.

"No, I can positively say this was meant for me. Shame. The walls in here were a pretty colour. I think I'll have to do a feature wall. That should cover it nicely. I hope I can rely on you not to mention this? We'll just let everyone think the vandal left when they realized there was nothing to steal."

She was positively amazing. There was nothing in her voice that showed how she was feeling about the message scrawled on her wall. I wanted to walk up and take her pulse, just to make sure.

"Sure. Though I'd have thought letting them know that there is this crazy person out there stalking you wouldn't be a bad idea. People like Rob are handy in a crisis. He's all tough and built and well, tall." For some reason people always laughed when I mentioned how tall others were. Like I didn't have my own unique perspective.

Sure enough, Jonelle gave a dignified snort and arched an eyebrow at me. Okay, so she looked positively giraffe-like to me, too. But Rob would top her by a few inches.

With amazing speed she was beside me and had a hand clamped on my upper arm. The strength in her fingers was frightening. "I don't think I require a bodyguard, just yet. I'll deal with this."

I looked down at that hand. I sought out her eyes again and saw steel. "Okay. If you know who's responsible, and can fix our stupid gate, no harm no foul."

She let me go and I rubbed the spot she'd held. I tended to bruise pretty easily and knew I'd be getting one in the shape of her fingers by the end of the day.

"Let's get a coffee, shall we? You want to come out for one, or would you rather stay in?" She was obviously been considerate about the state I was in.

"I'll make us one, that'll give me a chance to put a wash on as well. I don't normally look this bad."

What did she care what I looked like?

I led the way back to my unit, fraying the sleeves of my jumper even more. I was suddenly vividly aware that it was freezing cold and my feet were numb. It was funny how being with Jonelle made me more aware of my body in some way. She certainly made me conscious that I hadn't showered before running over to Donald with my amateur sleuthing. Crap.

Rarely one to lock my front door, especially when I was only over at a fellow apartmate's place, I barged my way through into the kitchen.

Each apartment was set up along similar lines and Jonelle made her own way around. I was glad to see in some respects she was typically female. She went from room to room, sticking her nose in just like I would. I felt we were on an even footing. I also realized she had neatly removed me from her apartment without appearing to do so.

Was she afraid of any more messages lying around? I left myself a mental note to watch where she went when she left here, though my memory wasn't the best thing to rely on. If Jonelle went straight back to her place, I'd know I had been put out for my own protection.

I smothered a grin. It was beginning to sound positively like a mystery. And I had a nose for this sort of thing. At least, I liked to pretend I did. It lent some colour to my rather indolent life.

I stood irresolute in the kitchen. Here I had a grade A guest, someone who gave off 'classy' in almost tangible waves. Someone you would be loath to serve instant coffee to. I looked up at the top of my cupboards where my percolator sat in its wrappings.

Jonelle finished her inspection a lot quicker than I would have. She appeared beside me and took up the same position I had, staring at what appeared to be the ceiling. But she knew, all right.

Within seconds she gave a laugh and said, "I'm happy with instant, you know. Percolating is something people who have the luxury of leisure do. I dump a lump of coffee in the mug and it's good to go, if I drink coffee at all."

My shoulders slumped with relief. Aha, a fellow coffee fake like me! It was lovely to be able to drink the truly good stuff, but at the same time, I was kind of addicted to the crappy coffee.

So I boiled the kettle and put instant coffee into two mugs. It's the simple things that make a home.

"So, what is it you do, Jonelle? And where does the name Jonelle come from? It's unusual, wouldn't you say?" I added milk and a spoon of sugar. "Oops. Sorry. How is it you take you coffee?"

"White and one."

Thank goodness. Man, anyone would think I'd never been a hostess before. I could almost see my mother's toes curling with my slack attitude.

I took the coffee into the lounge area and sat opposite my guest. I caught a glimpse of the time and nearly had a heart attack. It was only 8:30am on a Sunday! I was amazed at how alive my body felt. It must have been all the unaccustomed sleeping it had done the night before.

She sipped for a moment in silence then came back to my questions. "I think I am what you would call a mongrel, should you be so unkind, and also a dog breeder."

I watched her talking and got the distinct impression she meant 'should you be so *stupid*'. The longer I was in Jonelle's presence, the more I was beginning to feel out of my depth, which was kind of in the shallow end of the pool at the best of times.

"My parents travelled a lot," she continued. "I was born in Austria, but we moved straight away, so I don't have 'Sound of Music' type memories. My mother is a bit French, a bit Israeli, and a larger part Australian."

She grinned at my face. "My father speaks seven languages and made me learn them all as well. But he manages to speak them all with the accent of a local, so I'm not too sure what he is and he has never seen fit to enlighten me."

"Wow." I latched onto the one piece of information that I found the easiest. "You speak seven languages? I have a hard enough time getting English right; I can't imagine the mangled state of anything else I attempted."

She shrugged: the natural unconcern of the truly adept. How I generally loathed people like that. It kind of made her more mysterious, which was weird and distinctly unsettling.

"Actually," she set her coffee mug down and sat back, long arms stretching out along the back of the lounge, legs crossed in those flowing pants. "I speak about ten languages now and would like to find the time to learn Icelandic. But right now that just isn't possible. You asked what it was I did?"

I found it unnerving that as she spoke, Jonelle didn't look anywhere else but my eyes. It was as if she was holding the conversation right at my insides. I'd heard the saying 'window to the soul', but she may have been taking that a bit to heart.

"Yeah, I find it interesting what other people get up to,' I said, which was technically true. "Because I kind of just bum around, though for the last few months I've been learning to Sign. I wanted to get good enough to volunteer at the riding for disabled. Anyway, you were saying?"

"How interesting, I Sign. It helps when you need," she paused, "to be quiet."

I wondered what it was exactly she had to be quiet *for*?

"I could help you out. It'll give us both someone to practice with." I nodded. "That'd be great."

A strange silence sort of hung over us then. I didn't know what to say, a very unusual circumstance.

Eventually she got up in one smooth move and put her mug back in the kitchen. "I have to get going. But it was nice talking to you. I'm sure I'll be seeing you around when I move in. I'll get that gate fixed for you some time soon. We don't want any more visitors, do we?"

I gave a start. I'd totally forgotten about all that. So much for my finely honed detecting instincts, they appeared to be resting. A sharp meow from the laundry reminded me I'd also forgotten my new flat mate. Damn it.

Somehow Jonelle was out and heading off before I got myself together. I didn't realise till she had disappeared out our malfunctioning security gate that she had left without telling me what it was she did for a living, or looking through the rest of her new apartment. What was that girl's story?

A persistent meowing from the laundry had me shelving those interesting thoughts. I let Smudge out and he pounced on me. Going to the kitchen to get him some milk meant carrying him half way up my pants, little claws latched deep.

Tiny baby purrs kept me company as I started on my own breakfast. I felt that seeing I had bothered to get up so early, the least I could do was follow through on this health kick and have something a little more substantial than a liquid breakfast.

Then it would be, um, the couch for a few hours? I was at a bit of a loss really. Leaning my hip against the counter, I watched Smudge lick his bowl clean. Well, technically it was one of my dessert bowls.

Munching on toast, I thought about what I could plan for the day. The rest of the apartmates, except for Donald obviously, wouldn't surface for ages, so I felt kind of out of it. What did a person do at this hour? How did normal people go about filling up the extra hours when they got up before midday?

The phone rang.

Now, normally it would have safely gone to voicemail and I could have screened it when I got up. However, I put my lack of foresight down to disorientation. I actually picked it up and said good morning. There was silence.

Then: "Is this Fiona? Have I got the wrong number?"

Bugger. It was my mother. I was not equipped to deal with her any time before say ... well, anytime really.

"Sure it is. Hi Mum. What you up to this fine and lovely spring day?"

See what I mean? I became this vibrantly cheerful and falsely poetic person who in normal circumstances would make me ill. I took the phone with me through to the laundry and loaded the washing machine one handed. There was a lot to be loaded. When was the last time I had done this?

"Young lady, it's your grandmother's birthday today, or had you forgotten?" Damn Skippy I had. "Lunch is at our place and I expect you to be here. Twelve sharp, you know how she hates to eat late in the afternoon. And try to wear something nice. And you can bring someone if you want to?"

She had that nice querying tone, the one reserved to show that she was very interested but trying not to be, and still knew it was an interest doomed to failure.

I mean, just because my sister and brother, Joy and Delight, had managed to get themselves hitched and were popping out the next generation in a lovely race to see whose brood could expand the fastest, didn't mean that I had to join them.

My mother would beg to differ.

My siblings' actual names were Janet and Derrick. Normal and boring, not the least bit as fun as Fiona. It was always delicious calling them 'Joy and Delight'. They hated it.

We all have to have special moments in our lives.

"Okay okay. I'll be there. What should I bring?" I glanced at the pair of fawn coloured pants as I threw them into the wash. Hmm, could they last another day? I always seemed to want the clothes that need the most washing. It was like this fatal attraction I have.

If it was unavailable, then it was *exactly* what I wanted. I often wondered where this ridiculous notion came from. It certainly wasn't my perfectionist, neat freak mother. She puts all her clothes in the wash as soon as they were used – even for only an hour! After some internal debate, and a quick sniff, the fawn pants were discarded.

"Bring a bottle of bubbly. You know how much she loves to drink that stuff. It makes her feel positively 'decadent', she tells me often. Ah. As much as I love her, I do so wish your father could have taken her out somewhere. Mother-in-laws can be a handful especially when they get older. Not," she added hastily, just in case I was feeling I couldn't handle the responsibility of a mother-in-law, "that it's too onerous. She's been a tower of strength for me over the years, since I lost my own darling mother."

I had to cut that off. Once she was into the full blown 'I miss my mother' stories, we'd be there all day. Ruthlessly I dove in over the top. "No problems, I'll bring some French stuff, she likes that best. And I'll wear something appropriate. What is she again? Seventy, right?"

"Yes. It's a special occasion and I would so love it if you could bring someone, dear, I'll set another place if you'd like. We haven't met any of your friends for ages really."

I hit the 'go' button on the washing machine and went back into the sunny front room. Smudge had curled himself (itself?) into a little ball on the couch in the sun. I glanced out of the window and saw Jonelle was back, squatted at the security gate, tools spread around her. Lord alone knew what she was doing, but she looked competent. Amazing how reassuring someone with tools can be.

A wicked idea crawled into my mind.

"Absolutely, Mum. I'll bring someone. Set me another place. I look forward to introducing you two."

Sometimes I wished the little imp inside would just shut up. Mum, predictably, was ecstatic and just about had my wedding planned by the time I got off the phone.

I hung up and dumped the phone, and raced out to grab Jonelle before she left. She was just standing up and replacing her tools into her bag.

Waving one hand like a magician she indicted the gate. "There.

No surprises coming waltzing through that gate in a hurry. Mind you, I'll have to give you all a new key; this lock is a bit different to the other one. Would you mind handing them all out? I have some place I have to be." And she dumped a packet of keys into my hand.

I felt my stomach slide. I hoped her elsewhere to be wasn't for long. Twelve noon suddenly didn't appear to be that far away. How did anyone manage to achieve anything? Before you knew it, the morning was over. What a terrible thing to discover at twenty nine.

"You busy for lunch? My mother is always at me about not bringing anyone and I saw you out here, and I kind of said I would bring you. Though she doesn't know you're you, if you know what I mean." Why did this woman turn me into a blithering idiot?

Jonelle's cool smile was noncommittal and I winced; I hoped, internally. Things were not looking as promising as I had hoped.

"If I am deciphering that correctly, you mean you've mentioned that you will bring someone and allowed your ever hopeful mother to believe that this will be a male someone? And now you are afraid I'm going to say no." She looked helpful. That sort of 'trust me I can make things better', kind of helpful.

I crossed my fingers behind my back.

"Yeah, that sort of sums it up. Please God tell me you aren't offended. It's just my mother can be so ..."

Jonelle actually laughed. I could get to like this woman!

"So much like a mother. I do understand. Just give me the chance to make a call and re-arrange something, then I'd be delighted to meet your parents. Is Sunday lunch a weekly event?" She flipped open her phone and started to press some numbers.

"Not really. Not that I'd go, that is. I'm sure Joy and Delight do every chance they get, but this time it's my Gran's seventieth birthday. We have to get there by midday. Is that going to be a problem?"

By the time I got to the end of that, whoever she had rung had answered, and she gave me that preoccupied smile those on the phone get and held up her finger, indicating I guess, wait a minute.

Then she started talking in tongues. At least that is what it sounded like to my uneducated ear. It was harsh and rather guttural whatever language it was. Not exactly what I had been expecting. What was this woman's deal?

A couple of seconds later she clipped the phone closed and nodded. "Just give me a bit more than an hour and I'll be back. That'll make it," she tipped back her sleeve and revealed a sports watch, "about 11:30. Is that going to be plenty of time for you?"

I agreed - after all she was doing me a huge favour.

So back it was to my place and a quick shower, which turned into a soak as it always does with me, and then I was ready for the monumental choice of clothes.

I stepped into my wardrobe and riffled through the clutter. In there somewhere was an outfit that would say 'happy birthday, here is a new friend and don't touch me little children'. It was a lot to ask of a piece of clothing.

Eventually I emerged, like a butterfly from its cocoon. I glanced in the mirror. Kind of more like a moth really. I did the makeup bit and stepped back to get a good look.

Sometimes I liked to imagine that I was someone like Jane Russell, one of the sexy old time black and white stars, but who was I kidding? I'm not fat, just sturdy. Or curvy; depends on the day of the week and how cruel I wanted to be to myself.

And I *was* pretty curvy. More Marilyn Monroe than Russell, I think, as wasn't Russell the tall one? I have all this thick, dark honey coloured hair that never behaves itself, chocolate eyes and thin lips. I always wanted thick pouty lips, and painted mine to an inch of their lives. But it didn't make them any fatter. I surveyed the ensemble, as my mother liked to call it, and gave myself the nod of approval.

At exactly 11:30 Jonelle was knocking at my door. I had a bottle of French champagne, something I had en mass in storage in the laundry fridge. When I opened the door, I was surprised to be greeted with a massive bouquet of flowers. Somewhere behind them was Jonelle.

"I thought it would be nice if I gave your grandmother something. We can say it's from us, sort of combined, right?"

"That'll give Mum something to think about. Sure, if you don't mind. We'll give her the flowers and champagne together, and give my mother a heart attack. Let's go. I'd hate to be late."

Some twenty minutes or so later we pulled up outside my parents place. They still lived in the home I grew up in and that wasn't because I was too stingy to buy them something better. Mum never wanted to move.

I paid for some upgrading and changes, like the additional bathroom and rumpus room for the kidlets. At least the place had the room for the extensions. Though the back yard was considerably smaller than when I grew up there.

I smiled a little sickly at Jonelle. "Welcome to the little house of horrors."

She swung long legs out of the car. "Chin up. It can't be all that bad. I've faced worse."

The front door was open by the time we got there. Mum was waiting, a small, but always polite, frown between her brows. After all, she couldn't upset a guest, but I could see her struggling not to demand where my new boyfriend was. She wasn't ready to accept I had deliberately misled her.

"Hi Mum. How are you? Hope all is good. Where's Gran?" I pecked the air just near her cheek.

"Your grandmother is out the back with Janet, Peter and your father. Are you going to introduce me to your friend?"

"Oh that's right. Mum, Jonelle. Jonelle, my mother, Mrs Hilary Page. I hope you don't mind Mum, but Jonelle is new to the apartmates and I wanted her to -" I stalled. What had I wanted?

True, the rest of them had met my parents at some stage, but to choose to bring one of the apartmates to my family home? That was unheard of. Who knew what I'd been thinking.

Jonelle flashed that smile at me and smoothly stepped into the breach.

"I know Fiona and I are going to be good friends, and that was proven when out of the blue she told me I should meet her parents. It's a special day to meet a new friend's folks, and on a birthday, too. Please accept my thanks for letting me come."

Mum was flustered and before we knew it, the three of us were out the back and swamped with relatives.

"Jonelle, this is my older sister Joy and her husband Peter. They have four of those brats running around, Tennille, Leigh, Clarissa and Rick. There's an extra, Joy? Who's that? Anyway, this is my Dad, Paul and his mother Sandra." I stood at the back door which led on to the new decking (courtesy of me) and pointed everyone out.

Joy walked up and held out her hand. "Janet," she said firmly, frowning at me in the way older siblings perfect over the years. "The extra one, as you put it, is our niece Julie. Peter's sister had to go to her in-laws for something and we're looking after Julie for the weekend. Now kids, stop pulling Potty's ears or she'll bite." Turning back to

Jonelle she asked, "How do you know Fiona?"

I watched the five kids try everything from ear pulling to actually riding Potty to make her turn nasty. Potty didn't have a nasty bone in her body. Half Newfoundland and half St Bernard, my folks had had her for the last ten years. I wasn't really paying any attention to the 'getting to know you' talk from Joy. But that changed when my Gran came up.

There was a lot of fuss made and flowers and champagne exchanged hands. Gran leaned towards me and whispered none too quietly, "You are a very naughty girl. Your mother was running around telling us you were finally bringing a young man to see us."

I winked at her. She understood my mother better than anyone.

Two minutes later the front door opened, making Potty give a half hearted bark and then Delight and his brood descended. The Joy and Delight troop got married very young and they'd being procreating up a storm ever since.

Carleen has a lovely set of droopy breasts and flared hips to give a lie to her mere thirty two years. Six kids in twelve years. Six! Admittedly one set was twins so that kind of meant one pregnancy for the price of two kids, but hey. What a factory.

I'd never been able to keep a goldfish alive. Though, now I had a kitten. For a second I got a cold panicked feeling; I really didn't want to kill Smudge. Then it passed. Surely a cat was more self sufficient than a goldfish.

There was again the mutual hugging, yelling at kids and introductions. Obviously Mum had thoughtfully called Carleen and told her I was bringing company. So the way her eyes widened, and the not so subtle nudge she gave Derrick, was explained.

The Twinnies were my favourite, Carleen and Delight's only girls, and last of the brood. They couldn't answer back, they still pooped their panties and yet whenever I picked them up, they were beautiful and smiled all the time. I adored them. But that really didn't mean I wanted any for myself. Mum was nuts to wish me onto any unsuspecting child.

Finally we were all sorted into a seat and lunch was served. Dad managed to say grace then everyone dived into their food. In the silence of munching came the piping voice of Leigh.

"Aunty Fiona, why is your husband a woman?"

I just loved six year olds.

There was a pause. I can't say there wasn't. Overheard by little ears, Mum's story had obviously warped into me actually *bringing* my husband. I didn't know what colour I was, but I could see Joy's flushed face and imagined mine was a similar shade.

Jonelle leaned passed me, as Leigh was way down the other end of the table, and gave him the benefit of a shark-wide smile. His eyes nearly popped (even at six), as did every male between me and him. "My guess is she got mixed up and went to the wrong church, don't you think? Let's hope the stranded bridegroom isn't too unhappy with his replacement."

There was a little sigh of relief from the adults. At least the guest wasn't upset. I grinned. Some mix up. Mum was giving Dad a frowning hint to change the topic. My parents: the incredible homophobes.

Leigh kept his eyes on Jonelle as he ate and played for the rest of the time we were there. Well, to be fair to him, everyone did.

Later, sitting between Gran Sandra and Jonelle, I watched the kidlets playing and felt peaceful. No one had mortified me by bringing up anything more radical than Leigh's little slip over the table.

"What is it you do then, young lady?" Gran leaned towards Jonelle.

I snapped out of my thinking and watching to hear the response. After all, I had asked her the same thing and she'd carefully side stepped it.

Jonelle, who had been politely watching Little Mark get led around on the back of Potty by Leigh, who was determined to win from her another of those smiles, turned to Gran.

"I'm semi-retired, Mrs Page."

"Stuff and nonsense, call me Sandra. When you call me Mrs Page I keep looking for Fiona's mother. She became more of a Mrs Page than I ever was. Plus, Paul is a much nicer Mr Page than my husband was. So, retired from what?" She asked, taking Jonelle's hand. The older generation really did seem to think they could say and do anything they wanted.

Jonelle was pretty good about it. She just raised her eyebrow at me over Gran's head. I shrugged; she was on her own in this.

Gran gave a very unladylike whistle. "What exactly is it you say you retired from? These are hardly the hands of an office worker. You have some serious calluses' here. So, what's the deal?" she looked at me "That's how the younger generation puts it, right?" I loved the fact that she tried to be hip.

Jonelle gently disengaged her hand. "Well, I was in art. I bought and sold artworks around the world. Sometimes I have been known to do my own. But now, I spend more of my time at home. I don't socialize all that much, generally speaking."

She spoke that last sentence straight at me, as though warning me not to think that coming out to a family 'do' would be an every weekend event. I felt like explaining to her it wasn't for me either.

"Speaking of which, I have so enjoyed myself, but I think I really do need to get going. There are a few other things I need to get done before Monday morning and I can't put them off anymore."

She rose gracefully to her feet. Goodbyes were scattered willy-nilly amongst my gathered relatives, then we settled into my zippy little convertible and were on our way home. There was a peaceful kind of silence. I was busy thinking about how Jonelle moved conversations away from what she did for a living, which was interesting.

In a large family where they told everything about everything to everyone, I wasn't used to other people's reticence. I had only met the woman yesterday and just because it was normal for me to go happily blathering on about whatever, that didn't mean that was her way.

I took a quick peek at her from the corner of my eye. She appeared to be lost in thought. I looked back at the road for a second to correct a slight tendency to wander to the left, then flicked my eyes sideways again. Much to my chagrin, Jonelle was watching me. There was nothing worse than been caught out peeking. She grinned, all wolfish and predatory.

"You certainly have a big family. Why aren't you a good breeder too?"

I shuddered. Good thing I liked her, or that sort of question would have her walking home.

"I've tried hard to keep a low profile. I did have one serious relationship. But I took him to one too many family do's and he dumped me on our first year anniversary. Well, he was sleeping with someone else at the time, so perhaps it was mutual. Mum's never forgiven him, or me. What's your excuse? Or do you have a family tucked somewhere?"

Jonelle laughed. "Me? I don't think so. Never had the time or inclination. I'm not really family friendly." She shook her head and smiled. "I'm much too busy for all that nappy changing stuff."

I nodded. I could so see that. I couldn't imagine the elegance of her trying to change nappies, or feeding breakfast to children who were more likely to cover her with it.

"Not for me either. While I'd never admit it to Delight and Joy, or their spouses, I am constantly amazed how well they can balance everything."

"So, how did you end up so fabulously rich and them so not, if that's not a rude question?" Jonelle sat half sideways to study me as I drove. I found that a bit unnerving. She had too much of a direct gaze and while I wasn't looking at it, I could still feel it.

"A rude question? Just you wait until you've lived with us all for a while. There is no such thing as a rude question. We work hard at making sure everyone knows everything, so if you have any secrets at all, be prepared to unmask."

I caught her expression out of the corner of my eye before the habitual smoothness came down. She looked … wary. My sleuthing senses started tingling. I filled her in about my strange old relative who had left me every penny he'd made and how I could live on the income it provided for the rest of forever.

That got us back to the apartments, where she promptly left me.

Chapter Three

Funny things, Tuesdays. They had that suspended 'between the real days', feel about them. That was why the major cinemas put on cheap tickets; to try and make people come out of their homes even though they would have to go to school or work the next day.

That Tuesday I was meeting Brad in town. He had suggested a dinner and movie, but I couldn't commit to that sort of thing. What if we didn't like each other? What if and this is of great importance, we ran out of things to say and the rest of the meal was a total disaster?

You had to think about those things when you were in a dating spiral. I'd been trapped too many times in nauseating conversations that seemed to go on and on for the whole evening when all I wanted to do was get the bill and leave. So now, I went for a coffee and if that went well, I'd see a movie. That way I had a little exposure to their conversation and a movie length time with their company and the chance to grab a quick drink afterwards if it went well.

I'd met Brad through a mutual party acquaintance, who shall remain nameless to protect their identity. We were having an absolutely debauched time at his place drinking too much and I even walked into the spare room to find my jacket and found two couples hard at it. It was a wild night. More couple sharing than I ever wanted to witness again.

Anyway, Brad arrived stag like myself, expecting just a wild fun night and landed beside me as we were the only two with no one to share. It was quite embarrassing at first, but we muddled through a conversation and it worked out we both didn't know the guy very well and we probably wouldn't be advertising the fact we'd come to one of his parties. Before long, Brad walked me home.

Through four suburbs, no less! In Canberra's spring! The man had courage. But it meant we had done the talking part of my dating line up, so movie was next. Personally, I wanted to get to the rip his clothes off stage – fast. The man was sweet and smart, and from the way he filled out his shirt and jeans, I knew I'd be really happy with the outcome.

But I had to stick to my little dating rules, otherwise where would I be? There were steps and protocols I wasn't prepared to do away with because that way led to some unsavoury choices in the long run.

However, when I arrived at the cinema complex and spotted my date, my mouth literally watered and dating protocols slipped seamlessly out of my mind. Here was my own little slice of heaven all parcelled up and ready for me to unwrap. There could have been a slight drool factor. But I was quick to wipe it away. No need to totally embarrass myself.

He was dressed in faded denim, with a black knitted top-thing under a black leather jacket. He looked like main course. Suddenly the movie seemed a bit superfluous. But he'd already bought tickets; the man was a dream. No lining up for me.

"You look lovely. Hope you don't mind, but I got the tickets already. Is this okay with you?" He flashed me the name on the tickets. Not only bought them already but bought tickets to the latest girly flick.

Main course *and* dessert.

"That's great. I've heard fantastic things about that movie." There, how was that for scintillating conversation? Was I a riot or what?

Well, the movie was okay, though nothing to write home about. Brad agreed it was pretty formulaic. And I agreed to going for a drink after the movie. I was moving along my dating steps faster now.

I was almost humming with anticipation when we had finished our drinks and Brad had started the 'got to make a move home' sort of talk. I was in my own little zone. If it was possible, I think he'd have *smelt* my intentions. I may have dribbled down his shirt at one stage. He was just too delightful.

He led me out of the pub and walked me to my car.

"I had a lovely evening." Brad lowered his gaze to my lips.

I held my breath. Had I buffed them with the old toothbrush and Vaseline before I left home? I couldn't exactly lick my lips while his gaze was fixed on them just to make sure.

Come on, come on, I panted, in my head. I couldn't hold my

breath forever.

And then he did. He lowered his face slowly to mine and brushed my lips frustratingly gently with his own. Luckily, for the sake of my blood pressure, he didn't pull away from this, but dipped closer for a nibble. I sighed out in relief.

His lips were warm and soft, but firm. No sloppy kissing from this creature of heaven. I leaned into his firm bulk and gripped his jacket. Mainly, I would have myself believe, to keep my balance, but also, if I was honest, to make sure he didn't escape.

It was delicious and I shut my mind to everything. He was tall and lean and so damn strong. He took hold of my upper arms and braced me against him, deepening the kiss until my legs threatened to cave in. Then he moved me back a fraction and smiled down into my eyes. I wasn't capable of focusing on him. It was all a warm and fuzzy blur.

"Thanks for the evening, Fiona. I have to go now, but I'll call you tomorrow, okay?"

That certainly jolted me back to reality.

Huh? What happened to being swept off my feet for a mad passionate night of unbridled sex? Somehow someone had messed with my script. My confusion was all too apparent, because Brad gave a little chuckle (Christ, how humiliating).

"This'll all keep, Fi." He leaned down and kissed me once more, then propelled me to my car. "We'll make plans for Friday, how does that sound?"

A long time away, was how that sounded. But I couldn't say that now, could I? I mean, without sounding like a temperamental brat. So way before the witching hour, I was driving home with enough pent up sexual heat to immolate the car.

Fine, so he had helped me stick to the whole 'no sex before at least the third date' rule. But they were my rules! I was free to change them at any time and I had planned on this being one of those times. Who was this man to go about turning things on their head?

There was a part of me, of course, that was amazed and delighted to have found someone who was a gentleman and tucked me off before midnight. How sweet, that part of me was crowing.

Shut up, the majority of me told it. I mean to say – who was in control here? A bleeding heart romantic: or me?

I parked my car in the basement and took the stairs two at a time until I came out into the courtyard. Of course, not been a fit being,

I had to take a rest there and do some deep breathing to help the dear old body cope with the explosion of energy released. Standing slightly bent over, hands resting on knees, I cast an eagle eye around the apartments to check out who was home and who I could possibly bug. It was way early for me and I couldn't imagine settling in for the evening at a mere 11:30pm.

However, while my apartmates were happy to party hard every Thursday – Sunday, some nights of the week they usually went to bed at a reasonable hour, or were otherwise occupied.

Take the dim light shining under the blinds of Shaun and Fernando's place. They always had 'date' night on Tuesday. Their place was off limits on date night. They cooked for each other, drank wine and discussed anything that was on their mind.

Good on them.

There was light in the window at good old number 9. Yesterday furniture had started to be moved in. Jonelle had the keys in a happy arrangement with Simon and was moving in as her lawyers and their lawyers did their 'thing'. That was what I liked about how civilized we all were.

I hadn't seen much of her, even though things had been arriving pretty solidly for two days. It was pretty cool, just to sit by the pool and watch. I had idly wondered which art pieces had been her creations.

Now, I stood up and hesitated. Should I go bother her? But I was too wired to sit at home, and no one else looked interrupt-able, and she was the newest and most interesting. My nose for news and horrid curiosity landed me on her doorstep, knocking quietly.

The door swung open, a lot quieter than when Lorraine and Simon lived there and I wondered idly if she used WD40? I jerked my eyes from looking at the hinges and up into Jonelle's face.

She had her hair out of the habitual bun, but tied up into a pony tail. Even wearing sloppy painting clothes, Jonelle was headily attractive and my inner bitch snarled.

Her hair, now I could fully see it, was a shade of darkest black, almost blue, something I had always assumed only people in storybooks could get. It was thick and straight and had a healthy sheen which made it look like inky water pouring over her shoulder. Did I mention the inner bitch? I nodded at the paint roller in her hand.

"Midnight message painting over?"

She grinned. "You'd never know anyone wrote a thing. How

about you? Can't sleep?"

She moved away from the door, beckoning me in with a jerk of her head. I followed her into the defiled bedroom. The far wall, once home to red paint and warning messages, now glowed warmly in gold. Somehow, with deep walnut furniture and amazing art, the gold made everything look priceless. I admired her taste. It was rich, elegant and tasteful.

I wandered into the room, picking up things and putting them back. Having been trained by my house proud mother, I made sure they went back exactly as I had found them.

"Nah. I can't sleep before midnight anyway. But as it was, had a date and just got back." I turned over a voodoo-looking mask, checking for the made in Taiwan sticker and found nothing. Jonelle came over and took it out of my hands.

"Comes from Africa and costs $15 000US. It was very hard to find." She smiled at my gaping face. "I'll be hanging it once I've finished the wall. How was your date?" She swung back to her painting, but not before I caught a glimpse of a small frown. Had my careless handling of priceless art offended? I tucked my hands into my pants.

"It was fine, great in actual fact. Only thing is, he kissed me good night and sent me home. Imagine that. I was all ready to break a rule and take him home but instead he just says lovely evening let's do it again Friday! What is with that?" I stood irresolute. Could I actually sit on any of this stuff or did I have to hop from foot to foot like a naughty school girl?

Jonelle dipped her roller into the paint tray and noticed my dilemma. She indicated the bright cushions scattered around the floor. "Take a cushion. The sofa is just for show. It was a gift from my mother. I think it'd collapse if anyone sat on it, but the cushions are for sitting on. They're actually very comfortable." She went back to her wall. "So you wanted to break your rules with this boy?"

I snuggled down on a massive cushion, nearly a metre across, and yawned. "Yeah, I thought it would be a fun idea. It's been something like, I dunno, months since I last had great let's talk about it type sex. I'm dying here and I was all prepared to let him off the next date and get down to it. Instead he tucks me into my car and toddles off. Is he even human?" I played with the fringy bit on the pillow case, squishing my nose up in disgust.

"There. It's done." Jonelle stepped back from her wall and

displayed the finished product. Then she turned to me, roller safely in a water bucket.

"From everything I know about the dating game, it looks like you actually caught yourself a nice boy. Isn't that what girls all over the world are looking for?" She came and curled up next to me on another cushion.

I half lay back and she pushed another one behind my back against the wall. Ah, the comfort of it all.

"Well technically, I suppose. But it was still a bit of a shock. And I am so awake, I couldn't imagine going to bed, as I had planned to not be, if you see what I mean. So, what else you have planned for this evening?"

She laughed and stretched. It was like watching one of the big cats arching itself in the sunshine, minus the sunshine of course.

"There are a few boxes left I wanted to get unpacked." She rose and held her hand down to pull me up.

Jonelle was far stronger than I expected and when she gave my hand a tug, I found myself lurching to my feet mere centimetres from her. With our height difference I kind of found myself tucked in under her chin.

I tilted my head back and caught her glance. There was a second's pause. Like a swift intake of breath, then I moved back a fraction.

Was I getting caught up in her magnetism? I certainly was, which felt a bit freaky. Up close she smelled of spice and woody things. And her strength was undeniable. With the tailored clothing she generally wore, or this bulky painting outfit, it was hard to tell but underneath, Jonelle was packing some serious muscle.

With the light behind her and standing so close, I was suddenly unnerved. Her face was in shadow and her eyes were hooded. She didn't bend her head, more just looked down at me, standing there so perfectly straight and still.

Was I intimidated? Damn Skippy.

It was a long time since someone had stood over me and made me realise that five foot two is really short. And there was almost something in the room, like an undercurrent of tension and a hint of malevolence.

And then, it was gone. She moved away from me and smiled, and I gave myself a little shake. Sometimes my imagination was way too strong.

"Come through to the kitchen. I'll make us some hot chocolate if that's okay and you can help me put kitchen things in drawers."

Just my luck, the interesting rooms had all being unpacked and I was left with the kitchen. But there was something uniquely feminine in the poking of noses in someone else's kitchen, so I wasn't going to complain. The alternative was going across the way to my place and watching crap TV for an hour or two until I could settle for bed. These late nights were going to kill me one day, I suspected.

In companionable silence we made chocolate and settled some utensils into their new home. Even here, in the kitchen, there was artwork. The walls were a lovely sunflower colour and Jonelle had hung a vibrant painting of electric blues, yellows and greens on one wall. It was a painting of a bunch of flowers in layered oils and really leaped out at you. I loved it.

"I think this is wonderful. Who is the artist?" I ran a light finger over the paint, it was so real looking.

Jonelle glanced over. "That is mine. Paint and I are good friends on some days. Glad you like it."

I stared. I'd say paint and her were good friends. "Do you sell this stuff? Because if you do, put me on the waiting list!"

"I don't sell, I make. And then when I find a piece that fits with a person, I give." She grinned at me. "You're more a scene person. Don't worry, if I find the time, I'll paint you a scene in the same style." She banged close a cupboard. "There. Last thing in and I think it's time for a relax, don't you? You are more than welcome to join me?" She raised her eyebrow at me.

Nothing was removing me I nearly told her. She was the first thing to spike my curiosity in a while and I wanted to find out what it was that she did to 'relax'. We moved into the lounge. It was dimly lit with down lights and a dragon lamp in the corner. There was a plasma screen TV on one wall, a long low Japanese style dark wood table surrounded by more cushions and a low, what looked like green velvet, lounge against another wall.

Jonelle indicated I was to make myself comfortable and out of a dark wood cabinet, discreetly in the corner, she drew a burner and some incense sticks. Lighting the incense, and a whole stack of candles placed throughout the room, she switched on the stereo hidden in the entertainment unit. Soft pan pipes drifted through surround sound.

I sank into the pile of cushions and closed my eyes. I didn't know what she did to require such deep relaxation, and I didn't care. Right then all that mattered was the fact that my body felt weightless and I was drifting on a cloud of sweet smelly stuff.

There was a rustle and Jonelle joined me on the cushions. Peace. May be there is more to doing nothing than I had suspected.

I nodded off and the next thing I knew, there were birds calling and a sliver of sunlight had found its way through her blinds and straight onto my face. I blinked in this bright light and flicked a glance at my watch with a bleary eye.

"Crap! It's 7:30!" I sat bolt upright.

There was something awfully wrong with my world. This is twice in one week I had opened my eyes before midday.

I looked around me, wondering where the hell I was. There was the faint smell of lavender and I couldn't place it. I never burned lavender. Mind you, after the mind numbing sleep I just had, perhaps I would start to.

Just then Jonelle came into the room, a silk robe belted around her waist and a steaming cup of coffee in her hand. Everything fell into place and I realised I had fallen asleep on the floor, half on a cushion and half off. A soft woollen blanket was resting over my legs. My mouth felt dry and I glanced down to make sure I hadn't drooled all over her lovely pillows. Phew.

Jonelle placed the mug on a coaster on the table. "I thought you could do with some of this. I figured you'd be up soon."

"Are you mad? This counts as distinctly abnormal behaviour, being awake at this hour. Ahhh, thanks for the coffee. It's real!" I sipped and blinked. This was not instant stuff. "Am I keeping you from anything?" There was that curiosity killed the cat thingy.

Cat. Oh boy. Smudge! I nearly spilled my coffee. "I have to get home!"

Jonelle stared at me. It must have been comedy hour since she met me. "Are you okay? I don't have anything on at the moment, though I need to get to the gym at some stage. What's up?"

"My kitten. I haven't been home to feed him and I don't think he likes the kibble I bought, so he is probably starving. Oh, why did he have to land on my window ledge? I'll end up killing the poor bastard." I bolted another mouthful or two of coffee, burning my tongue and stood up, trying to fold the blanket on the crease lines.

Jonelle waved my attempts aside. "Go. Feed the kitten. I am sure

I'll catch up with you later." She looked away. "We'll have to have lunch some day."

My little heart gave a tiny lurch. What? Little Miss 'I don't socialise' was asking me out for a lunch date? Well, okay. I would counter offer.

"Sure, but we need to do the welcome to the Grangelands. I'll try and get the crew together for a BBQ this weekend. How does that sound?"

I didn't imagine it. I swear I didn't. But I believe she gave a delicate little shudder. Perhaps she really was averse to mixing.

"Sounds good. Let me know when you have a time booked in."

And that was it. I was outside, on another bloody crisp spring morning, letting myself back into my apartment, to be greeted by the yowl and pounce of Smudge.

Chapter Four

Inow had Wednesday through to the weekend to fill up and I was more than capable of doing so, thank you very much. Though not if I kept adding more hours to my days.

I filled Smudge's bowl with organic milk, his favourite, and checked off my calendar. I had an appointment at the Vets for him later that day. The promised trip to the supermarket had seen me return with a lot of Smudge-y things and realising I was making him a permanent member of my family, I had made the Vet trip a priority.

Smudge was now the proud owner of a kibble bowl, a milk bowl, a water bowl, collar, lead, bell, blanket and a million little toys which rolled, rattled and squeaked. He was far too energetic and still hadn't learned how to use his litter box properly, which made for interesting morning deposits in strange places. He had elected to sleep with me and nothing I did could persuade him otherwise. This also made me aware he could have worms, or other nasty bugs, and I was looking forward to getting him checked out at the Vets.

It was also bill day, so I had to go through the mail, check what had accumulated and pay them. Plus, I would check out my investments and in general make sure my funds were looking healthy and fat. I tried to force myself to do this every Wednesday, otherwise they might cut off my phone.

I curled up on the lounge and flipped through mail while booting up my laptop. I'd have to go through countless emails, as well. Hopefully Shelley would have sent me one from Greece. She was a dear pal who was set to inherit daddy's millions so naturally spent her life on perpetual holiday, being an only child. She'd been away now for a whole year and I was living vicariously through her adventures.

I was too lazy to go join her. I'd seen a big portion of Australia when I was the back packing pauper. Then I went mad when I first inherited and shipped myself around the world at a dizzying pace to see vast chunks of it. I no longer wanted to traipse around alone and the actual getting from A to B part of it had worn thin. I didn't mind holidaying in a Tuscan chalet. I just loathed sitting in airports and on planes.

Curled up as I was in the front room with the blinds wide open, I could see the whole courtyard. With Smudge purring on the seat beside me, I realised I was really lucky. Julie, who only worked part time, would be home soon and that would mean our regular Wednesday lunch together.

Julie lived in No.5. She worked as a doctor's receptionist and loved it. She came into her money by the freakiest method. Every one of us had money one way or another. Some worked hard, like lawyer Donald and accountant Rob, others inherited it and still others won it.

Julie won lotto. I still pinched myself over that. I mean, who really won lotto?

Anyway, emails and cheques for bills all done, I stretched. "Well Smudge my lad, at three you are off to the Vets and right now I am going to crack open a bottle of white wine for Julie and myself. Want some more milk?"

As soon as I moved, he was up, pouncing and pawing, demanding attention. A few minutes later while I was in the laundry feeding Smudge, the front door opened and Julie hello'd me.

"Anyone home? Where are you, girl?" We loved to be informal.

"Feeding the cat. There's wine open in the fridge and pasta from the Deli ready in bowls."

"You'll not believe it. There was this patient today, I tell you, the biggest hypochondriac I have ever met!" Julie trailed into the laundry with two wine glasses. "She was determined she had some terrible disease. 'Wasting, I'm just wasting away Doctor! You have to save me.'" Julie leaned her slight frame against the door and laid her hand across her brow in high dramatic fashion.

"I can't possibly go another day without some form of medication. You'll know what is best to do for me Doctor, I know you will." She snapped out of it. "You know what he gave her? Sugar pills. And she was all beaming and telling him he was the best thing and how much she appreciated the care he takes of her. Silly old bat. Not a thing wrong with her – she'll out live us all."

I took my glass and she reached down to pick up Smudge. With him purring in her arms, milk forgotten in the pursuit of a greater pleasure, we strolled back out to the dining room. Julie pushed aside papers and general crap on my coffee table once she dumped Smudge on the floor. I brought the bowls of pesto pasta in and we were set. I had barely sat down when Julie asked "What do you think of the new apartmate?"

"Well, she seems nice enough," I said cautiously. Nice was so open for interpretation after all. "I was thinking of having a BBQ on Saturday for a kind of welcome to living at the Grangelands-type thing. And maybe if any of the others wanted, invite Simon and Lorraine. You know - a farewell for them. It *is* just last weekend since they left, after all."

Was it only that long? Only a few of days and how much difference they could make.

Julie was nodding enthusiastically. "That's a great idea." She waved her fork around. "We should zap together a plan and invite everyone this afternoon. Oh. Do you know if anyone has their new contact details?"

I frowned. "I suspect if all else fails, then Jonelle will be the place to go. She would be in contact with them concerning the unit, wouldn't you think? Anyway, that can wait. I'd say, BBQ starting 11:30 with nibbles and drinks with the boys doing their meat thing, *with plenty of salads for Heather.*"

Laughing we finished the sentence together. Heather was our only vegetarian, an abnormality we had tried in vain to cure her of.

I scrounged round for a pen and paper to make a list. Julie rolled her eyes. "Fi, how hard can it be? We all know our roles by now. Who brings what and stuff. Just shove a note under everyone's doors and they'll fall into line."

I held my pen defensively. "Well, I'll still need it to write the notes, so there." I glanced at my watch. "Crap! I have to get Smudge to the Vet. Here." I delegated. Well, perhaps I wasn't as compulsive about lists as I thought I was. "You write and shove, so to speak. Let yourself out. I've got to catch that cat."

Why is it whenever you need to hurry, animals seem to know it and make life hell? Smudge thought it was a game and it was a long ten minutes later before I emerged from the bedroom, hot and sweaty, triumphantly clutching my rascal kitten.

The trip to the Vet meant worming, a flea treatment, some shots and absolute knowledge that Smudge was a boy. The Vet thought he was about ten weeks old and I was to bring him back soon for further shots and then for the chop.

"Sorry, my lad," I told him, snuggling my newly sanitary kitty under my chin. "But you are going to be half the man you used to be as soon as you are old enough. No toms wondering around my place."

A little too close for comfort that. There were no toms, human or otherwise. Oh well, it wasn't Friday yet. If Brad did end up calling like he said, I'd invite him to the BBQ Saturday and see what the Apartmates thought of him, which was always a good measuring stick. Seeing as half the women were truly beautiful, I'd found it a great litmus test. If their eyes and hands strayed, they weren't the man for me.

I struggled through Thursday to arrive breathlessly on Friday, hoping Brad wouldn't let me down.

What amazed me was the new - getting up before 8am - Fiona had stuck around. I was up playing with Smudge when the phone rang. I glanced at my watch. It was a hair's whisker off eight. I was half expecting it to be my mother. I hadn't heard from the family since Sunday lunch. But it was Friday and I knew silence couldn't last forever.

"Hello?" I was a bit wary. After all, no one I knew, or wanted to know, would call me at this hour.

"Wow that was warm and welcoming." Brad's voice came dancing down the line.

My feet hit the floor, sliding off the couch. Bugger! Today yes; but not at this hour. I hadn't managed to drown myself in caffeine yet and felt remarkably dull witted.

"Um, hi. Sorry was expecting someone else - along the lines of my mother," I added hastily in case he thought I had another man tucked up my sleeve. That may have been flattering, but hardly the way to embark on a passionate affair.

"Well, thank heavens I'm not your mother. What are your plans for the weekend?" He lowered his voice in a very sexy manner and I wondered if it was for effect, or if he was in the office and didn't want people to hear him.

"Funny you should mention the weekend. We're having a farewell, welcome BBQ tomorrow and I'd like you to come." Don't mind if you do, an evil little voice in my mind chortled.

"Farewell and welcome, hey? How could I refuse? What do I bring and when I do arrive?" I liked his economy of speech. I was verbose enough for both of us.

"Just bring something to drink, and we start at 11:30. Some of us sold their place and the newbie has moved in already so it's a bit of both, you see? Anyway, I was hoping to see you again." I was in no mood to be subtle. "I enjoyed Tuesday's get together a lot. A repeat performance would be nice." How could I politely say I wanted to jump his bones?

"Mmm. Me too. If I drink too much at your BBQ, I won't be able to drive home," he murmured.

Be still my beating heart, was all I could think. The man was going to kill me. Lust oozed down the phone lines and my toes did their obligatory curling thingy.

I'm addicted to beginnings. The bit when everything is hidden behind oblique words and messages, and the thought of what could happen makes my stomach flip over. Somehow it was always better than the getting to the 'done' part and realising it was as big a flop as the last guy. The silence extended and I thought – oops my turn to say something.

"That would just be too bad, wouldn't it just? Good thing I have a spare room…" I smiled around my words so he could understand from this message there was no way he would ever get to see the inside of any spare room.

He laughed, but ever so gently and warmly and wickedly. I imagined my face, the grin a mile wide. The drought was over. Tomorrow I was getting some, come hell or high water.

"See you then." And he was gone. Just like that.

Smudge came over and pounced on me and I tickled him. The glowy feeling had to sustain me through the day, which it managed to do quite nicely, thank you very much! It also helped me prepare for the mad party we had planned at the local pub in Kingston. Some of my non-apartmate friends were rocking up to fill me in on how their week had panned out and to help me flirt with the male species. I would be on my best behaviour now that I was going to see Brad again.

After grabbing barely adequate food-age, I toddled off to The

Batch and Haddock. The original owners were straight out from England and feeling homesick for some of the weird names they have over there. As a local pub it was damn fine. It often had live music and sometimes a DJ. I loved loud music and alcohol.

Stephanie and Grillia were already there. No one knew where Grillia got her name from. She was an orphan and we don't know what her heritage was, but they were a mixed bag, if her strange but compelling looks are anything to go by.

"Fiona! Over here. Shove off!" This last was aimed at an already intoxicated man who had mistaken Grillia for a girl who needed company.

Grillia loved them and left them with such amazing regularity I wondered where she got the energy and why hadn't the entire known male populace of Canberra woken up and run away?

"Fi!" She flung her arms around me with abandon. Perhaps it was her zest for life and full on love of people which had the men drooling.

I crushed her back and wiggled onto the stool she had managed to score for me. Steph was far more laid back and merely nodded. She was generally pretty sombre and tonight she appeared more so.

"Hi Steph. What's the g-o?" I had to ask. She'd be insulted if I didn't.

Her overly made up, cat eyes winked up at me. "I'm doomed to be alone and an old spinster like you. Josh dumped me. He said I was too unhealthy and morose. I ask you. That's my trademark."

For half a second I saw a flicker of humour in those eyes, then they were lowered to her drink, which was nearly empty.

I glanced at Grillia, who shrugged. They must have covered this already. I felt behind the times.

"I'll get us all another, shall I?" Well, technically it would be my first, but who was counting? "And pretend I didn't hear that little jab about me being an old spinster. I happen to have news on that front myself." And I flounced off with a smirk at their astonished faces.

I struggled up to the bar, which was already packed even though it was only seven thirty. The Batch and Haddock was very popular, which was a good thing. There was a bad element, as my mother would call them, which hung out at the Batch on occasion and being there on a slow night brought you to their attention.

Tall groups of leather clad muscle men, drinking their way into an early grave. Though the grave they were headed for could be bought with something other than alcohol, I feared. I kept well clear of them and if I happened to meet the narrowed gaze of one, I ducked my head and scuttled off. They were very intimidating.

I managed to get back to our table and dumped the three bourbons down. Doubles: it was a doubles kind of night. Steph was in no mood to be sober. Well, that wouldn't trouble us for long.

"So, when, why, and how?" The usual interrogation when someone was dumped.

I got way too much information about how dull their sex life was, how monotonous he was and that last night he had come over only to tell her she needed to get a life and not to suck his dry. Grillia gave me rolled eyes. Steph was actually a very giving person. Just not to too many people. Obviously Josh hadn't been one of the receivers.

"He had the nerve to say I needed Prozac!"

I struggled with this. He was lucky not to have received a punch to his groin for that comment.

The problem was Steph never had direction. She dropped out of Uni three times. They only kept taking her back because her parents paid up front. What a waste. She had wandered through her twenty five years with no goal. Mummy and Daddy had to bail her out of many a trouble spot. Grillia and I tried to help her. She wasn't stupid and every now again, I caught her eyes and knew the person inside was laughing at us.

'You need Speed, not Prozac, something to give you a jolt. But we don't have any, so down the hatch!" So we saluted each other and sank half our drinks in one hit.

After that, it was business as usual. Grillia kept her eye out for potential one night stands and I pretended to help her out, while day dreaming about Brad. Steph drank herself to a standstill. And that was quite a lot.

I tried to lighten the mood and told them about Brad's charming not tonight dear last Tuesday, and the trip to visit the folks. But Steph didn't want to be jollied.

At 1:30am Grillia took pity on her and piled the both of them into a taxi. Rare that Grillia was going home alone. But they lived close to each other, so it made sense to share the taxi fare. I, on the other hand, could walk home. Just a few blocks, and my warm and snugly bed awaited me. Getting there three quarters tanked was going to be interesting.

I wandered along in a haze of fumes and good will to all mankind. I hadn't gone too far when I heard footsteps behind me.

Now, even in my befogged state, I knew this was not necessarily a good thing. It was very late, dark and reasonably cold. No one sensible would be out. I hastened my 'not quite steady' pace, wobbling erratically in my silly heels. I always cursed them when I was drunk, but adored them when I was sober. I promised I'd never wear another pair of shoes higher than a blade of grass, then the alcohol would wear off and I knew that someone my height couldn't be fussy.

There was a very masculine cough behind me and I turned my head a little to try and see who was there, without looking like I was looking, if you see what I mean. I saw two shadows, large and dark. I required no second invitation to panic at the best of times and my heart rate took a giant surge. I was being followed. I couldn't run in these pathetic shoes and under the amount of influence I was under. That made sense to me.

So I stopped. I turned and I waited. Better to meet my doom head on. I sometimes wonder where I get these ideas from.

"Hi," I said stupidly, blinking owlishly at my two stalker people. They coalesced out of the darkness into two of the leather clad muscle men.

This was getting worse and worse.

Running now seemed a grand option, if I could possibly have taken it. The whole 'too late now' thing was singing in my mind, making it difficult to concentrate on the two men.

"Hi yourself, sweetheart. Saw you stagger out. Thought you may need some help. Going our way?" The larger (if that was possible) of the two leaned a little closer, leering at me and pouring beer fumes in my face. Having only touched bourbon all night, the beer was like a slap.

"Um, positively sure I'll be okay on my own, thanks guys." Hadn't I always told the girls not to engage these guys in conversation?

"Positively sure you won't be, love. Let's have a nice little walk together, shall we?" I found my arm taken in a gentle but firm grip. I gave it a test jerk but the grip tightened a little, and the man on the other end of it just gave me a small contemptuous smirk. Like I was a little flea he could swipe at any minute.

The other came up on my left and I was suddenly not quite sober, but certainly not as drunk as I had been. My heart was pounding in my ears and I felt weak at the knees. I was a good foot shorter than these boys and who was I kidding? Wherever they were going, I was going too.

Chapter Five

Hi fellas. This a private party or can anyone join in?"
I heard the words from the other side of a frozen and terrified fog. My feet were numb and my gentlemen friends were half carrying me. I forced open eyes that had sealed themselves shut in an effort to pretend I wasn't there. Standing only a few metres away was a vision.

Jonelle leaned with elegant grace against a light pole (the globe was on its way out, but I knew it was her). She was wearing a long black cape, or coat, I really wasn't sober enough to tell, and her hair was in its habitual bun. I had never been so glad to see someone in my whole life. It didn't matter she was 'just' a woman; she oozed capability and I sagged with relief.

My companions obviously felt a bit differently about the situation. The one on the left, for simplicities sake let's say Dumbass One, grinned. "Well, look at that. A party built for two. Sure, you can join Doll-face. Deeelighted."

I felt like saying, 'I don't think that's what she had in mind', but my mouth wasn't connected to my brain yet and so I stared dumbly.

Dumbass Two let my arm go and moved towards Jonelle. I can't say I was a reliable witness. I was giddy with relief and a heavy dose of adrenalin from the previous fear. I was also drunk; I was not too ashamed to re-iterate that point. But Jonelle sort of swayed away from her pole, and moving with her cat speed, Dumbass Two was suddenly on the ground giving a massive bellow, clutching his shoulder and his jewels in alternating agonies.

Dumbass One dropped me and I slid softly to the ground not that far from Dumbass Two. One dived at Jonelle, but she was too quick. A slip and a weave and he was diving at thin air. As he passed her on the way down, Jonelle delivered a slicing kick which knocked him flat. From their prone positions they looked up at her. Jonelle kindly flicked on the torch she brought out of her pocket and shone it on her face (strange, I thought to myself, I would have shone the light at them).

There was silence. Then Dumbass Two or was it One, groaned. "Bugger, it's you. Hasn't someone killed you yet?"

"Better men have tried and failed." She grinned. "Now run off, little boys, and go play in some traffic." Her almost affectionate tone changed and I could feel the icicles dripping from the words. "But remember, she's with me and if any one of you breaks so much as her nail, we'll find out who the better man really is. Understanding me?"

They rose up and while she didn't stand as tall as them, she looked far more deadly. I sat in the dirt and watched the fake bravado in their stance and her relaxed loose limbed 'I can kick your butt anytime' bearing and knew where I'd place my money.

Dumbass One flicked her a half salute and they melted into the shadows. I was left alone with my new friend. She reached down and hauled my sorry carcass back onto its legs. I felt a little zap from her hand. Boy she sure packed a wallop. I wasn't too steady on my feet, but she stepped back and allowed me to find my own balance. Perhaps that was for the best.

"So, any particular reason you're wandering around alone in the dark with those two?"

I glanced at her. It was hard to make out an actual facial expression, and impossible to judge the tone of voice. Was she condemning me for being stupid? Well, I would too when I woke up in the morning. Right then all I wanted to do was to get home and find my pillow. Oh, and have some sympathy about my narrow escape.

"It's not as though they are my usual Friday night special, you know." I think there was a chance I sounded a bit snippy.

In fact, I must have, because her teeth flashed in the dark in a grin. "Yeah, I wouldn't have thought so. The Batch boys are not the sort of attention you should be attracting."

"How do they know you so well? And how did you *do* that? I wanna learn."

At that she laughed.

"Hmm. It's kind of years of practice, my dear, but as to the other question? I use to come down from Sydney a lot. One of the reasons

I moved. Needed to be closer to some business interests I have down here for a while. I met quite a lot of people at the Batch and Haddock. It's a good thing I was on my way there tonight."

"Bit late for a drink isn't it?" I staggered along beside her, hating the fact that she was clipping her long legged gait to match my all over the place totter.

I still sounded childishly snippy.

"Finished off some business later than expected and thought I would pay a visit to what is now my local." She gave me a look. "Kind of good timing, really."

I huffed to myself. At least I thought it was to myself but from the little sniggers she was giving I guessed it wasn't.

I was tired and thoroughly grumpy when we got back to the Grangelands. I was no closer to figuring out how an arts dealer came to do business in The Batch and Haddock and the hangover was starting early. All the adrenalin had kick-started the process. It sucked.

"You right?" She took my key and got us through the gate and into my place.

I felt distinctly not all right and curled up on the couch. Jonelle stood at the doorway, clearly uncomfortable with sticking around. But I wasn't going to let her off. Somehow in my muddled state she should be stuck entertaining me.

"Sit." I told her and was surprised when, with a raised eyebrow and amused twinkle, she did so. She moved my feet along a bit and sat down on the couch where Smudge made his sleepy way into her lap.

"Tell me a story about yourself. I feel like I've known you forever and yet I don't know you at all. Are you coming to the BBQ tomorrow?" I realised I hadn't actually ever asked her and she was kind of the guest of honour.

She leaned back and half closed her eyes. "Yes I'll be there. It's nice to be surrounded by friendly people for once." That sounded kind of blunt and she must have noticed, because she continued quickly. "I have been too busy lately to be very social."

"That must get lonely," I mumbled.

I got a flash from those eyes and her lips twitched. "On the small occasions I actually get time to think about it." Her response must have surprised even herself, as those lips then pressed firmly together as though warding off any other outbursts.

I rolled over so I was on my back where I could see her without twisting my eyes out of their sockets. I snatched a pillow to rest on, pulling my knees up. "So, why does an art dealer hang out at The Batch and Haddock, and know people like the two Dumbasses?"

"The Dumbasses? That's a great name for them." She laughed. "Oh, you'd be amazed with how many artistic types hang out in the strangest places. And let's just say I have the strangest of contacts. People like your two try not to bother people like me. It's fun really." She swung sideways so she could watch my face.

"What are you doing with your life, Fiona? You're not a stupid little rich girl. Why are you playing at being one?"

If she'd wanted shock value, she was pretty on the mark. While the Apartmates are blunt, none of them had ever questioned what I was up to before. It was like if one of us had to think too deeply about the path they were on, we'd all have to. And that might lead to things like deep and meaningful plans for the future.

Jonelle kept her steady gaze locked on my eyes and I couldn't wiggle out of answering. It wasn't fair when people cornered you after you'd had too many.

"I don't know. Sometimes I think I should be doing more and my life has a lack of meaning. Then I sit down until that feeling goes away." I tried for a smile and only got a flicker back. Damn tough audience. She was onto me.

"You sound like my mother." I didn't think insults would work but I had to give them a try. All I got was that infernal raised eyebrow. "I don't know, I tell you! I hate to study, I don't want to be a journalist, which is all I'm qualified to be. I read and play and watch telly. Now I have a cat. The whole 9-5 thing would piss me off no end. What about you?"

I had the sneaking suspicion that Jonelle wasn't the sharing type. And I wasn't far out.

"I don't mind being disciplined. Nothing worthwhile comes to those who play all the time. And I don't mean money. It's soothing to have things in place to do each day, otherwise you'll wake one day and realise your life is over."

What a pleasant thought. Suddenly it was all too much and I wanted to sleep. Why had I invited her in again?

She watched my thoughts scrawl their way across my face. It was bloody unfair the way people did that. I needed poker-face lessons or something.

"What interests you? What could your hobbies be? Are you reliable? Can you work a computer?" She fired off a series of questions. My mind was slowly shutting down for the night, but I got the feeling she wouldn't let go until I answered.

"I like animals. I wish I could knit or make stuff with my hands. And yes I do know my way around a computer. There. Done now? I need to sleep." I pouted.

She rose with tireless ease and nodded. "I'll talk to you tomorrow. We should discuss a job you could do for me." Then she walked out. Just like that.

I couldn't process everything nor could I be bothered to move. Luckily for me, the heater remote was on the floor nearby and I dragged it closer. When the right heat was pumping through the vents, I slipped into mixed dreams of large men and fighting cats.

I struggled awake with sun on my face. Heavens, at this rate, I'd become one of those early morning risers who were horribly chipper at some ungodly hour like now. I used to loathe those types of people. Always singing and dancing and making breakfast. I didn't remember what breakfast *was*.

I was just about to roll over and make the sun disappear with the thick curtains I had installed for just this purpose when I remembered: Brad! Today.

Not exactly coherent thoughts, but it was early. I magically transformed into an awake person, leaping off the couch and dashing – get that – dashing into the ensuite. Time was a-wasting and I needed to bath, wax any excess fur off, moisturise and all those other things women did when they knew someone other than themselves would be in their bed that night. Had it really being that long? I tried never to think back to the dreaded time I spent with Jason, or was it Nathan or Paul who had been last?

I had a track record of bringing home non-keepers. Hence the instigation of my dating rules, which wasn't helping right now because there was no one to enforce them and look where I was. Right back at the beginning: two dates in and already about to leap into bed with the fellow.

There was coffee to make, wax to heat and then a luxurious soak in the tub for a while, a further cup of coffee keeping me company, as was an intrigued kitty. Though I didn't think I should let him get into the habit of being in the bathroom with me. He was young and impressionable.

At eleven o'clock I was just about ready. The only thing that remained was the actual getting into clothes. I chose flowing cream pants and a bulky chocolate pullover which I had been told brought out the depth of colour in my eyes. With hints of makeup, trying to emulate the tasteful natural look of Jonelle, I was ready. Just as well because I could hear the masses getting everything set up.

Sure enough, when I emerged, the long collapsible table was out and a cloth of some description had been thrown at it. Literally. No one had straightened it yet. The BBQ was out and fired up. Every Apartmate was lugging their various choices of food out.

We all had whatever we were best at. Julie was desserts. No one could whip up something sweet like that girl. Warwick and Cheryl always brought lamb. Wazza's dad owned a sheep station out somewhere, and they brought a lamb back once in a while. Carmen and Kylie from No.7 loved chicken and marinated two or so chooks' worth of pieces for everyone.

Rob cooked and his flatmate John did drinks. Too many nights behind a bar and he was too good to pass up. Fernando and Shawn usually made the table up – generally with lovely things, and incense and flowers. I didn't see them in evidence.

Todd, from No.3, was the steak man and Heather of course, brought salad. Amy (when she was around), Donald and I, known for our inability to cook, marinade or basically get anything done that was connected to these things, were the pre-eating nibbles. I, of course, had gone to the Deli. A beautiful platter of antipasto and assortments had been in my fridge since yesterday, and I was amazed it had survived so long.

Donald had platters of biscuits and cheeses and dips. But we had nowhere to put them. Where were those boys?

"Dunno," said John, when asked. "They came out with the cloth at one stage then disappeared again. Seeing as you never know when they'll be at it, I didn't want to find out."

I grinned. The rest of the boys were very, *very* heterosexual. The idea of what went on with Shawn and Fernando made them a shade of green, no matter how close they were.

I trotted across to No. 4. With one loud thump, I let myself in. I found them arguing over table dressings. Whether they had used the silver and gold last time and it was the red and green time, or should they save the red and green for Christmas? I rolled my eyes and mediated. Gold and silver won.

We all straightened the cloth and helped them set up, which was accompanied by more bickering as we didn't do it right. The only person we were missing was Amy. But she was at the Academy doing police stuff, so who knew when she'd get back?

Then the front gate bell rang and Lorraine and Simon were there, laughing and chatting, looking remarkably well considering they were broke and not a part of us anymore. Jonelle had obviously been out because she came up from the car park dressed in gym clothes. With a promise to be quick, she disappeared inside for a shower.

"Does it weird you out to see someone else going into your place?" To the point as always, Fernando offered Lorraine champagne and questions.

Lorraine refused, pregnancy and all that, but took a sparkling mineral water off John instead.

"Sort of," she replied, with a small twitter. I could feel a frown settling on my features. I thought I would miss this woman? Not a chance. Just having that twitter back in my space had me wanting to run away.

"The settlement period is not even close to being over, but she was in a hurry to have a place to put her things. And it's not like we needed it! Still, would be interesting to see what she's done with the place," said a bit wistfully, looking over at No.9.

We were all mingling and talking over the last week, mainly pumping Lorraine and Simon for news, when the front bell rang again and my heart gave a little leap. It had to be Brad. And sure enough, it was. My mouth watered.

Once let in, he greeted me with a hug and quick kiss. I felt a little shivery. Then it was on to introductions, and exchanges of pleasantries like what people did for a living (a big thing in Canberra culture) and they all got to size up my new man.

A few minutes later Jonelle emerged from her unit and joined us. Once we were all holding a glass of some sort, Rob held up a hand for silence.

"Let us say best of luck to our departing comrades and we wish them well with the new life and family." We all raised our glasses and drank to Lorraine and Simon. Then Rob once again held the floor.

"And here's to our newest member, Jonelle. May her reign be long and sure! And may we find out all the dirt on her as quickly as possible, and make our lives interesting once more."

There was a general "Hear hear" to all this then we went back to our own conversations.

I didn't want to appear to be crowdy or needy, so I left Brad to sink or swim, and wandered over to the table for more food. I was always hungry after a blinder. I was kind of half hoping and half dreading the next conversation with Jonelle, so I was not the least bit surprised when she arrived at my side.

"Roughing it?" I smirked. "We aren't a bad bunch really. But we're nosey."

Jonelle shot me an oblique look.

"You're all nice people. I feel very welcome, which is the whole point of today, so well done." I deserved that condescending tone, I really did. "I haven't lived in such a friendly block before," she added as a sort of apology.

I loaded my plate up with salad and a few pieces of the lamb. "Yeah, it took me all of a week to figure out how much fun it would be to live here. Mind you, it was a slightly different crowd back then. But I love it now and wouldn't swap the nosey buggers for anything."

I looked over at Brad who was in deep conversation with Donald. I was glad to see him fitting in and generally making himself agreeable.

Jonelle followed my gaze. "How long have you known him?"

"A couple of weeks. Though this is officially only our second date, I think it's going very well. What do you think?" I watched her closely for reaction.

"I can't really say, Fi. I haven't spoken to him yet, though he looks nice enough. Don't let him take advantage of you, is all I can say." Then she changed the subject. "How are you feeling this morning? You had quite a scare last night."

I tried to smother my embarrassment. "I'm fine. I recover well from too much alcohol, and lucky for me you were there. Look." I felt like grabbing the bull by the horns. "Did you mean it when you suggested I come and do some work for you?"

I had to admit it was mainly curiosity which had brought me to this question. She was an enigma and friendly in her own way. Plus, sometimes you just knew when you clicked with someone that they would be a part of your life. I felt I clicked with Jonelle. She was a constant tickle in the back of my mind.

"Sure. There are heaps of things I just don't have the time for. You could take on the role of my personal assistant, if that was okay with you? It would mean some pretty boring tasks until we got to know each other better. But it would get you out of the house and involved with life again."

I tried not to show my hesitation. It wasn't that I didn't want to know her better. I was just a tiny bit afraid that I would come out of it looking a bit stupid. What if she asked me to do things I didn't know how to?

I nodded, filling my mouth with succulent lamb. At least she wasn't rubbing my nose in my condition of the night before. Small mercies, but I was grateful.

We all brought our cordless phones and mobiles out to the table when we had one of these gatherings. It made it easier in a way, but harder in that we had no idea of whose was whose. A phone was ringing in the background, but I didn't pay it any attention. I was engrossed in the fine art of eating and wasn't going to pause for anything.

"Oh, hi, Mrs Page. It's Heather. Yeah, we're all sitting around together and Fi couldn't make it to the phone in time." Heather lied like a pro.

What a time for Mum to choose to break our happy little silence. Jonelle gave me a grin and faded into the crowd, chatting with people and generally making her way over to Brad. Hoping she was going to check him out for me, I dumped my plate and accepted the phone off Heather with an unhappy grimace. She grinned back in sympathy. They had all met my mother.

"Hi Mum. How's it going?"

"Hello, Fiona dear. I hope this isn't a bad time?" You can't tell your mother that 'ever' was a bad time.

"Nah. That's fine, Mum. How's everyone? Gran get down to Melbourne okay for her weekend with the others?" I wanted to keep the peace. I was trying to be a decent daughter, no matter how many of my-not-so-decent buttons she pushed.

"Nah is not a word, young lady. No is English and we are still an English speaking country, regardless of the government."

My mother: the great political thinker. She blamed the government for the influx of non-English speaking people, and she blamed them for the colour of her non-dyed hair (possibly I exaggerate again).

"Okay, Mum. Anyway, to what do I owe this unexpected pleasure?" I heard a snort behind me and knew one of the gang was finding my end of the conversation amusing. Good for them.

"Well," she was hardly mollified, "I was just calling to make sure you are okay. It never enters your head to actually phone your mother once in a while to let us know you are fine. Potty got hit by a car the other day." There was a brief pause and I held my breath. Potty was my favourite member of the family.

"She's okay, but a bit bruised. The man driving claims to not have seen her. I ask you! Not see Potty? Why, she's the size of a pony. I think he was concentrating on other things. Mary said she had seen him driving past on several occasions in the last few days. Though why, I can't tell you. He's a stranger and has no family here. Mind you, of course I didn't ask him what he was doing hanging around our neighbourhood, but I do think it is strange and a bit rude. You know, to hang around and then to drive over poor Potty." Boy she could master the understatement and still talk a million miles an hour.

"I'm sure he's not stalking anyone in the local neighbourhood, Mum. Just so long as Potty will be okay now." I was trying to be soothing. Jonelle was back and giving me a narrow-eyed stare as she actively listened in. "I have to go now. Give me a call and let me know Potty's progress." I hung up. There was only so much I could take after all.

One way or another, everyone knew Potty, so there were general commiserations about her being hit. Jonelle stayed in the background until I was relatively alone, trying to finish off my lunch in a dignified manner while standing next to Brad. It was hard to maintain the aura of mystery when stuffing one's face with lettuce and tomato. Not being the most elegant of eaters, it tended to destroy my credibility once a man saw me woofing down my food. It had been equated with a snout/trough … well, you get the picture.

"Trouble?" Jonelle asked me when my fork was on the way back up.

I dropped it regretfully back onto my plate. "Not really. Some bloke bruised Potty, though I can bet his car didn't come off all that lightly. The lady opposite says she's seen him hanging around all week, sort of checking the neighbourhood out. I think they're worried he's a thief of some kind. Though now Mum's made it clear they all know he's around, I'm sure it'll be the last they see of him."

Jonelle just looked thoughtful. I couldn't imagine what she found so interesting about Potty's assailant, so I went back to eating.

The afternoon passed slowly even though it was great fun. Fun in that it was lovely to have us altogether and Simon was in good form with witty comments about everyone.

But slow because I was conscious of the evening creeping up and the number of glasses of wine and spirits Brad was *not* having. I didn't want him drunk, but I also didn't want to see him drive off into the sunset, either. I wasn't so sure of myself that I could safely assume he wouldn't.

Not if Tuesday night was anything to go by.

Eventually though, it started to get dark and things were getting interesting. Music was put on and everyone danced around the pool. Though the alcohol had been available all day, now it was truly flowing. For once I stopped myself from getting caught up with it. There was no way I was going to make a fool of myself, or fall asleep, or throw up – the height of bad manners on a first sleepover date!

Sometime around nine Jonelle excused herself and went out. She obviously had plans which couldn't be moved, though she had had no way of knowing the party would be an all day event. Slowly, after ten thirty, others started to either head out, or go to their units. Seeing as there was no chance of rain, anything that didn't require a fridge was just left for the morning clean up.

I took Brad's hand and led him to No.1. I did a quick mental leap around the unit to make sure I'd left it in decent condition. After all, he'd never been inside it. When he'd walked me home the other week he'd simply made sure I was in the security gate and left.

Smudge, who had been partying with us, wandered in after us and made straight for his newly made up bed. He was one tired little kitten.

Brad shut the door and swung me round to press my back against it. Now this, I thought dreamily, was more like it. We kissed for what seemed like a forever. I explored every millimetre of his mouth and face. He nibbled his way down my cheek and neck. My legs threatened to dissolve.

With a groan, Brad pulled me roughly up into his arms. Really, it wasn't as difficult as it sounded. He was about six foot two and I was, well, a bit smaller. But still it was very romantic and I twined my arms around his neck and smothered him in kisses.

"Which way?" He managed at some point, standing there unsure of the layout.

"Second door on the right." And we were off. He made sure he closed the door with his foot, so Smudge couldn't find his way in, as I had mentioned the kitty was spending his nights with me once he got sick of his own bed.

I was glad of the effort I had gone to before the BBQ. We collapsed onto the bed in a cloud of soft perfume and my skin felt velvety and delicate. As first impressions go, I was counting on this being a good one.

A stripped down Brad was one hell of an impression itself. He had a washboard stomach and long defined legs attached to a fine butt. And everything else was in place and in working order.

The next few hours were well and truly something to write home about, in a manner of speaking. He knew all the buttons to drive a woman's body and it was well after three in the morning before, exhausted, we fell into sleep.

Mornings after the nights before were always a problem. I sometimes lay awake wondering if the other person was lying awake wondering. A very circular kind of thought pattern indeed. What if they were hoping to make a speedy exit? What if last night hadn't been for them, what it had been for me? What if it had been *more* and I was left with someone who wouldn't go away? You can see my dilemma.

I woke at seven, the new normal for me. Try as I might, I couldn't get myself back to sleep. I put it down to not being used to someone next to me. I peeped over at him. And found a pair of sparkling green eyes watching me. One long, strong arm came out and wrapping around me, dragged me closer. Before I could warn him about morning breath, I was been thoroughly kissed and I didn't think morning breath was on his mind.

By the time I managed to get into the shower, my bedside clock was switching over to nine.

The warm water helped to ease some of the more pleasurable aches I had accumulated. It was the smell of hot water hitting instant coffee which drove me out to get dressed.

Brad wandered into the room as I pulled on some pants and a

top. He handed me a mug of coffee. "Noticed that your percolator was new, so I thought I'd just get some instant, that okay with you?"

I grinned.

"Do we have plans for today that I should know about?" he asked, sitting on the edge of the bed, dressed only in the towel he'd borrowed for his shower.

There was a warning shout in my head. Plans? Us? But then I told myself not to be silly. Of course he'd think we would be doing something today. It was only natural. He was in my place, naked, after spending the night. I wasn't about to just turf him out, was I?

I combed through my hair and thought.

"I don't know. We could go do brunch at Manuka except we're way too early and would have to call it breakfast. I'm morally opposed to breakfast. I suppose we should start the clean up and then sit around the pool for the usual chat after-party thing. Then it'll be time for brunch."

He laughed at me, a deep sexy laugh which had me eyeing off the bed again. He caught the direction of my eyes and stood up. It was very sexy to have a man stand close and tower above me, *especially* if he was muscular and handsome. I tilted my head back and smiled up and up at him.

He grabbed my chin and raised me onto my toes, while lowering his mouth to mine. Mmm. Didn't they say everyone should have one thing they did very well in this world? Brad could be my one thing.

He broke away slowly. "I couldn't do you justice again, right now. You've worn me out, you wild hussy. I'll get into my clothes then we can get out there for clean up."

"Mind if I watch?" I stepped back to allow him room.

He had turned to find his clothes but shot me a look over his shoulder. "I would be very disappointed if you didn't."

So I did. I think he made sure to put his clothes on very slowly. Tease. Then we went out into the sun to see about cleaning up.

Smudge had woken up as well and voiced his immense displeasure at being locked out of the room all night. I hoped that this wasn't an indication of Brad not liking animals, but tossed it out of my head because nothing was going to be allowed to spoil my morning.

"Where's the new girl? Wasn't she introduced as Janelle or something?" Brad asked, as he folded some chairs.

There were a few things going on with that conversational

introduction. One, he didn't remember her name properly which was a plus. Two, he remembered her at all, which considering he was supposed to be mentally only thinking of me, was a minus. Not only that, three, he was asking after her whereabouts only moments out of my bed. Did men never learn anything? There are rules and etiquette surrounding these things!

"Jonelle. I heard her go out early this morning. I have no idea what time she got back last night. She must have the stamina of an ox for all the sleep she gets," Donald informed us as he wandered up.

He was obviously taking a break from the scintillating work with the law to help out with the party clean up.

"Stamina, huh?" Brad raised a brow, but shot his eyes to me and winked. "There seems to be a lot of that going round."

I blushed. For heaven's sake. Donald looked at me, then at Brad. He smirked. I ask you. My legal counsel smirked at me. I had to thump him. It was mandatory. He gave a yelp and ducked. The rest of the crew looked over. He picked me up, empty coffee mug and all.

"Hey! That's not fair. Put me down. Brad!" I appealed to my man, who backed away with hands up palms out.

"Don't look at me. I would never get between you and the law." Everyone started laughing and cheering. Donald edged me closer to the pool.

"Don't even think about," I warned in my ultra dangerous voice. Of course it was totally ruined by the quiver of laughter and thus, totally ignored. For one brief second I hung suspended over the icy blue water and then I was plunging into its embrace.

Swimming in Canberra unless the pool is heated to at least 28 degrees is about as practical as a nun dating Fabio. Our pool was scheduled to have a solar heater installed sometime next autumn. It had not been a top priority as we were too lazy during winter to bother with it.

My breath whooshed out in a long stream of bubbles. I could almost feel my skin contract on impact. I felt like I was falling through icicles. I came up spluttering, arms flailing around almost in a panic. It was a most unpleasant way to be completely woken up. I had just had a lovely warm shower after completely satisfying sex. If I lived, Donald would die.

I stood up; it wasn't all that deep but still it reached my chin. The rest of the Apartmates were in various stages of peeing their pants with laughter. Brad took pity on me and hauled me out. I still had enough mental capacity to admire his strength. I stood shivering in the cool air with my coffee mug still clamped in one hand. I had my priorities.

"Come on, let's get you into something dry," Brad murmured under the laughing comments thrown our way.

Jonelle chose this moment to arrive, with me standing there sopping wet in Brad's arms. She'd obviously had a heavy work out at the gym. Her pants and top were dark with sweat and her face was pink with exertion. She took us in with one of her long-eyed looks.

Brad glanced up and grinned. "You look as though you should have a dip too."

Was it his grin, or his tone of voice? But suddenly my bright and cloudless day was not so bright. I was a jealous girl by nature. I get that. So I tried to make sure I bit my tongue and didn't let it show all that often in bitchy comments. But at that moment I wanted to leap around howling. I wasn't upset with Jonelle. I was just upset that whatever she had, I didn't, because the warmth in his grin was not imaginary.

I then remembered how Leigh and Delight and even Dad had reacted to her. I had laughed to myself at how spouses would be ticked off and now I needed to laugh at myself. It was just harder to do when it was my turn.

Right then I realised I really liked Jonelle. That I wanted to work for her and try to puzzle her out and possibly be her friend. Why? Because I knew that it wasn't her fault, the impression she made and that she would never use it against someone like me. I got this by the look she flashed at me. Just one look, but I grinned at her in vast amounts of relief and acknowledgement. She held my eyes for a minute and whatever she read there made up her mind too. She gave me one sharp little nod and then she came forward to chat with everyone else, laughing with them at my condition, and in general fitting back in with the mood.

Brad took me off and I showered quickly to get the feeling back into my body and threw on some classic chic clothes. Blue jeans, brown leather knotted belt, RM Williams boots and white button up shirt.

I stepped back outside, ready to make the usual brunch type offers. Even Jonelle was coming, as I could see her fiddling with a lovely leather handbag, standing with Kylie.

"Okay, let's go get ourselves something to eat!" Todd was always thinking with his stomach.

Chapter Six

I was a teeny bit glad when Brad headed off. I wanted to sit on the couch and process all the events of the last twenty four hours. I wanted to be left alone. Too much sensory input and I needed time out to go through it all. Plus to be strictly honest, I loved to sit in the sun and do nothing.

The sun was getting low on the horizon, but I knew my day wasn't over. Jonelle had bumped into me on the way to Manuka and told me we'd have to have a chat about my new job. I was excited in a way. I was all set to head off on a new adventure.

Brad and I had parted on a good note. I was happy how things were going; it was okay that he couldn't help eyeing Jonelle off. As long as that was all he ever did. The Apartmates had given him their praise and seal of approval.

I sat watching Smudge chase a dust bunny across the floor, sipping hot chocolate and feeling pleasantly like I wanted to crawl into bed. It had been a thoroughly satisfactory weekend.

There was a soft tap on the door and Jonelle stuck her head around. "You mind?"

I motioned her in. I was too comfy to move or say anything to break the peace. Smudge did his little dance when he saw Jonelle. He hops backwards on his hind legs, waving his front paws wildly in the air. Then, once he's lost his balance, he grabs the tip of his tail and jumps up and down in excitement. Of course, then he feels the need to pounce, which is exactly what he did, making for Jonelle's shoe laces.

She picked him up. "You are such a good boy. Aren't you, you sweet thing? Such a good boy." And she rubbed her nose on his tummy which elicited high purrs of adoration.

"Have you quite finished flirting with my cat?" I asked stretching myself, before settling even deeper in the cushions.

She sat on the floor, her back against the couch opposite me. "Nope. Never." Her eyes twinkled at me while Smudge's little paw batted at her mouth. "Hope he hasn't been in the kitty litter for a bit. Ah well. I don't get sick, which is a good thing." Then she became more businesslike. "Shall I tell you a bit about the job?"

I guessed I was committed. I hoped it wasn't too demanding, being a natural sloth. But I nodded to get her started.

She laughed gently at me. "Such enthusiasm. I am not an ogre, you know. And you might find yourself enjoying the work and then it won't feel like work at all, will it? Stop that."

This was said to Smudge as he tried to climb up her shoulders. His claws were little, but needle sharp and he had no idea about depth. Jonelle brought her attention back to me.

"Basically it'll mean spending loads of time with me and doing things for me. I want a fully capable and well rounded Personal Assistant. You'll be coming to the gym with me, taking the clothes to the dry cleaner, ordering food, catering, keeping my diary, answering one of the phones, typing stuff, possibly doing some research. Booking flights if I have to go anywhere and probably coming along if required. You'll be run around gal, house gal and hopefully friend all in one."

She watched me for reactions. I was too tired to give facial clues. The brain wasn't processing the words, but I did get the last bit.

"I think I can handle that. The friend part. It will be nice to have a strange friend like you." I heard my words and my eyes went round. But Jonelle just laughed, no offence taken. "I meant, you know. You aren't exactly like the rest of us, are you? I don't know what you do, but semi-retired art dealer isn't the only thing."

She shrugged. "Let's see how you pan out. I have been working mostly alone for a long time. It's not easy for me to think of including someone, trusting them. I told you about the big brother type in my life? Well, at some point I decided that I wasn't much of a team player and moved away from the whole Big Brother watching over my shoulder routine. Since then, I've mainly worked alone."

She wasn't looking at me now. Her words were low and her head was bent over Smudge. "As we get to know each other it may be easier to introduce you to some more of the work I do. But trust is something we need to build, right?" She looked up.

"Yeah, I guess. On both sides." I wasn't all that comfy with the conversation either. Deep and meaningful wasn't my middle name. "Oh! What are my hours going to be like?" I dreaded the nine to five as much as the next person. More so than some.

"How about we play that very much by ear? Tomorrow morning is gym at six. Other things may or may not pad the rest of the day out. Flexible." She decided on. But I think she had left me behind on two words – gym and six.

"I can't get up at six! And I certainly can't go to the gym. I don't think I can jog a hundred metres. I'd shame you." I looked hopeful.

"Don't you have any gym clothes, is that it?"

Well, I kind of did. They sat happily on the shelf in my cupboard and made me feel guilty whenever I looked at them. They'd been bought a year ago when I had been trying out the idea of getting fit and healthy. As with a lot of my small projects in life, it didn't last and they never actually saw the inside of a gym.

I had the best of intentions, I really did. But somehow it never quite worked out. I see someone else doing something fun and think – oh I could do that! But when I actually get down to the doing part, it was never as fun as it looked. Those healthy people had been doing it for years. They were fit. Which meant they could jog, row, hike, bike and ride with a smile on their face because by then it was *easy* for them. Me? I'd start at the bottom and feel every step on the ladder upwards. So I generally hopped off, and went to lie down somewhere till the feeling went away.

I hadn't seen Jonelle in anything but loose fitting clothes, but I could imagine with the amount of gym work she obviously did, the tone-iness of her would be extreme. If tone-iness was a word, which technically I didn't think it was, but Jonelle would personify it. Would my rounded flesh handle been held up next to hers? Ah well, in for a penny, in for a pound – or a stone should I say…

"I'll come get you just before six, okay? Right now I have to head. Bit beat and need an early one." She got to her feet and plonked Smudge on my lap before heading out the door.

"It looks like we're off to bed early too, mister. Early mornings may be okay at your age, but trust me, the older you get the harder they are." I took him with me. No need to make him spend the night in his bed when I had perfectly adequate queen size he could romp on.

Did six in the morning roll around quicker when you knew you had to get up for it or was that just my imagination? I felt I had barely put my head on the pillow when the radio came on and I blearily discovered it was five forty five and counting. The cat was of the same opinion as me. He sat up in shock at having his morning disrupted in this vile manner, then with a hiss, left that side of the bed and curled up on the other: would that I could do that, too.

Instead I struggled up and crawled into a blastingly hot shower. The jets stung me they were so powerful and I tried to wake up. My system wasn't prepared for such a thing. Anything that had a five before it was just insane.

I made my way out of the shower and found a towel. At that stage I was still operating with my eyes closed. Somehow I was dressed and in the kitchen making a coffee when Jonelle knocked on the door. I opened it spoon in hand. She actually took a step back and laughed.

"Count yourself lucky that this is a spoon and not a knife." I made my way back to the kitchen.

Jonelle followed. "You can't have coffee! Your stomach will be awash with it when you're meant to be working hard. Now, put it down."

We had a standoff. I grimly held onto my spoon and mug, but she took the coffee tin as hostage. I narrowed my eyes and tried to do 'deadly' stare. Jonelle started to giggle, then it became a full on, mouth opening belly laugh. I was justifiably insulted.

"Mmmfpth," was all she could say. She held onto the side of the counter, little tears running down her face.

"Come on, it isn't that funny." I tried a small feint to get my coffee tin back, but she palmed me off like a football player. And giggled some more. Eventually I got snitty and put my mug down. I wasn't getting anywhere and if I had to be up at least I could regain some dignity and squash her like a bug. "Aren't we meant to be somewhere, little miss perfect?"

She grinned. "Sorry. But I've never seen someone so keen not to let a morning coffee slip her by. You should have seen your face. It was mutinous."

Well, scratch the whole deadly thing then. Mutinous huh? Man, I thought only little kids could be mutinous.

So we were off after a little hiccup. If I'd thought to delay her and possibly put the torture off a little, I was in for a big disappointment.

Jonelle didn't do put offs.

The gym was half full. Obviously there is a whole city of crazy people I didn't know existed, getting themselves out of bed and bashing their heads against a brick wall. At least, that was how I equated the gym.

Jonelle was greeted with grunts from some of the guys as she led me to some free weights and bench presses. I eyed them off. What exactly did she expect me to do with them?

It appeared she wanted me to lift them.

Repeatedly.

Who devised this method of getting fit? Who was the very first person who decided that yes, getting people together in the one room to stand or sit around lifting heavy objects would be classed as a bona fide method of getting fit? Where were they so that I could kill them?

I discovered that I had no upper body strength. None. After a set of ten reps, as these gym type people call them, of a twenty kilo bar, my arms disintegrated. It was woeful. Jonelle had put me on my back to do bench presses. When she put weight plates on the bar, I couldn't lift it, so much to her amusement I made her take them off and just lifted the bar.

All twenty kilos of steel.

Ten times.

Over and over, just like some kind of medieval torture.

"I think I'm starting to hate you. Just a bit." I puffed at her while I thought about dying.

She grinned. "That's the idea. When you know you hate me, my work here is done. Now, another set please."

"Don't you have some torture you can go inflict on yourself?" I didn't want to go through another set, not ever. Would it be impolite for me to quit my job already?

"Yeah, I have my workout to do. But I wanted to get you settled and into a routine first. Something you can just go on with eventually without me. And no, you can't quit." She showed yet again how easily she could read me.

She sat down on the bench beside the one I was gasping on.

"Look, I know that it must be painful. When your body isn't used to something like this, it's never easy to make it perform. That's why we'll start it really slowly. I would never put you into a position where it could permanently hurt you. We'll work you up to something slowly and before you know it, you'll be coming for runs around the block with me every day."

The visual I got to accompany that statement was enough to make me nauseous. Who was she kidding?

"I'm not cut out for this. I am more of a 'snuggle and marathon sex' girl. Can't we count that as my exercise?" I pleaded.

Her eyes took on a distinct twinkle. "And how would I know that the requirements of time and energy spent had been met?"

Let me tell you, the visual that went along with that comment gave me my cardiac exercise for the next month. With a snort, she leaned back on her seat thingy and went to work on her own bench presses.

It was cool in the gym, so we both had our full tracksuits on. I imagined that would change as the morning wore on and then I'd be shown up as the jelly belly I was. However, I was kind of curious as to what she was hiding under all those clothes.

Sure enough, as we moved through some more exercises and came to the cardiac ones like rowing and steppers, we both lost the suits and I was left feeling open and vulnerable. Why were gym clothes always so bloody tight? I mean, for the lifestyle I had I wasn't really that bad. But when Jonelle stripped down to her painted on second skin, I wanted to run and hide somewhere convenient.

She was lean. I mean really lean and had clear muscle definition. She had a scar on her arm which looked nasty, but I didn't want to ask about it. Her legs were sculptured and looked like running for the next three hours wouldn't be out of the picture.

I sweated and strained through what felt like a lifetime but I was told it was only one hour. Then we dashed off so I could shower and change. I had an appointment at my accountant's firm. Somehow Jonelle made me agree to come back to her place after.

At lunch I sat in the sun and day dreamed. But for once it wasn't about the daytime soaps. I was thinking too much of what I was going to be doing that afternoon! Jonelle, the work I would be doing and what I might find out about her was intruding on my thoughts. I wasn't going mad – I was interested in something! I had something to look forward to other than sitting at home with the telly.

What had I been doing with my life and how much time had I been wasting, if one structured morning later I was eagerly looking forward to the next instalment. I had to shy away from those thoughts. They were altogether far too serious.

I knocked on Jonelle's door. I wasn't as comfortable in this situation so I wasn't about to just walk in. Not, that is, until I heard her call out to come in.

Not a lot had changed. There were a few more art pieces and decorations hanging on the walls, but I wasn't really an art buff so had no idea if they were real, expensive, or just good replicas. She did have a strong preference for warlike imagery, with decorative native spears and shields and daggers. A touch strange, but well within the normal range, so I wasn't too put off.

"Hi." Jonelle popped into the room from the kitchen with two steaming mugs. "I thought it would be nice to relax for a moment. You've had a longer than normal day."

Did it have to be so obvious? I took the mug gratefully and sipped. The smell should have warned me. There was none of the pungent coffee aroma.

"Bleck! What is that?" I couldn't spit it out. That would be rude and I had nothing to spit it up in. I swallowed and tried again, because I was a natural blonde and a glutton for punishment. This time I wasn't expecting the strong taste of coffee, so I wasn't as horrified. It wasn't that bad, just, well, not coffee.

Jonelle watched me, sipping hers easily. "It's called green tea. It helps with getting rid of your toxins. After all that exercise, I think you need to cleanse your system a bit. Keep at it, it'll grow on you." And she finished hers up as if to prove a point.

I eyed my mug suspiciously. Apart from the occasional glass of water because I knew that at some time someone had told me it was good for me, I kept my liquid consumption to alcohol and coffee.

"Are you sure you're not trying to poison me? It doesn't seem right." I watched with sick fascination as she poured herself another mug full from a pot which I had thought was purely decorative, but obviously was full of the vile stuff.

Jonelle giggled. I couldn't get over that. I had never thought to hear such a wonderfully female and girlish sound out of her, but there you go. People amazed me all the time. It meant I lived in a world full of surprises, which wasn't such a bad thing.

"If I wanted to poison you, something in your coffee would be a better bet. You would've swilled that down a lot faster. Come into the spare room." She led the way. "I've turned it into an office and it's where you'll probably be spending a big chunk of your time from now on, so I wanted to make sure it suited both of us." She was acting kind of nervous, worried about whether or not I would like it. I grinned to myself. She was human after all.

The spare room was lovely. She'd taken the built in wardrobes out which made the room appear to be so much larger. I was suddenly re-modelling my own place in my head.

It was light and airy, with the old waist high window, looking out over the park, knocked through and made into a bay window so the whole room was lit with natural light (where had she found the time for all this? floated through my head). There was a long desk going along one wall and down the second wall. It had two computers on it and a laptop attached to one of them.

There were also books lining the third wall beside the door. There were filing cabinets under the desk, as well as drawers. She had it all planned out. Above the desk were two framed antique-looking guns. They reminded me of the period dramas I watched where they spilled gun powder down the barrel before they could let it off. Framed up in wooden boxes with glass fronts and hanging on the wall, they had a certain charm about them.

She watched me looking at them. "If they make you uncomfortable I'll switch them over to something else. I have a Monet in my room. It could come in here?" I shook my head. It was her room and seriously they weren't scary, less so than she was, half the time.

"Nah. Always thought guns were pretty sexy actually. Never thought to have them as a wall decoration, but there you go. Which one's mine?" I forgot the wall hangings and moved over to the computers.

Jonelle pointed to the one not connected to the laptop. "That one. Guns aren't sexy, you know." She paused.

I could tell she wanted to give me a lecture about guns and safety, but something seemed to hold her back.

"We'll go through some stuff, but I need you to feel free to ask any questions along the way. Some things may appear to be a bit strange, but I live a strange life these days and you'll get used to it all."

Well that blew my secret theory that she'd not want any questions asked, right out the window. See, surprises from people all the time. One day, I would even surprise myself. One always lived in hope.

We settled in behind our computers. "They're networked, so everything on one is on the other. Some things are password protected, so you won't be able to get into them. Don't worry; they're just tax and personal items. I keep most of my clients on the computer because they still contact me from time to time for one reason or another." She was scrolling down lists of people and dates and coded job numbers. Then she stopped at a diary. "This is probably what you'll be using the most. That way we'll know what the other is up to and where they are doing it."

It was pretty full. Each day had blanked out spots for gym, meetings, scouting (what was that, I wondered?) and travel. There were quite a few visits to Sydney coming up. But none of them really spelled out what she was doing there. They had a job number and that was it.

"What do you actually do? If I am going to be helping you out here, shouldn't you tell me stuff?" Not me at my most eloquent, but suddenly I was impatient. There was all this interesting stuff going on and I had no idea how to extract the information out of her.

She still held back. "Look, give it some time. Just run my day for me and as things come up I'll try to fill you in. A lot of it is sensitive stuff, people who like to keep their privacy. I can't just leap in and mouth off about their interests because I like you and we get along, now can I?"

I grumbled. That was the whole point. How was I going to be able to work only knowing half of the juicy gossip? It was frustrating, but she was pretty immoveable.

So I trolled through files and printed stuff off and created existing client file lists and stuffed them into my cabinet, to make myself feel useful and on top of the ball game. Sometime later, I asked, "Would you mind if tomorrow I brought Smudge over? He'll be lonely all by himself. He's not used to me being away during the day."

"Of course! Go and get him now if you like. He'll be great fun to have around. You can take him in the car if you have to go out as well. There is nothing worse than coming home to a pining pet." Then she looked at the time. "Actually call it a day. It's been a long one. Staring at a computer screen all afternoon is never fun."

I got up and stretched. I was amazed to discover it was five o'clock. I'd been trying to decipher codes (with little success) and get clients sorted into files for hours. It was little wonder I was hungry and stiff. But still, if I was honest, today had been the best day in ages. And I hadn't once wondered who had been on the Ellen show. That said loads to me.

"Dinner?" It seemed natural to ask. "I'll go feed Smudge and we could go out somewhere." I tested my aching muscles. "But if we have to go back to the gym tomorrow, maybe we can make it an early night?"

Jonelle smiled. "Sure. Give me a moment then I'll come and get you."

And that was how my first day as an employee went. I still had very little idea of what it was she did, or I'd be doing, but at least I had been out of my place and doing ... well, something.

I felt some level of accomplishment and like I was back in the real world. I hadn't even realised I'd missed the real world. I knew some of the Apartmates thought I was slack, but they didn't seem to mind what I did. And I had allowed myself to trundle along like it was okay for a twenty nine year old to be retired and wasting every day.

In reality, now I had spent a day doing something, I could see how bored I was! Yes, actually bored. Always waiting for one of the Apartmates to come home and fill me in on their adventures, not having any of my own. That wasn't living, it was 'existing'.

I let myself into my place to feed Smudge. I hadn't had a total epiphany and thus everything would change in my life. But at least I had had a nudge in the right direction. Perhaps Jonelle would end up being better for me than first thought?

Pretty prophetic musings, it was to turn out.

Chapter Seven

Dinner proved to be at a small French restaurant tucked away out of sight. It was sweet and secluded. There were romantic looking couples staring at each other across candles and I felt a little uncomfortable as the waiter settled us into our seats with a knowing look.

She ordered in fluent French, which shocked the waiter who was Australian and had no idea of a word she said. I giggled to myself. That sure wiped the knowing look off his face. Jonelle suppressed her annoyance and repeated herself in English. It was just entrée and some drinks. I opened the menu and started to read.

"Well, that was the first day out of the way. Not too bad?" She hadn't even opened her menu.

"It was fine, though the gym will be the death of me. I didn't learn anything new about you though. The numbers on your old jobs didn't match any notes I could find." I looked up.

Oops. Now she'd know I had spent some of my afternoon snooping. But her face wasn't registering any surprise or annoyance.

"You'll get to know the system, when you need to know the answers. Right now, it's nice just to have someone around the place. I haven't had a business associate to work with for a while." The waiter brought us the wine and poured. When he left she sipped and continued. "What sort of pay do you want?"

I was shocked. As if I needed to be paid. But I held my tongue for once. My busy little brain tried to work out the very best sort of remuneration for the situation. Was the question some sort of test or trick? She couldn't help but be aware of my monetary situation.

"How about information? You know I don't need the money and it would be an insult to take any. But I really enjoyed today. Oh, I know

I'll whinge about things and make your life hell when you want me to be at the gym instead of in my warm little bed. But it was amazing." I paused, trying to do the impossible and sort out my thoughts before they became words.

"I've spent so much of the last couple of years running away from doing anything. I didn't want to be relied on, or to set my day by a boss' expectations. It's a big weight off my mind, that key to freedom if I ever need it... but at the same time, I never realised how vacant my life had become. It's been great being the party girl and having that side to organise for everyone. Only, it was one dimensional. I'd wait until they came home to have someone to talk to. But now having my own day to think about, I wonder what I've been doing?"

I fiddled with the stem of my glass and continued.

"So in answer to your question, I would like information. It doesn't matter if I can't talk to the Apartmates about it. I can discuss it with you and I can think it over. That'll be enough. Lessons in some of that kung fu thingy you did the other night. Lessons on my sign language and maybe one day, you'll end up telling me more about what those files mean."

Jonelle was watching me. I mean really watching me. Sometimes I've had conversations with people, but they weren't really listening. They were thinking about making it look like they were interested, while they waited for me to shut up, so they could keep talking (a long wait most of the time). Jonelle weighted every word I said, as though they were important and mattered.

The silence dragged out and instead of easing it, she lifted her menu and began to read it. I felt a little itchy under the skin, but followed suit. I looked around the dimly lit little restaurant. It was warm and I couldn't imagine a better place to sit and have a chat with someone who was fast becoming a close friend. I realised, sadly, I didn't have many of those, Steph and Grillia notwithstanding.

The waiter then intruded, wanting to take our orders. I was happy to get to the food part of the outing, because I was starved and wanted to get home to stumble into bed. Sitting around in a warm place was making me sleepy.

After the waiter left Jonelle leaned back and closed her eyes briefly. When they opened they focused unerringly onto my face.

"I'm glad to hear all that. I was worried that perhaps this change in the way you live would be too great. But I could see that brain of yours shining out of your eyes and you weren't allowing it out to play. I took a gamble and it's paid off. I like that." She smiled.

We spent the remainder of the evening gossiping. I filled her in on the Apartmates and some of our adventures. We laughed and enjoyed a few too many glasses of wine, at least, I did because I wasn't driving and she kept her wits about her.

She drove us home and I made my way back to my bed. Staring at my ceiling which glowed faintly with its stars, I felt exhausted but so relaxed. My mind swam back through the day and I smiled sleepily at the ceiling. I hadn't once turned my telly on and yet I felt better than I had in months. I also had a friend. Albeit a strange, fascinating and potentially problematic one, but hey, it was a really good start.

As I slipped off into sleep, I thought bugger! I haven't heard from Brad.

Tuesday morning dawned. That is all I want to say about that. It came and it went, the morning that is, in a cloud of aching muscles and more gym work and light teasing from Jonelle. Every muscle I owned and even a few I never knew I owned, was awake and screaming. She promised that within two weeks my body would have found a nice place of comfort and it wouldn't be quite as bad. Hmm. I told her what she was doing amounted to torture and that if I was to die, I'd come back and haunt her for the rest of her life. She found that very amusing, which was insulting.

When I finally struggled back to her place after lunch, I was glad for the chance to sit down. Smudge spent the next half an hour wandering around making himself acquainted with the sights and smells. I managed to find the diary on the computer without her help and worked out what I could do for the afternoon. She had 'pencilled' in (if you can do that with an electronic do-dah), for us to go through some basic sign language at some stage that afternoon. Jonelle was a long way ahead of my basic training.

By that evening I was drop dead tired again. Who would have thought that lazy old me would enjoy being put through the wringer? She had me researching the prices of different art works from around the world, where they were and what sort of security they had. Mind you, that gave me a twinge. I wasn't too sure how exactly she planned on using the information, but I wasn't entirely naive.

"I don't just go pinching things, you know," she said when I brought that up. "Unless, of course, the commission is just way too sweet to say no." She grinned at my obvious discomfort.

"No! I used to when I was younger and I hope that you don't hold that against me. I needed to make a name for myself and build some capital. Now I've achieved that, I only protect my investments or placements, and steal back something which shouldn't be where it's ended up."

That left me a little dumbfounded and floundering. I found it hard to impose the image of cat burglar and art thief over the super sleek and elegant woman sitting in front of me. But I realised everyone had a past and I had to get over it if we were to be friends. Though she was what she was and I needed to think about how far I was prepared to get involved because if she went down, who was to say what I would be implicated in?

It had to be the strangest internal conversation I had ever had to date. It wasn't often people confessed to me how they stole things every now and again.

I went home at five thirty, sore and tired and thoughtful. It was fun and a bit of a lark to do this research, but what if she did something really silly with it all? I shook that thought out of my head. She had made it this far, why was I worried?

"Fiona!" Rob was coming home and greeted me as I opened my front door. "You didn't come out with us last night. Where were you? We had a few drinks down at the local, but no one could find you." He came up, slipping his tie off as he did.

"Sorry. I've started doing a few things for Jonelle and we went out to dinner to talk about it all. She has me going to the gym as well! Me! Can you believe it? What are you all up to this evening?" It wasn't unheard of for us all to troop down to the Batch and Haddock early in the week, but it was rare.

"Nothing. I guess everyone has their own things to go on with. What about you?" Rob leaned against the wall, tie dangly in one hand. He was a cute big boy, but not my type regardless of what we had first thought. When Rob had moved in I thought I had felt a zing, but after a kiss or two we both realised that it wasn't going to work.

"Me? A hot tub, loads of food and then my bed. Preferably with a good book but I'm up for anything." So we still flirted. It was good for the soul.

He grinned. "Aren't you meant to be meeting Brad for a movie?"

Shit! I'd totally forgotten. Bugger damn. I was in no fit state to be going out. I had the mental capacity of a goldfish and the muscle tone of a hundred year old turtle. I wanted my bath, dinner and bed in that order. I flashed Rob a panicked grin and rushed inside.

Was there an easy way to call someone you'd slept with a couple of days ago and tell them you didn't want to see them? Without damaging their ego or the potential relationship, that is. I did want to see him again, but I couldn't hold my head up.

Finding the phone I noticed my voice mail had a message. It was Brad.

"Hey there, shame I couldn't catch you. I'm really sorry about this sweetie, but I have to work late. We have a presentation tomorrow in Sydney and I need to be on top of it, then get some sleep before catching the six thirty plane. Can you forgive me? I'll call you tomorrow, okay?"

Well, that worked that out. I was half way down the corridor when I realised – he'd just dumped me for our first post-sex date! What an ass. It didn't matter I was about to do the same thing. What matters was *he* did it. Boys weren't meant to do that! I was filled with a brief rage. What was he saying about me?

At some stage my brain switched off. I couldn't cope with thoughts. I was way too tired.

Stumbling through my routine, I managed to make it to bed before I fell asleep.

When the alarm went off on Wednesday morning I nearly smashed it. There was no leaping joyously out of bed. No feeling that I was on top of the world and could look forward to the day with warm and fuzzy feelings. Oh no! More like, I was ready to break things and burrow under the bed for the next fortnight. It was me who put me in for this, wasn't it?

Finding clothes, even finding the kitchen, seemed to be too big a deal, but somehow I managed. I was just sipping some lukewarm water, Jonelle having told me that cold or hot water wasn't all that good for the stomach, when the phone rang. Who in hell would call me at this hour? It was exactly, I glanced at the clock, 6am. Could it be, my little heart lifted, Jonelle calling from her bed saying she wasn't coming?

With that happy little thought in mind, I pounced on the phone. It was my mother! I felt a sudden cold chill. She knew never to call me before at least eleven. Whatever she had to say could not be good at this time.

"Fiona?" she asked, as though there would be any other person picking up my phone at this hour.

"It's me, Mum. What's happened? Is Dad and Gran okay?" They were the only two at a certain age I could think of, apart from Mum herself, who was obviously not sick, as she was on the phone. My powers of deduction were incredible.

"They're all fine." She sounded put out by that fact. "It's Potty. We thought she was only bruised by that careless driver, but it must have been more than that. We woke up this morning to find dear old Potty dead outside, near her water bowl. Can you come over?"

Potty! I sat down sharply, a hole opening up in my stomach. A lump formed in my throat. I hoped she hadn't been in pain, but if it had been internal injuries then it was likely. And the great big brave goof hadn't tried to tell anyone. A tear slid down my cheek.

"Sure Mum, I'll come over now. Put a blanket over her and I'll take her to the vet."

I hung up and just sat there for a little while. I remembered Potty as a puppy. Already at eight weeks old she was the size of a terrier; all fur and large floppy paws and ears. She'd been the cutest thing we'd ever seen.

Potty had come to live with the folks and we all visited more than ever. The kids loved her and as she grew so did her protective tendencies. She could smell a family member from a kilometre away, but heaven help someone who wasn't family coming into her zone. The whole street became her zone and the neighbours loved her as well. She never needed walking. Mum and Dad just opened the front gate and she took herself off around the neighbourhood for a stroll. It was a guaranteed sight at seven in the morning, the big shaggy dog trotting along waving her tail like a plume. Now all that history and glorious nature was dead. It was unbelievable. If I could have found that driver, I would have killed him myself.

I was so locked up in my own thoughts I had forgotten Jonelle and our date for the gym. There was an insistent pounding on the door and I just stared at it wondering who it could be. Eventually I walked over and opened the door and an exasperated Jonelle came waltzing in. The amazing thing was, she knew straight away something was wrong.

"What? What's happened?" Her eyes scanned my face.

"I have to go home. Potty's dead." My voice quavered.

"Let's go. I'll drive, shall I?" She didn't even hesitate, but was out the door dragging me by my arm as she went.

We sat in silence the whole way there. I wasn't in the mood for conversation and she respected that. The strange thing was, when we got to my old home, Joy and Delight were already there.

The front door was open, as was custom when Mum was expecting us all home, and Potty would have warned against any intruder. I closed it behind me, a sad reminder that the place needed to be locked up now.

The family were in the back yard, sitting, sipping coffee.

Lying near the corner of the house was a great lump under a tartan blanket. I walked over to pat her goodbye. Jonelle followed, though strangely enough she wasn't so much interested in patting Potty, as in studying the ground around her and the water bowl. She even took some of the water in a little glass bottle. I watched in a detached manner, thinking she had to be the weirdest friend I had.

Joy spoke up. "Has anyone seen that car again? I think we should report him to the police. You just can't go around running over people's pets and getting away with it."

"It's hardly his fault, Janet. Mum and Dad should have had Potty examined. While she was a large dog, a car can do damage and a vet would have been able to tell if the internals were okay," Delight countered.

Mum raised her head in indignation. "I can't believe you'd blame us. We loved Potty and if there had been any indication of a problem we'd have done anything to save her!"

Dad patted her shoulder, as ineffective in grief as he was with most shows of emotions. I could see this deteriorating, as per usual, into a family blame session. Everyone had taken Jonelle's appearance in their stride and saw no reason to continue the charade of happy families they'd portrayed for her benefit last week.

"There is no reason to blame anyone. It won't help her and we all have work to get to. I'll organise something with her vet and we can have a ceremony this weekend." I tried to head them off, but all I managed to do was to focus them on me.

"Since when do you have a job?" sneered Joy, at the same time Mum was wailing she wanted to keep Potty's ashes and have them scattered in the garden. I groaned internally but took up the baton. It would be unheard of to allow Joy to say something like that without a comeback.

"As of yesterday I have a job and I'm late for work." I frowned at Jonelle in warning. Just because the lateness I was experiencing was for the gym part of my job didn't make it any less important – for now. I could change the rules as soon as I left my family behind.

There was dead silence. I would have keeled over laughing, if Potty hadn't being lying less than ten metres away. They were looking at me as though I'd suddenly grown another head. I felt a bit annoyed, but I really can't blame them.

"Well," said Mum. "Well, indeed that is good news, dear. Will your new boss mind very much if you dealt with Potty first?"

No 'what doing and who for', or any of the usual curiosity. I thought I'd managed to harden my heart against my mother's indifference to what I did with my life (except the marriage thing, like that was all I was good for), but perhaps I'd never really succeed.

Without looking at Jonelle, I replied, "Nope, I'm positive my new boss won't mind in the least. But can I borrow your Rover? I can't possibly take Potty to the vet's in my car there just isn't physically room for her."

Joy's face turned back into the sneer she seemed to perpetually wear around me when she wasn't trying to impress anyone. "Got your boss under your finger all ready have you? Or is it a mercy job?" Then in a complete change of topic, she kept going with, "If you had a proper car and not that toy, you'd be able to take Potty to the vet's without leaving Mum and Dad car-less."

Meaning I supposed that I was selfish and always thinking of my own needs. I had given up trying to figure out what Joy was on about a long time ago. Most of the time we got along to some degree, but like me, she wasn't good in the mornings and like Dad, she wasn't good with the finer emotions. Well – any, really.

I tried to keep eye contact with Jonelle to a minimum. But there was a little kernel inside which was bubbling with laughter. Mercy job? Under the thumb? I was glad that at that moment none of them had any idea of who my boss really was.

"Look, the faster I get moving the quicker we're all on our way."

It wasn't my morning to be diplomatic it seems. But it never was, so why that should come as a surprise was beyond me.

"Fiona! Mum and Dad have lost their companion and all you can think of is how fast you can dispose of the *body*?" Delight wasn't much use in the support stakes either.

Jonelle stepped smoothly in. She, at least, was awake. "I'm sure Fiona just wants to have all the organising over with, so you can grieve as you need to. Allow me to help anyway I can. Come on, Fi."

And she dragged me over to Potty, as though I was a puppy myself. Potty weighed in at more than I could comfortably lift myself. Moving her was going to prove interesting, but move her we did. It wasn't dignified, seeing as she was an awkward weight, but we managed to get her into the Rover.

I felt terrible driving her away. Like somehow there should have been more to it all than a sweaty fight to get her into a car.

"You know she was at an age to be considered old for a Saint, don't you?" Jonelle sat next to me, staring out the window.

"I know. But it doesn't make it easier to think she would have died soon anyway. At least that would have been old age, not some stupid man in a car!"

Jonelle hesitated. I wasn't watching her, but I could feel her hesitate. "You saw me take some of her water. Fiona, what if she wasn't just hit by a car? What if she died of something else?" She was feeling her way forward to another conclusion and I didn't like the way she was thinking.

"Stop it. Stop talking like an idiot. Of course it was internal injuries resulting from the car accident. What other possible explanation could there be? And I really don't know if I want you to answer that question." I pulled into our vet's car park.

I turned to face Jonelle. Her face looked a bit strange, kind of strained at the edges.

"Look, if I'm right, then we may have a problem. I didn't want to get into this before I had a lab check out that water, but I can't see Potty not telling someone she was in pain. And what about the stranger that was hanging around? Why? He turned up the day after we had lunch there. Why have they never seen him before and why did he hit the one animal on the street that looked after your place? Why, in other words, is your parents' place now left without its home warning system, in a street that has a fifty kilometre zone, where a driver could see Potty coming a mile off?"

Chapter Eight

I got a sinking feeling. The one that said I really didn't want the answer to any of those questions. There was also a little bit of me wondering when she would burst out laughing and say "Gotcha!"

Except she didn't.

"Why would someone want to get rid of Potty? It doesn't make sense. You're too used to covering your tracks and now you're paranoid."

She shook her head.

"Think about it. I come over, and then a man shows up, and then Potty is killed. If someone wanted to do some investigating into your background, or the connection between me and that house, the first thing they would do would be get rid of the dog." She kept her eyes on mine. "I know I would."

There was that sinking feeling again. Really more of a sick feeling, but I went with sinking.

"Are you trying to tell me that Potty may have been killed because of you? And me?" I had to admit it, my voice didn't do emotions well and it squeaked. She nodded.

"Are you completely insane? At least you didn't mention this in front of the others. They may have killed you themselves. Seriously, you can't go around blaming yourself, you haven't even analysed the water yet."

Where was all this coming from? Was it the grief talking, because I couldn't see me getting the courage to say these things to her in normal circumstances. And suddenly talking like I understood things like 'analysis' and 'water content' - what would I think of next. I was beginning to get a high from the cloak and danger business, and I wasn't even in it.

"I didn't want to alarm you, or them. But I think it could be a possibility, one we can't ignore just because it would suit us."

Was it possible to get all warm and fuzzy because someone was including you in their conversations, even if it was about killing a family pet? I liked how she just assumed that now I was working for her; I could handle all that sort of stuff. It was nonsense of course, a coward I had always been and a coward I would always be, but it was flattering.

"Let's just get Potty cremated or whatever they do for animals. Then we'll worry about the rest of it." I hopped out of the Rover, hoping to end the conversation. I should have known that Jonelle wouldn't be put off that easily.

She came around the back with me. "I think what we need to do is get your parents' a house alarm. Something that can't be shut off with the mains." She helped me lower the back and rearrange Potty so we could get her out. "But you need to get a vet and a trolley first."

I gave her a dirty look and went inside. Wendy, the vet nurse I kind of knew, looked up. "What's up?" she greeted me with casual indifference. She was obviously tired. It was a twenty four hour surgery.

"My parents' dog Potty died last night. I was hoping you could..." I'd been about to say give her an autopsy, because wasn't that what they did in the movies? But Jonelle had followed me in and interrupted smoothly, again. Man, she was good.

"We need to find a place that will cremate her, but thought you may be able to hold on to the body until something could be organised?"

It turned out our large and friendly veterinary surgery was also the local animal burial people too. A little voice inside told me that that was a little too handy. 'Oh sorry Mr and Mrs Smith, looks like Jaspar died, but we can cremate him and hold a wonderful service for the mere cost of...' What?! I was astounded. They were going to charge me what, to cremate her?

"I could put her in the ground for less. That's obscene!"

"Yes, but would your parents like her buried somewhere something else could dig her up, or would they prefer a discreet scattering of the ashes?"

She had me there. No way was Potty going to be left somewhere another dog, or fox, could dig her up. Still, if I ever needed money I could set up in opposition and make a killing. No pun intended.

Things were sorted out, a time arranged for Potty to be decently made into ashes, and Jonelle and I drove back to my folks place.

"So," I asked her on the way, "why didn't you want me to have an autopsy done on Potty? Wouldn't that have cancelled out your worries?" I shifted down a gear and it ground, making the whole vehicle shudder. I wasn't the best transmission shift person.

"I want to test the water. Where I intend on getting it done won't have paperwork or anything like that. Who do you think they'd report the findings to? You, or your mother? The last thing we need is for your parents to be freaking out about what killed their dog. I don't mean to sound mean, but your mother comes across as just a bit of a drama queen."

Funnily enough I wasn't upset; she had pinned Mum perfectly and Joy, for that matter. They'd live off the idea of Potty being murdered for the next hundred years.

"Okay. Until you have had your man do the analysis that's the end of the subject."

How cool was that? I sounded as though I knew what was going on. 'Your man' was pretty slick of me and I suddenly had this yearning to find one of my mates, possibly Grillia, and tell her how professional I was. I felt invigorated and thriving. There were things afoot and finally my Nancy Drew and Spider senses were not going to waste. I had cross genre detecting senses. It was quite possible I was getting carried away.

We dropped the Rover off, but didn't hang around mainly because I could tell Jonelle was getting pretty antsy about the water and her gym time; but also because Joy was still there and I really didn't want to get into it with her. It was easier by far to make myself scarce for the next little while. At least until they had forgotten I had a job and left it alone. There were questions I wasn't ready to answer. Like what I did – because lord alone knew the answer to that one.

We went straight to the gym, seeing as we'd both being dressed for it before Mum called. While it was just as hard as the other two days, I managed to get through my routine without putting myself or Jonelle to shame, as far as I could tell. Then it was home to have a shower while Jonelle took the water to whomever she had to do that sort of work. I glanced quickly at my voice mail.

I was surprised to see the little light flashing. Brad's voice filled the apartment. "Missed you again! Unless you are sleeping through this, which is a valid choice too. Off to the presentation so may try once more beforehand. Hope you're going great." Hm. Two calls in less than twenty four hours and not hangs ups. Both were actual messages. I hoped I wasn't looking at Mister Desperate and Weird.

I was making myself a coffee, knowing that all I would get was green tea at Jonelle's now I was on her health program (like it or not), when the phone rang. I rolled my eyes at Smudge. "Not again! I know I'm good, but the boy must be obsessed."

I picked up the phone. "Hello there you." I said with a smile in my voice.

"Are you Jonelle's new contact? Stay out of the way, Rich Bitch." I could hear the capital letters.

My hand shook and my voice did too. "Excuse me? How did you get this number? It's unlisted."

I felt the phone company had let me down. I had gone unlisted when professional sob-story people kept calling me asking for money. Unfortunately my fortune had made the papers and while I was a bleeding heart for lost dogs and legless horses, I couldn't finance all of them.

Then the name hit home.

"Jonelle?" I asked my caller. "Who are you?" My mind flashed back to the red paint on her pristine walls and I hung up, shaking.

I had only just managed to pull myself together, Smudge rolling on his tummy purring as I kneaded his fur, when the phone rang again. "Go away. I don't appreciate your hassling me."

"Sorry to hear that." Brad's deep voice murmured in my ear.

I had to go and find Jonelle, so his timing sucked. I made some vague reassurances that he'd caught me at a bad moment and I was glad that he had successfully pulled the presentation together and good luck for giving it, but could I call him back?

I waited by the window on my couch, strung out even though I was safely locked in my home. As soon as Jonelle showed her face up the stairs from the car park I ripped open my door and raced over to her. I must have looked like a mad woman because she froze and gave me the blank inscrutable face.

I pounced, grabbing her arm and propelling her into the apartment. She could hardly get the key in the door fast enough. I knew she was being polite, allowing me to push her around. If she decided not to go anywhere, I wouldn't have been moving her for love or money. Once the door was closed however, she brought us to a halt.

"Okay, mind telling me what this is all about?"

"I had a phone call." There I went again, losing my cool.

"Can I guess that it was your boy from the other night?" She raised a cool eyebrow, disentangling her arm from my deranged clutches and moving to a safe distance.

"No. Well yes, he did call but I put him off. But that was after the real call. Not that he was a fake call, though. Ah, bugger it. For once I would like to sound like a normal human being when explaining myself to you!" I snarled, pacing, getting back the shakes remembering the menace in the voice.

Jonelle took pity on me and moved me to the sofa. The green velvet sofa which I was loath to sit on because I was sure it was antique and I would ruin it. But she was firm and I sat. She pulled up a pillow and sat crossed legged at my feet. Looking up at me she said, "Okay. Deep breath. Relax. Whatever has upset you can't harm you in here. Nothing can. So tell me in your own time."

It worked. I looked into those stormy grey eyes and felt the firmness of her touch and thought to myself, no *way* was anyone getting to me in here! I took a deep breath and told her.

"I swear it must have been the same guy who painted your wall. He used the same tone and words and how *did* they get my number?" I looked to her to provide the answers, somehow knowing she was the one person who knew – well, things.

Too many things for my comfort.

Jonelle was frowning. Seriously frowning and those eyes had turned pale and frightening. I was glad she wasn't mad at me. At least, I assumed she wasn't mad at me.

"Finding unlisted numbers isn't that hard for the right people. I could get your number easily, too. The interesting thing is they have connected you to me so quickly. I don't like this, coupled with the Potty thing." She looked up at me again.

"Perhaps," she mused, "I should make a show of kicking you out? That would confuse them."

I opened my mouth and a little squeak came out before she laid a cool long finger across my lips. I could feel its pressure and that 'something' did a little twist in my stomach again. Life would be much easier if she kept her hands to herself at all times.

"Nope. That won't do. I don't think I can do that. What exactly is your hold on me, Fiona? I think, instead, I need to pay some nasty boys a little visit."

I closed my mouth. And she removed her finger. What could I say? She held a fascination for me too? Of what nature I really, I mean *really*, didn't want to know. And exactly what was she mixed up in that required a 'visit'? More and more questions were piling up and truth be told, after seeing her eyes fade into pale slits of scariness, I wasn't too sure if I wanted to know the answers.

She rose up and paced away from me, all long legs and lethal cat-like grace.

"There is just one more move I have to make, before I can take these annoying flies out of my ointment." She shot me a tight smile. "Seems my reputation is preceding me. Sometimes that can be handy and other times, like this, it can be downright dangerous. It'll teach them to keep their mouths shut."

I was confused. I had been harassed by some threatening jerk-off, my new friend was mixed up in something not so savoury, even more so than just art thievery and I had dumped Brad's call like a hot poker which was something I'd have to make up. My world was piling up around me faster than I could cope with. Plus, she wasn't making all that much sense, and did I really want her to?

There was a sneaking suspicion in my mind that whoever Jonelle was, I might not want to get mixed up with her further. At the same time, I was beginning to realise it was too late. People already were associating us together. Now, without her eagle eye to watch out for me, where would I end up?

"Ah. Who are these people, what do they want, what do you *do* exactly and who has to keep their mouths shut? I don't think you are just a retired art dealer. Art dealers don't have threatening messages painted on their walls." I looked at her with clear eyes for once.

And took in everything around me.

The new security lock on the gate; the new double glazed glass which had arrived for her windows yesterday (or was it bullet resistant?); the heavy duty lock on her new metal inlaid oak front door. My gaze swept around the room, gathering evidence. My new highly suspicious mind took in the 'art' daggers hanging on walls, the mounted 'antique' guns and I came up with a very different picture to the one I had willingly allowed myself to see.

Then I turned my wide eyes back to the owner of this fort.

She was standing still. Poised; as though about to take flight, watching me with the same hooded and wary expression tightening her face I'd seen once or twice before. I took in the flowing pants; a fashion must for her, the flat heeled boots and loose shirt. What sort of weapon could she hide in all that loose clothing? I looked at the way her hair was always back and out of her face, as though it was easier for her with it out of the way. And lastly, her strength, her power and the way she could come across all nice as pie, then turn into the barely leashed predator with a look.

I took a step back and scuttled sideways, closer to the door.

She grinned, that wolfish smile which was all teeth and gleaming eyes.

"Do you really think you could get out the door fast enough?"

Gone was the pretence at menace. It was solidly in the room gliding around between us, stroking along my skin, making me quake.

I am a total scaredy cat. No use pretending otherwise. I wasn't about to kid myself and I knew with utter certainty I wasn't going to be able to kid her. Whoever she was and whatever she was mixed up in, my detecting was going out the window. I didn't care. All I wanted to be able to do was walk out that door and not wet my pants. Sure, she was the first interesting thing in my life in a long time. But truth be told? I could do without discovering the answers to her mystery. I really could.

I stood there, barely breathing, eyes locked with the coldest gaze I had ever come across. Was this my friend, I wondered. Was it possible she would hurt me?

Chapter Nine

The tension was killing me and the need to visit the bathroom was close behind it. Just when I thought, I'll laugh that should make it ease, the door bell rang.

First thought was since when did she get a door bell? They weren't standard issue to our apartments. Mind you, you'd think I had better things to occupy my mind.

Jonelle gave me a serious look, then went to the door and peeped through the little hole. "Shit. What is he doing here?"

She wrenched it open. Standing on her doorstep was a lanky man, whose limbs looked as though he had cobbled them together from a spider. They were long, hairy and seriously thin.

He walked in. "Lovely place you have here, Jonelle. Nice to meet you." He nodded at me. "So, what's been happening? Where's our painting?"

I almost felt Jonelle groan. But that could have been my imagination. It wasn't my imagination though when she brushed passed me two things happened. She rolled her eyes and I felt my skin contract, like a pleasant shock or something. Get a grip, I told myself, the woman was half way to threatening you a minute ago and now you think she's flirting with you?

I needed therapy.

"Phil, I'm working on it. I told you to trust me. There were things I have to do before I can move on this. I know where they are, if not exactly where they have put the painting. Are you sure they didn't do this just to piss you off?" She moved to stand a finger's width from my shoulder.

Was she protecting me or was she making sure I didn't bolt? There wasn't much chance of that. I think at some stage I froze to the floor.

I lived a quiet, blameless life. Now, within a small space of time, I was dodging my own dating rules, visiting my parents, sleeping on pillows in a strange woman's house, receiving threatening phone calls and getting trapped in a room when all I wanted to do was go home. Could someone please say "out of control" really fast for me? It was absurd. I did the usual pinch myself to make sure I was awake trick, but the scenery didn't change.

"Now Jon, don't get excited. I was in town and thought, hey! I know who has moved to Canberra. Why don't I look her up? You don't want visitors? Don't give out your address." Phil cruised around the room having a good old look.

An explosion of air tickled my neck. She was obviously a lot closer than I'd thought and that gave me a sliver of disquiet down my spine.

"I haven't just given out my address to you for a social visit. It was for emergencies. You are, after all, my client. Believe me; no one else will be getting it at all. Now, I'm kind of busy here. If you want an update, I suggest you phone."

I wouldn't want that clipped tone pointed in my direction. Mind you, I was looking at more than a clipped tone if this Phil was to leave. And it looked like he was about to.

"Sure Jonelle. Sure. Just tell me, when are we getting our painting back? The wall is so bare without it, you know?" Phil had stopped his rambling and now looked her straight in the eye. He wasn't cowed by her tone at all, and I wondered where he got his balls from because truth be told, he didn't look all that courageous.

"I'll go and have a chat to them in a couple of days. Something else will have fallen into place then and it'll be all systems go. Now, please let me enjoy my day in peace!"

And just like that, he was gone with a mere nod again in my general direction. I didn't try to sneak out behind him. Though the majority of me was still a bit shaky, there was that little bit that was too nosey, too curious, to allow all these things to happen around me without knowing what was going on.

Jonelle closed the door behind him and I was back in the spotlight. But instead of ending whatever it was she had begun, Jonelle leaned against the door and laughed. It was infectious and before I could help it, I was laughing too, though Lord alone knows what about. I think I was laughing from reaction. After all, it wasn't my imagination – she had been threatening me, hadn't she?

"Okay." She straightened and the laughter faded, though humour still twinkled in those eyes. I made sure there was space between us. Cold comfort though that idea was, I hoped to give myself a bit of room to move.

"I have to go. There is something I urgently need to take care of now." She held up her hand. "I know you'll have questions. I just don't know how much of them I can answer. Sometimes you are best not knowing, Princess. Really you are."

I could stand it no longer. "What do you mean, not knowing is best for me? Someone threatened me on my unlisted phone! You threatened me, too. And this Phil guy. What is his deal? I'm in this now. You chose me to work for you. They think I'm in this anyway, and that is as good as an invitation. You're just going to move me sideways and hope nothing happens to me? That never works. Don't you watch movies? I need to know … stuff!"

Come to think of it, where had *I* got my balls from? On loan from Phil?

Jonelle stood there, uncertain. But I wasn't just about to disappear and I think she knew it. I had my stubborn face on.

"Okay. It seems you need to know a few things. If I can't trust you with this, Princess, your life will not be worth living."

"Now, why don't I think you're joking?" I asked her.

She grinned, once again on an even keel. "I never joke about making people's lives hell. They may not take me seriously when they really need to. Here, pull up a cushion and make yourself comfortable."

"Comfortable? You are joking, aren't you? A moment ago you were looking at me as though I was entrée and you want me to be comfortable?" I shook my head at the absurdity of it all.

"You have a point. But still, when I am going to make you entrée, Princess, you'll know about it." She gave me a new smile. One I hadn't seen before, with just a touch of the flirt behind it. I gulped. Who was on whose menu here?

I settled on the cushions and she joined me. Knee to knee we faced each other. I wasn't so keen on meeting her eyes, but I thought it was the sort of thing someone detecting would do. After all, eyes are windows to souls. Though whoever came up with that had obviously never looked into Jonelle's, because they were giving away nothing.

"Let's see. What can I tell you? Phil has employed me to find a painting that was stolen from he and his wife, Diana's, home. This marvellous piece of artwork was originally placed with him by an art dealer you now know, several years ago." Jonelle raised her eyebrow at me.

Man, they had to be the most overworked brows in history. But they got their point across. Phil got his picture from her. Okay, now what else? I nodded to keep her going.

"I promise my clients discretion, protection and a life time response system. They call me if there are any problems ... because not everything I acquire for them is totally viewed by the law as being theirs. I was an art procurer, not necessarily a dealer. I was paid a lot of money to put certain art works in the hands of certain people. Though sometimes," she mused "it was legal, which kind of spiced it all up."

I coughed. Some company I was keeping.

She snapped back to the present. "Sorry. Anyway, someone got upset about Phil having this painting and took it. I'm getting it back for him. I can't believe how slipshod his security measures are, even after I left him explicit instructions. Some people always believe they're beyond the reach of thieves." Here she smiled. And I couldn't for the life of me imagine ever meeting anyone who thought they were beyond the reach of *her* hand.

Then she shrugged. "I have one place I feel vulnerable, which is why I need time to sort it out. Then there is you."

She brought her wandering gaze slap bang into mine. Her eyes were warm pools of grey and her lips curved up. I was a bit freaked. I was beginning to get the sneaking suspicion that Jonelle's interest in me wasn't just for my scintillating conversation. I wasn't too sure I wanted to travel this road. But how to make her jump tracks?

She probably read my discomfort, because I didn't have the face to be a spy. "They appear to have linked me with you in a business capacity, thus far. This means you're safer than if they think you're my friend." Added a little sadly, "It isn't always safe to be considered a friend of mine, which is why I don't socialise all that often."

"I'm safer as business, because they think I'm as tough as you?" She nodded. "Let's go with that then. I like the idea of being the tough bitch for once."

Though I had to pray it was never tested because that could get interesting. It was funny how neither of us mentioned her just not having anything to do with me.

"Are the baddies really, um, bad?" I wanted to clear that up.

She laughed. "Not these ones. They like to play pretend, but it's pretty much bluff. Still, I like to be safe. And I have two more jobs in the pipeline which means I have to tidy some ends up. Plus," she mused, "one never knows when the past could catch up with you. There are a few people from way back who I'd prefer not to reconnect with. The person hanging around your parents' place is something I need to look into, too."

I was curious. What did she have in her life that could be used against her? Would she just answer if I asked? There was only one way to find out. Funnily enough, she didn't take umbrage. It was like we were in our own little cocoon and this was confession time.

"I don't see much of my parents unless I go to them. But there is someone who is vulnerable." She hesitated and I remained silent. This was a big deal. "You know? I had your background checked."

The change in conversation threw me. Then I caught up.

"What?"

She didn't look shamefaced about it. "It was necessary if I was to feel I could trust you. Mind you, you have an outstanding parking fee you'll be hauled into court about if you don't pay it soon."

Bugger. I'd forgotten about that. I tried to make a mental note to remember to pay that either later today or tomorrow. She stood up and held out her hand, but I struggled up without it and she grimaced at my independence issues.

"If you aren't busy, you can come and help me tie off my loose end?"

I must have done my imitation of a guppy again, mouth flipping open and closed, because she laughed, a light-hearted sound. "It'll be nice to have someone come along. Perhaps you can go back at some stage. I won't be able to until I have to move again."

All this cryptic crap was going to drive me to drink. Did the woman ever speak in whole sentences? But, as it happened I didn't have anything else to do, so she had the perfect person to follow her around. It was in my job description, right?

We drove off in her car this time, as we'd been using mine up to this point. She had explained it away by telling me hers was in for a service. And once more my internal envy machine snivelled in impotent jealousy.

She had a Maserati. The cat's pyjamas of hot cars. Still, if she was looking to be inconspicuous, then she was certainly going out of her way to stuff that plan. It was sleek, silver and the yummiest thing I'd ever seen. I stroked it before I got in and caught Jonelle sniggering to herself. Well, in my defence I had never blown that much money on a car.

I sat back and lapped up the luxury. It could handle and had power to boot under that hood. It kind of growled in a very low down tickle kind of way. We sped along the wide, simple streets of Canberra until we floated out of town. She pulled into a long drive way and parked her flashy car next to a garage. Then she opened said garage and pulled out in a Toyota Camry. I stumbled after her. It was the sort of car my folks had: a get-lost-in-the-crowd sort of car.

And get lost we did. Round and round, back and over and finally pulled into a nursing home miles from home and an hour later. I was feeling remarkably car sick. I could only guess that whoever or whatever she had stashed in this home was worth bucket-loads to her.

"No one followed us. I would have picked out anything that stayed on our tail." She took me into the foyer, and a nurse smiled and nodded in recognition. We took a left hand corridor and through some more twists and turns arrived at a pretty nondescript door. Here she paused.

"You have to be quiet now, until you're accepted. You'll understand. Loud noises freak her out." And with that she stepped into the room beyond.

I followed close behind. There was no way I was letting her out of my sight.

The room was more than hospital issue. There were large double glass sliding doors opening onto a little patio which was fenced in. No one was going midnight strolling here. Seated on one of the chairs in the sun on the patio was a thin and fragile looking girl. Lank dark hair hung down her back and I could see her shoulder blades through the top she was wearing.

Jonelle moved out to join her. The girl turned her head in a jerky fashion, then relaxed when she saw who it was. In profile, I could suddenly see the resemblance. This was Jonelle's weak spot: her little sister.

She went closer and stroked the hair back from her sister's face. The girl smiled a huge, almost vacant imitation of Jonelle's own grin. Jonelle leaned down and kissed her forehead.

"Hey sweetheart, got someone here for you to meet." She looked up and waved me in.

The girl leaped out of her chair and hid behind Jonelle. That way I got to see her face to face.

She could have been as beautiful as Jonelle. Once upon a time and in a different universe. As it was, some of Jonelle's features were unmistakeable. But the rest were a sad destroyed mockery of the vitality that was Jonelle.

She'd been in a very bad accident. Her face had a long deep scar line all the way down the left hand side and her mouth twisted down like a stroke victim with patches covered in burn scars. The eyes, which on Jonelle glowed with inner fire and intelligence, took me in, but reflected nothing. Not a lot was going on. The terrible expression 'lights are on but no one is home', flashed through my mind, even though it felt disloyal to Jonelle to think such a thing.

Her sister, her look-alike who wore her face, was mentally disabled in some fashion as well as the disastrously bad accident. I wanted to cry. Instead, of course, I walked over and smiled, holding out my hand in friendship.

"It's okay, Jodi. She's my friend. See?" Jonelle stepped forward and took my hand. I felt the familiar zap, but allowed the situation to sweep it away. "Her name is Fiona. This is my twin sister, Jodi."

I felt my world tilt a little. Her twin: the mirror image, the copy. I couldn't imagine what it would be like to know that this person could have been the closest human to you, but instead to always look after them and shield them from the outside world. She had a twin, and yet was completely alone. Poor Jonelle, I thought to myself.

I tried to talk to her. I really did. But I had no experience with this sort of thing. I rambled more than usual. Which was quite an amazing feat considering the amount of crap I managed to come out with at the best of times. It was a relief when the visit was cut short by Jonelle's phone going off. Another cryptic conversation in another language ensued, and I stared out at the impossibly bright sunshine, feeling lost and alone.

Jonelle wound her conversation up and gave herself a little shake. "We have to go, sweetie. I'll send Fiona to come and see you again sometime real soon, okay?"

She nodded at me, the signal to make my goodbyes, which I did. Then we were back in the car and headed into town. For the first kilometre there was silence. Then Jonelle burst out with, "It took me ages to get her a place there. Close, but not so close someone would find her." She looked over at me, fingers tight on the steering wheel. It looked as if she was trying to strangle it.

"I wish I could come and see her more. But I am pretty sure no one knows she exists and me continually visiting, well that would be too obvious."

"What happened to her?" I asked quietly, trying to make myself small in the seat, but still wanting to know the answer.

Jonelle slowed her throttled driving, and turned off the main road. It looked like we were going back to get the Maserati, but once again we were going to do it covert style.

"Somehow during our birth she lacked oxygen for too long. Madeline never really went into it with me. All I know is Jodi has been like that, mentally, all our lives. Because we travelled so much, she had the best care in Switzerland and we changed her name early on. I think Madeline didn't want her too closely associated with us, even then. Which has helped me out now, as no one knows I have a twin, as far as I know."

"When I came home to Australia and thought I'd try to make it my permanent base, I moved her here too. I was taking her for a drive one day when someone lost control of their vehicle and crashed into us." The hands were once again throttling the steering wheel and her voice was strained. The blame game I knew well.

"I escaped but went back into the car for her. It was too late to prevent the damage you can see now, but at least it saved her life. I checked out the other car. It was a hire vehicle for a couple on holidays. They were both killed."

She glanced over at me swiftly as she took a corner way too fast. "I followed back into their history a long way. I wanted to make sure they weren't a hit, because if they were, someone out there knew about Jodi. I couldn't link them to any of my known ... associates, or stakeholders. As far as I could tell, they really were what the hire company had them down as. Mr and Mrs Lang on their second honeymoon. Believe me, if I could have asked them for any information, they'd have talked to me. But they were pretty much charred messes. Their car exploded."

I sat there trying to absorb it all. It was kind of scary. It didn't matter if the people responsible for the car crash were dead. What mattered was her first thought had been 'what if this was intentional?'

That piece of information made my stomach queasy in all the worst possible ways.

Who did she know who would want to kill her? Surely not just over some stolen art. There had to be more, and did I really want to be involved with that?

While I had as strong a self preservation streak as the next person, my curiosity was stronger. I thought Jonelle would work pretty hard to see I didn't come to any harm. Seeing her sister made me aware that harm was subjective and not always preventable.

"I think I need to know some more things." I kept my eyes on Jonelle's profile and noticed her mouth turn up in a smile.

"I always thought you would," she responded.

"The most pressing is can you keep me out of harm's way? And then, in order, what sort of harm are we talking about, who is going to possibly bring about this harm and can I trust you?" I never really did think about things before I opened my mouth. Even as I heard the words coming out and forming in the air between us I realised they were all wrong.

I should have trusted my instincts about her. She eased back the acceleration and answered me directly, for her.

"I can't promise you no harm will come to you by being my friend and working with me. Not everything I do walks the line of legal and the people I deal with aren't always the nicest. Sometimes things happen that are out of even my control. I would never put you into a position where I felt things could get messy, but if you continue working with me, there is going to come a time when the call will be yours and the outcomes totally in your hands. I hope you can deal with that. Not everyone makes the right decisions when crunch time comes. And sometimes there are no right decisions, just ones we make at the time and have to learn to live with later."

I was to remember that at the end.

Learning to live with the decisions one makes can be the hardest thing in the world.

"Most of my actual clients wouldn't be harmful unless I failed in the job they set me. The only harm would come from those I work against. Like if I am on a body guarding gig, then they may be after my client but get me instead. You've seen the scar I have. It's a knife wound I received many years ago. Stray knives and guns are part of my job sometimes, yes. But should you be in any danger? I wouldn't like to think so. And lastly, yes you can trust me. I have to trust you, don't I? I think it can be a two way street."

I sat and thought about it. Sure, it appeared as though she was trusting me. But she still wasn't telling me enough for me to feel exactly comfy.

"Why can't you just come out and tell me stuff? I will be less likely to make mistakes if I knew what is going on most of the time."

"It's because I don't want you to be in danger that I don't tell you," she sounded exasperated.

"If you hadn't asked me to work for you, I wouldn't be in danger!" My voice rose. This was so circular. It hadn't been all that long and all ready I was looking for ways to wiggle out of my employment. Though I had noticed she mentioned working with her, not for her.

"Living anywhere near me can be a danger! I like having someone around I like and trust. It's different. But the danger comes from getting too involved which is why I am deliberately trying to keep you from the dirty work! If you just stay in the office or did the little tasks I ask of you, nothing should ever happen to you."

"Phil has seen me now, in your place, just hanging out like friends do. Tell me he's no danger to me."

I was getting picky, but suddenly I was seeing our relationship in terms of a car crash victim. Her sister may already have been mentally disabled, but the visual was more disturbing now her face was a tragic mess. My panicky mind was wading through mush, as usual.

Her breath exploded out in a sigh.

"Yes, Phil has seen you. And as soon as I have finished the job for him, he'll forget you. On the whole, he knows that going after someone in my life is the fastest way to," she gave me a look, "a lot of trouble. He's currently on my good side. It's a good place for him to be and he knows it. Don't fret about good old Phil. Don't fret about most people you meet through me, they know I'm a worse enemy than they would like."

"Yeah, that is *so* reassuring," I sulked.

Couldn't she see this wasn't making me feel any better? After all, she was talking about who was afraid of who. Just because she was the bigger gun wasn't much help to me. It all sounded so far out of this world. Sort of like, my brother is bigger than your brother so nah.

Jonelle ground her teeth. "No one will be coming after you. You manage my paperwork for heaven's sakes! You won't be coming out on jobs with me, will you? You're quite safe in my place. There are triggers and alarms everywhere. No one can get in without me knowing."

"You're scheduled to go to Sydney tomorrow. What are you going to do if the alarm goes off then?" I was feeling very petty by this stage.

"I have a local guy who handles those things," she replied shortly.

By the time we got back to the office, or Jonelle's home, depending on which way I was looking at it, the morning was well and truly over, and half the afternoon as well. So much had happened since I crawled out of bed at five forty five - I was exhausted.

Jonelle waved me off. "Go rest or something. There's no need for you to come and sit at a computer for a couple of hours. Eat and sleep. I'll see you tomorrow morning."

Ugh. That meant she expected us to go through the gym thing even though she was due to fly to Sydney. I was too physically tired to wonder what she was up to there. I just wanted to crash out and forget big chunks of today.

Of course, that was when I remembered I was supposed to be calling Brad. I put it on my mental to do list, beside the parking ticket. One week ago the idea of calling, or seeing Brad, had been the most exciting thing I had going for me. All of a sudden, he was becoming a hassle - just something else I had to do or fit in to the day.

How had my priorities changed so quickly? I felt a bit disturbed about this. I was the person to whom social engagements were supposed to mean something. And there I was putting off, *jettisoning*, my potential man because of my new job.

I was unrecognisable to myself. Who was this woman, coming home late afternoon after a busy day, head full of knowledge and mouth too tired to speak? It was scary and the most bizarre part of it was, I quite liked her!

I turned the phones down and fell into bed. I didn't want to hear about Brad's presentation, nor receive a call from Mum detailing how things were going to go at the ceremony on Friday for Potty. I most certainly did not wish to receive a call from my mystery man who would probably just abuse me anyway. Even Smudge wasn't fed. He got an abstract pat on the head and then I was out like a light.

I slept the clock around and woke up feeling fresh and alive at five in the morning. I hadn't realised there was a five in the morning.

My wandering mind picked over the previous day, as I showered and dressed for the gym.

What delighted me the most was, I could get a cup of coffee in before Jonelle appeared at my door so she'd never notice. That was wishful thinking at the best of times, because as soon as the kettle whistled, I heard a familiar thump on the door. What was her problem, it was like she had been watching for my front lights to come on.

"Morning sunshine. That's not coffee I smell, is it?" Larger than life and full of frisky beans, Jonelle came in once the door was unlocked.

I hunched my shoulders, which could in principle be either positive or negative; she could take it whatever way she liked. The main thing was, she was early and I had my coffee in my hands, no way could she get it off me this time.

She perched on the bar stools overlooking the breakfast bar. Leaning her elbows on the bar she cupped her face with her hands.

"I just got a phone call. The scientific mind is never asleep. According to my sources, Potty's water contained traces of ibuprofen and metaldehyde. Both of these things, taken in the dose which was indicated by the ratio of water to poison, would cause Potty to slip into a coma and die. Someone knew their poisons, because both of these things are accessible around the house and thus it could be explained as an accidental death. By anyone, that is, except your parents. Who like a lot of people who love their dog, don't leave those sorts of things just lying around. The poisoner wouldn't have thought they'd have the water checked."

"Without you there, it probably would have just been tipped out. So they were almost safe." Poor Potty, she'd never done anything, except love her family and guard them just like she was meant to. In the end that instinct had caused a loony to kill her off.

"What do we do with this information? I don't think the police would be interested in a dog murder, though we can run it by Amy if she ever gets back."

"Amy?" Jonelle's voice hardly changed at all, but I was beginning to know her and I picked out the caution. "Why would your Amy be interested?"

"What, you didn't run a background check on all the Apartmates? And she's not my Amy as much as she is the flatmate of Heather in

No.2 and it so happens, she's a police officer. Lowly at this point in time, but we have great hopes for her future."

I watched Jonelle's inscrutable face become more and more blank, while her eyes whirled with thought.

I grinned. "It should prove interesting when she asks you what it is you do, don't you think?"

Jonelle glared at me. "It's not funny. She could be a liability."

I did *not* like the way she said that. I returned the glare.

She softened.

"Though it could be a benefit once it's more widely known I live with a policewoman handy. But this police gig is pretty new, isn't it?" she added. I bet she even knew what time everyone went to bed. So much for pretending she hadn't known what Amy was.

"Let's leave that. Right now we have to work out what that guy had to do with anything and how much trouble my folks are in without their dog. I think that is a little bit more important than whether or not Amy is going to uncover any of your deep and dark secrets." I was getting a bit impatient; fear always did that to me.

"Not a lot, I don't think." Jonelle absentmindedly picked at the grapes in my fruit bowl. The gym appeared to be off the agenda and I can't say my body wasn't pleased, because that would be a straight out lie.

"Whoever he is, he'll probably go in one day and check it out. The most he can do is link the fact they are your family and thus have little or nothing to do with me. But it gives him leverage against you, which suddenly ups you as a player in whatever game he's playing. I won't know what that is until I see who he is."

I stood leaning against the fridge, coffee mug in hand, thinking. The flashing time on the microwave read five fifty. My world was standing on its head.

"What we need to do is set up some sort of surveillance and get his photo. That way you can see if you can identify him. Perhaps I can do that while you are in Sydney? I've forgotten, how long are you going to be away?"

Oh how much did I wish I could tape the conversation and play it back to the rest of the Apartmates, or my family, or *someone*. I sounded so sure of myself. Time enough later for the severe reality check I was up for.

"Only a couple of days, I'll be back Saturday morning. You'll have to come and collect me from the airport. Surveillance sounds a great idea. But be aware it's nothing like the movies."

She gave me an indulgent look. Humph. I'd show her. I'd get the photos and have the perp half way identified by the time she got back (we were way off in lala land now, me and my imagination, but that was cool with me).

"I'll give you some passwords for the computer. If you *can* get a photograph, you can run it through the database I have stored and see what you come up with. If I've crossed paths with him before, then we'll know about it."

I wondered what else she had up her sleeve, but all things considered, perhaps it was best not to know. There would be nothing worse than the apprentice going hell for leather while the master was away. We all knew how that turned out for a certain cartoon mouse.

I finished my coffee and we headed to the gym (no, it wasn't forgotten). It didn't matter as much to me now. I thought, hey, if I get into a bad situation doing my new important surveillance work, it would be nice to be able to run away really fast rather than very slowly. So I pumped those weights with new vigour and stepped that stepper with, well, a bit less vigour and lo and behold by the time I got to the treadmill, my vigour had all drained away leaving me pooped. But it was the thought that counted, right?

We got back and I headed for the shower. A brief stop with Smudge, feeding time for the poor little guy who missed his dinner last night, then I found a black tracksuit and I was back at Jonelle's door. She opened it and burst out laughing.

"What?" I looked down at my snazzy midnight suit which, by the way, could have passed as Ninja material, and then back at her. "This is perfect for skulking."

Still sniggering she took me to the second spare room.

"Yeah, perfect if you want to stand out like a sore thumb! It's bright and early, for heavens' sake, not the dark of night. What would your neighbours think? Surveillance doesn't mean sitting low in a car at midnight hoping to pop out at the right time. You have to have a plausible reason for hanging around. Make something up, appear casual, relaxed. It's your home street; you'll never get away with secretive. Be a little realistic."

I pouted. I'd had high hopes about this surveillance gig. Sneaking into the kitchen for an illicit cup of coffee, flash-less cameras.

She was right, it wasn't like I imagined, or the movies made it out to be. Jonelle sent me back for smart casual clothes, after she had unearthed some cameras from the spare room. Those, at least, were like I thought they would be. One was of highlighter thickness and shape, the other was a tiny little thing I was afraid I'd lose.

But once I was at Mum's, it all went downhill. For starters, I couldn't think of one single reason why I would be there. I walked around for a while, my heart racing thinking, 'I wonder if that is him?' every time someone drove past, and taking what turned out to be a load of useless pictures. Then once I'd done one lap of the street, feeling heady and scared, I was suddenly bored and less convinced that this was a great idea.

It appeared to be less of a good idea when Mum came home just as I slipped inside for a quick coffee. We all had keys still and Mum was always going on about how we were free to treat the place like home. But in reality, we needed to book well in advance, as she wasn't a spontaneous person.

I'd barely put the kettle on and settled the instant coffee into a mug when her car rolled into the driveway. Damn it. How was I going to explain this? More to the point, how was I going to get out without listening to hours of Potty this and Potty that. I wasn't in the mood for a day of endless tea and reminiscences. I had important work to do, and while I wasn't at liberty to discuss it with my mother, it would have been nice to drop hints about it. That way she might take my new job seriously. A part of *me* wasn't, but it would be cool if she did.

How could *I* take myself seriously? Here I was, little miss know nothing, trying to do the whole secret agent thingy with cameras and a surveillance database. It was beyond ludicrous.

There was no point in attempting to hide. After all, the kettle would be still warm and there would be a mug out. So I got down another one and made her a cup of tea while she got out of the car. I nearly spilled hot water all over the place when I saw what was in her arms. Another bloody puppy! That was certainly quick work, Potty wasn't even an ash yet.

She brought the squirming little thing right into the kitchen before she noticed me. "Oh! Fiona. You scared me half to death. What are you doing here at this hour? Aren't you meant to be at work?"

She deposited the puppy on the floor and I took in details. It certainly wasn't a St Bernard or Newfoundland. For which a part of me was grateful. While I loved Potty, finding friends to mind her had been a bugger. Also, her sheer size made her impractical for two people at retiring age.

This one was more in character. It was pretty tiny, had long crinkly ears and soft browny red fur which curled in silly places. I squatted down and greeted the new arrival. It licked me with great enthusiasm.

"So, what is it? And what do we call it?" I tweaked its ear and it fell over in a squiggly spasm of delight.

Mum watched, frowning slightly at its lack of manners. "So many things you forget about having a puppy. Mostly the mess." She recalled my questions. "Oh, it's a Cocker Spaniel and I thought we'd call him Puddle."

My folks had the strangest idea of what constituted appropriate names for animals. The pup would grow out of making puddles, but Puddle he'd stay forever.

I petted his tummy, then got up from the floor to finish my coffee.

Mum went about putting away some other shopping, while Puddle wandered around making sure there was nothing edible at his height.

"So are you going to let me know what is going on or not? I thought you told us you had a job?" She put a water bowl down and Puddle immediate sat in it. I was relieved to notice it was a new one.

"What did you do with the old bowl?" Ever the curious one.

"You mean Potty's? I didn't think it was appropriate to make Puddle drink from her old bowl. It was in terrible condition, so I threw it away. Why? Were you attached to it for some reason? Because if you were, it's in the garbage and let me tell you it is just not sanitary to get it out."

There, see? Nothing is easy with my family. One simple question from me and suddenly it was like I actually was looking for the damn thing and wanting it for some sinister reason. I wondered briefly if it was like walking through a minefield with every family.

"I was just wondering. I think that is the best place for it." Because heavens knew how I'd have explained accidentally throwing it away so Puddle couldn't gnaw on potentially lethal plastic.

Mum was still looking at me. That 'you haven't answered all my questions' face mothers get and I couldn't stand.

"I do have a job, but this morning I'm free, as I'm doing something later for my boss," liar liar, "and as I was in the neighbourhood I thought it would be nice to stop by and have a cup of coffee and now you're home, which of course makes it even better because we can have a chat and I was wondering if anything new had happened around here and well, with a new puppy obviously it has!"

Try saying all that in one breath. It had to be done. Sometimes she wouldn't let me finish an explanation and sometimes my own guilty tongue ran away from me. It sucked to be the youngest.

Mum went back to sorting stuff out. A never ending hobby of hers, I came to the conclusion. Talking to me over her shoulder she said, "I'm glad you have a job dear, it's more rewarding than sitting around talking to your friends all day. I hope you get to do some interesting things."

I didn't have the heart to tell her that would be the understatement of the year. Things may have started out slowly, but that was all about to change.

"Do you remember that man I was telling you about? The one who accidentally hit poor, old Potty?"

I held my breath. Allow nothing I do or say to put her off from what she is about to say, I prayed. Instead I just nodded and grunted, like it wasn't all that interesting to me.

"Well, I saw him again, when I pulled in just now. Reading a newspaper on the park bench waiting for a bus he was, but let me tell you, he wasn't fooling me. It was definitely the same man. Now what is he trying to prove? We all know he's got a car."

I tried for restraint. But all of me just wanted to sprint out of the house and run down to the bus stop. It didn't matter if he knew I was on to him, what did I care? As soon as I had that snap shot, he was a done deal.

I started to sweat lightly. I hadn't expected to actually see my man so soon. Jonelle told me that surveillance was usually long and tedious and filled with too much coffee and not enough sleep. I wanted to call her and tell her what an amazing spy I was going to make. But caution told me that calling her in Sydney before I got the shot was possibly counting my chickens.

I took a few long swallows of my excruciatingly hot coffee. I had made it with all the care and preparation of settling in for the long haul. Now I bolted it, thinking a scalded tongue was all in the line of duty.

"Sorry, Mum. I didn't realise the time. I have to run; I would hate to make a bad impression on my boss this early in the piece." She gave me a startled look. It must have appeared strange. I waltzed in, made general conversation and then ran out.

"Sure Fiona dear. Keeping the boss happy is very important in a job, especially when you have limited enough experience to fall back on." There was the kicker. "So off you go. We'll see you Friday when they cremate Potty. Your boss will allow you to come to the service, won't he, dear? And bring that lovely Jonelle. She was so kind the other day, helping you out with Potty. I think she is a lovely friend for you to have." Ah, how she liked to make sure I was well catered for with friends.

I so didn't want to tell her Jonelle was my boss.

Why?

Well, firstly she would get all huffy about me not having a proper job, just one off a friend. Then she would start to panic about me spending too much time with the one person. She also had this archaic idea that all bosses were men, simply because it was a world full of businessmen when she had last sallied forth to work for anyone.

While I loved to tease and frustrate my mother, I didn't have the heart to tell her that in the twenty first century the face of business was very different to her day. When I looked closely at the work my new female boss did, I really didn't have the heart to tell her anything at all.

"I'm sure I'll get the morning off and Jonelle would love to come, except she's in Sydney. I'll let her know she was invited." If I remembered; it wasn't exactly a priority of ours.

"Look, I have to run. See you tomorrow." And I leaned forward and pecked her cheek, an uncharacteristic enough gesture to earn me a stern look of reproof. I knew better than to touch her carefully made up cheek that look said. I had thought for a moment, it was time I tried harder with my family and my mother in particular. Mind you, that look reminded me of all the reasons that wasn't going to happen.

I tried to be cool and attract no attention. Slipping behind the wheel of the borrowed Camry (for anonymity purposes) I cruised down the end of the street only to see the bus pulling away. Well damn it! I had stayed chatting too long.

My heart started its fast and heavy rhythm. The only thing I could do was to follow the damn bus, even though that felt really stupid. My first day out on a job and already I was out of my depth.

How did you discreetly follow a massive orange and yellow bus while trying to see who was getting off it each stop? Detecting aside, my insecure demons were telling me I wasn't cut out for this and it was time to head home.

The only thing that kept me at it was the thought of Jonelle's face if I told her why I lost our man. Then it hit me. I hadn't asked Mum what he looked like. Or what he was wearing. Of all the people on the bus how the hell was I supposed to know which one was the right guy? Now I was feeling even worse. I took the first exit off the main road and headed to a snack bar. If in doubt, eat something. I had my curves to sustain.

I sat in the car and munched my way through a burger and nuggets. Not nutritious, but I didn't care. How was I meant to get this thing done without interrogating my mother and thus making her suspicious about what it was I was up to? I pondered for a while and then I had it!

Steph. A simple solution. Mum loved Steph.

I had absolutely no idea why or *how* they got along. It was totally off my charts of explain-ability. They just did. And they loved to gossip - about everything. I'd prime Steph and take her tomorrow in place of Jonelle for the funeral, then we could still be cooking with gas. Steph's morose way of being, but total need to know the latest on everything, was a balm for my mother. It just meant getting a hold of Steph...

I snapped open my mobile and scrolled through the address book. The amazing thing was I actually had my mobile on me. I never felt the need to stay connected like a lot of my mates did. Mainly because I was usually watching telly at home and anyone could get me on the landline.

"Steph! How are you?" Social chit chat was needed with Steph before business or she was likely to hang up.

"Mmm?" I think that was indication she'd had a big one and wasn't awake yet. I glanced at my watch.

Lord help me, I'd called Steph at eleven thirty in the morning.

It was a hanging offence. Funny how quickly things changed. Only a couple of weeks ago no one could have got me on the phone before midday either. Now I was calling my mates, not giving time a thought. It seemed important to get things done right at the minute and I wasn't going to waste the daylight hours waiting for Steph to wake up.

Funny, I could vaguely remember something similar hurled at my head by Mum …

"Sorry to wake you. Are you free tomorrow morning? Potty died the other day and Mum is holding some sort of service and cremation for her. Want to come?" If anyone liked a good funeral, it was Steph.

"Hey! Your old dog. That's too bad. Sure I'll come." Suddenly suspicious. "What time is this thing?"

"Erm, do you think you could be ready by nine thirty?" The cremation was at ten, but I had to fill her in on the information we were digging for. Hopefully this wouldn't mean a total confession as to why. I wasn't too sure what level of confidentiality we were dealing with here.

On the other hand, it was Steph. Who was she going to tell?

There was a not so subtle sigh and groan. "Yeah, if I must be. I'll wear … let me see, something black. See you then. Come and get me." And she hung up. Surprise, Steph would be wearing black. I wondered if the girl owned anything in colour.

Finishing my burger, I drove the car back to the garage where I picked it up. The mechanic there nodded, but didn't come over. Maybe he was paid not to show too much interest in the comings and goings of that particular vehicle. I was beginning to see patterns of suspicious behaviour where there wasn't any.

I climbed back into my own zippy little convertible and roared off home. It was only lunchtime and I had failed in my first assignment. Not, of course, that I was about to admit this to Jonelle if she called. There was always tomorrow and I wasn't going to give up until I had nailed that photo.

Grabbing Smudge I went over to Jonelle's. She had shown me how to disarm the front door. It reset itself once I closed it with a reassuring thunk and snick. The inside was free to be roamed around in, but the shell was intruder proofed. I felt safe and snug.

Putting on the kettle I wandered into the office to make sure the computers were up and running. The laptop was gone, but that was to be expected, Jonelle was sure to need that for whatever it was she was doing in Sydney. The other two were humming nicely, so I went to make myself some of that horrid green tea. Jonelle had hidden the coffee beans, so unless I wanted to unlock that door again and nab some from my place it was green tea, or other unmentionable herbal mixtures. I wasn't going to tell her this, but I was getting used to the green tea.

I brought the whole pot with me to the computer. In my bad old days I would have made sure it was my procrastination measure and used the opportunity to keep going back into the kitchen as often as possible. Now I had notes I wanted to read and actual things going on in my life, who had time for procrastination?

There were the last of the old files to print and code and label and file – Jonelle had had a stack of closed ones which needed to be sorted. It was the open and current ones I was more interested in, but I knew that any good sleuth needed to do their research so I was prepared to take my old filings more seriously this time.

Plus, I had access codes. I was hoping they opened more than the photo database so I could cross reference code numbers and get a fuller picture of what I was dealing with.

Smudge came in and leaped up on the in-tray. A couple of turns and he was a small ball of fluff, snoozing away to himself. The life of a cat: nothing but free feeds, sunshine, sleep and a bit of play if so inclined. And no one expecting you to be nice or friendly. A cat was allowed to have the manners that were so deplored in me.

I tried my access code in a folder labelled 2000 +. I was hoping to find what she had been doing in the last decade and bingo, it worked. Now I had a whole stack of files ready to be plundered, I felt kind of weird. There it was - the open door to Aladdin's cave or Pandora's Box, depending on your point of view, and I was almost reluctant to click on one.

What if I didn't like what I found?

Chapter Ten

I read the headings and double clicked on something called "Natasha". That sounded harmless enough.

It wasn't only harmless, it was actually quite boring. It was full of dates when she had made contact with the client, dot points on what was covered and a photo of the artworks in question. The whole transaction was legal and totally dull.

She had gone to Italy, talked to the owners, done a price analysis and put in a bid. From the correspondence, there had been a lot of haggling but eventually her client Natasha had walked away with the goods and a receipt for … how much? My eyes boggled. Just shy of two million. I wondered what the commission on that sort of deal was.

I kept scrolling. Remuneration was next on the list. It staggered me. What was even more interesting was the line underneath which was titled Retainer. There Jonelle had typed: For future security and on call problem solving. There was a retainer fee for the life of the agreement which in this case turned out to be ten years.

I needed to get that straight. She was earning shed loads for doing nothing? Just making sure she was available to quiet the fears of a paranoid millionaire. I was rocked off my feet; good thing I was sitting down. I wasn't a hundred percent sure what it meant by on-call problem solving, but I could understand figures and I was suddenly liking the sort of money she was making. The return on her investment, of time and energy, was staggering. And spoke to my financial soul like a beacon.

I closed the Natasha file and moved onto another one labelled Andrew M. This morning's little essay into her reading materials had to be more interesting than printing out old reports.

Pay dirt.

I knew I wouldn't be able to read these things unless she had deliberately wanted me to, so I wasn't feeling so bad anymore. This one was marked with a red flag. I didn't know her system of coding yet, but red was never particularly a good sign. So I skimmed down the details.

It looked like she had procured (love that word) some art for this Andrew fellow, which wasn't his to have. The people she took it from didn't have a right to it either. Man, weren't any artworks just bought through Christies, or whoever the famous art sellers were, anymore? Anyway, the original people she took it from, Peter and Paul, didn't like Andrew having their art.

Well, not Andrew per se, because they weren't really too sure who had it, they only knew Jonelle had taken it for someone other than themselves and they were mightily pissed about it. Her reputation had held them off for a long time about doing anything to retrieve their lost property, but lately they had been seen in discussions with a person labelled The Rose. Jonelle had highlighted that. I felt a cold finger walk down my spine. If she was highlighting that as a problem, then it had to be something to worry about.

But that wasn't going to keep me from reading further and I took a comforting sip of my tea.

The Rose was a muscle for hire, with brains, type of outfit, from what I could tell a bit like Jonelle herself. So this was not a good thing. There was a picture of him attached to the file. He wore an immaculate suit, with high polished shoes. His hair was beautifully cut and perfectly styled. Pity I didn't know his hairdresser really. He looked quite bulky under the suit jacket, but other than that, had nothing remarkable to make him stand out.

Except, of course, the cold, half-dead looking eyes. I wondered why he was called The Rose, in capitals like that, though perhaps I didn't want to know.

So far, Jonelle hadn't had any contact with The Rose and there was a query at the end of the entry. Perhaps he had been hired for another unrelated job, but she was going to keep her eye on the situation. The red flag now made more sense. It was linked to her electronic diary and kept popping up to remind her not to forget the possible impending doom. Really: not all that reassuring.

I closed that file as well and sipped quietly to myself. Instead of reading up on things that would only freak me out, I thought I would put my time to better use having a look through the photo database. That way, if I ever saw someone from it, I would *know* when to panic.

Once I had found it, after a few detours due to curiosity and a sad lack of really good navigational skills, I settled down to have a squiz. There were a lot of photos there and before long my stomach was growling. It was two. Time for a snack, too much time on the computer was bound to give me eye strain anyway.

I didn't want to hunt down anything at my place. I knew it was virtually empty except for some out-of-date chips and a few crusty apples which I made myself buy once a week because Mum always said 'an apple a day keeps the doctor away'. So I had an apple there for every day of the week though I never ate them. I knew that kind of defeated the purpose, but I had access to a whole range of yummy things like chocolate and the choice was clear to me. Simply put, who would chose to eat a semi crunchy apple instead of biting into the delicious thickness and goo of something like a Mars Bar? I was only human.

I opened Jonelle's fridge hoping it would yield something a little tastier than green tea. It was full – of vegetables, fruits and other disgustingly healthy options. My heart sank. Not to worry, there was always the phone. I dialled up my favourite home delivery pizza and had a long chat to Marty the phone boy. He knew me quite well.

With pizza happily on its way, I hunted around for some wine. Surely she wasn't a total abstainer? Aha! I found what I was looking for in the pantry. Stuck on the shelf was a note:

'Dear Princess, don't open more than one. I'll be back to check, you piss pot. Jonelle.'

Well bugger me! I stared at it with my mouth open. She was too clever by half.

Knowing my wines, I trolled through her selection. I didn't want to piss her off so I took something from the mid range. Settled with my wine, and pizza on the way, I went into the spare room. The front gate buzzer for Jonelle's number would let me know when my food arrived.

I hadn't had an opportunity to stick my nose in here. We had marched in, got the cameras and left again. Now I snooped. And she couldn't really object because wasn't she trying to train me into being a professional snoop? It was great to find a job that worked with my strengths.

I opened all the cupboards and discovered loads of electronic equipment. Some of it was hooked into each other and actually winking. So I left them alone. Who knew what they were monitoring? The others I picked up and took a good look at. I was still no closer to figuring them out. There were lots of little black boxes which looked like they plugged into other little black boxes. Probably a high tech wiz kid's dream, but lost on me.

There was a shelf full of boxes, some of which had locks and others which didn't, so I figured they were fair enough game. I opened the closest one. It was lined with velvet and had three knives in it, specifically designed to make the most mess, as easily as possible.

I was more the 'point and shoot and hope' that the target was in the right direction. I remembered trying to learn some sort of marksmanship a few years ago, but the instructor had yelled at me for closing my eyes.

Anyway, these knives had long wicked blades, with curved and jagged edges. All three looked like they could carve through human flesh like butter. I stared at them for a long time. They were concrete and physical proof that what Jonelle got up to was not always friendly and at some time required her to be downright scary: which she had down pat.

I closed the lid. I couldn't help wondering why it didn't have a lock on it. And if those knives had no lock and weren't considered dangerous enough for it, what was in the boxes with locks? I really needed to find another hobby other than snooping. Just then the phone rang and I jumped. Ah, the guilt of going through someone else's things. I let it go to her machine.

"Pick up would you? I know you're there, you made an outgoing call ten minutes ago to a pizza parlour." Jonelle's amused tones came over the voicemail.

I raced form the spare room and pounced on the phone. "Hi! Sorry, just um, working away." Could I sound less convincing?

"Mm." She wasn't convinced. "How's the surveillance going? You must have got him quickly to be back so soon."

"Oh, you know. Slowly. Thought I'd come back and make sure everything was okay here. Then I got hungry." Great, there was the guilts. And boy, she must have her phone hooked up to some snazzy stuff to know where I placed the call to. "How do you know so much stuff?"

She laughed; a lovely warm and normal sound. It helped. I hadn't even realised how much my imagination had been building her into a monster, reading and seeing the stuff in her place. Now, her laughter brought her back to mind. The fun interesting and capable friend I had – right?

"It's all very technical. But basically means I can tell what number you called. Don't worry, I don't mind. It's just the pizza will undo all your good work at the gym. No doubt there is wine to go with it?"

I wiggled in embarrassment. She knew these things and she wasn't even here. "Yeah, but I wasn't going to drink much of it. It's Thursday. I'll probably head out tonight with everyone, so I can't get sloshed this afternoon. I kind of lost my target."

"How?" the voice was still warm, not the least bit put out.

"I forgot to ask Mum what he looked like and then the one I think it was, jumped on a bus and I couldn't tail it taking everyone's photo as they came off now, could I? But it' okay I'm taking Steph to Potty's funeral tomorrow. She's my decoy. She'll get his description from Mum and then I'll hit the street again afterwards."

"Hmm. Can you think up a reason not to be at Potty's do? With everyone out of the house attending this thing, it'll be left open for our man to come back and have a snoop, if that is what he's up to. I would prefer to have you there."

I hadn't thought of that. How to wiggle out of it though?

"I already kind of said my boss wouldn't mind! I'm really sorry, that was stupid, without clearing it with you. I'll call Mum and make a different arrangement." I felt the size of a pinhead.

"No, that's okay. It's important to your mother and if you're already arranged it, I'll send someone else. That'll give the neighbours someone new to worry about."

Oh. I suddenly didn't feel so special. I remembered her saying she worked alone and felt a bit betrayed. Obviously not that alone after all. I'd forgotten she mentioned having someone nearby in case something happened while she was away.

"Oh? Anyone I should get to know?" I tried to sound casual, but I think my voice was probably as easy to read as my face.

"Don't get all pouty. There are quite a number of contacts you get to make if you've been in the business as long as I have. People who end up owing you a favour. Not people I would work with every day, but one off things like this? Sure. His name is Mike and he drives a Ford XR8, black with tinted windows. Just so you don't get him mixed up with the real target. I'll let him know you are the contact point in my absence, okay?"

I hated the fact she was trying to make me feel better.

"Now, I'm about to go into a meeting, but I'll call Mike first. I'll give him your mobile number so he can contact you, if he'd prefer to meet up first. Be careful. He's a charmer and will probably try to get you into bed. Though he may think you are off limits." She paused. "I'd like to cut this trip short, but there are a few people I need to see tomorrow night. Claire's just flown in from England, so I need to touch base with her. I'll call you again tomorrow. Keep your mobile handy." And she rang off.

I stood there holding the beeping phone. I was back in surreal territory and did the pinch test. Yep, still here and still me. I was having conversations about meeting more spy people and real life job stuff with my boss. This whole adult conversation and work related thing was something new and getting serious.

It was going to take a bit of getting used to but I think I was taking to it like a duck to water. Mind you, a blind duck who didn't know how to swim, but you get my drift. I wondered who Claire was; Jonelle had said her name almost as though I ought to know.

Hanging up the phone, I heard the outside buzzer go off. That meant I had to figure out how to disable the alarm system.

"Hold on, hold on," I muttered into the little voice receiver, flipping buttons and trying to remember codes that Jonelle had been stern about not writing down. There was a little click and I tried the handle. The door opened easily and I breathed a sigh of relief. Having no idea of have to turn an alarm off if I accidentally set one off, I was infinitely relieved to get out again without triggering it.

Paying for and grabbing my pizza, I was inside as fast as a rabbit. I was starving by this stage and I had to have some serious carbs. Glass of wine in one hand and the pizza box in the other, I settled into the pile of cushions and switched on the telly. It had been days since I had caught up with the soaps. Who knew what disaster had overtaken them in my absence?

That successfully wasted an hour and then it was back to the files. There were loads to read through. I wanted to be able to discuss real cases and names with Jonelle by the time she got back. The only trouble is, the red flags on things kept settling into my conscious thought and taking over. Two other files had flags, and one of those also pointed to The Rose. The guy had to be good, because two of her competitors were using him to find her.

What if he already had? I got a cold feeling that having Jonelle living in our apartment block could be potentially bad for our health. I tried to reassure myself by saying a professional wouldn't harm civilians, but you know what? That wasn't helping much.

The other red flag was more of a red wall hanging. She used exclamation marks and strong language. I read as I sipped the wine, finding it all a bit intimidating. Her client was a high class hooker and Jonelle had promised to protect her, for some reason, there was a bit of code work I couldn't understand there. However, whoever wanted that girl dead was not joking and Jonelle had woken up one day with a very cold client. Something Jonelle was not in the mood to forgive herself over. There were things like blood debt and other interesting phrases, which made me aware that my girl maybe walking on the very keen edge of sanity.

Whatever little Miss Blondie had meant to Jonelle, she was taking it personally that someone had wiped her out. The person who had killed Blondie was still at large. There had been no signature, no ritual which would explain who had done the deed, and I could tell from the numerous additives to the file, she wasn't about to rest until she had satisfactorily closed the case.

I looked at the name of the file "BB – unsolved". And I trolled through the photos attached. Blondie had been spectacularly lovely. Mind you, with the sums of money she was asking for a one night stand, she would have wanted to be special.

One line at the end of the file had me in a sweat.

'He has to know I'm hunting him. All I have to do is draw him out by finding the right bait."

I went back to Blondie's photograph. Give her red hair and a few less centimetres … the air chilled around me and my skin crawled.

What if Jonelle coming to this particular apartment block hadn't been mere coincidence? What if she had found the one apartment block which held a weak, unsuspecting kitten image of Blondie?

I sat back and thought about my fellow Apartmates. Then I looked back at Blondie. In my mind her hair was more titian, but there she was.

Heather.

I wanted my mind to shut up and shut off at this point, but it didn't. It went into hyper drive and none of it was pleasant.

In the end, I went home and drank another bottle of wine just to make the words in my head become a silence. Smudge and I watched stupid cartoony telly, sipping our way through too much alcohol.

I knew Heather. She lived here! With me! She was part of our Apartmates and that was enough for me. Was it possible that Jonelle was here, luring some maniac to come and kill Heather? My mind took another leap.

Bugger. I grabbed the bottle again. I remembered when Heather had a tragedy in the family. I clearly remembered her crying and saying her older sister had died; that while they weren't close since the sister went off and got involved in something the family didn't approve of, she'd still miss her. It had gone clean out of my mind. Blondie must have been that sister.

A knock at the door interrupted my contemplation, for which I could not be more grateful. I staggered a little when I got up. Boy, I hadn't realised my intake had been that high. I flung open the door to find a grinning Brad standing there. Someone must have let him in the gate. He stepped forward and crushed me to his chest, dipping his head to take my lips with his own. A part of me was still locked up in my own drama, but enough of me was aware of my surrounds to feel his pressing need for more than a kiss. The nerve!

I pushed him backwards a little. "Oi! Can you wait until I get on the same page?" Men, they really had no idea.

He grinned. "I just got back. The presentation was a major hit, we won the account, and I can see you have started the Thursday night celebrations a touch earlier than most."

I frowned at the bottle in my hand. How had that got there? I was sure I'd set it down somewhere.

"Yeah, well, it's been a long day and I wasn't expecting visitors," I grumbled, falling back so he could come in. "Though I think we are all meeting up around eight to head to the Batch and Haddock, if you want to come."

I tried to sound enthusiastic, but it was a hard game. My head was too full of disquieting and disloyal thoughts about my newly made boss, to worry about a potential new boyfriend. I followed him with my eyes, taking in the tight butt, long thighs and broad shoulders. On second thoughts, my body was reacting like a teenager.

I tossed the bottle on the couch, glad now of the screw top which went on so easily. When Brad returned from putting whatever bottle he'd brought into the fridge, I pounced.

Literally.

I took a flying leap and landed with my legs wrapped around his waist and my mouth firmly on his. I have to be blunt about it – the sex last weekend had been a marathon pleasure zone. Who in their right mind turned their back on that, regardless of the fact it might not be going anywhere?

He grunted with the collision, but held up under the assault. Now he knew the way into the bedroom I anticipated a smooth transition. But he surprised me – which really shouldn't have come as a surprise by now. He drew me down onto the floor of the lounge room, totally disregarding the open curtains and a curious Smudge.

Right there and then he slowly teased open my shirt, all the while kissing me so deeply I felt my head spin. When I was dressed only in a bra and knickers he allowed me to remove his shirt and trousers. Then we played and teased for what felt like forever.

My body raged; it was so on fire. He slipped his hands down the outside of my thighs and I ached. I could feel the mirror prints of those hands elsewhere and my body went crazy for him. I tugged urgently on his boxers and his teeth grazed my nipple. Just before I went totally insane, he lost the boxers and I scrambled out of my knickers.

I can't say the next couple of minutes had the most finesse. It was all hands and tongues, and bits and pieces. Afterwards, we lay panting in a pile of discarded clothes, sweaty and satisfied. Brad rolled over and gently kissed the side of my breast.

"I think I'll have to go away more often in the future."

There was a moment of panic from inside, where my little commitment phobic voice squealed, and then I quelled it and rolled into his arms. The future could take care of itself. There was no need to hurry matters.

We eventually struggled into the shower, where I used the stream of water to help sober me up. When we got out, I checked the time. Bloody hell, it was ten to eight. If we were heading out with the rest, we'd have to move.

Getting dressed and made up had never been so fast. The others were knocking at the door as I applied mascara. Brad went and let them in. It felt just a little weird having a man I had dated for a couple of weeks greet my friends at the door of my place like he belonged, but I quelled those thoughts too.

I was just grabbing my handbag when the mobile, strategically left on the coffee table so I would remember to take it, (which I had been about to forget), went off. I wavered. Brad was waiting at the door with everyone, watching me a little impatiently. But what if it was Jonelle with some vital information? Anyway – since when did a woman allow a phone to ring without answering it? I flung them an apologetic look and clicked it on.

"Fiona." I thought that sounded professional enough.

"Yeah, hi love. Jonelle gave me your number. I thought we should probably get in touch before tomorrow. Mike," he added almost as an afterthought.

So, this was the all out charmer Jonelle had warned me about. If his phone manner was anything to go by, there was no worry I would fall for his seduction technique.

"Hi. You've kind of caught me at a bad time. Can we meet tomorrow?" I tried to think of my schedule. "Early?"

I had to collect Steph by nine thirty in the morning. Once again there was going to be no sleep-in for me. I was enjoying the idea of being busy and important, but I think in the long run I was going to miss my mornings.

"Sure. I can swing by anytime. When are you free?"

"Could you make it about eight?" I could see the surprise in everyone's eyes. Damn. Now they were going to ask all sorts of questions about why on earth Fiona was getting up before noon.

Mike agreed that eight was fine and rung off. I grabbed a coat and smiled at everyone. "Let's go before all the seats are taken." I wondered if anyone could tell I was trying to deflect questions.

It never stood a chance really.

"Sooo, what was that all about, hey?" Todd asked, slipping his arm casually around my waist as I closed the door. "You up before half the day is gone?"

Brad frown at Todd's familiarity, but I was comfy. Todd was a loveable teddy bear, just not the sort you'd go out with.

"You all remember Potty? Well, she died the other day. Mum's arranged a funeral, would you believe, for some obscure hour of the morning." I wasn't about to tell them I had a meeting even earlier.

Brad came up on the other side of me and took my hand. What is it with territorial men? It wasn't something I found attractive to be honest. It said things like they were insecure and other things - like they saw you as their possession. But I was willing to let it go for now.

"So, who are you meeting at eight? That's a bit extreme. I hope that doesn't mean I can't stay." He ran his fingers down my arm. My body heated up and I flushed. Damn fair skin.

"I have to meet someone about some work Mum and Dad need done, then I'll get Steph for the funeral. You can stay, but I'll need to have an early start."

Then there was the general conversation about who Steph was seeing as Brad had never met her, and we were suddenly all there. The familiar sounds and smells of the Batch and Haddock reaching out to us and drawing us into its warmth. I wasn't the least bit surprised to see Grillia and Steph seated at our usual bench, trying to hold it against a tide of people demanding that two girls give up the massive space for larger groups. They looked very relieved to see us. We piled chaotically into the seat, waving away interlopers.

Introductions were done then rounds were bought. I noticed a slight coolness between Brad and Grillia, and my inner female sixth sense went into hyper drive. When was my life ever just smooth sailing? I made up some excuse and dragged Grillia to the ladies. Steph tagged along.

"Okay, tell me." Such was our friendship she didn't need me to ask about what.

"Bugger it, Fi. It's old news and nothing to write home about." She was doing the 'spare the friend any hurt' thing. I hated that. I narrowed my eyes at her.

Steph gave her a little nudged with her toe. "Out with it."

Grillia sighed. "I took Brad home about five months ago. I didn't know you'd ever met!" She held up her hands in defence when I growled and Steph gave her a stronger poke in the ribs. "Seriously, ages later when you mentioned this Brad guy, how was I meant to know it was the same person? There isn't a shortage of Brads going around, you know." She pouted at me.

How could I be angry? Five months ago I'd never heard of the guy.

"I've only known him for a little while. If anything, I should be apologising to you. You went there first, after all." I had to be fair here. Plus, did I really want Grillia's cast offs?

"No apology, please! It was just one night that happened a long time ago after far too many drinks." She looked down at her shoes and I caught the traces of a suppressed smirk. Her eyes came up to mine and I asked her what that was all about without a word.

"Oh all right. He's all upset and male about it because he'd drunk too much and couldn't perform, and when we woke up the next day I had a hangover so instead of letting him prove how manly he was, I kicked him out. So as I said, nothing to be worried about. We never, you know. There wasn't time or opportunity." She grinned wickedly. "Though I did get to check the goods out and I should think you are one happy little camper."

I had to laugh. She was right. There was nothing wrong with the overall package. We went out and joined the rest of them for a great night of alcohol and gossip.

Brad did come and stay the night and we did just sleep. We'd both had a few and I wasn't about to repeat Grillia's mistake and attempt anything which was potentially embarrassing.

There was no way I was going to the gym on my own, but I was still awake at five thirty the next morning. I stared up at the fading stars on my ceiling listening to Brad snore ever so softly next to me. I reviewed my day in my head and realised that once again it would be amazing if I finished everything before it ended.

Of course I could always work as long as I wanted to, as I had a 'flexible' working relationship with my boss, but there was going to be another evening out tonight. Everyone had agreed to eat out and head to the movies. Perhaps I would get in an evening without too much drinking, but was unsure if that was possible.

I gently pulled myself out of bed, hoping not to wake Brad. I was in no mood for sex and I knew he liked a morning romp. Smudge, relegated to his basket which had moved into my room anyway, followed me out into the kitchen. I closed the door after me so I could turn the lights on and still leave Brad to snore away to himself.

The kettle was happily singing to itself when I had managed to get Smudge patted and fed to his satisfaction. I was getting the feeling my life was going to be run by a small feline for the next ten years. Already, things were getting moved around for his convenience. Bossy little thing, for all he came up to my ankle.

I made the obligatory coffee. I wasn't at the point I could forgo the morning cup or two. If I spent any more time with Jonelle, though, I could see me getting bloody green tea instead. Distasteful thought.

Coffee and breakfast down, I needed to have a shower and get dressed. I would just have to brave the Brad.

I totally get having morning sex. I just couldn't today. It was only an hour until Mike was due to rock up. Anyway, didn't Brad have a job to get to?

I dived into the shower, and was out and towelled dry before he had managed to raise his head from the pillow. I found an appropriately dark and sober outfit while he watched from the bed.

"Don't you have to get ready for work?" I tried to sound casual, but really, sadly, I just wanted the place to myself.

He stretched. "Yeah, but it was more fun watching you. Mind if I grab a quick shower? Then I'll have to head home to get a change of clothes before the office."

I waved him permission for a shower, and headed back out to the kitchen. I felt awkward for some reason about seeing him all naked. Like a belated sense of shyness.

A few moments later the outside buzzer went off.

"Mike here."

Damn. He was early. I hit the release button and a short time later he was at the front door. I opened it warily. I didn't know this guy from Adam. Standing on my front step was a man slightly taller than me with a perfect face and body sculptured in miniature; he couldn't have been more than five foot six.

He leaned against the door frame and grinned at me. I suppose it could have been charming, if I wasn't already out of sorts with men in general.

"Fiona, I take it?" Quite clever for a man, really.

Then Brad came out of the bedroom and loomed at my shoulder. There was the whole 'man eye man' thing that men feel the need to do and I was ready to blow my top. I had a depressive girl friend to pick up, a dog to bury, a family of emotional children to survive, and possibly a murderer stalking my familial home. Dealing with the egos of two men was beyond me.

I snorted. "Puh-lease, you two. Get a life. Brad, go to work. Mike, get in here and allow me to discuss our *business* without the whole neighbourhood watching."

Even stressing the word business didn't seem to help and I sent away a rather put out Brad muttering about business at that hour and a person's home not being a place of business. I left him to it and dragged Mike into the unit.

The whole time he didn't lose that annoying grin which made me want to wipe it off his face. So I got down to business real fast. The less time I spent with him, the better. I wondered what the hell Jonelle was thinking, having this annoying short man as an associate. Yes, I could be very vertically politically incorrect. The virtue of being small was I could pay out anyone of a similar stature.

"Jonelle just wants me to keep an eye on your place and take a whole lot of useless pictures of any man hanging around, is that right?" Mike asked, as his eyes roamed around my place.

"Yeah, that about sums it up. Make sure that no one breaks in, okay? Then get the pictures to me as soon as you have them." I wanted to make a head start on identification if at all possible.

"No problems. So, how do you know Jonelle?" The grin had gone, to be replaced with an almost knowing smirk. I rudely glanced at my watch. It was time for him to be moving on.

"Jonelle is a business associate. I think that is sufficient information? Anyway, Mike, I need to be heading off now, so if you don't mind, we can head out together."

That was one way to make sure he was on the other side of the security gate by the time I left. I wasn't putting it passed him to have a snoop. My front door was no security job.

I practically pushed him out, then dashed around to my car. I would be a touch late, but Steph would just have to cope. She was probably still sleeping anyway.

But she surprised me. Instead of having to drag her sorry butt out of bed, she was awake and waiting out the front for me. As I pulled up, she slid into the passenger seat, her face a stony mask. This was going to be fun.

"Hi Steph. What's up?" I was almost loathe to ask, but sometimes you did unpleasant things.

"Fi. It's my stupid frigging brother." Steph generally hated to swear, though when she did, it did a trooper proud.

I sighed. The last thing I needed today was a temperamental Steph. "What's happened this time?"

She hunched forward, wrapping her arms about herself like a

child. I did feel for her, but seriously, the lease was under her name, why she didn't just kick him out was beyond me.

"He found me with Tamara. I was just trying it out, I swear. Men just don't seem to like me all that much after a while. So I thought I'd give girls a try and you know Tamara has always had a crush on me."

Yes, I knew that. But that didn't make it okay. Tamara was a real mental case - I wouldn't want my sister dating her and I was sure Nathan didn't either. I was pretty certain Tamara did hard drugs, and she was freakily attached to Steph. It was crazy stalker land with her.

"Crush," I said cautiously, "is such a mild word when it comes to Tamara. I'm sure Nathan was just looking out for you." I didn't like Nathan taking his sister for granted, but if this was about Tamara, then maybe he had a point for once.

"He threw her out! Physically I mean. Picked her up under one arm, grabbed her clothes and tossed both out into the street. She was shrieking at him and he was yelling about a cocaine sniffing little whore and I was crying, and I think sex with a girl isn't all it's cracked up to be and I just wish last night would go away but it keeps playing back around and around in my head."

And probably would for a few days yet I felt like telling her, but what would be the point? The trouble was, now I was trying to get out there and find myself a life, it was going to become harder to find the time to pick up the pieces of my friends' lives.

"He may have a point about Tamara, don't you think? She's just not a healthy girl to hang around. You know how Grillia feels about her when she tries to come to girlie gatherings. And it's not because she's a lesbian, so don't go all righteous on me. Grillia doesn't care about that. She's more worried about the drugs and any horrid things she may pass around. Her history is pretty spotty."

I manoeuvred around a double parked car and nearly ran head on into another. Man, it really wasn't my day. I glanced at my watch. There was still hope of getting to the vet's in time for the main event.

"Yeah I know." Steph was despondent. "It wasn't like I was going to make a habit of it. I was lonely."

That was the problem, I felt like yelling at her. Tamara was the sort of girl who would use the loneliness to wiggle her way into any situation. She was rude, unreliable and quite frankly, a bit smelly. I couldn't understand how Steph could even go there, but there was something about experimentation.

I listened to a constant stream of Nathan-bashing as we cruised to the vet's and arrived right on time. We slipped into the crematorium and took the seats nearest the door. My family were all there, Mum and Joy sniffing not so quietly to themselves and anyone silly enough to sit with them.

I took in the flowers and soft music and wanted to roll my eyes. Personally I believed Potty would have enjoyed a booze up and a hole in the back yard. After all, she had managed to dig her fair share of them over the years. I only hoped my will would be consulted before anyone got their hands on my corpse.

It was over quickly. Then it was off to the house for some nibbles. Just family, Mum said, like there was going to be a sudden rush of well wishers and sympathisers. She conceded when it came to Steph.

We drove up and I noticed a Ford XR8 slink off as we did. At least Mike had been around. I was kind of hoping there had been no action, that way I wouldn't have to thank him. But another part of me wanted the photos taken so I couldn't manage to stuff it up.

"So, Steph, you know what you have to do right?"

"Sure. Get your mother talking about some strange man who ran over Potty and describe him, thoroughly. Why is that again?" I hated it when my normally self involved friends decided to get interested in details.

"Because I asked nicely! Seriously, I want to make sure I know who he is if I see him around the place. But don't tell Mum I am asking. Make out you are interested and, please, try to pay enough attention to be able to tell me."

She shrugged like it was no big deal and went over to Mum, who greeted her instantly with a smile and gracious hug. They would happily gossip for hours. Mum also liked to catch up on the rich and famous around town, people Steph's parents hung out with all the time.

I wandered around the outside of the house. I had no idea of what it was I was looking for. Something - anything - out of the ordinary. Puddle decided he liked me and came for the exercise. He was a cute little thing and I had no objections to his company.

Surprisingly enough, I didn't find anything. It would have been too much to ask to find my perp hiding in the melaleucas. At midday I figured it was enough time for Steph to have gleaned everything she was likely to, and made my way back inside.

"Time for us to head, hey Fi? I have a few things to do before we get together tonight." I had forgotten she was coming to the dinner and movie deal with the Apartmates and me and Brad. Grillia had declined, preferring a Friday night out scoping potentials.

"Yep, I have to get back to..." I stopped. Oops, Steph had no idea I had a job. I didn't want to get into that because I didn't want to get into elaborate lies with my mates.

Mum saved the day, probably inadvertently.

"Oh yes dear. You can't hang around here all day. Thank that lovely Jonelle for the flowers and we'll see you Sunday, won't we?" She tried to slip that in.

I smiled and kissed the air near her cheek. "Sorry Mum, Jonelle has invited me to spend lunch with her, seeing as I brought her here last week. Only fair now." She eyes flashed as I successfully wiggled off her maternal hook. She knew once I was out of the loop again, I was as good as free.

Tugging Steph away, I got us into the car. Pulling out on the street I asked her, "Well? What can you tell me about the man who hit Potty?"

Steph eyed me sideways. "You do know it was an accident, right? That he was really apologetic and while your mother doesn't like the fact he hangs around a bit and his story of checking out real estate is slim, it isn't a crime?"

She seemed a bit worried I was dreaming of revenge for the dog hitting incident.

"I just want to know a bit about him, that's all. I'm not going to stalk him or even let the air out of his tyres."

"Alright." She sounded pretty doubtful, but at least she was complying. "He drives a white Hyundai Excel. It got a bit of a dint where it came in contact with Potty on the passenger front. He has black hair, a small moustache and dark glasses. He speaks with a slight English accent but she didn't know what part, so don't ask. But I think you'd notice him if you saw him again, as he also has a scar on his left cheek. There. That's it." She wasn't interested and I liked that. I didn't want to arouse her suspicions.

"Thanks Steph. I really do appreciate it. I'll just keep a little eye out when I'm in the area is all. I don't think he can be that good a driver if he hit Potty." She couldn't possibly get too doubtful over that explanation, surely. Though she did give me a rather odd look, she let it go.

I dropped her off at her place promising to wait for her to come over tonight before we went to the restaurant, then I drove home. I had only just let myself back in when my mobile went off. I didn't recognise the number but took it anyway.

"Fiona? It's Mike. I have those photos on disk for you anytime you want them." How did he manage to make that sound like I would be agreeing to wanting him at the same time? Some men were enough to drive me bananas.

"I need those this afternoon; can you deliver them or get them couriered over?" I hated to ask, but I wanted to make a start on identification now I had a ballpark as to who I was looking for. Then I could match him up with Jonelle's database. It was all coming together and I was getting those vaguely excited feelings I used to get when an assignment was coming together well at university, only better.

"Sure, seeing as I have nothing better to do than make house calls," he grumbled.

"Then send it! Don't go out of your way, but I am sure Jonelle would appreciate the help." I couldn't bring myself to say I would appreciate it, as I didn't want him to take the proverbial mile to my inch.

With a few more grumbles, he agreed to be around in half an hour. I shuddered to imagine such a man so close to where I lived, and who actually knew where I lived. But at least it would be quick.

Sure enough, he was around with the disk in no time standing at my door grinning away like he had the cure for cancer in his hot little hands. Boy, if he wasn't so damned attractive I would have loved to kick his arse. A few more trips to the gym would be in order before I tried to kick anyone's arse.

"Thank you," I said stiffly, trying to not let him into the room, but he breezed through my defences. Some people have really thick skins.

"No sweat, Peaches. Glad I could help, really. Tell Jonelle anytime. Same deal."

Curiosity almost made me ask what sort of deal did he have running with her, but I didn't want to appear to be out of the loop. By the look he was giving me, I think he already thought I was below the bottom rung of any totem pole. It was creepy. "So, what's on the agenda for the rest of the day?"

"I have a few more jobs to do for Jonelle yet. Then I'm busy. Glad to have met you, but I have to go now."

"You work *for* Jonelle?" Finally he cottoned on to what I'd been saying. Wow – the man had major listening deficiencies.

His whole demeanour changed. No longer was he mister slouchy, sleazy guy. Suddenly he became mister astute, keen narrow-eyed guy instead.

"I thought you were just someone she was helping out."

What an insult! Didn't I look the part?

The extent of the change in him was amazing. Suddenly I could see what Jonelle was talking about. The intelligence and hardness in his eyes and face was hard to miss. I hoped that toughness could be taught because there was no way I had it. Couple how he was looking at me with his godlike looks and I thought that taking him to bed was not as far out of the target zone as I had first expected.

"No, I'm her new assistant. The work you were doing was for me, because I was otherwise engaged at the time, or I would have done it myself." There: hopefully that would put him in his place.

"Sorry, love. Jonelle has worked alone for as long as I've known her."

I thanked Mike again, and hastened him out the door. He was much better as mister sensible, but still, I had enough on my plate without adding sleeping with a work colleague. Finally he was gone, and I shut up and took Smudge over to Jonelle's. I had the trusty disk in one hand and a purry little kitten in the other.

The usual battle of wills with her door, and I was in. Putting the makings of green tea on, I went in to boot up the computer. I was looking forward to an afternoon of solitude and research. I was also going to look up news articles from the time Blondie was killed. Heather's sister was called Brenda, so at least I had a name for her.

So there I was, back at square one, hunting through files. This time though I loaded up my disk first to see if I could match any photos from it with anything in the files I had seen so far.

There were only a couple of handfuls of shots on there. Two of me, I think now he knew I was not a bimbo customer Mike would be regretting those. There was one of Steph. He had caught her wistfully looking into space. It made her appear very waiflike and fragile. The rest were of neighbours and one of a man.

And bingo! He had to be my guy. There was a wicked looking scar running from his mouth to just under his eye. He could have done with some makeup at the very least. There were things they could do with that.

I studied the shot. He was looking furtively over his shoulder while walking toward the folks' home. Mike hadn't mentioned anyone breaking in, so I could only assume he hadn't gone into it, only walked by. He certainly couldn't have acted any more suspicious if he'd taken out an ad. There was the little top lip moustache and dark glossy hair. He had powerful shoulders and a slight bulge under one arm. It hit me dully that it must be a gun.

My heart leaped into a race of its own.

I sat there and my hands got all sweaty. My eyes kind of blurred, because I was staring too long at the one spot. Rubbing them and refocusing didn't make it go away. There was a definite bulge under his arm. Just his right arm, which made him left handed.

A very handy thing to know about him, and yes that pun was intended.

Here was a man stalking my parents' home because of me, and he was wearing a gun. And he had a scar which could only have come from a knife or something along those lines. It was kind of like Jonelle's. This was scary stuff. I had never come in contact with the operational end of a knife or gun.

I got up and went into the spare room. Time to rectify that. I opened the wardrobe and pulled out the unlocked box. Inside on the velvet were the three knives, strong, silent, and deadly. My stomach clenched like I was going into an exam. They looked a lot more frightening close up than they did on screen. They couldn't get the menace of these things correct in the movies I'd seen. It was too remote and distant.

These were up close and deadly personal.

Chapter Eleven

I stuck out a finger and prodded one of them. It was a scary piece of weaponry; made more so because it was casually in the closet of my boss.

With one swoop, I lifted it out and gripped it firmly by the handle. I took a few playful swings and nearly embedded it into the wall. I jumped back until I was in the middle of the room. I didn't want to put it through anything. Hopefully not even myself. I took another practise swing then pretended to stab someone.

That jolted me out of make-believe-land. I was making stabbing motions with a deadly weapon! What on earth was I thinking? I hastily put it back in its box. Some things I wasn't meant to play with. I wondered if it had ever done any damage.

Back at the computer, curiosity over with, I opened her database of photos. While not as much fun as surfing through the files, it would be quicker. I had a dinner date to get ready for. I checked the diary for Jonelle's flight details and wrote them down. I didn't want to be late for picking her up.

I skimmed through the database. Then I found the search key. I put in black hair and facial scar. Two people turned up and one was my guy.

His name, I read, was Harry Francis. Not a name to inspire cold dread or even a licking of fear. However, his history description was. He was known to have killed two people in Jonelle's estimation and suspected of at least one more. He was the usual muscle of one Lilly Pigholt. He played bodyguard, henchman and frightener.

Only Jonelle wasn't frightened.

As far as I could tell, if computer text could impart a feeling, she was a bit contemptuous of this Harry Francis, but not to the point of underestimating him.

I searched under Lilly Pigholt. I wanted to know whatever Jonelle did about her, and why this Lilly would have set her watch dog on to me and my family. There was no clear link as yet.

Lilly Pigholt was a short, fat, nasty looking creature. She had a sly smile in one of the shots and fake brassy red hair. I would have thought 'poor girl', except this poor girl had set her killer onto me so my sympathy was pretty much zip. I scanned Jonelle's notes.

Miss Pigholt ran an up market brothel for politicians, and the rich and mighty. There was a discreet little appendix which told me one of her clients was a Bishop I had heard of in the news. Why did this piece of hypocritical churchman behaviour not surprise me when everything else did?

She had classy call girls out for hire and a brothel which kind of resembled a small and tasteful hotel from the outside. I'm sure it did on the books as well. I read through a few of her other clients, but they didn't mean all that much to me.

Harry was protection also for any girls sent out to new clients. At least she was security conscious, or maybe she was just protecting her investments. She was dodging the tax man (but really, who wasn't?) and had dabbled in the drug trade. She may or may not have owed some nasty people some money and Harry was designed to make sure they didn't collect. He was also supposed to keep an eye on Jonelle, according to the file. She was paranoid that Jonelle was out to get her because Brenda had been her hooker.

I stopped reading. Brenda? Blondie? Heather's sister had worked for the monster I was reading about?

Oh, what a tangled web. My head was swirling fit to burst. I closed up the computer. Easier to ask Jonelle if she was in the mood for a chat, than sift through this stuff. I had the beginnings of a headache and didn't want to think anymore. It was past time for my first drinkies.

Man, did I sound like an alcoholic. I *had* picked up a few nasty habits. But I didn't smoke, which was in my favour.

I packed it all up and took Smudge home. I was knackered. It was all the tension and unaccustomed thinking. I'd had no idea that working was so demanding. I settled Smudge in with his feed for the night and grabbed a bottle of wine. Whoever said it wasn't healthy to drink alone hadn't met me.

The phone started to ring just as I had taken my first sip. It was

Jonelle. Damn, how did she know I had the wine out? What was she – psychic?

"Yeah, it's me."

"My, you sound positively buoyant. Is it that bad?" She didn't sound all that great herself.

"I have two words for you. Pot. Kettle. What's happening in the metropolis of Sydney? Oh, and Mum says thanks for the flowers."

"I'm having dinner with my English friend, but I wanted to check in with you to see what has happened lately. No problems about the flowers."

"Well, Mike took the photos, I got them, went through your database and guess what? He has a name and face you know well. Harry Francis." I sat down with the wine. No need to be standing at attention. She couldn't see.

There was a hiss of breath. "So, old Lilly is still trying to cover her arse, hey? She knows I know Harry; she shouldn't have risked sending him. I'll be back tomorrow. I'll deal with Harry then. Just make sure your parents don't provoke him."

"That doesn't fill me with joy. You know just how provoking my mother can be." I had a sudden image of her rapping on his car window and demanding that he move right along. Damn. "I think I'll go spend the night at home."

"Sure, you go do that." She sounded very distracted. "Take something out of the safe. Here's the code." And she rattled off some numbers which she made me repeat back to her in sequence. If nothing else, I'd get a better memory. Then she hung up. At her most communicative best, I see.

I didn't particularly want to get back into Fort Knox again, but the cat in me was dying of curiosity about what was in her safe. So I trudged back over. Half way there I met Steph and Cheryl. Cheryl, Warrick's unmarried missus from number 8, greeted me like a long lost relative. I wasn't the only one getting a head start on the sauce tonight.

"Hey, we'll be heading off soon. Where is dinner at?" Steph grinned. Such an uncustomed facial expression I was almost sure it would crack.

"I can't make it tonight. I have to go and see my folks. Sorry, but something has come up." There was no way I was going to mention guns and henchmen. Mind you, how I was going to explain my sudden need to come and stay the night with the folks was almost beyond my lying capacity.

There were the usual groans and disclaimers. Cheryl told me to let my folks deal with whatever it was alone. But I wiggled and then stood firm. I couldn't let them spend another night with that man stalking them. It could be worse. I could be the one to provoke him into doing something we'd all regret. I had considered that possibility. My mother wasn't the only one in the family who could be impossible.

I let myself back into Jonelle's and then the safe. It was a big thing and inside were all sorts of different compartments, which had their own locks. I didn't even bother trying to figure out how to get into them. It was obvious what she had sent me there to get.

I wondered briefly if Jonelle had forgotten in her distraction who she had been speaking to. There was a gun, wrapped in soft cloth sitting on top of a whole stack of money. And cases of bullets. Even if I did figure out how to load the damn thing, who was I kidding? No way would anyone feel intimidated by having me waving a gun in their face. More likely, they'd laugh.

I took it anyway. The only way to familiarise myself with the machinery which came along with the job was to use them. There was the chance that I could somehow make myself feel big and brave and bad by sporting my new look. Accessorised by Jonelle.

The coward in me cringed at my flippancy. I could end up getting shot, she told me. Oh well, in for a penny, in for a pound. The life I was living before all this came along would probably have killed me with boredom before long anyway.

Locking back up, I took the car and headed over to the folks place. I had come up with an ingenious new plan. I hadn't actually done the stake out I had had planned with the photo thing. So why not do it now? There was absolutely no need for my parents to know I was around at all. I could skulk, professionally, and they would have dinner, and watch telly, and go to bed all the while their guardian angel (me) would be out there protecting them.

At the word dinner, my stomach growled scarily. Ah, slight detour, but no change to the overall plan. I stopped into a take away joint and stocked up. I was, after all, planning to be at this whole deal for many hours. Many long, cool, and hungry hours. I added a few nibbles to my purchase, then a take away coffee. That might help for a few hours, though there was no guarantee.

By the time I got to my parents' home, it was dark and getting quite cold. Spring! It was so changeable.

I parked around the back, where there was an alley that people used to gain access to the park down the road. The street light was out. That gave some sort of anonymity to my car. The only hitch to my plan, as I could see it, was that everyone around these parts knew whose car this was. So, to get around that, I parked so I could find a convenient bush to sit in. And if it happened to be near a Hyundai Excel with a slight dent in it, and a man with a scar and a little moustache, then so be it. Sometimes coincidences did happen…

I left some of my food supplies in the car. I could always come back for them, and I didn't want to give into temptation and eat them all at once. The coffee and steak sandwich I took with me.

There wasn't much in the way of cover, just the bushes in Mum's actual garden. So I climbed the fence and plonked myself down in the middle of them. There was a small hollow where we use to play, and now the nieces and nephews hid on weekends. It was a lot smaller than I remembered it. But with only one broken branch, I managed to stuff myself into the space provided.

I did recall this bit of my last attempt at surveillance. Boredom.

I would have packed a novel but there was no way to safely use a flashlight while hiding. The whole idea was not to attract attention and a disembodied light bobbing around in the bush would completely defeat the purpose.

So I settled in, nibbling my steak sandwich and sipping my fast becoming lukewarm coffee. I didn't think the life of a private investigator would really be my bailiwick in the long run. Computers pissed me off, but at least they were set up in the comfort of my own home. Or in this case, Jonelle's own home. Sending me out on location wasn't all I had thought it would be.

I still had my little pocket light, so I used this infrequently to check on the time, which seemed to go by really slowly when checking every five minutes. A few stray cars went past, the neighbours down the street had a screaming match over who's turn it was to put the rubbish out. Then silence settled on my little patch. Deathly, I am oh-so bored, kind of silence. By the time my watch was showing eleven, I would have been happy to have the house burn down. At least there would have been other people out here in the misery of it all.

I stared out of my hidey-hole. Mum came to the front door and let Puddle out for his evening pee. That gave me a little moment of tension to relieve the stretch of boredom. For a moment I thought he was going to come gambolling over to investigate why a member of the family was sitting in his bushes, but she didn't let him wander off. Then the outside lights went off and there was a general settling in for the night kind of feel about it. Around about then I got hungry again.

I struggled out of the bushes and dusted off. Looking shiftily around, I hopped back over the fence and trotted around to the car. While I was digging around trying to find something yummy in my snack pack, I noticed a shadow shifting along the walkway. The internal light of my car had blown its bulb about a week ago and right then, I was damn glad of it. Gently I closed the door and eased myself further into the shadows. My heart rate suddenly spiked and the weight of the gun, tucked into my pocket, felt impossible. I knew I was protected, if it indeed could be seen as protection, but at the same time, I felt naked and vulnerable.

I stalked the shadow glad for the sneakers I was wearing and the black clothes. I knew that at some stage, it would all come naturally, (at least that was what I was telling myself and who was I to contradict my own pearls of wisdom?), but right at that precise moment I felt more out of water than any fish in history. We trod in unison all the way down the alleyway, and paused outside my parents' backyard.

Was Jonelle testing me? Sending me out here on the one night that something actually looked like happening, or was it one of those freaky coincidences which stand out in your mind for the rest of your life? That was provided I had a 'rest of my life', after coming in contact with Harry Francis.

The gate swung open without a murmur and I cursed Dad's efficiency in keeping the damn thing well oiled. If only it had made a squeak, someone else may have heard it and foiling this dastardly plan wouldn't be left to jelly-belly me. I had goose pimples the size of mole hills and a quiver in my knees which threatened to turn me on my butt in no time flat. What I wouldn't have done for Jonelle's reassuring and competent presence right then.

I didn't want to follow too closely, as I'd seen those movies where the imbecile cop basically trod on the villain's ankles and it all turned very messy for the cop. So I waited for a bit and then poked my nose around the corner of the fence, and stared into the darkness of the back yard. The only thing I had going for me was knowledge of the layout of the yard.

Another good thing was anyone moving around it stood between me and the white decking. Though whoever it was crouched low, I could still see their vague outline and I slipped into the yard, a mockery of a smile plastered on my face. I only hoped that if it was Harry Francis I could get enough air to scream my lungs out. Right at that moment, I felt remarkably out of breath.

I crept up closer to my mark (that sounded far more professional than I was feeling). The light sensors flicked on. I had totally forgotten about them. Mum had them installed about three weeks ago and I hadn't been over in the dark since, so how was I meant to keep all these things straight in my head?

The person in front of me dived to one side. Not before I got a clear look at him. And it was a 'him'. A slight, young, red haired him, who when he saw me out of the corner of his eye, turned a freckle and pimple ridden face to gape at me. I had managed to surprise a wannabe burglar. How spectacularly courageous of me. If I had actually pulled out my gun about now would be the time I would secure it back in its holster and read the kid a riot act. However, being me, I had left the gun in my pocket, had no holster, and my heart was still racing and my stomach too churny to utter a word.

We stood there facing each other mouths open, eyes wide and deer-caught-in-headlight frightened. And that's how Mum and Dad found us. They usually read in bed for some time after they officially 'retired' for the evening and they had just turned the bedroom lamps off when the back lights came blazing on. This was enough to bring them both downstairs they told me later, especially when Puddle was yipping to himself, chasing his tail around their room in the excitement of having late night visitors.

Dad's gruff "What's going on here?" was enough to un-stick my young companion's feet and he attempted a dash past me.

I was having none of that though and stuck my foot out, just managing to catch him on the side of the leg. Enough to send him tumbling and I was on his back before he could blink. Which kind of sounded better than it was. I heaved myself in his direction and allowed my trembling legs to collapse. Nothing fancy.

Dad came down the back stairs. "Fiona? Is that you? What on earth are you doing here at this hour and why are you sitting on that young man? This isn't a game is it?" My parents hated the idea of 'adult' type games. If there were bigger prudes out there, I was yet to find them.

"It's not a game, Dad. I was just happening passed and I saw this young man coming up the alleyway. I thought it was suspicious and followed him." I leaned down and whispered in his ear "Who are you and what does Harry want?" Then I turned back to Dad. "Good thing I did, as look where he was headed. Straight into your living room from here, isn't it?" And please, I thought to myself, don't look too deeply as to why your daughter would be driving passed so late on a Friday night.

"I wasn't! I wasn't actually going to go inside. I'm not a thief." He wiggled under me and I wondered vaguely if I was really that heavy. He rolled an eye back to try and look at me. "Who's Harry? I don't know a Harry, I swear."

Dad and Mum were busily holding a meeting about what they should do with him. This had to be fast. "If you aren't a thief and you don't know Harry why are you here? Why pick this place?"

"I swear I'm not. Some guy came up to me and said, here's an easy hundred bucks. I couldn't turn it down. I lost my job at McDonalds today. All I had to do was sneak down the alley and into this back yard. He said it was just to piss his ex-girlfriend off. Is that you?"

I eased off his back and sat on my heels thoughtfully. Why would Harry ask some lowlife kid to steal into the backyard? It didn't make sense.

"What else did he say?"

"He said that if I got caught, I was to tell you he said hi and why don't you stake out your own place from the comfort of your couch? I don't think he likes you very much, lady." An understatement, if it was Harry. It had to be him and that made my tummy rumble in a very unladylike fashion.

The kid sat up too, eyeing me warily. Mum and Dad approached, now he was up and talking, as though any danger had to be over.

"Is everything sorted out now?" Mum was actually subdued. Having a total stranger prowling in the backyard would do that to a woman. We both scrabbled to our feet.

'I'm sorry. I shouldn't have taken the money."

"Money? You took some money? You've been into the house already?" The panic was back in Mum's voice.

Bugger. "No no. He hasn't taken any of your money. It appears as though it was a misunderstanding and a friend was trying to prank one of the neighbours, only goofball here got the address wrong. Silly boy." The last thing I really wanted was my parents to get into a round of questions, and something close to the truth wafting out.

As misunderstandings went, my parents were all too happy to see me deal with it. I shoved whoever he was out the back gate, locked it (something the folks never did) and came into the house. Now they were up, a cuppa was the least I could hope for. When my stomach obligingly went off, Mum set about making us all a midnight snack.

"I don't understand what he was doing in our backyard, dear. It was quite a fright to see you both, let me tell you. What did you say you were doing here again?"

Here came the thousand and one questions. It was very hard to distract my mother from the central point.

"I was over this side of town visiting a friend. Now you don't have Potty to keep watch I thought I'd just swing passed on my way home. I saw that guy slip down the alley and thought it looked suspicious." I wanted to get my hastily thought up excuse out as fast as possible. But it was not to be.

"Darling, if you thought he looked suspicious, you should have called the police. Or at least come and got your father. Following a man in the dark when no one knows where you are is very irresponsible behaviour. Anything could have happened to you." Mum gave me a frown, as though wondering at my sanity. Sometimes I wondered at it as well.

"Yeah, now I think about it, I agree. But at the time, well, it was all too fast. Then the lights came on and you saw the rest."

I gulped the hot tea, thinking about Harry's involvement. What sort of message was he sending? Was he just letting me know that he could get in at any point in time? It was all a little unnerving, and I wanted to get back to my place and hide until Jonelle came home.

But was he expecting me to do that and waiting for that moment to come into the house and scare my parents? I couldn't think straight anymore. Come to think about it, why on earth would he be interested in harassing my folks? My tired brain told me he could just be trying to make me jumpy; in which case he had succeeded admirably.

"I really have to go now. I have an early start tomorrow. Sorry for all the hassles and the late night interruption." I stood up and rinsed out my mug. I was tired and a bit sore where my shin had connected with the boy's leg.

I left the front way, watching the shadows for anyone lurking around and then went back to my car. I sat slumped in the front seat for a while, then opened a Mars Bar. I needed the hit of energy to get me home. As I dumped the wrapper on the passenger seat I noticed a slip of paper. My nervous system wasn't going to like my new occupation. My heart leaped into gallop mode instantly. How long all hyped up could I survive before I collapsed? I picked the paper up and shone my pocket light on it.

'Are you feeling lucky?' was the charming message on the front. I flipped it over. 'Because you're going to have to be' complimented it on the other side. That was enough me for. I shot my car forward. The faster I drew this madman away from my parents the better. Jonelle didn't have anyone left in her life to be targeted, but I did and that was now beginning to bother me – a lot.

By the time I arrived home I was shaking. All the flight or fight adrenalin had been pumping for too long throughout my system, and I was in overload zone. I pulled off my jacket and it fell to the floor with a thunk. Somewhere in there I had a gun shoved in a pocket. Too bad. I was overtired and it could be dealt with later.

I curled up on the couch and flipped through TV channels. There had to be something worth watching at this hour. I settled on a repeat of Star Wars. So hugging my comfort rug, watching my comfort TV, and petting my comfort kitty, I eventually fell asleep.

Chapter Twelve

There was an insistent ringing in my ears. I struggled against it, warm and secure dreaming of just how much Han Solo wanted my body. The strange part was I looked like a young Raquel Welsh, but hey I really wasn't complaining about that. But the ringing was getting on my nerves and eventually I woke up, leaving mid kiss. Damn it all.

I stretched out and grabbed my mobile which was the source of my headache. As I lifted it up, I noticed it was only eight in the morning. After the night I'd had – this was the height of rudeness.

"Uh," was the deep and meaningful conversational gambit from me.

"Where are you? The plane landed twenty minutes ago. I've given you parking time, but now I want to come home." Jonelle's familiar tones came out at me, a little stronger than usual. She wasn't altogether happy with me.

Bugger. I had slept though my appointment to pick her up. Now I was awake I could hear my bedside alarm going off. Due to crashing on the couch, I'd missed it. Smudge purred softly in my ear.

"Sorry! I had a long night and then crashed out in the lounge room, and the alarm is going off, but I was kissing Harrison of the Ford variety and it was really yummy," I garbled. It was lovely to be as articulate as ever.

There was an amused snort from Jonelle. "How can someone stay mad with you when you always sound so disorganised? Well done, quite a score. Considering you aren't even on your way, I think it would be easier for me to get a cab. I'll dock it off your non-existent pay packet." I could hear the laughter in her voice. I liked the sound of that so much more than the other.

I turned off the bleeping alarm and dived into the shower. As disagreeable as it was to be up at this hour on a Saturday, it wouldn't appear to be half as bad if I was scalded and coffee-ed up.

Not too much later Jonelle arrived at my front door. I had the second cup of coffee in hand and was feeling something akin to human. When I opened the door to her I discovered she certainly wasn't.

"What the hell happened to you?" Possibly not the best way to start the day with your boss, but I was no diplomat.

The usually immaculately groomed and sleek woman was gone. She'd attempted something close to her usual style but the clothes were rumpled, the hair wasn't smooth, and the face was ashen. Those huge almond eyes were wide and a touch glassy.

"Things weren't smooth sailing in Sydney. I'll tell you some time. So, fill me in on all the excitement of the last two days here."

She'd obviously stopped off at home and dumped the luggage as she had nothing with her. Strolling in, Jonelle picked up Smudge and while moving my jacket from its obstructing spot on the floor, found and rescued her gun from its bulging pocket. Then she retired to the couch. She kind of sunk there, too frozen and tired to move by the looks of her. I didn't want to pry though. I wondered what was on her mind, though it couldn't be good, by the look of things.

I curled up opposite on the recliner armchair and filled her in. The more I spoke, the more shuttered and serious her face became. By the end I knew that Harry's days of haunting me were over. Eventually my story wound down and she rose. There was going to be action and I wasn't altogether sure I wanted to be involved.

The decision wasn't up to me. "Okay. Thanks for all that. I'll have a chat to our lovely Lilly and see what can be done about her boy. I'll see you Monday."

It was all a bit of a letdown. She showed herself out and as quick as that I had my Saturday all to myself. Which didn't really mean it was mine to do with as I wished, because dollars to donuts, Steph would call and possibly Grillia.

I tried hard not to think of what was going on across the pool in Jonelle's unit, but it was hard not to. It was a part of my life now, and I was a bit put out that she had commandeered my problem and set off to fix it.

I was a scaredy cat but I was one with principles, damn it. By Sunday evening I was really bothered. There had been no communication from Jonelle and I hadn't actually seen her leave her unit at all.

I'd like to think it was concern for her that drove me over there, but if truth be told, and it must be, then it was probably one part concern and three parts interest. I knocked, but when there was no response I tried the door. It rocked me off my feet when it opened. What happened to the security conscious Jonelle I knew? Unless of course she was leaving it open as a direct invitation to the baddies to come stroll in.

So I did.

The lights were all off and the place was lit by dozens of candles and the TV screen. There was the heady smell of incense and I saw Jonelle curled up in the midst of her pillows, an empty bottle of bourbon on the floor and a new one open in her hand. I didn't know how much had been left in that empty bottle, but quite a bit if the state she was in was anything to go by.

She was still in the clothes she had arrived home in, her face was pale and lined. In that instant, as I looked at her, it came to me that I had no idea of how old she was and that perhaps we weren't as close age-wise as I had thought. There was an old, beyond-care look about her and when she raised her eyes to me, they looked ancient.

"So, you're back huh?" She took a sip of bourbon straight from the bottle. She'd paused the screen when I'd come in on a beautiful man I didn't know. "Wondering what happened to Lilly and our dear Harry?"

Actually I was more concerned now than curious.

"Does it matter? Look at you. Have you even left this place since you got home?" I started putting cushions back into place, straightening and tidying up like a mother. Anything not to see the destruction in her eyes.

She waved a hand around. "Nope. Just sitting here, watching my DVDs. Harry will have to wait." She nodded at the screen. "Lovely boy, huh?" She stared at him hungrily as though force of will alone could pull him through the screen into reality. She unfroze the DVD.

The man laughed and pulled a young looking Jonelle into his arms. He looked down at her then across to whoever was doing the recording. "You two; my Queen of Diamonds and my Ace."

"Ace?" Jonelle was laughing too, tossing her blue black hair back from her face, love and delight shining from her eyes. "That's not a flattering as Queen, you know."

"You know why we call you Ace of Diamonds don't you?" The man smiled and nodded off screen to the recorder again. The love in his eyes for the person off screen was intense and my insides wiggled with the embarrassment of witnessing it. There was a girlish laugh and the camera jiggled, set down by strange hands. On screen came two women.

Both beautiful: one small and delicate looking, and the other tall, more Jonelle-like. Harder, stronger and far more lethal than I had imagined anyone was capable of looking. But at that moment her face changed and a smile swept the harshness from her eyes. They came to join the other two. All four stood there, sharing something, a look, a feeling, that the camera had captured perfectly.

A group of four strong (and scary) people taking time out from whatever it was they did to connect. I felt really out of it. The man leaned down and murmured just loud enough to be caught by the mike.

"We call you Ace, because you're the Ace up our sleeves." The other two smiled at Jonelle, though there was the distinct impression the Jonelle-copy wasn't smiling with her eyes. "No matter where this new venture takes you, you'll always be the Ace up our sleeves."

The younger Jonelle nodded. "Don't forget you can contact me if you need to. I'll only be in Australia. It's not that far really." And they held each other in silence. Then the darker, stonier version moved back to the camera and the screen went blank. End of show.

I stood there, cushion in hand. What could I say to that? It was probably the most personal thing I'd ever witnessed and I wasn't too sure if Jonelle was still aware I was even there.

"Well, what do you think of that then?" Obviously she was. "The smaller woman is Claire. The other one is Amelia. She's not as lovable as Claire, but for some reason Jack ended up with her. Go figure. The man, Jack, was our Jack of Diamonds. Amelia is the Queen and Claire was the Joker."

She stopped and gulped more bourbon. I felt like I should take the bottle off her, but that was probably way harder than anything I'd endeavoured before. Funnily enough, her voice sounded coldly sober, like granite.

"Who came to see you in Sydney?" I was trying hard to figure this out. These three people had obviously meant the world to her and something was drastically wrong.

"Claire. A flying visit, to let me know the latest news and then she headed off again. I guess she'll be trying to hold Amelia together; if Amelia allows her." There was a pause and Jonelle finally turned her eyes back to me from the black screen. They looked like holes of hell. "Some time back Jack went on some mission by himself. Amelia was beyond rage. He managed to get himself shot and had been in a coma for ages.

"Amelia was becoming hell to live with. Didn't know if she was bent on revenge, or drinking herself to death. Claire was a little fuzzy on the details. She says it's a mess, the boss is furious. Everyone's touchy and Claire came to tell me personally. You see," she said taking another jaw breaking mouthful of the hard stuff, "Jack died the other day. So there is no going back and making it all right." She sat there and stared me in the eyes. "Something like this; makes me wish I had the right to help out."

"Don't you?" I nodded at the TV. "Looks as though you guys were all pretty tight. I should think they'd be grateful to have your skills back in the mix."

She snorted. "While Amelia is grieving? She'd put a knife in my guts soon as look at me. She and I - it's complicated. We were never as close as her and Claire. Too much alike I suppose – in some ways. Amelia is harder than I could ever hope to be. It's quite possible she's not altogether sane."

She paused and looked into space. I had a sneaking suspicion that my current employer wasn't what I would call normal either. I wondered briefly if that thought had ever crossed her mind. After all, what she did, and what she took for granted, was some pretty intense stuff.

"Also," Jonelle continued, "she was never very level headed when it came to Jack. No, I left that world a long time ago and went my own way. None of them would want me back at a time like this. I'm not a team player. I'm getting out of that sort of thing, not into the middle of it." She shrugged. She watched me with those calculating cat-eyes, which didn't look drunk at all.

"It's just a shock to think I'll never see him again."

Those words reduced the stony gaze to glossy unshed tears and suddenly she looked like every girl who'd lost someone dear to them and not scary at all. I bent down and took the bottle away from her; then helped her to her feet. We staggered into her bedroom and I gracelessly dumped her on the bed. I didn't have the physical strength to manhandle her out of her clothes, so managed to get her under the covers instead. I figured that when necessity got too great, she'd deal with it herself.

Her fingers closed over my hands, in a grip that felt like it could break them. "Don't tell anyone about this. It can't get out that Jack's gone or that I ... "She didn't finish the sentence but I got it. People like Harry couldn't hear about her drunken emotional state. It would be like wolves to a slaughter.

I tried to remove my hands. "It'll be okay. I'll stay in the spare room and when you get up you'll know how to make it all better again."

I felt like a child who was seeing their older sister or parent suddenly behave far too humanly. I wanted her to be the one I looked to for reassurance; I needed her to be strong. I felt surprisingly out of place and out of my depth watching this overwhelming grief lay the strongest person I knew so low. I left her there and slipped into the spare bed. I was at the end of my endurance what with Harry and now Jonelle losing the plot. Sleep crashed over me like a cruise liner.

It was bright and sunny by the time I struggled into the kitchen the next morning. There was no sign of Jonelle and I hoped this meant she was either sleeping it off or had gone to the gym without me. I think that last bit was wishful thinking on my part. I put the percolator on and allowed the yummy smell of coffee to remind my body that morning time meant functioning time. It was Monday. It was more than time to get serious about all the unfinished business and loose ends.

The smell must have wafted through the whole place, because it wasn't long before Jonelle came out, minus old rumpled clothes, dressed only in bra and knickers.

Good grief.

At some time in my life I would have killed for a body like that. Sleek, smooth, lean, tanned and so toned you could have bounced peas off her. Knowing a bit more about what it took to get to that point, I'd rather keep my curves. She stalked past me and filled a mug with rich coffee: then promptly skulled it down without the usual milk or even a cooling off period.

"Ugh." She shuddered. "That has to be the foulest thing out. It's like taking it in the vein. How are you?" She swivelled red lined eyes to me.

"Much better now I've slept. Ready to sort out the files, get a lead on whatever and set Harry straight about stalking me and my parents," I said with much gusto and fake know-how. "Are you up to it?" I felt I had to ask considering how she looked.

Jonelle sighed. I'd never seen her so, well, normal. "You can come out with me when I deal with Harry, if you think you're up for it. I don't want to inflame the situation, but Lilly's irrational fears have got to stop interfering in my work."

Just like that it was back to normal. The two of us might look unable to walk a straight line, but things were business as usual. And last night was a distant memory neither of us were likely to talk about.

Jonelle took us in her car. A new one, not the Maserati. That, she told me, had been sold and she'd had someone take it away on Saturday when she'd not been in the mood herself. Personally I thought she would have been more accurate to say she'd not been *capable*, but I wasn't about to get pedantic.

The new car was far less flashy and wouldn't raise any eyebrows. I was sad at the departure of the Maserati, it had novelty value, but of course wasn't something for the covert sort of work Jonelle sometimes did. So we drove to Lilly's flashy little whore house in a Nissan Skyline and raised no eyebrows at all

It was amazing just how much legal and illegal prostitution went on in this nation's capital. Lilly kept it pretty low profile. It looked like a sweet little two story motel, done in red brick and white paint with frilly curtains on the windows, while inside women were gaining their fortunes, or at least Lilly's fortune, on their backs. Jonelle laughed at my naivety and told me that a lot of them were S&M mistresses, and spent most of their time whipping their slaves and not actually having sex with them at all.

I learned something new every day.

We'd only just stepped in the front door when two large and aggressive looking men came out of the office. They obviously knew Jonelle and weren't taking any chances; they had batons in hand: thick, long, lethal poles of steel. Jonelle ignored them like they were simply shadows.

She turned to the little camera in the ceiling and smiled. "Come out come out wherever you are, Lilly. Time we had a little chat."

Who could resist an invitation like that?

I'd had my back to the staircase. But when I heard a cold laugh I swung round fast. Coming down the red carpeted stairs was our moustached scar face, Harry Francis. He clapped his little hands and smiled down at us as he descended. He made my skin crawl.

Luckily for me though, Jonelle was made of sterner stuff. Where I would have turned tail and run back to the car, she stepped forward, brushing off the restraining hand of muscle man one and going to meet Harry as he made it to the ground floor.

"Jonelle, my dear. Lilly would love to see you. She's upstairs right now, so if you and your associate could come this way I'll take you to her myself." Somehow he made the whole things sound so sleazy. We were, after all, in a house of business – so to speak.

Jonelle just shrugged and beckoned me over. I liked the idea of being her associate, but also hoped that it didn't mean I had to be a henchman. I didn't fit the bill.

We followed Harry back up the stairs and along a corridor, doors on each side. Behind a couple were definite sounds of activity, but I tried hard to block out the noise. At the end of the corridor was a huge boardroom-cum-office area. And seated at a massive walnut desk was the Queen Bee herself, Lilly Pigholt. She wasn't much different from her photo, though there were definitely more lines now. Her light eyes looked cold and calculating. I wouldn't want her to be my boss that was definite.

"Jonelle." She nodded in greeting gesturing toward two chairs opposite herself. Jonelle and I sat; me nervous and distinctly feeling as though I had stepped into the wrong movie, and Jonelle as comfortable as any cucumber had ever been cool. I may have started to love the whole idea of being this ultra smooth business girl, but interviews like this hadn't been on my agenda at the time of acceptance.

"I'm a very busy woman, Jonelle, so please don't waste my time with all this arrogant posing. What can I do for you?"

Getting down to business in a hurry.

"Don't pretend you have no idea what's brought me here. As much as it would save face to think Harry was acting alone, it's a highly unlikely proposition. That being the case let's talk about calling your puppy off because I am getting more than a little ... annoyed." Heaven help me making her annoyed.

"And speaking of puppies, Harry had Fiona's family dog poisoned.

154

I would have thought that was more the feminine touch, but there you go. Any comments, explanations?"

The air in the room seemed to cool and thicken with tension. My stomach knotted, reacting in its own cowardly way. I had a sudden urge for some chocolate. For a while there I had managed to forget the fact Potty had died. Not that I was heartless, but things were getting a bit beyond the death of a family pet, if you see what I mean. But at Jonelle's words, memory came sliding back and there was ice in my veins. After all, if a man could kill off a family pet just for being in his way, what would he do to the family?

Harry wasn't taking that quietly.

"Hey, I had nothing to do with that dog. Okay, so I hit it with the car once, and you should see the damage," Jonelle gave him a look and he held up a hand, "but I wouldn't have poisoned the mutt. I just assumed it was my lucky day, when she suddenly disappeared."

Some lucky day. As if we were going to believe that! I glanced at Jonelle. Her eyes were narrowed and she was dong that thoughtful thing. Well, I wasn't going to believe it, even if she was big on the benefit on the doubt.

"You know me, Jonelle. I wouldn't poison a dog. Bloody hell. I can get around dogs if I have to." There was disgust in his voice; as though the murder of an innocent animal laid at his door was the final straw.

Jonelle gave a sharp nod. "But if I find out differently, Harry, I'll come back and you shan't enjoy the interview."

"Not really lovin' this one," he muttered, standing back from the desk.

Lilly and Jonelle went back to eyeing each other off, like it was some sort of competition. Though to my eyes, Jonelle was serene with it and Lilly had what appeared to be a bead of sweat gathering on her upper lip. I wished I'd had the sense to let Jonelle come alone.

"Heard anything else about Brenda lately, Lilly?" I heard a small intake of breath behind us as Harry straightened up ready for whatever was about to come.

Lilly's face went motley red. She obviously wasn't too comfortable with the line of questioning. There was a slight pause as she gathered her thoughts. I couldn't imagine what she had thought Jonelle had come to talk about, but Brenda wasn't at the forefront of her mind.

"Brenda's untimely loss is still being felt here. There is no need to bring up that sort of unpleasantness now." Her lips thinned and her eyes met Harry's over our heads. I did not like the idea of that man standing behind me. But if Jonelle was okay with it then I just had to accept it. The hairs on the back of my neck prickled none-the-less.

Jonelle suddenly leaned forward and put her arms on the table between them. Lilly sat back as though Jonelle had attacked her. Harry was there beside the desk hand on a knife, before I could swallow. Not that I had any saliva left with which to swallow.

"Let us cut the crap for once, Lilly. As you said; no posturing. Brenda had something on you or your known associates. Something urgent enough to have her killed. She died on my watch and I *shall* be seeking restitution from whoever ordered the hit. The hit-man himself is a dead man walking. I have no interest in you or your shonky business here or elsewhere, unless it has direct relation to Brenda's death. So unless you have something to tell me, a name or a place, our business is over with. Harry can go keep tabs on someone else, as my associate here has had nothing to do with Brenda's case until today."

She sat back keeping her eyes level on Lilly but I could tell the knife in Harry's hand was where she was focused. If he so much as twitched, he was a dead man too. "Do we have an understanding? Do you have anything to tell me? That's all I want to hear."

Lilly flicked her hand at Harry and he folded the knife up his sleeve casually as though it had simply fallen out. She leaned back in her chair affecting casualness herself.

"Look Jonelle, there isn't anything else I want to add to what we've spoken about. Whatever Brenda was running from had nothing to do with me. What my associates get up to I can't help you with, I don't have any control over that. If I find anything else I'll be sure to give you a call." She turned those pale hideous eyes on me. "Harry won't be bothering you anymore."

And that was that. We left in silence, not speaking again until we got into the car. Harry made sure we were off the property before he disappeared. I think the getting talked about, and not consulted, had upset his ego. When we were on our way back home I breathed again.

"Thanks. At least I don't have that man to contend with. But why would he have been sniffing around me anyway? And if he didn't kill Potty, then who did?" I was rearing to go – one little high on my power trip of adrenalin.

Jonelle, driving with throttling hands on the wheel, gave a snorted.

"Eager aren't you? I think Lilly was just curious as to who the new player in my life was. Not that it pays to be too curious in this business." (I wondered if that was a jab at me), "I'm not really sure who would benefit from having Potty removed, if it wasn't Harry. And he's right, murdering a dog isn't his style. We don't want to be tied down to watching over your folks all the time, so I think I'll detail Mike to cruise past every now and again. Keep an eye on things. And I'm sure if something happens out of the ordinary, you'll be the first to know." She smiled slightly, probably imaging my mother calling out an SOS over nothing.

She may have had a point, but it didn't really help me feel any easier. Potty wasn't random, I was sure. But if Jonelle was happy to leave it all in the hands of Mike, then who was I to argue?

"So, what's next then?" I asked.

"Don't worry, there's plenty more work to do, now that we have put a stop to Harry's visits. I have to go to Adelaide to appraise some art works of Thorn Ridley. Someone I know in America has a real hankering for his work. I also have to check out some details of Brenda's murder. You could go over the file if you like. Perhaps you could turn up something I missed. Then I need to track down someone called The Rose."

Man, she was more vocal in one day than she had been the whole time I'd known her. This was a record of sentences strung together. But she had brought up quite a few things that were of interest to me. Not to mention, she was off to visit this reclusive, odd ball of a painter living in the Adelaide Hills. No one got to see Thorn Ridley. He lived on some massive property and painted like a demon. The press even had the dogs set on them.

"Thorn Ridley? Need company?" I could get to The Rose comment later. Right now I wanted to settle my first working trip. It was less intimidating than thinking of another confrontation.

"Sure, if you want to go. I knew him a few years ago and he has a whole stack of new works he wants to sell, which goes well with Hank who wants to buy. You can book some tickets when we get to the office." That was it. I was back to pulling teeth.

"Who's The Rose and do we really have to find him?" I was dying of curiosity but you know what? Not so much that I actually wanted to do the dying bit.

Jonelle pulled into the car park. "We kind of need to find him before he finds us. That would be no fun at all, trust me. It's all messy and complicated. To cut it short, I find him, we talk and then I put him down."

It sounded so reasonable when she put it like that. When did we get to the point that talking about putting a human being down (like a stray cat) was okay? Mind you, his dossier read like a who's who of criminal know-how, so was it really a bad thing?

"I don't know if I want to go to that interview." I tried for the light approach. Jonelle flashed me the shark smile.

"That's okay, I wasn't thinking of inviting you."

Well, bully for me then.

"Want something to eat?" At the mention of food, my stomach reminded me that breakfast had been a while ago and my imaginings of eating chocolate had been far from rewarding.

Jonelle was raiding the fridge and piling up healthy looking sandwich-type ingredients. That hadn't been the first thing on my mind, but better than nothing. When she retrieved a massive block of chocolate I was stoked. She noticed my grin.

"I love to eat something truly horrific after a face to face. I burn through a lot of fuel if under stress."

Could have fooled me that there was any stress involved. Well, that was the whole idea, she had fooled me.

"Does it ever get any easier? The whole having to be larger than life and playing hard ball with everyone, thing? You looked as cool as a cucumber."

She shut the fridge with her foot. "Well yeah, it gets a bit easier. I no longer feel like I'm going to puke if they pull a knife on me. The first time someone did that, Jack." She stopped and bit her lip. "I was very lucky that Jack was there and he prevented too much skewering of me. That's how I got my scar. A reminder of how far I've come and how one slip can leave you permanently marked."

As if she needed that. Her twin sister was a constant source, I'd have thought.

"I know more now about other people's reactions, how to handle a situation so it doesn't have to turn nasty. That doesn't mean I don't get myself into trouble. I can get myself out of it better these days, that's all."

I started to build myself a massive sandwich while munching on a small mountain of chocolate.

"What about The Rose? What exactly is his deal?" I shoved everything onto a plate and headed for the couch. I was no longer so concerned about sitting on the velvet.

Jonelle followed, mouth half full. One quick swallow and she could talk. "I've stayed out of his hair for years. We had one monumental crisis and he went away limping. It was … distasteful. Since then I've only kept half an ear to the ground as to where he might be. Not too long ago a client asked me to acquire some art for him. I knew Peter and Paul had it illegally and felt no qualms about taking if off them. They are a little miffed and I heard they may have hired The Rose to get it back and to teach me a lesson." She took a huge bite of her sandwich and munched contentedly. To my untrained eye she looked anything but concerned about the possible chance of The Rose finding her.

"And?" I barely waited until she had swallowed this time.

"I don't learn very fast." She smiled at me. "I don't think he needs an excuse to be more of a pain in my arse. Anyway, I was bodyguard for someone a few years ago in an attempt to get them out of trouble and shut down some meat markets. You know, women for money stuff. It would appear that the threat may be back and The Rose has been hired for the hit this time." She shrugged. "I rid my client of the last threat. I presume I'll rid myself of this one."

Such calm arrogance in the face of anything but normal circumstances.

"Who is he and why 'The Rose' name?" It felt so normal to be munching with my boss and discussing work related issues even though it happened to be murder and mayhem.

Reality was going to be so dull if I ever resigned.

"His name, as far as I have been able to discover, is actually Ben Rosa. He took the rose as a symbol and had a signet ring of a rose made. He has a tendency to burn a brand from that ring on victims. Either as a warning to them or a warning to others, if he kills them. It's all very petty and manly." Her lips curled in disgust. "I met someone who had the brand on them. It was messy. She was scarred for life. The man needs to be taught a lesson."

I shuddered. There was one thing I knew and that was I really didn't want to get caught by this maniac. A rose tattoo was one thing; a brand made by something that hot was another. Had I mentioned the coward angle yet?

Jonelle brushed off the crumbs and got up. "Time for some work."

I sighed. Gone were the long lunches and relaxing afternoons in the sun. Smudge was learning to spend more time over here than at home. Ah, how one's children grew up so fast.

Back into the office and I was booking flights to Adelaide and updating the Brenda file to include today's interview with Lilly. I also familiarised myself with photos of The Rose, or Ben as I now wanted to know him. I mean, Ben sounded so much more ... normal and less threatening. I didn't want to wind up in a dark alley with a strange man and not recognise him as foe not friend.

Eventually I'd had enough and packed it in. Too many faces to remember and baddies out there. Where had I been all my life?

Living so quietly, not knowing the dangers that by the looks of things, surrounded us all on a daily basis. Had I had my head buried in the sand, or did they just skirt around the average citizen? I can't say I had ever given the seedier side of life much thought. It hadn't touched me and I was glad of it. Now I was immersing myself in it, and today I felt the need to go home and have a very long and scalding hot shower. Things were going on in the world that made me sick.

I'd never considered myself a deep thinker. But this was getting on top of my surface attitude. Human beings had such rotten minds. I read in one file of a group who tortured their victims. Jonelle had them marked with 'extreme caution'.

Where are these sickos? Half of me wanted to set her onto them. Where do they get off treating another life like that? And yet, Jonelle talked about ending a human life, putting it down, as though it was common place. Like it was a mercy for them and the world at large. The lines for me were becoming painfully blurred and I was suffering a crisis of conscience or something. While I liked to believe that on the whole I was working for some sort of good guy, I was starting to wonder if there was such a thing.

Who made the rules and who was right? Was it ever okay to end the life of another?

I stumbled into my own unit and dumped Smudge on the floor. There was a bottle of wine that had my name on it calling me from the fridge and I hoped it would help to end the clamour in my head. I didn't want to be asking these questions because there was no certainty in them, and I was too wrapped up in my new world to just walk away.

I hadn't asked Jonelle about the coincidence of her moving into an apartment block with Brenda's sister. I hadn't asked her about a history of cases involving violence and how many of them could come back and bite us in the arse. I certainly hadn't touched on the fact that there was a furiously grieving, potentially mad woman, called Amelia out there.

I didn't want to think of what she had been mixed up with before she moved to Australia. Who were Claire, Amelia and Jack, and why did the thought of someone out there who could bring Jack down make me want to run weeping into some safe hidey hole? If Amelia was someone Jonelle didn't want to mess with, perhaps friends were interchangeable with foes and then, who was I?

I uncorked the Chardonnay, a much easier proposition than attempting to unravel the knots in my head. I checked the message machine and found one there from Mum and one from Brad. Neither did I feel up to dealing with so I took my glass, shedding clothes as I went, into the ensuite. It was time to scrub my skin till it bled. Who knew - it might even make me feel a bit better about everything. Though that was stretching the powers of a simple shower somewhat.

It was quite challenging to keep drinking and shower at the same time. But when it came down to it, I enjoyed that sort of challenge. Nothing got between me and my glass after a day like today.

Clean and steaming, I made my way into the bedroom. It was only Monday. No one to my knowledge had plans to go out and do anything interesting or stupid. So instead of making myself the human diary and co-ordinating an outing for everyone I dived into bed and crashed out.

I had actually been in the room with people who had no interest in keeping me breathing. I desperately needed to get a handle on this whole gun-toting business. I wouldn't feel quite so vulnerable if I had some form of protection around me at all times. Currently though, it would be more of a liability than protection. I needed some lessons – quickly. Those thoughts drifted through my mind as my body was pulled down into sleep.

I liked to think I had the same response system as the average person. Better, if truth be told (I liked to believe it was better anyway). So when I came struggling to the surface the first thing I noticed I was no longer comfy and warm. In fact there appeared to be a rather nasty draft from somewhere. I heard a muffled cough and came awake in one giant leap.

My eyes flashed open and I read the red glowing numbers on the clock by the bed. It was three am or as close as to not make any difference. The next thing I noticed was that it wasn't fully dark. Soft light made me aware of just how naked I was. And there were two men in the room not unaware of that nakedness too.

"Good evening Miss Page. I was wondering if we could have a chat?"

He sounded so normal. So ... well... polite. Who'd have thought?

Chapter Thirteen

I sat up, pulling the sheet with me attempting some sort of covering of the naked issue.

"Who are you?"

I tried for an even tone, but it kind of sounded like a squeak. I couldn't pull off casualness with two men in my bedroom at this hour without a stitch on – a sheet really not offering anyway near the protection I would have hoped for.

"Excuse me, how rude. Allow me to introduce myself. My name is Charles and my associate is Daniel."

What was with that? One day I was just Fiona and the next just about everyone I met had an associate and I was one too.

"I think we have a friend in common. You know Amelia, I presume?"

My heart nearly stopped. Jonelle said Amelia was unpredictable, but surely she wouldn't have sent someone all the way out here just to give Jonelle a prod using me? I nodded, more a stiff necked jerk.

"Good." His voice was smooth and oiled, like a machine. "No need for further explanations then. I always like it when people are up to speed. I was wondering if you could relay a message for me. I would very much like it if Amelia was to keep her grotty little nose out of my business. Ask her if Jack wasn't a big enough casualty for her? I need you to make your message to stay away sincere now, my dear. So forgive the necessary inducement."

Charles rose and nodded to Daniel who had been standing just that little bit out of the light. I wish he'd stayed there.

Daniel was big. Big and scary and lightening fast. I had only drawn the breath to scream when he had knocked the wind out of me and stuffed something vile into my mouth. Thrash I might, but his paw-like hand held my arms easily as he wound wire around them. Bound hand and foot, I lay there staring up at these men. In my vain attempt to dislodge him, I'd managed to lose the sheet and I was uncovered, vulnerable, and scared half to death.

My mind could picture all too well the sort of inducements these men could inflict.

The fact that I wasn't raped helped.

I didn't look at the clock when they left. I curled up into a small ball of misery and lay there until I could see the sun staining the sky. My hands and feet were still bound and I was still naked. They had taken their gag with them, but I was in no state to do any screaming.

I ached in every muscle and my face felt like a frozen mask of torment. If I was meant to be a threat to the others, I think they were about to fail miserably. From what I could tell of Jonelle's character, Charles and Daniel were about to be visited by the avenging demon. I was unsure of Amelia's response, as I'd never met the woman.

I waited, lying on my side, for Jonelle to wake up and come get me. That I had no doubt she'd eventually come knocking on my door showed the faith I had in our new arrangement. The weekend was over; it was time to hit the gym again. It was highly unlikely she would go without me, so all I had to do was wait until six am.

Sure enough, she was knocking on the door just on six.

By that time I could take reasonably deep breaths without feeling like I was about to puke, so I filled my lungs and hollered for her. One beautiful lungful of squawk from me and I *heard* her attack my door.

A few moments later she came barging into my room, door picking file in one hand and flick knife in the other. Decked out in the training suit of black she preferred for our morning torture sessions, she looked lethal.

I had never been happier to see anyone in my life.

The sight of me halted her in her tracks. She stood for one breathless second taking in my obvious lack of mobility, then she was twisting me free and wrapping me up in the blanket from the bottom of the bed. I started to cry. The pain in my hands and feet as the blood sluggishly moved back into them, and the rest of it was too much. I leaned against her strength and cried into the shoulder provided.

"That's right. Let it out." Jonelle soothed me like a puppy. I choked and hiccupped most unladylike. There may have even been a little dribble. I was definitely not okay.

"Thanks." I hiccupped at her. "I knew you'd come eventually and I was so cold and I couldn't move and they *beat* me."

I've never been beaten before. My parents only ever smacked us all once and as I grew older there had been no bully in my life who thought it was okay to do that. I felt red and raw.

Jonelle looked at me sideways. "Yeah, I think I could tell that. Let's get you over to my place, shall we? You need some looking after, the least of which will be a long spa to help soak some aches away."

I felt like groaning. Did I look like someone who was able to do anything as energetic as walking all the way to her place?

I swayed to my feet, feeling ill and slightly dizzy. What had they done to me? I'd never felt like this before, not even after a ferocious drinking session. Jonelle stood beside me watching my face as I tottered on my feet. With a disgusted grunt, she swung me up into her arms. The woman was seriously strong.

She carried me to the spa in her ensuite and dumped me and my blanket in a puddle beside it so she could run the water. I allowed the sounds of the water filling the bath to lull me, head resting back against the tiles. I didn't have any energy, so this was heaven; someone else taking care of me and making everything okay.

In my half fogged out state Jonelle peeled me out of the blanket and lowered me into the spa. After turning the jets on, she left me. I was glad as I wasn't too comfortable with the whole naked thing, especially considering the last few hours.

I allowed the hot water and the pressure jets to pummel me into a sodden mass of heavy flesh. If it wasn't for the thoughts running around in my head, I could've fallen asleep. As it was, the constant chatter inside my skull kept me conscious.

Eventually I could put it off no more. I stood up and grabbing a towel, faced the mirror. I stared at the image reflected back at me. One eye was partly closed and starting to bruise up. My jaw line was an unhealthy mottled yellow and red. My wrists had a thin strip around them which was testimony to the wire. It was raw and inflamed; I guessed the wire hadn't been too hygienic. My feet were in a similar state. Covering my body was a spattering of bruises already forming. I knew there were more to come by the sheer ouch I felt every time I moved. I was not a pretty sight. How was I going to cover this one up?

I towelled off and picked up the robe Jonelle had left for me. Wrapping myself in the luxury of fluffy terry towelling several sizes too big, I wandered out to find my hostess.

She was in the office yabbering down the telephone in one of her foreign languages. She wasn't happy and I knew it had a lot to do with me. Just call me self absorbed.

She saw me standing at the door and waved me in. A short bark later and she hung up.

"How are you feeling?"

As if she needed to ask; my face was one large pulsating bruise and my feet and hands felt like they were about to fall off.

"Fine," I lied, wincing as I sat down in my usual chair.

Daniel had been quite thorough in beating my butt too. It was hot with the drubbing it had received. She grinned tightly at my faked lightness. Hey, two could play at that game.

"So, now you're up; tell me everything." It was the order of a boss to an employee; not friend to friend.

I accepted the hot mug of green tea she passed me and explained everything to her. I left nothing out. From thinking she was here using Heather as bait, to Daniel and Charles telling me that their message was for Amelia. I even put in my own agonising over the rights and responsibilities about killing people. Especially now I was probably on the list. My mug was empty and I was drained by the time I finished talking. I felt hot and cold and itchy.

Tears were leaking out the corners of my eyes, but Jonelle's stony gaze hadn't allowed me to stop halfway through. She wanted the whole story.

I was glad they had bound my mouth with their foul hanky. Thinking back, I remember screaming in my throat the whole time. I sat back. It was all out on the table and now it was time for her to let me know what the hell was going on.

"Who the fuck are Charles and Daniel?" My language often slipped when under stress.

Jonelle raised her eyebrows but didn't comment.

"Well, I've been talking to Claire and she has no idea. Amelia isn't making any sense to anyone at the moment, but I'm sure she'll get the message. According to Claire, she's like a time bomb. She is making revenge her mission and the Boss sending her home to Australia to cool her heels for a while may not have been the best idea he's ever had. On the other hand, it may just make her calm down. A drinking Amelia is not pretty. Claire is happy to take any information we can send her, but wants us to stay as clear as we can. I told her not to worry – I have enough problems of my own to work through without taking on hers and Amelia's. Whoever they were, however, we can't take the chance they will come back. I'll be setting your place up like mine. That way no one will be getting in unless announced. I think this place needs a dog." She flicked through some paper.

"That's it? These people get in and beat me half to death" (okay I liked to exaggerate when it came to my skin), "and they just get to walk away? Like nothing happened?"

So much for images of avenging angels and all that jazz. I felt monumentally let down and suddenly boiling over inside with anger, which showed like a reel across my face.

Jonelle watched me. "Yes. I have a job to do. You have a job to do. Unless you don't want to come to Adelaide?"

I shook my head dumbly.

"Okay, so we got a bit slack and some idiots came in and taught us a valuable lesson. Like, for instance, my past can still reach out and touch us. We'll be more careful. But my hands are tied. I don't know what Jack was into and I don't know what Amelia will do. The fact that those in England don't know who these jokers are, is … worrying. But we can't allow that to interfere. We have to find The Rose; we need to match Hank with some paintings from Thorn Ridley; I have to find Brenda's killer and I also have the small matter of getting Phil's painting back to him. Which reminds me I have to go visit some boys about nicking it in the first place."

She laid her hands palm down on the table. I could see the tendons standing out with strain.

"Don't you think we have enough to be going on with? I retired from all that other stuff. I can pass on messages to Claire. Once Amelia is human again she'll get it. What she does with it is entirely up to her. If these guys are professional they won't come back. If they aren't, then I'll deal with them, my way. In the meantime, I don't like what they did, but I can't take it away."

I had forgotten about bloody Phil waiting for Jonelle to return the missing art. It'd been taken over by so many other events it was the least of my worries. And come to think of it, the person who called me and wrote the message on Jonelle's wall may not have had anything to do with Phil. I had assumed it had, but now I knew she was meddling in so many other issues, it could have been any of them – such as Brenda's killer, which was very disturbing because that would mean he or she knew where Jonelle lived and thus, possibly about Heather and me already!

Didn't she know any nice people? Even her so called pals from England were the stuff of nightmares.

"What about Heather? I don't believe you came here just because you liked the outlook."

I was ready for an argument and didn't care if I was treading on her toes. I was sick of not understanding and being swept up in the thrill of doing things that were *really* beyond my capabilities.

"I found out where Heather was living and made a ridiculous offer to Simon and Lorraine. Yes, I want to be close to her. Not only because she is possible bait, but because there is the slight chance that Brenda spoke to her and I'm not the only one who knows that. The person who was after Brenda and eventually got her, may well try his or her luck with the sister. I'll not lose two of them." Her voice was steel.

"But it's been ages! Surely if they wanted to get her, it would have been done by now?" I wasn't too sure of time lines but it did seem a bit long to hold out waiting to kill a potential threat. If I was the murderer of one sister and thought the other one might know something, *anything*, I'd have done her straight away.

Jonelle was nodding. "Yeah, I thought that too. But Brenda had been cut off from her family for ages. Even Lilly didn't know about Heather while Brenda worked for her. It wasn't until the funeral did she cotton on. Heather came; she sat alone, with a thick black veil and didn't draw any attention to herself. I overheard her talking to Lilly. Lilly ran into her accidentally and said something like poor dear, did you know her? And Heather muttered, 'she was my sister', and left. Not much to go on and I was the only person close enough to hear.

"Without a description of her, a name or anything about Brenda that could lead me to family, it took me a while to find the sister. As Heather is safely alive, I can place odds that Lilly didn't really order her sister killed because she was the only other one to know about Heather. We both know she wouldn't want one of her highest earners dead. I just can't imagine what Brenda knew that was worth dying for." Jonelle bit her lip.

It obviously pissed her off to have something under the 'I don't know' banner. That I could understand.

But the little fact that these bozos had beaten me didn't seem to factor in high enough. I wanted them to be pulverised, and my struggle with ethics and morality was fast disappearing. If I could set Jonelle, or even this unknown Amelia, onto these men I'd have happily done so.

I didn't know what that made me; a psychopath or just a normal person with a taste for power and vengeance, but I was willing to explore it. I didn't have any skills when it comes to the fighting part, but hey – allow me to introduce my friend Jonelle and let her kick your butt. I daydreamed of saying that to Charles and Daniel. It felt amazingly good.

Jonelle stifled a yawn. It seemed even tough girls got tired. I wondered what she'd been up to all night while I was getting the stuffing beaten out of me, but thought twice about asking. I wasn't too awake myself. At least I wasn't being forced to go to the gym. My face would have scared the other fanatics.

"I wish I could make it better, Princess, but it's impossible. Whoever they were, they'd be long gone by now. But I have been asking around and if anyone knows anything, I'll hear of it." Jonelle eyed me sympathetically. Well, at least she was taking it seriously. I couldn't ask for more than that, really.

"So, what's on the agenda for today?"

It was only Tuesday and I'd booked flights to Adelaide tomorrow, so we had a whole day to kill before we could get away. I dreaded meeting any of the Apartmates looking like this, but I knew it was inevitable. And there were the messages from Mum and Brad on my machine which I hadn't looked into yet. Probably invites to things I wouldn't feel up to attending. Like the movies tonight with Brad. Who would venture out in public with a face like mine? There were limits to make up. Hiding the swelling and the multi coloured hues was going to be interesting on the flight as it was.

She rifled through some paper. "I have a contact to go talk to who may or may not tell me something about The Rose, depending on how co-operative I can make him. Other than that, not a lot. I do need to go see some of the Batch and Haddock's patrons about that stolen painting for Phil, otherwise he is going to come visiting again and I really don't want that."

After last night my body cringed at the thought of any more action for the time being, thank you very much. And while I agreed with it on principle, I still thought the idea of being swept along in events too swift for my thought processes was kind of fun. Hey – I was a child of the X generation. We liked things fast and disposable.

Though we preferred our lives not to be the disposable item.

She was off to visit people of untold origin, but by the looks of all the paper on her desk, I would be filing.

"Need company?" I asked.

Anything was better than having to sit on my sore old butt and shuffling bits of paper covered half the time in a code that I couldn't even read.

Jonelle raised her eyes from the paper she was reading.

"You feel up to it? Mind you, your face would be a good inducement to anyone to have a chat to us." She grinned. "If they see you up and walking around they'll think you are made of pretty tough stuff."

I liked the idea of a compliment in there somewhere and nodded. I felt up to something. I needed to be out there making sure I wasn't always the target.

When we were safely settled in her car (my arse complaining wildly about the seats) I asked where we were off to. I wasn't too sure if we were off to see the Batch boys or The Rose contact. Either would be scary.

"We'll stop in to see Tomas from the Batch and Haddock first. As far as I could tell from Phil's place and the people I've spoken to, the painting was taken by Tomas and at least two of his cronies. Why is beyond me. They don't have anything to do with the art world to my knowledge. But I'll ask. Mainly, I just want the painting back. You'd think they would know me well enough not to have been so stupid. And if they were the ones dicking around with paintbrushes and your phones, they'll wish they hadn't."

Tomas lived, if one could say that, in a horrid little town house which smelled like someone hadn't cleaned in way too long. The constant barking of a large dog inside may have helped with the overall effect of neglect and bad boy gone sour. Jonelle wrinkled her nose.

"You'd think he'd show some self respect. I'm beginning to think they either want to tweak my nose, or they did this for someone else. Can you see someone who lives in this having a hankering for artwork?" She snorted.

I didn't think I could open my mouth to speak without retching. The pain was thumping in my skull and the smell wasn't helping. Jonelle suddenly stopped.

"I'm totally not thinking straight. This smell – what's it smell like to you?"

I looked at her blankly. It just really stunk as far as I could tell.

"A dead body, that's what it smells like. Tomas isn't going to be too helpful I shouldn't think." She sighed in annoyance.

Well, I could see how it was a small vexing matter. Though possibly more so for Tomas. My stomach threatened to heave. Now I knew the cause of the smell; it really wasn't helping.

Jonelle glanced at my face. I knew it had to be pretty pasty. Added with the bruising, a frightful mix. "You don't have to come in, you know. There's obviously a dog which may go nuts and a body. Your call." She waited.

The choice was kind of out of my hands. It had been since I met her. From that first moment when we made plans for a business relationship – it had been leading to this. I was about to see my first ever dead body – unless she was wrong.

"Let's go do it." I firmly told my stomach to pull its head in, the last thing I needed to do now was to throw up all over my shoes.

Jonelle rapped on the door. We had to at least make some show of hoping someone might answer. The only response was increased barking. Jonelle withdrew a gun from under her left arm. How had I missed that? Her other hand went to the door. It was unlocked and I cringed. There was no hope for old Tomas now.

"Right, when we open this the chances of a dog attack get slightly higher, though he sounds in a back room of some kind. So let me go first." As if I needed an invite. What, she thought I was totally crazed and would just barge in, in front of her?

She withdrew her hand and took a chunky piece of metal out of her pocket and screwed it onto the end of the gun. It was the first time I'd seen a silencer and it hit me; this was serious.

"I can't hear him behind this door, but if not this one, the next. Let's go." And she pushed it open.

If I thought the smell outside had been pretty bad, the smell inside hit me like a steam train. I threw myself out of its range and threw up in the flower bed. Jonelle shot me a filthy look. Not like I could help it, I tried to tell her without actually opening my mouth at all.

The windows and door were shut holding the fetid air inside. We walked into a large family room which led off to the kitchen. Standard town house. Not much in the way of extra space. I couldn't believe the neighbours hadn't reported the smell.

There was a scrabbling behind one of the doors down the corridor to the right. I could only hope the dog hadn't been locked in the same room as the body without any other food … I shut that image away before I threw up the rest of my stomach, and more besides.

Jonelle was edging around the place, studying stuff. I didn't know what she was looking for and didn't really care. This was more real than I had expected. I had thought a civilised chat, a few threatening words and out the door with a painting in tow. What I hadn't counted on was someone in there before us making sure Tomas wasn't talking to anyone.

We stood at the doorway of the main corridor. There were three doors off it, each probably leading to a bedroom or bathroom. The one closest to us held the dog. The smell was so strong in general, it was impossible to tell which room it originated in. I wasn't in any hurry to find out, but Jonelle was. My guess was she didn't want to be found here. Not that I blamed her.

"I need to shut that dog up before the neighbours actually do something about it."

And she thrust me backwards and shut the door which connected the bedrooms to the main living area. There were a few more moments of barking, then silence. My skin prickled. It was worse than the constant noise; that deep dark silence. Then the door opened and Jonelle stepped out with her hand on the straining collar of a Dalmatian. It was thin and obviously thirsty as it took no notice of me, but dragged Jonelle to its water bowl. It drank it dry.

"Hold him. Tomas wasn't in that room, thank God. I'll go check the others."

Jonelle handed me the dog and went back into the rooms. The dog and I sat and eyed each other.

"Well, you aren't all that scary. Just noisy. Guess you wanted out and didn't know how else to talk to anyone, hey?" I stroked his nose and he flopped onto his stomach, grovelling for the attention.

Jonelle came striding back in.

"Tomas is going to be no more use to anyone. What a bugger. Mind you, I can't see this being about art. Tomas was a heavy drug user and by looks of things, his place has been tossed. Either he couldn't pay or someone wanted his stash. I'll make some inquiries about that later. Right now, we have to go see someone about The Rose, then I think we'll have to go drinking at the Batch and Haddock to find the rest of Tomas's group. This is getting messy. And far too many people all around me keep of winding up dead. I do not like that."

Her voice was velvet covered steel. I had no doubt she disapproved of all these dead bodies greatly.

"Can we take Tomas junior here with us?" As I stood up, the Dalmatian did as well.

He leaned against me, as though glued. I didn't think he wanted to be left there. His delicate canine nose probably couldn't take the smell anymore than I could. Jonelle looked down at him.

"Sure. Grangelands needs a dog anyway. A sort of communal resource roaming around at night, unless he's a sook." He ducked his head under her stern gaze.

"Oh stop picking on him; can't you see you scare him?" I crooned down at him and he raised puppy eyes to mine. I caught Jonelle rolling her own. "Shall we get the hell out of here? I really don't want to be sick again."

As we left, Jonelle scuffed some dirt over my sick. "Don't want any particularly bright eyed boy in blue to analyse that, do we?" I hadn't given the police much thought.

"They're going to know that someone was here. The lack of the barking dog for one. Neighbours do remember some things and that would be one of them. Should we put him back?" I shuddered to think of it.

"No. I'll deal with cop questions. They don't like me much, but I generally get around them." She amazed me. Friends with the police. Or at least, on uneasy terms together. Nice one.

"Can you swing me free parking forever?" I asked facetiously as I stowed our new dog in the back of the car, not an easy task in a Skyline.

"Somehow I don't think my influence goes that far. I could probably *get* you a series of parking tickets," she mused, grinning at me.

It is truly frightening to think she could go in and see a dead body, and come out cracking jokes. I didn't think my constitution was that strong. Not by a long shot. She waved a little packet at me.

"Guess what I found?"

I had no idea.

"Where did you get that?"

She glanced at me. "In Tomas' … underpants."

I gagged. "You rifled through his *undies*? Through a dead body's undies?" Man, she was a sicko.

She grinned at me. "I once overheard Tomas say that anything he wanted to keep safe, he kept with his most prized possessions. It doesn't take Einstein to know Tomas only had his balls to be obsessed about. And really, considering the look I got of them, they were nothing to be proud of. Though that could have something to do with the whole dead aspect."

She looked at the packet in her hand. "I think my hand and this packet could do with a good bit of sterilization. You'll have to drive. I could not possibly hold onto anything I may ever come in contact with again, with this hand."

So saying she took the passenger seat and one handedly put on her seat belt.

I shuddered. There was always an ick factor. Taking the driver's side, I pushed the dog's head out of the way. "So where exactly are we going now? And do you have any idea of what that stuff is?"

Jonelle sat in thought for a moment. "We need to get to The Rose contact sometime today, but I think this substance has to take priority. I don't know what it is, but I know of someone who can find out. We need to get to the clubhouse and find the Chemist."

She gave me directions and we were away.

While I wasn't much on knowing where I was going ahead of time, street names not meaning all that much, when I actually get to a place I was more than capable of putting two and two together.

"We're going to the *bikers'* clubhouse?" I think my voice broke somewhere in that sentence.

There were loads of places a good girl's mother tells her never to go to. You know; out late at night alone, a party with only boys, S&M houses (sorry Lilly, but already been there now!) and top of the list was never to frequent clubhouses notoriously known to house scary people like The Hellhounds. The clubhouse in question was called 'home' to The Hounds of Hell. It wasn't a pretty place and certainly not somewhere I'd choose to go even in the middle of the day.

"Are you nuts? Even the police don't go there." I didn't think I could stress that enough.

There just wasn't any way we were getting in there and out again unscathed. But Jonelle was, well, Jonelle, and wouldn't take no for an answer.

I pulled the Skyline into a parking space across the street. As much as I'd have liked to stay there with the motor running for some sort of high speed getaway, I suspected I was expected to go inside. I was a part of the team and I could hardly let her go in there alone. I climbed reluctantly out of the safety of the car and shut the door in the dog's eager face. I was already getting attached to the pooch.

Smudge, of course, was going to have a fit.

We crossed over and Jonelle led us into the clubhouse. It opened into a bar, which was full of smoke and men. Not exactly what I had been hoping for.

There was the buzz of conversation, the deep and constrained violence sort of thing. The type of tension that came when too much testosterone was in one room with nothing to balance it out. Couple that with the bikers' hard attitude and leathers, I felt the urgent need to be somewhere that was elsewhere.

Unfortunately that wasn't an option as they spotted us pretty much as soon as we came in the door. As heads came up to see who would enter this most sacred of places, conversations started to peter out.

Jonelle led the way across the bar floor. Of course the man she wanted to see had to be on the opposite side of the room. As we passed, anyone left speaking shut their mouths quite suddenly.

I had a prickly feeling tickling me between my shoulder blades and I felt a touch faint. It wasn't a congenial atmosphere and Jonelle appeared to be thoroughly enjoying herself. I think she could be suicidal.

In what was now total silence we came to stand in front of a table with five men seated playing some sort of card game. They folded their cards onto the table, watching us with narrowed eyes.

"You have a nerve, coming in here." One's eyes flickered from Jonelle to me, taking in my swelling face and barely concealed winces. "And bringing in the hired help. We all know about your little toy, Jonelle."

Well, that put me in my place. Could they have been the people to leave rude warnings for me and Jonelle? I wondered if Jonelle was even worried about those incidences any more. Bigger things had swept them away, even though I was still hung up over the fact someone got my private number…

"Yeah, that's me. My one nerve is full of spunk. Give over, Matt, and stop trying to be the tough guy." Then she ignored him and turned her attention to a slight guy with glasses. "I have to talk to you. Coming?"

She started back the way we had come. Another man stepped in front of her and she stopped, frowning.

"You so do not want to get into this right now. I've had a bad day, my colleague is a mess and I'm a bit pissy. Now get out of my way."

If I heard that level of threat aimed at me – I'd be getting out of the way. This guy just didn't get it. He stood there watching us with a half smile on his face and arrogance in his pose which kind of yelled 'hit me'. So she did.

One minute I was standing next to uptight but peaceful Jonelle, the next she was moving and the guy was falling. Can I say not the smartest thing she'd ever done?

We were in a room full of big tough men. Who obviously didn't like her and I was sure had various weapons stashed in loads of handy places. I just stood there, my mouth open, my one good eye almost falling out of my head. I didn't want to die in a bikers' den. I just couldn't see me managing to run out of there.

Three more heavies waded on in and before you knew it, she was ducking and weaving and laying them out. Two had knives, but she ignored this threat and disarmed them, with ease.

At least, she made it look easy, but it couldn't be. She was breathing evenly, but still heavily for her, and there was a light sweat layer on her face, though that could have been because the room was stifling. Unlike the Batch and Haddock boys she had rescued me from whom she had left able to walk away in a fashion, this time she wasn't playing. All four men were down and none were going to be walking away until they woke up.

And me? I was still standing there mouth hanging open. It had all happened so fast I hadn't being able to move. The Chemist guy she'd asked to come outside didn't look all that happy.

Jonelle surveyed the room. Every man was on his feet and several held knives. I think the guy who played at barman was also holding a shotgun, but he was holding it below the bar level so I'd seen only a flash of metal. The sweat that a minute ago had been hot and icky was suddenly cold and frightening. The whole place was frozen in one big ball of animosity. My stomach threatened to crawl out my mouth, with my heart a close second. All my aches hit me afresh making me want to cry. Or was that the atmosphere?

"We're leaving," Jonelle stated in a flat voice.

Her eyes swept the room looking for the one person who was going to deny this fact. Her muscles were tense and one hand slowly flickered and a knife slid down her sleeve into her palm.

A few of the guys' eyes acknowledged her knife. If empty handed she could put four of them to sleep, they seemed to say, then an armed Jonelle was a bigger threat. Though not as big as at least fifteen more armed men around us, I'd have thought. I tried to watch them all and Jonelle at the same time. I was less than useless and probably more than a little bit of a liability. How could she threaten them and keep me safe too? I was hoping it wouldn't come to that.

Suddenly a back door opened and two men came out. Both wore the same leathers as the rest, but one had some fancy Hellhound head branded on the forehead of his scarf. This then, was the chief Hound himself. Boy, did I have something to tell the girls when, or if, I got out of there. My brain was feeling more than a little fried.

All the Hounds had turned their eyes to their leader. This was about to get very interesting. He couldn't back down in front of so many. Not that I knew one little thing about Hellhound politics, mind you. I was just playing the odds.

"Jonelle." His voice was deep and more than a little scary.

At the same time, a contrary part of me shivered with excitement. It was deep and sexy too. What have I said about my inappropriate moments? The man could have us torn limb from limb with one word and there I was thinking his voice was truly sexy.

He was too. Tall, broad and more slender than any biker I'd ever seen, he glided over the floor in a long limbed stride, blue eyes twinkling and five o'clock shadow making his face hint at dangers. I think my insides liquefied.

Jonelle stiffened even more, if that is possible. "You? With the Hellhounds?" Her voiced grated. I was momentarily distracted from the overall threat hanging in the air enough to childishly smirk inside.

It amused me no little bit; the fact she didn't know everything. Seeing whoever this guy was in the midst of the Hounds had been a shock, or at the very least, a profound jolt.

The man touched her shoulder and nodded to the door. "Shall we take this outside?" his words parted the assembled bad guys and suddenly I could see a pathway to freedom.

I leaped at it. I stumbled, walked, half ran or threw myself depending on whose side of the story we were talking about here, in the general direction of the doorway; followed by the insufferable sniggers of the boys inside. I didn't care. Well, I told myself that I didn't and right at that moment? - all I could think about was saving what was left of my hide. Another beating would probably finish me off. The side effects of having a boss like mine.

I stood outside in the pure cool air and breathed deeply. It hurt every waking bruise, and I wanted to curl up and howl, but at the same time, all that space and fresh air were the best things I'd ever seen, tasted or felt in a long time.

There was the car; only a small dash across the road away and freedom was assured. I could relax; well sort of. I was followed after all, by Jonelle and Hellhound number one. Great. They obviously had a history and as I was becoming all too chillingly aware, a history with Jonelle never appeared to be full of chocolate and flowers. The woman was a magnet for the untrustworthy and downright depraved.

Outside in the sunshine he was even better looking. There had to be a catch; no biker was meant to make my legs turn to water. I had to get it through my head that he led a bunch of unsavoury characters and most probably came by any money he did have through ways I hadn't even thought of. I settled back to listen.

They faced each other neither too comfortable now it was just the two of them.

"It's been a long time, Jon." His voice, away from the audience, was deep and well modulated; as though he had been given a private school education.

It really didn't fit with his image and if I closed my eyes I would have been in raptures. As it was, one was swollen over and the other on high alert lest we got mobbed.

"Not long enough. What are you doing here, Will? These are not your sort of boys; I'm surprised they haven't eaten you alive." She looked at him and took in the glint in his eye and the hard jaw line.

"Then again, I guess you've come a long way since then."

Wherever and whenever 'then' was. Why was it I always felt I was one step, or more, behind the eight ball? I hardly knew the woman, but I was already thigh deep in her lifestyle and connections. Which was, as I can attest, not good for my health.

"Hmm, not exactly North Shore anymore, Jon. But then again, neither are you. Where I am right now suits me for … right now. If I need to extract myself I'm sure I can." He lounged confidently against the side of the building.

Jonelle shook her head, then shrugged.

"That's just delusional and you know it. Even as their current captain, you wouldn't be able to just resign. You know that. But that's not my problem. I just want to talk to the Chemist and then I'll be on my way. And no hassles for him if he does me a favour." Jonelle narrowed her eyes at Will who smiled, all innocence. Except I didn't think he'd been innocent for a very long time.

"Sure Jon, no problems. You deal with the Chemist and no one will bother him about it. I'll make sure it's an order, okay? Now, aren't you going to introduce me to your friend?"

And he turned those deep eyes to me and his smile became distinctly… hunter-ish. Something crept along my spine, and it might just have been fear or pure sexual umph.

If I thought Brad had toe-curling ability; it was nothing compared to this man. I felt his eyes sweep over my whole body and I wanted to get naked on the spot. Heat scorched up my neck and all over my face, and he laughed a low and dirty chuckle. It was that whole 'my face can be read no matter what' thing. It must have shouted at him to strip. Well, it was a very good idea, except I was one long bruise and in no condition to do anyone any good at all.

Jonelle snorted, watching us both.

"Will Malone meet Fiona Page. She's a personal friend and colleague, Will, so try to limit the ideas that are racing through that head of yours. Fiona, you have more sense than that."

I would have loved to have been able to differ, but my tongue was stuck to the roof of my mouth. She was always warning me about people and introducing me all the same. What was with that?

Will took one of my unresisting hands and brought the palm to his lips. I got a low down tickle and all but snatch it back like it was burned. No one person had the right to be that sexy *and* I was meant to be on the job. As in a *professional* something with Jonelle, though an as yet unnamed something because I had no idea what my job description was. But parading around making an even bigger fool of myself wasn't on the agenda.

Perhaps I was just a distraction for her worst kinds of associates. I liked that idea, as I had never once seen myself as a distraction before. While I was quietly musing on that idea, Jonelle had dragged the Chemist off and was talking to him rapidly, slipping him the packet she had extracted from Tomas. Will watched me with hungry eyes. He wasn't the least bit interested in what Jonelle and his mate were doing. Once we left I had no doubt he would be having a long chat with Chemist about every word Jonelle had said. Knowing this, I hoped Jonelle was being her usual verbose self.

"Now, why is it I've never seen you around before, sweetheart?" Will leaned just that little bit closer to me and I breathed in Lynx after shave. Something that was totally edible.

I dared to raise my gaze from the chest that was blocking my view of Jonelle to meet his eyes. They were many inches above my own and twinkling in a delicious way which made my mouth curve up. I couldn't imagine any man less likely to fit the image I had of a bad boy than this one. He was dangerous looking sure, but there was a clean cut edge to him which belied the stubble and leathers. He looked like he could wrestle with a crocodile to prove his manliness, but at the same time recite you poetry.

"I don't usually hang out in places like this." I waved my hand at the clubhouse looming behind him with its air of menace.

He looked back at it and grimaced. "Yeah, well it's not exactly my home away from home either."

He brought his gaze back to me. "Don't get me wrong though, they're my boys and you'd do well to remember that."

As if I would forget. He wore the Hounds Head. They owned his soul until they could sell it to a higher bidder. Not something which filled a woman with thoughts of picket fences and the pitter patter of tiny feet. He could come across as all sweet and misunderstood as he liked, but he had the backing to wipe me from the face of the earth. Looking into those eyes, I found it very hard to concentrate on that thought.

While Will looked set to give my blood pressure a hard time, Jonelle came back. I was in two minds as to whether that was a good thing.

"Okay, time to move. Chemist will call me with results." She pushed Will out of the way, and for a second he grabbed her hand and held it to him. They studied each other and then moved apart.

"Another time, Will. Don't let them take everything you have."

Then she was leading me back to the car and putting him out of her mind.

I slid into the driver's seat once more and watched Will watching us.

"You two go way back, huh? Is there anyone in this sort of dodgy world you don't know?"

She glanced at Will, then gave her attention to me. "Too many. Though knowing them doesn't always keep you safe from them. Will and I once had a thing when we were working the same deal a long time ago. We went our separate ways when the deal ended. Neither of us are particularly people persons. Long term doesn't work in our industry. Now let's get this dog home."

And she shut me out again.

We got the dog back home and I put him on a rope tied to the pool steps. Jonelle wanted a guard dog for the place, well now we had one. I eyed him dubiously. I think we would have to come up with a better name than Tomas Junior, because that could be potentially confusing. He also looked as though he was in need of about half a dozen good feeds all in one. He stood most pathetically, hanging his head, breathing the fresh clean air and trying to look cute. At least he had the last part down pat.

I left him there temporarily and followed Jonelle into her unit.

"What are we going to do now Tomas is out of the picture? Surely he didn't get killed over a painting he may or may not have had?"

I put the kettle on and found the green tea. Did this woman have me well trained or what?

"I don't think so. Whatever the reason for Tomas' demise, it didn't have anything to do with Phil. Those two were way out of each other's leagues. Nicking a painting was all Tomas was good for, if that. No, I'd say it was whatever we turn up in that packet. The room he was in had been gone over thoroughly. Someone knew Tomas had it and wanted to get it. But frankly I don't give a damn. The only interest I had was his connection with Phil's painting. Once I've got Phil's painting back, I may free up a bit of time for Tomas. Right now though, I need to find out who he was working with and go talk to them. Phil is getting antsy."

She appeared to be quite cool about it. But I could see her in my mind: tucking her sister out of harm's way, putting Phil in his place and sorting out Lilly. I couldn't see her letting Tomas's early demise go un-investigated. That wasn't her style.

The thought that she was just be trying to protect me from more dead bodies floated across my mind.

Bingo.

"Aren't we off to see a man about a Rose?" I handed Jonelle her tea mug and took a sip of my own.

I'd let the Tomas and Will thing go for now. She obviously didn't want to talk about it. The trouble, as I saw it, was my boss had ego issues. Letting someone else deal was not her thing.

It could wind up getting us killed.

Chapter Fourteen

Half an hour later, we pulled into a driveway of an immaculate home in the suburbs. Jonelle turned to me.

"You don't say a thing. You just look and glare if you can. If this guy does know anything about The Rose he may be too scared to let me in on it. So we have to be scarier."

I could believe it. She looked grim to say the least: grim and determined and deadly.

Jonelle knocked on the front door, all the time watching everything at once. I needed to learn how to do that. I, on the other hand, just stood there allowing my pain to make me cross and thus attempting the glare she wanted. If anyone touched my face or my butt it wouldn't be too difficult. Any painkiller magic was fast wearing off and I just wanted to head to bed. I certainly didn't feel up to demanding answers out of a possible associate of a psychopath. Nerves of steel I did not have.

The door was opened by a small Asian woman who had a broom in one hand.

"Yes?" She spoke with a slight accent.

Jonelle leaned forward. "I'm looking for Gavin. Is he home?"

"Who wants to know?" The lady with the broom was not intimidated, even with Jonelle leaning over her.

Some pluck. I'd have turned tail and hidden in the closet.

Jonelle was sick and tired of evasion. I think she may even be afraid that if she lost any more time someone else would die. So instead of answering she pushed the door open and walked in. This elicited a flood of invective and a broom handle across her shoulders. She caught it as it bounced and jerked it from the woman's hands. Her eyes almost shot sparks.

"Don't ever attempt that again. Now go get him and then get out of here."

They watched each other carefully, then with a sniff the maid disappeared. Jonelle led me into another room, watching all the time.

"Do you know this place?"

"Nope, but it is pretty much like all the houses out here. And I want to have a quick look around before our host comes in and distracts us from seeing anything important."

She continued her search, poking her nose behind pictures and into the tops of lamps. I stood awkwardly at the doorway. I had no idea of what she was looking for and didn't particularly care. So long as I didn't get in her way, everything would be okay. A noise behind me nearly gave me a heart attack. A man in training clothes was coming our way, a frown of serious annoyance on his face.

"Jon, someone's coming."

I didn't even stop to think about the shortening of her name, it felt natural. She flashed me a surprised look and then was standing in the middle of the room as if she had never thought of snooping.

The man came steaming in and checked at the sight of her. His face went a little pale before he turned to me. If he thought I was the easy touch out of the two, one look at my face kind of persuaded him differently. I felt like asking didn't he know of the 'don't judge a book by its cover' thing? Because the cover of this tattered book said a much different thing to the insides.

"Gavin." Her voice was almost gentle. "I think we need to have a little chat, don't you?" Her smile was so reasonable. You could almost imagine curling into the palm of her hand and purring like a kitten.

He sighed. He actually sighed. Poor guy. If he was mixed up with The Rose, then I guess he was used to these kind of talks. I would be too, one day.

We settled ourselves on various couches and Gavin was left facing us. Because I had to sit, I glared, the whole 'my butt is one big bruise' thing was getting me down.

They make it appear so easy in the movies. Someone gets thumped and the next day they're running around solving problems, and whacking people back. I didn't see how they did it. I needed another soak in the hot tub and possibly several days not moving. I wasn't enjoying traipsing around after my fearless leader pretending I was a knowledgeable sidekick. Plus my nose was still out of joint that nothing was going to be done about my attackers. All they required was one good hour in a room with Jonelle and they wouldn't be hitting any more defenceless women. But she wasn't concerned about them at all and I felt more than a bit miffed.

I tried to bring my focus back to the conversation going on around me. It was difficult because of the pain and the pain killers I had managed to dry swallow just as we went into the place. They were making me feel even vaguer than usual and that was saying something.

"Look, all I've heard is that The Rose is out here from America and is looking for you. He is supposedly working for some drug mob, but seeking you out is kind of personal. He's pissed off that you managed to get some art from a client of his. It looks bad for his reputation not to have taught you a lesson already."

Jonelle raised that eyebrow and looked dangerous. Gavin added hastily, "Just repeating what I've heard. That's all. Don't take it personally. You know I'm out of the business now, I just hear things sometimes."

"Yeah, out of the business. Gavin, you have at least three pieces in this room right now which total up more than you could make in ten years. Once a thief always a thief, unless you're just housing them for someone else. Then you are even more stupid than you look. If this is a side job for The Rose or his associates, you know someone will come calling for you eventually. You can't stay in this sort of business and be a spineless git. They'll eat you alive."

Jonelle rose and stretched. She looked in the prime of her life and Gavin was a shadow in comparison. Mind you, she certainly stopped looking so relaxed when he pulled out a gun.

I grunted. Were there any places we could go where someone didn't want to shoot, stab or beat on us? Jonelle lowered herself back onto the couch she'd just vacated.

"What on earth are you doing?" she asked slowly, eyeing the gun.

She may have been all John Wayne when it was a knife - after all, it could only be thrown once and she could see it coming. But a gun? There were unlimited bullets with a whole range of soft bits they could hit. And the distance between them was a problem.

Even Jonelle had to be wary of a gun. Toted by a sweated, half terrified weak man; I suddenly smelt disaster.

Ours.

Gavin gave us both a sickly grin, as though he was trying to convince himself he was in control.

"Not such a loser now hey, Jonelle?" he smirked, but there was sweat running down his face. That trigger hand looked mighty shaky to me. Not a very reassuring thought.

"I wonder how long I can keep you before The Rose makes contact and I can hand you over to him?"

I was definitely sure I did *not* like the way this conversation was going. Was anyone allowed to just walk away in the middle of this sort of thing?

Jonelle sighed and turned to me. "You know, trying to clean up my messes so that I can retire just keeps on getting harder and harder. I just want to put my feet up and take in some sun. How about you?"

Seeing as this was the first time I'd heard any real plans for retirement, I couldn't really say. She certainly hadn't come across in anyway shape or form as someone who was just cleaning up the edges. But hey, what did I know?

Maybe she'd decided Canberra was a nice sleepy town and perfect to do nothing in. Then again, considering everything that went on in this town unbeknownst to most of us, maybe not.

"Sure," I answered, trying to keep my mind and eyes off Gavin's twitching fingers, and the gun shaking in his hand. "Why not? Retirement round about now wouldn't go astray."

I hoped that this was some big game she had going. You know, waste a bit of time, unsettle everyone and then WHAM, she'd save my bacon. 'How' was up to her. I definitely had no ideas coming through.

Gavin giggled. I swear the man was on drugs.

"I can't miss from here and then you'd both be retired. Get it?" The twerp giggled again. He was getting on my nerves. "You're stuck, Jonelle. There is no way you can get out of this now. I have the gun."

And he waved said gun around as if to prove his point. I was getting less and less comfortable with the idea of being holed up with a gun toting manic. The guy was clearly unstable. Not something you wanted in your average gunman. Jonelle would have been holding that gun with firm and steady hands. Really reassuring that would have been. With someone as panicked as this guy, who knew what might get hit.

"Would you mind not waving that around? You might hit something important and then where would you be? A few art pieces less and some very unhappy customers." Jonelle sounded ... irritated.

"They're my art works!" He twitched and gibbered. "No one is coming to collect them, they're mine! They can't take them off me." He was reduced to muttering "They can't, they can't."

Jonelle looked at me, a faint smile on her mouth. What did we have to smile about? So much for this man being a professional. It looked to me as though life had been just a touch too stressful for him.

Jonelle leaned forward, her weight shifting onto her feet. Gavin stopped muttering to himself and straightened up.

"Don't think you can move. I know how you work. Just lean back and be quiet."

He needed the silence to think. Of what to do with us, no doubt. I didn't think capturing someone like Jonelle had been on his to do list. It would be kind of like grabbing a tiger by the tail. How did you let it go?

Jonelle relaxed as far as she was able. I could see her mind running a million scenarios over, and I hoped they all ended with both of us whole and alive. I'd hate to add a few holes to my already sore and sorry carcass. This standoff couldn't last forever. For one thing, our host seemed so close to losing his mind the difference wasn't enough to matter very much. A few more minutes of this unsettling silence and I would probably lose my mind as well.

Finally Jonelle made her move. She sat up suddenly, freaking both Gavin and myself out, and then said, "Gavin, I don't think The Rose is coming today."

"He never said he was. I don't get to speak to someone like that, you know. One of his lackeys told me to ..." He stopped, voice frozen in his throat.

Jonelle uncoiled and lunged in one swift movement. While he had been talking, the gun's deadly little snout had dipped and swayed, moving away from pointing at her. His concentration on other things, Jonelle took those few precious seconds and moved like a spring.

I knew she was fast. I even suspected she was half animal, but to see her leap at him that way - ! One minute she was watching me, her eyes taking in his movements in that uncanny way she had of looking at two places at once. Then wham! She landed just about on top of him, smashing the gun to the floor. One hand slipped to squeeze his throat and he was out like a light.

"Great. One of these days you're going to give me a heart attack,"

I muttered, greatly relieved to be out of gun range, but still quivering from over excitement.

"He shouldn't have told me no one was coming today. With no one to offer him aid or to distract him in anyway, I had to take the quickest opportunity I could. Well at least he let us know one thing." She stood, gun in hand, unclipping its magazine.

"He did?" I was confused. Was it just the medication I was on – or had this day being surreal? "What exactly did we learn from this?"

I watched as Jonelle dropped the gun next to our unconscious host and pocketed the bullets. At least he wouldn't be able to say we stole it. Small comfort.

"We know that Gavin here still likes to dabble in art, though he remains the worst judge of art I've ever met. We know that The Rose is coming to Australia, if not already here. And we know that Gavin would love to join the big boys, but so far they think he's a joke, which by the way, I would agree with. Only someone has let him play with the idea that he could join them, and he's gone and got himself a gun. We also know that he's on something."

She toed the lump that was Gavin. "Something that has made him quite unhinged, which of course, could be any number of drugs of choice. Though I never picked him for someone who would become an addict."

She shrugged, mind already onto more interesting things.

I followed her out into the afternoon sunshine. I couldn't believe that it was only day one after my attack. She really knew how to pack a day full.

"Where to now?" I slid into the passenger seat with barely a wince.

Right now I was floating somewhere to the left of Pluto. There was a good chance that I had overdosed on those pills before we went in there. But seriously, who was to care?

Jonelle gave me a glanced from the corner of her eyes. Well, maybe there was my boss. A sad thing when I started getting smashed on prescription drugs in work hours. Mind you, that would teach her to have a cupboard full of prescription pain killers. Kind of gave me a clue as to how many times she got seriously hurt.

"I think I'm taking you home to bed. You look mainly in need of a strong dose of coffee but barring that, a sleep. Me – I have work to do." She held up a hand.

I think it was to stem the flood of my protests, but there weren't any. Not one. I didn't even bother to open my mouth; it wasn't working all that well anyway.

"Nothing you can help me with, Princess, so home it is for you." She shot the car off from the curb and swung it into the main stream of traffic headed into town. Not that Canberra had much traffic at the best of times.

"You know what?" she mused, navigating around a truck. "Altogether far too many people know that I am a) living in Canberra and b) living at the Grangelands. I find that disturbing and very annoying. If they are at all tied up with Brenda and the mysterious reason she got killed, as I am sure at least one group of our would-be stalkers are, then it shan't take them long to discover Heather. Now, you may be thinking here, isn't that what she wanted? To draw them out and all?"

Jonelle flashed me her predators grin. I nodded my head; at least I think I did, it may have been simply I couldn't keep it straight on my neck anymore. But she took it as a nod.

"I know that's what I started out thinking, but now I know her and I want to actually enjoy living somewhere people can't intrude on, I am getting a might bit pissed off that every Tom, Dick and Harry knows where to go. Problem is I'm not so good at keeping a low profile. My reputation precedes me and I'm not going to spend my whole time making sure no one follows me home. It's too exhausting.

"Just think, now I have come out in the open and settled in one place, the phone lines are burning hot and voila! The Rose is coming across from America or wherever he plants himself these days. Coincidence? I think not. Do I want to meet up with him again?" She paused, speeding between a slow Ford and an oncoming motorbike. I closed my eyes.

"Well of course I do. He is a shitty little blip on my horizon. But in my own time. And why did Tomas have to die so inconveniently? I wanted to ask him who painted on my wall and who wanted him to steal Phil's painting! Oh and where is the damn thing?"

She thumped the steering wheel in angry frustration. I hardly thought it was the steering wheel's fault, but then again I'd never heard her talk so much, so I wasn't about to butt in and tell her so. Stringing a coherent sentence together wasn't on my agenda anyway.

Jonelle flung the car into the car park and screeched to a halt. I breathed a small sigh of relief. At least we had managed to get home in one piece. It was a struggle to keep my eyes open and I was more than happy to let Jonelle manhandle me into my apartment. I waved at her vaguely.

"I can take it from here. Go do whatever it is you need to do and I'll see you tomorrow." Something about tomorrow rang a bell. "Aren't we off to Adelaide tomorrow?"

I was vastly impressed with my ability to keep our movements in mind.

"Hmm?" She was obviously preoccupied. "Oh, yes. I'll come past around noon and see if you are fit enough to catch the flight with me. Try not to get into any more trouble. I've got to go out."

And she disappeared back in the direction of the car.

All I wanted to do was head for bed, but I could see Tomas Junior tied up at the pool side watching my every move with sad puppy eyes. I needed to make sure the poor thing was taken care of first. I wandered in a semi lucid state over to Julie's place. If anyone would be home, it would be her. Tomas would need to be walked, fed and in general, looked after.

"Hey there Fi," Julie answered my knock in her boxer shorts and singlet. I glanced at my watch. It was only just past four o'clock, an unheard of hour to be about to go to bed, or just get up.

"I think I'm coming down with something." She correctly interpreted my look. "Did you leave that poor thing tied up today?" Getting passed the whole bed clothes wearing thing, she nodded at Tomas.

"Yeah, that's what I wanted to talk to you about, though if you are about to go to bed too, there's little point is there?" I think I sounded slightly slurry even to my own ears. Julie's eyebrows climbed higher, especially now she had rubbed the sleep from her eyes and got a good look at me.

"Good lord Fiona! What the hell happened to you?" The usually urbane Julie: master of the vernacular. "You look like a bus hit you."

"I probably sound like it too." The whole snippy tone was back in my less than coordinated vocals. "I'm loaded with pain killers and need to get some sleep, but I'm worried about Tomas there, and I needed to see if someone would walk him and feed him while I conk out. Would you mind taking care of it?"

While I was loath to ask, I didn't really see that I had many options. "I have had a kind of accident, as you can see, and really can't stand up for much longer."

"You poor darling. Is your car okay? Of course I'll take care of … Tomas you said? What a bloody ridiculous name for a Dalmatian. But we'll talk about that later," she added hastily when I glowered at her.

There was no way I was going to correct her assumption that I'd been in a car accident. Better that than the alternative. I couldn't see me telling the Apartmates, oh yes, by the way – I was broken in to last night and beaten halfway senseless. I didn't think that sort of conversation would fill them with feelings of safety and warm tingles. So I smiled and assured her that I hadn't been in *my* car and that it was fine.

Oh, and of course we could all discuss the naming rights of our new apartmate – I wasn't about to make sweeping name calling judgements. But right then and there, I was more concerned about getting to bed and could she please just make sure he got fed and watered?

Julie didn't particularly like my tone, but as I was looking like the end result of two trains colliding at high speed, what was she going to do? Say no?

So I toddled back to my place – toddling being the most appropriate word I could manage – and downed another painkiller (one for the road) and tumbled myself into bed. The sweetness of oblivion beckoned from my groggy state. But as it was, I slept for barely hours before I woke up with the sinking feeling that I wasn't alone.

Never been prone to nightmares, I was surprised this woke me. Even as I child I was far too realistic to think of all the bogeymen that could come and get me. I could be a drama queen in other areas of my life, but the idea of some fantastic horror living in my closet or under the bed wasn't one of them. But that night I lay in bed and sweated on the thought that someone was lurking in the deep recesses of my home, breathing ever so quietly and waiting for me to drift back into sleep.

So involved and elaborate became this fear, my heart rate doubled. I could hear it. The silence, the tension: *something* waiting in the walls, breathing through my space. I lay still in bed stretched flat on my back, sheet and blankets clutched in my hands under my chin. I strained with ever fibre to hear and see better and clearer in the dark. I opened my eyes as wide as they could go (as though that was going to help penetrate the blackness) and I breathed one tiny breath every few moments; as though eventually they would breath at the odd moment I wasn't and I would catch them out.

I didn't turn my head to look at the glowing red clock. I didn't move at all, so I had no idea of how long I lay like that. It felt like an eternity. What if any slight noise covered their next move?

I lay there in petrified sweat; stiff, tired, and aching. I held my breath for long moments then expelled it gently. I stared into the corners of my room with eyes seeing nothing.

Eventually the faint edges of dawn smudged the horizon filling in the emptiness of my room with pale tinges of grey. There was nothing there. A peaceful Smudge slept on a pile of my clothes in one corner, oblivious to my sweat soaked fear. My chest of drawers sat in squat glory in its corner and the walk in wardrobe door stood open.

Other than that I was sincerely, happily and vastly alone. At that point, I relaxed my stiffness, felt every ache and pain like it had just been freshly visited on me, and groaned aloud. If this was recovery, bring on the morphine.

Was this what working for Jonelle and being her friend had reduced me to: a quivering mess of jelly who saw nightmares in every corner? I seriously doubted my sanity and choice. Well, probably not seriously. The lure to do things that were just *that* side of the line had me in its grip.

Come on, who hasn't thought wouldn't it be amazing to be able to play with guns, pretend to be a black ops guy and hang out with the toughest people in town? Long nights lying paralysed with imaginary ghosties and ghoulies was not, however, on my agenda. Neither was waking up feeling as though everything inside me had been pulverised.

I needed a new hobby.

With another groan I pushed myself into a seated position. Smudge woke up and gave his cute little morning yawn, then yowled in demand of his breakfast.

The body didn't recognise a night of terror as an inducement against the need to eat. Now it was getting a regular breakfast, the first thing my stomach did every morning was voice its own desire to be stuffed with something hot and delicious. Sure, a healthy fruit smoothie or bowl of cereal might have been more the sort of thing Jonelle had in mind but I was a rule breaker, and hot croissants or other delicate pastries from my ever helpful Deli were more my style.

I couldn't turn my stomach off and it eventually drove me to my feet in search of something to eat.

Everything was lit in a grey fog, like a curtain, and I made my way into the kitchen more by habit than by vision. Smudge kept up a constant stream of chatter, telling me how he had spent his night and the wonders of the dreams he'd had chasing mice. I sorted out some kibble and milk for him, then went in search of something a little more to my taste.

I took an apricot Danish, an instant coffee and an almost out of date yoghurt back to the bedroom, and thought about putting some clothes on. It would require effort, as would packing and it was all too much for me right then. I would've loved to curl back up and settle down for a long day of crap television, comfort eating and a good pandering to my various aches and pains.

Failing that, I'd have to pack for a couple of days and around two in the afternoon, haul my sorry carcass into a plane. Would they let someone who looked like me *into* a plane? I stuffed the last of the Danish into my mouth and opened the wardrobe door wider, so I could stand in front of the full length mirror hanging on the inside.

Dressed only in a pair of briefs, I had a really good look at the startling results of the last forty eight hours. I had thin red welts banding each wrist and ankle from my makeshift cuffs. They burned a little, but on the whole I felt they were getting under control. I had finger bruises all down my arms where Daniel had held me with one hand, while beating me with the other. I had bruises and a tear mark down my ribs, where the skin had been too thin and his knuckle had broken through. He'd considered the slight show of blood quite 'distasteful'.

But the worst was my bottom and my face. I had harboured this strange idea he was going to leave my face alone. It would be so obvious and I always thought 'baddies' didn't like to be obvious.

How little I knew.

I guess if they beat up their wife, visible bruising was a bad thing; but beating up the opposition? Even if she didn't realise she was the opposition? That was an entirely different story.

While I could see out of both my eyes, there was a shocking amount of yellow and purple bruising around one and it was still puffy. The other was a bit better, wide and wild, with shading around it and a tender, puffy cheek under it. My split lip had scabbed over, but was swollen and nasty looking. How, I wondered staring at the mess that I happened to call 'me', was I going to explain this to, say, Brad or my parents? No chance of running into someone I knew in Adelaide. Thank God for that.

I noticed that there was the faintest hints of ribs and hips bones. I turned sideways.

"Smudge! Congratulate your dearest Me! I seem to have lost weight."

I pirouetted, slowly, where I stood. It made my aches wake up with a vengeance, but to see a little less of me was worth it. Jonelle was making some sort of difference.

I dressed in loose relaxed wear, not wanting anything that could rub on my aches. Then I swooped up Smudge to spend some time playing. I hoped that Julie wouldn't mind yet another of my animals foisted onto her, but I could hardly take him with me.

Just before midday I took him over and thanked her for looking out for Tomas as well. She'd decided the dog was going to be called Manny, quite a ridiculously superior name for such a sook, I thought, but I let it go. Smudge didn't think much of Manny at all, so I left them behind squabbling over who had the rights to the 'comfy' chair. I was glad Julie had to arbitrate, not me.

Jonelle arrived at my doorstep at exactly twelve o'clock. Didn't the woman know about the whole fashionably late deal? She had one small carry bag and eyed my, let's say, more extensive array of travel gear.

"It's just for a couple of days, sunshine. What are you packing for? Cannes?"

I smirked at her. Ah, sarcasm at this hour. What a woman. With a toss of my hair I sauntered passed her, wheeling my luggage.

"Wheels make them so much easier, don't you think? Anyway, I have to be prepared for any eventuality."

She shrugged on a snort and led us down to the car. My poor little convertible sat dejectedly in its corner. It'd been a while since it'd gone out for a run. A taxi could have been in order, seeing as we were taking a plane but no, Jonelle was more about convenience and control than not paying the parking.

"So what's new in developments?"

Part of me would be content to know nothing, but that part wasn't very big, and kept on getting smaller and smaller as time rolled on. After all, I needed to know this stuff so I didn't walk into any more … brick walls. Or have to invent another car accident. That was most demeaning.

Jonelle hurled the car around some of Canberra's notorious roundabouts.

"While you napped the afternoon away, I paid a visit to some of Tomas' closer buddies. If someone like that could be said to have close buddies.

"One is a fairly well known thief and he told me that stealing Phil's picture had actually been a spite thing for him. Apparently Phil had done him a perceived wrong some ten years ago and he's never forgotten nor forgiven." She rolled her eyes at me.

"Lord, some of these people need to get a life. More often than not, it's these stupid revenge attacks that get them caught. Well, he nicked the painting because Phil paid so much for it. He decided to use male logic and if Phil was willing to pay so much it must have meant a lot to him, so it was fair game. It's safe in his house."

She grinned as we pulled up in the long stay car park of the Canberra International Airport.

"Let's say, it was safe in his house until I came along. It is now locked away in my place and there it is staying until I can get it back to Phil. Such a lot of hoo-hah for a piece I don't think is worth half as much as he paid for it. Oh well, it takes all types of art lovers I guess.

"Which clears up the missing art piece, but not what, why and who killed off old Tomas. Nor does it explain why the guy clammed up for a while after he told me Tomas had helped him. He then tells me Tomas boasted of another art theft he was involved in."

She shook her head, the small warning lines between her brows forming in a frown.

"I don't know what's going on, but it is beginning to sound like there were two art pieces! I have one, which was Phil's. Tomas was a side kick for that one. But Mick told me Tomas was bragging about being the main man on another heist. So who's painting did he steal and why was he trying to get my attention by flashing the information around town?"

"Mick was also mightily shocked to hear of Tomas' early demise, which means it's being kept quiet. But, interestingly enough, only when he heard it was murder, not the actual death bit. It seems Tomas had been hitting the drugs pretty hard and all his mates knew it was only a matter of time before he OD'd on something he couldn't handle."

I shuddered. What a life. Your closest mates knew you were on a one way spiral out of control and did nothing to help. I wasn't prone to introspection or any of that mushy stuff, but I tried to make a mental note to give all the Apartmates a huge hug when I got back from Adelaide. I'd like to think they'd notice and care enough to intervene if I was headed for implosion.

"Lovely people we mix with," I muttered, half to myself.

Jonelle flashed me a look. Her eyes rested on my face. My beat up, blue and black face. They softened fractionally.

"Perhaps getting you involved in all this was more of a mistake than I first thought. It's not really the sort of thing you were born to, is it?"

"And you were?" I shot back.

Was she impinging on my detecting senses? Brat. Sure, I was out of my depth more than half the time. I'd never known so much crap was going on right under my nose, and more than once I had been gripped with a paralysing fear of all things around me – but that didn't mean I wanted out – did it?

What made her so sure that she had been born to do this sort of thing? Was there a human conscience thing she had missed – after all, she talked of murder and mayhem with a casualness that took my breath away. I sure as hell hadn't been born to do *that*.

"I think I was. My parents have always been involved in … similar sorts of things. It was kind of a family business. I moved into the Agency to learn as much as I could. Falling in with Claire, Amelia and Jack was like coming home, I guess."

She locked eyes with me. Deep dark grey pools of unfathomable, well, unfathomableness?

"I may not be the sort of person Amelia has become, but never doubt for one minute I have it in me to be of a *comparable* nature."

Did I look as though I'd argue that fact??

"So no matter how badly you may get beat up, in the long run, I can and will protect you." She smiled grimly. "There are missions and missions, and I am not going to fail to protect you like I did…"

She stopped and walked off lugging her small bag, muscles quivering under her tailored jacket.

I may get beaten to a pulp, but I wouldn't necessarily get killed or brain dead she was telling me.

Like Jodi. Like the failure she saw in her inability to keep Jodi safe.

I was going to be the surrogate sister, the one she could save at all costs. Briefly I wondered if that had been one of the overall reasons she had agreed to take me into her life. She saw it as a chance to redeem herself from the failure to care for her sister. Not very flattering, but could explain her unprecedented closeness to myself. Though why she'd chosen me was still anyone's guess. I shied away from the idea that the sparks I felt when she touched me might go both ways and mean much more than I was prepared to accept.

Realising my internal struggle had made me fall behind I jogged, pulling my wheeled luggage behind me. It hurt, but it was amazing how potent certain painkillers really were. I looked a fright, but the pain was a twice removed buzz.

I hadn't been in public since my unfortunate beating. The looks I was getting weren't helping very much. What was it about people that made them look at a car wreck, and ogle someone whose face was all smashed up? I felt a little exposed. I caught up with Jonelle and checked in.

"Does it always feel like this when you get beaten up?" I asked the first thing that popped into my head. Good to see I hadn't learned to curb the connection between my thought processes and my tongue.

Jonelle led the way to the waiting lounge.

"They went very lightly on you, all up."

I didn't think she meant to be a callous snot, but really. You couldn't say something like that when looking at a crash victim like me and be taken seriously. I must have been gaping with a look of intense incredulity on my face because she half smiled.

"If they meant to give you a real pounding you'd have been in hospital. The things those types of people are capable of would leave you cold. Trust me. You served as their warning, but you were allowed to walk free. Walking being the operative word. They could have left you unable to function - they didn't. Thus they were forgiving. Be grateful."

Sometimes she spoke in a way that made me want to throttle her.

There was a little voice in my head telling me she spoke with authority, but whoever listened to little voices in their heads? Didn't that way lead to madness? I struggled on in her wake braving the stares, and dreading to sit down for however long it took to get to Adelaide.

When the edge of the painkillers wore off, I popped a few more. I didn't think there was a body on that plane who'd have begrudged me those pills. Jonelle sat in the aisle seat and read something written in one of her foreign languages, which I think she did just to piss me off. So I shut my eyes and pretended to sleep. Which turned out not to be such a pretence as my body was happy to oblige, considering the lack of sleep I'd been indulging in.

I'd never been to Adelaide; never driven in this strange, but beautiful city. And never been used as a pounding board before, so all in all, I was content to sit back and allow Jonelle to get us a car, pack me into it and drive us to the motel. A million star motel where I could get a massage, a spa, a sauna and room service.

Okay, I was rich, but while I never *did* anything, which could be seen as an indulgence in itself, I'd never allowed myself to pamper me. And it felt bloody marvellous. Forget the saying that money can't buy happiness. It was bliss and you weren't getting it on the average salary.

While I indulged, I could happily say I had no idea what Jonelle did and unusually for me, didn't care. It was late afternoon before I came back down to earth. I'd been pummelled, sweated, scented and now lay supine on the extremely large and puffy lounge, sipping white wine and munching inelegantly on strawberries. All was so right with my world I could feel the wine swimming round in my head – a lovely glowing feeling.

Perhaps that was the mixing of alcohol with pain killers, but I didn't care. Jonelle'd been gone for hours and for once I wasn't watching the clock wondering what I was missing out on. It was the last thing on my mind in the blessed out state I was in.

I was half dozing and half watching crappy TV when Jonelle came barrelling into the room. By the looks of her, she'd been at the gym. Didn't the girl ever rest?

"So you're back in the land of the living, huh?" She swooped down on me and snitched my glass of wine, gulping the rest of it in one long swallow.

My squawk of protest only served to make her give me her shark grin. Obviously the gym had given her a shot of endorphins, thank you very much.

"I'll grab a shower then we'll go somewhere for dinner okay?"

"Do I look as though I can get out for dinner?" The wine, the meds and the hour long massage were all making my bones melt. Standing, I could see, was going to be a problem.

Jonelle eyed me and shook her head.

"You know what? You are *such* a lush. For someone who wants to get ahead in this game, sometimes actually keeping that head level wouldn't go astray. How can you possibly think when you cloud the issue with that stuff?"

I frowned. That was coming on a bit harsh, wasn't it?

"I've seen you drunk." I protested.

Possibly not the most diplomatic response, considering the only time I'd seen her drink more than two glasses was the disastrous night when she'd been watching the home DVD of Jack and Co. I shouldn't go around reminding her, but as usual I thought about my words half a second after they were out of my mouth. I cringed inside but all I got was a raised eyebrow, and she disappeared for a shower. Got off lightly, I thought.

Sitting up a little straighter I managed to snag the room service booklet and cruised the menu. Why did they always put the price of room service through the roof?? It wasn't like it cost them all that much if the Chef was already doing dinners at the restaurant. In my befuddled state, I found this a very complex mystery.

I managed to peel myself off the couch and wandered to the bathroom door. Yelling through it, we came to an agreement as to dinner and I placed the order, plus another bottle of wine. Well, there were limits as to what I was willing to give up, and the wonderfully euphoric feeling I was experiencing due to the mix in my stomach was not one of them. I was sure she'd have another glass or two, after robbing me of mine.

In no time at all we were seated at the table, out on the balcony, eating steak and sipping red. Jonelle was wrapped up in a silk dressing gown which flowed softly when she walked, but clung to reveal the outline of knife at wrist and gun strapped to thigh, when she didn't. Even here, behind deadlocked doors, in a motel under a false name, she was prepared for anything. I knew I should've found that comforting, but it was unnerving.

"What have you been up to since we got here? You disappeared soon after my massage arrived." I bit into the steak and blessed Australian chefs.

She shrugged. "You looked as though you needed the break. I was a bit harsh. It was a nasty beating you took and unwinding the kinks seems to have done you the world of good."

Across the candle lit table her eyes met mine and they were softer than I'd ever seen them. I prickled with a hint of suspicion. What game was she playing at now? While she wasn't ever mean to me, she wasn't nice and cuddly either. Her mercurial moods kept me on my toes.

"Yes well, that's lovely. Nice for you to see how horrid it all was. But where have you been?"

She was dodging the question, so I had to press the point. My curiosity had been on holiday for a couple of hours, but it was back in full force.

"I spent a bit of time catching up with some contacts, trying to find out as much as I can about the drug trade and see what was happening here. I haven't been out this way for some time and I enjoy showing my face at unexpected moments."

"Though," she conceded, "this sometimes leads to awkward situations. Especially when they think you're dead. But anyway, I discovered there is some large American operation nosing its way onto our shores. Need to get up to Sydney and have a scout around on that point."

She frowned at herself. Boy, I'd love to have her work ethic.

"I also put a call through to Thorn Ridley to see when he can spare some time for us. We'll drive up to his place tomorrow. I need the commission for this sale to come through so I have more working cash."

I thought about the files I'd gone through with her commissions, retainers and other various lump sums. I couldn't see the need myself. Though once you get used to having so much coming in, it was hard to scale back.

She certainly had expenses. Keeping all her informants and contacts happy couldn't be cheap. And while I was prepared to pay my own way, I was still probably an extra expense as well.

"He doesn't want us around for long. Not one to socialise, that man. But a quick trip, a few phone calls and before you know it, Hank, my dear American, will have his next Ridley. Then we'll get back to Canberra. I hate leaving things in the middle of the plot. I also want to be around when, or if, The Rose comes to town. If Gavin was correct, someone should be arriving soon. I just can't imagine what would be so important that The Rose's elite are involved." She picked up her fork and went back to eating.

Me? I was interested to know many things. Like who killed Tomas and what for, why was Gavin even in the circle – the man was clearly unhinged. What was the Chemist's results on that white powder? And who had killed Brenda and why? I didn't even want to think of what had happened to Jack and why two men had seen fit to come after me because of it.

If Amelia was scarier than Jonelle, why had the warning come through me? Perhaps she had no friends to intimidate, which was a very sad thing to ponder on. Which made me the weakest link and I didn't like to think of *that*.

"If more than just The Rose turns up, can you handle that?" I didn't want to appear to be a Doubting Thomas, but just how many dangerous men could she control at the one time? There had to be a limit and I wasn't in a particular hurry to be around when it was met.

Jonelle swallowed and laughed.

"Don't fret so much. They'd have to bring his whole five for me to be worried. And they won't. Before we get to the fulfilling of any contracts, The Rose is arrogant enough to want to sit down and let me know, formally, that there is a contract. Me, I prefer to just make them disappear."

She grinned at my shocked face.

"I have tried hard not to be too blunt with you. But I think it's beyond time to let you hear how it really is. I don't play fair. I no longer have the backing of the organisation in England. I have to make every encounter with hostile people count. Them or me. No second chances, no hesitations. The first time I hesitate could be the last time. Not something I'm willing to risk."

She sipped her wine. "Though I am curious as to any information The Rose can give me about Tomas' murder and the powder I found. If our Rose, Ben, has the answers, he'll talk before anyone does any disappearing acts, believe me."

The sudden ice in her voice had me convinced. But I could also remember Amelia's eyes and it was starting to sink into my head that while Jonelle was scary to me, there were definitely people out there who took it into depths I couldn't begin to imagine, and really didn't want to. Still, part of me pitied this Rose character no matter what it was he was supposed to have done.

We finished our meal not discussing work. I was determined to change the subject as the added alcohol was fast putting me into the realms of not being able to concentrate and I didn't want to miss anything important.

When the dishes were all stacked outside the door waiting for collection and I'd settled myself in one of the double beds, my mobile rang.

"Hello?" I was pleasantly pissed and feeling very docile.

"Fiona? Where are you? I came over to say hello and ran into Julie who told me you'd been in an accident and looked like Frankenstein, and your place is blacked out." Brad's voice was flatteringly filled with concern.

My toes wiggled under the covers. When I drink too much, I felt infatuated with everyone. Even more so when I knew how marvellous they were between the sheets. I hoped that didn't make me some sort of trollop.

"Hi Brad! I'm okay. Just took a flying visit to Adelaide. Sorry – were we meeting up?" I'd forgotten when we were set for our next date.

"Well, I'd been hoping to take you out tonight." He'd dropped his voice into low and seductive overdrive. Not helping with my whole being in another state.

"Shame," I whispered, trying to be flirtatious, but after one and a half bottles of wine I was probably missing my mark somewhat.

"I'll definitely be calling you when I get back into town." I gave a giggle, again skipping the sexy point and moving straight to ludicrous.

"Fiona? Are you pissed?" he asked suspiciously.

Not that he would ever be far wrong with a question like that.

"Possibly," I answered. Short and hopefully without slurring. It was time to wrap it up. "Look Sweetie, got to run, but promise to call as soon as I get back."

"Why are you in Adelaide?" came the question I'd been dreading.

It wasn't as if I had a good excuse really. I mean, why *was* I in Adelaide?

"Just visiting some friends. Spur of the moment. You know how it is." Probably not, but then again he wasn't a rich lay about either.

So I ended the phone call and turned the mobile off. What if my mother called as well? Jonelle was laughing quietly to herself, but I wasn't going to address the issue with her.

I took my pissed principles and went to sleep.

Chapter Fifteen

Is there ever a good morning to wake up after having so much wine the night before? I shuddered into consciousness at stupid o'clock and my head roared awake barely moments later. I knew there would be sunlight somewhere out there, but I was damned if I wanted to find it.

Somewhere really close someone was murmuring into a phone and my stomach curled when I realised she was ordering breakfast. If only she'd learned to drink her share of the bottle, I wouldn't be feeling like this. Wasn't there something in a book about rules? Didn't one automatically grow up at some point and stop putting oneself through this? I'd missed that vital lesson.

Moments later I visited the bathroom and felt light years better. Once again, my amazing metabolism spirited the alcohol out in rapid succession. Glad to be me, I came back into the room. Jonelle was sitting reading a paper and the blinds were now pulled back to give me an uninterrupted view of Adelaide.

"So, when are we off?"

I slipped into the chair opposite with a fine disregard of the fact I'd been upended over the toilet bowl less than one minute ago. Life's like that.

"As soon as we've eaten. It's not far to the Hills, but a bit further to his actual place. We'll be back in town this afternoon. I've made sure we have the first direct flight out of here tomorrow morning."

Great, another early morning.

Breakfast was fruit and muesli (was she trying to kill me?) and then we were off.

Adelaide and its surrounds were lovely, though I didn't remember a lot of detail. Jonelle drove and I dozed. It wasn't like I needed to know the exact location of Thorn's place. I couldn't see me trundling up there to see him without Jonelle. So I switched off and let the scenery wash over me. Not very spy like behaviour. But one hyped up crazy person in the car was enough. She was *humming* to herself, threading the car through traffic and out into the hills of Adelaide.

Thorn's place was off the main roads and across bumping dirt tracks. Well, the man did like solitude and his own company. What was the saying about the madness of genius? Paintings by Thorn Ridley, I'd read in the news once, could go for anything up to $500,000 depending on their size. It would be rather nice to have a talent like that.

Sometimes if I stopped and thought about it (which I tried hard not to very often) I wondered what it would be like to have a talent. Something that was uniquely my own, and others valued. I had a lot of money and the freedom to do pretty much whatever I wanted, but no one was going to pay to see me dance, or sing, or buy something I'd drawn. When I died, the most lasting impression I'd leave would be a sizeable dip in some brewery's profits. It was sad not to have something that was just me, which was probably why I didn't think about it all that much.

Jonelle pulled the car into a sharp left and over a cattle grid. A few more moments and we were drawn up outside the most extraordinary place I'd seen. Admittedly I had a narrow education in the art of dwellings, but it was pretty amazing.

The side of the hill had been dug away and the house had been lowered into the hole left behind. It looked very energy efficient and the turret built on top made entirely of windows was the ultimate for an artist. It sat, low and squat and made from what looked to be mud brick. Jonelle grunted at my wide eyes.

"He built it himself, with a bit of help from an environmental engineer he knows. He's very proud of the house and you may get a tour – so don't say no thank you. While he is reported to be quite strange, I think you'll find Thorn Ridley an exceptionally sane person. It suits his need for solitude to be on the record as crazy." I kept my opinions to myself.

We'd only been out of the car a few seconds when a cacophony of sound reached our ears. Yeah – need for solitude and quiet huh? The man lived with a whole pack of dogs. I liked dogs, I really did. Hadn't I shed a few tears over Potty? But they had to have a place and they had to be, well, not en mass for heaven's sake.

No one was going to come onto his land without an invitation. Lined up in front of us all teeth and raised hackles, were two Great Danes, a Cocker Spaniel, a Doberman Pinscher and a Bull Mastiff. If I was the fainting kind of person, now would have been a good time to let go. Jonelle stepped forward, with inbuilt confidence and hope.

"Sit," she demanded sharply.

None of them did, but they backed off a pace. Ah, the voice of command. I'd have sat. There were many sides to this woman. She was a thesis all in herself. Though was that for the school of communication, psychology, or science?

"Boys. Behave." A new voice: sudden obedience. They wagged tails or stumps depending on breed, and I got my first glimpse of a legend.

Thorn Ridley was sixty eight years old. He'd retired from the world of art shows and tours when his wife of thirty years died when he was fifty. From then on their home here in the Hills had become his main base and one he was loathe to leave for any reason. I'd done my research and Googled the man.

Thorn and Patricia Ridley had two children. One died with Patricia in the car crash which shattered his life. The other one, Leila Ridley, lived in Sydney and never had anything to do with her eccentric father. She'd been overheard saying at one point he should just pop off and leave her the money as he was an embarrassment. Relations were cool to say the least.

So there he stood. Six foot four inches of thin, gaunt, but surprisingly fit old man with thick grey hair, chocolate eyes and palms the size of dinner plates with long elegant fingers. He might come across as cantankerous, but there was a real depth of thought behind those eyes, which surveyed us both from under heavy lowered white brows.

"Thought you'd never make it, woman," he told Jonelle, coming to greet her.

With ease he lifted her in an embrace and kissed both her cheeks. I got the impression this was a liberty anyone else would have been floored for. Setting her on her feet, Thorn stepped back to have a good look at her.

"Bit peaky aren't you? Not as robust as I last saw you. Getting old like the rest of us, hey?" He smiled down at her, and then turned to me. A frown settled into the lines of his face. "Who have we here?"

"A friend, Thorn." Jonelle's voice was soft, for her, and shaded with affection. She reached out and grabbed my hand to pull me closer. I refused to react to the usual flutter that came with such contact, and ignored her discreet smirk.

"Fiona, Thorn. A friend and associate, Thorn."

He took my hand and raised it to his lips in a very old courtly gesture. "A pleasure, my dear. Do come in and see my home."

Deep brown eyes twinkled down into mine and I was lost. Vaguely I was aware that Jonelle was finding my total capitulation amusing, but I didn't care. The tour of his home was an honour. He'd certainly given it every touch of class and homeliness.

After a healthy lunch of fresh garden greens and chicken which I shuddered to discover he'd slaughtered himself from the chicken coop in the garden, it was down to business.

We were seated outside on a flat stretch of green lawn to the side of his homemade house. The sun was pouring its heat down on us and my stomach was gurgling happily around way too much food. Eyes closed, hands resting down on the warmed fur of a couple of dogs, I could hear the other two as though from a long way off.

"Hank is very keen to acquire another of your larger paintings, Thorn. He's got a wall, twelve foot high by fifteen foot long. Ideal for a repeat of *The Summer Fling*; if you have anything like that, of course." Jonelle was quietly intense and persuasive.

I peeped out of my half shut eyes and saw Thorn lean back; he was clearly enjoying himself, discussing his art and bargaining for a price, as was Jonelle. It was a nice change from racing around checking up on people who may or may not feel the need to kill us at some stage. A friendly peaceful insight into what it was she did for a living; as opposed I guessed, the things she seemed to do for fun. It continually struck me as strange to think of the heart pounding moments as fun, but I was sure that was exactly what Jonelle would do. With my twinges and various aches and pains, the idea of sitting in the warming sun and haggling held a lot more appeal.

I half dozed for a little while, then Jonelle shook me by the shoulder.

"Time to go, lazy bones." She was all smiles and relaxed cat-like grace.

Thorn bowed over my hand again. "If you ever want to model

for me, Madonna, you let me know. Though," and his eyes twinkled, "please allow time for healing first."

I blushed. He hadn't made mention of my bruising until that point. It wasn't as though I thought he hadn't noticed, but it still made me feel badly about it all.

The dogs came with Thorn to see us off and then before I could blink, we were on the road back into town.

"Did you get what you came for?"

Jonelle kept her eyes on the road as we talked. "I used his fax and sent Hank a shot of the painting. He loved it. So we did the deal. Hank never cares what he pays for these things, but I got him a bargain really. Thorn was happy as well. So all round it was good for everyone."

I tried to pin down some of the murmurs I'd overheard, but I couldn't piece it together and didn't want to ask what the price ended up. Whatever it was, she seemed content and that meant the commission had been worth her while.

By the time we reached Adelaide I was starving again. Well, lunch *had* consisted mainly of salad and a bit of undernourished home grown chicken! I was ready to go another round. Jonelle left me ordering up a storm from room service and disappeared in search of the gym once more.

When she came back it was to be greeted by me munching on Lindt chocolate.

"Isn't this where I came in last night?" she asked amused, helping herself to a glass of wine and wandering out to the balcony. To actually keep the conversation flowing I was forced to leave my comfy chair and follow.

We stood leaning against the railing, sipping wine and watching the sunset. I was peacefully sleepy, something I always got after a day in the car. Jonelle, I could see, was the opposite. She was wired and the session at the gym hadn't relaxed her.

"I guess the whole bargaining experience hypes you right up, hey?"

She looked over at me, the last rays of the sun catching in her eyes, making them glint. There was something so wild and almost elemental about her standing there, wind tearing at the always neat bun of hair, grey slanting eyes shooting sparks and muscles coiled with the day's excitement.

"One of the reasons I left the English organisation was to pursue my art dealings with greater attention. It wasn't just that I wasn't a team player. Because if that was the criteria, none of them would join. They're all very headstrong about how things get done." She turned back to look out over the city.

"I just knew I wanted to be able to paint and deal with other artists. It was important to me not to just do the work I was trained for, but to explore the other possibilities with the gifts I had."

She was silent for a moment but I didn't want to break the spell, so didn't ask anything else. Eventually she spoke again.

"I didn't want to just be the hired gun. And no, Amelia, Claire and Jack weren't like that either, but they were happy doing what they were doing. They left their families and could live with that. I wanted to be close enough to always be there for Jodi should she need me. I *needed* to be here. Does that make any sense? And they needed to be where they are, until now that it's all been blown to hell with Jack's death."

The last of the wine disappeared

"I like the buzz getting a great deal gives me. It's a vastly difference rush to stalking your..." She grinned at me. "Prey. But there is something clean about it. I like that. And it was mine, you see. None of the others were into that side of things, though Amelia loves art. So I had something they didn't and I wanted to keep it clean. Though, of course, when things are stolen or threatened, I can use my other talents to protect the art and the owner. It's fun."

See? What had I said about her thinking that all this danger and stuff was fun? Bloody bizarre.

We could talk like this and apart from the topic, it all sounded so normal and sensible. But I could see the heated flush of excitement on her cheeks and the hints of the animal inside lurking in her voice, and not for the first time I questioned my role here.

All right, so she wasn't mad or anything (I thought). But was she entirely with me; on the side of the straight, narrow and relatively normal? My friends and I didn't speak of hunting prey or being a hired gun. It just wasn't a part of my vocabulary until a few short weeks ago.

Which was as terrifying as it was stimulating, because that meant I was stepping off my little path and heading into the jungle. Good thing I had my own partly tamed jungle cat as protection. It wasn't a thought that made me sleep any better at night.

After all, as with any wild animal, were you guaranteed that they wouldn't turn on the people around them?

Jonelle had swung round and was now leaning with her back to the view, watching my expressions. Her eyes were in shadow and my skin started to feel all tingly. It was impossible for me to read anything that went on in that woman's head.

"Go get some sleep, okay? And stop thinking about it and over analysing. I'm not crazy, I don't take insane risks and I *do* know what I'm doing, most of the time. I'm going out, but I'll be back in the morning in time for our flight."

She walked past me into the room, putting her glass down and grabbing a jacket. "Don't wait up."

Jonelle waltzed out the door leaving me with the sinking feeling she knew I'd been thinking she was slightly unbalanced. Which was fine only if she didn't decide to do anything about my treacherous thought patterns.

I ate my way through the piles of room service I'd ordered, then crawled into bed to fall asleep watching The Maltese Falcon on pay TV.

Six in the morning was no time to be woken up by the Road Runner. I drew a pillow over my head, but that didn't erase the inane sound of his beep beep. Why oh why couldn't that stupid coyote just eat the little bugger?

I raised my tired old head and glanced over at the other double bed. It was empty and by the unnaturally neat state, she hadn't come in at all. Not that there was anything bigger and badder in this city than my boss and best friend. Still happier if she'd come back.

A long hot shower and several extra strength cups of coffee later, I was feeling more human and laughing quietly at the cartoons, as opposed to throwing things at the screen.

It was seven thirty before I heard the key being swiped and Jonelle let herself into the room. She was slightly rumpled and there were dark smudges under her eyes. I was dying to ask what she'd been up to, but the hint of dried blood on her right hand knuckles killed that impulse stone dead. Sometimes not knowing anything was better than knowing everything. And those were words no one heard from me all that often. I studiously ignored her hands and focused on the TV as though it held the secret to the Universe.

"You should probably grab a shower before breakfast gets here."

I tried for the casual and off hand manner.

As though I was totally cool with the idea of her coming home at that hour looking as though she'd beaten a brick wall senseless. I went with the idea of a brick wall because it was easier to think about that than the idea that out there was someone who had pissed her off sufficiently to deserve the mess they would now be in. I could hear my mother telling me I would get tarred with the same brush and that she really wasn't a nice type of person.

Bit late for those warnings though.

I glanced up as she went passed to the bathroom and her eyes flicked to mine for a second. I couldn't read them well, but she was still sane and my friend; I could see that much.

She was walking with the loose limbed grace usual to her. The coiled heat of last night worked out by whatever she'd being up to. I was glad for the sake of her and myself. Saddened, however, that it had taken the obvious violence of the evening to achieve it.

I could see that narrow and safe path I had walked for twenty nine years some way behind me. But I kept on walking towards whatever excitement lured us both down the darkness Jonelle offered. Her eyes moved passed me and the moment was broken. Thank goodness really, because anymore of that fantastical nonsense and I'd have fallen off the bed laughing.

Breakfast eaten and bags packed, we paid the bill and took the hire car back to the airport in preparation of the flight home. Jonelle was even more withdrawn and quiet than ever. And my own thoughts were of such a nature that it was all achieved in relative silence.

Whatever she'd been up to, it had released some of her demons and now she just wanted to sleep, something she did all the way back to Canberra.

We were back at the apartments before too long and she left me with a casual: "I'll come get you for the gym tomorrow."

I felt like squeaking some form of protest, but I knew that wouldn't work. It was Thursday. One more day before the rest a weekend could offer me. Instead I waved her off and shut the door.

It was meant to be a shutting away of the world, but as with so many of my plans it wasn't to last for long. The phone was crowded with messages. Some from Mum, Steph and Grillia, all which reminded me I had had a life before I met Jonelle. Others included Brad, Julie and freakily enough, a soft and deep-voiced message from Will. I hit rewind. Will??

"Fiona. I've been thinking of you. Wouldn't it be interesting to see what direction our thoughts were to take us? Leave Friday night free, okay? I'll pick you up at seven."

I nearly hit rewind again, but knew that that was probably a little obsessive. If Brad wanted to see me as soon as I got back, then it was just conceivable I'd be free tomorrow night. It would require some manipulation, but anything was possible. And it wasn't as though I'd like both of them to rock up at the same time. That'd be confusion and angry testosterone everywhere. What a mess.

It wasn't hard to convince Brad he needed to come over tonight and leave me free to 'be myself' on Friday night. I have no idea what 'being myself' was meant to mean, but it was sufficiently female and opaque that he didn't question it. Silly boy. Did my conscience feel the weight of wiggling my life around so I could see Will with no one the wiser? For a moment I felt a twinge. Then it left me. I wasn't, after all, in any way shape or form tied to Brad. That was the sop I gave my now silent inner voice.

After organising my social life to my specifications, I trotted over to Julie's. I couldn't believe I could move so well. The massages and saunas and spas had done me the world of good. Though to look at I was no oil painting, the movement was a far cry from a couple of days ago. Perhaps she really had been right – about them not giving me a hard time.

Julie was home relaxing by her TV. I could see her through the window. Smudge was dozing on her lap, getting absent minded pats, while Manny lay stretched out at her feet. I had barely tapped at the door when deep barks erupted and Smudge let out a yowl. It was very satisfying to have been missed, regardless of the species doing the missing.

"Sit down and shut up!"

Obviously Julie had reached the end of her babysitting tether. The door was flung open and I was pounced on by three wholly relieved creatures.

"Oh thank God you're home. That dog is quite mad and makes me *walk* him! And your cat..! The less said about his washing habits in my bed the better. How are you?"

All delivered at high speed while I was scratched, licked and hugged in various degrees of welcome.

We settled in for a catch up. Though of course, there were limits to what I could tell her. For the first time I shuddered at not being able to tell one of my closest friends exactly what my adventures entailed.

How could Jonelle live like that? Constantly telling people half truths, or no truth at all! I sat with Julie and navigated a minefield of questions and comments which were innocuous, but full of potential hazard. No wonder Jonelle didn't have any friends. They demanded a response and they pried into your life with no regard for the secret buttons they could be pushing.

I wouldn't have them any other way.

Without exploding any of the realities of what was happening around me, I spent a wonderful afternoon without, I hope, Julie sensing my hesitations and reservations. I struggled out of there an hour before I was to meet Brad, with pets in tow. I felt like I'd been through a wringer.

Smudge was delighted to be home, pouncing his way around the furniture and in general getting under my feet. Manny was a little more subdued, seeing as he'd never made this place home before. Plus, I could see a few scratches on his nose. Smudge had made his presence felt.

Leaving water and some kibble in the bowls, I dived into the shower to do the obligatory shave and scrub. Once dry, I covered my newly de-furred body with scented oil, and chose the laciest and briefest matched set of panties and bra I owned. Brad, I decided, was due a heart attack. It was always good to feel the power of being a woman! A sleek black clinging dress topped the whole she-bang off. I felt like a million dollars.

Okay, so it was going to take a trick of light to make me *look* a million dollars, considering everything was starting to go yellow, but clothes maketh this woman. Even so, I packed the foundation on and drew kohl around my eyes, and did every trick I knew to highlight the best bits and shadow the worst. It would be touch and go, but alright in a candlelit restaurant.

"What do you think, hmm?" I pirouetted for my two boys.

Smudge yawned and went back to cleaning himself. Manny lay his nose down on his paws and raised adoring doggy eyes to mine.

"Okay, at least one of you is a fan. It means more treats for him and starvation rations for you, you ungrateful wretch."

I laughed, picking up a protesting Smudge and rubbing my nose in his soft tummy fur. He patted at me with his paws, but there were no sign of the needle claws, so I forgave him.

A moment later the buzzer went.

"Crap!"

I dropped Smudge back on the bed and did one last check in the mirror. There really was nothing more I could do. He'd notice. He'd have to be blind and *stupid* not to notice, but at least I could move without feeling as though my bones were coming apart. Thank God for small mercies. If I hobbled to the front door and winced my way through dinner, there would have been more than just questions. It'd have been a bloody Spanish Inquisition.

I let him in. Standing with my face in shadow, it was easier to pretend to the unknowing that everything was fine.

"Fi! Come here." He swung in the front door and gathered me into a hug.

Okay, so that stole my breath away and not for the right reasons. A crushing hug from a man the size of Brad was interesting at the best of times. Right then, it only served to highlight just how freshly healed I was … Ouch!

"Brad!" It was more of a gasp than a tender or sexy moan, but hey, who was judging?

He set me back onto my feet and stepped a little away. All the better to get a good look at me. I could have warned him, possibly should have, but didn't. He, in turn, gave a gasp of his very own.

"What the hell happened to you? This the aftermath of that 'small' accident I heard about?"

I think he could have been a little more subtle than that. I mean, I was wearing an actor's load of makeup.

"It's okay and nothing for you to worry about. Let's just go out and have a wonderful dinner."

I took his arm and tried to tug him out the door. I should have known that wasn't going to work. There was just no way someone my size was moving a man anywhere he didn't particularly want to go. He dug his heels in and turned my face up to the light.

"All right! But it looks worse than it is. Just a bingle. No other damage."

Was this making me a good liar or what?

Brad leaned down and kissed my nose.

"It's the only place that doesn't look like its being mangled. Hope you don't hurt too badly all over."

His voice had slipped down an octave again and I wiggled. He was just so damned sexy. How was a woman supposed to stay on an even keel around this lad?

He smiled lazily, knowing damn well why I was wiggly. Arrogant swine. Then he took me off for dinner. Which was lovely and I didn't feel like I was on display too much. At one stage I went into the ladies to check the damage in the harsh lights they always seem to have in there. Apart from a slight yellow haze to my makeup and a bit of puffiness, I thought I was pulling it off. Or maybe that was my delusion talking, and the bottle and a half of wine we'd consumed so far.

Around eleven we caught a taxi back to the Grangelands. For some reason it was easier to do than the usual arguing about going back to his place. At least home had seen a vacuum cleaner in the last two weeks. Maybe. I couldn't rightly remember that aspect of cleaning, actually. I made one of my mental notes to vacuum sometime in the near future. I never knew what happened to my mental notes – they seemed to disappear in the cyber space of my brain. But at least I made the effort to make them. There just *had* to be brownie points in effort.

Coffee, the usual beverage of choice at this hour after a few bottles of wine, was left cooling on the kitchen bench. There were more immediate and pressing matters to attend to. Like a completely gentle, yet demanding man in my bed.

He stripped me slowly, exclaiming softly as he uncovered the bruising and grazes down my ribs. I'd forgotten them. They were a distant ache, muted by the pampering and the alcohol. Who said alcohol wasn't good for you? My head swirled and I felt weightless. I stood in the middle of my room, naked and coated in bruises. And I'd never felt sexier. Brad was on his knees in front of me and I was worshipped as the goddess I was.

As the fire built inside, Brad swept me up and I was snuggled into the pillows. Sometimes, there were real compensations to being so short.

I remembered talking to Grillia once about the whole feeling small and fragile thing. Being considerably taller than myself, she told me it took a giant of a man with loads of muscle to make her feel even remotely fragile, which kind of limited her dating pool to a puddle.

I was lucky. The average height of a man was still several inches taller than me so my dating pool was more of an ocean. Even so, if the guy was six foot or over (as was the case here), I could be made to feel like a tiny bird, which was delicious. See? My mind was running away from the action; even when that action was burning up my central nervous system.

Brad had the largest hands. They were warm and firm and were callused in all the right places. For a man who does marketing, I wondered briefly how he managed to get callous on his hands. But that thought flew out the window as those hands stroked down my body leaving trails of fire in their wake. Bruising be damned. I was in heaven.

He took his time. Long drawn out moments were spent at my breasts, making them tight and achy. Small damp kisses trailed down to my belly button. My stomach muscles contracted and fluttered. He rumbled a chuckle, breathing warm air over the skin's dampness. I shivered. It was so intense. Had I known he was capable of delivering such passion? Deep inside, my muscles clenched and I rolled away on waves of pleasure. The man was a treasure and he was, for the moment, all mine. At times like this, I could learn to pray.

He rose up, using his arms as supports either side of my head. I was open and welcoming, but still he teased and hesitated.

"Brad. You're killing me."

It was a breathy sigh and those words released him. He rode me at a gallop to a breathtaking finish and shuddering, we finally lay quiet. Considering the decidedly loud moans and groans, I was very glad we'd closed the bedroom door. An indignant cat or a defensive dog was something moments like this could well do without.

Brad rolled over and took me with him so I was sprawled across his chest. I could feel his heart rate beginning to slow, and every ragged breath he was taking. I lay with my dark honey hair spread out over his chest and shoulders, feeling my breasts squish against his chest and every inch of him spread out under me. It was delicious. Something I could well get used to. As that random thought floated through my head I got a jolt.

Hold on a little there! It was just great sex. No need to get too carried away with it all. Sex was sex; getting used to having someone around was, well, stepping off a cliff with no parachute. And no one did that for fun, did they? I tried very hard to make my body move. It was the principle of the thing. I couldn't stay all snuggled up comfortable as all get out, getting used to the whole thing. I had to preserve my distance.

But principles were so much easier to maintain when faced with a cold empty bed, or life. It was an entirely different matter to make them count when I was held softly across the still damp chest of a man who could play my body like some form of string instrument. Try it. Principles are just about *impossible* to pin down under such circumstances. So I mentally gave them a heave, as I slipped effortlessly into post climatic sleep. After all, a comfy pillow is a comfy pillow and no one should knock one back.

The alarm shrilling in my ear was the first conscious event I could piece together after my mind lost the fight with my principles.

In my sleep I had slipped off Brad and lay curled up at the far corner of the bed. I actually hated to be touched when sleeping. I liked my space – in oh so many ways. The alarm was right next to my face, glowingly telling me that it was five forty five in the morning and I needed to get my butt up in time for the gym.

With a hearty groan, I flung one arm out and thunked it down on the snooze button. It was tempting to turn it totally off but that was dangerous, and I knew that Jonelle had no problems with breaking into my home and dragging me out of bed. Not something that I would appreciate with the butt nakedness of us right then.

So with a quick peck on Brad's stubble encrusted cheek, I hauled myself out and into gym clothes. A shower, a coffee and any other normal wake up methods would have to wait until after (which makes no rational sense to me, but there you have it) we got back. Which could be hours, seeing as Jonelle appeared to be in the punishing frame of mind.

"Where are you off to?"

Brad had woken up sufficiently to raise himself on one elbow and watch the proceedings. He looked so delicious, hair ruffled, stubble darkened cheeks, and sleepy half shut eyes. I checked my watch. Nope, no time to indulge in some fancy, quick, wake-up sex. Damn it. Jonelle's time table was going to be the death of my love life. Though, there was always tomorrow morning.

Except, I reminded myself, I was due to be out with an entirely different type of creature tonight. And I was *not* waking up beside him. That way would lead to all kinds of complications – or at least, someone in my life who was scarier than Jonelle and I was not going to invite that!

"Got to get to the gym, Mister Slugabug. Some of us have a physique to maintain, or gain. Help yourself to a shower, breakfast and anything else before work okay? I'll catch up with you over the weekend." I turned to go.

Brad was a lot faster than I thought such a large man could be. I had only just finished the invitation to help himself to anything else and he was out of that bed, and I was swooped up by a very naked, very aroused, male person. Giggling, I was dumped back on the bed and my gym pants reefed to my knees.

"Brad! Behave. I'm being collected in," I took a quick peek at the bed clock. "In five minutes!"

Plus, I was forced to admit, minus the alcohol of last night, the idea of bedroom gymnastics was awaking every known bruise, ache and graze known to my body.

"Plenty of time," was the muffled response from a face buried somewhere in my hair over my left shoulder.

And I felt him slip inside me and move with deep impatient thrusts. My body's various aches set up in a distance chorus, but I was ready for him. I had been since I woke up. In mind shattering speed we reached climax together, a scant three minutes after he entered me. Lying there, I was aware of the click as six o'clock was finally reached and the alarm sprang once more into life. Brad groaned and rolled onto his side, and I readjusted my clothing.

"Damn it! No time to shower. I'm going to smell of sex, you heathen! They'll all *know* and Jonelle will never let me live this down."

A faint voice told me I was worried about Jonelle knowing I had just had sex for a lot of different reasons, not all of them concerning her verbal annihilation masquerading as jokes. Something to do with feelings and sparks and that odd look deep in her eyes she could get. But I shied away from that, yet again; there were places I could go with my imagination and then there were places that fear allowed me to hide from.

Somehow I didn't think Brad was feeling the least bit remorseful. He had a self-satisfied smirk on his face and a sheet slung, barely, across his hips. My kingdom for a camera.

However, before I could act on such a thought, there was a

hammering on the front door, accompanied by meows and barks. I wondered how they'd coped being locked out of the bedroom all night. I opened the door and both cat and dog almost bowled me over in their excitement. Sniffing, they jumped up on the bed to check out the stranger in their domain. Manny followed Smudge, but he was careful to keep his eyes away from mine. He was unsure of how much liberty he could take as yet.

I left Brad to fend for himself and went to let Jonelle in. I wasn't going to have her come charging through using a pocket knife as a key.

"Morning! Shall we go?"

I moved passed her as fast as I could, hoping I was down wind. I couldn't smell myself, but that didn't mean anything. Onion eaters rarely realised just how strong they smelled either. I should have known I was doomed to failure. One long arm snaked out and I was snagged before I'd even cleared the door frame.

"You are looking more than a little guilty this morning."

Her eyebrow rose, eyes dancing. I was learning to hate that eyebrow. I should pay more attention to shaping my own.

I could have come up with something glib. After all, in the past week I'd managed to find a marvellously deceitful streak within myself. There was something totally convincing poised on my tongue. Only to be swallowed whole as an only clad in boxer shorts Brad sloped into the kitchen to put the kettle on. He stretched, knowing full well two women were eyeing him off. Muscles rippled and butt cheeks clenched. Something tickled me low down and I felt the overwhelming need to bite, but all that came out was an inarticulate squawk. He was better than breakfast.

"You up to the gym? Or have you had your morning workout?"

Jonelle's tone hadn't changed. Her eyes still held humour and the brow was up. But somehow, I just knew. You know, there was just a little twitch before she spoke, before everything was as it had been. It is a very weird feeling when you realise that your boss/friend/apartmate was jealous.

And not of you, but your boyfriend.

A feeling I could do without because this friend was mixed up with so many of my other feelings – mainly of fear, and wariness and caution and over the top adrenalin pumping excitement of the almost-going-to-die variety. So one more feeling was pushing my limits. But I looked into those stormy grey eyes and saw only calm. She wasn't the type to ever take a step when the direction wasn't clear.

I glanced at Brad.

"He's just showing off. I'm all ready to go."

I stuck my tongue out at him, as I closed the door.

"Let's go."

If she wasn't going to say anything, then who was I to? Anyway – my ability to judge people and get it right was phenomenally flawed.

"What have you been up to since yesterday morning?"

I felt safe with this question as I could see no recent telltale signs of renewed violence. Plus, there'd been so many things needing following up, I would have been surprised if she'd gone to bed or anything normal like that.

"I had a chat with The Rose."

Holy mother of everything.

The Rose.

In town.

Chapter Sixteen

I stopped. Walking, breathing, thinking.
  You name it, I stopped it.

There may even have been a slight break in the evenness of my heart beat. Thinking of him anywhere near me or Jonelle, well, it brought out the best in me.

"You did what with whom?" I asked numbly.

She took my arm and helped me get started again in the direction of the car.

"The Rose. Remember? The man we really wanted to say hello to and then bury."

She felt real. Solid. But she sounded terribly remote; like the person who had just been joking was from another life entirely. Multiple personalities be-damned.

"Yes, but wasn't he meant to be in America? You know, as far away from here as is possible? On route, but not actually in the state, or city?"

Nicely, safely the other side of the world, I thought to myself. Somewhere I didn't have to worry about.

"I'm sure he was. But now he's here. He's working for a new player who I don't know personally, but I am led to understand is very involved with everything happening around here. He wanted to 'catch up' as he put it. Which we did.

"There were a lot of oblique threats and comments which I had to play along with pretending I actually knew what he was talking about, but in the end he headed off to Sydney. So I'll be up there this afternoon for the weekend."

Yes, like that followed. Couldn't she just stay here? Nice and safe, like I said, far away from the action. Especially when she had just admitted to not really knowing what that action was!

She must have caught some of that on my face because she added for my benefit, "I know he wants me dead. His sense of 'fun' allowed him to hold this meeting, with his henchmen watching me closely so I got no idea of having my own fun. But I want to put a few of tricks in place so he stays put in Sydney, and as far from me and what I am doing, as possible."

"I also caught up with the Chemist afterwards which helped with the holes in my understanding."

We settled into her car and headed for the gym. I was glad for the seated position.

I grumbled at her. "You know what the trouble is? It's going off without me. It's like I'm your safety net, or pin or holster or whatever you want to call it. The scariest thing we've had is a gun pointed at us."

Which, come to think about it, was pretty scary.

"Or sitting across from Lilly with her watchdog behind us. But apart from that, cruise-y stuff. I just shouldn't let you out without a leash."

Although I wouldn't be tying the end of that leash to myself. Not got a death wish.

Jonelle flashed me her predator grin. My toes curled. Things were back to normal.

"Do you want to know what's going on, or are you just going to prattle all day?" she asked, but the tone was mild and full of the solidness it had been lacking. A vast improvement and relief.

"Sure, hit me with it. Not literally." I added, correctly reading her smile for once.

"Well, the stuff that was with Tomas is a new synthetic drug which is reportedly sweeping through the US and Europe. It's called 'The Way' and is supposed to show its user the 'way'. To what, I can only imagine. To stupefied wonders of another world or whatever drug users seem to find appealing. Anyway, it's potent and requires a delicate touch or it is very easy to OD. Mind you, wherever it takes them is worth the risk, Chemist tells me. It's that good." Her face twisted for a second. I got the feeling drugs weren't Jonelle's thing.

"The Way is being manufactured by a group calling themselves Phoenix – rising from the ashes. Which leads me to think some of its members must be from a previous organisation with a sense of warped humour. I'll try to find out if anyone has been sacked or moved on recently. Though generally speaking, to leave that sort of organisation means you're a dead man. But you never know."

She stopped speaking to manoeuvre the car into a spot. She continued as we walked towards the gym entrance.

"They're looking for a local distributor and loads of people are trying to outbid each other and move into the new market. Gavin was trying to be a Canberra contact, though I think they now know just how unstable he is. Sydney's up for grabs too. The Rose is over here to talk to some people about The Way."

Then we were inside and the gym, while not crowded, was not the place for that sort of conversation, which sucked. It was my worst kind of nightmare. Half the picture, a tantalising tease of what it was all about, then enforced silence! I was full of questions and had over an hour to stew in my juice.

Impossible woman.

It wasn't as though Jonelle didn't know, either. The whole workout she shot me little smiles and words like "patience" and "curiosity killed cats". I could have shot her myself. Everyone gets their jollies their own way, but hers was driving me nuts.

I had to take it easy. It'd only been five days since I'd been put through the mangle and while I was healing pretty quickly for me, I didn't want to push it.

The painful path of the minute hand swept its way around the hour. I was bursting with the need to know. Everything. Which wasn't novel, but enforced silence could be considered torture. I was breathing deeply and fast, with beads of sweat trickling down my face and between my shoulder blades.

So okay, I was taking it easy. But that is a relative term and Jonelle wasn't about to see me slacken off just to get fat and lazy again. Bruised and beaten was not a good enough excuse not to put in *some* effort. My body grunted its way through a mile or so, on the treadmill as a warm down. Things felt decidedly jelly-like, but I wasn't going to admit to it.

Finally, Jonelle gave the signal I'd been watching for. The 'let's go and hear the rest of what's happening' signal. Well, it was more of a commanding hand gesture and then leaving, but I got the drift and followed.

She was laughing before we even reached the car.

"You should see your face! It's been so very hard to keep a straight face."

"Glad to keep you amused. Now get back to the point. What else did you find out?" I wasn't feeling in the mood for anymore of her stalling tactics.

We slipped into the car and Jonelle backed us out.

"Okay. From what I can gather, Tomas snitched that small packet of The Way when he was over at Gavin's, possibly to on-sell this other piece of art which is still floating out there and bugging me to bits. That would explain how it was on his body. Now if Gavin mentioned who took his sample, I imagine retribution would have been swift. Seeing as the murder was handled very ineptly I think they probably sent Gavin to do it himself. To test if he had the balls to be effective. Now he's stuffed it all up by making me suspicious, failing to get the stuff back and alerting the police who will be sniffing around, they'll probably take Gavin out of the equation."

"At least," she mused "that's what I'd do."

We drove for a moment in silence. She may have been considering how to quietly rid herself of Gavin; I was mainly thinking about how to keep my skin intact.

"Is that it?"

I wanted to make sure I hadn't missed anything. After all, she was known to skip bits. Bits that could leave me open to some form of retribution. From lord alone knew who, these days.

"Practically. One last thing."

She paused and glanced over at me, those jealousy making full lips pursed in thought. What – she thought telling me was optional?

"And … that would be?" I prompted, trying to keep myself sane.

"Amelia's come home now." There - it was out.

I sat back in my seat.

It was the end of November. I'd only known this woman and her associates for a few weeks, but those words put a chill down my spine.

Amelia was home. Amelia was Australian; thus it meant she was here, in the country. The woman who Jonelle kept a distance from. Who Jonelle described as harder and stronger and scarier than herself. Was here. Close enough to reach out and touch us. No wonder my hot sweat chilled. So did my heart.

"Here? As in, Australia?" It was best to check before I started to panic.

Jonelle grimaced.

"Actually, Amelia is here, as in Canberra. Her family comes from here. The boss sent her back and wasn't taking no for an answer. Claire called to give me a heads up. I expect she'll make contact at some point. If she's still keen to destroy the people who killed Jack and believe me, she will be, she'll want to hear all about the Rose, the Phoenix and anyone else I may find suspicious. Claire says Amelia is determinedly under control, but somewhere in the vicinity of alcoholism."

She shot me a nasty little smirk.

"You two may have more in common than you imagined."

I chose to ignore such a low remark.

We parked next to my car and she turned to me.

"Things are moving faster now. There are more new players involved and still loads of questions. And they are dangerous players. Never underestimate our own associates either. Amelia is a loose cannon, for all Claire believes she's got it under control. If we step in between her and a perceived target, we could end up in a body bag."

"Jesus! Do you have to be quite so blunt?" That trickle of sweat down my back had just become a river.

"I need you to realise how serious this is. And understand why I am leaving you at home when I go to Sydney to check this story out. You need to stick around the Grangelands and be close to locking yourself in my place if need be. Plus, I want you to carry - all the time."

"Carry what?" She'd lost me somewhere around body bags.

"A gun, you idiot!" she snapped, exasperated.

Well, there was no need to get snippy. It wasn't as though I was up on all the jargon now, was it? She'd dragged me into this mess; this foreign minefield and now she expected me to be au fait with the lingo. All right, so that wasn't necessarily fair; I'd kind of wiggled my way further than she'd expected into this game we were playing, but hey, was I in the mood to play fair? I rather think not.

"I need you to carry a gun and be prepared to use it. If I'm out of the city they may come snooping around and I don't want them to find you. Plus, there are other people out there, not just Phoenix and The Rose."

Did I want to hear this? More people?

"Who am I looking for, exactly?"

She looked up and locked eyes with me. "You've never met them, but you'd know them. They want to hurt me somewhat, or have I failed to mention they are not the sort of people you take home for cookies and cream? I upset someone some time ago and the stakes just went up enough to excite a whole range of interesting folk."

Damn, I hated it when she called them interesting. It could only mean dangerous.

"I don't intend on letting them collect. I don't even want them to know about you. But we have to plan for anything. Now, let's go get showered."

End of discussion. She left the car and I followed, my head whirling.

I grunted a 'see you later' and went in for a long shower. I needed to think. I was savagely out of my depth. It had started as a game. Something to while away some of the long tedious hours of my day. A little research, a bit of filing and a new friend to talk to.

It hadn't lasted like that for long and I had welcomed the intrigue. The idea of walking in the shadow of someone who could do and was more than prepared to do, things I had only ever seen on TV. Or read about. Someone whose life was a real serial of danger and heady men of amazing attraction.

I'd played with the idea that this was a world I could navigate, even though in terms of length of stay, I was a baby. The game had taken me off my path of carefree harmless interaction with the rich and decadent, and slammed me down the road of caution and fear and violence. Where my heroine went out and stalked bad people to release her tensions, and talked of ridding the world of scum over green tea and cucumber sandwiches (okay so I was lying about the sandwiches).

Suddenly, it was do or die time. The real chance to get mixed up with people who would normally have me shivering under my bed and I wasn't too sure I could go through with this. A part of me was indignant that she would think to leave me behind. How could she have such double standards? Throw me in the deep end, and yet keep me coddled at home.

On the other hand, the majority of me wanted to save my skin - being a deeply selfish creature who preferred to look after myself and have everyone else looking after me, too. Like a cat, I loved to curl up on a comfy couch and sloth in the sun. Putting me deliberately in harm's way for the sake of someone else was completely foreign, and my self-preservation warning lights were all lit up. It was crazy to see me in the role of, well, anything really.

But I was enjoying some part of this whole experience. I just couldn't put my finger on what it was.

My lovely shower came to an end. I wasn't too sure what, if anything, Jonelle had planned for me to be doing the rest of the day, so I dressed for anything and wandered over to her place, trailed by the inevitable pets.

She must have seen me coming, because the door was open and the kettle bubbling when I arrived. Jonelle herself was sitting in the office phone clamped to one ear, fingers busy on the keyboard of her computer. She was muttering into the phone, nodding and shaking her head. I left her to it and prepared the green tea, after locking and arming the door. There were going to be no surprises on my watch.

"Thanks."

She'd ended the call and was standing at the kitchen doorway, faint frown lines creasing her brow. I took stock of her over my mug. In the harsh morning sunlight, the worry of her lifestyle and the all night violent romps she put herself through, I suddenly had a sinking feeling. Just how old was Jonelle? Could she keep up this punishing way of life long enough to find all her answers and get free of all the people who wanted her dead?

"You're thinking too much again. It'll give you lines." Like she could talk.

"Whatever you're worried about now, it won't happen. I may not be able to read your mind, but worry speaks volumes on your face." She accepted her mug of tea and motioned me to follow her into the lounge.

"When I go to Sydney, I'll be following up some other issues I'm involved in. Nothing that need concern you, but another reason I can't take you. They'd be shy of talking around a stranger."

Funny how I'd assumed that everything she was involved in revolved around what we were working on. It was hard to see past the immediacy of The Way, the Phoenix and The Rose, never mind Lilly and Francis, her friendly neighbourhood hit man. But of course, that was my egocentricity speaking. She'd been working before I came on the scene and would be long after I chickened out and exited stage left.

My disappointment, or whatever, must have shown. Jonelle leaned over and gripped my arm for a brief moment. A veritable avalanche of emotional outpouring for her.

"You'll have to stay and keep an eye on Heather, okay? The chances of her staying hidden gets less and less the more players come on the scene. *Someone* has to know Brenda had a sister. Someone will assume she told Heather anything that was on her mind. Perhaps you might even get out of her if she does know anything."

"Yeah, me, the secret Inquisitioner. Didn't you say she hadn't seen Brenda for a couple of years?"

"Well, that was her story. But she'd moved to Canberra only a few months before the funeral. I checked," she added to forestall my instant question. "There is no good reason why, unless she moved to be closer to her sister. Heather left a well paying job in Sydney, where her family was situated, to move to a slower town, with no family, for no apparent reason. *Unless*, she was here to support Brenda and get close again. They were the only children. No other siblings to talk with and two parents who sound very unforgiving and controlling. I have a hunch Heather knows more than we think and I want that knowledge to be ours, not theirs. And I want it sooner rather than later."

Boy, her personality could be forceful when she wanted it. I could feel her compelling me with her eyes and words alone.

"All right! I'll stay. You go do what you have to. I'll see you Monday. I'll spend some time with Heather."

I knew I sounded petty, but I couldn't help it. There was so much more to her and what she does that I was shut out of. I hated being kept in the dark.

So I finished my tea and Jonelle packed for the weekend. I rinsed the mugs.

"I'm off. Speak to you when you get back."

Jonelle had moved over to the small table near the door. She had her wrist knife out and was giving it a quick sharpening with what I had presumed was an ornamental rock. Sometimes even I was amazed at how far wrong I was. It made me remember her comments in the car.

"Why are they trying to hurt you this time?"

"I have something they want."

"Wouldn't it just be easier to give it to them?" I asked her, seeking the path of least resistance – watching her sharpen the knife I knew was illegal.

Jonelle stopped what she was doing and looked at me.

"It's mine and I'd rather not part with it." She smiled slightly and went back to the knife.

"Well, what is this wonderful thing they want so badly?"

She stood, sliding the knife up her sleeve and seamlessly into the harness attached to her wrist. Walking to the door, she turned back to me, tapping her head.

"This," she said, one of her rare and more glorious smiles sliding across her face.

I paled. A bloody silly expression, but I could almost feel the white spread up as my blood drained down.

"They want your head?"

"Preferably unattached, but with body if that's the only way they can get it." Jonelle watched me watching her. "Don't look so frightened. This isn't a movie. The bad guys don't have a secret weapon. They are only men, and men bleed and die like the rest of us."

Plus, a little voice in my head clamoured to say, who said they were the bad guys? Who was to say the woman standing less than four metres away from me was the good guy?

Once more, a sense of menace stole into the room. Not for the first time the little part of me which cried at scary movies and had a better sense of self-preservation whimpered something about predators and running and hiding.

As usual, Jonelle took my traitorous thoughts from my facial expression, and her eyes gleamed like a demon.

One easy glide and she was inches from my wide eyes.

"Don't worry little one, I'll take care of you."

Somehow that warm message made sweat spring out all over my body.

And then the doorbell rang.

"You expecting someone?" I asked, as Jonelle swung round in a flash.

She shook her head and eased her wrist knife out of its sheath. That, more than anything, totally freaked me out. Who did that sort of thing?

She went over and peered out the peephole.

"Shit."

One word, but it said so much really. If whoever was out there could obtain so much feeling from Jonelle, then I wanted to go home. She disconnected the alarm and swung the door open.

She was tall. Possibly an inch, or so, taller than Jonelle. Dark hair, olive tanned skin, brown eyes. She carried herself with the lethal grace that was second nature to these women. There was the overall statement of power, muscles and throttled violence. She made my skin turn to ice.

There could be no doubt as to the identity of this woman. Even if I hadn't seen a much younger version of her on DVD, I'd still know. If not by the contracting of my stomach muscles, then by the alert hum in Jonelle's body, mere inches from my own.

This then was Amelia.

The dangerous, not-quite-on-our-side, Amelia.

Chapter Seventeen

A melia."

Jonelle's voice held no inflection. She wouldn't know if she should be welcoming or ready to slam the door. I was voting slam door. No one took any notice of me.

"Jonelle. Heard you were in town."

She eyes slipped to Jonelle's hands and her lips twisted briefly.

"You greet all your visitors with a knife up your sleeve?"

The knife came out and was laid on the table. Amelia watched, her eyes the only movement, and they appeared flat and devoid of humanity. Not someone I would like to meet alone. In a dark alley. Or basically anywhere Jonelle wasn't. She flicked her own wrist and laid a matching knife down next to Jonelle's.

My, weren't they friendly?

"Who's that?"

Those eyes glanced at me and I wished the floor would eat me alive. They raked through me, taking in the bruises, my stature, my lack of anything remotely like their presence and dismissed me in a second.

Jonelle scowled.

"No one you need to know. You should go home now."

She hadn't taken her eyes from Amelia, but I just knew that last bit was for me. So I went. Amelia swayed to one side and I scraped through the gap without touching her. They disappeared inside as soon as I was out of the way.

My pets, who had dashed out when the door opened, and I made our way a bit shakily back to home. It may only have been across the courtyard from Jonelle's, but it felt light-years removed. The meeting I had just left was one of those things which would normally have me crying under the covers.

So it was back to my TV, the comfort of a packet of chippies and my two housemates as company. It was around then I remembered – crap! I had a date with the devil that night! The handsome, but decidedly wicked Will was due to pick me up at seven. That did leave me several hours to get myself into some form of delectable shape, but one could never start too early. And pampering me was a good way to get my mind off the clash happening across the building.

I kept getting a flash of her eyes. While Jonelle could be expressionless, Amelia gave new meaning to the word. Losing Jack may well have helped her to lose her mind.

Had I been expecting Jonelle to come and say goodbye before she loped off to Sydney?

Maybe.

She'd become a big part of my life so quickly. No, I had to amend that. She'd allowed herself, and invited me, to become a large part of each others' lives. I readily assumed she would come and debrief the Amelia thing with me. It was a rude awakening to see them walking out together, carrying Jonelle's overnight kit, heads down deep in conversation. I felt remote and shut out.

I played with Smudge and Manny for an hour. Smudge was easy; he just wanted to chase his favourite ball of string around. Manny on the other hand, wanted ear rubs, tummy rubs, a squeaky toy and hinted at his leash.

Well, why not? A walk would do us all good and keep me occupied until the earliest possible moment I could contemplate getting ready. Smudge picked his string up and followed along. I knew he wouldn't be able to keep up, but I could always carry him home when his little legs ran out of puff.

I walked the animals to the oval and let Manny off his leash. Throwing a tennis ball for him and the string for Smudge, I soon had them running around in all directions. It was the easiest way for me to exercise them without raising a sweat.

After half an hour of this, we all lay down and I counted the clouds. I must admit, they weren't so good at cloud counting and promptly fell asleep. I day dreamed of going overseas and meeting up with my group of mates over there. We'd hang out at the Ritz in whatever city we liked. We'd go to all the right parties and find men born of wealth and position. And whatever else we did, under no circumstances would we meet up, talk to, or hang out with, anyone who had eyes of fire. Life, I thought, would then be very simple.

"Well, that's shutting the stable door after the horse has bolted, as Mum would say," I told the boys.

Their ears flicked, but nothing else happened. I tried again.

"Time to get up, you lazy louts. I have a date tonight because I didn't have the courage to tell him I was already seeing someone, and somehow I have to get through it in one piece. That'll be fun."

I hauled myself onto my feet and Manny came too. Smudge refused, so I carried him home.

At home I filled the spa with hot water. All right, so I'd had a long shower that morning after the gym, but I had gone walking since then. I didn't want to get involved with Will, but I also had standards to maintain. I wasn't about to go out looking only half the woman I could be, regardless of the bruising.

So I soaked for ages, allowing the warmth and the jets to relax the rest of my bruised muscles. Things weren't looking as bad as Monday. I healed very well; a mild compensation for bruising so easily.

I had to dress for the occasion. I could reassure myself I wasn't giving him mixed signals if I stuck to conservative and reserved. So out came the trusty high necked, long sleeved dress of a deep shade of brown, which said a million things, none of which were 'jump me'. While I found him superbly attractive, I'd just had the evening of a life time with a man who may or may not be someone I wanted in my life for some time. I wasn't about to do my usual thing and stuff that up.

At exactly seven, Will was out the front at the security gate. Instead of buzzing him in, I went out. I wasn't too sure what would happen if I let him into my apartment. I had all these good intentions, but I wasn't known for having the backbone to follow through with them.

He was dressed in black trousers, dark blue shirt and dark blazer. He looked so edible I almost swallowed my tongue. I was greeted with a kiss on the cheek and a red rose.

"You look about as wonderful as a woman recently beaten up can be."

His eyes gleamed with mischief. I wasn't about to bite. He could tease all he wanted.

"Thank you. Where are we going?"

I felt like asking 'what exactly are we doing?' Of course I was a glorious picture of womanhood and of course any man would fall under my spell and want to take me out (well, in my dreams). But I had the sneaking suspicion Will was a businessman and I knew something about his sort of business these days.

"I thought we could go to the Tower."

He held open the car door and I slid inside. It was a late model Mercedes and everything smelled deliciously of leather.

The Tower sounded good. It had a lovely view of Canberra, a revolving restaurant and usually full of people. It was the alone aspects of this date which were going to prove to be interesting. I wasn't sure of his angle and suddenly I wished I'd told at least one person who I was going out with. Possibly even Jonelle.

Then I remembered her walking out talking with Amelia and my internal bitch growled. No way was I going to explain my every move to her! There was the slight chance he just wanted to date me. But if it came out that he just wanted information, well two could play at that game.

"Marvellous. I love the Tower."

I tried to purr; after all it is far easier to catch a bee with honey than vinegar someone once told me. I didn't think I was qualified to play the siren, but was happy enough to give it a go. I flicked him a glance out of the corner of my eye and caught the edges of a smile. Well, that was something anyway.

In a machine like the Mercedes it didn't take long to get there. Will leapt out and came to open my door. Usually I'd have not waited, but if I was going to play the femme fatale then I had to be prepared to be waited on. I fluttered him a smile through lowered lashes.

What was I getting myself into? There was usually a price associated with this sort of behaviour. One I was not willing to pay. I wondered what Jonelle had done (apart from kill people) in the name of getting information.

In the lift, Will took my hand and stroked my palm. It was a gentle gesture, which would have been reassuring coming from anyone else. If he was hoping to lull me into a false sense of security, he was badly mistaken. My stomach was fluttering with a whole herd of butterflies (are they a herd?) and I could feel my brain starting to kick into overdrive. At least it was awake.

"Mr Malone. Madam. A pleasure again, Sir."

The maitre d' was a picture of genuine service; I wondered if he knew what Will did for a living. We were shown to a table well away from the other customers. For the show I was about to put on, and hopefully the gleaming of some relevant information, I was glad of this.

Did plans always go awry? Or was it just me?

I was determined not to be the patsy. That instead of being the one pumped for information, I would do the ... er... pumping. So okay, the terminology left a lot to be desired. But the gist of it was I wanted to have something to tell Jonelle when she got back. I was sick of being one (may be two) steps behind all the time. It would be nice to be the one with the news.

My evening wasn't what I expected. Will determinedly turned the conversation from work every time I tried to press. He would smile that lovely charming smile, but give nothing away. Nor did he ask for anything either. I found us talking about skiing, and horse riding, and times at the beach.

It was terrible! How could I possibly stay on the alert and hoard information if the silly man wasn't even trying? Didn't he know the rules? People on opposite sides were meant to be a bit rougher with each other.

I tried the siren thing: the demanding woman, the toy, everything in albeit my limited arsenal. All he did was twinkle at me and move the topic on. So I started to drink. Lovely, sweet wine of the best vintage.

At eleven Will helped me to my feet and took me back down the elevator. This time there was no gentle hand holding. I found myself backed into the corner, regardless of the security camera, and Will's hungry, hot mouth descended onto mine. I felt the cold metal sides pressed against my back. I could feel his hands, holding my shoulders, pressing me back and his body blocking me in.

Then all I could feel was his mouth. All my senses zeroed in on that one thing. Firm lips and a probing tongue which invited me to play.

I was two bottles down. My body was surviving on leftover hormones from the night before and this morning's romp. I was only human. I gave a protesting little groan, then grabbed a handful of his shirt and pulled him closer. Bees, honey, and vinegar, went swirling through my mind and I applied myself to being the honey pot.

He was breathing hard by the time the elevator bell pinged for the ground floor. Eyes glittering, and faint pink on his dusky cheeks. Well, perhaps we didn't have to be that deep a honey pot. I slipped out and set the pace back to the car. Will caught up and swung me round so I crashed heavily against his chest. My siren call hadn't elicited any information, but it was getting me into a bucket load of hot water.

Somehow we made it back to the car. I even made it with all my clothes intact. Will gunned the engine and drove us back to the Grangelands at illegal speeds. The alcoholic fog that had enveloped my mind was swept away. I glanced over at him. He was driving in a mildly throttled manner which made me think I was in bigger trouble than I'd even been before. I wished Jonelle was at home: that *I* was at home. I had stepped off the cliff with a lion and if his claws didn't kill me, then the landing at the end just might.

Will's hand left the wheel and he snaked his arm around my neck. I was hauled in for a snatched kissed.

"Will! Not at this speed."

My heart was racing, fear spiking it wildly.

He laughed low and screeched the car into the visitor's car park. I was pulled roughly into his lap, witness to his heady need. What was it with men? I cooled my instant response. I had to get out of this. He opened the car door and somehow I found myself in his arms, being carried to the gate. Bloody hell.

But that's when his fortunes fell apart. Thank God for small mercies. We made it to the gate, me dodging more kisses, when sound hit us like a ton of bricks. There was a party going on in the courtyard, and all I had to do was make it inside and I was safe. He changed directions mighty fast.

"Will. Stop it. This is ridiculous. Put me down." I thumped him across the shoulders.

"You spend all night teasing a guy, what were you looking for? A medal?" He slanted a look at me.

How much did I hate humble pie?

"You were meant to be putty in my paws, not rearing to go."

He put me down and I straightened my dress.

"Look, I was so sure you would want the inside scoop to Jonelle, I was determined to get the low down on you first."

I could feel the heat rising in my cheeks. Damn it all, this was worse than I imagined. Subtlety thy name was not Fiona. I had to make a clean breast of it.

"You weren't meant to be quite so aggressive, you know." I hoped that tone was right. It was meant to be indignant. Who knew what I hit. Probably more like terror.

He stood there in the street light looking down at me. Thinking. Then with a mercurial change of mood, Will Malone threw back his head and burst out laughing.

"You thought I was going to dig for information? Honey, I know Jonelle. I've worked with her. You probably know less about what is going on around here than I do. Why on earth would I be here to gather information?"

All right so when he put it like that, I felt like the biggest fool in history. The man was linked with a large club of dangerous men and I'd had the enormous ego to assume he wanted information. Well, at least I hadn't had the ego to assume he wanted *me*! Which, as it turned out, was the case. Wonders never ceased. How was I meant to know these things?

Will shook his head.

"Sweetheart, believe me, I wasn't looking to find out anything except if you were half the handful I thought you might be."

I caught his eye. He was desperately sexy. He leaned down and kissed me softly.

"You call me if you change your mind, okay?" And all that masculinity walked back to his car.

"Wait!" There had to be compensation for my elevated heart rate. "If I know less than you, you tell *me* something."

Anything would be better than thinking I found out nothing except he wanted to make crazy hot sex with me.

He turned back. "Who was Brenda sleeping with before she got killed? Find your Mr X and there you just may have the solution. The question is, was she killed because of who she slept with or for an entirely different reason?"

He opened the car door.

"Jonelle is fixated on Brenda knowing something that got her killed. I'm all for a one tracked mind," he flashed me a grin, "but what she knew may not have anything to do with this new drug at all. Just because it would be convenient and Jonelle found some on Tomas doesn't mean anything. Cast your net wider." Then he was gone.

I stood in the shadows uncharacteristically thinking deep thoughts. What if we had it all wrong? Maybe I needed to be looking at this from a different angle, one Jonelle couldn't see because, as Will said, she was all wrapped up with Jack, Amelia, The Way and The Rose. What if Lilly and her boy, Francis, were protecting something else entirely? And just how much had the Chemist told Will?

Enough for him to make sweeping statements about people he shouldn't have known anything about. Information was leaking out everywhere. I needed to go back to Jonelle's files and re-read Brenda's case. She'd mentioned I should do that a while back, but I had never gotten around to it. Hey – I'd been busy! I'd put it on my 'to-do' list.

I set those thoughts aside and went in. The laughter and music flooding out of the courtyard was an irresistible lure; the two bottles of wine Will and I had partly shared (mainly because he didn't drink all that much) had been washed away with the adrenalin. Now I was ready for the post-Will party. I'd survived: scathed but okay.

Everyone was home. And I mean everyone. Even our elusive Amy. Plus Grillia and Steph and, more surprisingly still, Brad. He saw me come in and ducked his head a little. I'd warned him I needed to be alone! But I was so glad to see him, my hormones still pounding through my system, I couldn't be mad.

"Fi!" Grillia came over and thrust a glass into my hands. "Where have you been? Amy came back early, and I brought Steph over to see you and you weren't here!"

The rapid fire of Grillia could only come from way too much alcohol. They'd been at it for a while then I could surmise. I took a gulp.

"Hey." It was Steph. "What happened to your face?"

I'd forgotten no one had seen my new face.

"Accident. Minor, and I feel heaps better." I turned to Amy, as the other two drew me deeper into the party. "What's going on? Isn't your police course three months?"

With all the illegal activities floating around here, the last thing we needed was a cop.

Amy skulled down more colourful liquid.

"Well, it was. But I took myself off that. I don't know if I'm cut out to be an instructor after all."

Amy was well-heeled, but had always wanted to save the world. So she'd become a policewoman and was continually doing courses to improve herself and make her a better cop. Her edge was slowly being lost and I didn't think it would be too long before she resigned.

I gave her a hug then made my way through the rest of them to Brad.

"Sorry. I just couldn't stay at home and I came over to see if you wouldn't mind getting together after all. Heather told me she'd seen you go out earlier. I hope you don't mind that I stayed." He looked a little sheepish and very adorable.

Reaching up on tiptoe I gave him a smacker of a kiss. It was the least I could do, really.

"Not at all." I had plans for him later.

Later was a whole lot later. In fact, we stumbled into my apartment somewhere on the shady side of four. My plans had long since run out of puff. But I'd had a very interesting evening.

After the first shot of alcohol from Grillia, I'd filled my glass with lemonade. Everyone danced and sang and in general, made loud fools of themselves. I, on the other hand, stalked my prey.

Heather stood leaning against the side of the BBQ area. She had a drink nestled in her hands, but as I watched she barely took a sip. She was laughing at the game of Rider going on in the pool. The boys had paired up and each rider was trying to push the other from the shoulders of their 'horse'. I wasn't too sure about the rules of alcohol and pools, but it seemed harmless enough.

Eventually, with lots of stops, to be gawked at or commiserated with about my face, I made it round to Heather. I leaned next to her, trying for a sense of camaraderie, laughing with her at the boys.

She looked at me. "Hey Fi. Nasty face girl." Everyone had to be a funny man.

"How are you Heath? Haven't seen you in ages." I tried for the smooth subtle lines of conversation that had never been my forte.

She giggled.

"You're too busy with your newest toy, or two." Huh? She'd lost me.

"You know, Brad and Jonelle. Everyone sees how inseparable you've become with them." She looked sideways at me.

Bugger me, had they really?

"Well, we should break that. What about you and I go have lunch tomorrow? We could have a good old gossip and shop till we drop. I haven't done any retail therapy for ages and I think, of anyone here, I really deserve it."

I hadn't had time because of my two *toys*, as they put it. Anyway, if they knew the truth, I was more the toy in these games than the other way round. But I wasn't about to tell Heather that now, was I? It would destroy what credibility I had left.

Heather took a long swallow and stood up. I realised that she may have been sipping this drink, but it was far away from her first. She positively swayed as she left the strength of the wall.

"Sure, lunch tomorrow. See you then, Fi." And she wondered vaguely off in search of some more lubrication.

Yes! I'd hit the jack pot. Heather was all mine for several hours at least, in a hung over and vulnerable state. If I couldn't capitalise on that, then Jonelle was free to sack me.

So while I stumbled home at four and couldn't do my 'toy' justice, I went to sleep with that warm glowing feeling which told me I had a reason to be getting up in the morning. Once more I was on the case, hoping that my inexperience would still lead me to the answer.

Ten o'clock in the morning is a hideous hour if you went to bed at four. I struggled into consciousness, feeling the weight of Brad's arm slung across my chest. Peeling it off, I made my way into the ensuite for a shower. My eyes refused to open and I had a lovely dry mouth full of residue fumes. But I had a lunch date and it was one I wouldn't miss for anything.

There was no morning sex. Even though we might have had more time, Brad was still zonked out when I was leaving. I left a note on the counter telling him I was out with Heather and I would be back mid afternoon. Even without much sleep, I was feeling wide awake. Like the thrill of the hunt was flooding my veins.

Heather was barely awake, but still quite happy to head for the shops. Kingston and Manuka offer some classy and very expensive boutique style shopping. It wasn't until I was in the first shoe shop did I realise how long it had been since I'd done anything remotely sane - like shop. It was delicious.

"Fi!" Heather was finally conscious and in full shop mode herself. "Those shoes are gorgeous. You have to get them."

Though of course neither of us could think of one single thing that bright orange, three inch suede heels would go with. But she was right, no matter how hideous that may sound, the shoes themselves were lovely. I tottered around the shop, feeling I had finally joined the rest of the world in my elevated inches.

Three pairs of shoes later we left. I loved going out with a fellow shoe nut. I just couldn't see Jonelle entering into the spirit of it all.

"I think I need coffee before we try anything in the clothes line." Heather steered me towards an outdoor café. She plopped down in the sun. "We should do this sort of thing more often." She grinned at me. "Unless you can't tear yourself away from Brad."

I snorted. That sort of comment didn't deserve a reply.

"Is it serious?" she asked, while studying the menu.

What was it with my friends? They just couldn't keep their noses out. It conveniently slipped my mind the many times I'd pried into their lives.

"Well..." I wasn't too sure of the answer to that question. But suddenly having a girlfriend right there to unload on was too good to pass up.

"I thought it would be nice to have someone around, you know, it can get lonely now that what's his name is gone."

I really couldn't bring to mind who my last guy was. Brad and Jonelle had slipped into my consciousness and thoroughly pushed out everyone else. Minus the bumps and bruises, and the sheer terror of the idea of the knives and potential injuries I could sustain, it had to be the best month of my life. Sad thought that, in some ways. My life had been *that* devoid of anything remotely considered interesting...

"Now he's been around quite a bit and I'm starting to think it would be kind of good to keep him." That sounded a lot like he was a pet. "He's fun and we have a good time together. And the other day, I thought wouldn't it be nice to wake up to this forever?" I leaned forward and whispered that to her, like it was a monumental secret.

Heather smiled. "It's not such a bad thing, you know. I often wish I'd married David when he asked. Being alone as I wanted to be at the time has more than lost its appeal. And I am a fair bit older than you."

Well, when she said fair bit, she meant four years. I guessed a thirty three year old had a different perspective than someone at twenty nine.

"I remember Dave. Why exactly did you give him his marching orders?" I could remember that too, but asking gave me the lead into the conversation I was hoping for.

Her face closed up and became sad. I could learn to hate myself.

"My sister had just died and I wanted to deal with that. Dave was keen to move to England for a few years and earn pounds. He left shortly after I refused to marry him. I was kind of a mess, if you can remember. Loosing Brenda and then Dave. If I could have the time again, I'd go with him. I needed the support, which I wasn't getting from anywhere else."

"What about your parents? Couldn't they have stepped in and helped you?"

I was a bitch and then some. But how else was I going to show I was made of serious stuff if I couldn't interrogate my own mates with a hard heart? You had to start somewhere and at home was as good a place as any.

Heather was shaking her head.

"They refused to speak to me when I told them I was going to her funeral. They never agreed with her on the choices she made and never mentioned her at home either. They warned me I was on my own." She looked up at me from her intense study of the table. Her eyes were glittering and hollow.

"Someone who loved her had to be there. Nothing she'd ever done in life could justify letting her to go to rest alone."

She was silent. I bit my lip. Maybe this wasn't something I wanted to follow through with. The pain in Heather's voice was still so real and raw. Her parents sounded a right royal pair of bastards. So, chicken that I was, I changed the subject. In moments we were back to laughing about shoes and shopping, and Brad's capacity in the mornings… though her eyes still had that haunted look in them which made my stomach lurch.

"Okay, the next leg of our morning is clothes, then lunch."

I was determinedly cheerful, dragging Heather to her feet before we'd totally finished our coffee. I didn't want to sit there and try to figure out another way back to the former conversation. That way would lead to me wanting to cut my own wrists.

Both of us got new suits, several shirts and knitted tops to match. I even managed to score a lovely new handbag which was truly a darling. It didn't matter that I had a closet full of them, when a new one came out that made me ache to hold it I had to buy the damn thing.

"That's it! I can't do anymore. We've got to have lunch." Heather put her foot down when I picked up my fourth shopping bag. "Fiona, how can you possibly have enough space for anymore of this stuff?" She looked around my bags. "Your place can't take it all surely."

"You'd be surprised how much I can shove into the spare rooms.

But you're right of course. We need a break. Lunch and then I have to go and see a friend of mine who works in Mitchell." Her eyebrows went up. "It won't take long, I promise. And I hate having to end a day like this all on my own."

Okay, so that was lame. And I didn't know anyone who worked in Mitchell. But I knew that Brenda was buried out there, courtesy of Jonelle's informative files. So, I wouldn't be able to live with myself, but what was new? Not finding anything out to report to Jonelle wouldn't leave me feeling wonderful either.

Lunch over we headed back to the car. It took quite a bit of coaxing before everything fitted into my convertible, but finally we were off.

What was it with me and trying to be clever? My heart rate was climbing and my hands were slippery on the wheel. I had to make this appear natural. Heather had to think she was just handing over casual information which wouldn't be used by anyone in particular. Times like this made me wish I had that poker face after all.

I drove us to Mitchell. Mitchell is an industrial suburb. Gardening needs and car servicing and other such things. Not a lot for a rich playgirl like me. So I hoped Heather wasn't thinking too clearly. What she possibly thought I'd have to do there was beyond me. So I drove round a bit and found a shopfront that was open.

"Won't be a second." I leaped out before she could offer to come with me.

I could almost feel the stiltedness of my walk. My whole body was shouting that I was making this up as I went along, but when I glanced back, Heather had her head leaning on the rest and her eyes closed. Great, she was half asleep. I'd have to do some fancy driving and wake her back up before we passed the cemetery or it'd have been for nothing.

I wandered into 'Red's Autos' and looked around. Truly nothing there to excite the shopper in me. I rushed back out again. I didn't care to think what the guy behind the desk was thinking. Heather was still resting her eyes, so I shouldn't have bothered.

Jumping back into the car, I slammed the door to give her a jolt. The whole thing was up the proverbial creek if she wasn't awake.

"Do you have to be so loud?" she grumbled.

Well, yes.

"Sorry Heather. When we get you home you can sleep the rest of the afternoon." I took off. "Do you know if we have any plans with the gang tonight?"

I was going for the whole relaxed and natural, cool as a cucumber approach.

We swept through the deserted streets, heading right to the cemetery. The road went passed the front gates. There was a roundabout there which gave me the perfect opportunity to brake and creep.

"Have you been to see your sister?" Casual, keep it casual.

"Not for ages actually, would you mind?" Heather indicated the left hand turn.

Perfect, hardly any subterfuge needed. So I slammed on the brakes and swung into the quiet serenity of the immaculate lawns and sculptured gardens. Not a lot going on, for which I was grateful.

Parking the car in the empty car park, I let Heather take the lead. I had no idea where Brenda was actually buried. As it turned out, nowhere. Heather led me to a plaque set in the ground. I think Jonelle's files needed to be more specific.

"Brenda always told me that she didn't want to take up a lot of space. So she was cremated and I scattered the ashes down by the sea. She'd picked this plaque out as something she might like, six months before she died. We were just laughing about it, but she seemed kind of resigned and sad at the same time."

Heather knelt by the marble and ran her fingers around the edge. "I should have seen she was in trouble." There was a slight catch in her voice.

My self image took another dive.

"What happened to her?" I whispered, trying not to break into the moment, but using it nonetheless.

She sighed, sitting back on her heels. "I shouldn't tell anyone." Heather looked up at me. "Though, it'd be nice to tell *someone*. You won't tell anyone else, will you?"

Ah, the promises that were dragged out of me. Of course I would and how was I going to make her believe otherwise? My lying little face would dob me in straight away. So, novel to the situation, I chose not to lie at all.

"Well, you know me. I'd have to tell at least one person. But that was all."

Heather half laughed. "Yeah. And a month or so ago I would

have thought it would be Steph or Grillia, but now I guess it will be Brad or Jonelle. Would you mind very much if I asked you to only talk to Jonelle? I don't want some random man involved and I won't feel so bad if it's a woman."

I didn't put the words in her mouth. They just came pouring out, like a gift. Permission to tell Jonelle everything she was about to divulge. I wasn't going to let her know that Jonelle was the one person who could do anything about it, and was more interested than all of the others put together.

What Jonelle was and who Brenda was to Jonelle, well, that was something only Jonelle could tell her. So I sat in the sun warmed grass with Brenda's sister, who had tears glittering in her eyes, promising her faithfully that absolutely no one would hear about this from me except Jonelle, and prepared to listen to whatever it was Brenda had told her.

Heather crossed her legs and we sat, Indian style, across the plaque from each other.

"I came to Canberra because I knew Brenda was here. I got a phone call from her telling me she was sorry for all the trouble she'd caused at home and she would like to see me again. I'd always missed her. I'd been angry, but not at what she was doing, more at how it had affected the family. I was younger then and wanted everyone to get along. I couldn't believe our parents were still so adamant about her not coming home."

She looked at me. I tried not to let it show on my face that I knew anything about what she was telling me. I only hoped my eyes didn't give the game away.

"You see, Brenda had become a hooker. And some time in there, they'd managed to get her hooked on drugs. I was never too sure what it was, she didn't talk about it."

I was pretty sure as to what it had become. The Way danced in front of my eyes, dazzling me. This was priceless information. Even so, I was aware that my friend and apartmate was struggling with terrible emotions. It cut me to be the cause, but I tried to salvage my pride by convincing myself Jonelle was the one person who could avenge any wrong. What Heather was telling me was, in the long run, the best thing she could do.

"She called our parents in the beginning, all the time. I know that if they had only forgiven her and let her come home, she wouldn't have turned to the drugs. I couldn't understand why she'd become a hooker at all. So when Brenda called me and wanted me to come to Canberra for a little while to visit, I did. I wanted answers and I certainly wasn't going to get them sitting at home."

I imagined how emotional that reunion had been.

"I turned up and she installed me in a motel. I didn't want to ask where all the money came from, it felt embarrassing, but I knew that was why she had brought me here. To talk about it and see if I could get the folks to relent. What could I tell her? They had taken her photo out of the family albums? Seeing as she would never come home again, I thought that was something she didn't need to know." Heather's eyes pleaded with me.

"You did right, Heath. How could you tell your sister something so horrible? You protected her from that, at least."

I wondered what sort of parents they were. Some people didn't have the right to bring up lovely, independent little people. They ended up making screwed up and not so independent big people.

Heather smiled at me, though her thoughts were obviously somewhere else entirely.

"Thanks. I couldn't do it and I'm glad I didn't. There was enough pain without adding to it. I hadn't seen her for some time. The changes in her were amazing. Brenda had always tended towards slightly chubby, tall and elegant, but chubby. Her hair was more red than blonde, like mine. The woman who met me off the plane had had all the fat carved off her. Her facial bones were visible and everything about her looked elongated and refined. Brenda had dyed her hair a beautiful platinum and she wore such obviously expensive and stylish clothes."

She twisted the blades of grass through her fingers. I resisted the urge to glance at my watch. It wasn't as though I had somewhere I needed to be. It was more the case of wondering how long she could hold it together enough to tell me the rest.

She continued her story.

"We spent a couple of days just hanging out. I think she was officially on holiday, if you could call it that. She was jumpy and laughed sort of strangely. But eventually she told me how she wasn't just a hooker, she was the prize in a particularly good 'stable' as she called it. She was the number one call girl, and made herself and her Madam loads of money.

"Gentlemen, and I use that term loosely considering half of them were married or otherwise occupied, came from all over and paid big bucks to spend a night or two in my sister's arms. She told me some horror stories and how her Madam had hired this tough guy, called Francis, to keep her safe. However, the one time she thought about leaving, they'd spiked her full of drugs and now she had a habit the lifestyle was feeding. I felt so sorry for her. But she didn't want me to. Brenda was very happy to be making so much money. It was like a retirement plan she couldn't retire from. It broke my heart.

"She helped me get the place at Grangelands. I couldn't have afforded it by myself. She told me it was an investment for her. She asked me to stay. I couldn't say no and our parents were already mad at me for coming to visit, so I stayed. She worked a lot of hours, but I did get to spend time with her." Heather's voice became wistful. It was obvious she still missed her big sister a lot.

"In the end, we didn't have as long as I'd hoped. Nowhere near the forever we'd planned. She started to lose even more weight. It was weird. I asked her what the matter was. But she was too jumpy to talk about it. I knew she had loads of clients who were breaking all sorts of vows to be with her, so I assumed it was one of them giving her a hard time. I begged her to go to her Madam with the problem. And she only laughed. I guess it was silly. If they were paying the market price, why on earth would the Madam make waves?

"Just a week before she was killed, she called me in a panic and begged me to meet her. I was to be her insurance, against what I didn't know."

I tried to look shocked and must have succeeded.

"Oh, you didn't know how Brenda died? Someone murdered her in the end. I wasn't told all the details by the police, but I think she may have been with a client, as I overheard the question of rape and the disinclination of them to pursue that aspect because of what she did for a living. Someone had had sex with her and then strangled her to death. And they used a condom so there was no DNA. Just her - naked, roughed up and very very dead."

I was glad I hadn't read that. I may not have had the courage to push Heather to tell me all about something like that if I had known in advance. Who did these things? Well, obviously male people who had different ideas of what was acceptable. Somewhat like Jonelle, but without the conscience I was hoping she had.

I wondered briefly what the worse thing she'd ever done was, then turned my mind off it. That was something I really didn't want to know. And it wasn't something I could very well come out and ask her either. I mean, what did you say?

'Excuse me Jonelle, but after listening to Heather talk about how her sister died, I was wondering how you kill the people you go after?' Not a conversation I was ever going to indulge in, though maybe I should.

"Anyway, the day she called me -" Heather was back on the true confessions and I brought my wandering attention home to the conversation at hand.

"I met her in a park and she made us sit as far away from everyone else as possible. I'd never seen Brenda so wired. It was frightening. I wanted to calm her down, do something, but I could only listen. She had this client. Two actually. One was a priest and the other was in a bike gang."

Bells rang in my head. Maybe Will wasn't as far off track as I'd thought. And maybe he knew a lot more than he had let on and was sitting back laughing his head off. He could have saved Heather all this trouble, and me for that matter, by just confessing what was going on right from the start.

"These two men knew each other well and somehow they both knew about the other seeing Brenda. It was a game, a joke, that they could share someone, them being on opposite sides as they called it. The Hound and the Priest. Brenda told me that one evening, after she had spent some time with the priest, the hound turned up. For extra money, they shared her with the other right there. She told me it was a bit weird and made her uncomfortable, but they wouldn't take no for an answer.

"Afterwards, they started talking. She went and had a shower, but she could hear them when she got out. They were discussing a bishop and how the priest wanted this bishop removed. She heard them say how easy it would be to drug him and take photos of him with Brenda. And if that didn't work, perhaps the hound could do the job more permanently.

"They were very involved with their plotting. Brenda glossed over a lot of it, but I think they were explicit on times, days and what should be done if something else didn't work. They left together, but Brenda remembered seeing the hound look back as the priest closed the door. She said the look on his face promised her another visit; especially if she mentioned a word of it. He put a finger to his lips, then pointed it at her like a gun. She'd just overheard plans to have a man framed for using a prostitute, if not murdered outright.

"I could see she was shaking and scared. They'd paid a lot of money, and her Madam was looking to match them up together with Brenda soon. Brenda was terrified that the hound would silence her. She didn't think anyone could protect her from him. She told me she hadn't even mentioned this to her boyfriend."

Whoa! I really needed to get back to those files. A boyfriend? I couldn't picture it myself, but I guess it was something that could happened. Though if she was working so many hours, it was amazing she had time (or inclination) for a boyfriend.

"Boyfriend?" I had to ask. After all, what if I got back to Jonelle's and there wasn't anything in the file about a boyfriend? I would be the only one with this vital information.

"She told me she'd been seeing a guy called Craig. He was upset about her career choice and was working hard so she could get out. He wanted to provide for her. Which was very sweet but old fashioned, in Brenda's eyes.

"According to Brenda, Craig was strong on the idea of them not having sex until she'd changed her profession and become a 'virgin' again, by sleeping alone for six months. She found that quaint."

Really? I would have found him a freak. But then again, after meeting the kind of people she had through her job, I guess Brenda was looking for salvation. Even through some nutty bloke she picked up. But it gave us a new avenue to explore.

Heather had a small tear slowly leaking down her cheek. It followed the lines of her face and stopped on her jaw. Then it dropped to the ground. I watched in fascination.

Reading a file and listening to someone personally involved were two such separate events! It was all so raw, and real and personal. I wanted to find a hole somewhere and crawl into it. I couldn't imagine ever becoming hardened to this; open emotion and prying into someone's personal pain. For that matter, I didn't want to become hardened to it. I reached across the plaque and took her white, cold hand. It certainly wasn't fake sympathy, but somehow I still felt a fraud.

"She didn't happen to mention either of the others by name, did she? You know the priest or the hound?" I tried to give my voice just normal curiosity, not the burning fever of importance that was sitting behind it.

Heather wiped her eyes with her other hand. "She was trying hard to say everything, but nothing. She didn't want me to get into trouble. After that meeting, I didn't hear from her for two days. I was a bit frantic when I couldn't get her on the mobile number she'd given me. But I did speak to her once more before she was killed."

I was almost panting in frustration. I hated this – couldn't she just get to the point before I caved and took us home for an afternoon glass of wine?

"Just a few days before I found the police going through her things, Brenda called me. She said she didn't have much time, but she wanted me to know she loved me, and she knew I had risked everything with the family to come and live in Canberra with her. She told me that no one knew she had a sister and she had left everything she owned to me, but secretly through her lawyers, so I would be protected. I thought all these precautions were stupid and I told her so. Brenda just laughed at me and told me she was going out with the two of them once more. The Madam wanted her to get the double money. She told me that the hound was the right hand to the top man and she didn't think she would be seeing me again. It all sounded so melodramatic."

Heather's voice sounded now as though she was seeking forgiveness; for not taking it all more seriously and leaving her sister to die.

"She said she'd been speaking to another friend she knew and that person was hell bent on keeping her safe, but she hadn't let on who or why she was in trouble. Only to me. And she wouldn't tell me who this other person was. Somehow, Brenda had got herself so mixed up with all these horrid and wicked people, and the drugs, she just didn't know where to turn or who to trust. And when I went to her funeral, and saw the people who came and looked into their eyes, I agreed. Who could you trust out of them all? I didn't push and I'll regret it forever. I just told her not to be silly and I'd talk to her tomorrow, except there was no tomorrow. And I've been too scared ever since to tell anyone." Little beads of sweat had gathered on her forehead.

Was I in any position to blame her? If I didn't know Jonelle, and had just heard all that, I probably would have put it down to an overactive imagination. Except Brenda was dead. And it looked like Will's main man, whoever that turned out to be, was the reason. Him, and some faceless, nameless priest.

Knowledge was a powerful tool. And Jonelle was the person Brenda had turned to who hadn't been able to save her in the end. Someone she could have trusted with the whole story, but had played dumb with and it had got her killed.

I vowed to confess about my date with Will and this whole conversation to Jonelle the minute she got home. It was too scary to imagine the sort of trouble I could get into without her. I wouldn't make the same mistake as Brenda. I'd trust her. I'd throw my lot completely in with Jonelle, and make sure she kept the Devil and his playmates as far away from me as possible.

I was very cold. Death was walking beside me and had been now for a month. I may have started out with some strange ideas of how this game was played, but there were people dying and that cut away the delusions pretty fast. I couldn't back out and I didn't think I wanted to; but I knew it wasn't an amusement any more. It was for real and for deadly earnest; these people were playing for keeps. I felt a little queasy.

Heather suddenly stood up.

"I think we should go home. I'm really not comfortable sitting out here all alone. I don't think they know Brenda's sister is in town, but what if they find out? I go to work, I hang out with you lot and I stay at home."

I hadn't really noticed, but now she mentioned it, I never did see Heather just going out visiting people. It was like house arrest.

"I know it's not a great way to live, but I can't seem to leave the last place we hung out together. And it's not like I can just go home to Sydney. I don't know what the police told Mum and Dad, but they haven't tried to make contact with me, even now she's gone."

Some people hold grudges! I didn't think she was wrong though. Lilly might not know if someone out there knew what was going on, but she would be more than happy to have me or Jonelle lead her to Heather. Then, there was the hound himself and the priest.

"Aren't you just that little bit sick of hiding? If you can't go back to Sydney, what about somewhere else you could get lost in? Say Melbourne or the rest of the world?" If someone wanted to stay lost, surely it couldn't be that hard?

We walked slowly back to the car.

"I had thought of leaving, but everything about Brenda is here. Plus, it scares me to think like this, but wouldn't it be nice if I could find out who these bastards are and have some justice done?"

We made it into the car and yes, I was starting to feel a bit safer, but not with that last sentence hanging in the air.

"Just how were you expecting to put a thing like that into action? No, I think it's best if you let it lie."

I wanted desperately to let her know that Jonelle would soon be on the case and Will Malone was set up for a very awkward interview with her, but my tongue was tied. Plus, there was no point in raising her hopes if we couldn't get anything done about it in the end.

Chapter Eighteen

Driving back to the Grangelands was a very subdued affair. Maybe she was thinking hard about everything she'd said to me; and regretting that choice.

Me? I was watching my mirrors, making sure no one looked to be following us. Mind you, what was I going to do about it exactly? The greatest weapon I had was my phone and Jonelle was, to my knowledge, not exactly within hollering distance. I didn't think I could use the car as a weapon; the idea of impact with a soft squishy human body made my skin crawl. I had a long way to go.

"Thanks for the day out." Heather turned to me as we pulled up in my space. "And for listening to all that stuff. I've hated not being able to tell any of you. I just hope you will limit that knowledge as well."

She looked drawn and suddenly much older than her thirty three years. I felt like a mole. She leaned over and gave me a hug then jumped out. Our one on one time was over and it was time to put our normal faces back on for the world. We grabbed our various shopping bags, then decamped for our units.

It was late afternoon and I'd have preferred to head inside for a nap, but duty called. I had a dog to walk and because everyone else had slept the day away, there would be a party for sure this evening. I just didn't know where. I hoped it wouldn't be here, so if I needed to come home and sleep I could escape the noise.

Manny greeted me with the usual over enthusiasm. At least someone in my life would never be sick of the sight of me. No matter what I did, Manny would love me, as long as I fed and walked him. So that's exactly what I did, after dumping all my bags in the spare room to be sorted out later. This time I left Smudge at home, as he was contentedly curled up watching his own tail.

What with the gym in the mornings and now a dog to walk, if I didn't get fit soon it wouldn't be for lack of trying. Then there was stress and trying to eat more healthily, though that came in fits and starts. It was quicker just to munch whatever came my way.

It was getting on toward five thirty by the time Manny dragged me back into the apartment. Smudge had flaked out, his tail no longer enough to keep his attention span focused. Manny went over and stuck his long nose into the ball of fur, receiving a tiny swipe in greeting. It was nice to see how my newly made family was getting along.

Steph was sitting by the pool smoking with Todd and John. I waved, but needed to feed my guys first. Once they were happily chowing down on the best Pal and Whiskas could offer, I went out to join the others.

"What's the happening thing tonight?"

My body groaned, but quietly and on the inside. The party girl who'd ruled the roost was nowhere to be seen these days. I thought about her for a brief second and tried to think of what she'd be up to. But I could hardly bring her to mind and I didn't really miss her.

Steph blew some smoke in my general direction.

"Not a lot. I think some of us are headed down to The Batch and Haddock for a couple of quiet ones, but after the lateness of last night, it won't be a huge one."

It looked as though it wasn't just me who was finding the long hauls a bit too much. I was eternally grateful.

I glanced over at Jonelle's place, but the blinds were drawn and the place had an empty and unloved look about it. She hadn't come back early and it was silly of me to wish she had. There was too much for her to be doing in Sydney or wherever Amelia had taken her. There was that little part of me that wished my inner bitch wasn't such a loud voice in my ear. I couldn't even say; 'I'm sure Amelia was a nice person', because it was exactly the opposite.

"You coming?" Steph asked, idly watching Todd in that somewhat predatory way she had sometimes.

I tried not to giggle. Who was the sillier one? Steph caught my eye and shrugged.

"It's been a while."

All of a couple of weeks since the last one threw her out. The girl was mad. Then there had been that brief shocking entanglement with

Tamara. The devil in me came out to play.

"How is Tamara going?" I asked quite loudly.

Both Todd's and John's heads came up and round real fast. Steph shot me a deadly look through half closed kohl thick eyes. I did giggle then. Settling myself in the recliner next to Steph, I allowed myself to relax. I hadn't realised until then how much Heather's story had wound me up. It was lovely to sit and not think, watching my male Apartmates surround Steph and demand gory details about her woman.

Shortly more of us arrived and by the time seven rocked around, most of the usual suspects were all assembled, some in better condition than others. Brad had left me a note saying that he was busy after all and would swing round when he had the chance.

I wasn't too fussed. I wanted to take it slowly and not jump into anything that could be misconstrued as commitment, because that way would lead to my mother getting involved. Something I wanted to put off for as long as possible.

I was actually a bit nervous about going back to The Batch myself. Not many people knew that Tomas was dead, but his mates would by now. I hoped the ones who had helped him liberate the paintings didn't connect me with Jonelle.

I linked arms with Rob and allowed him to walk me there. He was a bit surprised by my clingy attitude, but I wasn't about to explain. Better off letting everyone think I had a crush on Rob for the night, than running into someone on my own. I liked the way his arm felt heavy and muscled under my hand. Comforting.

The Batch was packed. The noisy crowd spilled out the doors and over the pavement. A live band was thumping away inside and it was only seven thirty. A bit unusual, but we soon discovered that the Hounds were having a birthday party and had invited their favourite band to play all evening.

If I'd been nervous about running into Tomas' mates, the idea of accidentally bumping into Will or worse still, whoever was second in command, was truly terrifying. I wouldn't be able to cover up the fact that I knew something. Will would ask me all sorts of hideous questions. Who had I been kidding? I couldn't hold out if they asked me questions. I wouldn't even reach the toenail pulling stage.

Rob looked down at me. "Fiona! Loosen up, woman. You're practically taking my arm off."

I gulped. And looked at where my hand had been. Finger nail marks scored his skin.

"If Brad hadn't been around nearly every day for the last three weeks (gross exaggeration) I'd say you were half starved."

He grinned down at me, but there was a question in his eyes. Rob liked to look after me.

"I'm fine and no, I'm not starved. He's taken excellent care of me. I'm just a bit jumpy." I cast around in my mind for something to attribute this to. "People tend to gawk at my face you know. Big crowds aren't a great place for Frankenstein's Monster."

No one could quibble with the idea I might find people staring at my face a bit awkward. Suddenly I wished heartily that the evening was over. At least with Jonelle I didn't have to play let's pretend, something I wasn't up to.

We pushed our way through the throng up to the bar. For one heart stopping moment I could see through the crowd and locked eyes with Will. He was seated along the far wall, surrounded by other Hounds. But if this party was being held for his second in command, then I would assume one of the guys next to him was that man.

I glanced over at Heather. While I knew her well enough to put her face to the picture of Brenda and immediately say 'family'; would one of Brenda's clients do the same? That thought held distinct possibilities and yet how could I say anything without giving the game away? It wasn't as if he'd be looking for Brenda's little sister. I resolved to just keep an eye on her and anyone remotely gangster-ish. Not a very encouraging thought when half the bar was in that league.

Julie came up to me at that moment and distracted me from Will, which could only be a good thing.

"I think it's almost time for us to find another bar to haunt. Look at this place." She glanced around in disgust. "It's full of the type of people we try to hide from."

I could see her point.

"But Jules, it's not usually and we can walk home from here." Not usually… I suddenly had a heart attack.

Sure, there were a few muscle men and strange types here at one time or another, but not usually the entire pub in one hit. A cold chill crept up my spine. Had Will brought the pack out for the hunt?

I was suddenly very aware that Jonelle was a long way away, and my lovely and large bunch of friends were less than adequate protection, from anything, let alone what Will could throw at us. I swivelled my head around trying to find him in the crush. The seat he'd being in moments before was startlingly empty. I could feel my palms getting moist. I would much rather know where the devil was, than have him sneaking around. It was greatly unnerving.

"Looking for me?" a familiar deep voice murmured in my ear from the other side.

I jumped; no I leapt, into the air.

"Shit! Are you trying to kill me?"

Stupid question, considering. What was I going to do if he said yes? My heart was never going to get used to this sort of treatment. I was wearing it out. I remembered reading somewhere that everyone's heart has a certain number of beats they can expect it to take in their life time. If that was the case, I was using mine up at the rate of knots and I was potentially cutting years off my life. What a waste.

Will's warm hand came up to steady my poor frayed body. I was swaying on my feet faintly resembling a madwoman. Round about now I was beginning to realise just how much I was coming to rely on the stable (if you could call it that) and incredibly strong presence of Jonelle to get me through the day. A bedrock in my wonderfully chaotic world. Mind you, the *reason* it was chaotic was the same woman, but I wasn't going to let reality get in the way of my ranting.

Will's breath was dancing on my cheek as he leaned closer to hear and be heard. As yummy as the man was, I was all for my own personal space, thank you very much. He'd taught me a valuable lesson about trying to match him pace for pace.

"You'd never see me coming if that was the case, Pet." Now, where did he get off calling me that?

I swung around to face him, a startling manoeuvre considering how close he was. His eyes were mere centimetres from my own. Deep, endless blue eyes with a deceptive twinkle. I kicked him on the shin. At least that made him step back a bit, albeit with a laugh.

"You just keep your distance, Mister Will Malone." I tried to sound scarier than I looked. "What's all this mean anyway, taking over our pub with your hoodlums?" Perhaps that came across far more prim than scary, but my vocals would come good one day.

Will leaned against the bar; a place opening up for him as if by magic. It wasn't as though anyone would get in his way. Not here, not tonight. All the Hounds were wearing their colours and Will had the Head Hound bandana on as well as a leather jacket depicting a massive hound's head, with flames coming out its mouth, wearing a crown. It actually looked kind of cool, in a very rough way; though I would rather have dropped dead than let him know that. I wasn't going to be giving Will Malone any leeway from here on in, if I could help it.

Which was debateable.

He looked so relaxed and at home, I feared for the future of our pub.

"Gavel needed a place for his party. I needed to keep an eye on you. I wanted to see if you'd had any thoughts about Brenda since we last spoke. But I couldn't just come over, so this looks better."

His eyes left mine, and wandered around the crowd. He, like Jonelle, had the ability to look in every direction at the same time.

"Gavel?" I tried to keep my cool.

"Yeah, my second in command, if you will. Not that we have ranks exactly.' He smirked. 'The big guy with a bald head and the hound tattoo on his skull."

Will nodded as if in conversation, but pointedly toward the corner he'd just left. I half turned my head to follow the line he was showing me.

That, then, was Gavel. Oh goody. At the same time I thought, what the hell was Brenda thinking sleeping with him? Oh, so okay she wasn't given a choice, the whole paying customer thing but still! At least now I could see why he had to pay for it. No self respecting female would go near that.

Gavel was huge. At least six foot five and wide with it. No lean strength there; just plain brute force. He'd scrapped every strand of hair off his head and had their signature hound's head tattooed there in colour. It was most disturbing. Along with that, he had other tattoos showing from under his T-shirt and whenever he spoke or laughed, a gold tooth could be seen flashing in the light.

Boy was I looking forward to handing over all my information to Jonelle and possibly taking a very long holiday! Well, okay, probably not the holiday, but I didn't want Gavel to see me talking to Will at any cost.

I stood up to the bar and ordered a drink, pretending that that was the only reason we were standing so close.

"I've thought about it. What exactly were you hoping I would uncover, Will? Afraid that the truth of the matter may just be closer to home?"

I shot him a quick glance from the corner of my eye. He was frowning at his glass of what smelled like bourbon and Coke. All around me was the heady smell of a multitude of alcohols.

Speaking as though discussing something with the bar itself, Will continued our conversation.

"I knew Brenda. She was a nice enough kid. It's a sad thing what happened to her."

I knew hedging when I heard it.

"Will, stop treating me like an idiot. You know something. You're afraid of something and don't want it to be true, so you sent me out hoping that I would discover something to the contrary. Well I didn't. Whoever it is you're afraid killed her, really did. And I don't know why it bothers you. I'm sure you've known quite a few of the people killed around here."

Okay, so where had I suddenly got the courage to say these things? Where, in my cowardly soul, had such strength come from? It was an uncharacteristic outburst.

Will's frown deepened and he looked down at me, making my knees knock. But I'd started it and I wasn't going to let go. I had to get a confession of sorts from Will himself.

"I *think* you are forgetting who you're talking to," he muttered.

I tried hard not to laugh. Possibly more of a hysterical snigger, but either way not appropriate.

"Come on. You can't seriously expect me to stand here and report like a foot soldier. All right, so the crack about killing people you know was a little extreme, but why are you so bothered about someone in your crew topping a hooker?"

Did I sound like a cool customer or what? The sudden desire to pee my pants had nothing to do with it.

Will gave a little sigh. "I think one of my boys may be getting mixed up with something a little more dangerous than normal, is what I'm thinking. I don't want traitors or turn coats on my team. According to my American sources, a group called the Phoenix is starting to rear its head and become quite vocal. And, contrary to the ideas of some, they are not just about drugs. It's about power and politics and corruption. At all levels. And if one of mine has been meeting agents of this group and Brenda knew about this? Well, I'd like to know, is all. Brenda was someone I knew, someone I valued and she was shit scared of one of mine. I can't move on this. Some of my boys," his tone was sour, "don't trust me very much. So, have you got me proof?"

Funny how someone so tough could actually be as vulnerable as the rest of us. Moving without proof would have him killed just as surely as it would me. I felt like I was a little closer to having something in common with him.

Well, that would explain the priest. I'd been wondering what a hound had in common with a priest. I guessed the Phoenix wanted their priest in play, so had to remove the Bishop, or Cardinal or whatever it was Heather had been talking about. I was no expert on the hierarchy of the Catholic Church.

But I got the sad feeling I was about to become one. Jonelle would have me looking into what possible strength they could gain by having a Bishop removed.

"I don't think what I have would be constituted as proof exactly." To say the least. Heather wouldn't stand up to any rigorous questioning. "But I know who is concerned, a little bit of the why and a whole stack of more questions." I half smiled. "Every time Jonelle leaves me alone, I find more questions than answers. It's a hobby of mine, I'm afraid."

Will's lips quirked. "You're doing all right, for a baby."

I gave his shin another nudge.

"You have to crawl first, Pet. What Jonelle was thinking introducing a novice at this stage is the question I would love answered. Though looking at you could be answer enough."

I *think* that was a compliment. Back handed and roundabout as it may have been.

"Let me know when Jonelle gets back, okay? We should all get together and have a ... chat. But right now, I need to be seen to mingle." He grabbed his drink and pinched my ass as he walked off.

Annoying, but too yummy to stay angry with. I slapped my hand to my offended posterior and felt a slim piece of cardboard in my jeans pocket. Sneaky bugger. Slipping it out, I discovered a mobile number with the words, 'my private line' scrawled underneath. He'd been waiting for the chance to do that; pre-planned notes and all.

One day I would have forethought like that, knowing what situations I wanted to manipulate myself into.

I popped it into my wallet, knowing that in my back pocket was a bit too easy for everyone else to find as well. Though if there was anyone else who wanted to check out what I carried there, then they knew too much as it was.

I made my way over to where the Apartmates, with Steph and Grillia, were huddled. We looked a sad and small bunch beside the strength of numbers floating around us.

"I don't think we should make it a long night. In fact, let's just finish our drinks and take some back home." John looked around, plainly uncomfortable with the Hounds and their raucous goings on.

I was not going to blame him. Now Will had had his chat, I wanted out as fast as possible. There was also the need to get Heather away. She knew who the Hounds were and was practically frantic; I could see it on her face.

Moments later she came up. "Fiona, I have to get out of here. It's the Hounds I was talking about. Somewhere in this mob is the man who threatened and probably killed, my sister. What if they know who I am?"

I didn't want to tell her that if that had been the case, she'd almost certainly already be dead. No point in using facts to freak her out.

"It's okay, Heather. We're just leaving. This crowd doesn't suit any of us. Come on you lot, scull it down."

I threw the remainder of my drink down my throat. No point in wasting good bourbon just because we were panicked. I didn't want us to make a mad bolt for the door because that would make us obvious. On the other hand, I didn't want to waste one more minute either.

So out we scuttled, making no eye contact and trying to be unobserved. My heart leaped for one second when a big man planted himself in front of me and Heather, but Will smoothly stepped in and offered the guy a drink. The chance to drink toe to toe with the head man himself was too good a bribe and he cast me one last hopeful look before he followed Will to the bar.

As if. What was with these morons? Where did they get the idea that someone like me would be keen on someone with a beer gut, green tattoos and possibly a criminal record? Steph, one could understand, but me? It was insulting.

We trudged back to the Grangelands feeling a bit put out.

"I can't believe they took over our pub! Don't they have a doghouse somewhere to haunt?" Carmen had opened her bottle of whisky and was sipping out of the top as we walked. Not a great look but who was I to judge? I could guzzle the lot down, feeling as I did just then.

"Yeah, they do. But sometimes everyone needs to mingle with us commoners." Donald smiled and slipped his arm around Carmen as she stumbled.

Back we came, through our gate and then we spread out and relaxed on the deck chairs. Fernando and Shawn opened up their unit and soon Norah Jones came pouring out into the night air. It was going to be a lovely mellow night after all.

Heather was as twitchy as all buggery. She paced around the pool, staring at nothing, muttering into her glass. I watched for a while, then left my chair to catch her on the next round.

"Heather. You have to settle down, you'll attract questions." She went as stiff as a board. "No one tried to stop us leaving, we're home, the gates secure and Manny is happily... er... patrolling."

I watched my dog happily sniffing at Todd's crotch. Well, you can't have everything.

"That big man. He tried to stop us leaving. What if it was because he knows I know and now they'll all know?"

I thought I had problems with the English language.

I took her arm and led her to a corner, smiling like a fool at everyone in reassurance. As though Heather had had too much and needed to 'talk' as women do.

"Heather. Get a grip." I couldn't believe this was the same woman who'd been so cool since her sister's death. It was a complete makeover.

"That big man just wanted to score. Get laid. You know, not top you or anything. Don't fret so much. Just because I suddenly know some stuff doesn't mean anyone else does, but they'll sure as hell guess something is wrong if you don't pull it together. What's wrong with you?"

"It's like, I've had this big secret for so long and no one to talk to about it and now I do, and suddenly I just can't keep it inside anymore. My sister didn't just die. She was murdered. She wasn't a secretary, she was a hooker. And she knew something that killed her and now you and I know that same thing. Doesn't that bother you?"

Heather's wide eyes stared into mine.

"Well, it does *now*," I snapped crossly.

Boy, the girl was going to do my head in.

"If you want me to freak out, then you are going the right way about it! There is no need to go crazy. Nothing has changed from yesterday. Just keep going on as though nothing's the matter."

Except everything had changed; I suddenly knew things and Jonelle was going to be blown away with how professional I was. It didn't matter that I wasn't talking to her; that I was pissed off she'd cut me out to go wandering off with her old pal, and sometimes nemesis, Amelia.

That didn't matter at all now I had the goods and wanted someone to tell me I was marvellous. Though there was no guarantee she'd do that, considering my disastrous date with Will.

Heather looked suitably chastised.

"I'm sorry Fiona. It's just I've felt so alone and now I'm not. But on the flip side, now I've opened my mouth, I feel someone might have overheard, so I'm extra jumpy. Once you talk, nothing remains a secret."

I knew that.

"Please keep your word. I'd even prefer if you didn't say anything to Jonelle. Or if you have to, could you leave my name out of it? Just, you know, someone you know well. A friend of a friend of mine kind of conversation."

That part was easy.

"Sure, I promise not to mention your name at all."

After all, Jonelle knew who she was and her history better than I did. She'd know straight away, no names mentioned at all. The relief on Heather's face made me feel a bit of a heel, but not enough to come clean.

"So now we can go back to the rest of them and be cool? Just relax?"

She nodded. Thank God for that. Out of the ordinary behaviour was not something I was out to encourage. Bloody women. (And yes, I could see the irony of that, if you please).

I love a good party. And I love a mellow one. Okay, so pretty much any time we all got together was a good time. It was great to lie back with the Apartmates and watch the stars wheeling overhead.

At some point in the night I fell asleep on my deck chair. All the late nights, the alcohol and the tension caught up with me. I slipped in and out of consciousness; the delicious warmth of late spring, friendship and booze wending its way through my system.

When I came fully into myself again, the horizon was just staining grey and everyone had returned to their beds. I was the last man standing, well sleeping actually, out in the chairs. Manny was sprawled across my legs, head resting on my tummy and Smudge was on my chest. A nice hairy blanket. I guess no one had wanted to mess my little nest up.

"Off, brats."

I gave Manny a gentle shove and took Smudge up into my arms. Sitting up was interesting, but there was no immediate throb of hangover head. Thinking about it, I realised I'd been so worn out I'd only had four drinks before sleep overtook me. Unheard of, but I felt better for it.

I took the boys and headed in doors. It was Sunday. A day of rest and relaxation so no need to get too worked up about anything. Nothing much happened in Canberra on a Sunday, though I could always head down to the Markets. Something I hadn't made time for in ages.

Moments later I was out to it and thoughts of the markets were swept away with happy happy joy joy dreams of me and Viggo Mortensen getting together on the banks of some beautiful river. The man was seriously the hottest thing on legs. Sometimes I loved my mind.

I didn't, however, love two hungry wanting-to-play housemates who, thinking I'd slept enough, commenced a game of tag across the bed and down the other side and back over around one in the afternoon. So okay, they had a point. I'd been at it, the sleeping thing, for some time now. But was it cause for that sort of behaviour? Was that just?

"Knock it off!" I roared, attempting some order in my own home. "Domestic anarchy is not allowed, so bugger off, you little shits."

Incorrectly assuming this was an invitation to play, Smudge came bouncing across the sheets on stiff legs, fur standing on end. I had to admit, he looked adorable. Mind you, not so adorable when he pounced and butted my nose with those paws.

"Leave off, would you? I don't know where those paws have been, but I can give it a damn good guess. And don't you start," I warned Manny as he stood by the bed watching, tail going so fast I was surprised it didn't just fly right off.

His head lowered for half a second, but instead of taking me too seriously, he leaped onto the bed. Smudge turned his attentions to

Manny and between us all, paws, hands and feet, we landed on the floor. I was laughing too hard to care.

We traipsed into the kitchen for whatever we could find for nibbles. Then set up on the lounge for an afternoon of stupid re-run movies, chips and water. Yes, I was probably letting the side down, but I was feeling remarkably dehydrated. It was the most peaceful and pleasantly relaxing time I'd spent in ages. I couldn't even muster up the energy to wander around the markets. I didn't get any further than my couch and all of us were terribly pleased.

It wasn't until six the next morning did I realise that I hadn't seen the lights on at Jonelle's at all, which meant I could sleep in. It also meant no gym and blissful non-agonising beginnings to the day.

Only, my whole system was tuned to these mornings now. So I tossed and turned for a while then heaved myself out of bed.

"It's no use," I told Manny. "I can't sleep thinking about what I should be doing, and my body actually wants to get up and do stuff."

Was this the fitness person's utopia? When the body looked forward to expending its energy? Stuff of legends.

My gym clothes were in a ball of disregarded cloth in the closet. I gave them a shake and on they went. Hmm. Possibly time for a wash day. They were more than a little stinky. But they would pass. Absently patting my boys, I headed out for the gym. It was amazing I actually remembered where I was going. I was greeted with grunts and a few small waves.

My workout was considerably less than usual, I had to admit it. But I deserved brownie points for going at all. There was no sign of my mentor. I could only imagine she was out there somewhere pumping iron with her new best buddy (or old best buddy, if you looked at how long they had known each other). I threw myself into a new round of weights; annoyed at my own petty jealousies.

It wasn't that I needed to have Jonelle all to myself. That was even pettier than I usually was. It was just – she'd dragged me into this mess. Made me aware and then just when things were interesting and potentially dangerous, headed off to play with one of her old toys, leaving me floundering in the deep end. At least, that was my interpretation and I was sticking to it.

Back at home I showered and changed. Then set about doing domestic things such as the wash, a quick vacuum and change of water and kibble for my boys. I wondered briefly on why I hadn't heard from Brad, unusual even if it was only a call, then continued with my spring clean.

Feeling virtuous by five in the afternoon I was exhausted. Everything was spotless; two bags were ready by the door for my Salvation Army drop of clothes I possibly shouldn't have bought in the first place, the pets' beds had been aired and toys even washed. I hadn't been this domesticated for ages.

I wanted to go over and get stuck into research mode, but I was suddenly unsure about letting myself in. While nothing had been said about any change in our relationship, I was feeling a might bit uncomfortable about it all. So instead I kept myself busy and stared at odd times out the window to see if I could spot her coming home.

It wasn't until the sun had set and I'd managed to eat my way through a box of chocolate chip cookies that I saw the front room lights go on across the pool. I gave a little jump. So she was back, huh? Better late than never. Though I liked to think that wasn't an option, but who knew?

I waited impatiently for my summons to war. But it never came. She must have known I'd be waiting. That I'd want to catch up and talk and go over things. Possibly even stick my nose into whatever Amelia and Jonelle had been up to. Still, there was a deathly silence from No.9.

There was so much to go through, didn't she realise it was crunch time?

Okay, so that was more than a slight exaggeration. But I wanted to work up some enthusiasm so I could march over there and bash on the door and let her know all the things I had been up. And not think it was a waste of time.

Around ten, I lost patience. Leaving a snoozing dog and cat, I went over to rap on her door. Trying the handle, I found it was unlocked. Disregarding my earlier fears about walking into her place, I flung the door open and prepared for a fight.

Chapter Nineteen

There was only one other time I had seen her house like this: when she'd returned from Sydney with the news of Jack's death.

Candles burned everywhere; incense rose in soft swirls of smoke to the ceiling, making the place smell of woods and wet pine trees, and Jonelle sat curled up on her cushions sipping one of her brews. Her head came round as I burst in.

"About time you got here."

There was no smile on her face, but her voice was relaxed; not tense nor destructive. I relaxed a little. Perhaps it wasn't going to be as bad as I'd thought. She waved me over to my own pile of cushions and I sunk into them. Beside her were a pot and another mug. I helped myself without an invite, knowing it would be the green tea.

"So. You're terribly quiet." She smiled then, a small quick flicker.

"I've only just got here," I responded sipping my tea.

"Yeah, well that doesn't usually matter. You'd have exploded by now with news. What's on your mind?"

I raised my gaze from the tea mug to her eyes. They were serious, yet held the old affection and amusement just below the surface.

"You know damn well what's on my mind. Where have you been? What have you been up to and where is Amelia? Tell me all the *news!*"

Jonelle flung her head back and barked a laugh.

"See? Now that is more like it. No way were you going to hold that lot of questions in." She settled back more comfortably.

"Where do I start?" she paused and held it. I twitched, trying not to be too impatient.

"There, I was waiting for you to bust a gut." She smirked.

Shit. Damn it all, I would love to be less predictable.

"Amelia is staying round for her family. While that does mean she is in town for the next month or so, I doubt we'll have too much to do with her. The boss wanted her to spend Christmas with the family in an attempt to humanise her and make sure she didn't run off and try to follow Jack's trail. I think everyone is afraid that she'll be killed too, though that could be a merciful release for her and for those around her." She paused, thinking, searching her mug for answers.

"What's wrong with her?" I had to ask. Having never lost anyone I loved deeply, I was ever the curious one.

Jonelle glanced at me. "Amelia has a bad temper, has the sort of skills in unarmed and armed combat that make me shiver, and now has lost the one thing that could control all that ego and aggression. What do you think is wrong with her?

"There is, simply put, no leash anymore. Not, I must add, that she is a bad person. She's just a warrior without a war. A loose cannon - and she's in my backyard. It makes me twitchy. I'm not in a space where I want to take on a whole stack of bad guys, but she is likely to drag them here, because if she discovers anything that links anyone to Jack, she'll be off like a shot. It is," she tried to find the word. "It's disturbing, to have someone like that so close."

Huh. If *she* thought it was disturbing, how did she think I felt? It was like sitting next to a bomb watching it tick, not knowing when 'zero' would occur.

And I had two of them.

Jonelle, at least, knew herself and what she was going to do. I didn't.

"Anyway, she really isn't our problem. She's someone else's. I only hope whoever pisses her off needs killing because that's exactly what she'll do."

"You really do have the nicest friends." I was just a touch sarcastic. Not that anyone could blame me. I liked the idea of Amelia being overseas far more than having her walking around my home city. What if I ran into her? Hmm.

"What happens if we bump into her?"

"Amelia is more of a onetime work colleague." Jonelle wanted me straight on that. "And if we run into her, we nod, smile and say good morning. Then we move on. We've said all we had to say. And we both agreed that her being here has nothing to do with me." She saw my glare. "Or you. She has her own issues and demons to fight. While you and I - well we have a million and one things to be getting on with."

"You are not wrong." I was very relieved to hear that Amelia wasn't about to become a permanent fixture in our lives.

One crazy potential killing machine was enough for me to handle. I couldn't see my questions and less than qualified mistakes endearing me to Amelia.

"So, what else did you get up to while you were gone?" I asked.

I was saving all my news till last. I wanted to make sure it would *be* news. Nothing worse than me telling her everything only to discover she already knew it.

"Okay. Amelia's news really hasn't got much bearing on what we are doing, so let's not go there." I was more than happy to do as she asked in that matter.

"I didn't spend the whole weekend with her. A couple of hours and we were done. I found The Rose again and we had more of an in depth chat about things."

She looked away from me then. A shadow flickered across her face. I got the nasty suspicion that even second hand this wasn't going to be news I would enjoy hearing about.

"He has accepted a contract from some people I knew a while back. They want to collect the bounty on my head. I hate been vague with you, but the less you know about some things the better. We agreed to disagree about it."

"What's that meant to mean?" I was loath to ask, but I was still me. I had to know everything I possibly could.

Jonelle was silent. Perhaps I do push too much.

"It'll sort itself out," was all she had to say.

I exploded.

"What do you mean it'll sort itself out? I have spent the past month in and out of trouble, with my heart beating itself into an early grave, people threatening me, wondering if I was going insane to be hanging out with someone who views killing people in the way as a *hobby* and now I have another crazy person in town.

"You don't tell me anything, you have all this history with half the town's tough nuts, you go around leaving me behind and you pretend to care and protect me but when I *do* get all beat up you don't do *anything* about it!"

I knew I was stressing words and I knew it was probably driving her nuts, but I couldn't stop. I was stressed and sore and afraid.

"The whole city is full of people who know you and some who want you dead. We walk around with targets on our backs and then import more people from God knows what countries, to add to the mix.

"I've never been hit before or seen a gun or a knife and suddenly I find myself talking about killing and dying like it is just a matter of simple language! I don't know how to defend myself, I don't know how to hold a knife so I don't look stupid, and I am a soft target who can be used against you.

"I can't understand why I'm even here, because you're so professional and I am *so* not, why on earth did you allow this to happen? To carry such a liability around with you? I blunder into things and make your life even more complicated.

"I don't know if I even want to get to a point where half the things you know and talk about are simple for me, and yet I have never felt more alive than when we are doing stuff together. And I feel kind of fit and I don't want that to change, but it's all such a mess!" I paused.

I had to. I needed a breath.

Jonelle's eyes hadn't left mine for a second. I felt a bit trapped and more than a bit scared, but I couldn't have held any of that in for another moment.

"Anything else?" Her voice was low and controlled.

Not that long ago I would have wet myself wondering what she was going to do. At least we were passed that; I was no longer afraid of her reaction toward to me. But I still held myself in some sort of readiness. Her voice was no give away to what she was thinking. Neither was the rest of her.

"Nope. I would have to say, that right now, I don't have anything else to add to that rant. But give me a few minutes and I'm sure I'll do a better job."

She smiled slightly, taking more tea.

"There was a lot in that. Very hard to answer it all." Her eyes came back to mine and in the candle light appeared to glimmer.

"Do you really want an answer?"

My heart skipped. Yes, I really did, I wanted to say. But I was trapped in that gaze and no, somehow I really didn't. What had Will said? Looking at me was answer enough.

Well I *was* me, and I still had no answers.

She leaned forward and her hand fluttered mere millimetres

above my skin. Every hair on my arm and at the back of my neck rose up. My heart drummed in my ears and I was surprised she didn't comment of the noise of it all. Little flickers of ... well, something, slithered down my spine. A pulse beat started in my stomach and I found to my embarrassment, I was trembling.

She took her hand back and settled deeper into her pillows. The fever feeling under my skin ebbed away. I could learn to hate her. And I couldn't decide if that was because she didn't touch me, or because I wanted her to.

"I like having you around. And I won't let anything major happen to you. I don't like to lose ... anything or anybody. I'm sorry that I didn't go after the two visitors you had. I mentioned them to Amelia, but she had no idea who they were either.

"The Phoenix are relatively new players and none of their names appear to tweak anyone's memories, *if* that is who Charles and Daniel work for. They could have been anyone. I don't want to jump into a hornet's nest. There is only me, no backup. So I had to leave them. But I don't have to like it."

Her gaze turned fierce and I remembered that Brenda had asked for her help, just before she died.

"I can't help who and what I am, Fiona. I did get out of the organisation and move into art so that I could live at least a semblance of normalcy. It isn't easy, when you carry a reputation and have been trained in all sorts of different things. It's not like I have an MBA and can just go get a decent job. I have skills, I use them. I like to think I rein in my more - socially unacceptable aspects.

"But I won't change everything about me. I'm good at art dealing; I protect my investments and I help clean up undesirables. I'm not exactly open about it, but I don't hide the fact I'm different. I can't be too open; I'd be arrested, for God's sake!" She flashed that hot gaze at me.

"We have three problems, as I see it, that we should be working. Things from my past, people and issues are not important. What is happening now and the current events are what matters. If anything comes along that needs fixing from back then, I'll deal with it.

"Amelia, I'll handle. Anything at all like that is my business. I like having you here and enjoy having someone to talk to, but I want you only involved so far. I don't want you to be any more of a target than you are.

"Certain things from back then *are* scary. I try hard to keep you away from that. I'm looking forward to a certain level of retirement soon and don't really want the past to come knocking.

"So, I leave The Rose alone for now until I can get rid of him and not stir up too much trouble, because I really do not want the Fist to come looking for revenge and I'll leave Amelia alone because she may just kill me by accident. What we'll concentrate on is getting this second painting back that Tomas stole for some reason and finding out a bit more about Tomas' death.

"I don't want to go chasing the Phoenix until I know they are our problem. I also want to concentrate a bit more on Brenda's death and a few more deals that are coming my way. Not many more and I'll certainly be able to retire."

"Does Amelia want to retire?" A strange question, considering the lead she gave me into my news about Brenda's murder, but the dark and oddly tainted woman who was Amelia was very intriguing for me.

Jonelle's wandering eyebrow climbed again.

"I don't think Amelia would get the reasons behind retirement. I don't know, I have never asked her. I left because I wasn't as hard as I needed to be to keep going. I couldn't block out the things we saw or did. Also, my talents were more artistic. I like it more.

"However, there was another fundamental difference. I could see my future. I wanted it and I wanted to sit beside a beach and do yoga and read a book. I wanted to play in the surf and relax. I think that has driven me and kept me sane." She smiled at me. "Reasonably so, anyway. Amelia isn't like that. She doesn't think of her future. She just saw Jack. Being with him, and doing what they were doing, was her life. Claire is a bit more like me. And then there was Jack.

"He balanced us all. And we could talk about my beach dream, but Jack was a devil and loved the chase. The thrill. He was never going to retire. It was always a case of dying on the job." She was quiet for a while."So. What's been going on here while I was gone?"

I respected the total change of topic. We both could do with no more Amelia talk. Plus, I had exciting news of my own.

"Well, I found out a few things on my own." That came out all wrong. Somehow I sounded like a little girl at show and tell.

All I got though was an encouraging smile as Jonelle refilled our mugs.

"I went out on a date with Will on Friday night."

Tea flew out of her mouth. I've never seen her react so much. It was kind of cool – to blow her cool like that.

"You what?!" It was, almost, a squeak. I giggled.

"What on earth were you thinking, going out with Will? And what happened to Brad? And Will! Of all the men to play around with. He'll either eat you alive, or kill Brad or something. How can I *possibly* look after you if you keep on going off and pulling stunts like that?"

"I could hardly say no, could I?"

"Of course you bloody well could! It's not difficult. N-O. Bloody hell, you stupid girl. Getting yourself mixed up in trouble is one thing. Deliberately searching it out is another."

If it was possible for a human to self combust I think fumes would have poured out her ears.

"He called and told me to be waiting for him. I didn't have a contact number at the time to let him know it was impossible. Then, of course, I didn't want to."

"What?!" Same tone. "You actually wanted to put your head in the lion's mouth."

Her using the same metaphor, of Will as a lion, wasn't helping much.

"I thought it would benefit us if I could get him talking. I wasn't really sure what about, but he must know heaps of stuff that we don't."

She glared.

"All right. That *I* don't. It was a grand plan."

"One, I take it, that didn't work."

"Well, no. Not exactly. He doesn't talk all that much about interesting things."

I really didn't want to get into the action of the evening. It made my skin crawl with embarrassment.

"Will, my dear idiot, is a professional conman, and heads up a group of men with the warm and fuzzy name of The Hellhounds. What were you expecting? Him to come over all confessional? He ordered a hit on his own brother-in-law and held his sister as she cried. He's a hard and scary man, and I want you to stay the hell away from him."

"You know what would help? You telling me the worse and most intimidating thing about everyone we meet so I don't think they are going to sell me flowers. I know he leads the Hounds. I wanted information and needed to get it from someone, seeing as you're so open all the time. And why did he order his brother-in-law killed?"

She laughed.

"I was wondering when you'd get around to that question. Ken was a bad little boy and upset his bigger and tougher brother-in-law. The spoils of war, my little friend. It was a long time ago and Will wasn't a Hound then. Just a very mixed up young man. But don't change the subject."

Bugger.

"Well, I wanted to see if he would slip up. Which kind of didn't happen, but he did ask me why we were so fixated on linking Brenda with Tomas, The Way and the Phoenix. He told me to look closer to home. So I stuck to Heather and she told me everything."

So, okay that was probably a porker and exaggeration. But it got her attention. I felt like I was in the cross hairs of some scary gun of high powered velocity.

"Everything?"

Her voice had gone silky and rather smooth. The hairs on the back of my neck went up again. And not for any warm and fuzzy reasons.

"Brenda was being used by Gavel the Hound (now wasn't that a wonderful name to carry with you) and a priest. She overheard them talking about getting rid of a Bishop and putting this priest in his place. She was terrified that they would get rid of her as well. Then when I spoke to Will on Saturday..."

I didn't get to finish that sentence at that moment.

Jonelle growled in her throat and grabbed my wrist. I forgot about sparks and could only concentrate on the pain of her grip. The woman was a vice.

"You saw him again? What are you hoping for? A quick and pain free death or something?"

"Boy, if you'd just settle down you'd hear that it wasn't by choice. He was waiting at my local pub, hosting a party for Gavel actually. He used it as an excuse. I tell you, I don't think the grip he has on that lot is as strong as he thinks it is. He wanted to see if I had come up with anything.

"Mind you, he was expecting quick work, wasn't he? It just so happened I'd spoken with Heather and found all that stuff out. But

I'd promised her I would only tell you. She felt safe with that, more fool her. Though I did tell her I wouldn't mention her name, sort of just make vague references to a friend of a friend."

I kind of felt bad about that.

"Oh well. That wasn't going to last for long. Far too complicated a mouthful. So basically, Will was afraid that someone in his crew was talking out of turn with the Phoenix. Not that I know this for sure, but its sounds about right.

"He knew Brenda, quite well I'd say, did you know that? And why doesn't Amelia know about the Phoenix if we keep running into them? It's not like they're trying to be sneaky or anything. And why did you never mention that Brenda had a boyfriend?" I ran out of breath.

Jonelle was more relaxed now. She had let my arm go somewhere through that and settled back into her pillows. Thank God for that, because anymore of this lunging and grabbing business, and I'd be covered in bruises. Again. She looked thoughtful.

"I don't know about the Phoenix thing, I hadn't heard of them, until the other day, though Amelia does know about them, by the way. She's hot on their tail as she has some very real evidence they provoked Jack into coming after them and had him killed.

"Nothing about them, Brenda, Jack's death or anything is a certainty. Don't ever forget that. Sorry about not mentioning the boyfriend. I wrote it up in the file, but I guess you haven't gone back to them?" Her eyes twinkled at my lack of studying. Why would I, when working the angles was so much more interesting? (Would you get a load of me – 'working the angles'!)

"His name is Craig and at the time of her death, he was down the south coast. I talked to Craig quite a lot when she died. Of course, he was my first suspect. Murder is usually a lot closer to home than the average person thinks. Admittedly, the man has a complete Saviour complex, thinking he was going to 'save' Benda from her choice of lifestyle and rehabilitate her." Jonelle's lips curled. She was obviously not a huge fan.

"He was a stuttering, weeping mess, knowing she was dead. I went down the coast and checked out where he was staying. Yes," she held up her hand to prevent me interrupting, "complete with photos and impressive fake police ID. He really was staying in the Bright Palms Motor Inn for the whole weekend. There was even his signature and the waitress remembered how he prayed over his meal on the Saturday night. I couldn't link him to Brenda's death.

"But when I find the sick bastard who did her in, he'll wish his mother had never met his father." Her eyes were dark pitiless holes.

I almost felt sorry for Gavel and our mysterious priest. They were about to be visited by an Angel of Death. Or was that an Avenging Angel? Whatever. She was mightily pissed, was what she was.

"The Phoenix is starting to pop up everywhere. Fine. Let them come out. If it can be proven Jack knew them and they ordered the hit, they will have Amelia to deal with, which is enough for anyone. She can rope in the Agency and it'll be a fun little war for everyone to write home about."

Her lips curled in a feral manner. Wasn't a show of teeth a show of dominance in some animal cultures? She made me shiver when she did things like that. Most unnerving.

"What we're going to do is find Tomas' mates, get my art back, give it to whoever it belongs to and worry about the rest tomorrow. First things first. A trip to the old Batch tonight should help uncover some of Tomas' mates in crime. He didn't have a very large circle of friends."

My head felt all swirly. I knew she wanted to chase The Way. I knew it. How could she act so cool and put the whole thing in the to-do-later basket? I may have no idea about a lot of things, but I was fairly champing at the bit to have a crack at them.

I owed those sorry bastards; if it could be proven Charles and his Neanderthal mate were indeed from Phoenix. Rise from the ashes in my life time would you... mutter, mutter. I touched my fading bruises. I wanted them to feel my pain. Fat chance I guess.

"Can you train me?" I came out with the most extraordinary things sometimes.

"Train? Elaborate please. I thought the gym of a morning was enough for you?"

"Well, I think it is! Don't get me wrong, the whole getting up early is a killer. But I was thinking more along the lines of with a gun or knife or hands. You know, some sort of Kung Fu thingy."

"That was almost sounding remotely professional until the last bit."

I snorted.

"What were you expecting? A treatise on the use of your toenails in unarmed combat? Just answer me, yes or no?"

I thought that had come out just right, a clever mix of sarcasm and bravado.

She watched me with those uncanny cat eyes. "All right."

"Just like that?"

"Just like that. You want to learn to not get yourself killed and be an even bigger pain in my butt, then I'll teach you. It'll mean getting up at five."

Can blood really drain from your face? Was it humanly possible to turn into a pillar of bloodlessness? I could hate her (especially after that other unwarranted crack). I knew *that* was possible. People do it every day. Well, I just joined their ranks.

"Five, as in, in the A M? When do I sleep?"

She twinkled at me. Cow.

"Try going to bed before two in the morning sometime. It's a novel way of looking at the world. Or learn to go without as much sleep. It's not complicated. You want to learn – you get up and apply yourself. And no biting the instructor."

I really did need to control my facial expressions.

"Which means go home and get some sleep. Now."

"I hate that bossy tone you get." I tried out some A class whinging.

"That isn't going to get you anywhere. Out."

So I went.

Nothing much else I could do. I wanted to learn, I really did. I just wished there was some easy way to program all that sort of information into my head and into my body's reflexes without having to go through the actual training part.

As I got myself ready for bed, I wondered if she meant to take me with her when she visited Gavel. Would he spill his guts (literally and figuratively) about the priest and what they did to Brenda?

While some part of me shuddered to think of what she could do to him, I was strangely excited about the idea of going on my first real information recovery jaunt. If I could convince Jonelle I was ready to go.

"I shan't be convincing anyone of anything if I don't go to bed and get up at five a.m." I told a sleepy Smudge who had left the safety of Manny's paws to come and snuggle on my bed.

Five of a *morning* comes around a lot faster than I would have thought possible. One moment I was complaining to Smudge and the next, the alarm was ringing incessantly in my ear. Everyone had something to say about the issue. Smudge was the most persuasive however, because he could use claws.

"Let me go, you little shit. Next time I'll leave you outside." As dire a threat as I could come up with at such short notice. Not that it did me any good. He knew his charms.

I scrambled into a tracksuit and limped my way into the kitchen. I was tired, stiff, hungry and the whole idea had knobs on. There was no way I'd come up with this all by myself. Try as I might, I couldn't see how she'd manipulated me into it, though I was sure she was to blame somehow. Grabbing a carton of OJ, I gulped some down straight from its neck.

"No more of that." Jonelle leaned herself against the door jamb, comfortable and at home in my space.

I hadn't heard a knock on the door.

"There wasn't one. I let myself in just to make sure you weren't getting into bad habits." She took the carton off me. "*That* is a bad habit."

"How do you *do* that?" I grumbled.

"Let myself in or know exactly what it is you're thinking?" She smirked, head coming round the fridge door as she put the OJ back in.

"Both really. You suck. And it's too early for your smart ass smirky attitude."

See how far I'd come? I was quite comfortable in telling her off. Okay, well maybe not quite comfortable. But my knees weren't knocking and there was only a slight sensation of dizziness. I knew she wouldn't kill me for insurrection. She liked me. Didn't she?

"You forgot to lock up last night. You're far too trusting. Of the lock I put on that damn gate, and Manny telling you of anyone coming in. Where was he when I got here, hmm?"

Damn it, I hated it when it was so easy for her.

"And the other? Learn how to read people, my dear."

I had to cut her off.

"That was patronising! I won't be shunted out of bed, forcibly removed from my OJ, then told off like a child. I can read people."

The fact that I usually got my readings all wrong and it felt like I'd read Harry Potter rather than War and Peace, had *nothing* to do with it!

Laughing, Jonelle gave me a one armed hug. I nearly leapt out of my skin. I'd never seen her so carefree and affectionate. Her eyebrow quirked at my instant reaction. She let me go.

"I'm sure you can read people, but it only works well if you shut up and listen to them for five seconds. Really listen."

She ushered me toward the door, a non-touching usher.

"For most people, conversation is only two way because the other person is inconsiderate enough to want a chance to have their say. So they pause in their incredibly self absorbed ranting and wait for the other person to finish. Then they keep on going."

We headed to the cars, Jonelle talking the whole time. Ironic.

"People aren't listening, so much as waiting for the chance to speak. To really listen you have to not care about when you get to talk next. You have to be prepared to absorb the other person's ideas and words and they have to connect with you.

"You try to understand them, not just have them wafting over you like so much verbal garbage. Have your brain engaged, not thinking about what you are going to say next. That way you get an idea of what people are really all about. You get a sense of them. In you get."

She popped me into her car, then went around and got in the driver's side.

"You start to build up an idea of what that person is like. How they form their ideas and what their face or body is saying at the same time. Then you can start to sort of guess what it is they're thinking, while someone else is talking. You'd be amazed how many people say whatever it is that just wandered across their mind.

"In time, you can read faces quite easily. People can say a whole load more with their body than with their mouths. You," she added, glancing at me, "say everything with your face. It's like a printed book. Emotions, thoughts and feelings just floating on over it, out there for all who care enough to read. I make it my habit to check in on your thoughts by studying your face whenever we're together. Helpful for me and unfortunately helpful for everyone else as well."

"Well, piffle is all I have to say to that. I can't help it. It's just my face."

I felt oddly put out. Like my life was hanging out there for all to see. It was invasive.

"Then learn to think with quiet thoughts and an impassive face."

She said it like I had a choice in the matter. Jonelle sighed.

"It's one of the things we'll work on, okay?"

Fine, but I was going to enjoy seeing how she planned on making me a poker face.

We parked next to the lake.

Lake Burley Griffin is a massive body of water walking distance from the CBD full of gardens, bike paths, seats, pretty much the works. Jonelle took me to a flat grassy area removed from most of the morning walkers.

I laughed.

"You know, this would make a great movie. You drive me down here, I'm all friendly and jokey, then you do away with me. Here in the most isolated stretch you can get. No struggle, no mess."

I stood smiling out at the lovely soft rippling waters. Behind me the suburb of Yarralumla would be waking up; well, some of them would be; it was only five fifteen after all. I felt her move, then suddenly her breath was on my neck and my hackles rose.

"Who said you were safe?"

Her voice was a whisper.

Coming as it did out of the dawn and from her, I nearly fell into the lake. Her hands reached out and steadied me.

"Always be prepared for anything that could happen. I have friends, I really do. But I'm always aware of what they could do to me given the right motivation."

She stepped back and I turned, to catch that feral predator look on her face.

"Take Amelia."

Did we have to? Somehow that woman had managed to invade all our conversations since she'd arrived. It was more than a little annoying.

"She makes a good case in point. Stop fretting about her."

"There! What did you see?"

"Your face clouded over and you got a little pouty. You also had a flicker of a frown, just for a second. Why do you think everyone gets my full attention when talking? I like to really hear everything they have to say. And something like ninety percent of every conversation is non-verbal.

"Now, back to the original issue. Amelia. Don't get sulky. She is someone I would trust with my life. But right now, she's a little unstable and likely to be more of a liability than a help. So I'm wary and I keep a very close eye on what she does and says when we are together. Friend or no friend, she is dangerous."

She fixed me with her stare.

"Will is another case in point and one you would do very well to spend as little time with as possible. I don't think he wishes you any harm. I really don't or you'd be, well, harmed. But that doesn't mean he isn't dangerous for you. You're not ready to test yourself against someone like that, even if he does like you."

"I keep trying to tell you, I didn't mean to get involved with Will." That annoying eyebrow climbed.

"All right! So I thought... *think!* I think he's a hottie. I could possibly see myself wrapped around the man given any other circumstances. But there aren't any other circumstances and he told me we were going out and then turned up at my pub, and it wasn't as if I had to lead him on to get him there."

Okay, so I had, just a bit, even quite a lot. But she didn't know that and in my defence, it was only *after* he'd practically ordered me to have a date with him.

"You have guilt written all over your face. But I'll leave that for now." She came to stand beside me, turning us both so we looked back out over the water. "We're here to start your training. It's going to be a mangled job, as you are really old..."

I squawked. "Hey, look who's calling whom old, buddy."

She grinned.

"I started my training when I was three. You're twenty nine, right? And have never been made to do much physical activity until now. Not ideal, but we can work with that. What you need to do is basics and some calming stuff. So that you can think clearly at all times and not keep getting yourself into a pickle over everything that happens.

"I've seen you," she added when I opened my mouth about to defend myself against such a salacious attack. "You freeze, or worse still, panic and want to run. You don't think; you freak out. You don't control your body's desire for flight, you don't harness that energy. You let it escape you, leaving your body in fizzles."

"I'm not blaming you, idiot. But we need to try to work on some of that. And help you keep a level head. I've been watching you. You spend a lot of time joking and laughing life off. That's fine, but you also need to be quiet and at peace and have a few serious moments in your life. They can help centre you and create a well of energy you can call on when you need to." She stood with her legs apart and bent at the knee.

"Come on, copy me."

I groaned. It was bad enough when she set about destroying me verbally with all those comments about how I was this and that. Now she was going to make me squat and work on those damn thigh muscles. It was too early, I hadn't had anything to eat, and I was going to be stuck going to the gym straight after, I imagined. It was going to be torture.

"Look, you did ask. And I fully agree. I need you to be self sufficient. I'm not always around and I won't be living here forever.

"You need to be able to cope. Life isn't something you just throw away, you know. Learn to appreciate it, live it and get involved. Don't skim. It's like a good book. Skimming to get to the end only leaves you empty and unfulfilled. But read every page, get involved with the characters and suddenly when you get to the end, you're richer for it."

I stood with my legs apart, thigh muscles burning and stared stoically out at the water.

"Stop looking as though you are about to chew rocks."

Okay, so stoically had been a big leap.

"Be light, not so fierce. Be gentle with yourself and relax. Don't think about what your legs are feeling. They'll hold you up. That's what they do. Let your mind focus on the water. Drink it in; follow your breath, in and out. Don't think of words or action. Just follow your breath."

Yes, because that was so easy. Because looking at the water and following my breath and not thinking about how my thighs were about to stop functioning was going to make me a better fighter.

Was this what we were going to do every day? I'd go mad.

I stood there and made a go of it. I didn't lose myself in the moment. My mind was too busy thinking about Brad and Will and Brenda. I looked over at Jonelle, trying to gauge how much longer we'd be at this.

Her face was a mask; her eyes looked lost and full of the water. It helped that she had naturally grey eyes to start with, the cheat. Her breath was coming so slowly I had to concentrate to see her chest move at all. There was not the slightest tremble in her legs. Bitch!

"Look at the water, not me."

Her voice sounded far away, but still carried a note of threat. A harmless, friendly threat. I snapped my head back to view the water.

Bloody hell.

Eventually she rose up, bowed to the water and shook her limbs.

"I think that is probably enough for today. Of that anyway. The best things for you to learn are Tai Chi, meditation, balance and basic self defence. I want you to be able to disarm someone, probably not a professional someone, but eventually who knows?"

She grinned at my obvious surge at the injustice of her comments.

"We want strength and conditioning training. You'll be doing a lot of running, using the fitness balls at the gym to get core strength, and weights. We'll up your gym training to go with this. You'll be someone to be reckoned with soon enough."

I did like the sound of that. But my appeal came from the party animal, light hearted approach. That could all be ruined before I turned thirty.

We did some stretches, and basic Tai Chi. The whole time Jonelle kept up a running commentary about the whys and the hows and the what it was good for.

I attempted to follow what she said, watch the movements and keep an eye on what her face was saying. She wasn't the type of person I should have been practising on. Jonelle's face was no book; it was more of a slab of granite. Very frustrating. She caught me peering and sniggered, but didn't say a word.

It was quarter to seven by the time she decided enough was enough. I was covered in a light sweat. This new training was going to be a lot worse than just the gym work.

I wasn't home and showered until nine. What I really wanted was a long soak and a massage. Some of that Adelaide pampering wouldn't have gone astray. But Jonelle had headed off for a shower saying she'd see me in ten.

My stomach was aching for breakfast and as I dashed passed my kitchen I cast a longing gaze at the paper bag full of my Danishes. Smudge and Manny followed me back to Jonelle's, happy to have me home and some company.

"What torture do you have planned now?" I asked as I let myself in. Then I nearly swallowed my tongue. "Hello. What are you doing here?"

Chapter Twenty

Will rose in one smooth move. He'd been sitting on the floor, long legs spread out before him, and nearly given me a heart attack.

So much for all the calm I'd being learning about. I could hear Jonelle in the kitchen muttering to herself and most probably making the by now long familiar pot of green tea. Will stuck his hands in his jeans pockets for all the world looking like a teenager caught out. Jonelle came in.

"Don't hang out with him, huh? Too dangerous for the likes of me. But fine for you to have floating unchaperoned in your home."

I tried to keep my voice flat and businesslike. I think I successfully failed miserably.

Will grinned. "Too dangerous, hey? Why thanks, Jon. Nice wrap of my talents."

He glided over to me and planted a kiss on the top of my head. Pfft, I felt the need to kick him again and stick my tongue out.

Bastard.

Jonelle saved me the trouble, giving him a slap.

"Dangerous for her, not me, so back down." But her voice was light and teasing. See? I was learning stuff. Like if I looked into her eyes I could see the wariness deep inside and I knew she was prepared for whatever Will had coming.

"You said we all needed to talk, so talk, buddy. We've got work to do."

"I know. Look, we don't have to be on the opposite sides for this. There is such a thing as working together. Gavel has powerful connections, but I have suspicions he's aiming for my job and I'll be damned if I'll let him take it. We'd end up being the lackeys of any overseas connections. Well, they would; I'd be dead."

He tried for some levity but only got flat stares from his audience.

"Tough gig."

Jonelle settled on the pillows and waved us both to a pile each.

"As far as I can tell, the Hellhounds are not something I want to get mixed up with. Sorry Will, but when you chose to go down that road, you did it alone. They may well only be local louts, but if you're suspicions *are* correct, Gavel is attracting some international interest and I don't want a bar of it. I could dig you out if that is what you want, but if your loyalties to the rest of them make you want to stay and keep Gavel out of the top job, then don't drag me or Fiona into it."

Will was not looking happy. Not sad, more a touch annoyed. Could I leave now, please?

"Sorry, Will. I'm aiming for a nice comfortable retirement and all I want to do is tie up some loose ends, then bugger off into the sunset. Like all good heroes get to do."

She gave us a tight smile.

"I think this all comes round to your loose ends. I can't touch Gavel, you want to find out if he killed Brenda, then you can kill him too."

How can two people make killing someone sound so reasonable and almost like a plausible way forward?

"I'm not trying to prevent your retirement, though there are going to be enough impediments to that, trust me. What, you think you can just move and none of this will follow you? People will always want you to sort things out for them, or want you dead. You don't think I don't know about the price on your head?"

The air suddenly got a lot thicker. Magic words, 'price' and 'head'. I could *feel* Jonelle curling herself up ready to spring.

"For fuck's sake, Jonelle, if Will wanted to collect on that reward, he wouldn't be telling you about it."

I was trying to be the reasonable one, but my language slipped somewhere.

Their eyes were locked and they were too busy bloody 'reading' each other to hear.

Will broke and smiled. "She's right."

Well, someone listened, that was a start.

"I'm not here to cause trouble, Jon. I don't want their reward. But there are a few people out there who will. It won't take them long to find you. You aren't keeping a low profile. Everyone knows you live somewhere in town. Just watch your back. The Hounds know we aren't picking up the contract, but what if Gavel goes on his own merry way?"

"Why are you so keen to point me at Gavel, Will? Who or what are you hiding? If you really wanted him dead he would be, without pointing the finger at you. Why set me up to do your dirty work?"

Jonelle's needle like attention hadn't wavered.

Will shrugged.

"You know why, Jon. I can't have anything to do with the death of a fellow Hound. And before you say it, yes it would bother me to think they were after you instead. But you can look after yourself. I hear Amelia is in town. Let her loose."

He looked far too calculating and relaxed. I had my suspicions about the man, but now? Why had Jonelle agreed to meet him here?

"Amelia isn't some sort of weapon I point at people." Jonelle's voice was icy. "Will, for old time's sake I'll not push the issue seeing as I am going to be having a chat with Gavel either way."

"Chat? I think it'd be better for all if we just agreed to do away with the man." Will finished his tea, and rose. "I know he's trouble but I can't pin anything on him. Help me out Jon, and get rid of him before he hurts someone else, like Fiona."

Jonelle's eyes cut to me. There was a flicker as we stared at each other. Will knew what button to push.

Protect and destroy were missions Jonelle knew all too well.

I wanted to tell her that just because I'd been beaten up and her sister was a mess, it wasn't her fault and it wasn't as if she'd been asleep behind the wheel. She looked back at Will.

"Gavel won't be hurting anyone."

It was a simple little statement, but kind of read like the man's obituary.

Will nodded.

"I'll owe you. The Hounds will owe you when the fool doesn't drag us into some sort of Phoenix puddle. I'll let myself out."

Which was nice of him, but Jonelle went with him. Just to make sure he actually left.

I finished my tea, but was still majorly upset so I found my way into the kitchen. There had to be something there to eat. I had done altogether far too much on an empty stomach. Jonelle came back in just as I was rifling through her cupboards.

Instead of feeling guilt I asked her, "Don't you have anything interesting in this place? It's all salads and health bars, and tofu this and tofu that. No wonder you always want to murder someone."

"I'm not going to murder anyone. If it makes Will happy then he can think that. I intend on having an uncivilized chat to Gavel. First, though, let's go out for breakfast. I think we deserve it, don't you?"

Moderate tone: sensible suggestion. Was this my Jonelle? Seeing as body jacking wasn't possible, I had to safely assume it was.

Out we went again. This time, however, Jonelle visited her safe in the spare room. She caught me staring.

"I think we'll go straight from breakfast around to Gavel then on to find some of Tomas' mates, don't you?"

"Isn't that a lot to take on for one day? Shouldn't we stick with just one mission?" My palms had sprung up with that annoying sweat. "Don't you want to drop me off home first?"

"I don't want you out there loose. You can stay in the car." She slipped a gun into her waist band. That wasn't helping.

"I think I'm going to get indigestion. How can you possibly eat when thinking about what might happen?"

She looked at me.

"I don't think about it. Gavel will be home or not home. If not, he'll be at the Hounds' house and I'll find a way to get him out of it. He'll either talk or he won't. It should prove interesting."

We went back down to the cars and headed to Manuka for breakfast.

"Interesting?" There quite possibly was a squeak to that. "You are talking about some form of ... of interrogation and you think it's going to be interesting. I really shouldn't be surprised, should I?"

"Not really."

I shut up. Breakfast wasn't going to be the mad orgy of pastry that I'd imagined. Instead, I sat there and picked at my croissant, sipping a milk shake and trying to concentrate on breathing in and breathing out.

Maybe I could follow my breath right on up into the atmosphere.

"Don't be such a baby. Eat your food and relax. It's not like I'm going to ask you to talk to him, is it?"

Jonelle, let loose off whatever crazy eating regime she normally had, was hoeing into a huge plate of eggs, tomatoes, mushrooms and other various vegetarian options. I watched in morbid fascination. She grinned at me around a mouthful.

"We all need to keep our energy up."

"It's not that I don't agree with you. It's just I think it's a little inappropriate. This could be Gavel's last meal."

Somewhere in there was logic. I think my brain was short circuiting. She shrugged those broad and muscled shoulders. Had I never really noticed just how strong she looked? I'd also never seen someone get through so much food in such a short space of time. Throwing down her napkin, Jonelle rose to look down at me. Her eyes were hooded and careful.

'Time to go, Princess." No more wiggle room; off we went.

Gavel lived on the outskirts of town, in a fairly new suburb. Houses lined streets not yet leafy, as the trees were all little and stumpy. I sat in the car, twisting the seat belt as Jonelle walked up to the front door. Not that wearing it was going to provide any sort of safety if things went pear-shaped in that house.

She rang the door bell and it was immediately opened by Gavel himself. It was obvious he was on his way out. What was also very apparent was the fact he had not expected Jonelle. Or anyone like her. His face closed over and he attempted to slam the door. Yeah, like that was going to happen. She was through the opening and inside before I could blink.

I sat there watching as the world spun harmlessly on its way. A couple of joggers went passed; a leaf fell off a tree. I wound the window down, but the only sounds were cars and the breeze. It all looked and felt so normal.

There was no indication that inside the house opposite, behind the bricks and the plain bland curtains, someone was going to be telling someone else all they knew about, I'd say, anything she bothered to ask him. She was still pissed that Brenda managed to get herself killed after employing Jonelle to see that it didn't happen.

So Gavel was in for a very unpleasant interview.

I sunk down in my car seat. Would there be blood? Would I hear a scream, cut off, and then she'd emerge? Hollywood didn't need to create special effects for violent scenes. People's imaginations were all the tools they needed. I couldn't hear or see a thing, but my mind was reeling with sensory overload. Even the silence left in the wake of a retreating car was more than I could bear.

Finally I had to get out. I'd just opened the car door when Jonelle let herself out of the house. She was wearing a frown, but there was no other sign of a problem. I shut the door again.

Guess I wasn't going anywhere.

"What were you planning on doing if you got out of the car?" was her first question as she let herself into the driver's seat.

"No clue. Just not sit here anymore. It was driving me nuts."

Jonelle glanced at me. "Hmm. Well that proved to be interesting." She pulled the car away from the curb.

"Well? That's it? You're going to sit there and tell me how interesting it was and not give me details?" I was more than a little outraged.

Jonelle laughed. Lord, the woman was steel; she actually laughed after that.

"I don't know how much detail you want ... but I'll tell you what was said. Gavel threatened Brenda. He had a very nasty time with her and petrified her half to death. But he did not kill her.

"And before you ask, yes I believe him. He comes across as hard as, but he isn't so tough. I don't think he's ever actually murdered anyone. He did, however, give me the name of our missing priest. Gavel, I do believe, is a little afraid of this man. Which means our lovely man of the cloth is not so peaceful and loving as he would have his congregation believe.

"He sounds like a very nasty piece of work. And has the balls to back it up. Sometimes I wonder what attracts people to the priesthood." She shook her head. "I snapped the neck of a Deacon once, overseas somewhere. He was molesting my cousin's son who was a local altar boy."

Her voice had turned to gravel. I didn't want to stop her talking, but really, I didn't know if I wanted to hear anymore either.

"Anyway, I'll go see this priest and find out if he can shed any light on the subject."

I watched the scenery go passed. I wanted to ask this one question, but it seemed almost indecent to do so. Finally, I couldn't help it.

"Jon, exactly how did they get to Brenda through you? How could anyone get through you?"

It was a valid enough question considering everything I knew about her.

I watched as her knuckles went white on the steering wheel. Possibly not the most diplomatic thing I'd ever asked, but it wasn't something she was just going to confess up to, was it?

"It was a while ago now."

She seemed vague on the timing, but perhaps she had other things on her mind.

"I knew Brenda slightly, Will introduced us. You wouldn't call us friends or anything, but I understood her and we had tea sometimes. Just so she could unwind and I suppose, I could too. We were people who knew the seedier side of things; but not really in each others' worlds."

She was silent for a while.

"If one or the other was strung out they could talk about it or not. We didn't mind. For a couple of weeks I noticed she was getting worse, you know, more jittery and abstract. Eventually she confessed that things were too much for her and she needed help. I promised I'd look after her." Not a promise she would have made lightly, I presumed.

"Brenda didn't want it to be too obvious I was looking out for her. She had a job to do, after all, and some clients wouldn't be happy with surveillance. Not that I cared about that. I staked her place out. But the night she was murdered I wasn't there."

Jonelle's voice was lacking in all emotion. However, I used my wonderful powers of deduction and could tell she was blaming herself.

"I'd just got a phone call from England. Jack was found and in a permanent coma. Claire was fuzzy on details, but it sounded as though Amelia had discovered him in Mexico and had in every specialist she could.

"No one held much hope of him ever recovering. I was stunned. That Jack had gone out alone, that someone had got the jump on him and he was comatose, possibly dying."

Her eyes left the road for a second to meet my own.

"I wasn't in any state to look after anyone that night. I went out and got trashed, and had a bar fight with some unfortunate bloke who got in my way. It was messy."

I clearly remembered how she'd been when Claire had told her Jack was dead. The alcohol fumes, the glazed eyes and hints of trauma. Really not surprised Brenda's murderer had managed to do the deed.

"Bit of luck they happened to choose that night wasn't it?"

She shrugged.

"Luck sometimes happens. I thought it may have been planned. But how would they know? It was crazy. So I'm thinking it was dumb luck and she wore it. I wasn't a pleasant person to be around at the time. Jack in a coma, my subject taken out."

I could well imagine. 'Not pleasant' was somehow a massive understatement.

"Speaking of everything I can't do, could you go and visit Jodi sometime this week? It's been a while and I like her to get visitors when I can arrange it."

Jonelle flipped the topic. I hated when she did that. It meant I couldn't keep prying.

"Sure. I'll go there later."

I couldn't say I'd love to because that would be a lie. There was something very depressing about watching someone with Jonelle's face, who wasn't switched on upstairs. It reminded me of how Jonelle could end up given her choice of occupations.

"We'll go back home and I'll sort out some outstanding art deals. We'll find the priest and Tomas' friends tomorrow."

I was surprised. It wasn't like Jonelle to duck an issue and take time off.

"You feeling okay? Oh and won't Will get pissed off when Gavel shows up?"

It had just occurred to me Will was expecting Gavel's obituary notice, not a fully functional Gavel to walk into the Hellhouse.

"Hmm? I'm fine, just sick of this whole mess for today. I have to get in contact with Hank and a few others. I still need to live off my commissions, you know. Will'll just have to deal with it. I wasn't about to start a war with either the Hounds nor whomever else Gavel may or may not be working for. Not until I know a bit more of what is going on around here."

She was practically growling in frustration. "There are too many people who could be involved. There is still that price on my head and other various annoyances out there. It's amazing how fast the past can catch up with you."

"Personally, I wouldn't know. There isn't anything in my past that could bite me," I grumbled. Not that I'd want something to come along and bite me, but really, things had been very boring until she came along.

It was late afternoon when I got back from seeing Jodi. Due to the complicated route Jonelle had insisted I took to make sure no one could link me to the nursing home, I was tired and grumpy.

I hated driving around in circles. I let Manny and Smudge follow me over to Jonelle's. The door wasn't locked again and I let myself in and went straight to the kitchen.

Jonelle came out of the computer room, stretching.

"Well, that's my bread and butter for the next few months. I needed to get some real work done. Now we can play."

She gave me that predatory smile, rolling her shoulders aggressively.

"Time we hunted down that painting, for what it's worth, considering we have no idea whose it is and will probably get nothing for it. I want one less thing on our to-do list.

"Tomorrow we'll go chat to that priest and I'll see just how closely he is linked to Brenda's death, the Phoenix, or anything else like that. I don't want to get anyone connected with Phoenix out here in force. Having The Rose floating around is bad enough. I can't believe he's still in the country and I haven't killed him yet. He's being awfully quiet. But anyway, if we can get information out of this priest without upsetting anyone, good for us."

"Don't you enjoy upsetting people? Isn't that kind of your job? Or hobby, should I say."

She gave me a look. One which kind of said, 'silly girl'.

"Don't confuse me with Amelia. I like to get things done with the least amount of fuss as possible. Otherwise it just gets messy and no one likes that. So, how was Jodi?" She opened an orange juice.

"Pretty much the same as last time. She perked up a bit when I told her I was from you, and kept trying to find you, but other than that not a lot happened. I chatted to her in a roundabout fashion, though I didn't know what I should tell her."

"Nothing. The less she knows the better. Because if she has a lucid day, you never know who she'll tell what to." Jonelle moved into the lounge room, dropping onto the cushions. "Now, unless you have plans with Brad, I was thinking we should go out for dinner and then head over to The Batch and Haddock to see who we can find."

Just like that she changed the subject. One minute Jodi, the next back on track. I liked to think it wasn't because she was cold and lacked humanity, but because she needed to protect her own feelings about the matter.

But sometimes lately, I was beginning to wonder about my assumptions.

Someone couldn't go around interrogating people and killing other people, and still be a part of the rational and normal world. Surely. She had to have something wired a bit differently in her head compared with someone like, say, me. To be able to switch between family and work as though nothing mattered, well, it came across as heartless.

But I still went along with it all. No one like Jonelle had ever entered my existence before and I was too wrapped up with it all to walk away. What if I missed something truly memorable? This was going to give me stories I could tell my grandchildren (presuming I had any) for years to come.

After dinner, we went around to the Batch. It was quiet after the revels of the weekend. But a few of the regulars still propped up the bar. Two in particular caught Jonelle's eye. After getting us a drink, she took me over to them.

"Hey there fellas."

She sipped her drink. I tasted mine and discovered that we were drinking lemonade – straight. I shivered, but played along. She probably didn't want to cloud her judgement, but I couldn't see why I had to go on the same drought.

"Jonelle."

At least one of them knew her then. He nodded and shifted a bit uncomfortably, but held his ground. I was impressed despite myself.

"Hello. I was wondering if I could talk to you or Tomas?" she asked blithely, as though she didn't already know Tomas was a footnote in history.

The straight face she kept was an education.

The one who hadn't spoken grunted and left the table. She watched him go, thoughts hidden behind that inscrutable face. Her eyes flickered to the other.

"Well?"

"Tomas won't be any help to you now. The cops found him yesterday, dead as a post. But I thought you'd know?" He eyed her across his beer.

"Dead, huh? Well I guess it'll be you helping me out after all." Somehow that didn't reassure him.

"What is it you want to know?"

He wasn't meeting her eyes now and I could see a fine line of sweat appear on his forehead. In my little bit of human-reading experience, that could only mean he had something to hide.

Jonelle put her glass down and leaned into him.

"I want to know where the painting is he had stolen. He was going to shift it to Gavin given the right time and opportunity. Or was he just keeping it to piss me off?"

Her voice wasn't strong or even particularly frightening, but the guy was visibly upset.

"Jonelle, I swear, what Tomas did on his own time had nothing to do with me. Leave me out of it."

"Now, you see, somewhere in there I am finding it very hard to believe you. Don't ask me why; must be my suspicious nature. I think, being one of Tomas' closest friends, you would have been along for the ride. You may even have the painting because Tomas surely didn't."

"So, you did know he was dead. Did you kill him?" the guy asked out of curiosity.

"Let's just say, Tomas knew better than to tweak my dial and now he won't be tweaking anything. So, true confession time for you, mister. Where is my painting?"

I was beginning to see where she got her awesome reputation from. I could see this man telling the next person how Jonelle had done for Tomas over a painting, and the story building and building.

Therefore, could it be possible she wasn't half the person I'd thought? Maybe most of her danger was in my head. Really, I couldn't even get *myself* to believe that.

The guy made as if to get up and Jonelle's hand whipped out and held on tight. She had him in some small complicated thumb hold and while he could probably break it with his other hand, he didn't seem to want to try.

"Settle down and start being sensible. You don't want to make this an incident. I just want the painting and then I'll not have to bother you again. It's really quite simple. Whatever reason you had for helping Tomas, and it really wasn't the smartest thing you've ever done, is now over. He won't hold you to whatever deal you had going. So 'fess up."

She sounded so rational and forgiving. If it wasn't for that hand grip and the slowly going white knuckles, I'd have believed her. As it was, I would give up the painting.

And I wasn't the only one.

"Wait, wait! Tomas just wanted to play silly buggers. He said if we could shift it through Gavin all well and good, but mainly he wanted to get your attention."

The guy looked embarrassed. "He had a crush on you and thought you'd come hunting it down a lot faster."

She snorted. "So where is it?"

"At my brother-in-law's place. He's a fence and agreed to hold it for Tomas until it was needed. Tomas knew you'd never be able to link Geoff to him."

"Take us." She nodded to the door and we all got up. "Time to leave."

She gestured for me to follow and marched the man out first. His mate watched from the other side of the bar without moving a muscle.

"I'm coming with you. Fi, follow in my car, okay? We'll take it slow so we don't lose you."

So in convoy we travelled away from inner city living to the southern suburbs. Geoff lived in a snug home with two kids' bicycles lying abandoned out the front. It all looked so normal; I would never have suspected stolen goods were pushed through the place.

We disembarked and bad guy number one (I hadn't been introduced yet) rang the doorbell. It was answered by a five year old. For someone who fenced stolen goods, the security of having his child open the door wasn't exactly what I'd been expecting.

"What cha want?" The child eyed us all suspiciously, chewing on whatever he was having for dinner.

"Mum, someone's at the door," he bellowed.

"Actually, we've after your dad, if he's home." Jonelle told him.

"Nah, doesn't get home till after dinner."

A woman appeared in the corridor behind him and he scampered off to finish whatever he was eating.

"Yes?" She wasn't exactly welcoming, but considering what her husband did for a living, one really couldn't blame her.

Jonelle had that official look about her and a visit from the cops wouldn't be something they looked forward to. She came closer and got a good look at us.

"Oh, Simon, it's you. What are you doing here?" Recognising at least one of her evening visitors didn't make her visibly relax.

"Hi Joyce. You remember that picture Geoff is storing for me and Tomas? I was hoping to get it from you, if that's okay." Simon was trying for the even tones of someone who was there under his own steam.

She nodded and opened the screen door. "Only two of you."

Jonelle motioned me to stay on the doorstep. I wasn't put out. The smell of their fried dinner wasn't sitting too well with me anyway. Amazing really, considering I used to eat that sort of thing all the time.

I waited, hoping the man of the house wouldn't come back until we were safely gone with the picture. I was tired and didn't need another confrontation.

In moments, Jonelle was back. In her arms was a small canvas covered in a sheet. Thank goodness.

"I'm staying here to see Geoff and explain things." Simon stood with Joyce, arms folded almost as if he was expecting Jonelle to order him back with us.

She shrugged. "Whatever you say. Thank you for the painting."

And as easy as that, we were back in her car, picture squashed haphazardly into the remaining space. Jonelle gunned the engine and we screeched away.

"Can you believe that?" The words fairly burst out of her. Temper and frustration flickered in everything.

"I hide Jodi, I try hard not to spook whoever stole the painting and took my time about it all, knowing that Tomas was only a point man and not capable of follow through, and it was all about getting my attention anyway! It was his own weird and twisted made-up concept that somehow I would come gunning for him – and what?" She wrenched the wheel savagely.

"Fall madly in love with him? I can't believe he even got it in the first place. A little weasel like that. And from the looks of it, it's a bad copy of something. A fraud, a fake!

"This hunk of junk," she jerked her head at the painting in the back, "could just as easily be burned. And I made all that effort because some two-bit stupid crook got the idea of luring me over for a one night stand! What? He played decoy on the robbery of Phil's priceless art, heard I was coming for it and decided to get another one done up so I would have to come 'liberate' it as well? What if I had come in and just shot him, and asked questions later? Was he that stupid?"

I kept quiet. Somehow I didn't think she was in the mood for any of my levity. As it was, I was more concerned about making it back in one piece. Jonelle driving in a temper was truly intimidating. A small part of me hoped the cops were out. Mainly to slow her down; not because I have a mean streak and wanted her arrested or anything.

Jonelle drove at manic speeds back to the Grangelands. Picture and woman slammed their way into No 9.

I stood irresolute, not knowing if I was to follow or leave her alone. After a few moments, I chose the cowards way and went back to my pets. She'd have cooled down and found her sense of humour by the morning, I hoped. Otherwise, we'd all be living in Hell.

Chapter Twenty One

I woke up as the sun poked its nose across the horizon. My pets snored softly around me but I couldn't find any more sleep. Not with so many things hanging over my head. Okay, technically they were hanging over Jonelle's head, but I wasn't getting technical at five am!

We may have all the stolen art sorted out, but there was a priest to go find in order to solve Brenda's murder and out there somewhere were people bent on getting Jonelle's head – dead or alive. With a description like that, I assumed they meant attached or unattached. Knowing the woman, the only way they'd collect was unattached.

For some reason it was easier to get up. My body was getting used to all the waking early business. I slipped into my training gear and sipped some water with lemon juice in it.

If I had to be healthy, I may as well get it right. At exactly five o'clock, Jonelle was at my door ready to take me to breathing classes and basic Tai Chi. Yes, I felt a goose, but at least I would be a fit and thoughtful one.

This time round, when we did the twenty minute meditation, I didn't lose myself in thoughts. Instead, I held my focus on the water and tried not to think of anything. I didn't want to plan the day so it was easier than I'd expected.

By the time we got to the gym, I was feeling relaxed and stretched out. I could learn to like the early morning sessions more than the gym ones. Though practising being quiet and actually listening to everything someone else was saying to me was going to prove hard. Half the people I came in contact with didn't have anything interesting to say, and the other half wanted to damage me or Jonelle. How did it get to this?

"Can you tell how much fitter you are?" Jonelle led the way back to the car, long limbs elegant even after a brutal workout. "You don't complain as much and you can lift twice as much weight as when you started. I'm proud of you." She flashed me a grin.

"I don't complain because I am lifting heavier weights and have no breath left," I groused. "But you go on being proud and I promise not to embarrass you too much in front of all your mates."

She knew half the bloody gym by now. Secretly though, I was happy with how things were going. I was noticeably leaner and firmer. Sure, things could still jiggle, but not as badly as they once had. One day I would be more comfortable in the awfully tiny bikini I'd bought in one of my silly moods. It was something that had hidden in the closet ever since, not game enough to show its face because of the remarkable *lack* of material.

"We'll start putting some target practise into our routine at some point soon. I would feel a lot more comfortable if you carried a gun and knew how to use it. As it is, you forget to take your bloody mobile with you half the time. I don't know how such a social creature as you gets away with it."

"I think you'll find in my old life I didn't have much reason to leave the house, so never needed it. Plus, sometimes it's nice to be un-contactable. Though," I hastily added seeing the frown beginning on her face, "in this line of work, not the most sensible option, I'll grant you. I'll make a bigger effort."

"I shudder to ask, but what exactly are our plans today?" Not knowing was worse.

Jonelle swung into the car park. "Well, we go find ourselves a priest and have a nice chat over cucumber sandwiches. You never know what'll come from that. I promise though, tomorrow we'll take the afternoon off and just relax. I think we could both do with doing nothing."

I liked the sound of that, a lot better than the idea of this priest thing. If we found the person who killed Brenda, didn't that mean we had to do something? Like vengeance or retribution or whatever the right word is. And that freaked me out more than anything.

Showered and dressed in pants, matching shirt and fashion sneakers (all the better to run away in while still looking good) I finished off my apricot Danish on the way out the door. Manny and Smudge followed along behind.

Jonelle met me at her door.

"Time to go." She eyed the boys. "With the gate locked they'll be fine to leave out. Smudge won't go far without you or Manny."

Little did she know! He'd found me by wandering off. I'd hate to lose him. With some misgivings we headed off, pets left to roam around the courtyard.

"So, where does this priest person hang out?"

Having never had a family which attended any church, regardless of how pious our mother could come across sometimes, I wasn't up on the whole personal arrangements of priests.

"According to Gavel, this one is intent on becoming the major priestly power here. So he lives in a seminary with a whole stack of other men, trying to oust the players and solidify his own base." Jonelle drove, yet again.

At least she knew where we were going, while on the whole, I never did. So I sat quietly and watched the scenery go by. My life was starting to make some kind of weird sense.

On the outskirts of town, there was a seminary which housed many of the local and in-training priests, deacons or whatever they're called when training. People could also turn up and spend a few hours, days or a month there, and live as traditional monks would have. Eat small meals made from home grown produce, that sort of thing.

I had always liked the sound of it. So peaceful, quiet and relaxing. Mind you, it appeared that even here, there was a hot bed of politics and intrigue. You couldn't escape that sort of thing in Canberra.

It didn't take us long to get there. Jonelle was on a mission and drove accordingly. By now I was used to this kind of driving though it is always interesting to see if we got to our destination.

"Have you had many car accidents?" I thoughtlessly asked, conveniently forgetting the one where her sister was nearly killed.

Jonelle's eyes flickered at me. She wasn't going to lose track of the road, which was one good thing.

"No. Two. Not enough for you to be worried about. One thing I always have had is quick reflexes."

"A handy skill in your line of work." I think my mouth was on autopilot. Or maybe I really was starting to become relaxed in her presence. Make for an easier time for my nerves.

She snorted. "Chatty today, aren't you?" Glad to see it wasn't lost on her.

"Trying not to think of what we are headed out to do. The things we may find out. The people involved. If someone like Gavel is a wee bit intimidated by this priest person, shouldn't we be just a bit more cautious than usual?"

My blood was starting to hum in my veins. A sure indication my nerve radar was on the increase.

"We're just here for information, kiddo. If the priest plays nice, then it'll go well. And if he is the one who killed or ordered the hit on Brenda then I'll deal with him myself. I don't think you should get out of the car, anyway. I mean, you're just about recovered from your beating, but let's not put your face out there for someone with potentially dangerous connections to have a gawp at, shall we?"

I was so used to my own aches and pains and fading yellowing bruises, I'd forgotten I'd received them from two people warning Amelia about backing down.

"I wonder where they got the idea that Amelia was a threat? She didn't even know who they were. But now she does."

"Sometimes smart and focused people can do some dumb and very lacking in foresight type of things. They were covering their bases and probably just passing through town.

"With Amelia not knowing them, they're safe for now. But now that Jack is actually dead, as opposed to lying around in some coma needing attention, she'll grieve, then they'd better be careful. I really don't want to get mixed up with it too much. I want to deal with the Brenda issue. I'm a lot older than Amelia. I don't have the time or the inclination to start another crusade."

I could never contain that innate curiosity. "Just how old are you?"

"Rude little bugger, aren't you?" But her voice was amused, not condemning. "Older than you by a long shot. Things don't heal so well my side of forty. Suddenly I don't feel quite so invincible. Hence the decision to start looking seriously at retirement. Amelia is only twenty eight or so. She's still playing at being the superhero which, mind you, suits her personality. She's a bit dark."

I felt like squawking. A bit? The woman could make the pit of doom look like a day in the park. Okay, so I was exaggerating again. I didn't know her, but I could guess. Everyone walked on eggshells around her, including her one time friend Jonelle. And Jonelle was no shrinking violet.

"In other words, sod off and I won't have to tell you any lies about how old I am?" I smirked at her.

'Yeah, in other words. We can safely say I'm not in my dotage, lucky for you. Otherwise, we'd be trying to sort this mess out using your youthful muscle instead of mine. And see how far that would get us."

"Cow," I muttered, affectionately. She grinned.

Then we were swerving into the seminary and the bottom fell out of my stomach. No more time for trivial jokes, we were on the job again.

Jonelle leapt out and strode off in the direction of what looked liked dorms. I could only assume Gavel had given her directions. Wise man. I sat hunched in my car seat, hoping no one would notice me.

I had kind of been hoping she'd take me on this one. I wanted to see exactly what it was she got up to when asking these things. I mean you didn't just walk into the room and say 'hey, you know that hooker you were seeing, how about telling me about her death?' Because I really didn't think that'd get her very far.

This time she was much longer. I kept checking my watch and the minutes slowly crept by. She wouldn't actually kill a priest while on holy ground, would she? If he pissed her off enough and wouldn't come up with anything good to say, she'd rough him up. But exacting her vengeance right there and then, well I'd like to think not.

Two whole stinking hours later, Jonelle appeared around the corner of the building. She was walking slowly, talking with a priest. What – she wanted to bring him all the way over? Yep, looked like it. Through my window, which I'd wound down because the car was stifling and I was bored, I could hear them as they got closer.

"So sorry Father Michael was not up to seeing you today." The priest was talking. "I can't imagine what laid him so low so quickly. And he does enjoy visitors from town."

So this one wasn't ours. Which could only mean Michael was and Jonelle'd done him in. Bloody hell.

"Not to worry. I'm sure I'll catch up with him another time. Do leave him a message. Tell him I'm always around and that he can feel secure in the knowledge that everything he's ever told me will stay in my mind forever." Jonelle's voice was smooth but I could hear laughter bubbling underneath. I was getting better at this reading people thing.

"Indeed, my dear. Father Michael speaks so well on so many

things. I'm glad to hear he has touched your life. Now I must be going back. God bless you."

I heard him crunch off up the gravel toward the buildings once again. I sat up as Jonelle let herself into the car.

"You've done him in, haven't you?" I blurted. My day for diplomacy.

She started the car and pulled it away from the drive.

"No, I have not 'done him in' as you so kindly put it. I've merely given him a few injuries which helped our discussion along nicely. And I tend to agree with Gavel," she added musingly. "Our Father Michael is not a very nice man at all. If he doesn't have strong ties to Phoenix, whoever they really are, then he surely will one day soon. Or he'll set up in opposition." She swung the car into traffic and picked up speed.

"Well? Are we going back to exact vengeance? Is he the man who killed Brenda?" I badly wanted to pee. All this sitting around waiting in suspense hadn't helped my bladder at all. The least she could do was put me out of my misery. The curiosity misery that is, not the permanent one.

Jonelle glanced over at me and met my eyes for a second. Hers were twinkling with humour. "Just exactly what were you expecting, Princess? Me to ride in on my white horse and teach the nasty man a lesson? It doesn't work like that. I'll have to check out his story and then figure out if I believe it or not."

I could have shaken her and I think she knew it.

"What, then, was his story?" I asked in exaggerated tones of patience that I didn't have.

She turned a corner too sharp and our tires squealed. My hands gripped the seatbelt a bit tighter. Jonelle laughed, savagely, but still a laugh.

"According to Michael, yes he was using Brenda as his paid bedfellow. Not unhappy to admit it. Not the least bit worried about how that might sound at all really. A smooth customer." She flicked us around another corner.

"He's into some sort of big time crime, I could tell that much. The way people who have something very nasty in their cupboards act when I come into their life; it never ceases to amuse me."

The things she found funny!

"He says he was out at a political dinner that evening and isn't into

302

hiring my type of person to do his dirty work. His words." She told me as I opened my mouth to object.

"I got the impression that he would enjoy doing his own dirty work. Though he would need to be a lot faster." She smiled the wolfish smile.

"We had a nice long chat about the sorts of things priests should and shouldn't be into, according to my rather narrow minded views of the priesthood. He'll be quite unavailable for some time. It was the least I could do." She was wearing that smile still.

"Now all I have to do is check out the political dinner story and ask around to see if there were any people like me in the neighbourhood. Because he just may have hired out. Somehow I don't think lying is a very big problem for dear Father Michael. Though lying down per se *will* be for a couple of days." She really did come across as very contented. Like the cat that got the entire carton of cream.

"He won't die or anything? You know, they could get a little upset if you start leaving corpses everywhere." I was still cautious. Perhaps less like a cat and more like a Doberman who didn't understand its own strength?

She blew out an exasperated sigh. "No, he won't die. He'll certainly remember me and not altogether fondly. Which may prove to be interesting in the long run. But his health will be unfortunate for the next couple of weeks." She looked over at me. "I had a personal score to settle with anyone associated with Brenda, remember?"

I gulped. Sure I remembered, and I didn't want to think of how my priestly friend was looking right now. "So where to now?"

"I think I'll drop you home. You can look up political stuff going on at the time of Brenda's murder. Then make some calls and see if our Michael was on the guest list. I'm off to see some people about other people."

How lovely and cryptic. Though I knew what she was on about. Trying to find out if there was someone in town who really shouldn't have been when Brenda died. Though I'd have thought she would have noticed someone like that in a small town like Canberra.

A few minutes later she dumped me off at the gate and took off again. Maybe she would have some luck in jogging people's memories, but I thought it was a waste of time.

Letting myself in, I was greeted by the boys who followed me happily into Jonelle's place. It really was becoming a home away from home.

I settled myself in front of the computer and connected to the internet. I was hoping something would jump out at me straight away. It was too lovely today to sit inside and the desk top couldn't be moved out to the pool area for sunny internet surfing.

I plugged in the dates surrounding Brenda's death and politics. It was an easy search if I narrowed it down to Canberra. There was always something political going on. That was the trouble though; he didn't have to put much thought into his alibi. He told Jonelle it was a charity ball for Labor held at the Arts Centre, which I found. Jobs like this were great, simple, easy and direct. Finding the right event and then the invited guest list, I eventually found our Father Michael.

There was even a picture of him with some of the political figures of the day. No way could he have faked that lot. He'd definitely been there. Mind you, now I was more aware of the types of people you could buy for the right amounts of money, there was no saying what he'd had done while he was busy being photographed.

There wasn't much point in me just hanging around waiting, so I packed up the computer and took my pets for a walk. For once, I actually took my mobile with me just in case Jonelle needed to get in touch while I was gone.

It was one of those magical days that Canberra could spring on you. November was over and December just begun. Summer, while technically here, doesn't come in full force until the new year. The sun was the only thing in the sky and a soft warm breeze was tossing leaves and blossoms through the air.

Manny was overjoyed at the prospect of a walk. He was practically dancing. Smudge, predictably, wasn't quite so enthused, but we dragged the poor little bugger along anyway. Never let it be said I allowed my cat to resemble Garfield. Though of course, after we had left him behind for the second time, I relented and carried him. He was still small enough to be a nice bundle of fluff and not too heavy. The vet told me Smudge was possibly part Persian but that's where his guess was going to end. Nothing like a mongrel for a cat.

I lay in the park, absently throwing the ball one handed and letting Manny gallop off to bring it back. It occurred to me, while studying the sky, that I hadn't heard from my parents, Brad or anything from that horrid Lilly and sidekick Francis, for a long time. Of course, when it came to the latter I was relieved and when it came to the first two, the simple solution would be to phone them. I didn't want to call either, but it was probably my turn.

I flipped over onto my stomach and hauled my mobile out. I thought about it and decided that the folks should get first dibs. If I lucked out and they didn't answer, Brad would be next.

As it turned out, Mum was home. "Hello? Oh Fiona! What a pleasant surprise. What are you up to dear?"

Sometimes if it's been long enough between calls or visits, we can sound genuinely happy to hear from each other.

"Hi Mum. Just wanted to call and see how you and Dad are. You know, make sure you two are coping without Potty and with the new one." For a second I had a blank. "Puddle."

"That's nice dear. It's still a large hole not to have Potty around. You know how much a part of everything she was. Mind you, the food bills, if I may be so crass as to say, are a lot lighter these days with only Puddle. He's doing well. Filling out as he grows up. You should stop passed sometime soon dear, so he gets to recognise family. The kidlets are round here all the time. They just love having a puppy to spoil."

Ah, the subtleties of my mother. In other words everyone, except me, had been around and she was trying to make me feel guilty. It would be so much easier if she just said 'get your butt over here sometime soon, young lady'.

"I'll try to pop over soon, Mum. It's just very busy right now. And I have to spend some time with my man, Brad."

Now where had that come from? I was trying hard not to let my mother or any family member get a whiff of Brad yet. But the excuse was too perfect. The idea of me actually dating would have my mother enraptured for hours. Still, it would be nice when I could learn to bite my tongue.

"Brad, dear? I hope we get to meet him soon?" The tone was right; that halfway between plea and demand.

"Sure, Mum. Any day now. It's just quite early in the piece and I don't want him to run scared meeting you all." There, put that in your pipe and smoke it.

"Oh, of course not, dear. We wouldn't want that. You take it nice and slow and I'm sure he'll come round soon."

And as easy as that I was off the phone again. Man, I should have invented a load of family-shy boyfriends years ago.

Next, was a call to Brad. Manny had given up on me, and flopped out on the grass next to Smudge. Tongue lolling, he watched the ball idly not too sure if the game was completely over. I scratched his ears and he closed his eyes in ecstasy. I only wish all the men in my life could be so easy. I tapped in the number and listened to the phone ringing.

"Hi there, you." Brad's deep and ultra sexy voice came down the line. Instantly my stomach muscles clenched. You'd have thought it was weeks since we last got together, not days. I felt all liquid and drowsy. The man was a tonic.

"Hi there yourself. Working hard?" I tried to put half as much sex in my voice as he could ladle into a few words. No idea how that was working out, but it still made me feel good.

"Yes. Very. I'm mostly in Sydney for the next few weeks. They might have to relocate part of the office up here." His voice, though still sexy, was now a bit hesitant. I wanted to leap up and howl.

What were they, whoever they were, thinking? We'd just managed to get past awkward into hot sex. I'd woken up thinking wouldn't this be great to wake up to for ... well a while, anyway.

"Does that mean your section is going? Or you, and is it definite?" Was there just a touch of panic in my tone of voice? I could only hope not.

He chuckled down the line. "Don't sound so grumpy, sweetheart. It's not the end of the world. It could be as simple as a couple of people or just until this account is taken care of. It'll only mean we get to pack a lot more into a shorter period of time." I could hear the smile in that voice. It made more than my toes curl.

"Well speaking of which, when are we likely to be doing that again, sir?" I kept the tone light. Nothing worse than sounding desperate. There may have been hints of a system in overdrive, but I tried to keep my cool.

"I'll make it down this weekend, okay?" Outright laughter. Bastard.

"Don't put yourself out." Ah dear, there I went, into snippy mode. What was it with Brad and Jonelle? Both of them could get me defensive in seconds.

"Honey, I never do. But seeing you is a treat and there are all sorts of wonderful compensations for not being around all week. I'll take hours to make you happy."

"With promises like that, mister, you'll need all the energy and strength you've got."

"Then it's a good thing I'm fit. Look Fi, I have to go. It's flat out here. And just remember, nothing's definite yet." And he hung up.

I lay there staring at my phone. Damn it. Just like that, the best sex and fun I'd had in ages could be walking out. Sydney wasn't that far, but could well be the moon seeing I was now a working girl.

Unlike a short while ago, I can't just flit up to Sydney whenever I wanted to visit a boyfriend. Now I had to plan ahead and make sure Jonelle was okay with that. Not that we were doing anything that could be construed as formal employment and it had rapidly become even less formal as time went by. But I was enjoying it, damn it, and I wasn't going to run out now it was getting gritty.

I knew I didn't want to run slap bang into murder and bloodshed. But on the other hand, I was kind of intrigued as to what someone like Jonelle got up to when let out at night, or during the day. I couldn't imagine what my friends and family would think about my new acquaintances.

Jonelle, in particular. I could see how she viewed the world. At least, I think I could see it. There were people who needed culling and there were those who did the job. I couldn't believe I just thought that! But it was kind of the way they lived their lives. The backbone of what they believed in. I guessed in the real world that would make Jonelle a dangerous criminal, but after meeting her and talking with her, I couldn't see that anymore. She was just this woman I knew, who walked to a majorly different drum beat.

I stood up. "Time to go guys."

I snapped my fingers at my lethargic pets. Smudge didn't even turn a hair, he knew he'd end up being carried. Manny raised his head, but had to ask if I meant it. He was out of puff, the hot sun and the ball game having reduced him to canine impotence.

"Yes really. Up you get. I'm not carrying you as well." I stroked his long silly dog nose. I had already fallen in love with these two chaps. There was no way I could imagine my life at Grangelands without them.

We wandered back slowly; taking our time because it was lovely and the phone hadn't rung. Which could only mean Jonelle wasn't back yet so why rush? I had the last hours of the afternoon to actually get some good TV watching in.

I hastened my pace. Hey, it'd been ages since I'd managed to sit down and just veg for several hours in a row. If Brad did take a job offer in Sydney, even only for a few months, looked like my out of business hours would be free again.

I wasn't in the door two seconds before I switched on the telly. We spaced ourselves out on the couch and dug in for some serious mental veg time.

Bullseye. They were running Buffy: The Vampire Slayer repeats. Cool. At one stage in my life, I was seriously considering doing martial arts in the vain attempt to pretend I could hack it as a Slayer. Now, of course, I knew a bit more about what was involved with getting fit and understood I had something like a snowball's chance in hell of ever doing it. It was nice to know my limitations.

Somewhere between Buffy staking a vampire and another such riveting event, I fell asleep.

When Jonelle arrived after dark, I was only just coming to. Smudge and Manny were insisting on going outside for their last nightly patrol and I was trying to think up something inspired to eat at nine o'clock, which was a lot harder than I thought possible.

"What happened to you?" Jonelle leaned in around the door frame, watching as I put frozen pizza into the microwave. "Are you really going to eat that?"

I gave her a glare. "Yes. I really am. It'll be warm and runny and cheesy. Want some?"

She shrugged. "Why not?"

I nearly fell over.

"I don't always eat just for my body's sense of health you know. Sometimes it can be all about the calories and the taste. Mind you, those days are rare." She smiled, but it was low wattage and looked tired around the edges.

I put the kettle on. It was altogether sadly comfy and domestic.

"So what did you turn up today?"

She laughed. "My toes? No seriously. According to my sources no one was around who could have pulled off Brenda's murder and would have, more importantly, for money or favour. That is not including our Will who may or may not know anything at all."

"Why don't you *ask* Will?" I made us both instant coffees. I didn't feel like I wanted to go to bed straight away and Jonelle looked as though she needed something to help her stay focused.

She followed my pottering with her eyes.

"I'm having my doubts and suspicions about our lovely Will. I can't put my finger on it, but something doesn't feel right. And believe me, when I get irritable, there is a problem."

"Do I look like I doubted you?"

"No, but then again you have a thing for Will and may not want to think him capable of throwing a spanner into our works. There is something just not right about his explanation and the reasons behind his need to get rid of Gavel. I think Gavel and Will have history, and Will is seeing me as a cheap opportunity to free himself of the hassle." She sipped her coffee.

"I don't like been seen as convenient."

Master of the understatement. And truly if you were up to no good could Jonelle technically ever be seen as convenient?

The microwave pinged and I removed our steaming pizza. Cutting it into halves, I put them on two plates and went to sit on the couch.

Biting into my half, filling my mouth almost to capacity, I was suddenly aware of how contented I was. I grinned. Whoever would have thought?

Jonelle waved her slice at me. "What's the huge smirk about?"

"Mufft, ffgrrt mph," I mumbled, articulate to the last.

"Didn't I come in at this point a few weeks ago?" But she smiled to soften the words. "I think I know what you meant and yes, it is companionable and I feel content with the situation as well."

Boy, she was good. But it may have had more to do with the snug atmosphere. The front door, which hadn't been fully closed, swung open and Smudge and Manny came in. There, it felt like the whole family was home for dinner.

"But back to your insult, I am *not* hung up on Will and I wouldn't let my feelings about a situation hurt your investigation." Well, I probably would, but I liked the sound of my story better and I was sticking to it.

"Plus, why on earth would Will want to throw spanners? Into our works or not?" I had barely finished the question when I had plied myself with another mouthful.

She swallowed.

"Glad to see you can think clearly when it comes to Mister Malone. He really isn't your sort. Better off sticking with Brad."

Yeah, well that's what she thought.

"Will may think he can help us out, but when it comes down to it, he's only thinking of advancing Will. Never forget that. Most people you will ever meet, either through me or just in life, may offer to lend you a hand, but they have a motive. And that may not have your best interests at heart. People, on the whole, require getting something out of a situation to actually get into the situation in the first place. Will wants something or has an angle; I just can't see what it is yet."

"That is terribly cynical of you, Jonelle. Fancy thinking everyone is out for themselves." I grinned at her. "I'm not totally stupid, you know."

Jonelle rolled her eyes at me. "Of course not."

I threw a piece of crust at her. "No one is going to believe you with a tone like that." I couldn't believe how normal and relaxed we were. "Anyway you might be interested to know that yes, Father Michael attended the gala he mentioned and there were even photos to prove it. This means he didn't kill Brenda and if your information is right, he didn't hire anyone else to do it either, which means we're back to square one."

I finished off the remains of my pizza and eyed her partly eaten half. She picked it up and took a massive bite, watching me watch it disappear. Bitch. I needed more food.

"I think we can clear Gavel and the priest. Mind you, I don't like them or what they keep implying the other is getting into. But being up to no good, regardless of how bad it is, isn't something I'm concerned with right now. If say, they head in the direction of the opposition, as Will would call such groups as the Phoenix, then they can be Amelia's problem and if she decides she doesn't like them, she can kill them if she wants to. Leaves me right out of it."

Sometimes, she was just a little too callous and it made my ethics shiver. Jonelle must have noticed my screwed up nose.

"Some people who are into the wrong things just need to be eradicated, like vermin. Don't think about. It's not our issue."

Easy for her to say. I couldn't just come out and ask her how many people she'd personally eradicated, but more and more I was aching to find out.

"So, we have The Rose working for sundry nasty people, while sitting happy as Larry in Sydney. We have two people here who are in the clear when it comes to Brenda's murder and no new suspect. I managed to get Phil his picture back and instil in his micro sized brain that people *like* Monet and he should be more careful in the future.

I have attempted to trace the badly done painting Geoff was hiding for Tomas.

"And believe me, in the cold light of day, it wouldn't have stood up to any tests for a fake, even from a hack like Gavin. No one appears to be interested and the work is so bad I can't be bothered putting the artist out of his job, so I burned it. I checked on Hank, who loves his new Ripley and I have a massive headache." Jonelle rubbed her temples.

"It would be nice if some of this would just disappear. The price on my head comes from a man who should know better, seeing as he was in protection and I have been asked to place a Dante Keystone with another client. Bloody stupid name for an artist if I ever heard one. So that about raps it up."

True, the name was odd to say the least, but the man was a legend. He painted, sculptured and made some sort of cook book series. People from all over wanted his works.

"What exactly do you mean by 'place'?" By now I had the right to be a bit cautious.

"I've been asked to liberate a particularly lovely piece from a very rich couple in Sydney. They may miss it, but they can afford to get another one. My client likes this one, which is not for sale. It should be fun."

I shook my head. "You have the strangest tastes in what constitutes as fun. How do you pick and choose your clients? I mean, wouldn't it be simpler to just go tell the other people for a sum of money I'll protect your art objects from ... er ... me? Then they don't get all unhappy and go to the police."

Getting caught was obviously not even on her radar.

"I make sure I'm not going to be hurting people I could use in the future or who need the money. And really, do you seriously think I'm as easy to catch as all that? I don't think the police even have a file on me." She thought about it. "Well, maybe they do, but it'd be pretty thin and no way they could use it to hold me on anything. I'm a clever little thing."

Getting up, I took her plate and mine back into the kitchen.

"Yes, you are. Now we have pandered to your ego and nutted out what is pending, do you think we could find something else to eat? I'm starving." I started opening cupboards randomly.

"I need to do some shopping. This is insane." Luckily we lived near a twenty four hours Coles. I grabbed my keys. "Let's go. I should probably get the boys something as well." I eyed them off. They looked pretty happy with kibble, but variety wouldn't be a bad thing.

"Sure." No arguments, no attempt to make me think of less food. Maybe someone had body snatched her.

We could have walked. In fact, after all that pizza we probably should have. But we didn't. Parking the car took longer than the actual drive, which said something about our laziness. But it was good to see Jonelle being like everyone else who just quaffed half a pizza.

After being so slack and just eating from a take away or at Jonelle's for, like, ever, it was marvellous to zoom around the aisles and stuff my trolley full. Every conceivable nibble, or tin, even some vegetables were loaded in. I wouldn't have to come out again for a week.

Three hundred dollars later, with bottles of wine and gin attached, we made it back to the car. Jonelle was laughing at my extravagance, but hey, now I knew she would actually eat real stuff, she could laugh all she wanted to. There was no way I was feeling guilty now.

"Anything else?" Jonelle eyed my stash, which nearly took up the whole trolley. "I'm sure we could balance something on top…"

I gave her a glared. "It's all essential."

She grabbed a box randomly. "Homebake Chocolate Chip Cookies, yes, I can see, all a matter of life or death. Cadbury Milk Chocolate." She began rummaging through my shopping.

"Hey," I snatched for the chocolate. I had priorities after all. "That's enough of that! Let go."

Here we were, two adult (I'd like to think) women, fighting over the contents of a shopping trolley, when we heard a polite cough. Jonelle let go and swung around, while I tried to keep balanced, now I had no opposing force.

"Jonelle. What a surprise." His voice was weak, thin and strangely high. Or maybe that was just because I was used to Will and Brad's masculinity.

I managed to get myself together and took a good look at our guest. Having now accustomed myself to Brenda's file a little more closely, I knew this man. It was Craig, the boyfriend. Though, if I hadn't known that in advance, I would have assumed he was a bit too feminine, if you see what I mean.

"Craig. What a surprise. How are you?" Jonelle pushed a box of biscuits deeper into the trolley, as though hiding her foolish behaviour would help. "You keeping well?"

I had never known Jonelle to make such banal conversation. Mind you, I rarely saw her talking to anyone who wasn't a gangster or involved with them somehow, so I was no judge.

Craig wrung his hands and his face twitched, as though he was trying not to let tears form and ruin the pretence of actually coping. "I don't sleep so well, Jonelle. I keep thinking of Brenda and wishing I could have done more. I should have saved her, you know," he looked at us earnestly. "She shouldn't have been out there alone, working in such a dangerous industry. She knew I would take care of her..." he trailed off, lost and alone.

While I felt very sorry for him, there was also a very strong part of me in disbelief. Brenda had been a very attractive woman. She couldn't have come up with someone better than *this*? Give him his due I probably wasn't seeing him at his best. Grief had washed Craig out. Lank brown hair clung to his scalp, large puppy dog eyes were rimmed with red and his nose was swollen from his last crying jag. The man was a mess.

Jonelle recoiled faintly. She too, didn't want to get too close to Brenda's boy.

"Have you found anything new?" He looked at her as though she was the second coming, all hope and expectation. I wondered how she coped.

"Nothing just yet, Craig. You know how sorry I am. I'll find who killed her, you know I will." Jonelle gave him a reassuring look – from a distance. No pat on the shoulder there. "You need to take better care of yourself, Craig. She wouldn't want you to fall apart."

There was a distinct odour about the man.

He shook his head. "I just don't seem to be able to do that. All I can think about is Brenda, crying out for someone to save her and me sleeping peacefully on the coast, not helping..."

"Don't blame yourself." Blame me. I could almost hear those last two words, though of course she never uttered them.

"Try to move on, Craig." She looked at me. "Sorry, I have to go."

Craig raised his eyes to me. And I felt a jolt. Red rimmed they may have been, but the venom in them was redder. Perhaps he hated me taking Jonelle's attention? I shuddered. The man was clearly becoming unhinged.

"I hope you find something soon," he spoke calmly to her, moving those eyes back to Jonelle. "Bye." He waved vaguely, and wandered off.

Jonelle watched him go through narrowed eyes. "He was never a great catch, but right now? I'd have to ask Brenda what the hell she'd been thinking."

I struggled for something nice to say. "Didn't you say it was because he stood for everything that she didn't have? You know - safety and values and um ... stuff? Sure, he looks no catch now, but did she really have that many choices?"

I mean, I wouldn't share my boyfriend with anyone, let alone half the city.

Jonelle shrugged. "He may feel better when I can close the door on who killed her. But let's not think about him tonight, yes?"

I was more than happy to comply.

Back home, we haphazardly piled it all into the cupboards. Then I fed the boys some pet mince. "That was exactly what they were looking for." I watched as they both wolfed it down. "Now, what are we going to have for seconds?"

Washing my mincey hands, I opened some chips, a tonic water to which I added some gin, and a packet of mint slice chocolate biscuits. We put our feet up on the couch and munched.

"So when are you off to Sydney?" I picked the conversation back up.

"I was thinking of heading up tomorrow, if I can grab a flight. It'll mean we won't have the day off per se, but at least we won't be wasting any more time. You should come. You could drop in and see Brad at the office."

I had mentioned how Brad was thinking of relocating to the bigger city. Jonelle wasn't as concerned as I was.

"Yeah, and get the brush off. He said he'd be back on the weekend. But I could snoop." I grinned. "You know, go by, poke my nose in and see where he'll be."

I liked that idea more. He need never know I'd been. So when he talked about the office next, I could visualise it. But I wouldn't see him, because he might think I was lonesome and needy.

"Surprises never work out, Fi. Take my advice and let him know you're coming. Men are not ones who like to be spied on." Jonelle helped herself to another biscuit. "God, these are great. It's been ages since I've eaten anything this fattening. I wonder if I could just add a thousand more sit ups and eat mint slice for dinner every night?" She held it out and studied it at arm's length. "I mean, how many calories can they have? Really?"

I flipped over the packet. "About a million." I threw it away. "But who cares? They are now a part of our every day diet and there will be no quibbling." I held up a finger as she opened her mouth. "Ugh. No quibbling I said and I meant it."

"Okay, but I'm not taking my dietary directions from you as a rule." And she finished off another one. Then she stood up. "I should go get some rest. Or at least pretend to. I'll come get you at five."

I waved her away. Flash Gordon had just come on telly. Old movie re-runs are another wonder of pay TV.

"Don't stay up all night, Princess. You'll be exhausted tomorrow."

"Yes Mum." I glanced up at her then back to Flash. "See you tomorrow."

Smudge came and curled up with me, but Manny headed for bed. At least one of us was sensible. He happily found his cushion in the bedroom. Nice to know he was cured of the need to sleep in the bed. He was just too big for that.

It was past midnight by the time I carried Smudge to bed. He curled up in one corner, tucking his little nose under his paws. I stripped and slipped under the sheet. It was too warm for anything else and while I was conscious of the fact I didn't want to be naked if people like Charles and Daniel came back, I had to live with the hope that Jonelle's beefed up security and Manny would provide me with some safety.

Chapter Twenty Two

I sat next to Jonelle in business class. I twiddled my seat belt, flicked through a magazine eyeing off celebrities in bikinis no one should be allowed to buy. It wasn't about the journey for me anymore, it was about being there. And everything in between was just filling.

"Would you settle? You're really starting to get on my nerves. If you are that worried about snooping on Brad, then call him." Jonelle growled at me.

"I'm not worried about snooping. It'll be fun. You know, I can see you but you can't see me. I can get a whole stack of the perve factor in. I just hate having to get there." I grinned at her scowl.

"Are we there yet Mum?" And stuck out my tongue. Yes, I was twenty nine, but no one ever said that any particular level of maturity came with the gig.

Jonelle rolled her eyes. "Sometimes you make me concerned about my own sanity. I actually chose to have you along."

"Yep. You asked, begged and practically demanded. So in reality, you only have yourself to blame."

And I settled back into reading the scandal sheets, a big smirk plastered all over my face. I was beginning to enjoy this new phase of our relationship. It meant I was more comfortable teasing her and not so wary about upsetting her temper.

Not long after, we landed and sorted out the luggage. Seeing as we were only meant to be staying a night maybe two, we were light on the baggage. Well, actually Jonelle didn't have much. Me – I had the usual half tonne shipment. I didn't know how she could call herself a woman and be content with something only slightly larger than a gym bag. And half of that would be given over to various tools of her trade.

"We'll stay in town and go to Vaucluse later. I'll hire a car or something." Nothing like actual organisation. I'd never seen her so relaxed and almost slap dash.

We ended up finding a suite at the Hilton. Tough life this working girl business. I left Jonelle poring over some maps or blueprints. I didn't want to ask, but I was pretty sure they were security prints for the place she was looking at busting into. How she got these things was beyond me and I really didn't want to know. Safer thinking she magicked them up.

I had some scouting to do. I knew that Brad's office had its Sydney branch somewhere near and I didn't want to wander into him accidentally. The whole idea was to be stealth itself. Something I wasn't all that familiar with, but I was getting there.

I hadn't been up to Sydney in a while so I was enjoying the sightseeing, watching the millions of people scurrying by, peering into shops and not so discreetly gawping at lovers in cafes. So it shouldn't have come as a surprise to see someone I knew. Well, it should, because Sydney is huge. But that it was Brad and he wasn't alone really rocked me.

I stopped and allowed people to stream passed me, bumping me and some even cursing my untimely stoppage. There, in a small café, holding hands and leaning into each other, was my guy and some woman. Brad had the same adoring grin on his face, but his eyes were soft and full of love and other sappy emotions. My heart started to pound and my skin came over icy. My eyes pulled over to have a good look at the woman.

Her legs curled out to the side from under the table, lean long expanses of them. Straight ash blonde hair fell around a small face with a fabulous smile. White teeth gleamed as she flashed them continuously at Brad. He leaned forward and kissed her – deeply and passionately, so as to leave no doubt in my mind they knew each other, very well.

There was something I had to do. I knew that I had to start to move and get away but somehow my legs refused to function. I couldn't be caught here, my brain screamed. But I stood and stared and drank in his lips locked with hers.

Eventually another passer-by practically pushing me out of the way got me moving. I struggled back toward to the Hilton, where there was some form of safety.

Had it only been a few days ago I had woken up with him and thought this was nice and how do I make it permanent? I pushed the button for the lift.

"Are you all right, Madam?" A concerned porter touched my arm briefly.

"Fine. Really, just going back to the room." I plunged into the lift, not caring what he thought. My brain was on fire. What was going on? Who was that woman? And why was Brad kissing her?

The lift pinged gently as it came to rest at my floor. Suddenly the door key, which was a infernal credit card look alike, wouldn't open. I was practically weeping in frustration by the time I slammed the door open.

Jonelle had gone. And for once I was more than grateful. There was a note sitting on the coffee table, propped up against the TV remote.

'Out. Back in time for dinner. Don't spoil your appetite.'

Too late. It was permanently spoiled. I flung myself into the lounge and stared at the wall.

"Bastard. Bastard! Who is that bitch?" I was practically growling.

Okay, I wasn't at my best. Probably not doing myself any dating favours by admitting to that type of behaviour, but I didn't care. My skin was crawling with ice and somewhere my stomach was curled up crying.

I was shaking. No denying it, I was not happy.

Why oh why couldn't I have taken Jonelle's advice and not gone snooping? Then I'd still be in blissful ignorance. I reached over and grabbed the telephone directory. I only had Brad's mobile, never having had to call him at work. And that was something I didn't want to use.

Flicking through the white pages, I came to his firm's Sydney listed number. I grabbed the land line and punched it in.

"Could I speak to Brad Morphett?" I practically drowned the receptionist out. I felt like screaming, but I tried very hard to achieve something along the line of a business tone. Somehow, I didn't think I was succeeding very well.

"Certainly, putting you through." She sounded a mite bit put out.

"Brad's office, Mandy speaking." A young and chirpy voice answered.

I almost ground my teeth. "Is Mr Morphett around?" Not easy

to play it cool.

"Oh I'm sorry, Mr Morphett's out with his wife right now. They're celebrating them getting pregnant. Can I give him a message?"

I think I heard the rest of that sentence. From somewhere else may be. At least, far, far away from here and now. I sat down. I hadn't even realised I was standing.

"He's where?" My voice didn't sound connected to me either.

"Out with his wife. They're very excited. They've been trying to get pregnant for the last two years. Can I take a message?"

Her young voice no longer came across so bouncy. She was starting to sound a little peeved. Probably aware that the information she'd just given out was not the most professional.

"No that's okay." And I hung up. I sat there with the cordless handset dangling in one hand while the other clenched involuntarily on the arm rest.

There were thought patterns you went through in moments of crisis. I was sure there were. I just couldn't get any thoughts to process, let alone find a pattern. Somewhere out in the city were two love birds cooing over their new family. And I was bereft of a relationship I hadn't even realised I was so attached to. One I'd had no right to.

I stood shakily and made myself a drink. A very strong double bourbon, light on the Coke. Married. Not only married, but now pregnant and married. I sat again. My legs weren't strong enough to hold me for long periods of time. I sculled the whole drink and hastily made myself another. This was no time to go easy on the alcohol. I didn't want the brain to actually function. Not that that was going to be an issue for a while.

There was this blank feeling in my head. I tried experimentally to put thoughts into the hole. Nothing came out. I was stuck on an image of Brad smiling protectively and lovingly into the eyes of his ... *wife*. Could we replay that bit please? And hit the wipe button. There was just no way you could wipe a wife. My brain kicked in.

Well, actually, there really was.

I'd gone through the better half of a bottle of bourbon by the time Jonelle came swinging in the door. She was wearing a little smile and carrying a bag of shopping.

"Hello there, Princess. Hope you haven't spoiled your appetite."

If there was a reason for this joyful tone, I couldn't see it. I stared stonily at her, trying to convey my inner misery so she wouldn't have to ask. She turned and took a good look at me when I failed to respond. This included a long sweep of the bottle, the Coke bottles, and the empty glass in my hand.

"Not a great day, hey?" She tried to keep the tone light, but her eyes narrowed.

"Brad has a wife." I told her flatly. I couldn't give a toss about my tone.

Her eyebrows climbed. Both of them. "Excuse me?"

"You were right. I shouldn't have snooped. I could have pretended it was all okay, except he has a wife and they are pregnant." I stopped.

I hated the raw and revealing tone in my voice. It spoke of loneliness and desperation. Not two things anyone wanted to admit to. I turned my eyes up to hers, flinching at the concern in them. "Can you get rid of him or her for me?"

She hesitated, then laughed. "You really do not know what you're asking." She took the glass from my nerveless fingers.

"I do! I want him to suffer. Make him pay. Isn't that what girlfriends are meant to do?"

"Yes, but I'm not the usual girlfriend and the things I could do to him both of us would regret. Now, don't be silly. And be glad you found out now, before you asked him to move in with you or something."

If I had been looking for sympathy or revenge, I could have done better with a fellow barfly.

"I can't believe you won't help me! What's the point of even knowing someone like you if I can't rely on them?" There was logic to my argument, if you were me.

She was next to me in two long strides. Her fingers had terrible strength when she wasn't pulling her punches – well, her grip. Her eyes were dark and piercing.

"I am not a toy you can take out and wind up and hope is pointing in the right direction." She watched my face and I could feel its colour seeping away.

"Good. Now, be glad I don't think you know what you're talking about in your state." Jonelle stood up and moved away, gathering Coke bottles and capping my bourbon.

"Sorry. I know you aren't like that. It's just … well, how could he? What sort of man has a wife like that in one city and someone like me in another?" A thought came through my intoxicated head.

"Does that mean he's been living here all the time and only coming to Canberra to help out, not the other way round? What a mess. The Apartmates loved him. How could we all be so wrong?" I looked at Jonelle for the answers.

She came and sat opposite my slug-like body. "I don't know. Perhaps he was thinking of leaving her and the pregnancy has taken that option away now. Perhaps he really is scum and wanted his cake and eat it too. Whatever the reasons, you know now. You can't go back to not knowing, and the only thing to do is get sober and move on." She waved her hand at my physical destruction.

"You want him to win? Lay you low by this and become a drunk? He's obviously not worth it, Princess. Have some pride in yourself." She came over and bent down.

"Sleep it off and tomorrow we'll have some fun. Then we'll take care of this job and go home. Life can be exciting without him you know."

Then with one of her amazing displays of strength, Jonelle picked me up. I wasn't a big girl. Plus, am really short compared to, well, nearly everyone. But still, it was an impressive feat to do with the dead weight of the intoxicated and from a bending position. She stood with what looked like ease and carried me to my bed. There I was laid down and the blankets wrapped around me.

"Have a rest, Princess. I'll go and sort your Brad out for you."

And she was gone. I fuzzily thought that probably I should have stopped her, or at least asked what she meant, but alcohol, disappointment and hurt crashed over my head and I went under.

It was sunshine, the hangover's worst nightmare, which brought me round the following day. A rather large beam of it was slanted across my bed and I wished Jonelle had thought to close the blinds last night. Or possibly it was my punishment.

With a groan I swung my legs over the edge of the bed and waited for the room to stop its slow loop. Even half a bottle of bourbon was capable of flattening me these days. My high tolerance for alcohol was seeping away the longer I hung out with veggie munching, and green tea drinking, Jonelle. I sat there gripping the mattress, head hanging low, eyes screwed up. I wasn't prepared to have a look at the day yet.

Though once I had purged my stomach, things were on the up again. I had a scalding hot shower and wrapped myself in the luxurious bath sheet provided.

Jonelle was sitting at the table, sipping what smelled like coffee and reading the papers. She glanced up as I wandered in wearing only the towel.

"You look almost normal. How are you feeling? Want a coffee?"

"Thank you, okay and yes please." I plonked myself down in the chair opposite.

I could see no need to get dressed, and swept my damp hair back off my face. First things first. A lovely hot coffee for my over loaded system. I smelled breakfast coming from the covered platters.

"Oh, you ordered! I thought we might have to do down for it." I reached over and took the covers off. Eggs, bacon, mushrooms, croissants, and bagels. The woman could have reached into my head and plucked my most wanted food stuffs right out. I tucked in.

Jonelle came back from the bench with a coffee. "Slow down, Wolf girl." She laughed. "There is plenty there for everyone."

I paused in my head long dive into food. "Dare I ask what you got up to last night?"

I briefly met her eyes, but hastily went back to studying my plate. Sometimes she could make me distinctly uncomfortable. On the other hand, my curiosity always got the better of me.

"Well, I took my much vaunted abilities," she was laughing at me gently, for which I was grateful, "and I found our Mr Morphett. I had a long chat to him and his delicious wife, and when I left he was baling himself out. To what degree he was to be successful I'm not sure. But I felt he was owed that much at least. Regardless of the new family on the way, he shouldn't get off scot-free."

She bit into a croissant.

Taking a large swallow of boiling coffee, I felt a bit better.

"Even though it must have been nasty for her, I'm really glad you did it. She needs to know everything about him if she's starting a family with him." I sighed. "It's kind of sad for her though. But thanks. Thank you for taking the time out to go do my dirty work."

I met her eyes and held them for a moment. They were softer than usual and still held the sympathy.

"It's never nice to be betrayed, Fiona. I do understand that and while I don't like hurting innocent people, she had a right to know. I only put things back on an even playing field. Now she has all the facts, she can do with them as she will." Jonelle finished off her food.

"We can have a day of play and sightseeing if you like. I also swung by our target and we can have a crack at it tonight. If you still want to come along?" Her eyes started to twinkle. She had that air of excitement about her again; the anticipation glow. Man, was she a weird one.

"Sure, I'll come along. Take my mind off things. How about we go see the Sydney Aquarium and perhaps do some shopping?" I glanced over at the bag she had brought in yesterday. "Or have you already been?"

She grinned, getting up to grab it.

"I actually bought you something I thought you might like now you are getting into all sorts of trouble with me." She opened the bag and pulled out a parcel.

I loved presents. I'd never been given a complete Ninja suit before though. It was completely black, with face mask, utility belt with one of those wire cables which you use to attach to things and abseil down them. A small very sharp knife and night bloody goggles.

"The night goggles aren't as handy as you'd think really. They limit your field of vision, but sometimes they are needed, when you know you have a small target and can't afford to miss in the dark."

She was like a little kid. The strangest things really did turn people on.

"Thank you. Really, it might mean the difference between escaping and being seen." After all, I only had my snazzy running suit which she'd already laughed at once.

"We'll try it out tonight."

Looking at my new cat suit, the gear that came with it, and having a specified target, made my stomach clench. It was nerves. I glanced at my watch. My palms went wet.

Jonelle noticed my expression. It must have spoken volumes because she gave me her most ferociously lethal grin.

"Hang onto your hat Princess, tonight we take your innocence."

That was less than reassuring.

It wasn't hard to enjoy myself in Sydney. But it got a bit harder when I spent the day alternatively dreading the evening, and thinking about my scummy ex-boyfriend. Though to be technical, we were never at that stage. We'd only known each other a month. But damn it, the sex had been so bloody hot!

We spent four hours in the Aquarium, wandering around watching

323

all the fishes. I'd always loved the sharks personally, so graceful and deadly. Now, though, I could see them reflected in my companion and it wasn't something I wanted to dwell on.

At lunch Jonelle took us to a quiet place with private dining rooms where she could lay out the plans for the evening and not get interrupted. Or overheard. Anyone listening in to any of her conversations would be in for a rude shock.

"Okay, here's the plan. Well, as much of a plan as I go by, which I usually only use when I have company." She smiled at me. "From what I overheard last night, they are going out tonight for a party. It starts at nine and they will be home very late indeed. Which suits me. Us. We'll get there about ten thirty and I'll disable the alarms. They have a dog, but let me deal with that."

Oh yes, I was going to argue the point. No, no, my dear girl, allow me. Pfft. Of course she was dealing with the dog. I was a passenger on this. I was the real novice here. Almost a liability.

"Don't you think I'm a liability?" Say what you think.

Jonelle looked surprised. "Well of course you are. You have been since I met you."

Her warm smile softened the whole blow.

"When I first thought it would be nice and ... er ... interesting to get to know you better, I knew there would be problems. You weren't fit and had no idea of the world I inhabited. But I always knew I could take care of you as well as myself. So don't worry about it."

I felt like putting in a query about Charles and Daniel and my lack of protection then, but thought better of it.

"But that's not the issue. I wouldn't take you on a jaunt where I thought for a second an amateur would be in danger, or put me in danger. This is pretty routine stuff. I take out the not so sophisticated alarms, put the dog to sleep and then we pop inside and take the Keystone. Easy."

Put like that, it sounded so simple. What on earth was I worried about? Gee, could it be all the things that could go wrong and the lack of a backup plan?

"What happens if the police arrive?" I was always looking on the bright side of life.

She sighed. "And why would that happen? They don't just randomly come over, you know. I can disarm the house in my sleep. I've installed systems like it a million times. We'll be fine. We're after

Keystone's *Mother and Child* sculpture. Once we have that, we come back to the motel and go to sleep. Tomorrow I'll drop the art to its new owner, collect the remainder of my fee and we fly home."

Why was I not convinced?

Spending money didn't even help take my mind off everything. When I was getting changed after trying on a lovely dress, I was struck with the thought that Brad would have loved that colour on me. And when I bought myself a whole matching set of beautiful lacy underwear, I smiled when I thought of his reaction, only to frown at the memory of his wife.

I'd get him out of my mind, but right then I was still in a bit of shock. I'd never had an affair with a married man before. Even though I'd been blissfully ignorant, I still felt guilty. I certainly wouldn't like the idea of sharing my husband with someone like me!

At six we had dinner back at the Hilton. We wanted to be seen going up stairs and everything normal. We peeled off and slipped out the back through the service entrance around nine thirty after a very filling meal which I'd had to struggle through. Jonelle ate with relish. I could feel my heart starting to beat too fast. Anticipation would be the death of me.

Jonelle took us every bloody back street known to man. I'm not sure if it was strictly necessary because only one other person should have known we were coming – and that was the person who had made the request in the first place.

We parked some way from the house and slipped along in the dark. I'd stripped off the street clothes she insisted we wear over the top and now padded along beside her dressed in the matching cat suits. Laughter kept bubbling up inside. I was nothing if not predictably inappropriate.

"Okay, you stay here for a second," Jonelle murmured in my ear, sending chills down my spine. Her breath tickled my ear and caressed my cheek. I wish she wouldn't stand so bloody close. Then suddenly she was gone and I wanted her back. I felt open, naked and exposed, standing in the bushes all by myself, waiting for the all clear.

Moments later, which felt like a lifetime, Jonelle reappeared beside me. Instead of talking, she touched my arm and motioned me to follow her. My heart rate notched up a bit and my breath started to come in little pants. Maybe I wasn't cut out for this cloak and dagger stuff up close and personal like this. I'd end up having a coronary. I wanted to say out loud I thought it was a very bad idea to bring me along and could I go back to the car and wait. Sit it out. But there was no going back.

Jonelle led me through the darkened gardens of some massive mansion. These people were not short a few bob. We passed a sleeping Doberman and Jonelle's teeth gleamed in the dark. I was never going to ask what she gave him and how she administered it. Though not asking something was against all my natural instincts, I kind of liked the idea of some blissful ignorance.

She'd obviously disarmed everything, as she let us into the house and no outside lights came on: nothing happened. I didn't know what I'd been expecting, but the ease of it all hadn't been on my list.

I could feel the sweat on my palms underneath my thin black gloves. We made our way through room after room and eventually came to a rather lavish formal lounge. There, pride of place, was the Dante Keystone. Jonelle waved at me to go collect it.

You paid a fortune for this sort of work. This sculpture was meant to represent the artist's impression of Mother and Child. I picked it up. To me, a philistine, it was a misshapen smallish lump of marble.

I waved my free hand at Jonelle and gave her a thumbs up. I didn't want to be too cocky, but how easy was it?

Perhaps being a crook was seriously overrated. My heart rate was now steady. Jonelle led me outside into the wonders of their lush garden. Playgrounds for the rich truly are spectacular and I stood for a moment looking around.

I couldn't believe it. Here I was standing in someone's garden by their pool holding a priceless artwork. One I had liberated (great word that) from their home and was about to make off with. I breathed in deeply. For a novice, this was heady stuff. I tingled and could suddenly understand everything Jonelle felt.

The thrill, the power, and the sense of disconnection with reality. I was out of time and out of place. No one could do this and not feel invincible. I felt like a warrior returning home with the spoils of some long forgotten war.

So okay, I had a marvellous imagination.

As I stood there, breathing in my victory over my nerves, I heard a faint plat and felt a zing as something went passed me very fast. I glanced up and made eye contact with Jonelle. She was looking very surprised.

She took a step towards me and held out her hand.

"Goddamn it. I've been shot."

I stared at her stupidly. And looked down at her side, where her hand was suddenly clamped. She was wearing black and it was nearly midnight. There wasn't a lot I could see. She took another almost staggered step.

"Shit." And her eyes went passed me, over my shoulder.

Everything kaleidoscoped around me. I could suddenly feel a presence behind me and ice trickled between my shoulder blades. I did *not* want to turn around. But I had to. I had to uproot myself from the paralysis and do something.

Turning I used the soft moonlight to look where Jonelle was looking. Turning, I opened my eyes wide and took a deep breath. Turning, I faced the chance of being shot myself.

Metres behind me, stepping out from the foliage, came the one person who could give anyone nightmares. I turned and found myself face to face with … The Rose.

Behind me Jonelle was swearing and she'd fallen to her knees, at least that what I assumed had happened by the thump I heard. I was too trapped in The Rose's eyes to look.

He smiled almost gently.

"End of the road," he whispered in the dark.

And I felt night closing in around me.

Somewhere as if from a long way away I heard Jonelle say, "Stay with me, Princess", but it was all too difficult. Fainting seemed such a logical step right at that moment.

I opened my eyes and felt myself falling, and the last thing I saw was The Rose's face peering down at me, eyes two large dark pools of destruction. Then I could see and feel no more.

Chapter Twenty Three

Subconsciously, I was fighting the inevitable glide back to reality because reality as I had known it was vastly screwed up. There were things I couldn't quite remember in my happy state and who wanted to upset the status quo?

Not me. I wasn't filled with a natural sense of courage and inner determination. Nope, I was more of a curiosity killed the cat person; an ask-questions then run from the answers type person.

Though I hadn't run fast or far enough.

My various aches and pains hit me first.

At least I was alive. Something to be thankful for considering the last thing I could remember was watching the merciless and frighteningly human-less eyes of The Rose coming closer.

My eyes popped open. Crap. Now everything was flooding back. Jonelle, The Rose, myself and some stupid sculpture by Dante Keystone which was *so* not worth getting caught over.

Double crap. Jonelle'd been shot. Shit.

I tried to move, to do something - anything. I needed to get to my feet and find out what had happened. Unfortunately I wasn't going anywhere. Not for the time being anyway.

My legs were not fully cooperative and my arms were only slightly better. I could feel a sting in my right shoulder which reminded me of getting shots at the doctor. So after I'd gracefully fallen on my face someone had made sure I stayed in that state by jabbing me with some form of sedative.

Well, bully for them.

Turning my head I could make out the vague outline of my surroundings. It was pretty dark in here, wherever here was. I appeared to be in a small cabin of some sort, but with the chugging going on I was getting a nasty feeling I was actually heading out to sea.

Now if I'd been a good little girl and stayed home in Canberra this couldn't have happened. However, now I was stuck wondering if I was headed out into the wide blue yonder. I could only hope Jonelle was alive somewhere on board my floating prison. What I didn't know about bullet wounds could fill an encyclopaedia. In the dark I hadn't been able to make out where she'd been shot and then everything had gone from bad to worse.

Joy for me.

My head was pounding in time with the engine. And as my thoughts became more complicated and awake, feeling started to return to my legs. One of my ankles was chained to the wall and the other swollen and sore.

I sat up and reached down to give it a rub. The movement nearly caused my head to fall off. I wasn't much of a sailor at the best of times, but to be stuck down here, with very little air and heat and noise on top of sedation? I was feeling more than a mite bit ill.

My ankle had been struck with something heavy. Whether this had been intentional or accidental when moving me in here, didn't matter, it was hot and puffy. I couldn't see me running off on it. I felt along the chain and came to a link in the wall. A long bolt; great, just what I needed, more complications.

My bedding consisted of a few blankets on the floor, so I threw them off and crawled as far as my chain would let me. I could smell diesel and hear the thump thump as the engine stroked along.

Lord knew where we were headed. There was no point in yelling. I could scream myself hoarse and not be heard over the racket going on.

So I sat in the dark and rubbed my ankles alternatively to restore the blood. I also gave the shoulder which had been jabbed a quick rub too. He hadn't been too gentle in his administration of the needle.

The more I got the blood flowing, the more awake I became. The head was still pounding, but at least I knew my brain was in there. It was the increasing need to throw up that was becoming a rather pointed issue. I didn't really want to do that on the floor, as there was nothing to stop it running into my blankets. Not a result I wanted to sleep in.

Eventually, I cuddled up in my blankets and had a good old cry. I was sore, tired, hot, and sick. No one knew where I was and there was a chance Jonelle was dead.

Why oh why had I allowed myself to get swept up in the excitement of her world? Couldn't I have left well enough alone and stayed in my daydreams?

At some point I fell asleep again. Exhaustion and the end result of the sedative combined to put me out.

When I came to, it was the lack of noise I noticed straight away. It was even darker if that were possible. Perhaps it was night time, though of course, I could be wrong. It had been known to happen.

I lay there trying not to catalogue my ills because thinking about them made everything ache even more. My stomach had settled and was now complaining about being hungry. I wished it would make up its mind.

I knew I was meant to be thinking about how to escape. Action movies show the heroine making plans. But it was far more difficult to do than watch.

Firstly, I didn't have a bargaining chip to my credit. Not one. I was no threat to whoever was manning this tub and they would certainly know that. I didn't want to think too closely on anything else because that all led me back to wondering if Jonelle was still alive, and what I was going to do if she wasn't. Probably die too. Not the most rewarding of internal struggles.

There wasn't a lot to *do*. I was growing increasingly bored with captivity. I couldn't believe I'd just admitted that to myself. In movies and books they made it out as so exciting; captives falling for their captors and great escapes happening. Me? I just sat there and stared into darkness.

Boring. But I wasn't the hero type.

It was getting to the point of sending me mad when I heard footsteps above. At least there was someone around. There was a bit of scraping and suddenly a hatch was thrown back and a face appeared. I'd been right about the timing. It was surrounded by darkness and stars.

"Are you awake down there?"

Now where oh where had I last heard that voice? Hmm, let me think. Oh that's right, just before I passed out. The person above me was The Rose himself. Brilliant. Was I ever screwed.

"Yes, if that matters at all. I'm hungry." Might as well start with the demands.

He laughed. "I can help with that."

And he lowered a ladder and came down.

Now in make believe land I would've had something up my sleeve and I would've hit him with it. From there I'd use a lever and unchain myself and find the key. But that wasn't the way reality worked. Not mine, anyway.

The Rose came over to me and unlocked the chain from the wall, then helped me back up the ladder. I was now on a leash with him on the other end. Not a comfortable position to be in, but at least I was out of that hold.

It was late and a cool evening sea breeze was blowing. The stars twinkled coldly in their sky and the moon shone down upon us. It was all very lovely and quite romantic.

Except for my companion, of course.

Minor details like that could upset the romantic scale somewhat. I leaned over the side watched the waves lap at the hull. I couldn't see any vague shape of land or another boat at all. And the moon really did make that possible.

"I wouldn't jump, if that's what you're thinking."

He'd come up behind me, dangling the end of my chain from one hand and holding a plate of something in the other.

I snatched the plate. 'As if. This bloody chain would drown me in a second. If you didn't."

There was a bread roll on the side of warmed stew. Not exactly summer fare, but lovely all the same. I started stuffing it into my mouth, almost afraid he'd take it back.

"If I wanted you dead, you would never have woken up, you stupid git."

Charming: how to wine and dine a woman in one easy lesson. But I couldn't argue with his logic. There was no way he could have missed.

"What about Jonelle? Did you want her dead enough?"

Was I out here on my own?

The Rose came and leaned on the rail beside me. Close up in the moonlight he didn't look half as scary as he had been rushing towards me in the dark. I tried not to stare, but couldn't help it. I was inches away from someone who was a real baddie. Sure Jonelle killed people, but they had needed it she assured me. This guy did it just for kicks or money or if they were in the way. I shivered. He turned those soul-less eyes on me.

"Do I make you nervous?" His voice didn't improve with setting. It was soft, creepy and vile.

"Of course you do. I'm stuck out in the middle of an ocean with a man who kills people, and I have no idea if I'm ever going to get home again and if my friend is alive."

Not making any mad assumptions, but I think he liked me. He moved a fraction closer. What had I been thinking before about captors and captives making out? Only in fiction. Because the idea of the creature beside me laying one hand on me made my skin crawl.

Not even to get myself off this boat.

He giggled.

"Jonelle was left behind. I left her at a rendezvous point waiting for someone who wanted to speak to her. I don't like to think of what they were going to do with her."

He paused, obviously loving to think about it. Which meant that I thought about it and knew it was the one thing I should keep out of my mind.

If he'd left her for any of those who wanted her dead, then a wounded and potentially drugged or tied up Jonelle was going to be in serious trouble. I began to hate the man beside me with a passion. Before it may only have been fear. Now, there was hatred with touches of anger and quite possibly still loads of fear as well. Hey, I was irresponsible, not stupid.

"So I'm sure you can forget her rescuing you, Princess." Eck, it really didn't have the same ring to it coming from him as it did from Jonelle. "So that just leaves you and me out here a couple of hours off the coast of I'd say, Narooma maybe, by now. Not really into navigation and we've come some way south." He smiled at me. "And you're not dead yet."

Well, that was reassuring. Not by much, but enough. The last he had seen Jonelle she wasn't dead and I wasn't either. Things could begin to look up again, except I was out here all by myself with a nutcase who just might want a piece of me. That was far less reassuring.

"So," I needed to grab this particular bull by his horns. "Why exactly am I here and not out there, swimming with various fishes?"

He brushed against me, and I tried very hard not to shudder with absolute fear and general loathing. He was *creepy*! Wasn't there a rule against that? Didn't the person who finally ran the heroine to ground have to be cute? Why couldn't he have been reminiscent of someone like Will? Being trapped on a boat in the midnight hour with moonlight and star dust and Will would have been bearable. Who was I kidding – it would have been bliss. This – well - this was a nightmare.

"I wanted to see why Jonelle was keeping you so close. Not a part of this are you? Not your usual situation? Why has Jonelle dragged you around with her? Close protection?"

Yeah, but for whom? Certainly not for her. But I was suddenly filled with a thought. If he was trying to discover how and why I was associated with Jonelle it wouldn't do me any harm to have him think I was hired to protect *her* from the head hunters, would it? He would gain some respect for me and stop trying to inch his way closer and closer. It was getting on my nerves.

"I can only hope my retainer doesn't get misplaced just because you jumped us." I tried an experimental sentence and waited to see his reaction to that.

He stared at me in the moonlight, then started to wheeze. All right, so laughter wasn't a great sign. It was demoralising to have my bluff called so easily. Jonelle always told me my face was a book.

"Honey, you certainly can invent well. I was thinking more along the lines of her romantic side, not work. Jonelle hasn't had a girlfriend in a long time and I was curious as to how you came into it. Plus, I wasn't too keen on finding out any information from Jonelle herself. She gets nasty when tortured. But you," he smiled lingeringly at me, "I was kind of hoping you'd just give me the info. And if you don't, it'll be loads more fun getting it out of you."

Any last thoughts I had about safety and security went sailing out of my head. The man was mad and I was about to be tortured. And he thought Jonelle and I were … not to my knowledge. I didn't even want to go down that thought pattern. It would complicate many situations in the future, providing I had a future.

"There isn't much I can tell you. She keeps running off with Amelia and having counsels of war. They aren't really the chattiest of people you know."

How well did he understand the dynamics of Amelia now she was home from England? Obviously quite a bit. He gave a start like I'd goosed him.

"Amelia wasn't with you in Sydney." It was a statement. "Jonelle would *not* have taken her as well."

What is it about Amelia that could frighten everyone? I smiled to myself. I now had my bargaining chip. I didn't know her from a bar of soap, but he wouldn't necessarily know that.

"Amelia will probably begin to ask around if we're late." I wondered how long I'd been out of it. Dare I ask? "I guess it'll depend on how long you kept me down there."

The Rose's hands were a little twitchy. Suddenly there was fun to be had at his expense, in limited doses. "I shot Jonelle last night."

So only one day down. I couldn't see anyone worrying about us in that amount of time. Though the Hilton might start to wonder where their paying guests had gone. Good thing we'd paid a couple of days in advance. Still, unless Amelia did, by some stroke of luck, call and find us out of contact, I was still stuffed and going to have to get myself out of this.

"How exactly did you end up in that particular garden?"

I needed to be the one doing the questioning. There wasn't a lot I could tell him and if my usefulness was so limited, I couldn't see me residing on this boat for any length of time. So the trick would be to keep him talking and try to find a hole in his security.

"The whole thing was a set up. The people who wanted the Keystone are friends of mine. I bumped into people I know who wanted to see her more than my clients do, so I set up the Keystone heist to get her away from Canberra and closer to a rendezvous with … well, the others. I kept a watch on the place and when you two arrived it was just too easy."

He smiled at me, obviously expecting me to be proud of him.

I tried hard not to think horrid thoughts about him. Jonelle always told me that whatever I was thinking showed immediately, so I tried to hold neutral thoughts only. Not so sure about my success, but at least he didn't hit me over the head or something similar.

"Why? You could have just come down to Canberra and shot her there." I could sound business like and callous too.

He looked surprised.

"Of course, but she's so paranoid. Surely you've seen her watching everything at once? It's *so* annoying. If she thought she was somewhere no one was expecting her, doing something she would consider fun, how much more surprise was it going to be to hit her then? Plus, I only had to take her a few suburbs to the drop. Easier all round."

"Who wants her that badly, but couldn't get her without you?"

"It's a contract thing. You wouldn't understand. They want her, I get a pardon." His face curled up in anger. "I think they over estimate how important they are these days. I don't need their pardon. I work for people they couldn't even dream about."

What was it with some people? Their ego was so far out of touch with the reality around them, they felt the need to continually stroke it themselves. So basically The Rose had been in big do-do and used Jonelle to get out of it. I narrowed my eyes. Somehow that was just a little too simple, even for him. He was a big scary killer, but seriously, I was beginning to doubt him in the upstairs department.

"You've had a nasty history all up with Jonelle, haven't you?"

Why hadn't I thought of that before? Here I was, stuck out in the middle of nowhere with someone who could provide me with all sorts of gossip on Jonelle. All right, it was probably going to be a skewed, but I could fill in the blanks. I looked around for something to sit on. It could end up being a long night and eating on my feet was bad for digestion.

"Um, Mister Rose, can we just move over there please?" I pointed to where boxes on deck provided something to rest on.

He took my plate and helped me hobble over, my feet not all that healthy still. Having his hand guiding me under my elbow made my skin contract, but there were limits to how far I wanted to antagonise him by pulling away.

"You should call me Ben, you know. We're going to be spending a lot of time together and The Rose is just a job title." And he tried another attempt at a smooth smile. I didn't have the heart to tell him he looked like an oily eel.

"Sure, Ben." I hoped my return smile wasn't as sickly as it felt.

I sat down rather heavily, anything to drag my arm out of his. From there it was easier to wipe up the rest of the stew from my plate. I tried to relax my clenched stomach muscles. Getting indigestion wasn't going to help me.

Ben sat opposite, but not far enough. What did he think I was going to do? Make a run for it?

I wanted to prolong the whole eating experience because it have me something to do with my hands. The more nervous I became the more my hands liked to either tremble or wave around in a crazy fashion. It didn't come across strong and independent when I did that.

"So," I mumbled around the last piece of bread soaked in gravy, "why are you so angry with her?"

There was something about darkness. It made everyone want to confess to deep dark secrets and people like Ben were no different to the rest of us. Midnight is a great hour for the deep and meaningfuls. Or anytime after a bottle of wine, but I didn't think my cruise ran to the finer things in life.

There was quiet for a while and for a moment I thought I may have gone too far. But then he sighed. Yes he actually did. I didn't know if he was going to try for the sympathy angle, but it wasn't going to work.

"I met Jonelle years ago. I thought we could work well together, but she would take risks that were just too far. It was like she was challenging everyone around her. She was newly out of the International Protection Agency or IPA, as they like to call themselves, and wanted to prove to the world she didn't need them."

Hello. What was he on about?

"Excuse me? Who are the IPA when they are at home?"

Ben looked over at me from the shadows.

"You really don't know a lot about the person you work with, or whatever the relationship is between you two. Amelia and the English team you mentioned earlier all work for the IPA. They're the crew that taught Jonelle her tricks or some of them at least. I always suspected Jonelle knew more than she let on. Like someone else had started her training years before the IPA took over, but she's never let on. Their big boss sends out his mercenaries and reaps in the cash." He snorted.

"They make out like they save the world, but they're no better than the rest of us. Sure, they do protection stuff for some of the high flyers in the world, but when all is said and done, they kill like the rest of us."

I wasn't too sure what 'rest of us' he was talking about, but the people I grew up with weren't in the habit of killing their neighbours. I knew I had to take what he said with a grain of salt, but still. There was a part of me that was beginning to worry about the close ties I'd forged with Jonelle.

Quite apart from getting me mixed up with murderers and the like, if she thought it was just like 'the rest of us' to go play protectionists, then we had a fundamental value discrepancy. I bit my lip for once and let Ben ramble on.

"They do all these sorts of tests to see if you can become a member. If you're good enough or at their level." He sneered. "I don't need their approval. I'm good at what I do and never needed any one to tell me so."

Somehow I doubted that. The more he sneered the more he made it damningly obvious that he'd wanted in pretty badly.

"So I left England and moved into my own things. But when I bumped into Jonelle years later I assumed she'd got over their elitism. But she hadn't, stupid git. I hate people patronising me about my work, you know? There's just no need for that sort of behaviour. We all have our preferred way of doing things. She doesn't get paid all that much more than I do for a job."

He frowned into the darkness. The past was still with him and it rankled. I could only hope that he wouldn't take that out on me.

"We were working on this job and while we had different employers the goal was the same. But she had to go off and make a big deal of everything. Two of the men working for me had some fun with one of the young women in the organisation we were closing down. My boss wanted them shut down because they were competition. Jonelle's boss or whoever she was working for, wanted them shut down because they were trading in all sorts of things the moral bastards didn't like, including flesh."

He was hardly pausing for breath and I wondered idly when had been the last time someone had actually listened to him talk. Who was going to actually sit still long enough? I, on the other hand, was a captive audience.

"Anyway, two of my boys enjoyed some time with one of the young prostitutes. She was only sixteen and wasn't all that willing now she thought she was being saved."

Funny that, but not exactly something I could explain to a man like him.

"Jonelle took exception and shot them. Both of them. It pissed the hell out of me. They were meant to be covering my exit. Bit hard to be doing that while lying around with their brains hanging out."

He was getting all worked up, as though the moment was coming back to him in vivid detail.

I could see how that would be annoying. But more to the point, he'd just let me know that, for sure, Jonelle had killed two people.

All in a good cause, I mean who hasn't wanted to kill a rapist here or there. But it was numbing all the same. It meant she was more of his world than of mine. A shadow slid between me and Jonelle.

It hurt to admit it, but up until that point I hadn't put much credence on her blasé attitude to death. Now I was going to have to try not to allow any sort of horrid judgements on my part to come into our relationship. If we had one. If she was alive.

"I managed to get out, obviously." He smiled slightly at his own poor joke. "But I couldn't forgive her. After all, what did it matter? The chick'd been paid for it for the last two years or so, what was one more day? Jonelle can be very unbending and unreasonable sometimes, you know." He stayed quiet for a little while.

"We had a massive argument over the whole thing. Threatened to kill each other. It was messy. But the years went on and things can be forgotten, except she kept pissing off people who employed me."

I felt like asking him if he'd ever considered getting paid employment by people with less Jonelle-like baggage. But wisely didn't.

"Recently I've become attached to a group of people who really have a passionate hatred of all things IPA. The fact that Jonelle accidentally annoys them just for being who she is hasn't helped. For the sake of old times, I offered her the chance to make things right last time I saw her. She laughed in my face and said she'd take her chances. So I set this up and she threw the dice." He grinned at me. "She got snake eyes. She loses. Right now I imagine that the mob that have her have cut off her head and sent it to their boss."

"Who did you give her to?" My voice came out thin and weedy.

"I left her with two of the guys out to collect on the price on her head. Fred and Larry are old cronies of mine. They'll take her or at least the vital bit of her, to Joker, the man after it all."

He said that with the finality of someone who assumed I had any idea of who these people were.

Not only did I have no clue, I didn't want to. I mean to say, who wanted to work with someone called Joker who demanded people's heads as trophies? But the vital information here was Jonelle wasn't out there looking for me. She was too busy making sure two idiots didn't decapitate her.

"Why would this Joker want a head?" I had to ask those things. It was like a compulsion. 'And what kind of name is Joker?'

338

Ben watched me with his sad crazy eyes.

"It's a nickname. Family name of Jockery, Joke, see? Anyway, a while back now, Jonelle killed his son. It was self defence, even I know that. But Joker wasn't impressed. Jason was his only son. Not the wisest thing she's ever done. Because she's such a clever dick it's taken him some time to uncover who it was. Now he has, however, nothing is going to save her. He doesn't have all that many people loyal to him since Jason died. But he can afford to buy her head if nothing else. There are always people out there like Fred and Larry who'll do anything for the right price."

Lovely people he knew. Lovely people I was involved with.

Okay, so killing a madman's son wasn't the smartest thing she could have done. But there were some people who were no loss to the gene pool and by the sounds of it, Jason's hereditary material labelled him as one.

I'd finished my meal and was sitting holding my plate. There was nothing to do with my hands and I was dreading having to go back down into the darkness. Not that I was afraid of the dark, but I was more than a little afraid of the man seated opposite me.

Ben finally got to his feet and stretched.

"I think we could both do with some sleep. It's," he checked his watch, "three in the morning. Time to go below, Princess."

I put my plate down and hobbled along with him to the ladder.

"Do I really have to go down there? Can't you tie me up or something on deck?"

I looked down into the hole I was expected to crawl and my knees felt weak. There had to be another way, surely. It just wasn't humane to lock someone up there, again.

What part of this man had nothing to do with being human hadn't I realised?

"You have two choices. The hold or my cabin." And he gave me that smile again.

To say I was surprised about having any choice in the matter was an understatement.

"I think I may just have to pass on the cabin bit. Tired, you know." And I slid myself down the ladder.

"It won't always be a choice," he muttered as he closed the lid over my head.

I sat in what was now total darkness. The promise in his voice quite took my breath away. Crawling, I made it back to the pile of rough blankets he'd left me. I wrapped one around my shoulders and huddled. There was something soothing about a good huddle. And boy did I need soothing.

I'd sat and eaten my dinner with a madman who was promising me I was next on the menu. I couldn't really understand why I wasn't up there already entertaining him in the cabin. Maybe he had better things to do this evening. Good for me. Though, technically, it meant I had only twelve hours or so until I faced that lovely possibility again.

Lying down didn't help. My mind just kept going over and over the last couple of days. What a mess. We'd being lured to Sydney for a fake job, and I'd gone snooping and discovered Brad's betrayal. I slumped even further into myself.

Lying in the darkness I could feel my throat tightening as the unshed tears threatened. There was something about having too much alone time.

Here I was kidnapped with a psychopath, my best friend about to lose her head and I was trying not to cry over a man who wasn't worth a tear. But it hurt. The thought that he could have said and done those things with me, and made me feel so warm and comfortable and all the time he was headed back to Mrs Morphett. What sort of person could do that? I'd had no idea he was married. It hadn't even entered my head that I should ask. Perhaps that was my naivety talking, but at twenty nine I'd never come across someone prepared to lie so deeply. Well, a man anyway. Jonelle was becoming a different matter entirely.

I stared into the blackness around me. Ben wasn't the most reliable witness. However, some of what he said made terrible sense, which shook me up. I had always known Jonelle was cut from a different cloth to the type of person I usually hung around with. It was coming home to me though, with only one conversation with the 'enemy', that she was even more deeply entwined in his world than I could ever have imagined.

It was altogether possible that my best friend and recent employer was slightly psychopathic herself. Not something to dwell on, but there really wasn't any other in-flight entertainment. And she'd been so arrogant she hadn't even investigated the job properly. Well, in her defence, it had *sounded* like a small nifty little robbery.

Somewhere in there I dozed off and got myself a few hours sleep. But they were fitful and I awoke to the same headache I'd had before.

I started to daydream about all the action movies I had ever watched. Why? Because one, it took my mind off where I was and the whole horror of what Ben might end up asking me to do (or telling) and two, who knew where I could end up getting some inspiration?

Truth was, I was waiting for Jonelle. And it looked like I would be waiting for a damned long time. There was only one person who was going to get me out of this and that was me. I had no James Bond. I couldn't sit back and hope for the best. The best would be not feeding the fishes, but feeding Ben's appetite instead. Now that was a joyful concept.

Light was filtering its way into my dingy little hold, and I could only imagine what time it was. My watch was frozen at eleven-o-five. Helpful to lose battery power in this situation.

The engines hadn't started up again, so either we were anchored or drifting on the currents awaiting Ben's decision on the future. Perhaps he was waiting for news about Jonelle's head before he made any moves.

That made sense. If there was a slight chance she was still alive, he'd hardly want to kill or torture me. The retribution would be swift and nasty. On the other hand, once he was given the all clear I was toast.

As Jonelle discovered to her amusement, I wasn't much of a physical person. The whole being able to intimidate by sheer presence, was never going to be my thing. However, now was the first time I was going to have to do *something*.

Anything!

There was nothing for it. Unlike the helpless Bond women who allowed James to come to their rescue without even remotely looking like they could manage themselves, I was going to have to single handedly get myself back to shore. Oh joy.

I glanced up. There was a rattle and suddenly sunlight came streaming into the hold. Ben's head blocked it out.

"Hey down there. Time for breakfast. Catch."

That was it. A bag was dropped down and the hatch slammed shut. The only conclusion I could come to was we were within sight of another vessel. That could have proved useful if I could have climbed up. Hauling my sorry butt over to the vague outline of the bag, I ripped it open. Small mercies: he wasn't going to starve me.

Inside was nothing to write home about. A lump of pull apart bread, not fresh needless to say, a chunk of cheese and a bottle of water. I'd been dead lucky the water bottle was plastic and bounced rather than broke. While I say it was nothing to get excited about, I was still excited. My nerves were all shot to ribbons and last night's dinner hadn't filled the gap the nervous energy was chewing through on the inside.

With that in mind, I managed to get through everything on the inside of that bag in a very little space of time. However, once done, it came to me I didn't have any bathroom facilities. And with a whole bottle of water inside me, the matter was going to be become fairly urgent.

As more light made its way into my space, I could see the bulk of the engines, a small cupboard, locked, and bolts and straps on the floor. I could only presume these were to tie down excess cargo. There was no little girls' room and with the roll and pitch of the ocean, I didn't fancy making a spot in a corner because sooner or later my blankets would end up wearing it. Okay, not the best thing to dwell on. But they didn't come up with the solution to body function problems in the movies. It was like their characters don't ever need to go, which wasn't going to work for me.

Time marched on. So did my problem.

"Oi! Ben." I tilted my head up and gave him a lungful. "Open up for a second, would you?"

There was silence for a moment, then the hatch was lifted and Ben's head poked through.

"No matter how much noise you make, no one's going to hear you, you know."

"That doesn't matter. I need to go to the loo."

That did matter. And I was willing to promise never to speak again if only he would let me use a proper loo. Without supervision. There were limits.

He gave a snort. "Can't you wait?"

"Till when? Not if it means dark. I don't think I have another twelve hours in me." So to speak.

With a long suffering sigh, he lowered the ladder.

"Come on up. But no funny business okay?"

As if. What did he really think I was capable of? Mind you, I would have to become capable of something really fast if I was going to get out of this mess.

I struggled up the ladder and blinked dazedly in the sunlight. It had to be late afternoon by the look of things. I wasn't much on navigating by the movement of the stars and the sun, but just about anyone can tell afternoon from morning.

"This way."

Ben took the end of my leg chain and started off to the stern of the boat. There was a little cabin and to my immense relief, a loo. Not big enough for two. Hardly big enough for one, so he had to stay outside.

"I'm going to be right outside the door, so don't get any funny ideas. Knock when you want to come out."

Great. Now I was going to get performance anxiety. There was nothing worse than having someone right there, over hearing everything you did. However, given the circumstances, I quickly gave anxiety the flick.

At least I had some privacy. I sat there and stared at the door. If it was mid afternoon, then darkness wasn't all that far away. With the night came the expectation of a duty call from Ben.

Not something I was looking forward to.

Seeing him in the light hadn't help with the appeal business. If anyone was destined to be a psychotic killer, then Ben was. He had that strained flat eyed look. Not one to take home to Mother. There was no way I wanted to be his nightly entertainment, so I had to think and do it fast.

"What's taking so long?" He spoke barely inches from the door.

"Give me a break would you? I've been cooped up for ages. Leave me be."

I frowned at the door. If only he would keep quiet, I might be able to come up with something that could help me. Looking around my tiny little space wasn't going to provide the answers I desperately needed. No inspiration was leaping out at me from the blank walls.

Eventually I knew that I couldn't keep him waiting any longer. There were limits to what a girl could get up to with no mirror and limited space. I stood up and flushed.

I could feel my heart rate starting to climb, a clear sign that some part of me was gearing up for flight. With it came the usual shakiness and near collapse. I could almost hear Jonelle telling me I was wasting all that good energy.

"The problem with you, Princess, is that you let all that adrenalin leak out of you instead of putting it to good use. Try not to panic so much and think about what you can do with any given situation."

Wise words, but not exactly helping right now.

I straightened my clothing and had an inspiration. What if I charged through that door and tried to hit him with it? I mean, if it only upset him I could apologise and say I was afraid of keeping him waiting anymore and hadn't realised he was so close. But if it did more than just upset him … there was a slight chance I could do something with this.

Leaning down I grabbed a handful of my leg chain. It could come in handy too. It was thick, heavy and perfect for walloping someone with. Then, before my courage took a flying leap over some nearby cliff, I reached out for the door handle and opened it with a rush.

I put every ounce of fear and anger and adrenalin into swinging that door wide open with a massive shove. It connected with the side of Ben's head and he gave a grunt, his knees buckling slightly.

I was out! My captor was leaning groggily against the opposite wall, holding his head, eyes a little glazed and unfocused.

Perfect. Before he could pull himself together and before I lost my courage totally, I swung my makeshift club at him.

He went down like a ton of bricks.

Waiting for some sort of reaction, I gave him a slight nudge with my toe.

Nothing happened.

I stood looking down at a comatose Ben, suddenly filled with a deeper fear. What if I'd killed him?

The temple was the weakest point of the skull and it was possible to whack it too hard. He wasn't moving at all. I knew he deserved it, what with the whole kidnapping me and possibly getting Jonelle killed business. But I didn't think I'd graduated into the killer stakes yet. The idea I may have killed someone, even this someone, made me shake even harder.

Kneeling, I dropped my chain and fumbled with his wrist. I desperately needed to feel a pulse. My own was going through the roof. Slippery with sweat, my hand found latched onto his wrist. I held my breath. Was I a murderer?

Chapter Twenty four

For a panicked moment I couldn't find it.

This probably said more about my lack of medical skills than anything else. Because after feeling like I was about to be sick, I encountered a measured heart beat. I sat back on my heels. Well, okay now I'd achieved something. He was out for the count but for how long? That really was the question. I'd have to move fast to make sure I was far away by the time he regained consciousness.

Frisking a knocked out psychopath wasn't fun. I had to get the keys to my chains and work out how to steer this boat back into harbour. I had very little idea of which way that would be. There were miles of deep blue all around me and not even a faint smudge on the horizon that could be construed as land. There were, however, some other vessels. Not close enough to hail yet, but at least they were something to aim for.

I slid my fingers deep into his pockets, shuddering at the contact with a snotty handkerchief. It wasn't pleasant, but it was going to be liberating. That was the basic plan, anyway.

Bulls-eye! Sitting back, I withdrew a handful of keys. Ben gave a groan. I froze. He wasn't meant to be waking up yet. I didn't know a lot about concussion, but I wanted to give him a better dose of it than that. The only problem was I wasn't really the ruthless type. Hitting a man when he was not only down, but distinctly out, seemed easier in the movies.

He groaned again, then subsided. I didn't know if he was faking it or not, so I gave him a sharp nudge with my toe. Nothing happened. I pinched his inner arm, a tender spot I'd discovered when Joy used to pick on me. Older sisters had to have some use.

Still the psycho killer made no move, so I went on faith he was out. I tried out every key until I heard the sound all prisoners live for. The snick of the lock turning. My manacles fell away and I scuttled back, lurching to my now unhindered feet. Freedom had never tasted so good. My ankle gave me a slight twinge, but I chose to ignore it for the greater good of being free.

I now had all my limbs unfettered. I swung away from Ben, then hesitated. There was the chance he would wake up soon if that groan was anything to go by. I held in my hot little hand a bolt and chains. Moving back to his side, I wrapped as much chain as I could around his arms, legs and waist. I then went in search of some sort of unmoveable object I could lock him to.

After much dithering, I found a thick iron hoop in one walls. Who knew what its purpose was, but it was perfect for tying people to. I made my way back to Ben and grabbed his arms. Moving him to the hoop was going to be the interesting part. He was bulky and now partly weighed down by chain. It would have made more sense to wrap him up after the move, but I was more concerned about leaving him free at all in case he suddenly sprung back into life.

Eventually I made it. The relief when I passed the end of the chain through the hoop and clicked the bolt through it - there was nothing like it. Having someone like Ben even within a few metres was bad enough, but leaving them laying around not under lock and key... well, it was death defying.

I took two large steps back and wiped my soiled hands on my pants. Touching him had felt unclean.

Part of me wanted to sit there and watch him sleep, just to make sure he stayed put and to see his reaction when he woke up, of course. I wanted to show him I was faster and smarter than he was. Well, I probably wasn't, but luck had been on my side and the victor always writes history to suit herself.

But I knew sitting around was wasting my precious time, so I clamoured to my feet and took the keys for a walk around the boat. I needed to find out how it was run and if he had left any handy maps lying around.

The boat had a little cabin as I'd seen the previous night. Inside up a tiny flight of stairs was what I assumed was called the bridge. I wasn't too sure of my nautical terminologies. It wasn't like any of the romantic steering rooms I'd seen in the movies. There was no large wheel or dial which had low and full steam ahead written on it. It was all high tech gadgets and a joystick like contraption which I could only assume guided us places like a Nintendo.

What would they come up with next?

I settled into the chair and found a key hole. Trying every key I held eventually one slipped in. But I didn't turn it on. Even I knew that was stupid. First step would be to contact someone and get some sort of directions.

Finding what resembled a radio I flipped a few switches and then paused yet again. What would I say? Oh, by the way, am stuck out here in the middle of nowhere having been kidnapped while out stealing something. Could someone please come and get me, and my killer companion?

It wasn't something I'd pull off. There would be questions and police and all sorts of things I wasn't ready to face. Apart from the fact I was still living in a world where I believed Jonelle was alive. If I sat down with the police and told them my story, she'd murder me herself.

I stared out the window at the deep blue sea. There was the slight chance land was just over the horizon and all I had to do was take what courage I had in my hands, and head – somewhere. I was well aware that whatever fuel my boat had could easily run out, leaving me stranded in my wide pond. And I wasn't rowing back to shore.

I sat, stared, and chewed my lip. As beautiful as the ocean was, it didn't give me a lot of answers.

With a sigh, I started to search the room for anything that could help me figure out which way I should point the nose of this thing. Lo and behold, I discovered a GPS.

I knew enough about them to get it on and read what it had to say. It was a simple one and for that I sent a prayer up to wherever they go. I zoomed out and found land not that far off to my right.

"Eureka! Now all I have to do is up anchor and we're away."

I glanced around self consciously. There wasn't anyone there, of course. It was just, I hadn't heard a voice in what felt like hours. Ben's hardly counted; he was a homicidal maniac. I wanted comfort and familiarity. The sound of my own voice made me feel better.

I left the bridge and toddled down to the end of the boat. I knew that anchors usually lived somewhere at the back. Sure enough, there was a chain dropping away into the water, connected to a winch. I pressed the only button anywhere in the vicinity and with a screech it started to wind the chain in. Leaving it to finish the job without me, I made my way back to Ben. Just wanted to make sure I was truly alone and he hadn't moved.

Sure enough, he lay against the supporting chains, snoring to himself. At least he'd moved from dead unconscious to what I could only assume was sleeping. And the snoring was indication of life, so I didn't have to get my hands dirty again by checking for a pulse.

Returning to the bridge, I turned the key. With a muted roar, the engines sprang to life. If he was only sleeping they'd definitely ruined that for him. They pounded away and reminded me of the nasty headache I'd woken up with the other day. I hoped Ben had one too. Bitchy, yes, but I was happy to be.

I swung my little joystick forward and jammed the stick marked 'throttle' wide open. The boat surged and I hoped I didn't flood her, if it was possible to do that with a sea going vehicle. I'd never tried to manoeuvre a boat and found the experience both exciting and frustrating.

My feet wanted to press down on an accelerator. Which was understandable, I was kind of in a hurry. Pointing the nose directly to land I eased her back against my screaming urgency. No need to push and run out of fuel. We weren't that far out. Just over the immediate horizon, but I had no idea which indicator was what, so I wasn't about to lose my head over speed.

My plan was just to go in and beach her, or get as close as I could with the motors hanging off the back. I could worry about where I was later. There was a coast road winding around pretty much the whole of Australia. If I kept on heading inland I would run smack into it.

Before I disembarked (how fast was I picking up these nautical terms?) I'd give the boat a thorough going over and try to find my mobile. The chances of it been here were pretty slender, but then again I would've said the chances of me ever getting away from Ben had had the same probability.

It wasn't long before land came into sight. At first it was just a little faint haze then it sort of bloomed. I'd never been so glad to see anything – ever. Well, okay so I was exaggerating again. There were times when seeing Jonelle, knowing she was about to get me out of a fix, gave me the same feeling. Relief, safety and all sorts of warm and fuzzies.

With a flick of my wrist I cut the power. We were close enough and I was more than happy to let us drift. There was a search to do and I wanted to check on my passenger.

Once the engines were silent I could hear my passenger. He was bellowing at me to come and let him go. As if. Would he have done that for me, I asked myself. I didn't think so. I wasn't a humanitarian. He could bloody well stick the indignity of it all.

I wandered over to his post, where chains were rattled at me.

"What the fuck do you think you're doing? Do you really think you can get away with this? Even if you ever get off this boat, I'll find you and kill you for it."

"Way to go. Threaten the one person who could possibly help you in your situation." I glared at him. "I could kill you now and then where would all your fancy threats be?"

He laughed. Yes, that's right, he actually laughed at me. I needed to perfect my whole intimidation routine.

"If you were the killing kind I wouldn't be trusted up like a turkey. I'd be dead. I'm no use to you and holding onto me is pointless. But you don't kill people. You'll just leave me here."

He had a point. I couldn't just walk up to him and crush his skull or something. Before, it could have been an accident. But now it would be premeditated and there was this line I just couldn't cross, even if it left me on one side and Jonelle on the other.

The only problem with my whole plan was – how was I going to leave him in a position to get help and not have him coming after me straight away?

"Where did you put my mobile?"

I hunkered down a couple of metres out of reach. Sure he was tied up, never stopped any of the baddies on telly from escaping. And there was the slight possibility that my chaining skills might not provide as big a deterrent as I hoped.

He snorted. "It'll be floating somewhere out there. " He nodded towards the side of the boat and the blue glow of water. "You think I wanted that going off all the time? Women and their phones. You'd have them glued to you if you could."

"You just threw away the latest in digital technology?" I squeaked.

Sure, I didn't know a lot about technology on the whole, but my phone could email, take photos, internet search – all manner of things I never used because I had no idea how to activate them…

Ben smiled a slow and decidedly icky one.

"Sure, what's a rich girl got to spend her money on? Go buy yourself half a dozen and you'll never run out of them."

"Smart arse."

I rose to my feet and plodded back to the bridge. Re-starting the engines I powered up and drove straight at the shoreline. No need to search. He may have been lying, but the chances were high that he wasn't. I didn't want to hang out in his scummy company any longer to find out. Interrogation was not my strong suit. I just wanted to get home and see if Jonelle had found her way out of whatever situation Ben had left her in.

Was that too much to ask?

It wasn't long before the engines got stuck in sand. We weren't that far off shore, but I wasn't looking forward to my swim. The ocean currents didn't shift here till at least February. The water was going to be icy.

I turned everything off and went back to Ben. He was my problem.

"Give me a number I can use to call someone who will come and help you."

I hated being the Good Samaritan, but I wasn't cut out for anything else.

"Sure, and then you'll just take that number and trace it and hand them over to Jonelle."

"You said she's as good as dead, so why worry what I do with it? I'm not going to untie you or even leave the key somewhere handy you could possibly reach in a few hours of effort. I'm not tricky like that. So the only thing I can do is alert someone you know to come and get you. Once I am back in civilisation and surrounded by loads of people."

He snorted. "Great hero you are. Just knock me out and leave me untied when you go."

"Perfect solution, except I could accidentally hit you too hard and you'd never wake up. Or not hard enough and you could fake it until untied then pounce on me." I shook my head. "I think I like my plan better. I can just leave you beached here and you can hope that someone will come along and get curious."

I stood up and glanced at the uninhabited coastline and the non-existent houses. "But I get the feeling you could be waiting for a while."

"Fine."

He wasn't happy with the situation but who was? Either way we played it, he was wasting my time. It was getting dark and I just wanted to disappear into those bushes.

He gave me a number. Then I walked to the edge of the boat.

"Hey! Just like that? Aren't you even going to leave me some water close by or food? It could be a couple of days before you get anywhere or they get back to me. I could still die. And drop the bloody anchor at least. I could end up anywhere."

There was a distinct note of panic in his voice. That gave me sad pleasure; nice to see that the killer was uncomfortable.

I went into the cabin and found a few supplies. These I took back to Ben and pushed over to him. I didn't want to get too close. He had to wiggle around to pick up the water, but I didn't trust him and was afraid to make things too easy. Before I left, I put the key well out of reach, but visible.

Sometimes, my inner bitch surprised me.

Back I went to the side, where I lowered the anchor and used the chain to crawl down into the water. Gasping, I let it go. I hated just hopping into cold water. I was more of a sit on the side of the pool until my body could cope, type of person. But I wasn't wasting time. Plunging in up to my chin, I started to breast stroke away from the boat.

The swell eventually began to help me, pushing me toward the shore, some waves tossing me along, others dumping on my head. By the time I was knee deep, I was frozen and out of breath. It was hard to stay calm, breathe, swim and keep warm at the same time.

I struggled onto the beach. Tottering I made it to the tree line. There, I plonked myself down, exhausted. I didn't realise how much nervous energy I'd been using till it was over. Not that this whole thing was behind me. I still had to figure out where I was and how I was going to get myself back to Canberra.

All I wanted to do was lie down and sleep. Oh and possibly eat something as well. Leaving everything behind for Ben had been stupid. It just seemed, at the time, that he would need it more than I would. Because he'd had a point – who knew when I would send help back for him?

But who was going to help me? I could have done with some of that marvellous competence Jonelle exuded. There were limits to my coping and I was at them.

So there I sat, on my lonely little stretch of sand, watching the waves rolling in as the sun set over the ocean. The boat rocked on its anchor just passed the swell of the waves. Somewhere on it Ben either waited or slept. Sleeping seemed a great idea. But I was still too exposed for comfort.

With a sigh and a massive heave, I staggered to my feet. Every part of me complained. With one last look as the sunlight disappeared totally, I turned into the bushland and made my way directly west. At least, I hoped that was my direction. Somewhere out there was a road. Any old road would do at this stage, I just wanted to find civilisation.

It didn't take long. In fact, as soon as I came upon the major highway, I kind of felt let down. Like here was my big adventure, my chance to prove how I could tough it out, and instead I found salvation less than hour in. I had no watch, so I couldn't be too sure of exactly how long I had been wandering around, but it didn't feel like ages to me.

I stood on the side of the road. There were car headlights coming my way from both sides. I had no way of knowing which one I wanted. Now I was out of the bush, I could see the lights of isolated houses and the glow further down the road of a town. Okay, that was going to be my target. A town would mean phone and help of some variety. At the very least I could reverse charge a call to someone like Julie at the apartments.

There it was again. The physical kicker when I realised I couldn't put a call in to Brad's mobile. What would be the point? Jonelle had already been there, exploded his life by telling his wife about me, and I couldn't see him wanting to come to my rescue. Funny that. But it still hurt. It was a pain I hadn't had time to grieve yet, due to the whole kidnapping incident which had claimed my attention.

Brad had managed to get under my skin. I'd started to feel comfortable with him around. I liked hearing his voice on the other end of the line. There was distinct future possibilities lingering in the air when we'd chatted and slept together.

At least, so I'd first thought. I stood there watching the cars getting closer, feeling tears threaten. He'd been playing with me and I hated him for it. At the same time, I felt miserable because I'd liked him so much.

I wasn't the sort who went out and started buying bridal wear.

There was a long streak of commitment phobia in me. At the same time, it hurt to think I was deemed as transient in everyone's eyes. Children scared me silly, but was I never going to have grandchildren to dang on my old and wrinkled knees?

Eventually the cars started to sweep past me and I straightened up, wiped leaking tears of self pity from my face and stuck out a thumb. Universal sign of 'pick me up, I'm hitch hiking'. It wasn't a safe sport these days, but I couldn't see many other options.

Several cars went past me without a pause. I was just about to start swearing when one swerved into the curb and pulled up twenty metres, or so, in front of me.

I made a heroic effort and dashed to the passenger side. The window came down and I stuck my head in.

"Heading for town?" The lady inside didn't appear to be threatening. For which I was very glad. "Jump in," she added at my affirmative.

I allowed myself to settle into the comfort of the seat. The air con was humming softly and I realised that while the sea had been freezing the air temperature was the usual December heat and my clothes, while not dry exactly, weren't dripping. Though I was pretty sure I'd leave a water mark on this lovely lady's car. Good thing it was dark. I didn't want her to turf me out.

"A bit late isn't it?" She turned her head to glance at me. "I wouldn't have dreamed of picking you up, except you were alone and my daughter looks about your age. The thought of someone driving past and not helping made me upset. So I did."

She flashed white teeth in a smile, hoping for some praise.

I couldn't disappoint.

"Thank you. I have had a real bit of bad luck and had my backpack stolen. All of my luggage, my wallet and address book. I was trying to get into town to give a mate a reverse charge call."

There, that sounded plausible enough.

"Oh, my goodness! That's horrible. Did you get a good look at them? I should take you straight to the police station. They can take all your details. You just can't let them get away with that!"

Bugger. What we had here was a true blue Good Samaritan, the sort who wanted to help even when you really didn't want them to.

"Seriously, it was my own fault. I fell in with a bunch of people I didn't know and they took me to the cleaners. It isn't a big deal. I just need to get to a phone and get some help."

I didn't want to clarify with her where we were headed. It would show that I not only lost everything, I had no idea of where we were. Some backpacker I'd look like.

A few minutes more of her trying to change my mind, and I was delighted to hit the township. Sure enough, Narooma it was. With some convincing, my new found friend finally let me out at a public phone booth. I waved until I could see her car no more. Thank heavens for that.

Okay, so whom to call? The folks would normally be the first people to call in an emergency. Sure, we had a strange relationship, especially my mother and me, but they were still my parents. However, I had no idea what I would tell them. Mum would be guaranteed to have a million and one questions which could not be fobbed off. Mates, on the other hand, were far more easily manipulated.

After much internal debate I settled on reversing a call to Grillia. She'd be the easiest to get a hold of anyway.

"'Lo?" Grillia, at her best. It wasn't late, but she was entitled to have the night off. Who knew what had been going on while I was away?

"It's me, Grill, Fiona."

"Fi! Where are you? That new girl has been bugging the crap out of us all trying to find out if you've made contact. I tell you, she's worse than you at questions!"

I could hardly hear her. There was a rushing in my ears and I felt the desperate need to suddenly sit down.

I started to shake.

Somewhere deep inside I'd convinced myself they (whoever 'they' were) had managed to kill her. I hadn't wanted to go through the whole let down thing. Why build my hopes up?

So to hear that she was there, making waves trying to find me was as though a huge weight was suddenly gone. The black yawning pit I hadn't even realised I'd been staring into closed up before my eyes. Bright spots of light flashed around my vision and for one horrifying second, I thought I would faint. Instead, I clutched the phone tighter.

"What did you say?" I whispered.

Grillia almost growled. "I said that new woman from your apartment block has been hounding us all like we're your keepers. Anyway, I thought you were off with her?"

"We got separated. Actually, could you pass on a message to her ASAP? Could you tell her I'm in Narooma?" I thought quickly. "Scrap that. I'll call her now. Thanks for everything Gill. Go back to sleep." I hung up quickly.

Just beside the phone booth was a bench. I managed to make it there and plonk myself down. I was short of breath.

Jonelle'd made it back. That much was stuck in my head, whirling around like a band gone mad. It was the music I wanted to hear. Of course, I wanted to be the sort of person who always believed in the best of any situation. That instead of pitying myself the loss of both Brad and Jonelle, I'd stayed a believer and held onto the idea that Jonelle was alive.

Yeah – then why was the news she was alive hitting me so hard?

Eventually my shaky legs got a grip and I went back to the phone. I asked the operator to connect me to Jonelle's home line. When she answered the operator asked her if she would accept the charges from Fiona Page. There was silence for half a second. Then she exploded.

"Of course I will, put me through. Fiona!"

I nearly wept. And yes, embarrassing to admit, but what the heck. Who's going to tell?

"Jonelle. Help me. I'm stuck in Narooma with no money, no watch, and no clothes!"

It ended in almost a wail. I felt remarkably ill. It could only be put down to reaction.

"Calm down." The voice of authority came down the line. So used to doing as she asked, I shut up immediately and even the sob disappeared back down my throat.

"I'll be there in a couple of hours. Stay put. Whatever you do, don't move or speak to strangers." Now she did sound like my mother. "Where exactly are you?"

"On the way into town, near the visitors' information board. I'll be sitting with the phones. How- ?" I could hardly bring myself to finish the question.

"I'm coming. We can answer all our questions when I get there. Don't think, Princess." There was sudden amusement in her tone. "Just sit there. I won't be long."

"Bring some extra clothes. I'm cold and a bit damp. Oh, and hurry would you?"

"Damp? Don't answer. We'll talk later. And of course I'll hurry.

Have you ever known me to drive any other way? See you."

She hung up. Well, of course there wasn't anything else to say. All I could do now was wait those long two hours until she arrived.

Leaving the shelter of the phone booth, I went back to the seat. It was a lovely, warm, balmy night, but the chill of my swim clung to me. It was aided by the fact I was quite possibly in shock. Too much had happened in the last few days and the resurrection of Jonelle, however temporarily she'd been a ghost, was the last straw.

I was glad. It was just too much to take in. The last time I'd seen her, Ben had just shot her. And I was kidnapped with the threat of being Ben's bed partner looming over my head.

Now I was free and Jonelle was, once again, racing to my rescue. It had a sort of Twilight Zone feel about it. There was little wonder I was feeling completely out of my depth.

Perhaps the mind numbing terror of sitting on a boat with a killer had finally seeped into my brain. The further I climbed into the situation, the more I worried about my immortal soul. Such deep thoughts did *not* keep me warm at night.

I sat in my dampness and shivered. I didn't want to think. Jonelle had expressly told me not to. And not doing what Jonelle wanted was a pretty silly idea. She had a wonderful knack of knowing when I wasn't behaving myself. But mainly, it was good advice.

I wanted to sleep, but every time a car came by I jumped. What if Ben escaped somehow and made his way to Narooma like I had? I peered into each one as they crawled down the street passed me. None of them contained my enemy and I sank back into my fog.

My eyes twitched with sleepiness. Eventually, the body needed to motor down so it could recoup. Just when I thought I would nod right off, regardless of the situation and my wet clothes, I noticed a man.

Nothing too drastic about that, except I knew him. I snuggled my chin deeper into my collar and peered through my lashes. Encrusted with salt as they were, this proved to be a bit difficult. But I could still make out the guy in question.

Craig. But oh what a vastly different 'look' he was sporting tonight! Gone was the grieving man who could hardly wipe his nose. His hair was washed and combed, clothes on straight and he had a distinctly jaunty spring to his step. There was a small posy of flowers witling tragically in his hand. Our boy Craig was obviously on his way to a date. I tried to smile, and think warm fuzzy things about this turn of events.

Good for him. Someone had come along and saved him instead of the other way round. She was good for him I noted, watching him tug shyly at his shirt collar. He'd even had his hair trimmed. While he gave me the willies, it was nice to see he'd made a bit of an effort. Perhaps all was not lost for the man.

Then, thinking about men, and things been all not lost, I managed to get lost in my own self pity and tossed Craig out of my mind.

Just when I thought I would pass out, the Nissan Skyline came roaring up and screeched to a halt beside me.

Tears leaked out of my eyes before I could gain control. Jonelle practically leapt out before the car settled. She must have done some pretty low flying to get there.

We usually weren't very demonstrative with the other. However, I think extenuating circumstances played a huge role. I stood up, feeling once again the strange weakness sweep through me to my knees (why does it always settle in the knees?). I didn't even try to move toward the car.

Jonelle closed the distance in her long-limbed cat-like stride and I was swept up into a hug that said everything.

It said, 'hold on, I'm here'.

It said, 'it's okay now, whatever is threatening you, I'll take care of it'.

But most of all it said, 'hello Princess, I've got you, you're home'.

I rested my head against her shoulder and cried like a baby. It was very exhausting.

"Hey, hey, settle down or you'll get me as damp as you." But I could hear the smile in her voice, so felt able to take absolutely no notice whatsoever.

Then I remembered she'd been shot and I jumped back.

"Your wound! I didn't hurt it, did I? Where were you shot? How can you even be here?" As usual, the master of the million questions in an articulate order.

But Jonelle knew me by now and took them in her stride.

"It wasn't as bad as it appeared on that night."

She handed me a track suit and quite regardless of the fact it was public, I stripped to my undies and bra and suited up. Jonelle turned herself slightly to the side to afford me some sense of modesty. It was soft and warm in my new suit, because even though the night was warm I was in need of the comfort of my clothes.

Jonelle then led me to the passenger's seat and tucked me in. Two seconds later she was slipping in beside me and starting the car again. We slid smoothly from the curb and she turned it, facing back the way she'd come.

"You went down. How much worse could it be? Oh. Of course you could be dead, so don't answer that question." Relief was messing with my brain.

I sat sideways so I could watch her as she drove. I kept telling myself that this was so I could see her reaction to things, but in reality it was simply me not wanting to let her out of my sight for one second.

"I blame myself entirely for the whole thing." Jonelle bit her lip and flicked her gaze at me. I would much rather she kept it on the road. She was driving at speeds best reserved for Oran Park, a speedway in Sydney.

"How do you figure? I personally blame Ben or The Rose or ass wipe as I am, for my part, going to call him from now on."

I could sense the anger in my words. I could afford to be angry and throw defamatory comments around. I had my strong arm sitting beside me again. It was amazing how powerful I felt when Jonelle was two feet away, which probably didn't say good things about me.

She gave a little laugh. Her heart wasn't in it. Obviously she was really down on herself. I guessed it was a matter of professional pride. Letting someone like Ben get the better of her would be like Pharlap getting beaten by the nag down the road.

Unlikely and certainly a sore point if it ever happened, which it had. So I could see her point of view. Though, to be fair, Ben was a professional in their work as well. He couldn't have got there without some sort of skill level.

She throttled the steering wheel as we whipped around a bend.

"I should have checked into the story behind the Keystone better. It was all too easy. That alone should have made me suspicious. But I was so sure of myself, so bloody *arrogant*."

She bit off the rest of the sentence. I didn't think there was going to be any sort of forgiveness any time soon.

"Nobody's hurt. We're all back safe and sound. So let's not get carried away shall we?"

Okay, so she'd been shot, the extent to which I hadn't been told yet. And I'd been dragged off by a psychopathic killer and threatened with all kinds of bodily harm. But it wasn't about the truth and laying blame. It was about making Jonelle loosen up on herself.

"I got shot on a job, which is enough to piss me off. But you just happened to be kidnapped on same job, which makes me the most incompetent fool out." Well, I could see my reassurances were starting to work their magic.

"Okay then. We'll play it your way. It's all your fault, you should have known better and Ben should never have been able to get the jump on you. I loathe the fact that that beast actually got to put his hands on me and you didn't protect me – yet again! And if you say something like 'I am not going to go after him right now', I think I'll resign my position immediately."

There, put that in your pipe and smoke it. Which really, had to be one of the most inane comments I could come up with, and I knew a few.

I didn't think Jonelle was denying any of this, which wasn't good for her psyche.

She gave me a black look.

"If you think for even a heartbeat that Ben isn't a very dead man for this, then you don't know me at all. He was actually stupid enough to *take you away!*"

Her teeth ground together. It was very satisfying. I loved the fact that when this particular woman said someone was a dead man, she wasn't exaggerating. Sure, that could come back and bite me in my morals, but for now, who gave a toss?

"Well, if you really want him, he's kind of tied up on his boat just off the coast."

I felt a small measure of pride in that accomplishment. I'd bagged the bad guy. Sometimes, it was wonderful to be me.

She slammed on the brakes and I shot forward, hitting the end of the seatbelt with a snap. On the other hand, sometimes it could be less than wonderful. There would be bruising.

Jonelle swung around and pinned me with her most predatory gaze. I squirmed. It was rather like being viewed by a wolf as supper.

"He's where, how?"

"I think we need to do a little bit of tale swapping. This could get confusing really fast." I took in her intensity. "Perhaps I'll start, shall I?"

And so I did. I sat there in the semidarkness of the car, lit only by the dashboard lights and told her everything I could remember. Which left out a lot, but she was there to fill those in.

"So, you see," I concluded, "he's still out there. At least, I damn well hope he is. Waiting for me to be a Good Samaritan and call someone to release him. Though come to think of it, he must have known the only person I would call is you, which means he knows his moments are numbered. Though, of course, he rather suspects you're dead."

I couldn't imagine sitting trusted up like a turkey waiting for someone like Jonelle to come along and dispatch me. Made me glad I wasn't considered a big enough threat to anyone to be immediately killed off. I was more of the 'toy' they played with before their meal. That had distinct eek factors.

Jonelle's gaze became slightly unfocused. I imagined the revenge-like thoughts running through her mind. Made me glad thoughts didn't come with pictures.

"Could you find the exact place you came out onto the road?"

She snapped back to the present and turned those cold grey eyes on me. At times like that, I questioned the existence of a soul.

"Well, I could try. It was dark you know. But it didn't take long to get into town. I could see the lights from where I stood. That certainly helped no end with the whole not so alone thing."

I looked out the window. It was all pretty much the same. Bush, road, car lights. Who could tell where my particular patch of bushland was?

"Get out."

Jonelle's voice was as cold as the grave. I hoped this was only in preparation of what was to come and not an indication of her true feelings.

"Excuse me? It's dark out there and I'm not a reliable witness. Potentially, we could have passed it already."

I had this sneaking suspicion that out there was the bogeyman and I wasn't getting out into the darkness. Not even for her.

Jonelle rolled her eyes. "We'll go back to the outskirts of town and go slow. And please, nothing out there is scarier than me."

"Yeah," I muttered. "That's what I thought last time out."

She'd turned back to drive the car, but that comment made her swing her head round again. Her eyes, hard and expressionless, widened. But instead of throwing me out, she grimaced and continued driving.

"Look, I'm sorry about that. Letting you down, getting you kidnapped, not killing Ben while I had the chance before."

Her words sounded good, shame they were bitten off like shards of glass. I didn't think Jonelle had ever had to apologise for something like that before. If she wasn't my friend, as well as my boss, I would've loved to watch her squirm. For once it wasn't me. But I had to take pity on her.

"I don't think you can blame yourself. You did happen to have a bullet in you at the time. And giving The Rose a chance wasn't a bad thing. It showed you really aren't like him, after all." At least, it gave that impression and impressions were what count in the world, right?

"A bullet in me shouldn't have slowed me down so much. It hasn't caused me much discomfort since."

Some superwoman.

"Then where the hell were you?" I smiled to myself in the darkness. Sometimes I just loved to twitch the tiger's tail.

Chapter Twenty five

She knew that. So really there was just no fun in the game. With a snort she pulled the car round so we were faced down the road again.

"I was trying to be all tough. Yes, it knocked the wind out of me. The stupid thing got lodged between my ribs. Not exactly death defying or anything, but painful and a shock. More so because it was the last thing I'd been expecting. It doesn't matter about the price on my head; I always thought Ben was smarter than that." She shrugged.

"I was knocked off my feet for a moment. It was enough for him to get the jump on me with a tranquilizer. Why he couldn't have used that first is beyond me. Probably wanted to make sure I'd wake up hurting, little shit." She shifted uncomfortably.

"They're bandaged pretty tight. Nothing that won't heal quickly, thank God. Ribs are close to the surface, so it's only a small tear of the skin."

So analytical about it all. I'd be a frazzled heap. Good thing no one shot me, then.

She stared out the window thinking.

"When I woke up I knew it was going to be a bit of a problem. Someone had done a dodgy job of tying my ribs up. The bullet was out, but I was leaking blood, luckily not a lot. More of a drizzle than a down pour." She tried to smile at me but there was no joke on her face.

"I was tied to a chair and there were two men talking somewhere nearby. They weren't very good at their job. I could have untied myself in moments. But you know me. I wanted to find out what was going on. People prefer to talk to me when they think I'm at a disadvantage.

"I don't know where they ever get the notion that it's a good idea to chat to the victim before they kill them. From movies I guess," she mused.

True. I couldn't imagine being stupid enough to sit around chatting while she was looking like she'd have me for lunch. It definitely had movie madness stamped all over it.

"They talked. Looks like an old acquaintance wants revenge for the loss of his son. Ben was sent to help those two fools collect. He'd have been better off to put a bullet through my head than to hand me over still alive."

"It didn't take long to convince them it was a very bad idea. Especially when they realised my hands were free. Bullet wound or no, they weren't actually going to take me alive. Why on earth would I want another conversation with Joker? The one time I'd met him was bad enough. I put it down to vanity myself. Wanting to gloat over me."

Fool. I could have told him it was a wasted effort: she never listens. Jonelle only seemed to hear threats or bluffs if they seriously impacted on what she wanted to do.

"So I disabled them and went back to Canberra. They were set to meet Joker or lackeys at the drop point." She smiled, tight and feral. "I plan on being there. It is time to get rid of this contract on my head once and for all."

"Good luck with that." Those boys could kiss their sweet butts goodbye. She was in no mood to be little Miss Sugar and Spice. I paused.

"When you say 'disabled' do you mean they'll be able to make that rendezvous or not?"

Cautious, I told myself, tread cautiously!

Those eyes narrowed. "You're *not* about to get all moralistic on me, are you? They were about to hand me over to get decapitated! I wasn't in the mood to check for vitals. Not," she added almost as an afterthought, "that there would have been any vitals to check."

Answer enough.

Two more wiped out of the equation. It was possibly meant to make me feel safer. It was beginning to fall short of the mark. And yes, that was more to do with my pesky morals than any real desire to leave the bad guys alive. Morals which only turned up at the worst possible moments. After all, they weren't in evidence when Charles and Daniel were beating the snot out of me, were they? But that was a different story.

"So, then what happened?" Better to get off any topics where we may happen to disagree.

"I got back to the Grangelands and as expected, you weren't there. I checked out everyone, though people like Gillia and Steph proved to be more complicated." She grinned.

"You have two very loyal friends there. They were very hard to question without raising hackles and suspicions. It hadn't been long, but knowing what Ben is capable of, I was a bit … frantic." She frowned. Admissions like that never came cheap.

"Lucky for you, and me, I suppose, he was more interested in chatting and I don't know – persuading me to move into his cabin?"

I was still a little unclear as to what he'd been hoping for. That I would just give up working for Jonelle and come along as his sidekick? As if.

She gave herself a shake, like a dog. Moving the subject along, she returned to the point.

"Now, can you please keep an eye out for anything that is familiar? I'd love to go and clean Ben up before we head back home." Nasty terminology.

So we progressed back down the road at a snail's pace. If another car came up behind us, Jonelle pulled over until their taillights were fading into the distance. I kept my eyes peeled.

"Stop!"

The car stopped dead. She had great reflexes.

"There." I pointed to a clump of trees. They'd stuck in my mind.

Jonelle pulled the car right over and tucked it into the closest bushes. She didn't want it to gather any attention while we were gone. Then she was out, flashlight in hand. I jumped out as well.

We headed into the bush. Before long we could hear the ocean and catch glimpses of the water shining in the moonlight. Jonelle snapped the light off straight away. No point in letting Ben watch our progress.

Jonelle took us right to the edge of shelter, just before the ground became sand and we'd be spotted from the boat. There it was, just as I left it, rocking gently on its anchor.

Moonlight played across the sea and the white beach, and yet again I was struck with how remote and romantic the spot was. I glanced at Jonelle. Her focus appeared to be wrapped up with studying the best way to get out there.

"It is quite peaceful." She cut her eyes to look at me, a hint of a promise in them.

All right, maybe not all her attention.

She moved off.

"Hey, aren't we worried about Ben seeing us coming?" I asked, as I followed over the bright white sand in my black as pitch tracksuit.

"No. Either he's out there waiting for rescue if he really thinks you're stupid enough to call someone he knows. Or he's escaped because he believes that maybe I'm not dead. In which case it doesn't matter anyway."

Good point.

I hesitated at the water's edge. I'd just gotten into warm, dry clothes. Did I really want to go through this again?

Jonelle barely paused before shedding her outer garments. Off came the slacks, off slipped the flowing shirt. She was left with a bra and panties. Of course, there was also the knife belts strapped to each wrist, the small hand gun at her ankle.

And a tight, one can only presume water proof, adhesive stretched across a patch on her lower ribs. Muscles rippled and her skin gleamed in the light. She turned to me.

"Coming?"

Egh. Not that I could refuse, of course. This was my crusade. As I shed my own clothes, Jonelle ripped the ankle belt off and took it to a tree. Looping it around a small branch, she left it there.

"Not water proof," she answered my unasked question.

Finally I joined her at the water's edge, dressed similarly in bra and briefs. Though of course, that was where the similarities ended. I glanced at the two knives.

"Quiet, but perhaps a bit messy." She'd mastered succinct responses to my non-questions.

"Messy?" That one had to be put into words.

I looked out at the boat. This was not going to be pretty. And I couldn't distance myself. No pause on the remote, no fast forward. It was here and now.

My heart jumped and my stomach took a swooping dive. No pretending my way out it; someone was about to die.

"You okay?" She wasn't looking at me. Her eyes were staring off out to sea, giving me my moment.

"Yes," I whispered, feeling anything but okay.

I took her in with a long look. In contrast to me she was ready to go.

Jonelle had perfected the warrior pose. She stood with shoulders back, stomach tucked in, legs spread in a 'knock me down if you can' kind of way. Head thrown back, long dark hair pulled into a tight pony tail, her body screamed a challenge.

I envied her the strength and surety. Every bit of her was toned. Long lean flanks, hard stomach and broad muscled shoulders. If Amazons had ever truly existed, they would have asked Jonelle to be their Queen. Unless, of course, they met Amelia … I shook my head. I was not ever going to think of that woman again. Well, only in my nightmares.

With a small smile, meant, in a parallel universe, to reassure me, Jonelle stepped into the water and I followed. No going back now. Waves pushed at us, but they'd flattened out since my earlier dip, so they didn't pose much of a problem. With measured strokes, Jonelle and I moved out to where I'd parked the boat. Moored, parked, kind of same/same really.

Jonelle moved smoothly through the water, making barely a ripple. Kind of made my shoreline blundering a few hours ago look a joke. This time I tried to keep myself as small as a mouse in the water.

When we reached the boat, Jonelle shimmied up the anchor chain, silent and sure, as deadly as the cat-like predator she reminded me of. I heaved myself in her wake, taking twice as long, with more than double the effort. Hey – it was my second time in the drink that evening.

I poked my nose over the edge and allowed my poor old body to follow in an incomprehensible puddle.

Jonelle was moving along the shadows one knife out, body tense and ready for anything. I finally got myself coordinated and padded after her.

"So, where exactly did you leave him?" Jonelle had peeped around the next corner and now leaned down to breathe the words in my ear.

My skin shivered and got covered in goose bumps.

"Just around this." I patted the cabin.

"Well, he's not there."

Jonelle stood up from her half crouch and walked confidently into the moonlight.

She gleamed. The water basically made a mockery of her underwear, leaving her naked and wet in the evening light.

I shivered.

Jonelle looked back and her gaze swept over me. I got the feeling my bra and panties were in the same shape. This time I flushed with embarrassment – I was certainly no warrior figure. We locked gazes for a moment and her eye glittered. My stomach tickled. Would she just learn to focus and leave my nerves alone?

I finally unstuck my feet from the deck and trailed behind her. I came up short when I saw the chain. It was hanging from the post ring I'd pulled it through. And the water and food were gone. So, unfortunately, was The Rose. The key which I'd considerately left out of reach must have wandered a bit too close.

I felt the surge of a wave rock the boat and had my answer. One surge too strong and slip; the key would have slid right across the deck to his feet. How ingenious of me. I'd handed him his escape on a silver platter.

"Shit," I articulated. "How stupid can I be?"

Jonelle shook her head.

"Don't beat yourself up about it. After a day in his company, I don't blame you for not thinking straight. He's out there somewhere, but I don't think we need concern ourselves too much with his exact locality. He'll come searching for us. I would in his position, especially when he doesn't hear from his two henchmen. Unless he's completely brain dead, he'll know by that simple fact I'm alive and he'll want to do the whole catch me before I catch him thing." Her teeth flashed.

"Then let the better hunter win."

I wasn't betting against her. I was more attached to my money than that.

So we slipped back over the side and made our way to the shore. Jonelle had vetoed the idea of keeping the boat. She was more than happy to let him come back and find it peacefully rocking at its anchor.

"Keeps him guessing," was her explanation.

Back on shore we gathered our clothes and walked back to the road. By that stage the prude in me had run screaming into the fine recesses of my mind. Who could be worried by the fact I was marching along basically naked, when I knew out there was a loony who wanted me dead? Even I could get my priorities straight sometimes.

By the time we had reached the car we were mainly dry so we

could pull our clothes back on. I was very happy to climb into them and the car. I knew I should've been more worried about the missing killer than I seemed to be. But at that moment all I wanted to do was get back to Canberra, shower, eat and sleep. Though her current record was a bit shaky, I had utter faith in Jonelle's ability to keep me safe. After all, she'd managed to get rid of her own kidnappers in a day, though shot and tied up, and tranquilized. I'd say she was still batting a hundred. At least, if we were to go with that analogy, she wasn't 'out' and I was pretty happy with that.

I missed a lot of the trip back to Canberra. Let down, reaction, exertion all conspired to send me into a deep comatose sleep. The fact that I was warm and comfy seated next to the one person in the world I trusted never to deliberately hurt me, helped. The swishing of the car tyres lulled me into sleep and into dreams.

Ben was chasing me with a large butcher's knife. He kept telling me that my mobile wouldn't work with the number he'd given me and I was a dead woman. I tried to hide, but everywhere I hid would dissolve and leave me exposed, and the chase would begin again. I came awake on a scream when he finally caught me…

Jonelle glanced over. Her hand was resting on my arm, shaking me gently.

"Wake up, would you? It's not going to happen."

"What's not?" I was dazed and disoriented.

"Whatever you thought he'd do to you when he got you. You've being muttering to yourself."

She moved her hand back to the steering wheel.

"Did I happen to mention he had a carving knife in my happy little dream?" I wrinkled my nose. "And that he left me with a phone number so I could contact someone with his whereabouts?"

She shot me a quick look. "Was that in your dream as well?"

"Nope." I fished out a sodden piece of paper. There was nothing but a soft blur of wet ink left.

"I wrote it down when I was on the bridge, to help me remember, though that wasn't necessary. With all those combinations you keep hammering into my head I'm starting to remember numbers quite well." I scrunched the paper up.

"Here's my mobile. Punch it in and see who we can talk to." Jonelle fished her phone out of the consol.

I flipped it open and dredged up the missing number from the depths of my memory. Quite a feat, if you ask me.

"It's going straight to voicemail, so they are either on the phone or have it off," I informed her as I waited for the message to click in.

"Will here, leave a message and I may get back to you if I feel the need."

I shut Jonelle's phone with a snap and dropped it like it burned. She shot me a concerned look.

"What? Who was it?"

I watched the lights of Canberra flicker passed outside. We'd come into the city while we'd been talking and now Jonelle pointed the nose of the Skyline toward Kingston. It may seem illogical, but I'd kind of been hoping that I would feel safe and beyond the reach of all the nasty things we were facing by simply coming home.

I'd been dreaming. Tentacles of reality were stretching out further every second.

"Well?" There was a particle of irritation in the word.

Now I was back here, I would have to keep in mind who I was dealing with. Employer, yes. Friend, yes. Something beyond friend, possibly.

A creature of infinite patience – definitely not.

"Sorry. It was one of Will's numbers. I got his voicemail."

There was a grunt from the driver. I turned my head to have a look. Sometimes it was hard to decipher those verbal explosions. I mean, was she surprised, angry, acknowledging Will's inherent duplicitous nature, or what? There was a slight frown between her perfectly plucked and shaped brows.

My inner woman got momentarily sidetracked by trying to figure out how she managed to get the lines so faultless, without even an errant hair to mar the effect. Then I got back on track.

"Are we surprised or annoyed?"

Sometimes it was best just to ask and get it over with. Showing my ignorance of a situation wasn't exactly something new.

"Pissed."

Wow! The one worder and what a word, from little miss cranky pants.

I tried not to giggle. I really did. After all, there were pointers on not completely aggravating your boss and I'd already filled up my quotient of inappropriateness for one day - week or year, depending on who was telling the story…

My attempt was a dismal failure and before I could control it, I was giggling helplessly. If anyone asked, I was putting it down to stress relief. In a couple of seconds flat, I was clutching my ribs and giggling like a school girl.

I risked a glance at Jonelle. Her lips were thinned, but when she caught me peeking, her eyes snapped with inner giggles. The type she was much better at, because trained professional hit-people didn't indulge in giggles in these types of situations. As far as I was aware. Not that I had vast swathes of experience in the matter, having known Jonelle for not even two months.

Which was no time at all and we're already sharing moonlight dips in our underwear. Whatever would it be next? On second thoughts, if I didn't ask those types of questions, I couldn't get answers I didn't know what to do with.

"Okay, so not a great word. But I am!" She sighed. "I had high hopes of Will at one stage. Ben has connections to a lot of rotten people in the world, but let's assume Phoenix is the major threat he can pull out of his hat. Will claims to us he wants Gavel out of the Hounds because of his rather tenuous link to someone who may be linked to Phoenix. See how far removed that sounds, even to us?"

She shook her head, and pulled up at a red light.

"Will told us he doesn't want the Hounds to get mixed up with external pressures. In fact, wants nothing to do with them at all. So why would he be getting a call from their hit man? So, if he's that upset about Phoenix coming into Australia and pushing their new drug, why would he be in contact with their muscle, The Rose or Ben as we now affectionately call him? It's not adding up."

The light changed and she gunned the car forward. I'd never buy a car off her second hand. She accelerated and braked with altogether too much gusto.

"Well, how about this for a scenario?" I loved to sound all important and with just a hint of knowing what is going on.

"What if Ben had Will's number from a previous incarnation as someone Will may have used for a job, because he obviously hired out at one point, consider his brother-in-law for instance. It wasn't the number Will gave me, so maybe it was an old one. And if Ben was planning on how to escape *before* I even got off the boat, he may have given me this number to make us think he was in league with Will. After all, he's pretty self-sufficient. He wouldn't sit around waiting for me to get him help, assuming he believed I would even try."

I struggled to express my thought patterns at the best of time. It was killing me.

"What if he wants us to be on the outs with Will for some reason and the best way he could see that happening was to make us think Will would come to get him? What if, and here we are a bit random, Ben actually wants us to eliminate Will *for* him?"

I tried to find out if my thoughts had too far gone by the expression on her face. Even in the orange glow of street lights I couldn't read it. Sometimes it was possible, other times it was like trying to read a book under the covers. At midnight. With no torch.

I stayed quiet. She'd have to think it through, then the only way to get her to share those thoughts would be to behave like a mouse. Not a squeak.

"Is it possible that Will was right? Gavel is in bed with Phoenix, whoever, and whatever, they stand for. Ben has the hit on Will to clear the path for Gavel, seeing as they all seem so dead set against dirtying their own hands with the blood of each other, and now Ben is hoping you'd do it for him if you thought Will was entangled with him somehow?

"But then again," I had to keep rationalising this, "how did he know you would be the one getting this message? According to his story, you were as good as dead and headless."

Now there was a pretty picture.

"I mean, it's almost as though he expected you to be back. Like he wasn't concerned that he'd handed you over tranquilised and trusted up. Maybe, he suspected you would end up killing those two men and he wanted them gone as well!"

My mind was on a roll, imagining all sorts of conspiracies. I mean, if a bad guy wanted one other bad guy dead, why stop there? He could be after the whole hat trick of opposition. There, nicely put, though probably more wordy than what Jonelle could manage.

More silence. I was beginning to suspect she thought I was crazy. Which, I was actually not about to contest. It all sounded pretty farfetched to me and I'd come up with it!

We pulled into the car park underneath the apartment block. Jonelle made no move to get out of the car. I could see by the glow of her really expensive, all purpose, all singing and dancing waterproof watch it was close to four in the morning. But somehow I wasn't sleepy anymore and I could see by the tense outline of her muscles, Jonelle wasn't either.

"You think I'm nuts and my theory is full of crap, don't you?" I was starting to feel slightly stupid.

"Actually, I was thinking that at least one of us has their brains switched on. My thoughts were at a slower pace than yours." She turned her sleek head and smiled down at me.

"It could be that most things about you run at a million miles per hour. Or the sleep you just had. Though there are a few too many deaths and conspiracies in there, overall. I can't see Ben wanting his mates dead."

I could see she was running at half speed due to the lack of sleep and midnight driving she'd just pulled. Along with bullet wound, the killing of two men and the worry. I mean, *I'd* known I was okay, but she hadn't. Of course 'okay' was a relative term, but I wasn't grading it on a curve.

Her eyes had dark circles under them and there were extra lines around the corners of her mouth which hadn't been there a few days ago. Deep inside of me there was a little voice busy denying my friend was getting old. This job of hers was aging her in front of my eyes. No wonder she wanted out.

There was quiet in the car. I pushed open the door and hauled myself out. Standing with it open I looked over the roof at the emerged Jonelle.

"Hey, would you mind terribly if I slept over tonight?"

Yes, I'd be thirty in a few weeks and slumber parties were meant to have gone out in the teens. But somehow the thought of been home alone, after the last couple of days – well it just did not appeal.

Her eyes started that faint, but unmistakeable twinkle. I gripped the car door a little tighter.

"Sure," she drawled. "I'm always up for some company."

I snorted. Take it lightly, she's only teasing you, I advised myself. "Thanks." Then I had a thought. "Who's been looking after my boys?"

I couldn't believe how neglectful I was! One brush with danger and my kitten and dog went out of my mind like so much debris. Smudge and Manny would not be impressed.

"They've been shared around. We weren't gone that long, you know." She gave a low laugh at my dismay.

"They'll feel neglected, regardless of how long it was, or wasn't."

I tried to sniff at her in disapproval, but couldn't be sure it didn't come out tearier than that.

"Well, I left them curled up on their blankets at my place. Once I got home, I raided your apartment for their things and took them with me. No one seemed to mind. As I said, they're fine."

"Your place? As in, full of antiques and cushions and knives and stuff? You can't leave two little boys alone with all that! They'll ruin it. Or kill themselves."

I turned away, slammed the door, and hurried to the stairs.

Jonelle was on my heels. "They know the rules."

She was distinctly laughing at me. I gave her a look. Yes, there is just the slightest chance I'd perfected my own 'look'. I could only hope that it was one of disgust.

She let me into her apartment and we were greeted with sleepy joy. I collapsed on my knees, hugging first one than the other. There might have been more tears but let's not get into that.

Then I looked up at Jonelle. Her eyes were hooded again and her face unreadable. I tried a smile and she gave a little start, then smiled back, face relaxing and the twinkle returning. Uh oh.

"So." How could one person put so much inflection into one teeny word?

"Shower, food, bed or chat, and what order?" The smile went wider, and it wasn't the nice gentle one. I was back to wondering who was on the menu.

"Shower than sleep."

My appetite had been left behind in Narooma. Or I may have been too scared to say the word 'food' when she was looking at me like that.

I made it back to my feet and she nodded to the main bathroom.

"All yours. I'll use the ensuite." She disappeared into the master bedroom.

I stayed in that shower until the hot water ran out. I washed sand, salt and the memory of Ben giving me the eye, right off. Amazing how fascinating swirls of water going down the plug could be. I nodded off standing up. But I came back to myself in a hurry when the water went to ice.

Leaping out I towelled off and wrapped myself in the fluffy bathrobe Jonelle always had handy. Not that she ever had guests. Hearing the depth of silence from the other room, I came to the conclusion she'd finished, and slipped into the guest room.

I slid between the sheets, totally naked. All my stuff was sandy and not bed worthy. A moment later there was a gentle tap on the door.

"Yup." Mistress of the concise.

"Can I come in?"

Who was I to say no?

Jonelle pushed open the door.

"You going to be all right? No more bad dreams? I'm only down the hall if you need me."

I half sat up, clutching the sheet. Some semblance of modesty wouldn't go astray.

"I'll be fine. Seriously. Smudge and Manny will make sure I'm okay."

I glanced at my two boys, Smudge curled up in kitten-y cuteness on the bed and Manny snoring on the floor.

She leaned against the door frame, eyeing them off.

"Yes, I can see how they would make someone feel safer. Well, you know where I am." And with one last little smile which sizzled, she backed out and closed the door.

I lay there in the dark, heart rate not in the 'rest' position. There were times, like now, I wish I wasn't as prudish as I was. Admittedly I had my pets, but there was nothing as reassuring as having Jonelle less than a metre away. Down the hall could be miles in my present state.

Which, I tried to convince myself, had nothing to do with her offer and more to do with my fear of Ben.

We all live in some sort of denial.

Chapter Twenty six

I'd had good intentions. Just a couple of hours nap then back up and into it. That way my entire body clock didn't fall apart in one swoop. A late night was like jet lag. If I didn't reset myself quickly, I'd end up back in the old patterns I was only just breaking out of. So there I was lying in Jonelle's spare bed after what I could only assume was many hours sleep, wandering what the time was.

Eventually I pulled myself out of bed and into the bath robe again. Immediately I noticed my two pets were gone. I must have been dead to the world not to have been aware of all this to-ing and fro-ing.

Leaving the room I was about to head for the kitchen when I heard something in the office. So I changed direction.

There were my missing pets, and Jonelle. Smudge had commandeered the sunniest spot, spread out on the desk, batting idly at a piece of paper Jonelle was poking him with. Manny was pretending to be above such silly nonsense sitting on the floor, watching them out of the corner of his eye. He jumped up and pounced on me when I appeared at the door.

"Hey, yourself."

I squatted down and hugged Manny. Glancing up, I encountered Jonelle's gaze.

"Sleep well?" she asked.

One last pat and I rose up and went over to give Smudge a cuddle.

"Yes, too well. I was so out of it I have no idea what the time is. My watch has completely stopped."

Smudge curled into my neck and started to purr.

She looked at her watch. "It's two in the afternoon. Glad to hear there were no more nightmares. I hope you don't mind, but the boys needed to go out a while back."

"Of course not. Nice to know they didn't burst a vessel." I perched on the desk. "What are you doing?"

She laughed. "I'm really not doing all that much. Most of all, as you saw, I've been annoying Smudge while I was thinking."

She stuck her finger in the ball of fluff in my arms. A little paw came out of it and swiped back at her. But its claws were retracted.

"If you can remember what you proposed last night, I've been thinking it over and can't see any other explanation. Unless we go down the track that Will is mixed up with Ben and that's something I don't want to even contemplate."

She frowned at Manny in concentration. Manny ducked his head. He wasn't a strong personality.

"Will isn't a friend these days, but he's not the enemy either. I wouldn't like to think of him as an associate of Ben's or anyone else remotely tied to the Phoenix. But lately I have been concerned I'm not getting the full story from him."

She picked up a pencil and started to roll it between her long fingers. It was more my style to have some sort of nervous habit.

"You're thinking of Brenda's murder?"

Jonelle nodded.

"We followed up Gavel and that priest, neither of which I feel killed Brenda. Don't get me wrong, both are more than capable of doing away with someone who gets in their way. But Brenda wasn't seen as a threat. She was paid to sleep with them and they knew fear would keep her in line. So who had motive and the opportunity?"

I was distinctly hoping that was a rhetorical question. Last night's effort on my behalf, all that thinking, was as good as I was getting. I wasn't the brains of the outfit.

"Ah well. I'm sure something will turn up. I think we need to go out and rattle some cages. Spook the spooky. Make lots of loud noise and see what turns up. At the very least, someone will come after us if they think we're investigating Brenda's death."

Hang on.

"Whoa there. Are you setting us up as targets? Is that what you are saying? Because I've only just lost the bruising from the last time someone used me as a punching bag and I'm not in an awful hurry to explore that avenue again. I thought we were doing the discreet thing. You know, on the sly and quiet like."

There, I liked that idea much better.

She smiled - the light feral one. I could see my peaceful afternoon slipping out of reach. When she looked like that the resting period was over. The inner beast was coming out to play.

"Sure, see how far quiet is getting us. We go have a *quiet* chat to Gavel and Father Michael, and all we get are the assurances they didn't do it. I'm not about to twitch the tail of whatever creature they work for by killing them. Though it would give me pleasure considering the choices they are making in their lifestyle."

I hated it when she talked like that. It made me aware of just how closely she wandered on the edge. Sometimes she appeared lost entirely.

"No, quiet is not the way to go. I want to cause panic in the heart of whomever it was that strangled my client. It annoys me no end that they have managed to get away with it for so long. Paybacks a bitch." She grinned. "And so am I."

No doubt; I wasn't about to argue.

"So." I slid into the chair reserved for the sidekick, which was currently me. "What are we up to?"

"Well, in two days time there is the drop off in Melbourne for me. I intend on being there - not quite as they expected, but I'm not here to accommodate others. It's only Monday, but I think a trip to the Batch and Haddock tonight wouldn't be out of the question. Up for it?"

At least she was asking.

"I guess so."

I didn't want to show much enthusiasm as I still believed a loud approach was suicidal.

Her irritating eyebrow quirked up. I hated that. I didn't have moveable eyebrows to express myself with.

"Well, it's not like I want to be the target again, okay? Just don't forget Ben's still out there somewhere bent on making me his toy." That was unsettling. "I thought you were hell bent on making him your next objective?"

She shrugged. "Wednesday will see me one step closer to that. I'm sure Ben will know about the drop point. He may even turn up to see why his boys aren't returning his calls. His curiosity will be killing him." Another grin. "You never know, quite literally, I hope."

Yes well. I wasn't going to pretend to lose sleep over the early demise of The Rose. But wandering around making a fool of myself at the Batch wasn't on my list of priorities either. Sometimes my job sucked.

"So have you made any contact with Will?"

Not that he would come on out and say 'sure, I'm a great mate of Ben's and would have come to his rescue at the drop of a hat'. At least, I'm hoping he wouldn't say that. But we needed to clear it up. Well, Jonelle needed to clear it up.

"I left a message on that number you called and asked him to meet us at the Batch. If the number is still something he checks at all, we'll be seeing him. Mostly I think, because he'll be worried about how we got it in the first place."

It never paid to be curious in this business. Something I was having trouble coming to terms with because I was the Cat personified – as in 'curiosity killed the'. Fill in the blanks.

But one thing I was learning very slowly was: bad guys chopped your nose off if you were silly enough to stick it into their business. So I tried hard to let Jonelle go first. If someone tried to chop her nose off they were in for a nasty surprise.

"I'll just toddle on home for the next few hours then. I desperately need clothes and some of my own things."

Like another shower and a gallon of skin care products. Salt water wasn't forgiving on my skin type. I felt as dry as the Sahara.

"Off you go then. Take Manny for a walk too. He's been pining for you. But be ready for dinner and then Batching by say 6:30."

I glanced again at the wall clock. Time was flying away as we sat and gossiped.

Snapping my fingers I brought Manny out of his musings and took them both back home. I wasn't sure if I wanted to go off walking. Kingston was pretty much a hub of activity at most times, but it seemed a little exposed. Like Ben could jump out at me at any moment and what exactly would Manny do about it? Lick him to death?

I'd had high hopes for Manny. As a guard dog for the apartments and myself, but he was turning out to be more of a lapdog wannabe. Gentle and afraid of upsetting anyone, he had a tendency to mope if left alone too long. Not exactly earning his kibble.

So I shelved the whole walking plan and settled them in front of the telly instead. It was re-runs of Lassie and while Smudge hissed and spat at the screen, Manny loved it.

I took my sorry dried out old bodkin and ran myself a bath. Into it went all sorts of oils and concoctions we women love to believe make the world of difference.

An hour later I was sleek (but a bit wrinkly) and ready to rock and roll. Applying still more moisturizer and hair conditioning I stood in front of my wardrobe trying to decide what I was going to wear for the occasion.

All right, so it shouldn't have been such a big deal. But the simple fact was who were we going to bump into? What if Will did turn up? A major league hottie was our Mr Malone. Then there were the miscellaneous cuties that sometimes appeared and I could technically be on the lookout because Brad was history.

That still stung, but I wasn't allowing myself dwelling time. Onwards and upwards.

A soft pink sleeveless top with white three quarter pants ended up been the 'thing', then make up and I was done. And it was only five by this stage. I could relax.

Out at the telly, my boys were watching some old black and white movie.

"You cannot sit on me Smudge!" I gave him a shove. The last thing I needed was fur on this outfit.

I settled in for some catch up TV. At 6:30 Jonelle was at my front door.

"Hello! Fiona! Time to go, Princess."

It's the small things in life. Having the pets to tease, Jonelle calling me Princess. It was back to normal and I'd only been home for a day.

With one last check in the mirror, I let myself out. Jonelle was immaculate as always. Black everything, sleek and panther-ish, I could kill for some of her poise.

We ended up at a local restaurant, mainly because neither of us could be bothered driving, but also because Jonelle wanted to be able to see the doorway of the Batch from her table. The woman was obsessed with business.

"I'm hanging out for some wine."

I disregarded the menu and opened the wine list. Ben hadn't exactly been Ritz-style catering.

"You know there is a term for you." Jonelle was reading the menu, a slight smile on her lips.

"If you say one more word I'll have to deck you. I know exactly where you're going with this conversation and I will dispute it."

It wasn't the first time someone had insinuated I was an alcoholic. I just happened to have a fine appreciation of beverages. Preferably ones of the alcoholic variety. There was nothing wrong with that.

Jonelle gave an inelegant snort.

"Deck me? Well, I do like the fact you've gained some confidence in your abilities, no matter how overrated they are."

True. When we first met, I was terrified of saying something that would upset her. Now, pretending like I was tough and knew what I was doing was becoming a habit.

"Well, don't intrude on my hangovers. They are sacred to a woman like me. Now how do you feel about a local white?"

My eyes travelled down the extensive list provided, listing the top one.

"I don't have any feelings for it at all," she replied.

"Did you just try to crack a funny? You amaze me."

I loved sarcasm. My mother was continually telling me it was the lowest form of wit, but I begged to differ. It was magnificent! It could be cutting and the best verbal tool.

"Just get your wine, and I'll order food."

Jonelle was in fine form tonight. Although her relaxed exterior was belied by the fact that her eyes kept flicking over the road to the Batch's front door. I knew our slow evening would float on out the window as soon as anyone she knew walked in there. So I had to capitalise on what time I had.

After dinner and wine were duly ordered it was down to business. So much for having a moment's breather.

"We need to be down in Melbourne by Wednesday night. The drop time is 11pm sharp. I don't intend on missing it and I sure as hell hope Ben turns up."

She must have seen the look of my face, somewhere around terrified by the feeling in my chest because she added, "Don't worry, I'll be there and this time I'll be ready for the bastard. There is nothing he can throw at me which will hurt you."

I knew she was trying to be reassuring, but she was failing miserably. If Ben was there and he didn't take us down, then she'd kill him and I was on my own little roundabout of terror and elation.

"Couldn't you leave me at home? You know, to file paperwork, file my nails or something equally absorbing? Look what happened the last time I was out on the job. We both got kidnapped. A roaring success that was. I'm much better at the whole home fires burning bit. Plus, shouldn't we be concentrating on Brenda's murder?"

Anything was better than the latest crazy idea. Me? Tagging along on a vendetta gig? And the wine hadn't come out yet.

Jonelle was shaking her head. "We can take some time out, go shopping in a truly cosmopolitan city and go to the drop point as well. It's perfect. All you have to do is pretend you know what you're doing."

"Will you promise on that?"

Her eyes slid sideways to the window again. Now, she could be checking on the comings and goings of the Batch, but I think she was actually trying to slide out of making any such promise.

"Jonelle."

I tried for a warning note. It almost came across like I meant it.

"I can't make a promise. I don't go back on them, but there are too many variables on a job to factor in for promise making. Just know that I am highly unlikely to put you in a position where I thought I might misplace you again."

I sighed. It wasn't worth arguing about. I would lose and subsequently feel a fool. She knew I was too interested in what I might get into next to really put up a fight. That made both of us fools, if you asked me.

"All right! I'll do it. But if something goes wrong and I end up Ben's play thing for the next decade, I quit! No more adventures. "

Fine, so I was a liar as well. It was the adventures that made this whole thing exciting. And the people I was meeting. Okay, so it was the whole package and while mind numbing fear was never my favourite thing, I was learning to cope with that. At least, I pretended I was.

"I'll get him. You'll feel as safe as houses."

She gave me a small smile.

Yeah, and pigs might learn to fly someday soon. The wine arrived and I took a hefty gulp from my glass. Sometimes it helped me to think clearly and other times I just needed it to make the thoughts go away. Like, how many ways I could get carved up for fish bait. Everything appears much simpler and definitely doable after that first sip.

"I'll take you out to somewhere really special and we can go to a day spa for totally outrageous hair and body care. Then just before you get bored, it'll be drop time and we can go see who bothers to turn up for my drugged or decapitated body. Now, doesn't that sound like a fun filled week to you? Not many employers could offer half as much.

"Joker wants to make himself a big name again in the field of threats. I plan to upset this crazy idea and put him out of business if he doesn't take back his contract. It should be fun."

But there was no real twinkle in her eyes and her words were flat.

Jonelle tried a smile on me. I wanted to say she couldn't charm her way out of this one, but then again, who was I kidding? She suddenly stopped her teasing and focused outside.

"We need to speed this dinner business up." Another pause. "Maybe we can do without the food part." Her attention came back to me.

I finished my wine in record time. "But I was looking forward to eating. You ordered some lovely food and a whole bottle of wine is going to go to waste."

That bothered me more than the food. I eyed the bottle off. Was it considered cheap and nasty if I took it to the pub with me?

Jonelle growled. "It's time we were over the road."

She snapped her fingers at a passing waiter. Probably a bit rude, but then again she wasn't in the mood for civility.

Food was cancelled and Jonelle put her foot down on my taking the wine with me. So empty handed and with an empty tummy, we crossed the road and entered the Batch and Haddock. I didn't know who she'd seen, but it was making her twitchy. A twitchy Jonelle was hard to live with.

"Exactly what is the plan here?"

It would be nice to know so I didn't end up putting my foot in it. Or doing the usual and opening my mouth about the wrong thing to the wrong person. Not that I knew all that many 'wrong' people. I glanced around. On second thoughts, I knew at least three in there all ready.

Sitting in one corner, pints of what looked like Guinness propped in front of them, were Gavel, Will and other assorted Hounds.

Great. Why had he brought the troops? Especially that particular troop? Gavel was one of the people I liked least.

Across the room, which was hardly full, being so early on a Monday night, were Tomas' mates Mick and Simon. They were sitting with a couple of fellows I didn't know. They didn't appear happy with the influx of Hounds, but then again who could blame them. Not me.

I wished they were anywhere but here, preferably in their own little clubhouse all warm and toasty. Some people had no place coming and mixing with us commoners.

Will noticed us straight away and gave a barely discernable flicker of his eyebrow. Jonelle didn't say a word, but took me across to the bar and ordered drinks. Once they arrived she turned to survey the room. She was controlled and calculating. Crap, was all I could think. Here we go.

"The plan, as you put it, is to poke a stick into the hornet's nest and see what we can stir up. Glad to see Will brought some familiar faces. That'll make things play out a bit better. And Tomas' old buddies are here too. Lovely."

Her eyes were tight and her voice tighter. I felt I should reach out and give her a shove just to make sure the Jonelle I knew was still inside. Maybe I would have except I knew that could earn me some sort of damage when she was like this.

"We know Tomas had connections with Gavin. That was how he managed to steal that package of The Way, our new designer drug of choice. Gavin was tenuously linked to Phoenix through Ben, as he wanted to get into playing with the big boys.

"As a test he was either sent to kill Tomas for the theft and retrieve the drug, or he told Ben who stole it and made the suggestion himself as a peace offering. He killed Tomas, made it as obvious as all get out that there was a search for something, and failed to turn up the package. Which I got my hands on."

She took a long pull on her beer. Yuk. How could she possibly drink that stuff? I gulped my bourbon. Much better. Strong too. It had to be at least a double which was unusual. On the whole Jonelle deplored my excesses and tried to minimise them.

"So I imagine when Ben gets the chance, Gavin will be made an example of. Which will mean I won't have to do it myself. Back to the point."

Jonelle never wandered unless it was for a reason. She was wondering aloud in her own way why Gavin was still fully functional.

"Tomas' mates may or may not have been aware of his new drug habit. We know that Mick was not surprised he was dead which tells me Mick knows a little something, though he was surprised it was a murder. He'd thought Tomas would OD first.

"Gavel, we know, is Will's number one threat in the contest for the leadership of the Hounds. Which means to me Will is walking a tightrope; otherwise he would have a firm hand on the reins.

"In its own way, that is reassuring, as I would hate to think of the Hounds owning Will that much. Gavel is also trying to bring the interest of Phoenix to his work by supporting one of their players, the priest? Not too sure about that link. Is Father Michael merely ambitious or does he really have connections to the Phoenix? Either way, Gavel is hitching his star to him.

"Will wants Gavel removed but feels his hands are tied re doing the job himself. Which is crazy and I wonder why."

Her eyes flicked around the room. There were a few other people in there, but I was unaware of any link they had to us.

"Will wanted Gavel dead before I talked to him. Which makes me think Will has something to hide and Gavel knows it. Or, he doesn't know anything and Will is playing a deeper game, which is sure to really piss me off when I find out what. Though Gavel spilled his guts quite considerably when I had my brief chat with him, nothing linking Will to anything suspicious came out. Shame."

She smiled and took another chug of beer.

"Why would you *want* Will to be linked to something?"

I was lost. Regardless of her little 'Will is no friend but no enemy either' speech, I knew they had a history and couldn't see why she was trying her best to paint him in a bad light. Unless it was because he showed an interest in me. And that either meant she hated to share him, or me. Which was terribly egotistical either way.

She slid her eyes sideways to mine. They rested there, then moved back to cruising the room.

"I don't particularly want to, but I have this itch which tells me Will is hiding something. It would be a lot easier if someone came up with something to tell me about him than me having to go to the source. That *would* get messy. My itches, before you ask, are never wrong."

I could imagine they had saved her life often enough. Shame she'd had no such itch before Ben tricked us and stole off with me. Sure I felt kind of over it, but sometimes when I wasn't paying attention, I could feel his slimy hands on me and I came over all nauseous.

An itch *then* would have been good. An itch over the scrumptious Will just seemed … paranoid.

"We know The Way is Phoenix's big gun in the usual drug wars. And that's about all we know of them. Though we are beginning to suspect Jack knew more than we do and they had him killed. Which, if we can prove it, will be enough to pull Amelia in and then they'll be her baby." Jonelle's smile became veritably shark like.

"Happy hunting is all I can say to that. If Charles and Daniel, your midnight visitors, are directly linked with Phoenix and they warned her off through you, then trust me, when she knows the whole truth, there are many and varied ways of unpleasant death that will be visited upon them."

I shuddered.

Sure, I had my own reasons to want Charles and Daniel smacked around. Daniel had done a fine job of beating me to a pulp under Charles' direction. I had no love for the dear boys.

On the other hand I'd met Amelia. Jonelle was right. If Jonelle was deemed scary by the majority of law abiding citizens, then Amelia was a demon. She walked like a tiger, had eyes like a shark and the abilities to match. I didn't like the idea of her being in Canberra, of her being on the planet, but if she was in your corner I guess you'd feel pretty safe.

But she wasn't.

She was just there, waiting for the chance to kill whoever had put the man of her dreams into his deathly coma and *no one* was safe until she knew who they really were. Because until then, everyone was a potential target. There were loose cannons and then there was Amelia. Scary, deadly and not quite sane (in my books). A lethal weapon perpetually half cocked.

"And what are we going to do with all this wonderful knowledge we've gained? And how come you think Jack and Phoenix are mixed up?" She had mentioned that before and I'd not questioned it, but this time I had to.

I was still not quite getting her picture. And my bourbon was drained. I waved it at the barman and got myself another. I watched carefully. Whatever reasoning she had, my request for a repeat of the first drink was a double.

I couldn't imagine why Jonelle wanted me drunk, but my mind was starting to fill in the blanks. In many and varied ways, as she put it.

She glanced at me and my glass.

"My chat with Amelia on our way to Sydney the other week where we both agreed Jack was on the hunt for someone new and with a name like 'Phoenix' you know, rising from the ashes, we are playing the odds. Just trust me, would you? Anyway, we need to find some answers to the questions our incomplete knowledge has raised. No one's talking, I'm tired and don't want to go visiting ever snitch in town, so we are here to be loud, obnoxious and hopefully someone will come to us."

"Yeah and try to do away with us – again." I pointed at my bourbon. "So basically you're feeding me loads of alcohol so I will be indiscreet. You think I may not be if left sober." I glared at her.

"Tell me I'm not right."

Well, I wouldn't but that's beside the point.

"You don't want to wave a red flag at anyone and I know that alcohol will loosen that resolve, so yes I was priming you to be my spokeswoman." She grinned.

With a sigh I finished it off. "Never let it be said I didn't do my job, tough as it may be. Fill me up."

My level of tolerance for alcohol had increased over the years. So making me a talkative drunk was a pleasant, but extended job. The bar was slowly filling, but it wasn't ever going to overflow on a Monday. For which I was glad.

The last thing I needed was this evening recorded by an acquaintance of mine and reported back to any of the Apartmates, Grillia or Steph. Then they would know I had a problem. Getting plastered on a Monday had definite alcoholic tendencies.

Will came over at one point, pretending to collect some more drinks from the bar.

"Jonelle. Fiona."

He gave her a flat look and me a charming smile. My internal organs did slow somersaults. The man could melt a woman at twenty paces. I happened to look at Jonelle. Her face was stony.

Okay, so not all women.

"Will."

My, we were a communicative bunch.

"I see Gavel is up and walking around. I thought we'd come to an agreement about him?"

Will faced the bar and put his money down. The barman started to refill his order. The guy had a great memory of what everyone had the first time round.

"You wanted me to put Gavel out of contention for your job. You never gave specific reasons, so I chose to ignore you. He's no immediate enemy of mine now I know he didn't kill Brenda."

She narrowed her eyes. Amazing. I didn't think they could go any further. I leaned closer and peered into her face. Just keeping an eye on them!

Teehee. I was starting to find myself very amusing.

Jonelle and Will stopped the glaring match and both turned to look at me. Perhaps I'd leaned too far. I blinked at them owlishly and waved my bourbon in her face.

"You feed me doubles, I can be doubly annoying." I grinned.

This was fun. She could hardly rake me over the coals for doing exactly as she'd ordered. So far I'd only managed to twitch her tail, but I could broaden my horizons. I switched my bleary gaze to Will.

"How are you doing, Handsome? Up for another trip to the Tower any day soon? Now I have no boyfriend, fake one that he turned out to be, I can basically screw anyone I want to."

Somehow I didn't think that as an invitation, it was quite as alluring as I'd hoped.

Jonelle snorted and rolled her eyes. Will on the other hand, tried valiantly not to laugh in my face.

"Fake boyfriend?" he asked Jonelle.

"Don't ask. He was married, long and sad story, which, if her current state is anything to go by, will get sadder with each telling. Will, Gavel is no threat to you. He's not half the leader you are, so why try to pin Brenda's death on him?"

So much for not going to the source. I looked at her glass. Had she been putting too much away as well? I couldn't tell from its level, but it looked as though she was still on the same one. I stuck my finger in it.

Warm – definitely the same one.

"Oi!"

Jonelle grabbed my hand and wrenched me out of her glass. Her long fingers closed over mine and I gripped them for a second before snatching my hand away.

"That's definitely out. No playing in the alcohol. Weren't you taught better manners?"

But I could see the contact had softened her, and a half smile tugged at her mouth. Thank goodness for that. It was vitally important, in my sodden state, not to allow the Jonelle I knew to disappear inside the iron shell of the professional.

I giggled and fluttered my lashes at Will. I hoped to distract him from her question. You know, prevent world war three. His hand slid down and caressed my thigh for a second, but he caught Jonelle's eye and placed it back on the bar.

"No fair," I complained. "He's open game."

One day I really was going to have to learn not to drink so much. Shame today was not that day.

Will leaned over and breathed in my ear which sent shivers down my spine.

"I'll speak to you later," he promised.

"Stop that, you tickle."

"Stop that, period," Jonelle growled. "Will. Wake up. She's more than half under."

"And you're attracting a lot of attention," I informed him. "To be fair I'm probably not helping. But in my defence, Jonelle, you did want me to attract attention and I think I'm succeeding admirably."

I smiled in what I thought was a truly winning manner. Somewhere along the way it got lost in translation because Jonelle scowled.

Will leaned back on the bar, suddenly in control. Whatever foul mood he'd been in; whatever knowledge he'd been about to spill was swallowed in one massive change of heart.

"Looking to make a splash were we, Jonelle?" He smiled. "Why would that be, I wonder? The woman who prides herself on silence and discretion only makes loud noises when she has no clue as to what is going on and needs to rattle some cages."

He was awfully smug and I felt the need to smack him.

Jonelle wasn't going to let him niggle her.

"Sure, if I shake the tree hard enough, some information may just fall out."

"Ooh, like a potato. Except they don't grow in trees," I rationalised. "So probably more like an apple?"

I tried hard to focus on them. But they were wearing matching looks of disapproval and amusement, so I allowed the whole focus bit to dribble away. Hey, they were lucky I was making any sense at all. I'd lost count of how many doubles I'd poured down my throat. Good thing Jonelle wasn't going stealthy right now, because I think my voice was closer to foghorn. Not one hundred percent on that. There was a growing buzz in my ears.

Jonelle patted my hand and turned her attention back to Will.

"So, talk to me Will. I can't help if you aren't straight with me."

He frowned.

"I've told you. The Hounds are in an unsettled period. If Gavel gets in, we head down a path none of us are ready to go. But I don't want to move against him openly. I just wanted a favour. Why are you hassling me?"

Will was getting huffy. Boy was he ever cute. Even while being a stroppy bastard.

"I'm not muscle for hire these days is why. Why don't you use you dear friend The Rose?"

Jonelle watched Will closely. I suddenly felt the need to visit the bathroom. At the same time I kept my eyes firmly on Will's face myself. This was getting mighty interesting.

He picked up the drinks the barman had put by his hand ages ago. "I don't know what you are implying Jon, but I don't like it. I thought we were mates. Ben is a dangerous fool and any association of ours was before he took my brother-in-law down with him."

Will's eyes were flat and nasty. Suddenly my previous invitation to him didn't appeal so much. He turned and took everything back to his table. The fact he'd stood talking to Jonelle so long had not gone unnoticed. There were a lot of questions going around over there.

Studying the group, Jonelle gave a little jolt. "Well, what do you know?"

"I'm hoping that's rhetorical becaush right now, I don't think I know anyshing," I slurred at her.

She turned that magnificent head back to me and rolled her eyes.

"You've done a great job, but I think it's time I cut you off. One of the boys over there is Will's little brother, Theo. William and Theodore Malone. I didn't think big brother would introduce little Theo to the Hounds. I'll just swing on by and say hello."

She plonked her beer on the bar, hardly touched. If Jonelle wanted to make a scene then here it came. I shuddered delicately. Either Will would have a fit for having to talk nice over his brother's head, or Gavel would throw something at us.

"Can I stay here?"

I leaned happily on my section of the alcohol damp bar. I could even end up taking a shine to the barman. He was starting to look remarkably edible.

"I don't know if meeting the rest of his family would help."

"Too late. Here they come." Will, seeing Jonelle's intention, had pre-empted her table visit by dragging Theo to us. Wise man. Who knew what Jonelle could come up with in front of an audience?

"Theo." She smiled: all teeth and power. "What has your brother been getting you into this time?" Jonelle glanced at Will. "You take your brother down with you, after having Kate's husband killed, and no one in your family will talk to you." Sometimes, she was no diplomat.

Theo put a restraining hand on Will's arm. Something I wouldn't mind doing myself. It drew my attention to the outline of muscle and sinew under his shirt sleeve. I was easily distracted when uncomfortable.

Nope, scratch that, I was just easily distracted around pretty men.

Brother Theo wasn't hard on the eyes either. It was like looking at a less hard, less defined Will. I watched them both from the vantage point of severe beer goggles. I would still pick Will over Theo, even if he came across as though he'd sooner knife you as kiss you. Call me crazy, but I was starting to develop a bad boy crush.

"Theo," Jonelle touched his arm gently as though handling a fine crystal piece. I could tell that in her own way, she was upset that Will had brought Theo into this. "Meet my assistant, Fiona. Fi, meet Theo Malone." She shot Will another dagger look. "Obviously the best of the Malone boys."

"Pleshed to meet you." I smiled at them all with great love in my heart. "You're both very dishy, you know that?"

Will grinned. "Stop it, Fiona, or you'll make me jealous."

Theo held out his hand, which I enjoyed shaking, then turned his attention to Jonelle. She did kind of commandeer people that way.

"Will is showing me around. It's about time I got involved in the family business, wouldn't you say?"

Had I thought he was the softer one? His smile was as warm as the Arctic. There was something about him though that made me struggle with an elusive thought. I gave up and just sat watching.

Will shook his head.

"I don't think you'll be following my footsteps anytime soon, but at least you'll be able to take care of yourself." The look they shared was a bit more than brotherly love.

Jonelle watched their exchange and kept her thoughts behind hooded eyes.

"You in town long?"

"Not too sure." The boys shared another look. "Probably not." Ah, the joy in the room could hardly be contained.

She nodded. "Well it was nice to see you again. Try not to get into any trouble while you're here, okay? Neither of us want to have to pull you out of the fire."

And she smiled to take the sting out of her words.

Smile or not, Theo nearly jumped out of his skin. Pink tinged his cheeks. Jonelle raised her eyebrow.

"All ready in deep, are we?"

Grabbing Theo's arm, some random drinks at the bar, Will started to head back to the Hounds' table.

"He's fine, just finding his feet in a strange town. Come on Theo, let's leave Jonelle to clean up Fiona." He flashed me a smile that melted my shoelaces and was gone.

Jonelle leaned once more on the bar. Her eyes stared into nothing. "You know what? We can go. I think I have some very unfriendly thoughts about our Will which I need to think through." She plucked the latest drink I'd managed to snag from my unresisting fingers. "And I think Will is going to have some explaining to do to the rest of his team."

She nodded at the Hounds. Gavel was eyeing us off, probably hoping that the things he'd spilled to Jonelle weren't the topic of her conversation with Will. A damp patch between my shoulder blades started to itch. His eyes promised me murder and mayhem.

"Fine. Going is good."

Who was I to argue? Most people who knew her wouldn't take Jonelle on face to face. But what if Gavel got the rather naff idea of throwing a knife or pulling a gun – at her or me? She wasn't bullet proof as far as I could tell.

I levered myself off the barstool and tilted. Only Jonelle's wonderful reflexes kept me afloat. The world was faintly fuzzy and had a distinct list. She wrapped one strong arm around my waist and basically hauled me to the door. One day I would look back at the guffaws that followed me out and smile.

At the time, I was keen to go back in and 'sort them all out'. Jonelle used a restraining hand to make sure I wasn't made into pulp.

Walking back to the Grangelands was a tough one. I staggered, continually pulling Jonelle off her stride. And she was sometimes so busy laughing she had no stride. Messy, one might say.

"Would you lower you voice? Do you really want everyone to witness your Monday evening debauchery?"

"Hey! It was your fault! I wasn't up for Monday night anything." But I gave whispering my best shot. "Tell me, what is it about Will you think you've learned?"

She opened the gate and pulled me through. "Hang on. I'll get you inside. Mind you, I really should wait until tomorrow. Chances are you'll forget everything."

She stole my keys and opened my apartment door.

"I never forget anything. At least," I corrected myself as she dropped me onto the couch beside an indignant Smudge, "not because of having too much to drink. *Mainly* just because I have a hopeless memory."

That made sense, to me.

Jonelle settled herself on the floor and Smudge landed in her lap. Manny came out of the bedroom to see what the fuss was all about, but fell asleep on the floor.

"Well, Will admitted a while back that he was friends with Brenda but according to Heather, she had no friends. Only business associates and we all know what business she was in. That being the case, can we assume Will was one of her customers? Which would explain his interest in the case and then raises the immediate question of how often they met, did she confide in him at all, and where was he the night she died?"

"That's more than one question," I observed. Clever little possum.

"Smart ass. They all tie in together. Because if he doesn't have a reliable alibi, then Will suddenly becomes a suspect, which begins to explain his motive for trying to get me to kill off Gavel without speaking to him first. A big mistake."

She fiddled with Smudge's ears, which earned her a smack from the paws. Changing tactic and blowing raspberries on his stomach didn't help.

My head floated somewhere in outer space. The world not only tilted now, but was slowly making circles around me. I couldn't decide if the sensation was about to make me throw up or go to sleep. It had been a while since I'd indulged quite as much as this.

Looking up, Jonelle caught my eyes, just before they closed altogether.

"Here." She plopped Smudge on my tummy. "I think we'll call it a night. I'll skip the gym call for you tomorrow and see you when you can move again. Then we can discuss my theory about Theo."

I grunted. Usually an open comment like that would have me demanding answers, but all I could do was fall head long into black out.

The joys of bourbon.

Chapter Twenty seven

I was sinking in fluff. Wrapped head to foot in purple towelling, I was being dandled in water upside down. I thrashed wildly trying hard not to breathe, but wanting air like a polar bear wanted the snow. And no, I had no idea where that analogy came from.

It took falling off the couch with Smudge dangling his paw in my mouth for the source of my nightmare to become apparent (though where the colour purple came from is anyone's guess). I was wrapped up in the fawn throw rug I sometimes remembered to put on my couches, with Smudge playing some sort of bizarre game with my swollen and decidedly icky tongue.

I'd probably been snoring and the chance to see what it did was too much for the kitten. But I could have done without the fur stuck in my mouth.

As soon as my body realised it was conscious it started to ache. Everywhere. In fact, I didn't know there were so many places to ache. I groaned. I wanted - no scratch that - *needed* to die. Was it only a month or so ago I was crowing about how my body could cope with any sort of punishment with barely a flicker of repercussion? How could I possibly have aged so much in a month?

It was more likely to be your new healthy lifestyle, a tiny voice told me. The lifestyle which was helping me to detox, but making me vulnerable to the effects of a great big heap of 'tox'. God save me from Jonelle's regime.

I struggled into a sitting position where I was immediately licked by Manny. He was glad I was still alive. That made one of us. I tried to think how many bourbons I'd had the night before and lost count. Doubles. I was amazed I wasn't paralytic.

"Softly, softly boys."

I used the couch as a lever and tried to heave myself to my feet. That disturbed everything and instead I lay back onto the floor.

"Give me another day or two," I muttered.

Then I glanced at my watch. Unless I was reading it wrong, I *had* missed another day. It had to be 4:30 the following afternoon. What had I been thinking? Not a lot, came that same little voice. I could strangle it.

Crawling I managed to open the door so my poor pets could get out. I sat in the doorway, letting the cooler air work its wonders. Something had to help and I was fresh out of any other ideas. Sometime very soon I'd be visiting the bathroom.

I could remember when I had yet to stretch my wings and go out to a pub. I watched my older siblings as they came home tanked, exhausted and grinning from ear to ear with stories to tell. While I would rather have died than let them know it, I'd been so envious, waiting for my turn to grow up and get drunk. It was like a rite of passage; every teenager needed to go through it. All the while, Mum would be lecturing me about the evils of alcohol. She made it sound like ambrosia. But every time Delight or Joy would swear, regardless of the stories they would tell me, they would never do it again. Every weekend. Like a litany.

Now, as I half lay half sat, in my door, I was struck by the thought I could hear Joy and Delight's words in my head.

"I swear, God, if you let me live through this, I swear I'll never drink again."

I had become my worst nightmare – my older siblings.

Just then, light and springy footsteps came my way. I didn't even bother to raise my head.

"The things I do for you. I think I need to get a bonus for hangover in the line of duty."

There was a reassuring and sympathetic chuckle from somewhere above me.

"Hi there, Princess." She squatted down to my level. "Sorry. You really do look a mess. Want some help back inside?"

Not waiting for an answer, she lifted me up and took me to the couch. But the movement was too much for the over loaded system. I struggled onto my own legs and ran for the bathroom.

Ten minutes later I could shakily walk back.

"Hi yourself." I lowered myself to the couch feeling drained, but human again. Perhaps I hadn't lost my touch completely.

"What have you been doing while I was sleeping?" I thought I'd magnanimously gloss over the acute details of the induced hangover.

"Well, went for a couple hours run. Needed to clear my head." That made two of us. "Then got us tickets for the last flight out tonight for Melbourne." She looked at the state I was in and shook her head.

"Maybe I should have tried tomorrow."

I growled.

"Fine." I resisted the urge to put my hand to my head like a tragedy queen, though I could feel the clammy sweat lingering there. "So when does this flight leave and why on earth did I agree to this?"

"I'll come back in an hour. Try to be human. And you agreed because, like me, you are a sucker for the danger." She did a terribly un-Jonelle like thing and stuck her tongue out at me. I would have retaliated with a similar gesture, but it was still furry.

"Don't forget, tomorrow is also drop off day, so we have to factor some time in for that between detoxing you in a health spa and some serious shopping."

Nice to know she was female underneath it all. Then she left me, for which I was eternally grateful. Like an actor she knew her entrances and exits. I dropped my head onto my knees. I hadn't asked her about Will and Theo. Considering my fragile state, I wasn't too sure I wanted to know her thoughts on the subject. Plus, I could remember some of what I'd been blathering about last night and the idea of bringing Will up was too much.

Once she was gone, I pulled myself together and took a long hot soak, ending with the jets on full cold. Now if that doesn't wake you up, then you have no pulse.

Packing proved to be interesting. So I threw something black, something casual and something reasonably formal in together and hoped the whole gig wasn't going to go on for too long. There were actual limits to my concentration, which needed to get factored in. Post large evening, I had the concentration of a gnat.

It was usually a treat to sit in Qantas Club drinking before a flight. I was sure many people had flown in states similar to my own. I defied them to enjoy the experience. I sat staring out the window trying to find a fixed point of reference I could study so as to keep my stomach in one place. Jonelle was very nice about it all, considering the whole thing had been her idea.

"Apart from deciding that Will was probably a client of Brenda's and thus a suspect in her murder, was there anything new that came out of last night which could justify feeling this way?" I had to ask, my mental condition notwithstanding.

She gave me a concerned look. "Knowing just how much and how fast you can put it away?"

I experimented with a snarl.

"Sorry. We were the centre of attention. And if Will thought he had trouble with Gavel before, talking to me for over half an hour at the bar isn't going to help his situation, which is fine by me. I want that boy well and truly spooked." She sipped the in-flight juice and made a face.

"He may come seeking help or the chance to offload his guilt by spilling the beans. Mind you, the one thing I took into serious consideration was the arrival of Theo on the scene. Why is Will bringing his little brother into the Hounds? And why was Theo so bloody nervous about saying a mere hello?"

I could see she was off on one of her rhetorical outbursts, so didn't interrupt. But at least that explained what it was I'd witnessed the night before. It was Theo's almost terror at having to greet Jonelle. He obviously knew her and didn't particularly want to renew the acquaintanceship.

People got that way around Jonelle when they had something to hide. Which begged the question – what was Will's little brother possibly hiding that would interest Jonelle?

Jonelle was continuing, rudely talking over my thoughts.

"The near panic in his eyes when I mentioned getting into trouble while he was here was a surprise. I always liked Will's family. Kate's marriage was a disaster, but she's nice enough. And Theo, well, he looked up to me and Will. I didn't think he would ever come to see me as something to be afraid of."

I could tell this was upsetting her. To have someone she liked, even if her feelings about his older brother were ambivalent, suddenly see her as a monster wasn't something she was going to accept lying down.

"I hope Will hasn't been talking out of turn. Not that Theo would have any delusions about me, but still, it's not nice." Sometimes she reacted in such a normal way to hurtful situations, I felt it hard to tie the two Jonelle's together. Then she shrugged.

"Oh well, if Theo has lost his puppy crush, then I guess it was just meant to be. Thanks for the help you were last night. Shame it didn't flush anything of monumental value out. Though we at least know that Will still checks the voicemail of the phone number Ben gave you."

I shrugged. "Glad to hear I could help. Maybe tomorrow I'll be up to thinking this was a grand sacrifice."

Then I plugged in my headset and tuned her out. I was still a little pissy that she was Miss Elegance while I was trying not to puke.

We arrived late and Jonelle drove our hire car into the city. I drifted in and out of wakefulness, barely registering Jonelle propelling me out of the car and into reception. The receptionist gave me a frown, but held her peace. Who knew what I would have said if she'd passed comment on my state.

Finally, though, after several hours of hell, I was able to collapse into bed and let the darkness claim me once more.

I focused my eyes on the bedside clock. A mere 6am. I scrambled out of bed. We'd booked the top floor suite which had two bedrooms linked by a lounge room. Jonelle was already there with breakfast wafting sweet smells in my direction. My stomach informed me it had been an incredibly long time since it last was fed. I helped myself to a huge plate of eggs, bacon, mushrooms and other assorted goodies, plus a scalding coffee. I felt marvellous.

"Okay then! When was it we were meeting these guys?" I asked around a piece of toast.

"Drop off is at 11pm. In the mean time, I've booked us massages, facials, waxing, and hair treatments to start at 9:30am. We can go shopping tomorrow."

She was flipping through the newspaper, skim reading, picking out little pieces of information.

"That is, if there *is* a tomorrow for both of us. Try to remember we are observing the drop point for your body, not some third party." I liked to get the story straight.

"Yeah, yeah. Don't get all twitchy about it. It's not like we can get into any trouble. No one will be expecting us, we'll be hidden somewhere discreet and I'll take care of the rest, if the need arises." She smiled, obviously delighted with herself and predicting the need to arise.

Her smile curled up at the edges and took the resemblance of a snarl.

"He really shouldn't have put a price on my head. I don't feel the need to negotiate with people like that."

I shuddered. Well, Joker may just have asked for it, whatever *it* turned out to be.

"Should we be talking tactics and all that sort of stuff, rather than sitting around getting our faces done?" I would much prefer to the female thing, but I needed to make sure that this time we were prepared. The last time we'd bungled it big time.

She stood in the middle of the room frowning. Uh oh. That was the 'in deep thought' look and who knew when she would actually get around to letting me in on them. I padded over to the kitchenette and started to make myself more coffee. There was no point in hounding her. Experience had taught me one thing. Jonelle didn't share unless she felt the need. A deep need. Otherwise everything stayed happily bottled up inside. The kettle boiled.

"Want one?" There was none of her usual green tea, so she'd have to do with my goop.

"Hmm?" She swung her head to glance my way. "No thanks. Thinking."

"Yeah," I muttered, as I poured boiling water over my substantial amount of instant coffee, "tell me something I *can't* see for myself."

"All right, I will."

One second she'd been over there and the next, she was standing right behind me breathing down my collar making the little hairs on the back of my neck stand to attention. I spilled hot water all over my fingers.

"Shit." I stuck them under the cold tap.

"Does it hurt?" Jonelle looked at me, her eyes far away and expressionless. What was this? A rite of passage? First knock me senseless with alcohol and then burn my fingerprints off. I scowled at her.

"Sorry." At least she sounded contrite. "I was preoccupied. You're right; we need to be better prepared this time round. Of course, this time it will be us doing the surprising. We'll get there ahead of time, just to check it out." Her eyes roamed over my body, neatly tucked into a pair of jeans and a T-shirt. "You can go ahead with the pampering. I don't think there is anything else we can do. I don't want you wired when we head out. But I'll expect you to carry these."

And she brought out a knife in a leather scabbard (here again I am playing with terminology!) and a small hand gun, holstered.

I backed away very fast, coffee forgotten. "No way! Both? Are you out of your mind? What use are they to someone like me?" I thrust my hands behind my back, as though this would save me.

Jonelle leaned forward, close enough for me to see the fine red lines in her overtired eyes. Her breath whispered across my cheek and my heart rose into my mouth. But instead of doing whatever it was I thought she might do, Jonelle reached around me and brought my hands back, placing the weapons of destruction into them directly.

"You *will* carry these."

There was no polite request in here. It was an order.

"The gun is for anything coming at you and the knife is in case they get through. Body to body, you don't need the gun. You need to stick that knife into anything soft. You understand? No hesitating. If something happens to me, then you get out. Shoot and stab whatever tries to stop you."

Her eyes were level with mine suddenly. They held a serious light with determination in them, rather than menace for once.

I gulped and closed my hands over her gifts. "Fine, whatever you say. I'll take them."

Who was I to argue the matter anyway?

"And later tonight, we can go out and have a dance. I would say have a drink, but I think your system has suffered enough for the time being, don't you?" Her eyes twinkled their usual insults at me. My insides may have been liquefied with fear, but at least she could laugh at it! "You can pick up a total stranger and make yourself feel every inch the single Australian woman."

Which of course, just made me remember Brad. I tried to turn away before she could see where my thoughts had travelled.

Might as well as hoped the Pope wasn't Catholic.

"Princess. He wasn't worth it. I know it's hard to let go, but start counting yourself lucky. You got out and now the world is your oyster again." She tried a smile, even though she was distracted by her own thoughts. "Brad was a fool and I couldn't bear to see you dating a fool." The eyes snapped back to me and sparkled in a very *un*friendly manner.

I grabbed my coffee and beat a hasty retreat. "So when should I be ready to head out?" There is nothing like a good change of the subject.

Behind me I heard Jonelle give a little snort. Let her think what she must. I was a natural born coward.

"If you could be finished with the last treatment say about 5pm, I'll come and get you for dinner. Then I'll grab what I need and see who we can run to ground."

There was something in her voice which made goose bumps pop out all over me. While we chatted away like friends and I sometimes thought I could do half the things she told me too, I had to remind myself of one elemental fact.

Jonelle wasn't like other girls and it could take just a small tone of voice to help jog my memory – don't tread on the tiger's tail.

I sat on the couch, which brought me round to face her again. But by this time I had my red face under control and everything was back to business.

"When do you leave me then?"

Did I say that everything was back to business? Somehow I always managed to put my foot in it.

Jonelle's smile was wide. She stalked over to me and watched me try to drink my coffee.

"Leave you, Princess? It'd never happen…" Her tone gave me all the rope I needed. Now I could happily go hang myself.

I wasn't that stupid.

I gave her the coolest look I had (which pretty much meant de nada) and settled myself deeper into the cushions. Business with Jonelle just needed a firm hand, I told myself.

"It'll be nine shortly and I think it would be best if I knew what the score is before we go out into the company of strangers. What the plans are." I hastily corrected myself. I was having a very bad speech day. Scoring of any sort was out of the equation.

"We get pampered, we eat a full and healthy lunch then get more pampering. I'll head to the gym around 3 and come back for you about 5pm. We eat again; shower, dress and I get us to the rendezvous point by 9pm." She was back to pacing, long legs eating up the carpet, mind furiously going through things I couldn't even hope to imagine.

"We see who has arrived and I try to find Ben in the cover of darkness. Then I kill Ben, maybe Joker, too."

I must have squeaked, or done something similar because she flicked me a glance. It wasn't as if she spoke like that all the time. Usually she was a bit more euphemistic. You know, 'have a chat with' or even possibly 'make sure they don't make trouble again.' But to come out so baldly with let's just kill them and have done with it … well, it made me feel a little pale.

"You would rather I leave them out there? I'm not in the business

400

of second chances, Princess. It's my neck or theirs. Or worse still, yours. That the ending you want? Being cut up by one of Joker's men, or being made into Ben's lap dancer and sex toy?"

I knew she was being brutal to make me see sense. But I didn't want to see sense. I wanted to just go and get my massages and hair care products, and then possibly hide under a convenient doona for the next two days. Who cared if it was the middle of summer – the heat would relax me. I looked down at the coffee mug in my hand.

"Look, I'm sorry if I'm a disappointment, but all this tough talk is something I usually only ever hear if I watch a particularly gruesome movie. How am I meant to react?" There may have been a touch of petulance in that tone, but I would rather hide that fact.

Jonelle came and sat opposite me. She leaned forward with her elbows on her knees and clasped her hands, studying them, not me.

"You come and see how it all plays out in my world for yourself. I will make sure you stay out of harm's way and I'll stay alert, so long as you don't go dancing around in the moonlight this time." She smiled at me to take the sting out of her words.

"All right." I still felt a bit shamefaced about that. Perhaps if I hadn't been crowing about stealing the damn Keystone, we might not have been caught. She only ever needed a moments warning. "But I'm not sure that seeing the world through your eyes is going to help me. There'll be messy stuff."

Probably not me at my most articulate, but try putting a coherent sentence together when faced with the prospect of seeing violence done in front of your eyes. For real. I was beginning to feel the strange need to visit the bathroom – and possibly stay there.

"Try not to think about it. Time is wasting; we need to get to the first appointment." Jonelle grinned at me and headed for the door. It amazed me how calm she was. I could try to emulate that calm by faking it, but underneath we both knew I was a quaking mess.

I usually enjoy being pampered. I mean, what woman wouldn't? A whole day to laze around and relax while other people slaved on you hand and foot. But there was an underlying tension. My massage therapist kept telling me to relax my shoulders. Jonelle would wink at me and then go back under her cucumber slices to totally enjoy herself.

Every time I closed my eyes I kept seeing Ben's face, a cruel smile on his lips while he tried to cut Jonelle's head off. It was most disturbing. What possessed me to head off into these things was beyond me.

Lunch choked me and by the time Jonelle headed off for the gym I was ready to climb the walls. I struggled to make it through the afternoon, jumping at shadows. There was just the slight chance that my nervous system wasn't built for this kind of adventure.

I made my way back to the suite around 4:30. I couldn't sit at the salon waiting for Jonelle to come and get me. The clock on the wall appeared to be travelling at an impossibly slow rate. And my head was filled with the kind of thoughts I usually avoided. Serious time consuming thoughts about how I was to explain witnessing the possible murder of these people to those mythical grandkids or even worse, the murder of Jonelle in front of my witless eyes.

Jonelle came sliding back through the door exactly at 5, to catch me pouring myself the third coffee straight.

"Hey, I don't know if that's a good idea." She frowned at me as she started to strip off gym gear heading for the shower. "You'll be more jittery than usual. I want you to be able to sit still for a few hours before the whole dancing bit, you know."

Off came the T-shirt and bike pants. Sweat gleamed on tanned skin and muscles rippled as she stalked over and took my mug away. Why couldn't she just stay clothed like the rest of us? Sports bra and panties didn't count as clothing. I tried not to think of the few extra pounds I may have gained over the last several days as my gym workouts had slackened off. I could feel that definite jiggle as I walked again. Dismissing it, I attempted to get my coffee back.

She laughed, dancing back out of my reach, holding it aloft. There was no way I could reach it at that height. Jonelle brought it down and took a swig. She scrunched up her nose.

"How many spoons of coffee are in this, Princess? It's strong enough to rot your socks."

I plucked it from her unresisting fingers.

"It tastes just fine thank you," I answered primly, scuttling my way out of reach. "It's only my third and it'll help me stay focused." If I didn't spend the whole night trying to find the most convenient loo.

"And, just in case you have forgotten, you aren't wearing any socks. Did your gym help you?" I hastily finished off the coffee just in case she decided to confiscate it once more.

"Perfect, thank you," she matched my tone with a smirk. Jonelle had a tendency to get too cheeky before a job. It was the buzz and high she exuded I found amazing. "I'll be focused and rearing to go as soon as we've eaten."

She vanished into the bathroom. Moments later all I could hear was the high powered jets of the shower.

Food of any sort was the last thing on my mind. The tiny bit of lunch I'd managed to get down had threatened to show itself all afternoon. I was in no hurry to repeat the performance. But past experience had taught me Jonelle would probably be up for a mammoth meal.

I went into my room and got changed. Somehow my lycra pink hotpants, okay for the dancing Jonelle was promising later, would raise an eyebrow or two at dinner and the rendezvous. The new ninja outfit fitted a bit more snugly than the last one, ruined with the sea dip escaping from Ben. Perhaps I really shouldn't have a private stash of chocolate bars hidden at my place.

It wasn't long before Jonelle came out of her room, decked out in black as well. We looked like some strange double act. She was carrying her tool kit and stuffing it with rope, a gun and extra rounds of ammunition. I couldn't help but wonder if she was expecting an army. That was not reassuring.

As she came to the door where I waited, she checked the flick motion of her wrist knives, pushing them back up her sleeves. Then double checked the gun strapped to her ankle, the one under her arm and the new addition. A knife strapped between her shoulder blades. Not the easiest thing to get at, but not something most people would check for. I stood at the door, mouth open at the arsenal.

"Planning on your own little war?"

She looked up.

"Don't be a smart ass." But she smiled. "This time I'll take as many of them with me as I can. Didn't you do girl scouts or whatever it is? Always be prepared."

She ran her thumb along the blade of the knife at her back before slipping it under her shirt. A thin line of blood appeared and she popped it into her mouth, eyes not leaving my face. I gulped. Real blood.

"So," Jonelle stepped forward and tucked my arm into hers. Everything zinged. "Are you all prepared for dinner? I know it's early, but I made a booking at the restaurant here. The chef does the best Crème Brule I've ever experienced. We'll share. No need to get a sugar high is there?" Her eyes several inches above my own glanced down at me and invited me to enjoy myself.

I tried. I could feel the humming energy tripping its way along her body as though she was plugged into a current I couldn't see. It made the hairs on my arms stand up and my heart rate spike. The actual muscles in the arm next to me twitched and flickered with the hum. She was so wired we could have lit up the city.

Apart from the fact we were going into a totally new environment, with at least two known hitmen attending, and no knowledge of the area – we were as safe as houses. It still didn't help with the eating business.

I wanted this, I told myself. I wanted to be a part of something more than boring old life.

What was there? Get up, go to work, come home, make dinner for the family and sleep. Was that all I had to look forward to as I got older? Becoming my parents, buying the house in some random suburb and popping out the children made to order?

I wanted to have done something more before that. Filled myself up with everything that could be offered. I couldn't do that by being safe.

So there I was. Sitting opposite someone who was everything I wasn't. I watched Jonelle laughing, eating her steak, talking with her eyes and hands, and waving her fork around.

I watched with some kind of disconnection, hardly aware of a word she said. This was the world I wanted to know. Something not quite safe and touchable. She sat there, this woman of flesh and blood, eating like a mortal and talking to me like I was one of them. But I looked into those eyes and saw something I'd never seen in anyone else.

They were hard bits of grey strength. Sure there was the potential for compassion there, and friendship. But she moved and talked and looked like something from another world. I shuddered slightly. Here was touching the sun. Here was something dreams, or nightmares, were made of.

I would be living. I would feel every inch of being alive and human. And this woman, this Amazon, could make me do that. I stared and stared. What power.

"Hello?" She snapped her fingers in front of my face. "Princess? Are you still alive in there?"

"More than you could possibly know."

Jonelle stopped. Another thing she had: a unique way of being totally still and absorbed in whatever was going on. She cocked her head to one side and looked at me. Then she smiled.

"Oh yes! Now that's what I'm talking about. Feeling alive with all of you and when you're dead, it won't matter because what a ride, hey?" And she winked at me.

Suddenly I found my appetite. Okay, so maybe we were still going to end up as Chop Sui. But at least I wouldn't go out *hungry*! For a moment Jonelle watched, then she snorted and dove back into her steak.

We ate and laughed from 6 till 8. Then before I knew it, we were in the car. Now was not the time to regret the dinner, but my stomach didn't work when clenched up. I tried to massage away my indigestion.

"So much for sticking my fingers up at fate and eating the last supper. How *did* they eat the Last Supper? Didn't it come back to haunt them? I mean, it's all well and good to want to have a glass of wine with friends and a light meal, but how do you keep it there when the leader gets…" I stopped.

Oops. Probably not the best analogy. We all know what happened to the leader of that particular group of supper attendees. I shot Jonelle a little peek.

She was smiling to herself.

"You are the strangest person to go out on a job with, Princess. Does that mouth of yours ever go to sleep? Or does it chatter away even when dreaming?"

"I don't know. I would say ask Brad, but seeing as that option is ruled out, I guess we'll never know. How much further?" I didn't want to talk about my sleeping habits.

"Anyway, I'm more of a find things out for myself kind of girl." Jonelle was in fine form tonight. She glanced at her watch. "Probably only another twenty minutes. Then we'll hide you somewhere handy and I'll check the layout. Then we wait."

"Egh. I hate the waiting game."

I thought about my night of recon at my parents place. The sheer boredom of it all could certainly put a girl off this type of thing.

"I don't think we'll have to wait long before something happens," she commented dryly.

I spent the next few minutes fidgeting. "What will you do with Joker?"

"Well, I have two options, as with most things, Princess. I can kill him if it comes to that and hope the word gets out, thus rendering the hit on me obsolete. If there is no one alive to pay, no one will bother with it." She turned a sharp corner and I was nearly flung into her lap.

405

She straightened me with one hand, pointing to my seat belt which I hadn't bothered with.

"Or I can reason with him and try to convince him that it is in everyone's interests to call off the hit himself. While that option works well in nirvana, we live in the real world and Daddy might not want his son's killer to be enjoying her life while he slowly rots in the ground. Though I can be very persuasive with that sort of thing."

"You are so ... picturesque. So basically, it's a let's hope all major players turn up and we can have a massive showdown, kind of thing."

"Basically. It doesn't pan out like this very often. Showdowns are tricky and mostly I like to avoid them. You never know who else is watching, waiting for the chance to spring out on the winner." She was slowing down and pulling off the road.

"Here we are. As far as we can go in the car, anyway. Out you get."

I stumbled out, legs gone to rubber. "Why on earth would you bother to hide this hunk of junk? No one's ever going to try to steal it."

Jonelle gave the car a quick look to make sure as little of it could be seen from the road as possible.

"Start thinking like a criminal, if that's possible. Not the sort that steals, but the sort that kills. If you were coming to some out of the way place to do some dirty dealings, and spotted a car parked within walking distance of said place, are you going to be suspicious?

"The first thing I'd ask those keeping the appointment would be what sort of car they came in. And if it didn't match, then I'd be thinking we had some other player hanging around." She came over and patted me down, checking I was carrying her recent gifts. "We don't want them to get worried about who else is out here now, do we?"

Her hands felt warm and strong and reassuring. For a second I leaned into all that muscle and allowed myself to pretend we were safe. Then I heard the unmistakable click of an automatic.

Jonelle was checking her weapon. It was out, the safety presumably off and ready to pump hard little iron pellets into the bad guys. I swallowed. Loudly. Her teeth flashed in the gloom. It was fast getting dark; made more so by the scrub all around.

"I don't like surprises." Then she led me into the trees.

Now, it had already been established I was no delicate flower when it came to stealth. I couldn't hear her moving; even though I could see her feet touch the ground. Me, on the other hand? There was something to be said for elephants. They were a nice, friendly, healthy grey kind of animal. A lot going for them, elephants. Can't say I necessarily like my similarities with them sometimes, but still … Jonelle turned back to me.

"Can't you try to be a little less attached to the ground?" she breathed in my ear.

"I *am* trying! We haven't practised mouse tactics yet," I muttered.

"Remind me to set you up some obstacle courses when we get back."

"Fine." I could be a really bad sport about some things.

We kept going for what felt like forever. Of course it was only fifteen minutes, but whose counting when walking towards potential death? Checking my watch all the time wasn't helping. The ground slowly rose and the moon sailed out from behind her guardian clouds. While this nicely lit up the world around us for viewing, it also made the pair of us visible.

Jonelle turned her head and brought up one hand. For a second I was too busy watching the eerie shadows, but then it clicked. She was using sign language.

Hmm. Perhaps I needed more practice.

"We're here," she signed. "Stay low and keep quiet. And whatever you do, don't get carried away if Ben turns up."

I gave her a glare. As if!

More than happy to stay out of the way thank you very much. I crouched down and brought myself level with Jonelle.

This was it.

No backing out now.

Chapter Twenty Eight

We were perched on the rim of a slight natural bowl in the ground. Joker had picked this as a handy little amphitheatre of his own. Who knew how many marksmen he had on the perimeter (there I was, getting into the lingo again!).

I was very glad of the quietly confident bulk of Jonelle leaning cockily against the tree next to my own. There wasn't a lot of room in the glade below, but the moon was strong enough to show two men standing just under cover opposite. They lacked the scruffy hedges Jonelle had positioned us near. Probably because they weren't worried about whoever was turning up, which was an unhealthy indication of their confidence in themselves.

There was a sort of general holding of breath. I glanced down at the glowing numbers on my watch. The minutes ticked away and 9:30 glowed serenely up at me. The two men waiting were talking quietly. Though not quiet enough, considering the layout of the amphitheatre. It brought their words to us on the breeze.

"Have you heard from them? Do you have any contact details? This is ridiculous!" Even to my untrained ear, the anger and impatience came through loud and clear.

The man speaking was slightly hunched and too overweight to be a hit man himself. The dangerous people I'd met so far all had a leanness about them and this guy really didn't. Jonelle's hand sneaked out and grabbed my arm. My eyes snapped to her.

"Joker," she signed at me. "Don't know the other guy. I'm off to do a routine scout. Stay low, stay quiet and don't show yourself no matter what happens."

She glided off into the gloom and I was left lying flat on the dirt, face peering through the scrub at the little clearing below and the men in the shadows opposite.

My attention was brought back to the tableau in front of us when there was a rustle in the surrounding bushland and Ben appeared.

Joker's man pulled a gun. I shrank back even further. This was about to get, as Jonelle would say, very interesting, and the sight of Ben made my nervous system start to jump.

"Troubles?" He sneered.

The obvious threat from henchman number one's gun went right over his head. It was as though he didn't see it. I glanced in the direction Jonelle had set out. They were a little too alike, if you asked me. She only saw the threats she wanted to as well, as though if they didn't acknowledge them, they weren't real.

Joker straightened up as much as he could. I saw a lined and bitter face before he turned his head to greet The Rose.

"You weren't meant to be here. I thought you handed Jonelle over to Fred and Larry? I told you years ago I never wanted to set eyes on you again."

Ben's shoulders twitched. I could see him tensing up.

"That was a long time ago, old man. You don't command the same respect anymore. You're the joke you're named after. Anyway, I don't think the boys are turning up." He smiled nastily.

Joker's man cocked his weapon. No one was happy here. Suddenly I was filled with an overwhelming need to close my eyes.

'What do you know about it?" Joker turned to his sidekick and motioned him to point his gun someplace else. "Let's not be too hasty, Dave."

The muscle nodded, lowering the weapon, but not holstering it. Everyone remained alert, sizing up the opposition. There were times in this whole escapade where I was all too aware of my amateur status. My knees were weak and my heart was threatening to climb out of my chest. But everyone else appeared cool as cucumbers.

"I would say Fred and Larry won't be making it as they never returned any of my calls." Ben's voice was flat and his eyes were starting to rake the perimeter. I got the feeling he knew Jonelle was out there. He dragged his attention back to Joker and Dave.

"Dave the only one with you? Because if I'm right, Jonelle is out there somewhere and you're going to need a lot more fire power to get out of here." He smirked, then raised his voice. "You hear me, Jonelle? I know you're out there. Let's talk about this and be reasonable, shall we? Nothing personal."

Sometime in that exchange, Jonelle had come back to my side. I slapped my hand on her arm. Signing as best I knew how I asked, "You aren't going to take him seriously, are you?"

For a panicked moment I got the distinct feeling she'd been about to step out of cover and have a chat! You know, just a quiet word with the lads. The look she gave me was enough to disabuse me of that notion.

"Are you mad? I've spotted at least two others out here. Stay put. I need to neutralise our guests. Let me borrow that." She slid my new knife out of my belt and faded into the gloom.

I crouched lower, wishing the hedges had steel coating. Somewhere out there, somewhere I hadn't even thought of looking, were two more henchmen, working for either side. Surely, when the bullets started flying, they weren't likely to aim at the dirt. I watched Joker, Dave and Ben trying to look in every direction. They couldn't pull it off like Jonelle did.

For a second I thought I saw a shadow flicker in the night between patches of darkness and moonlight. While holding one's breath generally worked in the movies, I was finding oxygen a necessity, so I drew in air and expelled it in little scared pants trying not to make any noise. If I concentrated on that, I figured time would pass and before I knew it, Jonelle would be coming back to get me for the dancing part of the evening. How long did it take to neutralise people?

I felt a soft tap on my shoulder.

"About time," I breathed quietly.

"Well, I wouldn't get too hopeful," came the very male response.

I froze. The first and possibly only comprehensive thought that flew through my head was, oh crap, not again. How many times can one person get caught and hung out to dry?

Because while Jonelle was out there; she was a little preoccupied, yet again. I turned my head to have a look at whomever it was that had managed to snag me this time.

Muscleman number two was of medium height and looked like wrestling bulls was not out of the question. Even with the dappled light I couldn't tell much about his facial expression, except he was smiling slightly. Damn. I hated being the funny part of an evening.

"Shall we?" He pointed with the gun I'd failed to notice toward where the others stood.

Not joining The Rose and Joker was top of my plan. I watched the nose of the gun. It dipped and swayed, taking itself away from me. All the better. When it was aimed as far from me as I thought it may ever get, I made my move.

"*Jonelle*!" I bellowed, loudly, clearly, and with just the faintest tinges of hysteria colouring the edges of the word. No need to be more specific, I think she could get my meaning from just that.

You'd have thought I lit a firecracker or shouted 'police!' The whole area suddenly went off. I flung myself to the side, as the henchman with his friendly gun made a grab for me, furiously waving his gun again (someone should give the poor boy some lessons in *aiming* it).

I hit the ground, wrenched my shoulder, but rolled. The most unfortunate part of the whole deal was the only way to roll when that close to a dip, is downhill, which, of course, led me to roll practically to Joker's feet. I lay there, out of wind, feeling faint with fear and self loathing, staring up at three comically surprised faces.

"Why, Fiona! How nice of you to drop by."

Ben was the first to recover. He smiled down at me, fingers twitching. I imagined he just couldn't wait to get a hold of me. Not if I could help it.

Joker nudged me with his toe.

"This is what all the fuss is about? You think Jonelle would miss her much?" He nodded to Dave, who assisted me to my feet.

I stood there feeling foolish. What had Jonelle said about staying out of trouble? I brushed some dirt off my legs. Anything was better than looking into their faces. Those flat, dead and scarily happy eyes that were probably laughing at my incompetence. Though it was hardly my fault the other dude had found me. Speaking of which…

Dave nodded at the new arrival.

"Bret. Almost lost her did you?" He smirked, as though nothing like that could ever happen to him. I hoped he was wrong.

"She wouldn't miss me all that much." I wandered where I was getting the courage to talk. "You know, easy come, easy go. And going would be good right about now…"

I tried to move sidewise, just to test everyone's reflexes. They were pretty good. Ben put a heavy and rather painfully tight grip on my shoulder.

"I'll take this one from here. Let's say the evening wasn't a total bust for anyone. I have what I came for," he flashed me a nasty grin, "and out there watching this whole show is the star. The one you wanted so badly. Feel free to bring her in."

Joker raised his eyes to the trees. "Jonelle. You have about three seconds before Ben takes your girl or I kill her. Either way, you won't be getting her back, so I'd come on out for a slight chance of her freedom."

Freedom was sounding good. There was little part of me that was a bit concerned. How much did my freedom rate here, I mean, in the grand scheme of things?

We all stood there, twisting our necks, watching the darkness waiting for the one thing that could settle this – Jonelle.

Ben leaned over and whispered in my ear.

"Looks like you're going to be mine after all, pretty lady."

Even having his breath on my neck made me feel sick. Like something evil and demented had crawled down my spine. There was nothing about him that was okay. I hated to think he might be right. Perhaps Jonelle was waiting for something to even the odds. I looked at the situation from her point of view.

There were four of them around me and who knew how many still out there watching things unfold. Though, knowing her, the other two she mentioned would be out of the game about now. I wondered how she'd missed Bret? Maybe she really was getting too old for this sort of thing. Me depositing myself at the feet of the enemy wasn't something I could blame her for, however.

The odds were stacked against us and I, for one, tried never to bet against the odds, an idea which left a rather sour and icky taste in my mouth.

There came a long string of words in a foreign language. It was Jonelle's voice alright. The words however could have meant anything to me, at least. It worked magic on Joker and his two henchmen. Joker gave them a nod and they took a subtle and discreet step away from me and Ben. I eyed them all a bit warily. Exactly what had Jonelle being proposing?

All was to be explained. Down from our previous vantage point she swept, into the moonlight and plain sight. I stood stunned, not even trying to move. I felt remarkably like a deer in the headlights.

Jonelle wasn't running. She wasn't even *looking* hurried. She came toward us with long easy strides, eating the ground, but not exerting herself. I gave Ben a little peep to check out his reaction.

He was watching her, gauging everything about her. He still had one hand clamped to my shoulder, so I gave Jonelle my full attention. There was no point in missing the action. Ben reached into his coat with his free hand. I knew he was going to draw a gun, but there was nothing I could do.

Oh, all right. Technically I could have done a million things, like you see in the movies.

Fall down, drag at his arm, hit him, yell, distract. Anything like that would have helped. But I dare you to have a go at that when a psychopath is attached to your arm. Then tell me what I should have done instead. As it was, I just stood there like a stuffed dummy and let it all pan out.

Fear was a powerful drug.

She walked up to us all like she was out for a Sunday stroll. I was half expecting her to start up a conversation, or stop. But she didn't. I almost missed it all.

And I think Ben missed it altogether. I have never seen anything like it. The confidence; the power.

Ben was reaching for his gun, pulling it free. Jonelle was walking at us, eyes locked on me. One minute it was all suspended around me. I could feel the air *humming*, and a bead of sweat started to trickle down my forehead.

A heart beat later Jonelle was within reach. But still she didn't stop. She was on the other side of Ben to me and as she went passed she sort of *leaned* into his body, using her body weight and the power from her stride to press him. Then she took two more paces and swung around.

Ben stood there for an instant. Hung from my shoulder.

"Well, screw that," he muttered, and let go.

That pesky bead of sweat rolled into my left eye. There had been no time for it to reach anywhere else.

Ben went to his knees. He grabbed his belly and grunted. Jonelle came back and looked down at him, every inch of her tense. Even in the soft light provided I could see her eyes. She looked up from Ben for a brief second and I met that gaze. I wish I hadn't.

Her eyes reminded me in some twisted way of Amelia. They were dark pools of something unfathomable and I really wasn't too sure if I *wanted* to fathom them. There was just a touch of wild animal in there, and the snarl on her lips did nothing to deter that image.

A tingle spun down my spine. There would be a reckoning about this – my association with this. But right then, with a reprieve from being the sex toy to a murderer, I wasn't overly fussed.

We both looked down at The Rose. He gave a soft defeated sigh.

"Fuck you, Jon. What did you have to go and do this for?"

He pulled his hands away from his stomach, and lifted the knife she'd filched off me when she'd gone 'patrolling', away from his shirt. It was coated in his blood and more pumped out as we stood there in the moonlight.

As no one did anything.

As this man's heart blood pumped away out through a hole she had twisted in his guts.

I forced myself to witness it even though I wanted to run. Or maybe puke. Possibly both, if I was truly honest with myself.

This, then, was the real bits and pieces of what Jonelle could get me mixed up in. I stood there and for the first time in my life, saw someone die. And it wasn't in the hospital, surrounded by nurses and IV tubes.

It was here, in the bush. Surrounded by trees; the only spotlight, the moon and the only people to watch; his sworn enemies. Not exactly on the top one hundred ways to go.

It couldn't have been painless. He gave a few heart wrenching grunts. Dying from a stomach wound, even one that was taking you quickly with lovely gouts of blood, as your heart beat uselessly trying to build up some blood pressure (like that was ever going to happen again), was not easy and painless. And I couldn't move. How could I? I had nowhere to go and Jonelle was standing like some iron maiden, tall and avenging-like, watching over every breath he took.

Joker and his boys had pulled back a little. I'd like to think it was to give the pair of them a bit of private space for the whole slayer and slain thing. But it might have something more to do with taking one look at Jonelle, arm rich with blood, knife now back in her hand and one foe down, literally lying symbolically at her feet.

She kept vigil until Ben rolled up his eyes and his heart gave out. Standing there, feet apart, knife arm held a little away from the body, head bent slightly as though deep in thought. When Ben refused to breathe again, Jonelle raised her eyes.

Nothing else moved. She brought her gaze up to Joker's and that was it.

"As much fun as this is."I gave Jonelle a glare, one she wasn't even aware of, took a couple of stumbling steps and was promptly sick all over my expensive Nike runners. Bugger.

I sat staring at nothing as the car purred, spluttered and coughed its way back into town. My shoes were in the boot; we couldn't leave them at the scene because of all sorts of incriminating evidence that could be found on them. Not the least, the contents of my stomach which would be enough DNA to start my own lab. I could taste bile as my stomach roiled not so quietly to itself. Sitting facing the window I watched the blackness of the night roll by outside.

Inside, somewhere deep inside, I could feel numbness stretching its fingers throughout my system. Numbness was good. Numbness was quiet and non-invasive.

Jonelle sat next to me, hands tight on the wheel, driving more by reflex than by any actual watching of the road. I could feel her eyes resting on me every few seconds. And I could sense the tension and concern filling the air between us. But I couldn't, for the life of me, look back at her and give her the reassurances she needed.

I was definitely *not* okay. So telling her I was would make me a liar and she'd see it straight away, anyway. There was also the little detail of me not wanting to talk to her. I knew that made me ungrateful. After all, she'd single-handedly kept me out of Ben's clutches and made sure her own head hadn't being forfeited. Quite the night's work.

This time we'd made sure the bad guy lost – everything. Game, set and match: Jonelle.

I peeled my eyes from their vacant night watching and dropped their gaze to my hands. I hadn't touched anything. I hadn't being capable of very much really and that was okay. At least, I thought it was. Though it was hard to think of the situation getting any worse; at least by standing in frozen shock and doing nothing, I stayed out of trouble.

Jonelle had taken me by the arm after she'd spoken at length with Joker, and brought me to the car. Like a child, I'd allowed her to open the door and push me gently into the passenger seat, where she clipped the seatbelt in place. While I'd kept my hands free of Ben and anything concerning his death, the fact was Jonelle had guided me with her own hands. Hands covered in blood, which now clung to my arms.

I watched in fascination as the wringing action of twisting my fingers in my lap set the handprints on my arms writhing in sympathy. I tasted bile again and willed my stomach to stay put. There were many things I knew I could be saying to Jonelle and would, once I had overcome this need to hit something.

But asking her to stop the car while I was sick, again, wasn't one of them. I clung to myself, hoping everything would stay where it was meant to, and went back to staring out the window.

The fact was she had needed to do what she'd done. I couldn't have gone back to whatever hell Ben was planning for me. So I owed her my life. But I could only see his face, lips peeled back in a snarl, heart pulsing its blood all over the ground around us. Not something I saw every day. I knew she'd had her small wrist knives attached. But she'd looked at me in the darkness, when she'd gone off for that second patrol and must have seen in my face the knowledge I'd never use my knife, so she'd taken it. It was heavier and longer, and made a much better weapon.

Now I knew just how effective.

I stayed locked in my mind, swirling thoughts running around, trying not to puke. Safest option, really. If I opened my mouth right then, I might have started screaming and never stopped.

Eventually we pulled into the car park of the hotel. We both were very conscious of the blood coating our arms. I had to look at her then. I met her eyes for a second then glanced back to the finger prints I was sporting.

"If we wear the jackets I have on the back seat, no one will notice. At least, not enough between here and our room." She shifted in her seat, twisting to pick up two jackets she'd thoughtfully provided earlier.

"Nice to know you came prepared." I bit off the words and snapped my teeth over my tongue. They'd slipped out on their own. I still didn't want to talk to her.

She snorted. "Some of us think ahead," she answered shortly. Not that I could blame her for the tone. I wasn't helping much.

I snatched the jacket she held out for me and pulled it roughly over the worst of the marks. There was nothing I could do about being barefooted; I wasn't putting my shoes on again in this lifetime. They could rot in the boot for all I cared. Though, knowing little miss super woman, my shoes and any other incriminating evidence would be far away by the next day.

Folding the edges of the jacket around my stomach, I leaped out of the car and headed for the lifts. Getting back to the room seemed the best idea I could come up with.

We rode the elevator silently and I practically pushed her out of the way, running into the room. I was in no real state to care at that point what Jonelle was planning to do. I made it to my ensuite and threw up inelegantly for the next few minutes.

I challenge anyone to see what I had and keep their stomach. Oh, unless they were cold blooded killers like my employer.

Washing my mouth out, I glimpsed my face in the mirror. Not exactly pinup material.

I was a ghastly shade of white, with high points of red on my cheek bones. My eyes were wide and staring; and starting to fill with tears. Shock. Reaction, I diagnosed. My eyes wandered from my reflection and came to rest on the toothpaste. Suddenly that was all I could think about. Wash everything off and clean my teeth. Get rid of the taste and smell of blood and vomit.

For the next few minutes I scrubbed my arms, until the skin ached. Then I attacked my teeth. I stood there, eyes locked on my reflection, while the toothbrush threatened to strip the gums right out of my mouth.

"You know, Princess, you'll make them bleed."

Jonelle was there, suddenly beside me, gently taking the toothbrush from my almost nerveless fingers.

"Too late," I mumbled, exposing seeping gums.

We both stood there and watched the blood fill my mouth and stain my teeth. I could hardly bare it. It was all too much.

Too much blood and sensory over-load for someone like me. Tears, held in my eyes for too long, trickled down my cheeks. I hiccupped loudly.

Jonelle put my toothbrush down and filled a cup with antiseptic mouthwash and water.

"Gargle," she commanded and I did.

Once the worst of the damage was halted, she took me gently by the arm and walked me to the bed. I allowed her to lie me down. Then she sat next to me, back leaning against the wall, long legs lying out next to me. For a second I wanted to move away. But the feel of her strength, the undeniable heat and comfort she radiated overcame everything and I curled up, putting my head on her thigh and cried like a baby.

Jonelle did nothing but stoke my hair and murmur things in strange languages.

Eventually I stopped. Had to really; there were no tears left and I could hardly breathe from the snot gumming up my nose. I sat up and finally met her gaze. Her eyes were dark and soft, not the least bit condemning, for all I had treated her like poison.

"Sorry."

"Don't be. If anything, I should apologise to you. I wasn't thinking too clearly. I just saw Ben holding you, threatening you and all I could think was – bloody hell! He's got her again!" She smiled rather ruefully at me.

"I wasn't going to allow that to happen, you know. I'd promised you he wouldn't get you. But I wish I hadn't killed him quite so dramatically. You shouldn't have had to see that." She bit her lip.

I shrugged. What else could I do? She'd just saved my life, and I'd asked for adventure.

"I'm okay."

Which was a blatant lie, but they were the words she was looking for. Even if she could tell when I was lying, it was better than saying point blank 'I think I'm scarred for life', now wasn't it?

Jonelle rolled her eyes at me.

"Hmm. I can tell. Just lie down and sleep. I think a bit of dancing is out of the question, don't you?"

I gave a little half hysterical snort. The idea of getting up and hitting the club scene made me giggle.

"I think I'd better lie down before I hurt myself." And I curled back up beside the bulk of her body. "What happened with Joker?" I was still me, and the ever questing curiosity was starting to flood back in.

Somewhere above me in the half darkness Jonelle gave a little laugh. "How about you rest now, yeah?"

"Not a chance. You can't get out of it that easily."

But my words were a little slurred, even to my own ears. I could feel her beside me, oozing strength, making me feel warm and safe. The shock of the evening was wearing off and in its place, I was feeling tired beyond measure.

"Tell me a story." It was, at least, a coherent sentence.

She sighed.

"You heard me speak to Joker before I came for you. I asked him to stay out of it; this was between me and Ben. He was too happy to comply. Joker was no friend of Ben's, which was in my favour. So that kept the worst of the problem at bay. I'd already neutralised the two others out there.

"Don't worry," she felt me tense up, "they won't be permanently damaged. Now it was only the four around you."

Jonelle paused and I opened one sleepy eye. I could see her dimly in the light but couldn't read her expression. She looked down at me and smiled slightly.

"I think the death of Ben was quite a shock all round, really. Joker is an old man. He watched and made his decision. Regardless of how many bodyguards he had there, talking it over and making sure no one else had to die, was a very good idea." Her voice held an edge. "It took a little to persuade him of that, but I do believe the contract out on me will be removed. Now, you need to sleep." She was quiet for a few moments.

Then: "I *am* sorry, Princess."

I could hear the reproach in her voice. She was going to beat herself up about this for hours, I could tell. But there was a little part of me which was not unhappy about that idea.

"It's been hard for you, hasn't it?" She sighed. "In the last few weeks so much has changed for you. You've being beaten, threatened, kidnapped, met some real lowlifes and had your world shaken up. I can understand if you want to go home and forget that any of this had anything to do with you."

Even though her voice was measured and her tone serious, I could sense the underlying hesitation and almost fear. Would I really leave her, was her concern.

I lay there, head shifted now to the pillow. Turning over, I stretched out on my back feeling my stomach muscles groan from their night of exercise.

Yes, in all honesty, it had been a hard time. But I was doing something hardly anyone in their lives got to do! Could I pass it all up just because I had watched a man die?

Well, yes. A big part of me right at that moment wanted nothing more than to leave. But I knew by the morning that part would be getting smaller. It was late, in the grand scheme of thing, in the day for me to be learning all this, but minus a few unpleasantries, I was having a ball. I was even getting fit!

"It was ... terrible to see The Rose die like that."

I had to tell her this. Anything else would be a lie and she'd know it.

"I don't know if I'll ever forget it." I felt her tense up. "But that doesn't mean I don't want to go on! I'm sorry for what you had to do. And probably, if I'm honest, will have to do again, but I like getting up every morning knowing something different, something exciting will happen to me today.

"Everyone walks through their lives, you know, working, playing and having families. They walk around blind to all the other things that they could be doing. We watch movies and TV, thinking wouldn't it be nice to be extraordinary? Wouldn't it be amazing if we were doing something wild and extreme?

"But we're all afraid to take that step. Now I'm not saying I'm not afraid. I'm bloody terrified half the time and just mildly pant wettingly scared the rest. But I don't want to go back to watching the movie, when I've lived it, okay?"

It was the best I could do for the moment. My system was in shut down mode after far too long processing too much.

Jonelle patted my shoulder. "I'm very glad to hear it," she murmured. "Get some sleep now, Princess and I'll see you in the morning."

She didn't move and in a few short breaths I could feel the tension leave my body and sleep steal in. It was very reassuring to have her so close by, even though in normal circumstances, it'd kind of freak me out. Then I couldn't think anymore.

Chapter Twenty Nine

Waking up from peaceful dreams into a world where I could remember someone dying at my feet was a bit confronting. But I managed.

Which was starting to give me some idea of just how cold hearted I could be. Instead of running screaming into the night, I was lying here contemplating breakfast, and then hoping we were heading back to Canberra to finish off other pressing issues. If only my family could see me now.

On second thoughts, probably a good thing they couldn't.

I stretched out a hand, but didn't encounter a sleeping Jonelle, which was not altogether a bad thing, either. Now I was out of the whole 'shock over deadly encounter' thing, I wasn't too sure how I would've coped waking up together. It was possibly a little beyond the employer/employee relationship. And even a bit further than our friendship would allow.

On the other hand, I wondered where she was and when she'd left me, because I hadn't felt a thing.

First things first, however, a shower was in order. Crashing out without removing my clothes had seemed a great idea last night, but now I could smell myself it was losing its appeal. I glanced down at my arms. The skin was raw and pink. That was one part of me I hadn't neglected.

Showered and dressed I felt able to handle anything. Well, with possibly a few exceptions like murder and mayhem. I hadn't had breakfast yet. They were more of an after breakfast thing. Humour; sometimes the only way I could deal with myself.

I made myself a strong coffee and mindful of my sore gums, took it out onto the balcony to sip it *very* slowly while watching the

Melbourne traffic crawl past. There was no sign of Jonelle anywhere, but that was of no immediate concern. With a touch of violence under her belt, the woman was probably at the gym to wear off the excess energy. She'd fairly crackled with it last night. A spot of danger was bound to do that to you. On the other hand, the only thing it did to me was make me sleepy. Horses for courses.

I was on my second coffee and starting to feel remotely like myself again, when Jonelle came through the door. She hesitated when she saw I was up, but came on through to the balcony to stand next to me.

"So." Love to be back to my conversational best. "You don't look like you've been working out."

She glanced at me sidelong. "Been out all morning."

Well that basically said nothing; I could *see* that for myself. The fact that she was wearing all black, *plus* gloves, made me a little nervous.

"Yes, obviously. Care to elaborate?" Sometimes I just didn't know when to stop even for my own good.

Jonelle snorted. "I waited until you were out of it and went back."

That wasn't what I'd been expecting.

"You what!?! Are you nuts? Isn't once enough for you? What if something had happened? How would I have known where you were?"

Not that there was a lot I could have done about it even if I had known, but logic wasn't my strong suit.

"You would have waited for a while and then gone back to Canberra, I should think."

She didn't know me all *that* well then. I'd have panicked, was what I would have done.

"I had to go back and clean up my mess. The last thing I need is a police investigation; they have a tendency to cramp my style somewhat." She tossed me a grin.

"I can't think of anyone who will actually miss Ben, so no one will report him missing in action for a while. But if someone was to find the body … well that would be a different matter. There are limits to how far I can push my luck. I'm no use to anybody rotting in a jail cell." What a peaceful image that conjured up. "Though let's hope his Phoenix connections are mythical, or we may have some visitors."

Reassuring.

"What did you do with it, er, him?" I didn't know if I really wanted to know, but I haven't learned the fine art of keeping my mouth shut.

"He's now officially not our concern. Don't worry, he'll never be found and the place where he died just looks like a nice open space for a picnic. I know what I'm doing." She sounded just a touch huffy.

It wasn't as if I was questioning her ability to dispose of a body. In fact, I was more than sure she was capable of it. I opened my mouth to ask again, but she held up her hand to stop me.

"Best you don't know, Princess. There *are* some things you really do not need to know. Leave it."

I grumbled into my coffee.

"What are the plans for today then?"

Jonelle gave me a quick smile, thanking me with her eyes. Eyes, now I came to see them clearly, which were dark and exhausted looking. I looked back at my coffee. I hadn't even asked her how she was. Made me a great friend to have around, didn't it?

"I was thinking we need to get back to Canberra. Melbourne has a bad taste right now, wouldn't you say?"

"At last, something we agree on. Let's get out of here."

While the idea of some cosmopolitan shopping in town wouldn't have gone astray, I was beginning to feel a distinct need to get home and surround myself with all things familiar. A few cuddles from my crazy pets would go down a treat, too. I wasn't totally over the events of the previous evening, but leaving the scene of the crime, so to speak, would certainly help.

Half way back to Canberra I leaned across to Jonelle.

"I have decided to not think about it ever again. That way it can't make me queasy. But before I put it in the too hard basket I thought I should say, thank you."

She looked at me, surprised.

"I don't know why you're so amazed." I grouched at her. "Anyone would think I was an ungrateful bitch." I caught the smirk and gave her a thump. "Anyway, you saved me from Ben and kept yourself from becoming headless, so all in all, a successful trip, wouldn't you say?"

I just wanted to put the whole deal behind me. Easy to say, possibly harder to do, but I was more than willing to give it a try.

Jonelle flicked her fingers at me. "I'm glad you're okay. And I'm quite pleased about not having to defend my head from every trophy hunter in Australia. Joker was waiting for me when I went back. Have I become *that* predictable?" She gave me a funny little frown.

"I think he would have known you'd not leave dead bodies lying around. And it's not as though he would want it coming to light either."

There, I was back to hard headed, side kick mode. By the time we touched down, witnessing a murder would be just another day's work. If I could convince myself, there was the ever so slight chance I might be able to convince Jonelle, one day… in the not too distant future.

"What did he have to say that you aren't telling me?" There was always more. Nothing could just be straightforward and wrapped up tidily, could it?

"You're learning, Princess." Jonelle gave me what passed for an affectionate glance, though I could still see the tiredness and lingering violence in her eyes.

"He had only one goon, so it was easier to talk. I was his unfinished business. He wants to retire to the peaceful life, but needed to see me out of commission for what I did to his son." She looked thoughtful. "I think it's a parent's role to be blind to a child's sins. Though, of course, Joker is not one to worry about a few misdemeanours. After all, he'd taught Jason most of his tricks. Sins of the father and all. But I explained a few things.

"Like how his darling boy had turned to dealing out torture and all sorts of wonderful punishment to prove just how big of a 'man' he was. I was meant to be the piece de résistance. You know, torture Jonelle, have your way with her and then kill her. Show the rest of the baddies out there just how pathetic the woman really was." She shook her head.

I couldn't see how anyone could be that stupid myself. But then again, I only had a one-sided point of view. If I was mixed up in these sorts of things, I wanted to make sure my weapon, meaning Jonelle of course, was bigger and sharper than anyone else's.

I certainly couldn't see some fool with acne making merry with her.

She smiled and I felt something slither down my back.

"Even Joker could see how that wasn't going to play out to his son's advantage. He is more of a small time crook, into protection and extortion, not rape and destruction. Children must be such a disappointment, sometimes. Anyway, to cut a long dark morning's work short, I agreed to not come after him in his retirement for putting the damned price on my head in the first place and he agreed to make sure everyone was aware of our terms, and we parted for the last time. Can't say I ever want to see him again."

"You didn't feel the need to ... er ... neutralise him as well? He doesn't sound like much of a loss to the taxpaying majority of society."

With a certain amount of space between me and dead bodies; and me and the actual action of neutralising someone, it didn't sound so scary anymore. Call me a hopeless hypocrite.

"Blood thirsty little bugger, aren't you?" Jonelle gave me a narrow eyed look. "He's retired. I can understand the desire to be left alone, and even for the whole revenge thing. Killing off a toothless old coot when peace had been established isn't exactly the sort of reputation I am looking for.

"He's no harm to anyone anymore, though I did warn him I never wanted to hear his name linked to anything other than bingo from here on out. He's not stupid. After a failed attempt on my life, he knows a reprieve when he sees one."

Glad to hear it. Glad to hear that the crazy man, with a psycho son, who used to run a protection racket, was no longer out for her blood. I peeped over at her. She was lying back, eyes closed, resting. She didn't look unduly worried or upset. Some people have either nerves of steel or no nerves at all.

Just like that, everything was straightened out. She must have amazing confidence in her reputation as a killer; because if I was a nut case and she'd done *my* son in, I wouldn't stop just because she asked me nicely.

"I can feel you thinking. Stop it, you'll damage something." Jonelle's lips twitched, but her eyes remained firmly shut.

"Bugger. How do you *do* that? No, don't answer." I growled. "How do you know he'll keep to his end of the bargain? You killed his son, Jonelle, not some random employee."

I tried to keep my voice low; we were, after all, on public transport. And I had no great inexhaustible supply of foreign languages to babble in.

She sighed and the eyes snapped open. "Can't a girl get any rest?" But she didn't sound particularly annoyed, so I felt reasonably safe.

"I know he'll keep his end of the bargain because I stabbed a man in front of his eyes and am more than capable of doing the same to him. You saw him. Apart from some hired help, who, by the way, he only hired for the night, he is all alone. No son, no wife, no nephews to take out his revenge for him. Not a massive threat.

"Plus, he's terribly unfit, dying of some cancer or so he tells me, and just wanted to make sure Jason was avenged. Though I could see he had his own doubts about the wonders of his son's temperament. I think I convinced him with enough threats and dire consequences that living quietly in the Mornington Peninsula for the remainder of his life, is as good as he'll get. The fact I knew his home address and other little interesting titbits about his life, such as the call girl he pays $300 an hour for, made him realise my resources are considerably more than his. Okay? I think I'm pretty safe from that side of my life." She looked out the window.

"Now it's time to land." And she snapped her seatbelt on firmly, shutting me out again.

Sometimes her resources shook *me* up, and I was supposed to be one of them.

With conversation a very limited commodity on the way home, I was glad to leave her and make my way to my unit. Manny and Smudge were on the loose, roaming the pool's edge. I had left out water and begged Julie to feed them for me. Seeing as we were only scheduled to be gone two days, I hadn't seen any harm in leaving them outside. I'd left Smudge's bed on my doorstep but he never used it anyway, so I don't know why I bothered.

I was greeted with loud affection and I barely managed to get my door open, what with licks and paws, and general confusion. I sincerely hoped that we didn't make a habit of the last twenty four hours. Or at least, if we did, Jonelle took care of things pretty much alone. Scaredy cat and other not so nice names sprung up in my mind. I couldn't change my character overnight.

I flipped on the telly, leaving it blaring as I took all my clothes to the laundry. I'd need to get some new Nikes as well. Washing them wouldn't have done any good, if I could have found them to wash. Jonelle appeared to have taken care of my shoes when she took care of the body.

A small part of me was just a touch curious about what she'd done with it; though not enough to find out. I was beginning to learn that my limited experience was not a bad thing in the long run.

Leaving the washing machine to make short work out of my clothes, I wandered back into the kitchen. Smudge and Manny were curled up together on the lounge watching whatever cartoon was making ridiculous noises on the telly, but I couldn't settle. My stomach was growling, and my head was starting to re-adjust to Canberra matters.

Like, I wondered what Will was up to and when were we going to be get back into the saddle with the Brenda thing? I pulled a Coke out of the fridge and popped its top.

Ah, fuzzy brown beverage.

I took my liquid refreshment into the lounge room and pushed my pets up one end so I could snuggle down on the couch with them. Smudge came over and after a few moments of happy paws, leaving little claw marks over my thighs, he curled up and started cleaning himself.

"Thanks, mister, just what I always wanted. A small man cleaning himself in my lap." So he washed and I stroked his fur, while Manny looked mournful, as there just wasn't enough room in one lap for a kitten and a fully grown Dalmatian.

I hadn't finished my can before there was a knock on the door. I glanced at my watch. Nearly everyone I knew should be at some sort of work. Well, except me and Jonelle, but I couldn't see her turning up already.

"Doors open." Face it, if it was a bad guy, they wouldn't have knocked.

Of course, my oldest and dearest friends, Grillia and Steph had no jobs to go to. Steph poked her nose around the door.

"Hey there, we're bored. What are you doing?"

It felt like a million years since I'd had the time to sit around and gossip with them. Waving one hand I motioned them in. Manny raised his head and gave a sleepy woof. But it kind of lacked in the deterrent stakes. Grillia smiled at him and stroked his nose.

"Hello there you handsome man. Give old Grillia a kiss." I watched in horrified fascination as she leaned down and rubbed noses with my dog.

"Do you have any idea where animals put those things, Grill?" Steph wrinkled her own nose.

Steph had a morbid fear of germs and anything unclean. The idea of kissing a dog would have turned her stomach. She plonked herself on the couch opposite.

"We haven't seen you for a while." She flicked back the black fringe of hair lying across her eyes. "Where have you been?"

Hmm. That was an interesting question. Not one that I could answer truthfully, so I hoped my lying skills had improved.

"Oh, around. You know, flying into different cities, playing at being important."

It was vague enough to be the truth and close enough not to catch me out.

Grillia gave me a look over Manny's head. Unlike Steph, who had a tendency to be a bit self involved, Grillia was more likely to need details.

"Where's Brad?"

There. In one swoop, Grillia had put her finger on the pulse. Sure, events in Melbourne, and prior to that, off the coast of Narooma, had sort of superseded the Brad issue, but I was still the walking wounded. My face was an open book.

"I think we need to go out for a drink. All in favour?" Grillia suggested.

Steph's face lit up. And they tried to tell me I was the one with the drinking problem.

"It's only 2pm. Let's watch a movie first and then head over to The Batch. I haven't seen anything in ages."

If I could drag them into a movie for a few hours, it would put off the telling about being dumped – for a wife.

Steph was easy to derail. As we walked down to the movie theatres, she chatted about a new man she'd just met, which was upsetting Tamara greatly. I raised my eyebrows.

"I didn't realise Tamara featured so highly that she could get upset?" Mind you, Tamara was crazy enough for anything.

I linked arms with them both, looking from one to the other. I was very glad to be home and to be out with my old friends. Sometimes the little things made up for the monumental cock ups I was experiencing.

Grillia giggled.

"Tamara didn't like Nathan telling her to get her sorry carcass out of his sister's life. She's practically stalking Steph these days. It's playing havoc with Steph's non-existent social life, isn't it baby?" Grillia gave Steph a friendly slap.

"She's impossible! I finally picked Pete up as protection." Steph rolled her heavily kohled eyes. "I think the relationship is on the rocks. It wouldn't be, if I could ditch Tamara."

"Didn't we tell you that encouraging that woman was suicide? Now look what's happening. Can't Nathan have another chat to her?"

I wasn't all that worried. Tamara was small bikkies. She didn't look capable of hurting anyone – not even herself.

"Nathan told me it was my fault, so I had to deal with it. Pete kind of agrees. At first he thought it was neat, you know, some girl and girl action." Steph squirmed, embarrassed. Prude: unlike me, of course.

"Now, after she's haunted three of our attempts at dates, he's just getting pissed."

Grillia and I teased her all the way to the cinema. We ordered super-sized Cokes and popcorn, with chocolate topped cones to go with them. I looked around a little guiltily. Man was I glad Jonelle couldn't see me. Reassuring myself, I rubbed my hand over the slightly emerging hip bones. They hadn't disappeared again, yet. All would be well.

Two and a half hours later we surfaced, overfed, but happy and relaxed. It was close on 5pm now, not too early to grab a bite to eat and make our way over to the Batch.

Walking along, sipping the inevitable Coke, I listened with half an ear to Grillia and Steph giving each other a hard time. I had to admit while my life was becoming more exciting with the advent of Jonelle, I missed the nonsense the other two provided. Who on earth but Steph could be in such dire straits with a lesbian stalker chasing off the current man? And Grillia, having slowly (or fast depending on your point of view, I guess) gone through nearly every single male and more than a few not so single, she could find locally, having to widen her search for interesting talent to include the little townships bordering Canberra?

It struck me how much I wish I could go into what it was that I had been up to the last few weeks. They would just about die from the jealousy; or quite possibly from laughing at me. But I wasn't getting pedantic. Sometimes *I* couldn't believe it was me and had to pinch myself as well. It would be simply the best if I could take my friends to work with me.

I stopped walking, Coke half way to my mouth. What a *brilliant* idea, if I may say so myself.

"Hey, you still with us?" Grillia had stopped as well, several paces in front of me.

"Ya-huh," I muttered, thinking at a million miles an hour.

It would be fantastic. They were both well-heeled and living the same sort of life style I had been until Jonelle came along and changed everything for me. For the better, I thought with satisfaction, consigning the last forty eight hours to the devil.

She could work her magic with Grillia and Steph as well. We could all work together, and discuss cases and go out on recon together (because alone it has to be the most boring piece of work I had ever encountered). My mind started taking leaps and bounds, imaging all sorts of perks having my best friends side by side with me every day.

By this stage we'd come to the local take away. Something quick and filling, then on to the Batch where I just knew my relationship, or lack thereof, with Brad would become the major part of our evening's dissections. Not something to look forward to. They could be very nosey, my friends. And not tactful. They definitely could use some social skills; both of them prone to attacking anything male within arm's reach. Then there was the fact that Jonelle would either terrify them, or encourage their more base natures.

I was fast revising my initial enthusiasm. By the time we'd scoffed down our kebabs and made our way to the Batch and Haddock, I had agreed with myself that involving my friends was one of my crazier ideas and I was never going to bring it up again.

We walked in, nodding to the bouncer as we passed. It would have been nice, once in a while, if he made a show of asking for our IDs. The sort of flattery I was starting to look for the closer I came to my thirtieth birthday. Sad but true.

"The usual?"

Steph took the very *un*usual step of taking the first round. She was more likely to sit down and tell us all her woes than go get a drink. Grillia nodded, then snagged me and a table.

"Okay, spill. You practically looked like death when I mentioned Brad, you've not said a word all evening, not even to bitch about the horrid film which I must say, is your speciality. You even have Steph off ordering drinks because you look like you need to complain more than she does, for once. That and the fact that Pete's a barman here." She shrugged at Steph's ulterior motive.

I wiggled on my hard wooden chair. What was it I had said about nosey? Somewhere between two months ago and the millions of questions I used to love and inflict on everyone, I'd gained a life that needed concealing, and constant prying was annoying. I felt like someone from the Spanish Inquisition.

"Brad's got a wife."

I'd meant to put it a little less blunt than that. But what the hell; tact wasn't my strong suit. It had occurred to me Grillia had missed out on being me by a few drinks. How lucky she was. The lack of Brad's performance on their one and only encounter had shuffled him down the line – to me.

"He's got a *wife?*" she practically squeaked. "Are you sure? I mean, couldn't you be wrong?"

"*Wrong?*" I mimicked her tone. "Of course, that's the problem. I'm wrong. I'm confused about seeing him kissing another woman than finding out they are about to have a baby. Oh, and just happen to share the convenience of a last name together as well. But yes, let's just say, I'm probably wrong."

Had that come across just that mite bit sarcastic or bitter?

Grillia eyed me warily. "Okay, so you aren't wrong, exactly."

"There is no 'exactly'. He's got a wife, he's moving back to Sydney now whatever job or account or whatever he had here is finishing up and back into wifey's arms. Well, possibly not into her arms exactly now she knows about me."

I didn't know if I felt satisfaction or guilt about that part. I knew he'd been an unfaithful bastard. Strike that. A *lying*, unfaithful bastard. But now they were about to embark on a family together and I'd ruined the exciting 'first' part of it all.

"I actually feel a bit of a bitch, letting her know." I nodded my thanks at Steph who had just arrived with first drinks.

Grillia leaned over and whispered the update in her ear. Steph turned her big soulful eyes on me.

"God, what a prick." Then she buried her nose in her bourbon.

I choked on my drink, torn between laughter and hysteria.

"Right you are, Steph." I chugged down the rest of my drink in record time. "Anyone for another?"

Somewhere between the beginning of that question and its end, possibly as the alcohol came to rest in my stomach, I remembered it was only a couple of nights since my total inebriation. I eyed the empties. Hmm, this could be the biggest disaster in Fiona-history.

Ah well. I needed to have a few drinks with my closest girlfriends, while they still were my closest friends. What with running off with Jonelle and not being around to gossip, they were starting to feel a touch like strangers.

"Three double bourbons. Sorry, make that two doubles and one single."

My stomach had roiled at the idea of another double. I'd have to take this slowly and carefully if I wasn't to embarrass myself terribly within a very short period of time. My helpful barman went off on his errand and I went back to perusing the rest of them.

Ooh! There he was. I took in a good look at Steph's man, or soon to be ex if Tamara wasn't brought to heel. He was quite spunky, in a quiet non-demanding kind of way. Who'd have thought Steph would look at someone like that? Perhaps that meant it was supposed to last. In that case, we really needed to do something about her stalker, and fast.

"Fiona, right?"

I'd just handed over a fifty dollar note when a familiar voice stopped my heart. Well, not literally and it shouldn't have, because while it sounded like Will, he'd not ask me if I was me, now, would he?

I turned slowly and found myself face to face with Theodore Malone. A shade shorter and a shade not as hot as his older brother, but still someone to notice in a place like this.

I smiled, but not overly widely. I'd had my fingers burned with encouraging a Malone and I wasn't going to make that mistake again, any time soon.

"Yes, that's right. Theo, isn't it?" I could play cool and hard to get, though.

"That's me. Here, let me help you with that."

Theo deftly hooked Steph's and Grillia's drinks off the bar with one hand and gestured for me to take the lead with the other. It looked damned impressive. While I was trying hard not to be too easily impressed these days, it's hard to stay business-like with a Malone.

I grabbed the last drink, which was luckily mine seeing as I would hate to foist a single on one of my unsuspecting mates, and shouldered my way back to our seats.

"This way."

What was Theo's connection with everything? How much did he know about Jonelle and Will, and what they get up to? I would hate to let any cats out of potential bags by introducing him to my friends and having the conversation wander where it shouldn't.

Which was awfully grown up and responsible of me, I kind of

thought.

"Um, Grillia and Steph, this is Theo, a mate. Theo, Grillia," I nodded in her direction and he deposited a bourbon in front of her, "and Steph."

And down went the other drink. They blinked, first at him, then at me. So okay, I wasn't immune to the man, but I had seen the perfect image and while Theo was obviously doing something interesting to the girls' heart rates, mine was safely tucked up waiting for the appearance of...

"Will!" *Now*, my heart kicked up a notch. Silly, huh?

As Theo snaked a leg around an unused chair hauling it to our table, his big brother arrived beside me. He didn't need to push through the beginnings of a Thursday night crowd. People just kind of parted for him. I only wished that I could stop my traitorous body from giving off enough heat to start a small bushfire by having him mere centimetres from me.

"Er, um." Now my conversational skills had totally exhausted themselves.

Theo and Will smiled slightly, and Will neatly took over all introductions. A good thing that, because I could have stripped naked for all the attention Grillia and Steph were giving me.

While Theo started giving the others a gripping tale of woe concerning his disastrous day, Will turned to me and we held our own conversation in murmured tones.

"Sorry if we crashed your party."

Will nodded ever so slightly to where Grillia and Steph were hanging onto every word Theo imparted. Grillia had given me a wink when Will commandeered me and there was no way to let her know that nothing in the world could be further from reality.

Will Malone was off my menu, if not before Monday, then certainly after my little drunken rampage. My toes did their obligatory curling in my stylish boots. I hated to think what he thought of me after that little episode.

"I hope you're fully recovered from the other night?" His eyes crinkled with inner humour.

Oh yeah, he was a right hoot.

"If you think I'm going to apologise, then think again, Mister. All in a day's work."

Liar. If I could have apologised without him laughing out loud at me, I might have tried to pull it off. As it was, I would much rather forget it. That and everything in the following forty eight hours.

"What are you doing here, again?"

Let's get this straight. I wanted to jump the delectable Mr Malone's hot lanky body, but that didn't stop me panicking about having him and his brother turning up on my doorstep all the time.

Will shrugged, taking a swig of his beer.

"Theo isn't a Hound and I would prefer to keep it that way. Limiting his exposure to them is probably the only thing I *can* do, seeing as he already has a passion for the bikes." He glanced over at his brother. "I was hoping one of you might turn up."

I could only assume he meant me and Jonelle. I would hardly see Grillia or Steph as his type. Giving myself a mental slap, I tried to remind myself *I* wasn't his type.

"What could you possibly want with us?" I tried to act the part; super cool and collected.

"I wanted to check on progress. You know, with all the information you were searching for and failing miserably at getting on Monday." He smiled down at me in a knowing manner.

Damn it, I could just wipe that smirk off his face.

"I'm sure you'll find out, sooner or later." My voice was remarkably chilly and I marvelled at the collectedness of me.

Will frowned. "Don't play games with me, sweetheart. Jonelle was on a mission and I saw her today; she looked incredibly pleased with herself. What's happened since Monday?"

His hand, one minute lying so quietly next to mine, slid over my wrist and gave me a bone crushing squeeze.

"Oi!" I whispered. "Hands off. The price on her head has been lifted, which is enough to make anyone leap for joy. Other than that, I can only assume she has a lead on who killed Brenda."

Well, of course, I couldn't really assume that at all, because I hadn't seen Jonelle since we parted after getting home. But seeing as that was the next thing on our list, I was hoping that might be the case.

I had no idea my words would have such an effect. Will was no Jonelle in the poker face stakes. He gave a little start like I'd goosed him. And I could feel the electricity wave down his body, almost as though he was preparing the fight or flight response to a threat. He gave the merest flicker of his eyes to Theo, then he was back under control.

Hello! I wasn't the expert, but something was very wrong. Even though I'd spent the afternoon breaking every dietary rule known to mankind, I wished Jonelle was here. She'd know what to do and say to get Will to spill his beans.

"I didn't realise she was so close to solving it? The police still have no idea." Will's tone was deliberately casual.

I narrowed my eyes at him. It was the best I could do. I would have to try this my way. Not that I technically *had* a way, but blundering had got me so far, a little further would be nice.

"The police aren't theoretically still looking, as far as I was aware. But why are you still so involved, Will? Anyone would think you had something to hide, but I would have put money on it you weren't using Brenda for her ... services. So come on, give. Why the desire to kill two birds with one stone?"

"Excuse me?"

I certainly had his attention now. There was a dangerous glint in his eye. I tried not to let that intimidate me. After all, Jonelle carried a whole range of dangerous looks around with her and if I let that start to bother me, then I was out of a job.

"You know. You wanted Gavel gone, because he's probably annoying you, which I totally get, mind you. I mean, the man looks like a thug." Could I dig my own grave any deeper? "For some reason you needed Jonelle to do the job; maybe because you owe her for something long ago, or she owes you? Or perhaps you wanted something on her – to keep her in your pocket?

"Anyway," I hastily moved along, watching his face darken with every word. "Jonelle was to do away with Gavel for you and you saw framing him for Brenda's death a handy way of making that happen. What, you thought Jonelle was so gun happy she wouldn't even *talk* to the man first?"

I was getting pretty involved with my own conspiracy theory here.

"And by getting Gavel killed for Brenda's murder, Jonelle would stop searching and the real killer would just fade into history. How am I doing so far?"

I took a large swallow of bourbon and Coke, nearly choking while my stomach cringed.

Will leaned down to me.

"I don't know where you get your ideas from, but I think you're pretty cute." He sat back, smiling. "Nuts, but cute."

He reached over and tweaked my hair.

But while he seemed happy enough to tune into the conversation around us, there was one thing I noticed. He had neither disagreed with me, nor had that lovely, beautiful smile come anywhere near reaching his eyes.

I half listened to what was going on around me, but for the most part, I found myself sweating. Jonelle was right. Will had something to hide. And whatever it was, I rather suspected it would be Jonelle who got it out of him. Unobtrusively I held out my hand. It had a big case of the shakes. He may not be as good at hiding his reactions, but Will Malone had a good line in intimidation – just like the rest of the deadly people I was associating with.

Lord help me. Because I was pretty sure I could not help myself.

However, I wanted to forget work for one night, so I put it all to the back of my mind and tried very hard to join in with everyone around me. If I didn't look too closely, it was easy to see a small group of friends catching up after a long day at work. It didn't matter that one of them was a gang leader, another an accessory to murder and one, an unknown factor. I sipped my drink and watched Theo through my lashes. I didn't know what his story was, but I was very curious to find out.

When Will next stepped in and took Grillia's and Steph's attention I leaned over to Theo.

"So, do you visit your brother very often?" A simple enough question, one would assume.

Theo gave a little start. "Er, not really. In fact, Will tries to visit us mainly. I guess he doesn't want to involve us with his associates too much, you know?"

He smiled at me, all warmth and gooey eyes. Some men should be kept on leashes.

If I thought about it, I probably wouldn't have asked the next question. Though, why should I start to think before I open my mouth now?

"Didn't happen to come visiting him a while back did you?" I thought about it and gave the month. Just to see what would happen.

I tried my hardest to be like Jonelle and watch both Theo and his brother. Just about impossible. I simply didn't know how the woman achieved it. Not that it mattered all that much. It was obvious Will was listening to me, and not to whatever conversational gambit Steph was dribbling in his ear.

Both of them snapped their heads up. They deliberately did not look at each other, which seemed to me even more of an omen than if they'd exchanged lingering looks of guilt. Like that, was it? I smiled inwardly.

Damn, I was good.

Then I happened to glance at Will and had second thoughts. I maybe making all the right guesses, but there was no guarantee I was getting out of this pub. His face was like thunder. Not so hot at hiding those feelings, darling Will.

Theo pretended to choke on his beer.

"Maybe sometime then. It's nice to catch up with family, wouldn't you say?"

And he did a very credible job of changing the subject. Considering my options, I didn't try to stop him.

I kept up with the conversation. I really did. Even though my heart was going pitter-patter and all I wanted to do was go find Jonelle. Watching my friends and my not-so-friendly male acquaintances, I came to the realisation that while I missed my friends and the things they did, my life had moved on. That gave me a jolt.

I was sitting here drinking my favourite drink, with my favourite people and *now* I came to the conclusion I needed to be elsewhere? I just loved my inappropriate moments. I watched Grillia flirt with almost professional ease with both Will and Theo. I adored her, and yet I was busy taking note of everything he said or didn't say, hoping to remember it all for Jonelle later. Since when did my life take me so far away from my friends?

I could only hope I hadn't changed beyond all recognition.

Eventually Will and Theo took their leave. Grillia and Steph both gave them their numbers, but Will's last words were for me.

He sat close, draping one arm along the back of my chair. Ducking his head, he brought his lips to my ear. His breath teased my frazzled hair; and didn't do much for my nerves either.

"I'm always lenient with you, sweetheart. But don't push me too far. You're mine and I'm not inclined to share you with Theo, so no more interest in him, yeah?" His teeth closed over my earlobe and he bit me gently. Every inch of my skin shivered.

Will leaned back, so our eyes could meet. I saw a thousand things in his, none of which I could read. He stroked my cheek.

"I know you're a free woman, so don't think that whatever you started the other day is in any way over."

Then he brought his mouth down on mine, hard.

If he hoped to drive his point home, or to wipe Theo right out of my head, he was sure doing a good job of it. He pressed his lips so tightly to mine I could feel my teeth quake. I wiggled a hand between us. I had hoped to push him away, but instead I found my fingers twisting in his shirt, wrenching him just that little bit nearer.

If that was possible. Which, somehow I doubted. Will gave a satisfied grunt and pulled back. A faint smile flicked on his mouth, then he and Theo were gone.

I sat still, a bit like a landed mullet. A thousand thoughts swirled around my head, but could I make sense of any of them?

"Wow," Grillia said softly, smirking at me. "Now that is what I call sizzle. Care to tell us your secret?"

I attempted to get my head together. I had this sneaking suspicion there was a loopy grin on my face, which possibly wasn't going to fade for the next, oh, several *hours*. The man had serious *punch*.

"Who knew you knew such interesting people," was Steph's rewarding comment.

"Thanks," I snapped at her. "He is pretty hot, hey?"

And there was the chance I'd steam up even a cold shower at that point.

"Brad really is out of the picture, then."

Grillia stepped right back to the conversation we'd started before being so gracefully interrupted by the sexy brothers Grimm.

"What, you thought I'd keep it going once I found out he was married?"

I didn't know if I was insulted or flattered. Grillia would only have been judging me on her standards and I did love the girl.

"Nope. He had to go. Though I had been hoping for a keeper."

They both raised eyebrows.

"Not forever," I added hastily, lest they start to think my commitment phobia was waning. "Just for a while. Longer than the last two. But no, back into the pond I go. It's getting depressing."

If my stomach wasn't in the middle of a revolt there was the chance I would have thrown more bourbon at it. Even thinking about the mess of my romantic life was enough to make me want to get good and drunk. My semi professional life may have taken off, but I was a girl who needed *loving*. Things were definitely on the lean side there.

"What about the delectable Will? He certain made a good show of wanting a piece of you. And I certainly wouldn't say no to a bit of *that* action."

Steph's eyes glowed; which for a woman decked out solely in black was quite a feat.

"He's off the menu, ladies."

How was I going to explain why? When underneath all I wanted to do was play some horizontal games with Will myself. I shuddered to imagine what Jonelle would think of that little piece of honesty!

Grillia nodded. "With the Hounds, isn't he?" She shrugged. "You could do worse. At least he wouldn't be clingy."

They both giggled. I glared at them. Back to normal then, was it? Except it wasn't.

Firstly, I didn't get drunk. I made sure the rest of the drinks were on me and I stuck to Coke. There were limits to even my stomach and I realised I'd just reached them. Plus, I wanted to watch the people around me.

Especially Will and his brother who had retired to a corner; where they talked, laughed and drank happily together. Though every time I looked over, I managed to meet Will's hungry gaze which was unsettling, to say the least.

And secondly, I didn't have much to say. I had no juicy gossip, no news, and no new disaster to share. Well, I had plenty, but nothing I was going to tell my friends. I realised why Jonelle didn't have social friends; just people in the 'game' who knew the rules and made no claim on her time.

At midnight I called it a night. I wanted to get home, because dollars to donuts that damned woman would be coming to get me out of bed at 5am.

"Sorry sweeties, I've got to run. See you all later?" Better if I didn't put a day to it. I could never tell one day from the next where I'd end up.

Steph, in mid-spiel about the wonders of Pete versus the excitement of someone new like say… Theo, broke off to give me a rather wobbly hug. Grillia was a bit more sober and told me not to walk home alone. I glanced over at Will. Yes, he'd noticed I was making 'leaving' noises. Somehow I doubted whether my walking home alone would be an issue.

I hadn't gone two steps out of the pub when I felt him at my back. Neither of us said anything until the pub and all its noises were a block behind us.

"Pleasant evening." Perhaps making banal banter was about to become my strong point, because there was not a lot I had to say to him right now.

"Fiona."

It was more of a warning. Will grabbed my arm and hauled me into his.

As romantic interludes went, it wasn't the worst I'd ever had. My body was practically humming with hormones. But as far as charming the birds down out of the trees, Will needed to work on his delivery.

Everything about him was hard. Muscles, angles, arms, mouth and attitude. When Jonelle had told me to play it safe with him, she really hadn't been kidding.

Now the lion was out of his cage and there was little I could do but go with the flow. I wasn't going to kid myself; the point of me asking him to stop had long since passed. Three date rule, be damned. If only Brad could see how far *over* him I was, right at this point …

Eventually I had to come up for air. With a monumental effort, I managed to push Will a few centimetres off me.

"In an alley, Will? It's not that far home."

His eyes glinted down at me and I tried to remind myself he was the Head Hound. But as warnings went, it fell remarkably short of the mark. Hell, a little spot of trouble was what I was looking for. Things had felt queer since Monday night. I felt out of my skin and having Will's hands roaming all over me was, well, guaranteed to help put me smack bang into it again.

I challenged any woman to keep a sense of detachment happening while playing fast and loose with the delectable Mr Malone.

Then, in one of his lightening mood swings, Will lost the wild aggression and gave me a heartbreaking smile.

"Whatever and wherever you want, sweetheart." He took my arm and turned us towards home. "So where have you and Jon been?"

I hesitated. There's the thing. Knowing Jonelle and Will were old buddies, or at the very least, had a lot of history together was one thing. But he played for the other side now. Technically, I presumed, that made him an enemy though we'd never really treated him as such.

Did that mean I could go ahead and tell him what we had been up to, or was it one of those diplomatic moments I sucked at?

He glanced down at me. Those eyes. I swear I could fall into them and never reach the bottom. Hypnotic, deep, challenging. I wanted to eat him up.

"You've been twitchy all evening, love. Don't tell me Jonelle hasn't got you in too deep; its written all over your face."

Damn that easy to read manual I call a countenance!

And then it was easy.

"We went to Melbourne because that's where Jonelle was meant to be and The Rose was there and he'd already kidnapped me once, so she wasn't going to let that happen again …" What is it with my story telling ability? Just one long jumble of nothing. Mind you, I got as far as the kidnapping part and Will stopped short.

He grabbed both my arms (as though someone was just about to come up and haul me away!) and jammed my nose against his broad, warm chest.

"She let *what* happened to you?" His chin was resting on the top of my head, which was fine, as far as it went. His arms tightened. "That bastard." I was left wondering if he meant Jonelle or Ben.

"In her defence, he'd shot her at the time. And now he's dead, so I can't complain."

Vivid images of the night of Ben's murder flashed through my head. I couldn't complain – but that didn't make the re-runs any easier to watch. Not so keen on the idea of any more action, either.

"Dead, huh?"

What was with these people? I'd just told him a man was dead and the reaction was zip! This was taking stoic to the extreme.

I gave him a little shake.

"Doesn't that mean anything to you? Jonelle killed a man last night, and he lay dead at my feet and now all I can think about is all his blood."

I hiccuped. Perhaps I wasn't as over it as I had pretended. It was never this hard in the movies. Someone killed someone else and then they moved onto the next scene, where they solved the mystery. It didn't prey on any of their minds – the death of someone.

Will lifted my chin so I could meet him eyes.

"Sweetie, if Jon killed him, he needed it. And if she hadn't, for the very fact he shot her and kidnapped you, I probably would have.

Try not to lose any sleep over him. Think of all the people he's killed or maimed, and try to see it as having done society a great turn." He smiled gently. "What, you thought Jonelle would just give him a slap on the wrist? Wake up, Fi, and realise who you're playing with. We look after our own and we don't put up with shit."

I shuddered. Damn Skippy they didn't.

"Jonelle's not like you." Pure idiotic stuff, but I had to make myself feel better. "She doesn't hang out with a group of people who sell drugs, or whatever it is your boys do, does she?"

I could pick my moments. Being held in the arms of the leader of said group was probably not one of them. But Will was graceful under fire. I mean, the bastard *laughed*.

"God, you crack me up. The Hounds are a lot more than that. But I think we've headed off track here. You'd be surprised at just how much alike Jon and I are. So don't fool yourself." He paused. "If things get a bit rough, come and see me, yeah?"

Then he started us walking again.

A bit rough. I like that, coming from a man who had his own brother-in-law killed. I tried not to snigger, just a touch hysterically. Both of them warning me about the other.

If it wasn't so serious, it would be a comedy.

We hadn't taken two steps through the gateway at home, when Jonelle exploded out of her unit. I admit it, I jumped. I think somewhere along the line, I may even have swallowed my heart. It certainly did a crazy hop inside my chest.

"Crap." I didn't know if I was upset with her for appearing and thus destroying my evening plans with Will, or worried she had plans herself.

She eyed us both. "Going somewhere, Will?"

"Jonelle! What a pleasant surprise."

How can someone say something like that but sound as though he wanted to drown her, at the same time? I took a wary step to the side. Getting mixed between them right then could be detrimental to my health. I cast a longing glance at the safety of my unit. So close and yet so far.

Jonelle raised her eyebrow. "I'm sure it is." Her eyes met mine. "Hey, Princess. We should probably talk. How about now?"

Will groaned. "You aren't her nursemaid, Jon." But her gaze didn't waiver.

"Alright!" He held up his hands and backed to the gate. Somehow on the way passed he managed to snag me. With a tug, I was slammed up body to body. I heard a sigh behind us. Lord alone knew what she was thinking.

"Another time, love."

And he was gone.

My body ached and hummed to itself. Was it possible to get burnout when you didn't actually *do* anything? I could kill her.

"Sorry." She didn't sound very sorry to me. "But what have I told you about that man, Princess? He's way over your head. You go all nuts over me disposing of Ben and you cuddle up to Will?" she snorted. "Talk about double standards."

"I was *trying* to cuddle with Will. Note the operative word of trying. Some*thing* keeps getting in the way." I gave her a glare. "That something had better have a damned good reason for needing to talk to me. At midnight, when I was all set to go off like a firecracker."

Some people had no sense of timing, or perhaps a little too much. Either way, I was grumpy. And I wouldn't sleep for hours. I went into Jonelle's place. If I couldn't sleep, neither could she.

I picked up a steaming mug of green tea. By the looks of the place, she'd being reading, drinking her herbal crap, enjoying the evening until she'd seen me come home with 'the enemy'. The least she could do was forfeit her tea. I took a strong gulp, eyeing her defiantly.

"Silly little bugger."

Her tone was affectionate. She went into the kitchen, where presumably the pot of tea was residing, because moments later she was back sipping from a new mug.

I settled on the cushions.

"What's so important then?" I wasn't letting her off the hook. If my evening had to be ruined, so did hers.

"I was worried about you. Where have you been all day?" She was casual, but I could see the lines around her mouth.

"Not with Will, if that was what you were thinking." I grouched. She gave me a look. "All right! Bloody hell. It's not that every moment of my day needs to be recorded, you know. I was out at the movies with Grillia and Steph. We talked about Brad being a prat and all men being arseholes and bastards, then Theo came over and it was uphill …" I caught her eye, "er … downhill all the way from there, okay? Happy?"

There was a touch of petulance there, but I wasn't in a caring mood.

"Theo was out with Will at the Batch, again?" Jonelle leaned forward, suddenly interested. "He's not gone home then?"

"Will said he didn't want to drink with all the Hounds with his younger and impressionable brother around, so they chose to finish his visit off at our local, rather than the clubhouse."

So okay, they hadn't been his exact words, but as good as.

"I gave him a few jabs about Theo and he got narky, then well, fuses were lit and I *was* about to enjoy the results of my labour." I jabbed at her, instead. Not quite as satisfying, but I had to go with what was on hand.

"What exactly got him so riled up?" I tried to look smug. "And I don't mean you, Princess. What did you say about Theo?"

She was trying for casual, but failing as miserably as I usually did. Curious-er and curious-er.

"I don't know." It seemed a long way back. I was still floating on a cloud of sexual angst. "Something about letting the real murderer of Brenda walk free if you had killed Gavel, and then I asked Theo if he'd been here then. Really cooked Will's goose."

I grinned at the memory.

"Anything else?" Jonelle's tone was suddenly sharp. I sat up.

"Nope. That was about it. Then he got all sweet and romantic, as boys tend to do when I'm around. Have I ever told you how I'm a femme fatale?" I was easily sidetracked, too. Jonelle growled warningly. "Oh fine. I don't remember; my brain's a little fried. Maybe, if I'd had the chance to clear it with a little bit of exercise, then you'd get a better story."

Heavy on the pointed references there.

"Ever think he may have known the best way to distract you would be to slobber all over you?" she snapped. Ooh, she was a bit touchy tonight. And maybe I'd had a few more drinks at the beginning than I'd thought.

"I'm beginning to think my suspicions about Will weren't far off. The Malone boys need to have a long chat with me, I feel."

"Are you trying to tell me, that far from finding me irresistible, Will was just trying to blow me off the scent of something even juicer than say, him?"

I crashed down to earth with a nasty jolt. And there, I'd been sure he was just after my body. Ah, the illusions of youth. But come to think about, I did remember his change of attitude came right after I asked Theo where he was at the time in question. I buried my nose in the tea. How embarrassing. Bugger.

Jonelle took pity on me.

"I'm sure he's after your body, too, Princess. He's usually a little more circumspect about it though, which leads me to think our Will is hiding something. Up for a visit with him tomorrow?"

"If you'd let things take their course, he'd be here tomorrow to pump for information." Among other things, I giggled to myself.

She rose and took our mugs to the kitchen. Coming back, I was shown the door.

"Glad to see you are bouncing back to your normal self. I'll come and get you around 5 then, shall I?" Ugh. Where was the reprieve in the face of extenuating circumstances? I gave a theatrical groan and she laughed.

"Out you go, girl. Get some sleep and I'll see you in a few hours." Put like that it seemed positively medieval.

"Yeah, yeah, see you then."

I staggered over to my place, where I was greeted by sleepy, furry love. There was something to be said for the let down of hormones. Now, all I wanted to do was get some satisfying sleep.

Changing into a T-shirt, I grabbed a glass of water and made it into my room.

"Shove over." I gave Smudge a push, as he tried to commandeer my pillow. Manny put his paws on the bed end. "Don't even think about it. Go sleep on your cushion."

He gave me mournful eyes, but slunk into the corner. Like he was hard done by or something.

With a bone cracking stretch, I flipped onto my bed and tried to make my way into sleep. Images of Ben; stroking my arm, smiling silkily, or dying, kept flashing across my retina.

"Crap."

I wiggled around a bit more and got a paw in the nose for my trouble.

"You stay out of my head, you hear?"

Enough was enough, after all. Just how many times could a serial killer steal my sleep? I think it was sometime just before dawn when sleep finally claimed me.

Chapter Thirty

Around about 5am, after approximately ten minutes sleep, visitors are an irritant. Or, if I was strictly honest, I would have to say, a bloody pain in the butt. There was one thing I was learning however and that was, if I was silly enough not to answer the door, Jonelle was quite likely to come right through it anyway.

"I'm coming, I'm coming."

I was more than half asleep. Not at my best, but she could hardly complain. I let her in and made my way back to bed. There I curled up, and pulled the sheet over my head.

"Go away."

"Now is that anyway to greet someone?" Her amused tones did nothing to endear her.

"It is when they come visiting at some obscure hour of the morning." I answered from somewhere under my covers. I clutched tightly to the end of the sheet, mindful of the fact she was quite likely to rip it off if she was so moved. Not that that was going to be of any use to me, as it panned out.

Jonelle peeled back my protection and peered closely at my face. It was only lit by the grey dawn light, but I was pretty sure my expression was self evident. I stuck out my tongue.

"Bugger off." Okay, so not quite the insult of choice, but the best I could do at that hour.

"Nope. I think you're faking." She brought her face down to my level. It was a bit startling to view her myopically close before a morning coffee. "Yes, definitely a fake. Out of bed, you. For death or disease you may get away with this, but for late night due to being out with the girls, you can run but you cannot hide."

I pulled the sheet firmly back into place.

"Okay, so you can hide, but you can't run. Same thing, different version. Up."

And she went out, presumably into the kitchen to feed the boys, as they happily followed along, chatting to her like a long lost relative.

I groaned. In part, she was to blame. After all, without her interruption I would have had mind blowing Will-sex, then peaceful slumber. As it was, I'd had a severe talking to about boys from my new bloody mother hen and then a disturbed sleep, where my mind couldn't determine if it wanted me to suffer Ben's demise, or the torments of unfulfilled hormones.

Either way, sleep hadn't been exactly of the energising variety. But that wasn't going to wash, so I hauled myself out of bed and into gym clothes. It was too warm already for the usual tracksuit, so I couldn't hide my slight tummy bulge. There was nothing worse than knowing every inch of you would be assessed the minute you walked out the bedroom door.

I looked down at my waist – just how much would Jonelle notice, and care?

A few moments later I found Jonelle, and my last chocolate bar, in my kitchen. She held it up like evidence at a trial.

"Having fun with these?"

"It's just the one," I groused, snatching it back and shoving it randomly into a cupboard.

She glanced at my figure in its second skin of coloured lycra.

"Just the one, huh? Come on Princess, I think it's time we got back into some sort of routine. Let's warm up by running down to the Lake."

She was out the door before I could open my mouth for a protest. Not that that would have done me any good, but I was forever hopeful.

With a grunt I followed, leaving Manny and Smudge to munch through the kibble she'd left them. I found Jonelle by the pool doing limbering up exercises which reminded me of some form of archaic torture.

"Are we sure you're doing it right?"

I eyed her stretched and contorted body somewhat dubiously. If she thought I was getting my generous curves into a position like *that*, she could think again!

She bobbed back up, a touched flushed from the exertion. There was a slight smile playing around her mouth, like she knew I was mentally killing her and she found it vastly amusing.

"Let's get you all stretched then, shall we?"

Stretching my muscles was not quite the task it was to make sure she was limber. The more flexible you were, the more it took to give you a full work out. Me? Dead easy.

While Grangelands wasn't that far from the Lake, it felt like forever when I had to run it. The woman wasn't much for the whole concept of walk/jog. The pace she set was designed to make me feel every one of my extra pound (or two). By the time we got to the Lake, I was red and huffing. I flopped to the ground.

"Ever heard of taking the car?" I was amazed I could form words.

Jonelle glanced over at me. I was lying on my back kind of spread out like a starfish. Something about wanting to die kept flickering through my head.

"Ever heard that running on a treadmill has made you soft for running on actual terrain? We only had to come four kilometres!"

"When you put it like that - don't!"

I opened my eyes and took in the sky as the sun's rays came dancing over the horizon. So okay, I happened to like this time of day now I was getting used to it, but that was an admission she'd really have to torture out of me.

"What happened to your get up and go?" Jonelle came and sat crossed legged beside my dying body.

I half rolled over and gave her a glare.

"Do you have to make it so easy?" I loved to joust, even at 5am in the morning. "It got up ... and went!" I did so amuse myself sometimes.

She snorted. "Sit."

I swung myself up and crossed my legs so I could feel the heat from her knee beside mine, but didn't touch. There were some lessons I wasn't going to have to learn again.

"Who was your dog last year?" I muttered to myself.

"With all the good intentions in the world, I couldn't equate you with a dog." She sat, immobile, staring out at the water. "We'll meditate, do some Tai Chai and then head to the gym."

I grimaced. A good book and some Oprah sounded better to me. Shades of old habits ...

"What are our plans for today, apart from killing me?"

I bit my lip. I was so used to joking with her now, the words just came out. But now … now I'd being there. Next to her when a real killing had taken place; could I just joke about? Would she just let it go as a joke, or would she get aggressive? I hated being back to the guessing game about her reactions.

She dipped her head and glanced at me from the corner of her eyes.

"No need to panic, Princess. We're okay." I felt my heart, ready to leap its way out of my chest, climb safely back into place.

"After the gym and breakfast, we're going to visit the Brothers Malone."

What was that I said about heart in its rightful place?

"We're what?" I squeaked. "We, as in you, right? We, as in me, will be doing something safe, harmless, and extremely innocent and non-life threatening, like playing Free Cell on the computer?"

There was an eternal optimist in all of us.

Again, that little snort of amusement. My day to play Court Jester.

"No, we, as in you and me, will both be attending this meeting. If nothing else, you can run interference with Theo by providing the humour for the occasion. Anyway, what happened to your curiosity? You don't want me filling you in on something like that, do you? I might miss telling you the best bit."

"That's not fair. You can't play to my weak points." Well, of course she could, there were so many of them to choose from. "All right, I'll go along."

Loved the idea that there had been any choice in the matter. Illusions: such powerful tools.

"Good. Until then, however, let's look at least like you know what you are doing out here." And she zoned out into whatever little world lived inside her head.

I glanced over, but all I could see was the sun's reflection in those eyes. To the average observer, which sad to say I was, it really did look like no one was home. I shrugged. May as well pretend I was doing the same.

The strangest thing about pretending to be quiet and peaceful; after a little while of staring at tranquil water and the sun coming up, I really did become quiet and peaceful. It was kind of nice to leave behind the incessant chatter of my brain and just be still. Not that anything like that was going to last for too long.

"Okay, come back now." Jonelle's voice reached me from what

felt like a long void of water.

"Huh?" I was not my most focused.

"We've been meditating for the last forty five minutes. If you're not careful, you'll become some sort of Zen Master." Jonelle gave a little snigger at her own carefully crafted joke.

"Haven't you got anything better than that?"

Forty five minutes? Wow, that was the longest I'd managed to fake anything. And I always thought it was a talent of mine.

Faking (or not as the case maybe) meditating was one thing, faking the next couple of hours was another. By the time I dragged myself back to the shower, my muscles were remembering why they'd hated me the first time I'd headed out with Jonelle. They were quivering masses of jelly. God, I'd kill for some sort of body double.

"It'd be kind of nice if you could go out and do it all for me," I told Manny, peeling off my lycra and diving into the shower.

So, I was teaching the boy a bad habit. Letting him sit on the bathroom mat, watching me shower didn't make me a bad mother, did it? Talking to him possibly made me a bit mad, but not bad.

"Now, if I had four legs, it may be easier. Though, trying to get them all fit and muscled could pose a greater challenge, I guess it would depend on my point of view. No, don't stick your nose in here. I'm talking at you, not requiring a general exchange."

I shoved Manny out of the shower recess. Sometimes he got a little bit too friendly. Though I had managed to break him of the need to sniff everyone in the crotch, which was a blessing especially when naked.

Dressed in denim shorts and a top as small as a woman my age could conceivably get away with, I wandered over to Jonelle's. I carried with me the ever present apricot Danish and hoped that this easy to consume breakfast wasn't going to be off my eating list now I had a few more bounces and wiggles in my step. The front door wasn't locked, so I let myself in and made my way to the kitchen.

"What is that garbage?" Jonelle kicked the fridge closed, while balancing soy milk, fruit juice and what looked like blue berries, or at least a dark berry of some kind, all at once. Maybe she'd trained as a juggler before turning to hit-man status.

I stuffed the rest of my Danish into my mouth. There was just the slight chance she may have snatched it. She rolled her eyes.

"Anymore of that sort of thing and I'll run you around the Lake, instead of just down to it. The kettle boiled. How about some green tea while I make us some real breakfast?"

"There is nothing unreal about a Danish." I flicked the kettle's switch, just to make sure the water was really hot. "There is, in fact, all sorts of gastric proof toward the reality of my Danish." I hummed a few off key bars, while adding hot water to the pot of green tea leaves.

"My stomach is inclined to believe in its reality so much so, there is going to be little room for whatever lovely surprise you have in store."

Plucking down two mugs from her cupboard, I loaded the lot onto a tray and made my way into the lounge.

"Voila. Green tea to top my Danish. You on the other hand," I gave the plates of fruit and yoghurt a rather sceptical eye, "are free to force that down your throat if you must."

"We," Jonelle stressed, taking the tray and placing it on the floor between two cushions, "are going to be looking into your diet a little closer from here on in." I wrinkled my nose.

"If you want to be fast and catch the bad guys, Princess, you have to be able to move like them." She held out a bowl. "Soy yoghurt and fruit. Keep you fit … and regular."

"Lord, do you have to be so icky? And did you see Joker? He had a figure that makes me look positively svelte. And while we're at it, don't you just love my choice of words?"

I took my bowl and gave it the evil eye. *Soy* yoghurt? What happened to the good old fashioned regular kind?

Jonelle took a large spoonful. "Svelte is a wonderful word, Princess. Let's try and apply it to you by say… the end of next year. Now eat."

Cow.

I obediently took a mouthful. It was truly foul. I choked.

"Jonelle! I can't. You're ruining the taste of my Danish!" I put the bowl down. "Nothing is going to induce me to eat that." I glanced up and met Jonelle's gaze. "Okay, so the word *nothing* was probably a little strong. In fact, could be easily interchanged with say, you, but let's not get hasty."

Had I mentioned how much of a coward I was? I ate the damned fruit. But there wasn't anything in the manual that said I had to like it.

Even sipping the green tea after was a relief. Anyone who's ever been force fed soy *anything* may sympathise with me.

Jonelle leaned back on her cushion.

"If I remember Will's waking patterns, he'll just be starting to think about getting up round about now."

Lucky Will. And – excuse me?

"Remember - his - what?" I nearly choked on my tea.

She gave me a decidedly enigmatic smile. Then relented.

"Will's a late sleeper."

Which just goes to show how much we would have had in common before she got me in her clutches. I loved sleeping in. The man was fast heading towards the heady heights of fantasy land. If there was only a slight chance I would ever get the chance to fulfil some of those fantasies, I would be more than happy.

"And you came by this delicious knowledge because there was no one to tell you to go home and leave Will alone?" I was still smarting with left over hormones and she tells me she knows all about his sleeping habits??

"Many years ago, I crashed at his place with him and the family. Before Kathy got married and things all seem to have gone to pot for the Malones. So don't fret."

I wasn't. Much.

Finishing up our tea, Jonelle went into the spare room to collect a few things. I had no intention of following her to learn exactly what it was she wanted, seeing as the spare room housed every weapon known to mankind. Possibly a slight exaggeration, but I wasn't in the mood to be factual. There was something wrong with the idea of mounting an attack on a man who was as sexy and into me as Will. By all means, I wanted to be over at his place, *especially* at this hour of the morning. But preferably from spending the night; not being a raiding party set on interrogation!

Rude: unpleasant and potentially dangerous if he was in a foul mood. 'What are your plans for this wonderful warm December Friday?' Oh you know, hunt down the leader of a gang and ask him all sorts of prying questions implying either he or his brother were murderers.

Nothing much.

Could I run and hide now?

Jonelle came back, dressed in combat gear of black on black. It kind of suited her, but made me quiver. She was expecting trouble then. She bent down and slid a thin blade into the top of her boot.

Rising, she caught my eye.

"Better safe than sorry, Princess, as trite as that may sound. He's faster and stronger than me if it comes down to it. He's younger and has the advantage of bulky male muscle. But I'm only saying!" Something along the lines of terror must have shown in my face. "It won't come to an argument. You know Will! He could charm birds out of trees and all those sorts of clichés. It'll be fine."

As reassurances go, it fell remarkably short of its mark.

She obviously knew where to go as a few minutes later we were in her car heading out at top speed. I clutched the door handle.

"Does it always have to be the Grand Prix with you?" I asked, as we hurtled around another corner. It was a shame, but the lights all appeared to be in her favour.

Jonelle laughed.

"You're sense of adventure is starting to fade. Why waste time sitting in traffic when we have the technology under the hood to get there a lot faster?"

She was relaxed and zinging with her usual spirit. The electricity in the air was starting to ramp up and I could feel the strange hum along my skin I get when Jonelle was in fighting form. I glanced down at my arms. Sure enough, the little blonde hairs were starting to lift. I could feel sweat break out between my shoulders and on my palms. Well, 'interesting' this was certainly going to get. Especially if Will woke up feeling how I did of a morning.

The strange part was Will lived in an outer village, on some acreage. Not what I'd expected. I looked around, taking in the small dam, willow trees, old farm style home and the massive hound dog wagging its tails at us. Really, not what I thought Will was all about. Appearances were certainly deceiving.

Jonelle brought the car to a halt. It was when I went to open the door the guard dog showed his real face. So okay, a Hellhound wasn't going to live without his own hellhound around. I slammed the door and sat still. Beside me Jonelle grinned.

"Believe me when I say, that one's bite is much worse than his bark."

Considering the dog in question wasn't making a sound at all; was just walking stiff legged around the car sniffing and occasionally growling, I tended to believe her.

I peeped out the window and met its eye. Gulp. As cross breeds go, it was a lovely looking animal. I took another peek. Yes, *he* was certainly lovely.

"So now what?"

Jonelle sighed. "When Will gets up, he usually locks Brutus away. One dog on guard at a time." She grinned. "Which means he's not awake yet. Or doesn't want visitors."

"What happened to your cool under pressure attitude? It's just a dog." I watched him watching us.

"I never said I wouldn't get out. Just do it without making any sudden moves. He is quite happy, well let's say not too unhappy, to have someone he knows go straight up to the front door. It's when you make detours that Brutus gets all antsy." Jonelle slid out of the car and stood quietly while Brutus sniffed her all over.

"Hey there, Brutus. Where's Will?"

At the sound of his name and most probably her familiar scent, Brutus gave one stiff wag of his tail. I crept out of my side of the car and he came round, sticking his nose everywhere.

"Come on. He won't complain if we both go to the door."

Jonelle led the way up the path and on to the veranda. I followed, I would like to say calmly, but the reality was more along the lines of praying Brutus didn't see me as breakfast. He wandered around us both, almost as though he was herding us, growling gently just to remind us he wasn't all show. I didn't test his reactions by putting a foot off the side of the pavers.

Jonelle rapped on the door and moments later Will opened it, dressed only in boxers. My heart nearly ruptured. It just wasn't right to have so much packed into one person. I'd felt all that muscle, more than once I was chuffed to say, but to see it without a stitch on! There was the drool factor again.

"Close your mouth, Princess." Jonelle muttered out of the corner of her mouth. I snapped my jaws together so hard I felt (and heard) my teeth clash.

Will smiled. Egh! I hated being the most obvious person alive.

"So early, Jon. Couldn't wait to catch up, hey?"

But there was wariness in his eyes. He wasn't stupid. The only reason she'd come out here at this hour was because of something we'd turned up. Namely, the conversation we'd had the night before. Will turned those startling eyes on me.

"Fiona. What a pleasure. Though of course, there was always a chance I'd see you this morning, one way or another."

His voice was low and husky. I could feel the amusement emanating from Jonelle and my toes curled with embarrassment and heat. Why wasn't my love life simple and straight forward?

He stepped back and waved us inside, closing the door after giving Brutus a pat.

"Good thing you didn't provoke him. He hasn't eaten anyone recently and must be feeling the lack." He grinned maliciously at Jonelle. "Now, coffee? Tea? Anything at all?" He led us through the hall into the kitchen. It was easy to see this room was central to everything that went on in the house. Just like farmhouses of old.

There was a long table half covered in the morning paper, a desk in the corner and a low settee next to a cold open fireplace. I loved it on sight. Though that may have more to do with the owner, but I wasn't getting technical. Will swept the table clean of papers, thrusting them into a corner on the floor. Then he filled the kettle.

"Such hygiene, Will." Jonelle nodded at the paper pile. He gave it a disinterested look.

"It'll get used. See?"

He turned from his domestic duties to lean back against the counter. Sure enough, two little kittens came scampering in from another part of the house, pouncing on the readymade kitty litter.

"Shame if I still wanted to read it, but it was mostly crap anyway, if you pardon the pun." Considering the use the kittens were now putting it to.

"Where's Theo?"

Nothing like getting straight to the point. I had temporarily forgotten our mission out there. Will had his arms braced behind him, weight comfortable on his hands, ready to move at any moment. But all I was registering was the play of muscle across that tanned expanse of smooth chest. Jonelle gave me a swift kick. Crap.

Will gave me a look that held distinct promises for another time, then turned his full attention on Jonelle. Playing me as a distraction might have worked with someone less professional, but Will knew who the real player was here and wasn't going to take his eye off the prize.

"Gone."

Her eye brow climbed. Here we go.

"All ready? From all accounts he was pretty comfortably settled in last night."

Did she have to bring my evidence into this? I liked the idea of being a partner, if it was of the silent variety.

"I don't like him to stay too long, for obvious reasons. I don't want him to form any close bonds of friendship down here. Either with the lads …," and he gave me a quiet look, "or with any of the women he meets. Having Theo come to stay permanently would not suit me, Mum or Katherine, at all. He's better off trying to 'find' himself in Sydney."

"How are your mother and sister, by the way?"

Jonelle leaned casually back in her chair, but I could see by the placement of her feet, there was no way she was relaxed and taking this all easy. Boy, I loved the atmosphere when we go visiting friends.

The kettle boiled and Will set about making us all coffees, not waiting for an answer to his question in regards to our preferences.

"They're fine. Katherine's even dating someone again. Mum hates him, but I think that's just on principle." He plonked our coffee down. "Shall we get to the real reason you're here, Jon? You don't really care what is happening in my family. At least, not in the past, you haven't."

He sat down opposite us, wrapping his hands around his mug. But no one took a sip and the strange tableau held for a moment. Both of them watching the other.

I snorted.

"Hello! Can you two at least pretend to remember you used to be friends?"

Not diplomatic, but she had brought me here to break the tension. I hoped that was why, because the only other thing I was particularly good at was running away and Brutus patrolling outside put paid to any thoughts of that.

Will gave me a dirty look, then he smiled.

"All right. You two are friends and guests in my house. Still, Jon doesn't come calling unless she wants something."

"Answers," she said slowly.

I watched Will's face. Not that that was going to be the keys to the kingdom. I still wasn't very good at this. But he wasn't trying to hide. There was wariness, but also almost a sense of relief.

"Will, you and Theo are awfully jumpy. There aren't too many reasons why you should be worried about me. But whatever has you and Theo hopping is more than a few problems from years ago."

I swung my gaze between them. More than sometimes I felt I'd come into the story more than half way through. They were definitely speaking of things not on my radar.

He shrugged. He wasn't about to come over all confessional. Such a shame really. It would have been nice to get out of there before lunch. I felt my heart tripping along in my chest. It would be nice to get out of there – period. Could I offer to go walk the dog?

"Talk to me, Will. Or I'll make my own conclusions and you won't like that. Let me help you."

Will gave a short barking laugh. "I am not likely to need help, am I? The Hounds take care of their own."

"Then why were you trying to off load Gavel onto me? Will, something has happened here and before I go treading in a pile of shit, I need you to let me in on it!"

Jonelle was practically growling, herself. I was amazed at the use of such coarse language. She really had to be upset with him. But she hadn't reached for any weapon, so there was hope for him still.

"Theo has got himself mixed up in something, hasn't he? What has that stupid little fool gone and done? Killed someone?"

Now, just about then, I could suddenly see what she was driving at and so could Will. His face went pale around his sexy no-shave shadow. There wasn't exactly anywhere on his body he could be concealing a weapon, but all the same I felt light headed with dread. The white knuckles gripping the coffee mug didn't help with my anxiety. I felt like taking Jonelle aside and telling her that most 'friends' didn't go around accusing each other of murder or its cover up.

Damn, these people would be the death of me.

She leaned forward, straight across the table at him.

"Tell me he didn't have anything to do with Brenda's murder and I'll walk out of here. But be sensible here, Will. For once, since I came back, tell me the truth because you won't be getting another chance. This is it. Talk to me, or if I find out what is going on and if any one of you is implicated, I swear, I will forget we were ever friends."

There was silence. I didn't know about them, but I held my breath. It was as though every moment before had led to this. I felt the need to eat copious amounts of chocolate, pee and run, all at once. How's that for an amazing feat? They just sat there and locked eyes for what felt like eternity. Then Will's shoulders slumped. This was it, then.

"You know there isn't anything I won't do for my family."

His voice carried all the conviction I needed. That plus the memory of him having his sister's husband killed, well, I wasn't going to contest the statement. Jonelle nodded.

"I'll tell you what you need to know, then. But if you try to see Theo about it, I *will* stop you, Jon. Okay?"

His voice was deep and carried a note of finality that was extremely scary, for all we sat in the bright morning sunshine. It felt like midnight. My skin crawled.

Jonelle watched his face for a moment.

"All right then. You talk to me and I'll keep Theo out of it. But you have to tell me everything, Will. I can't help you if you don't."

Why was it we both were so keen on the whole truth and nothing but the truth? Right about then, I could have done with about five minutes of half truths and some of that Grand Prix action of hers.

He sat forward, leaning his weight on his wrists. Our coffees were getting cold and I think I was the only one who noticed. There is nothing worse than cold coffee. I wrinkled my nose.

"Theo was here back then. You were right last night, Fi."

It sounded as though he was forcing the words out over rocks. I didn't suppose someone who could call themselves Head Hellhound was used to true confessions, unless they were someone else's.

"He was just turning twenty one and was a virgin, for fuck's sake!"

Both of them snorted. I failed to see the significance. So what if he was a little slow on the up take of those good looks? Good on him. But hey, what did I know?

"Kate told me this over the phone. You know, 'little brother Theo is coming down to visit you and oh guess what he's never been with a woman. And by the way Will, he's getting even more buried in his books and can't you do something?' I didn't mind the idea of him being a reader. But when he got here, Christ on a bike Jon, the boy could hardly talk to girls at all!"

They shared another moment, half smiling. This was *worse* than pulling teeth. At least that was quicker.

"The lads," such a refined word for such a distinctly unrefined bunch of men, "laughed themselves stupid. So I thought I'd lend the poor bastard a helping hand and called Brenda. I asked her to come out and 'pretend' to fall for him and take him home. I wanted to pay her top dollar, but she said she'd do it as a favour."

"So we bumped into her after a few drinks. She came and joined our table, and started a conversation with Theo. Well, she was a looker, our Brenda, and Theo isn't hard on the eyes."

Ah, such is the power of the understatement.

"Things went great. As they left, Brenda gave me a wink and I drank to their health. I spent the rest of the night thinking my little brother was being well taken care of."

Will was quiet for a long moment. Jonelle used all her patience and didn't push. Obviously, we were not kindred spirits on that issue.

"He went back to Sydney the next day. He was quiet and angry and brittle. I didn't ask. I was hoping that things with Brenda had gone well. It wasn't until a few days later that I found out she was dead. And yes," he held up his hand to forestall her questions, "I did go up and talk to him. Theo was beyond angry that I could think he had anything to do with her death. But he wouldn't tell me what went on between them. Not that I wanted details, but I wanted to make sure of him." The distrust that lived with Will and Jonelle every day was enough to give a normal person ulcers.

How did you ask your own brother, politely, if he just happened to murder the hooker you'd arranged for him to meet and get taken home by? I was glad Jonelle was quite sure I wasn't ready to be the person asking the questions. The mind boggled, was what it did. Boggled.

"What would you have done if it was your little brother? I'd killed Ken. Kate was getting her life together, Mum was, well, she'll always just be Mum. But I couldn't see Theo ruined because I set him up with a hooker! I wouldn't allow it, Jon. And then I found out you were looking out for her and she was a pet of Gavel's ... Well, shit. I hated the idea of lying to you, but I wasn't turning Theo over to you, even to just 'question'."

Jonelle gave a start.

"What? You thought I'd *make* him tell me? Will! I played with him when he was a kid! You didn't think you could trust me with the truth? You can't possibly think I'd torture Theo. Christ, Will."

I could see she was insulted.

Will growled. "How could I risk it? You aren't the same person you were back then. All right, so you are no Claire or Amelia -"

Why did it no longer surprise me that everyone used Amelia as some sort of yard stick and that everyone knew her so well? Who were these people that go bump in the night? It was worse than saying the boogie man would get you. What a small world these murderous types lived in.

"- but we aren't exactly playing for the same team, and I'm not grading on a curve here. Just as you couldn't trust me, I couldn't trust you. The last thing Theo needed at the time was a visit from you. He's still just a kid, for all his bluster. And the damn thing has scarred him for life."

"He seemed quite okay hanging out with you and the 'lads' the other day." Jonelle sounded awfully unconvinced.

Will shrugged. "He's learning to cope. But he hasn't dated since and the damned fool is talking of becoming a priest, a love of bikes notwithstanding!"

Well, then. Case closed, he'd obviously lost his head.

Locking all that potential up in a priest's collar would the sin of the century. I gave an inarticulate grunt of dissention. Jonelle's eyes flicked sideways at me. They may just have held a fraction of humour, but I couldn't tell.

"Jon," he was playing the earnest card. "Don't make Theo out to be the bad guy here. Whatever went on between him and Brenda had nothing to do with what happened to her. You know that. You know that Theo couldn't kill anyone, regardless of how bad the night went. He's sworn it wasn't him. I had to believe him. But it's changed him beyond all recognition. I don't know if he means to become a priest just to hide all that coldness, or as punishment for the sex. I can't get through to him."

Will was angry and distressed. He sounded convincing to me.

"I'm sorry Will. I'm sorry that Theo had a hard time with the hooker you pushed in his direction. I'm sorry that he didn't like his first sexual experience and that whatever happened has scarred him for life. But scar or not, she *died*, Will and I will talk to him about it. Am I making myself clear?"

Ah, she knew the art of a well placed accentuation. I was suddenly very glad not to be in Will's position. I ran my eye over him. Well, not in but *on* was sounding good. She was also using up a lifetime's worth of 'sorrys'. I could foresee her *not* apologising the next time I got kidnapped. Hell. I take that back. No need to jinx myself!

"Will. I may buy the whole Theo didn't kill her thing, but why try it on about Gavel? And I do not buy why you waited so long to tell me. Since when have you been afraid of me?"

He stood up and hunched his shoulders, crossing his arms tight. Jonelle gave a start and I saw her fingers twitch. Any more sudden moves on his part and she'd be bringing out the big guns. I couldn't blame her. I was feeling decidedly twitchy myself. I liked these two people. It felt all wrong to be watching them circle each other like a pair of dogs.

The advantage he might have thought being half naked won him was suddenly gone. Distracting though his beautifully carved body maybe; facing Jonelle with very few stitches on would be more intimidating than usual. I felt sorry for Will. What a way to wake up in the morning.

He stood with his back against the counter again; leg bent and foot resting easily against a drawer handle. But even I could tell that a position like that was far easier to push off from if Jonelle had any sudden ideas.

"You weren't there, Jon, so don't tell me how I should have cut it. You may have been looking after Brenda and even sticking your nose into The Batch and Haddock every now again. But you were based in Sydney, with some interesting trips overseas yourself."

Will's eyes glinted at her. I loved hearing back stories about my new best friend from the opposition. I felt like I was in a tennis match, eyes swinging from one to the other.

"You would come down and spend a few hours with Brenda and renew your contacts here, then bugger off again. I'm surprised you left the main part of surveillance on Brenda to someone else."

Here was news. I turned on Jonelle, surprised myself.

She frowned.

"I kept an eye on her, but you're right. For a large chunk of my time I was elsewhere, which was how she wanted it. As it was, I kept a closer eye on her than Brenda was comfortable with. But losing her, finding out that Canberra had a few more things to offer than politicians, brought me here, in force, for now. So I'm in your backyard now, Will, and I'm not going anywhere. I'm not a good guy."

I squawked and she added, "And I'm not a bad guy either. So don't think to hide from me."

Will snorted. "You're just a bit of everything, as you always were, Jonelle."

We sat and watched him fight over his thoughts. Whatever he was or wasn't telling her must have been big, because he was silent for some time, thinking. Jonelle didn't rush him; she just sat quietly, hardly moving more than enough to take a breath. I wish I had that sort of control. As it was, I wriggled on my chair, hating this more and more.

Finally he straightened up. He'd reached his decision and I could feel the air temperature lower a few degrees. So did Jonelle. She let one hand slide casually down her hip; things were going to get interesting, or messy, depending on who did the talking.

"I'm no longer that young man you could intimidate and who needed your approval, Jon. I'm sorry, but that's all you're getting out of me. I have my own problems and I head up an organisation you openly despise, if not oppose. So I don't have to come over confessional."

With his stubble and the sudden power crowding into all the visible muscle (of which there was considerable), Will looked very dangerous – or edible, if you were me.

"Theo had a one night stand with someone who was killed within twelve hours or so of his visit. That doesn't make him the killer and I promised him my complete silence on the matter. I was amazed when you moved here and started up enquiries again. Just let it go; even having you here made Theo sweat, and he likes you!" Will frowned, remembering, I guess, his conversations with Theo.

Jonelle looked at him through narrowed eyes.

"Okay, Will. I'll take your word for it, but next time Theo is in town, he'll tell me himself. I am the type of person who finds neat endings hard to believe."

She was so not kidding. Me? I would take the unhappy little scenario Will had given us and been glad to close the file. What was her issue?

"That only leaves me one thing to clear up."

There is just the slight chance that in a former life the woman was a terrier. Will, who had partially relaxed, stirred at this. It was like he was being hunted by some great big black panther. With a voice like raw silk, she continued.

"Why Gavel, Will? What is in it for you if I got rid of him?"

Well, now, that was probably more the point than tying Theo in knots, really. Why Gavel, indeed.

Will gave a little laugh. I despaired. They were as mad as each other. All this talk of death and half hidden threats hanging in the air, and he could still *laugh*. Though there was the ever so slight chance I could become immune to it all, I would like to think I wouldn't laugh at it. He caught the look on my face.

"Sorry, sweetheart."

But he looked anything but sorry. He'd moved on; Brenda's death and Theo's role, however small, was over and he'd pushed it to one side. I thought of the death of Ben. Would that I could push that so easily out of *my* head.

"Gavel." Will came and sat down again. The tension in his muscles had vanished and there was the twinkle back in those gorgeous blue eyes. Jonelle was busy noting the changes too.

"He hates me. I'm too clean, too easy, too 'nice', I think his complaints are." Will turned his charm on. "Think so, ladies?"

Jonelle's long legs could reach the other side of the table. He received a swift kick.

"Hey! Anyway, when Dillon was killed, the former Head Hound," he explained when I looked blank. "Gavel thought he was a shoo in. But he just doesn't have it and he found out no one thought he could do the job. It was probably the worst insult for him."

Will grinned.

"He tried to have me conveniently killed and I rubbed his nose in it and its all nice little politics. But he bugs me, even though I have been asked nicely not to harm the stupid fool, sooo, I figured, hey wouldn't it be nice if my old mate Jonelle got rid of him for me? "

Jonelle was not exactly a happy camper. "And the fact that the Hounds would then be after whoever killed him as a vengeance gig, didn't enter your head?"

"Yeah, but I run the Hounds. So just how far would the investigation into his death have gone? Nowhere. And I could have been happily sitting with my boys when it happened, so they'd not think of me. It's not like I'd hire the hit, after all." He grinned disarmingly. "So, hey, I thought Gavel's in bed with the Phoenix – Jonelle is sure to jump on that. And the younger, more feisty Jonelle would have." He looked a little downcast, but then philosophical about it. "It could have worked."

"Only if you're a naïve idiot," she muttered. "I'm not reckless anymore, Will! I think more than we used to."

"More than Amelia does, is what you really want to say." He grimaced.

"What is Gavel up to?" Jonelle went back to her questions. I felt like giving her a kick myself. We had our answers. Did we really need to baby-sit Will too? I glanced over at him, catching his eye. Will winked. All right, I'd probably baby-sit him for free.

"Nothing I can't handle, Jon. Seriously, we've had some pretty big deals going on so I've been distracted, but now I can concentrate on things in my own backyard more, he's my problem."

Jonelle sat there and studied him. I felt a few drops of sweat slide down my back. She wasn't happy about any of this and her hand was still mere inches from her knife. If Will knew her as well as they both pretended, he'd know that as well. There wasn't any room in here for my awkward sense of humour. So for once, I kept my mouth closed. It was painful.

"Basically, 'stay out of it Jon until I call you'. Is that what you're saying?" Her tone was grim, but her hand came to rest on the table top.

"Exactly. I either can cope with Gavel, or I can't. Sink or swim, it's my neck."

"Okay! And what a pretty neck it is too. I think that's got it sorted? How about we head now?" All right. Me staying quiet was not going to continue for any length of time, who were we kidding?

They both gave little jumps. It was as if I had been forgotten while they'd done the whole stare each other to death, thing.

"Hello! Could you at least pretend I'm a part of this?" I grumbled.

Jonelle laughed. So they were insane together. Now she was laughing. I shook my head. She reached over and patted my arm. Every single hair on my body rose. The room was crazy with the hum of electricity and bottled in violence, laughter notwithstanding.

"She's probably hungry. She gets like that when I take her visiting." Jonelle shared a look with Will. "And no, no matter what you are about to say, you are not on her menu today."

"I wish you would stop talking about me as though I'm a child you have to take shopping at the Mall." She could really piss me off!

Jonelle turned serious for a moment.

"Will, I know I was swearing all kinds of blood for Brenda's death. I accept the responsibility of sounding like a blood crazed fiend. But I'm hurt to think you wouldn't have come to me, and would have dragged Gavel into it." She looked at him. "If there was anything that was going to show how different and how far we have separated, this is it. I'll leave you be. And I won't cause you too much drama. But stay away from me and mine, okay?

"Canberra is a small town and while some things can be kept a secret for a long time, events will out. So keep your nose clean and away from me. Or I may just have to cut it off for you."

I blinked. It wasn't her usual oblique threat. It was an out in your face, take me at my word, kind of threat.

Will had gone a little pale, but nodded. "Nice to know where we stand, Jon."

"You chose to get mixed up with the Hounds, Will. To lie to me and watch me chase windmills. As I said, I play it straighter these days and I don't go off half cocked, no matter how angry I get. Brenda's death just happened to coincide with... well." She stopped. Jack's coma and subsequent death was not something anyone really wanted to talk about.

"I know, Jon. I heard about Jack and I know Amelia's in town and yes, I'll be keeping out of her way." He looked sad, and old, for a moment. "It makes you pay its price, doesn't it?"

She stood up. "Yes, it really does. Which is why I'm working towards leaving it all behind and I won't be dragged into anything that'll stuff that up. Take care of you, Will. I guess that's what you're getting best at. Come on, Princess. We got what we came for."

Somehow, I doubted it. I looked at Will's remote, sad face and Jonelle's cold reserved eyes and wondered what exactly we'd come for.

It certainly hadn't been for the severance of a mateship that went back however many years. And it hadn't been, to my knowledge, to unmask baby Theo's sexual parlour games. Wretchedly I wondered if by making this my world, I was going to age myself too fast. Will couldn't have been more than thirty five. Who had done and faced what he did, at thirty five? Looking, for a moment, older than the grave.

We never did have those coffees.

Chapter Thirty one

Jonelle was quiet all the way back to the apartments. I couldn't blame her; I wasn't in the mood for talking myself. Though some part of me knew we'd have to lighten up soon or self combust.

I made a silent vow not to look for conspiracies from here on in. If I hadn't being overly interested in pushing Theo's buttons, we'd still be hunting a murderer, but without the distressing side trip. Not that there was even a slight chance I'd keep a promise like that.

I invited myself back to her place without as much as a nod from her. I just happened to bring Smudge and Manny with me. In order to bring back her humanity, I enlisted my pets' help. There was something about cuddling fur and rebuking a dog who tried to eat your cushions, that breaks the ice.

Jonelle curled up with Smudge, tickling him on his tummy. I made the tea and brought it out to the lounge. Manny made himself scarce. If he hid under the coffee table and just poked his nose out for the occasional pat, everyone was happy.

Making sure we could both reach the tea mugs, I settled myself into a cushion opposite Jonelle.

"Are you really going to ignore Will forever?"

Nothing like the subtle approach. But then again, I wasn't going to try for a diplomatic mission to a foreign outpost.

Sipping her tea, Jonelle took a moment before answering. Obviously there was a lot to think about concerning our recent interview, but I needed to get to her thoughts and feelings on the matter. I was never going to win any awards for patience.

"Probably not. But he needs to see how serious this all is. He isn't playing at keeping the home and hearth safe. He's playing for big stakes, with lives to be won or lost." She frowned. "But I've known him for many years. So no, I won't totally cut him out. A history with anyone for someone like me is too much to throw away."

Which could have led me into all sorts of pointed questions about Amelia; but I had no desire to go there today. If she could try and retire, and not let Amelia waltz into her life, who was I to query the rationale behind it?

Then she smiled.

"A fat lot of use that would do me, anyway, what with my assistant's ridiculous infatuation with the man."

I threw a coaster at her, which she neatly fielded.

"It's not so much an infatuation, as a desperate need to get him out of my system. Which you have not been helping!"

"And a good thing too. Now you know just how deceitful the man can be, perhaps you'll start to see some sense in that direction."

Yeah and pigs were about to learn the ancient craft of flying, too. I smiled non-committedly and went about finishing my tea.

"I can't get over the fact that Will or Theo didn't tell me about the whole set up. And why is Theo so upset?"

I was hoping these were rhetorical questions. The type I could just sit back and ignore. Because I'd had enough of any sort of question, for at least the next century. But she was looking at me with that faint air about her that said 'well?'

I shrugged. "Not being an expert on the Brothers Malone, I can't rightly say. But I would imagine that Theo isn't too happy with anything to do with that night." I warmed up to my subject.

"I mean, look at it from a purely sexual/egotistical way. I'm a hot guy with a low self esteem when it comes to women. Or, at the very least, some idea that when I actually sleep with someone, it'll be someone I care about and not just a random one night stand. Keeping myself for something wonderful." I put my mug down and stretched.

"I come to visit my older, wiser and hotter brother." I grinned at Jonelle's expression. "We have this great night out and half way through, this amazingly attractive chick comes over and totally ignores my hot older brother, something that just never happens, and zeros in on me. I am buzzed. This is it! A woman who hasn't fallen for the lure of the Will. We talk and laugh for ages. She lets me know that going home together is the one thing she would love more than anything. I'm here with Will and a couple of the Hounds. I can't back down and I'm not too sure I want to. She's the most out there chick I've ever met. So we go to her place. The night is an amazing adventure of firsts." I really could see it panning out like that.

"Then somehow, it comes out that she's a hooker and my brother set me up. There is a nasty taint to all we've said and done the whole night. Every word she has said comes with a price tag. Every action; practiced on the richest half of the population. I'm humiliated. I know everyone in the pub, and the Hounds, knew what was going on. Inside, I can't cope. My hero has made me a laughing stock. So Theo may come and visit, but he holds his heart and his feelings wayyy behind a cold wall where Will will never find them. How's that sound?"

Jonelle nodded slowly. "You know what? I have the sad feeling that you're probably right, which makes me want to throttle Will for the mess he's made."

"Or Brenda," I murmured.

"What?"

"Well, come on. It's not like Will was in that room. Somehow Brenda let it be known what she was. Will wasn't going to tell, was he? So she must have. And Theo has a complex and Will was angry, and you don't think Will killed her for letting Theo know, who is now blaming Will, do you?" Now that was a nasty thought. Because that would make Will the murderer of a scared and lonely woman, and a very big bad liar too.

"Your mind leaps around like nothing I've ever met before, Princess." Jonelle's lips twitched. "It had crossed my mind, however. But no, I don't believe that Will took the rejection he is getting from Theo out on Brenda. He is a lot of things, our Will, but he isn't petty. Though he may have been quite angry with her for letting the cat out of the bag, I think it is more his style to go rant at her."

Well, yes. I have seen him when he was angry, or at least, annoyed. Ranting was more his thing. And I wasn't too keen on pushing him as our next suspect, because then I would have to do some very deep soul searching about my feelings for him. And that was to be avoided at all cost.

"Well, we've done the only thing that was on the list for today. Talk to Will. Does that mean I get the rest of the day off?" There was always hope for a quick check in on my favourite soapies. Not something I'd had much time for over the last few weeks.

She stretched like a mountain cat. "Actually, let's just get the hell out of here."

I looked at her. "As in...?" It was best to be one hundred percent sure; making assumptions was bad for my health.

"As in, slow poke, stopping past Coles for some travelling nibbles and heading down the coast for the day." She looked thoughtful. "Or two. We've had our heads buried in work for ages. It won't hurt us to sit on a beach and think about Christmas. It's not that far away, you know."

How could I forget? In a few weeks times I would also be turning thirty. The big three-zero. That was going to take some getting used to. I would no longer be able to say I was an irresponsible twenty-something. Which seemed a shame, really, because that sounded much better than a thirty year old who just wouldn't grow up.

"You going to be around for that?" I asked her casually.

"Probably. My family is pretty scattered and I don't like to take my problems to wherever the folks are. I'll go visit Jodi and have a quiet one." She had a slight frown on her face, like a she'd had too many of those sorts of Christmas' already.

"You could always come to mine." Might help deflect the constant pressure to get married, have the two point five children, and be a proper grown up, for once. Though that could be asking for minor miracles.

Jonelle raised her eyes and gave me a look. She wasn't stupid. "Running interference? Haven't we done that before?"

"Yes, and look at how well that turned out. They were so worried about how you fit into my life they left me alone for a whole afternoon. It was bliss." Of sorts. "You can spend the time making friends with Leigh. After all, he was a great fan." I smirked. She had as much love for the overwhelming magnitude of children in my family as I did.

"Ask your mother first this time, okay? It's Christmas. They might not want a stranger. But thank you for asking."

"If I tell them you have no family in the country, they'll practically beg me to bring you. I must give my family their due. They hate to think of anyone being alone." And so did I. What a way to spend Christmas Day.

"Well, we'll settle that out later. For now, let's get the hell out of here."

I liked her plan. A day of sun, surf and sand. Perhaps it may just manage to chase the shadows in my head far far away.

We piled into my zippy little car and roared off to Coles. We couldn't make a trip to the coast without suitable munchies on the way. Diet or no diet. I only hoped the bikini I packed wasn't going to look too ridiculous.

"Maltesers and Jaffas." I threw them into the basket. "Loads of water, and..."

Jonelle grabbed me by the arm and dragged me into the next aisle.

"Hey! What was that all about?"

"Craig. I don't particularly feel up to spending the next few minutes feeling bad about how little progress I've made on Brenda's murder. We're taking the day off, remember? A little bit of Craig goes a long way." She poked her head around the corner and jumped back. "Damn. He's coming this way, but I don't think he saw me. Come on!"

I tried to smother a grin. She was acting as demented as I sometimes did. But I allowed (as if I had much of a choice really) myself to be manhandled down the aisle in an attempt to make it safely to the other end. I allowed myself one peek back around Jonelle as we sailed around the corner.

"Funny. He's back to normal." I screwed up my nose. The glimpse I'd had of Craig was pretty much the same as the last time we'd met him in Coles. Not the almost respectable creature I'd seen in Narooma.

"What do you mean – 'back to normal,'" Jonelle peeked at our quarry. "He's pretty much same old same old, to me."

"I saw him while I was waiting for you in Narooma. Didn't I tell you?" She growled. "Um, must have slipped my mind. Anyway, he was all dressed up, with flowers. I'd say he was heading out with a new girl. He was bright eyed and almost happy looking! In fact, the haircut made him look..." I trailed off.

Haircut! How stupid was I? I popped my head around the corner too.

There he was. Red eyed, six o'clock shadow (ahead of his times) and long lank hair. I ducked back. I know my eyes must have been like saucers. Jonelle was looking very thoughtful.

"Funny he never mentioned a twin, isn't it? A twin who just happens to live down the coast. I wonder what else he has been keeping from me?" Even I knew that the question was totally rhetorical. Her eyes had become glaciers.

"We're taking the day off." I made a rather futile snatch at my sun, surf and sand. It had sounded so ... comfy.

Those eyes swivelled round and drilled holes in me. "I now think I would prefer to have a quiet word with Craig, wouldn't you?"

Was she kidding? The moon was looking good.

"Have we mentioned lately how much I am a coward? I don't know if we've stressed that enough." Craig was wandering closer. Like a lamb to the slaughter. Though, if we were thinking the same thing about him, he wasn't particularly lamb like and the slaughter may well have been over. I took a step backward.

"How about I go buy these things?"

"Fiona!" She was amused and exasperated. "I'm hardly going to beat the man in the supermarket!"

Well, true. How silly of me. But she could easily kidnap him in the supermarket and take him off somewhere. And she'd need my car to do that and then I'd have Craig DNA in it and all sorts of horrid fantasies about crime scene investigators travelled through my head.

"Let's just see what he has to say. We can even invite him home for a cup of tea." Her eyes glinted with her own special brand of humour. Oh joy.

"Craig." She'd stepped back into the aisle, neatly snagging me and the shopping basket on the way. I guess it gave her a legitimate reason for been there. "How are you?"

He gave a start. "Jonelle! You gave me a fright. I … wasn't expecting to see you." Canberra was a small place, but I could manage to *never* run into any of my family, so it wasn't as strange a comment as it sounded.

"Coles is my local supermarket these days," she smiled, wolfishly.

I could almost see Craig resolve to do his shopping elsewhere. This reading people gig wasn't so hard after all.

"How … how are things?" I wondered at his nervousness, then took a good look at his shopping trolley. There was a lot of alcohol and mixers to be seen, and not a lot else. Craig took note of where I was looking and went a fiery red.

Jonelle tutted. "How is your brother these days?" Nothing like the direct approach.

Craig gave a little jump. "Which one?"

There was more of them out there? I shuddered. What had his mother been thinking?

Jonelle's eyebrow climbed. "Why the one in Narooma, of course. The one down the coast."

He shuddered. He actually did, as though it was too much to bear.

"You did fail to mention the fact you have a twin, you know, Craig. Rather remiss of you, don't you think?" Her voice was smooth as silk. My stomach growled, in nervous anticipation.

"I failed to mention that?" His voice cracked. It was kind of like a mouse facing a large and particularly hungry cat. "I didn't think it would be relevant."

Jonelle rolled her eyes to me. "What is it lately with men hiding their brothers from me? I am not in the habit of eating them for breakfast." She turned her concentration back to Craig and all humour disappeared. "Though I may start to make exceptions."

"Well, I … um …. that is," he paused. He definitely had a captive audience. I was all ears. "I had, er, have two of them, you see. I mean, we're triplets. Not twins."

He looked almost apologetic at correcting her. As I would too. Ho hum.

"They both live in Narooma. I much prefer them to, you see."

Well, no I didn't see. That was the whole point of asking questions, right? To help uncover what we couldn't see? The man was a twitching mess. And I thought I had family troubles. I got the distinct impression that Craig was not his brothers' biggest fan.

Jonelle gave a long suffering sigh. "How about we all go back to my place and have a cup of tea?"

And there went the beach. I gave her a disgruntled glare. One she neatly avoided. Craig wasn't much happier than me.

"I … er … that is, I really need to be going."

"It wasn't so much an invitation as a polite way of saying you and I are going back to my place for a chat. Though I try very hard not to be impolite and demanding."

First I'd heard of it.

"Oh, right. Um … okay then." Craig abandoned his trolley and turned to leave. "Only I have an appointment later this afternoon, so I hope this won't take long."

"So do I, Craig, so do I," Jonelle purred.

He swallowed loudly.

I made the tea myself. It wasn't that I wanted to miss out on anything going on in the other room, but seeing as Craig was so nervous he could hardly talk, I didn't think that was much of an issue. He needed something to wet his dry mouth more than I did.

"Tea for everyone." I brought the tray in. Scary how much like my mother in one of her more stilted social gatherings I sounded.

Craig grabbed at his like it was a lifeline.

"Now we're all settled," Jonelle gave me an oblique look, "shall we talk about your brothers?"

He tried a smile. "Must we? I've done my best for years not to talk about my brothers. Even pretend they don't exist. Though, of course, I pray for them every night," he added, as if to convince us he wasn't a truly bad person. I didn't think I'd ever prayed for anyone.

Which might explain a lot.

"You were down the coast when Brenda was killed." Jonelle leaned forward, allowing Craig the chance to see just how coiled and spring-like she really was. As if the man had any doubt she was trouble, with a capital T.

His Adam's apple jumped of its volition. "Yes."

"This would go a lot faster if you put some effort into your responses."

"I don't know what you want me to say! I was down the coast. I was at a motel. I had dinner there. I stayed the night and then came back. A day later I went to see Brenda and found the police instead." His eyes glittered with unshed tears.

Either he was a world class actor, or he really did miss her. Or he just regretted killing her.

"You know all this. You asked me then. You even went to the motel and made sure I was there."

"Yes, which I did all in the belief there was only one of you!"

"Not my fault you didn't know the rest," he muttered.

"Actually, it is," her voice was soft. "I didn't do a full background check on you. Why would I bother? Why would I waste the time? I'd placed you far away from the scene of the crime. Maybe I was slack, maybe I was just old and tired, but I *am* making up for it now. You either tell me all I want to know, or we will be turning your family life upside down."

We would? I had a bad feeling I was suddenly going to be doing a lot more work. The beach slipped further away.

His shoulders slumped. "Whatever. It hardly matters now, does it? She's gone and I could have saved her."

Those words took on a lot more significance, now.

"How could you have saved her, Craig? Were you really down the coast?"

"Yes, it was me in Bateman's Bay. Really. I was supposed to be meeting one of my brothers. John. They usually do everything together and go everywhere together, so to be asked to meet just John, was …

unusual and I thought, a good thing." He swallowed a lump of tea.

"Why? What makes that a good thing?"

I was as interested as Jonelle, though probably not for the same reason. Me; I was just curious.

Craig wouldn't meet her eye.

"Together they can be … bad news. John used to … he used to kill animals. You know. When we were little, he'd experiment. Like this one time he put the cat in the dryer with a couple of rocks just to see what would happen. He stood in front of it and watched the cat go round and round …"

I felt the tea swirl lazily in my stomach. Animals. Nothing more defenceless. Well, possibly children, but I wasn't going there. I thought of Smudge and his cute little nose and my stomach roiled.

"And?" I snuck a peek at Jonelle. She sounded so impersonal. Her face was shuttered and hard.

"He weighed this puppy down once …"

She held up her hand. "Not 'and … tell me more of your brother's sick and twisted tales.' I meant 'and how does this fit with what I want to know?'" she shot me another look. It rather said 'sorry for having to make you hear this'.

I was sorry too.

"He got treatment, but I don't know if he ever got over it or just became cleverer at hiding his experiments. Then there is Peter." He shifted nervously.

It wasn't too hard to see that his brothers made Craig into a jibbering idiot. Poor sod. I wasn't much better with my family. Though luckily for everyone concerned, there was only one of me. Two would be bad enough. But three - !

"Peter is the eldest. I'm the last one. Which they have always made sure I never forget, like I was an afterthought. There was quite a gap between me and John. Time wise. It made them closer and me the third wheel. Peter is sort of the mastermind. He tells John what he should be doing and what to and how to think, and things like that. He is a sick and nasty man." Craig clutched his mug tighter, as though by mentioning his name, he might conjure Peter out of thin air.

"They don't like women. They don't like men. They only like each other."

Eew! Well, unless he didn't mean that like I thought he meant it … which could happen. Not everything in the world was about sex. But still. Eew.

"They think all women are Eves and all men have the weaknesses of Adam."

"You weren't brought up strictly religiously by any chance, were you?" Jonelle asked.

"Yeah. Can you tell?"

Well, he could have stamped 'maladjusted religious nutter' on his head to make it a bit easier, but it really wasn't necessary.

"It might be a little obvious," she murmured. "Keep going."

I could see that Craig was actually finding this quite cathartic. While talking about his brothers clearly made his nervous and scared, telling someone, even Jonelle, about their predilections was a relief.

"Of course, I forgive them and make every effort to be a good brother to them."

Oh, how kind of him. I could almost see the sanctimonious waves of righteousness radiating off him. Me? I thought they needed to be locked up and the key thrown in the deepest darkest waters imaginable. Animals …

Potty was an animal … Blackness threatened the very edges of my reality. I threw up my head and gave Jonelle a panicked look. She nodded at me reassuringly. Whatever had frightened me, she seemed to say with her eyes, she would make sure I got the chance to ask about it when he slowed down in confessing.

"I always wished we'd been closer. So I told them I was seeing Brenda. I was so happy. Not many women dated me." He looked a bit confused at this announcement, like it was a shock or something. I could have explained it to him, but didn't have the heart.

"She was so eager to know how to save her soul. She'd pray with me and hold my hand and ask me to forgive her."

Jonelle growled. He gave her a frightened looked.

"It took a while before she told me what she did to own such an apartment and a BMW and her jewels. I was shocked!"

Horrified, one might say, by the expression on his face. The thought that his loving woman was paid for sex was, well, beyond his comprehension.

"It was quite disgusting to think I was dating a common hooker, though she assured me that she was not common, but very expensive." His nose wrinkled in distaste. "We prayed a lot harder to save her soul after that confession, I can tell you."

He was winning no brownie points with his narrow minded point of view. I was kind of interested to see how he would cope if Jonelle got confessional.

"Stick to the point." She shifted edgily. Patience was not her friend.

He coughed. "Anyway, we agreed that her profession was no way to make a living and she was to leave it immediately! Though, immediately was taking a long time."

I doubted her employers would have helped her along with her request to retire. Her drug habit wouldn't have either. I wondered if he knew of that little piece of news.

"I told my brothers I was seeing a lovely woman, but they had been right. All women led a man to sin. She was, after all, a tempting piece who would have taken me to bed, had I not told her we would wait until she had been cleansed of her sin first."

There was no doubt that whatever insanity led his brothers to torture animals hadn't skipped over the last triplet either. There was a fanatical gleam in his eye when he mentioned cleansing and sin. Poor Brenda. Even if she'd tried to move on and get another boyfriend, I suddenly doubted he would have just 'let' her go. There was too much 'saving' to do.

"I explained what she did. They were amazed I would date her. I told them she just needed to be cleansed of her sin and we would get married," he faulted. There was a chance he hadn't realised how evil his sick brothers really were.

"John called me two days later. He wanted to meet me and talk about getting help for Peter. Without Peter there to lead him astray, I thought John might be prayed for. I agreed to meet him. He never showed. When I found out Brenda had been killed, I knew." He paled. "I just knew I should have saved her. I asked them. They came and visited me, and told me that I was going to keep my mouth shut and they had tasted all I had not and found her wanting." A tear slid down his cheek.

"They gloated about having sex with her and how she had begged for more. I refused to listen. She wouldn't have done that. She was going to come to me and get my help to save her soul. They should have left her alone!" Craig was staring at Jonelle, eyes wide and soulless themselves.

"I told John he wouldn't have done this without Peter. So I killed him."

Now there was a twist. I dropped my mug (fortunately it was empty or I could just see Jonelle killing me).

"You what?" I asked, stupidly. Just needed to make sure of my facts.

Jonelle had straightened even further. Her fingers twitched and I could see the tip of her wrist knife peep out of her wide loose sleeve. Now we knew Craig wasn't just a passive religious nut but a murderous one, it was only sensible to take precautions.

It also helped explain his continued drinking problem. It was a lot harder to get over the murder of your brother, especially when you did it, than just the death of your girlfriend.

He looked at me. I much rather he hadn't. I couldn't see if there was anyone inside those eyes. They were frightening in a sick way that Jonelle's could never be.

"I loved her. She was *my* soul to save. While John strangled her, I knew he would never have come up with that idea himself. He certainly would never have had sex with her. That was Peter. Without him, I could save John's soul. So I went to Narooma and took Peter out in the tinny and shot him, and pushed him into the water."

He made it sound so easy!

"I don't think it would have been as easy as all that." Jonelle unconsciously echoed my thoughts.

"Oh, but it was!" He sounded terribly eager to show her how clever he had been. "Peter always thought I was a bit slow. And believed I would never do anything to hurt my older brothers. When I offered to take him out fishing, he laughed and agreed. I shot him in the back."

Coward. Nice family. He was making mine look positively friendly.

"I couldn't let him see the gun. And I couldn't let him talk me out of it. I needed to do this. For John, for me, and for Brenda. So you see, Jonelle, I made it all right."

That's what he thought. Somewhere in there, I was sure he thought his logic was going to mean something to her. I just couldn't tell what. Her face was a glacial wall.

"So Peter's been dead this whole time? So who killed our dog and why?" I had to ask.

Craig shrugged. "John did. I thought he was doing well, you know, without Peter. He was getting out. He never asked me where Pete was. He started to act like it had always just been us. No one asked. I don't think there are that many people who knew there are three of us." He smiled, as though he was proud of the accomplishment of this deception. "Our parents are dead."

He said it like you would say 'I eat fish'.

"It was great! He found himself a girlfriend. Though I don't know how long that will last. I eventually started to ask him to come and visit me. I didn't think it would be a problem. Do you remember when I bumped into you at the service station?"

I looked over at Jonelle. I certainly had no recollection of that meeting.

"You were back here, Princess. I was on my way to inspect Simon and Lorraine's apartment. " She correctly interpreted my quizzical look. "Not long before we found out about Potty's death, actually." She looked back at Craig.

"Yeah, you didn't see him, but John was in the gents. He saw you and asked me who you were. I didn't want him to think you were another girlfriend! There was a chance he might … well. I wasn't too sure he wouldn't have tried to kill you, too."

Would have been interesting to see him try. Jonelle gave a little snort, which indicated she thought so as well.

"I told him about you telling me Brenda had asked you to look after her. And how you were interested in her murder and I'd covered for him. He got a little obsessed about it all. It wasn't until later did I realise he'd followed you home and then he must have seen you talking to Fiona and … who knows what goes on in his head? I'd had to go to work, leaving him that day to his own devices."

Or just plain vices. The whole family were a bunch of raving nutters. I'd hate to have met the folks.

He might not know what John had then proceeded to get up to, but I did. That was the day before the red writing had appeared on Jonelle's wall. The day before I saw a figure sneaking off into the morning dawn. The day before I'd asked Jonelle to come home for Sunday lunch. He could have followed us there and he would have seen Potty. A large and friendly animal, just waiting for his type of experiments. I felt sickened. Jonelle reached over and patted my knee. I must have looked as green as I felt.

"So, he followed us and decided that Potty was fair game, hmm?

Sounds like a *very* reformed character to me." Jonelle's voice was gravel.

Yeah, totally rehabilitated.

Craig shrugged. "It was just an animal."

Something akin to a moan came out of my throat. Just an animal. Was killing twice over too much to ask for this man?

Jonelle gave me a sympathetic look. "How about you stick around in town for a few days, Craig? I may have some further questions for you."

He rose, with a huge smile. "So you understand? You can see how it all happened. And Peter won't be hurting anyone anymore. I took care of it all for you, see?" He sounded like a small schoolboy caught out in a misdemeanour, trying to make it all right again.

Jonelle led him through the door to the gate. I sat where I was, stunned. When she came back I nearly pounced.

"You're just letting him walk out?? What are you thinking? He covered it all up! He killed his brother, his other one killed Potty … it's all my fault! Potty died because of me! It had nothing to do with you, or Phoenix or Brenda's death. Not really. Just me!" Somewhere along the way I may have crossed the line over to hysteria.

"Snap out of it, Princess." Her voice was gruff. "You can't blame yourself for the actions of a madman. He was tailing me, not you. Potty was just … collateral damage. Sorry, but if Craig had been the one to tail me, the animal hating brother wouldn't have had the chance. So lay the blame on me. I didn't spot the tail. And as to letting him go - I had to. I could hardly kill him here, could I?"

Well she had a point. Killing someone in your own home was practically drawing the police a map with a large X on it. Even I wasn't that stupid. At least, I hoped I was never that stupid.

"What are you going to do then?"

Or didn't I want to know? I was still smarting over the guilt. My entire involvement stemmed from that day when she came over for lunch. If I hadn't been so keen to give Mum a fright, John would never have tailed her to my place and Potty would still be giving the Twinnies piggyback rides. I felt ill. Allowing one of the main problems to waltz out the front door was disheartening, to use a mild understatement.

"I know where he lives. I now know John lives in Narooma. And if I am any judge in character, our Craig will be setting off to visit said brother very soon, possibly to tidy up any further loose ends.

What's another brother, between murderous friends?" Her smile held no humour whatsoever.

"So, you're off to the coast then? Not exactly the day we had planned." At least *someone* was getting close to a beach. It was just a shame about the circumstances.

"I do believe I am. Most probably alone, unless - ?" She raised her eyebrow at me.

As though there was going to be any doubt about that. No way in hell was I heading off to Narooma with Death as my travelling companion.

"You can safely assume you'll be going solo. As much as I love the idea of spending the day with you, taking on two psychos wasn't on my agenda. Sorry."

Not that I was very sorry. Maybe just a fraction. But I couldn't see me going along and holding her knives or gun between brothers. There wasn't enough sleeping pills to deal with *that* little bit of insomnia.

She shrugged, making her way to the spare room. "I'll be back tomorrow. This shouldn't take too long. I want to make sure John backs up Craig's version of events. I am heartily sick of brother's trying to fob me off, one way or the other. This time, I'm making sure of the facts and not leaving anyone around to do anymore harm."

There it was: the momentary twinge of my conscience.

"Shouldn't we like, you know, tell the police or something?" One had to ask these things. It was mandatory. Police did have their place, even in her life, surely. Not that these two boys would be any loss to the gene pool. Whoa! Now I was even sounding like her.

Jonelle's head came around the door. "Bit late for them, don't you think? If they'd done any sort of investigation they'd have found out about our triplets long before this. They have more resources. But putting it down to work related, well, they were just lazy. Plus, they won't charge them. They'll be put into some psychiatrist's care in an attempt to rehabilitate them. Not my scene."

She wasn't kidding.

I bit my lip. Sometimes it was easier than pointing out someone *else* could have discovered things a bit quicker too, if she had tried harder.

She came out. "Don't stick around in here all day. Go out. See the girls. I'll let you know when I get home. See you."

And that was it. She was gone.

Chapter Thirty two

I couldn't believe it was still Friday. That only that morning we'd toddled around to Will's and everything had been downhill since then. I checked my watch. Damn, I'd missed lunch.

Wandering back to my own apartment, I realised that there wasn't any hope of me stomaching food anyway. Not with the massive cloud of anxiety and guilt hanging over my head.

When it came down to it, what had been a perverse friendly gesture, right back when Jonelle was new to Grangelands, had become the very moment things had started to unravel. If it hadn't been for the little imp in me that wanted to upset my mother, Jonelle would have gone to whatever appointment she'd cancelled that day, and Potty would still be gambolling around the backyard.

I slipped inside and curled up on the couch, clutching a pillow. Sensing the mood, Smudge and Manny lay on the floor, eyes watching me in morbid curiosity.

How was I ever going to explain it to the family? Scrap that, there was no way I was every going to explain anything to the family. The less they knew about how my world worked these days, the better. *I* wasn't even sure how things worked. It was thoughtful of Jonelle to allow me to keep myself in the dark just that little bit longer. The mind boggled at exactly how she would persuade Craig to take her down the coast, if he hadn't already left.

For once, I reined in my need to know and went back to old habits. Getting up, I fetched the latest bottle of white wine from the fridge, half gone already, and some chips I'd somehow managed to hide in the back of the pantry. This done, I turned the telly on and settled in for an afternoon of movies and alcohol. When the world was too scary, it was time to do the simple things that reinstated old patterns.

I drank from the neck of the bottle.

Somewhere between two thirty and six o'clock I caught a nap, which enabled Smudge to feel free to curl up on my tummy and Manny to steal the remaining chips. A good thing they didn't get into the wine.

A constant thumping on my door drove all remaining thoughts of sleep out the window.

"I'm up!" Lord, how could I not have noticed how loud my neighbours could be?

Amy stood waiting less than patiently for me to open the door.

"Boy, aren't you the hard one to wake up these days? You do know," she continued, pushing past me and throwing herself on the couch, "it's Friday night?"

She eyed the bottle, still a quarter full. "What time did you get started?" Unscrewing the top, Amy stole a quick mouthful.

I rubbed at my eyes, suddenly feeling every day of my nearly thirty years and snatched the wine back. Hey, there was sharing and there was sharing. My need was greater.

"Didn't get much sleep last night." Mild understatement. That, and the hideous wake up time and subsequent stress levels; I believe me being in any way conscious was a miracle. "What are we all up to tonight?" I'd been out of the loop for too long.

"We're heading down to Madame Wu's for a quick bite, then over the road to The Batch. You up for it? I handed in my resignation and want to celebrate."

"You quit the Force?" Not that this came as a massive surprise, but we'd all been hopeful that Amy might actually settle into something. Okay, so it was hypocritical of me to think it would do her good to have a career, but look at me now. I was even developing work ethics, so wonders might never cease. "That's a shame. I thought you were enjoying yourself for a while there?"

She picked up the chip packet and gave it a shake.

"I wouldn't if I were you. Manny has had his nose in them. And while he has a very pretty nose, I can't vouch for how sanitary it is," I warned her.

"Fiona! When are you going to learn to put things out of their reach? Yuk." She threw the packet back on the floor. "Too many rules. Plus, there is this great cruise I saw an ad for coming up and if I didn't resign I wouldn't have been able to go. I have no leave."

She shrugged. Glad to see her priorities were as screwed up as mine.

"I met this great bloke and we're hoping to head off for a few months overseas. You know, cruise and then party in Europe. Whatever."

Ah, the idle rich. Love it when Daddy was footing the bill. I wondered what happened when Daddy ran out of money. Or decided that signing cheques wasn't all he could be doing?

Not my concern.

"Sounds like a plan, anyway. When are we heading out?" Anything to take my mind off what may or may not be happening in Narooma.

"You have time to wake up." Amy grinned. "Be out the front by seven." Then she departed.

It took the remainder of the hour to have enough coffee to feel fully functional, a shower and get dressed. Friday nights couldn't be hurried.

Unfortunately, it wasn't a resounding success. I was distracted and uneasy. It didn't help that I couldn't shake my feelings of guilt, regardless of Jonelle telling me it wasn't my fault; and knowing there was nothing I could do now. Beating oneself up after an event was fairly unproductive, but gave my mind something else to worry about, apart from the all consuming dread of what was going on down the coast.

At eleven, I pleaded exhaustion and went home. Everyone agreed I was not my usual party self and could do with the extra sleep. I hated to leave them while there were good party hours left to be had, but my heart wasn't in it and I retired to bed.

Mixing alcohol with a sleeping pill wasn't the best prescription, but it certainly helped my brain to stop over analysing everything and I slept like a log.

I came back to consciousness slowly, with a wicked headache and dry mouth. Squinting, I managed to make out the glowing red digits on my clock. Nine. I dropped my head back onto the pillow. Only nine? I'd hoped for oblivion to take me right through the day. Better that than allowing my overactive imagination free rein.

There was no way I was going to try her mobile. The scary part of that would be distracting her at an important point. Though, I had to concede, if she'd left her mobile on at a crucial moment, she'd only have herself to blame if it rang.

How my mind wandered.

It was no use. I was now awake and no matter how forceful I was about it, my body was determined not to go back to sleep.

"Morning boys." I acknowledged the two sets of eyes watching me reproachfully from the doorway. "You all need to go out, right? Give me a mo." I wasn't feeling the least bit zippy.

Pets taken care of, I put the kettle on. Health kick notwithstanding, I was going to absorb copious amounts of coffee and there was no Jonelle around to force feed me green tea. I was standing in an oversized T-shirt, which served as a nightie, staring out the kitchen window sipping scalding hot coffee, when the door (unlocked so the boys could go out) burst open.

"Shit!" I put the mug down, holding my Tee off my body, a large coffee stain spreading from chest to hem. Looking up, I stared.

Larger than life and radiating sun-like energy, Jonelle grinned savagely at my clumsiness.

"Poor Princess. I do manage to give you more than your fair share of frights, don't I?" She didn't look the least bit sorry. "What's for … brunch?" Consulting her watch, she moved into the kitchen, pushing the joyful pets to one side.

"You're back." A piece of useless information, but there you go. Her sudden arrival had rendered me verbally incompetent – again.

"What a clever little mother you boys have." Jonelle petted Manny and gave me a condescending flicker of her eyebrows. "Got back a few moments ago. Thought you would be up for a visit. Though I can see you haven't been out of bed for all that long." Disapproval added to the condescension.

"Clothes!" I squeaked and dashed back to the bedroom. Crap. Bugger. Though of course, she wasn't going to give me detention for being slack. But my skin crawled with embarrassment. She'd caught me just out of bed, mid coffee and in my nightie! Life, I reflected, was always trying to catch me unawares and have a good old hoot at my expense.

Executing the quickest change in the history of - well, me - I was back in the kitchen moments later. Jonelle had raided pantry, fridge and cupboards; finding the last of the mint slice biscuits, mini frozen pizzas (now happily cruising around in circles in the microwave) and a packet pancake mix, which she was reading with studied concentration.

"Do you even *have* a flat-bottomed pan?" She didn't look up from the directions.

Nothing said 'I have had a rather fraught twenty four hours' better than Jonelle eating junk food. I was glad of the distraction.

"Never let it be said I don't have all the means for making actual food. That I prefer to eat takeaway has more to do with the fact that *eating* actual food I have made may lead to potential hospital trips, than the lack of food making materials."

I produced said pan and put it on the gas. Try saying that mouthful three times very fast.

Jonelle added milk and gave the pancake mix a good thrashing.

"Have you even slept?" Watching someone else make food wasn't proving to be as distracting as I'd hoped.

Grey eyes, rimmed with red, met my own. "There was a little more to do than I had expected. I'll sleep later this afternoon. Starving now. Must eat." Vocal, as well. This was getting worse and worse.

A few minutes later we took plates of pancakes, syrup, biscuits and scalding coffee into the lounge. Late morning sun was pouring in the windows and we sat opposite each other, legs tucked out of the way. Animals sat, ever hopeful, as close as possible.

"Now, are you feeling up to telling me what went on?" I shovelled another mammoth-sized mouthful of pancake in.

She shrugged. Sugar tended to make me jumpy, but Jonelle just absorbed it and went on her way. But the hot sun on her back was turning her into a giant sleepy cat.

"We'll never have to worry about the Brothers' Grimly again." A rather bald statement of fact. "Not," she added, studying her pancake thoughtfully, "that we were particularly worried in the first place, were we?"

Well, not too sure which 'we' she was talking about, because this particular 'we', as in me, had been. They had been completely insane. Thinking it was okay to do these things and that by more murder, everything would just work itself out. If that wasn't something to worry about, I wasn't too sure what was.

"I take it from that lovely comment Craig and John are… um." I stuffed a mint slice biscuit in my mouth. It was Saturday morning, not gone noon. That, in my books, was way too early to ask someone if they had spent the night murdering anybody. You just couldn't say 'death, murder, slay' when it was only Saturday morning.

Several weeks ago, on a Saturday morning just like this one, I had walked unsuspectingly into Lorraine's unit and met this woman. Back then, the only thing I had to think about was whether or not my shoes matched my handbag and if The Young and The Restless had been cancelled for more cricket coverage. Now, there were no Black Eyed Peas on my telly, in fact the telly wasn't even on. And the only thing on my mind was 'let's not give me indigestion by raising subjects better off left unsaid'.

Though, of course, I never take any notice of myself.

Heavy lidded moody grey eyes met my own.

"Details, Princess?"

"Some," I agreed. Though not as many as my innate curiosity would like. I hesitated over the next mouthful. "Do you ever think I'll really 'get' your world?"

She snorted. "I don't think you'll ever want to. And that is a good thing. Paddling on the edges until I retire isn't a bad way to be, Princess, unless you want more?" Again with the piercing look.

Did I? I thought about seeing the blood pumping out of Ben; of the sting and mind numbing pain of the beating given to me by Charles and Daniel. Did I really want to be so deep into the darker side of things that those things would be okay? That Potty's death would only mean 'collateral damage'?

"Not right now. I think I can safely say, it looks good on telly and reads well in books, but living through fear and pain and death isn't all it's cracked up to be." I grimaced. "So give me the censored version."

Jonelle smiled, though it was tired and almost listless.

"Craig was packing things up at his place when I arrived. He was taking a prolonged holiday down the coast, he told me. According to Craig, he could see how leaving John alive might 'provoke' me into retaliation, so he was going to see if there was anything he could do to make John disappear. I didn't quite understand whether he meant disappear as in kill him, or just disappear from my vicinity. I wasn't interested in his logic.

"So we went to Narooma together. It was a long and sick trip. He had some very warped views on how he could save people's souls."

She wasn't in the business of saving souls, but that didn't mean Jonelle hadn't got some of her own seriously warped and macabre views, herself. Wasn't there something in the Bible about throwing stones while living in glass houses? I diplomatically kept my mouth closed around those thoughts. No need to poke a stick at the tiger.

"I didn't want to muck around with this. We went straight to John's beach, well, shack really. He was there. Actually getting himself ready for a date. He was doing a Craig, and was determined he could save her soul. Though I think he was just getting himself all worked up so he could kill her. Needed a bit of lead time, now there was no Peter to give him a push. He had the taste for killing. That real deep seated psychosis that made him feel the power of God through handing out Death." She rubbed her hand across her face.

She must have felt that herself at some stage, but again I kept quiet.

"I couldn't hand them over to the cops. I sat with them for hours, listening to their story, the intensity and insanity of it all. They happily showed me pictures of the three of them and worked on the idea that Peter had been the bad apple, leaving them now to be okay with his disappearance, as they called his murder. Singularly, they were mad. Together? They were enough to make me sick."

I'd seen Jonelle in loads of situations, but the pale skin and bleak eyes I could see now, well, it just made me sad. Many years ago, a mother must have held three little boys and thought 'here's to the future'. Now look where it had got them. And I could see how tainted Jonelle felt just by listening to them. But I didn't reach across the space and pat her knee reassuringly. I was slow sometimes, not stupid.

"So once you made sure that what Craig told us was true, what did you do?" I had to know.

"I asked John for another cup of tea, and while he was out of the room, I -" she paused. "I suffocated Craig. Quick and simple. Something his mother should have done at birth."

Well, there went my happy little family scene of mother and children.

"Then I went out to the kitchen and did the same to John. Quiet, relatively painless, and easy for me. They didn't put up much of a fight. It was as though they were expecting it all to end. Like they had to pay and were happy to settle their sins. I even took the mug they served me tea in, so nothing was left behind that would show I'd been there."

At least she was considering the DNA angle, which was something.

"It was after midnight by that stage, but it wasn't hard to find the boat the boys used for fishing. I had my inflatable with me, which I towed so I could upend their boat and make it look like a simple drowning, if anyone ever found it. No one is going to be finding the bodies. I took them out as far as I could and threw in lots of bait ..."

Her eyes met mine. "Do I need to tell you how many sharks came to the call of blood and fish guts, Princess, or can I finish this food and go to bed?" Her voice was as dark as her eyes.

"That's all, thanks." Sometimes I hated the remarks I made. *That's all, thanks* - like she'd just handed me another cucumber sandwich.

We ate in silence until our plates were empty.

"This whole thing wasn't quite what I expected."

Jonelle jerked her head up and caught my eyes with hers. They were dark and shadowed with age, with tiredness and with a sort of loneliness. I stared at her.

"What had you been expecting?" she spoke slowly, as though dragging herself away from her thoughts.

"You know, the hero rides in, asks all the right questions, and saves the day. And in all the books the hero is righteous, strong, unequivocally for the good side," she smiled a little at that, "and to my knowledge, always a man. Well, generally a man in our male oriented society."

Her lips quirked.

"How would you feel about a hero who is sometimes right, could ask all sorts of right *and* stupid questions, who may end up making a small difference in the overall picture but not saving the actual day, on the day? Oh, and this hero happens to be a woman?"

"I think," I told her, glancing down at my hands, then back into those eyes, "that I could certainly live with that."

Jonelle kept looking at me for the longest moment. Then her eyes twinkled.

"Well *living*, Princess, is the whole idea. But not something I'm willing to place a life time guarantee on."

I laughed. Relief; her eyes looked human.

"Welcome back," I murmured and she acknowledged the hit with a small tilt of her chin.

"What are you going to do with the Phoenix and Amelia, and the nefarious Gavel who likes to hang out with the priestly type?" After all, there was taking a break, having a rest, and then there was falling into a pit of gloom.

"You know what, Princess?" Jonelle put her mug down. She leaned back deeply into the sofa and lifted her feet onto the coffee table. Folding her arms behind her head, she contemplated the ceiling.

"There's always tomorrow," she said.

The End

www.ingramcontent.com/pod-product-compliance
Lightning Source LLC
Chambersburg PA
CBHW072015020726
47501CB00006B/1820